BLIND TRUST

BLIND TRUST

CLOVER JEAN GARDENER

CONTENTS

DEDICATIONS

to **my wife**, who poured la croix on my head to get me to stop panicking and finish publishing the first edition of this book.

to **arri**, who edited this twice, refused payment, and still points out my every typo.

to **everyone who has bought a copy of this book's previous edition**, and were very kind about it, despite the obvious errors in formatting.

to **you**. i hope you're having a nice enough day.

Note for the Reader

Dear Reader,

This book contains references to sexual assault, child abuse, suicidality and self-harm through mild physical injury and substance abuse. No sexual content happens directly on the page, and the child abuse is implied and takes place in the past. There is a running theme of psychosis and dissociation. It is my hope that all of this is handled safely and and with care, but please take the same care of yourself as you read.

Best Regards,

cjg

Then and Now

"Lark?"

"Yeah, Eddie?"

"I can't sleep."

"Me neither. I'm too excited!"

Eddie...

Scott?

I'm so tired.

I know. It's been a really long day. Just close your eyes and try to

rest.

Overture

Eddie Gallows woke up in the middle of the night on his twelfth birthday aching so terribly that his first conscious action was to choke back a scream. His instinct was to call out for help, but even in the daze of broken sleep he knew that would only make things worse. So instead he scrambled, bleary-eyed, out of the smothered embrace of his covers and sat up, panting at the blank wall ahead of him.

There was a dream, perhaps. A memory, or the presence of something that felt like it. Something already blurry with concrete details fading by the minute, but leaving behind an intense feeling of wrong wrong *wrong*. When he touched his face his fingertips came back wet with fresh tears, even though his chest didn't heave and his eyes didn't water.

There were things he was supposed to do in times like this – sigils, chants, spices and candles. The single wooden shelf hand-built above his bed by his father before he left was already bending under the weight of textbooks for classes he wasn't old enough to take yet. Opening one and following orders would, in theory, make this better. But, filled with the wisdom that only comes from a decade of not succeeding to die, he knew no spell on paper could make his heart stop hurting.

No ritual documented could drive him to the hospital.

He shifted in bed and settled his feet against the cool of the hardwood floor, which grounded him somewhat. Eddie made sure to step carefully, as if She could be listening from directly outside the door, and he didn't allow himself a full and satisfying breath until he was safely positioned on the window seat looking into the backyard.

Outside was a still and empty snapshot of snow. The oak tree growing for as long as he'd been sentient was stricken of leaves and wrapped in a loose shawl of white. Things grew in Shreveport throughout the year, but on vacant winter nights like this, it would be easy to think no life could ever have a chance of surviving.

What he found himself waiting for, objectively, should've had no way of happening. And yet it wasn't long before it did, as it had every year before. It came with a flutter, a tremble, and suddenly there was a bird on the tip of the branch closest to the windowpane. It was a small, fat thing colored in shades of brown, with a tuft of feathers atop its head. As soon as he saw it, Eddie felt his jaw relax and his shoulders loosen.

A small smile touched his face. He was so tired.

Eddie settled his face against the glass, moving slowly so as not to frighten off the small creature watching him. As he did whenever they met, he quietly wished he could find a way to bring the bird inside where they could keep each other company all the time. But he knew, as a child in an environment like this, he was unable to provide a home suitable for a being that special.

It was much better to be grateful for what he could get.

"Hi, Lark," he whispered.

The bird stared back. His little head cocked to the side.

"It's my birthday today," Eddie continued, the only time he will say this with any element of pride or pleasure.

The bird hopped a little closer to the window. The gesture was knowing – almost human – and as soon as Eddie let that thought in it was like trying to toss an egg through a brick wall. Because there was

something else

wasn't there?

In his mind he felt a sweltering heat that made his bones bead with condensation. Eddie had a distant memory of dark metal webs rimmed with faint, oceanic light. He clenched his jaw to swallow back the feeling of missing something very important. It looked so cold out tonight. Eddie hoped that his layer of feathers
would be enough to keep the bird warm.

Warmth. Eddie hugged his hands around his bare and shivering arms and rubbed them back and forth, wincing softly as he touched the sore spots.

Another year. Another year, likely just an extension of the one before. A continuing seep of something poisonous and radioactive that only he could feel.

But now was not the time to think about that, because Lark was here. Eddie turned back to his dearest friend and smiled apologetically. The gesture of perceived goodwill cracked, bit by bit, before it fell completely and left him far more tired than he was before.

Eddie sighed. He ached then, near-madly, for something soft and comforting. But that just wouldn't happen.

"This used to be different," he whispered, "didn't it?"

Outside the snow picked up, a billion minuscule ghosts drifting from the sky. The bird would stay there long after Eddie curled up on the window seat and went back to sleep.

When the boy would wake up a few hours later, in a room stark with cold daylight and obligation, he
would be alone.

First Movement

The new chef at the Fairy's Den was absolutely ruining the jambalaya.

Edgar knew it, but he kept silent for a variety of reasons. For the most part he wanted to stay clear of the ire most chefs were capable of when faced with even a critique-shaped observation. He was also pretty curious to see how the situation would progress unimpeded. Would this paid professional figure out what Edgar learned in the first week of his high school culinary course? Or would he ultimately blame someone completely unrelated to the issue?

He stayed back and watched as the new lead of the kitchen and the Den's long-time sous chef argued over a bubbling cauldron of disappointment and what now had to be overcooked rice.

"Your broth is off, dumbshit," the head chef said to the sous chef, who definitely knew the jambalaya was made from a boxed broth base. "It's not thickening. I don't know what you did wrong."

Cornstarch, Edgar thought to himself.

"I can get another box from the basement," the sous chef offered wearily. "We can start over."

You wouldn't have to if you added even just a tablespoon more of cornstarch and water.

Edgar reran a load of clean dishes through the sanitizer to buy himself some more time to watch this trainwreck. Michael, the owner, seemed very pleased with his choice of the new head chef – even using that semi-bragging tone of voice when describing the man's training and expertise in Cajun cooking. As soon as he heard that, Edgar had a feeling that the new boss of the kitchen was exaggerating his achievements in the way culinary people do when trying to get jobs from people unfamiliar with the industry.

And while he wouldn't consider himself to be *friends* with the sous chef, they were amicable enough for him to be certain that she knew how to handle a majority of the menu on her own. That's exactly what she was doing after the last head chef left, and while it did no favors to her mental health, at least the food was good. Though she was no longer doing two jobs for one wage, she now had to physically stifle her knowledge to appease the ego of a Cajun cook unable to grasp the basics of Cajun cooking.

The sous chef glanced in Edgar's direction. He cringed and quickly looked away.

"New guy seems fun."

He snapped out of his daze and looked over at Katy Delaney through the order window. She flashed him a smirk as she buttoned up the blouse of the awful, professionally-seductive uniform that the Fairy's Den assigned to their staff of mostly young women.

In clubs and themed restaurants across New Orleans, it was commonplace for the server to be some college girl dressed almost too provocatively to comfortably serve food. Edgar appreciated that the Den had slightly more dignity than most other establishments in the area. Still, it was rough to look at.

Katy was around his age, slightly older than the other servers. He worried about her less than he did the others, as she was capable of defending herself and any of the other servers that may need it. If someone got drunk and stupid enough to forget the city's unwritten rule of "look, but don't touch", she did not hesitate to grab even the toughest-looking customer by the collar and practically throw him out the door.

Edgar's seen it happen before. Given his inability to properly measure his drinks, no matter how often he studied the recipes, he'd gotten people drunk enough for it to happen on a pretty regular basis.

He watched silently as she split her honey blonde hair into pigtails. *Ugh.*

"Don't make that face," she said. "I need the tips."

"Does that really work?" Edgar asked.

Katy considered her reflection in the metal of the counter and touched up her lipstick. "All it costs is my dignity. But as long as I can pay for Wilford's special food then it's worth it."

Edgar remembered Wilford, that ratty Persian cat that Katy obsessed over. He always knew Persians to be graceful, regal felines, but this loose sack of fur and bones looked more like something you'd pull out of your dryer vents before dry heaving and immediately washing your hands.

Katy loved Wilford in a way that she once described as *maternal*, which certainly gave Edgar conflicting feelings about his own upbringing.

The sanitizer trilled to signify the end of its run, but Edgar didn't move. He was lost in thought, his mind pulling him in two different directions.

"Eddie," Katy chided in a sing-song voice. "You aren't allowed to judge the cooks until you finish your prep work, you know that."

"I *am* prepping," Edgar insisted, still not moving. "I'm doing dishes."

He said all that, hoping she would take him at his word and move on with getting ready for her own shift. Of course, this strategy only worked about a third of the time, and this particular moment was not one of those occasions. Katy crossed to the double doors and pushed her way into the back of house, coming to examine what Edgar ended up with after forty minutes at the dish pit.

Edgar started to bow his head like he was taught to do in the presence of authority. Then he cringed again, threw a few insults at himself, and forced his line of sight to be level and upright.

Katy whistled low and nodded. "This must be twenty – maybe even *twenty-five forks.* Do you think we have enough people on staff to handle that kind of business?"

Edgar wanted to volley back the comment and found that he had nothing clever to defend himself with. He tried to fill the silence with anything when the sous chef approached. She muttered a weak "behind" as she passed them, disappearing down the hall towards the basement

stairs.

He caught a glimpse of her just as she rubbed the ball of her hand across her damp, defeated eyes. His chest tightened briefly in a way that he didn't know what to do with, but luckily went away almost as soon as he noticed it.

"Katy," he said. "You know about cornstarch, right?"

She didn't answer. Edgar assumed he was not being specific enough.

"Like – do you know how to use cornstarch?"

"You need to get laid, Ed," Katy said. "Or – pick up a new hobby, maybe. Something that isn't – whatever you'd call what you're doing right now."

She stepped back past the doors and towards where the staff kept bins of rolled up silverware. Edgar knew he could very well leave the conversation at that. Despite that, he followed close behind her, speaking in that half-whisper used exclusively for complaining under the guise of tact.

"It just makes *no sense* to me that they would..." he scoffed, then quickly lowered his voice. "I mean, this is food we'll be serving to people who have *never* been here, and if they eat...I mean, would *you* come back here? *I* wouldn't."

Katy hummed softly, stacking two bins of roll-ups on one arm and a few serving trays on the other. He continued to follow her to her section, leaving both hands free to gesticulate his outrage.

"Michael bought this historic building downtown, spent all this money revamping and remodeling it, and now he's calling people from *all* across the land to come down for *mediocre* jazz and *soupy jambalaya?"*

He scoffed again as he watched Katy start to light the candles on each table.

"I mean, is it so hard to staff a place like this with qualified people?" Edgar said, posing a mostly-rhetorical question.

"I don't know," Katy responded, unaffected by his ranting. "If they did you'd be out of a job."

"What's that supposed to mean?"

She stopped and straightened up, casting him that *big sister* look that she only gave when she was about to say something undeniably combative.

"That new guy isn't a good cook," Katy agreed. "But *you* aren't a good bartender."

Edgar felt his face flush with a weird, defensive, embarrassed outrage. "I am a - *fine* bartender," he said, stiffly.

"You muddle your cocktails with a fork."

"Yes, Katherine. To break out the juices."

"It bruises your mint leaves. That's why all your mojitos taste like rusty toothpaste."

He still attempted a cool and unaffected demeanor, but now found himself completely unable to meet Katy's eyes. "Well, what *else* am I supposed to muddle stuff with, if not a fork?"

She furrowed her brow. "It's called *muddling* because you use a..." Suddenly the neutrality in her eyes flickered. "Do you know what a muddler is, Edgar?"

"Of course I do," he said immediately.

Don't ask me to elaborate, he mentally pleaded. *Please don't push for more details. I cheated on my ABO training exam to get this job and still somehow got two questions wrong.*

Katy looked him up and down, from his unbrushed, rusted curls to the slip-proof shoes that he *may or may not* have stolen from the lost and found. She gave him the kind of look that suggested that she knew he didn't drink nearly enough water today and had no intentions of starting now. Katy believed in taking care of herself, doing things like *applying scented lotions* or *washing her face with more things than water.* A person like that must see someone like Edgar as a large collection of red flags in the shape tossed loosely into the shape of a thirtysomething "Independent Adult".

She reached out a hand and rustled his hair, "You need a haircut," she observed.

And just like that, Edgar Gallows was once again right on the money.

It was a Thursday night at the Fairy's Den, so not much was expected to happen. The Jail Birds, the restaurant's mediocre house band, would don their striped prison costumes and play the same set-list they played every show. Edgar would nurse a headache and try not to look too outwardly disgusted as he listed the same three points of interest to tourists who claim to want to "see the city", and yet still spend their time in an establishment like this one.

Edgar wouldn't consider himself a cynic. He was sure his view on humanity would be a lot sunnier if he didn't work a customer-facing job. Especially one with nearly no repeat customers, which meant constant conversations with customers too new to realize how bad Edgar was at bartender small talk.

It was hard not to ignore Katy's observation while he was doing "prep work" at the bar, which was his personal industry speak for biding time and looking productive until someone decided they were ready for a mid-tier night on the town. He cut lemons. He cut limes. He cut them in a variety of shapes, none of which looked totally right at this point.

No. He would not let himself fall into a crisis of ego at the shove of someone regularly dressed like a magician's assistant.

In an attempt to correct – to over correct, even – Edgar decided to focus every ounce of attention and motivation on finding the exact right place to put the bucket where he threw his dirty rags throughout the night.

"Hey Gallows," Jess – Katy's favorite server – called out, leaning up against the bar and lowering her voice down to a conspiratorial hush. "Do you have any idea where tonight's musician is going to be sitting after the show?"

Edgar raised his brow, still anxiously shifting the bucket from near the sink to by the Red Bull fridge. "I don't know, Jess. I thought they usually relegated themselves to the green room between sets. You know, where people can't hear their opinions."

"The Jail Birds aren't playing tonight."

What a dumb thing for one human being to say to another human being. What a tragedy that it was the exact type of statement that fit perfectly within the context of Edgar's life.

He shifted his eyes to her and saw Jess fully relaxed, one hand supporting her head and a dreamy
smile on her face. This, he realized, was the first time he had seen her authentically smiling.

She noticed him staring and either didn't notice his reaction or didn't care. She just broadened her grin.

"I met him upstairs after clocking in," she said. "He said he's passing through town and Michael offered to give him a venue to play in for the night."

"That...doesn't sound right," Edgar stated bluntly.

Once again, Jess ignored him. "He's a pianist. I asked if he knew any Philip Glass and he said he'd play something from *Metamorphosis* just for me. Isn't that just...?"

Jess left her question hanging in the dusty air and then punctuated her nothing with a soft sigh. By this point Edgar was absolutely certain that something here was very, *very* wrong.

Michael Sinclair, as a business owner, believed in finding what the best clientele wanted and catering to them exclusively. He knew the tourist culture of New Orleans better than anyone Edgar ever worked for, so there's no way he would attempt to pair their overpriced cocktails with surreal, minimally-composed piano pieces – even just for one night. It just wouldn't happen. The people that came to the Den wanted cookie cutter, "Authentic" culture, which usually didn't go much farther than frozen beignets and songs that tell you what type of train you should take.

Hint: it's the A one. It's always the fucking A-Train.

What was even weirder than all that was the way Jess in specific was reacting to this strange new musician. She was very open to anyone who asked how she never really felt anything in terms of romantic or sexual attraction, throwing around a bunch of labels Edgar was too afraid to admit to never having heard before. Jess also had a husband, and was quick to say that her self-described *marriage of convenience* only had room for two.

To put it plainly, there was absolutely no reason for her to be literally drooling over this man the way she was. She was so deeply infatuated that she didn't notice as Edgar got closer and reached out a hand.

"I'm going to touch your face," he said.

"Hm?" Jess let out a small laugh. "Okay, sure. Whatever."

He hesitated for a moment longer, and then touched her chin and tilted her head up for him to get a better look. She didn't look sick. There were no obvious marks on either side of her neck. He was about to give up entirely when he became aware of something new happening in her eyes. The thought was vague, as if obscured by fog, and it was hard to grab hold of it for long. But when he focused hard he could see that the near-black of her eyes were vibrant with a dark blue glow.

Edgar pulled his hand away in a sharp recoil. He looked around the room, the hairs on the back of his neck stiff and buzzing with paranoia. People were starting to trickle in for the night. There were so many potential points of entry, so many corners just perfect for hiding in.

If Edgar knew that this was the type of thing he would have to deal with today, he would've eaten breakfast.

What could he use? There was his paring knife, obviously, but the angle might be wrong. A straw from the container on the counter might work. Maybe even a beer bottle if he held it in the right way, though depending on the situation it ran the risk of shattering entirely in his hand.

He kept Jess talking while he looked. "Uh – what'd he look like?" He said, feigning playful curiosity to feed into her delusion. "Probably handsome, right?"

"*So* handsome," Jess purred.

"Cool. Great. Elaborate?"

She opened her mouth to speak and suddenly paused. Her brow furrowed, and then she laughed.

"What is it?" Edgar said, growing increasingly concerned.

"It's so weird. I – I can't really picture his face," her expression was lucid for only a second before slipping back into a lovesick reverie. "It's his eyes, though, they're so...*blue*. Bluer than anything I've ever seen before," she was able to focus on Edgar long enough to notice something about the man. "He's got the same thing you do, I think. His pupils are all, uh..."

"He's got a coloboma," Edgar confirmed dully.

Jess perked up, then melted back almost immediately. "Right! That's what he called it! He told me it has something to do with, uh – magic. Or something," she lowered her voice into a playful mutter. "And I was like, '*you're magic*'. I don't remember what he said after that, but...*mm*."

She trailed off, staring wistfully off at the middle distance, just completely enraptured. Edgar clenched his jaw and tapped his fingers against the leg of his pants, debating what exactly he was supposed to do now. When he left Shreveport, he assumed he was separating himself from magic for the rest of his life. There was an Academy in the business district in New Orleans, but it wasn't a university and he knew they had little interest in Edgar as long as he didn't try and register in their system or access their resources.

The last thing he expected was for a genetic witch to breeze through town with some sort of *intention*. Because that's the root of all magic, isn't it? Intention. And he knew it was a bias, he *knew* it was one of the only remnants of his mother's control that he was still unable to shake off, but he did *not* trust genetic witches.

There used to be more of them, according to the research he'd done when she wasn't there to watch him. In more modern generations their population has dwindled significantly, and there were now only a handful of colonies across the United States, and even fewer established witch towns. There were some more alternative members of the Academy in Shreveport that had tried to get Edgar to visit a witch town when he was younger, but every time the subject was brought up, his mother would immediately shoot it down.

She would vent to the older members about the new indoctrination tactics of keyholes. That's what the more traditional Academic witches called their genetic counterparts, and it was always said with some measure of disgust or pity.

Keyholes. Edgar absorbed it as a child before he really understood the connotations, and once he connected the dots
he would sometimes repeat it to himself while he tried to sleep at night. Or when he cowered in a corner after ruining an incantation. Or even just as he brushed his teeth and stared reluctantly into his own reflection.

And still, years later, the word flashed into his mind. *Keyhole.*

He felt a rippling, sparking burn at the base of his neck. Not a new feeling, though it was unpleasant nonetheless.

"Uh, I have to go in the walk-in," Edgar said a little louder than he needed to convince someone not paying attention. "I have – my limes. I cut all my limes. I need more limes... that are not cut."

Edgar paused for a moment, checking to see if his terrible excuse would pass without protest. It was immediately clear that it would, and he nodded to no one and slipped to the back of house.

All of Edgar's jobs so far have been in restaurants, and up until now he spent most of his time in the cluttered underbelly, washing dishes or prepping meat and produce. It was exhausting work, incredibly over-stimulating, and at any point there was a chance someone would yell at

you for reasons downright incomprehensible. Still, it was ideal
work for him.

He could never do what Katy did. From the bar he would watch her
go from table to table with a carefully-composed smile, making minute
adjustments to suit the energy of each individual party. She understood
people, the menu, and had beyond a basic grasp of the restaurant's
point-of service system. The fact that so much knowledge could be contained in the body of one person was beyond reason.

No, Edgar Gallows was built for the kitchen. He knew it, the scars
and burns accumulated across his hands and arms echoed the fact. He
had no inherent worth here, but every night when he got home with
his leftovers nabbed from off the line, he proved to himself what he was
capable of creating. Unfortunately, to progress in his career, he needed
professional experience that he did not have. And in the meantime, he
still needed money. Bartenders make better tips, anyways.

In theory, at least.

It was easy for him to navigate the weird corners of the kitchen and
find his way to the walk-in without running into any of the cooks. He
knew he could only hide for so long before some patron lost patience
with their own sobriety. Still, if he could take ten minutes in a quiet
space by himself, he could formulate a plan to grab Katy and get out of
there as quickly as possible.

Edgar ducked inside the walk-in and allowed himself just a moment
to enjoy the quiet. He leaned slightly against the door and took a deep
breath, shaking his hands as he exhaled in an attempt to gather his
nerves. Slowly, his heart rate calmed and the burning at his neck lessened. Edgar relaxed slightly and, finally, opened his eyes.

He immediately let out a startled yelp, one that escaped in a register
he did not know he was capable of making. It was embarrassing, especially since he now knew that he was not alone. There was a figure in a
green tweed suit sitting limply on the floor, his back up against a stack
of produce boxes. He was loose and awkward in the way that a child
might be when you've neglected to give them something to do but still

insist they go off on their own. His head was lowered slightly, and Edgar couldn't quite make out his face through the veil of long and tangled black hair that covered it.

When Edgar made his stupid squeaking gasp the man looked equally as startled, and he scrambled to his feet in a way intentional enough to keep his face out of view.

"Sorry," the man murmured, turning to look anywhere but directly at Edgar. "I didn't mean to bother anyone. I was just looking for some quiet."

"You aren't supposed to be in here," Edgar said, one hand still clutching the inner knob of the door and the other palming for a tool he did not have.

"I know – actually, I guess I didn't, but I assumed. I..." the man twisted a lock of hair in between his fingers in a way that made it immediately clear where the tangles came from. "Listen, I have a soundcheck in about an hour. Can't I just stay here? I saw your shift board of how many people are on staff tonight and I..." He grimaced and did the closest thing to facing Edgar without actually looking at him. "Please?"

He fidgeted in place, and Edgar took the silence that followed as an opportunity to give this man the once over. His suit, while nice at first glance, was ill-fitting if you looked at it closely, and thoroughly out of style. He had the hair of someone with a first-draft manifesto, and while his shoes looked fine at first, Edgar was almost certain they had Velcro straps.

Is the biggest threat of my life really a man who doesn't know how to tie his own shoes?

What was closest to him? He took a quick look around the space while the man in the suit shifted from side to side. There was a box of carrots, but Edgar would have to get closer to access them.

What else? A dry erase marker just out of arm's reach. A broom that would maybe work, but likely prove too unwieldy.

Think, Eddie, his mind reeled. *You have to think of something.*

The man stifled a yawn into his fist. "'S okay, I get it," he mumbled. "I don't want to get you in trouble."

"Show me your face," Edgar demanded, hesitantly.

"I'll just be outside on the loading dock when Mister Sinclair gets here. Sorry."

He took a single step to the side, and without missing a beat, Edgar grabbed a baguette of bread from the box on the top shelf. It was high enough to send a shiver of pain down through his bad shoulder, but he didn't let that stop him as he stepped forward and jutted it harshly in the man's direction. His lips opened and he released an incantation. It was a rush of sound, speech without a discernible language.

It still came out of him so easily. As if no time had passed since the night he left home.

The effect was a force that grabbed the man's hair and yanked, forcing his head up to look Edgar face to face. He did so with a wince and whimper that was soft, yet audible enough to cause Edgar to drop his bread and take a flinching step backwards.

Edgar felt his mind fracture in a moment of fear and confusion. There was a voice speaking that sounded like him, yet felt long unfamiliar.

It's *him*. He's here and you hurt him.

Why would you ever choose to hurt him?

I don't understand you.

Edgar rubbed at his eyes like it could somehow silence the strange intrusive thoughts. It helped a little bit. He blinked at his feet until his vision refocused.

The man in the suit was perfectly average looking. He didn't look like a supermodel, or a hippie elf, or anyway else Edgar might've expected based on how other people described genetic witches. He looked pretty much normal - although clearly pretty haggard. He was both sunburned, dark-skinned, and somewhat gray with pallor. The man was short like Edgar – maybe even slightly shorter. And much like Jess described, he had large eyes hued a deep navy blue that glowed noticeably.

Even from a distance Edgar could see the coloboma. Each pupil dragged down, almost as if seeking something impossible to fully grasp.

The man's eyes were just like his, and as he saw them Edgar tried to ignore the sensation of some long-abandoned part of him absolutely screaming for attention.

Time crawled to a standstill as the two stared at each other, wide-eyed and unblinking. Edgar waited for the thrall to wrack through him.

He knew what it felt like to have someone reach inside your brain and manipulate the folds like keys on a piano. Doing so with magic would be new, but still – it should be easy for someone like him.

Edgar waited, and yet nothing happened. The man did not hurt him. The man didn't even try to move. He just looked at him.

After about a minute he finally blinked a few times, which drew attention to the fact that he hadn't closed his eyes up until that moment. He lowered his gaze and let out a shuddering breath, then hesitantly darted his eyes back up to Edgar.

He stared at him like he was waiting for something to happen. When it apparently didn't, he smiled. His eyes welled up with tears and Edgar felt more compelled to run away than ever.

But he didn't. He stood his ground, staring down the man to keep him contained through the will of his own eye contact.

"Who are you?" Edgar said.

The man's smile widened for a moment before being forcibly restrained. He wiped a visibly shaking palm across his eyes and faced Edgar again with a bit more cheer.

"Hi," he said. "I'm – I'm Scott. It's...*so good* to meet you."

Scott held out a hand in his direction. Edgar stared down at it, and then up at him, and eventually Scott pulled back and huffed a small and nervous laugh through his nose.

"You're a witch," Edgar stated.

"I – I am. I am!" Scott motioned towards him, perhaps without realizing. "And so are you, right? Dual wielding, even."

"What?"

"My sister isn't technically Academic, but she's self-taught. So I've seen my fair share of wand stand-ins," Scott tapped the pads of his fingers together, one after the other. "Not like what you just did. It's really - I mean - *wow.* You're impressive," he flashed Edgar an unnervingly easy smile. "You must be very strong."

In an instant Edgar felt prouder than he had ever felt in his entire life, followed by a wave of shame so intense it practically made his knees buckle. He quickly lowered his head, and then shifted his entire body so that he was fully faced away from Scott. Because this was just too weird. What was he supposed to do in a situation like this? To say it was out of his pay grade implied that there was some higher force stupid enough to grant him a wage.

With that thought in mind, Edgar pushed open the walk-in door and escaped back into the kitchen.

"Wait wait wait *wait*," Scott whispered sharply, following directly behind him with almost imperceptible steps. "I want to talk to you. Can we talk? I'd love to –"

"Leave me alone," Edgar said, his tone more pleading than demanding.

"But -"

"Gallows!"

That voice could freeze Edgar in his tracks quicker and more effectively than any incantation. He stopped immediately, hands clenching, jaw clenching – just generally tightening himself into something small and ready for conflict.

For a moment he forgot the presence of Scott the Weird Sad Wizard Lunatic, because Ian the Floor Manager was standing near the dish pit with a look in his eyes that could melt steel.

"Uh, hey, Ian," Edgar said, head slightly bowed. "Is everything okay?"

"You wanna' tell me what I'm looking at here, Eddie?"

There was no good answer here. Dishes. Sanitation equipment. The residual effect of being raised by an abusive narcissist. *Help.*

Ian pointed at one of the vats of liquid hanging by the sanitizer.

"You changed the cleaner last night, right?" He asked with the soothing

hum of an enraged rattlesnake.

"I...I..."

"You hooked it up to the Wash 'n Walk. Luckily I caught it before anyone else got here. Did *you* notice, Eddie?"

Edgar's head dipped even lower, and he felt his face flush red and hot.

"It's an easy mistake, I guess," Ian continued. "It's only a different shape, size, and color liquid than the actual fucking sanitizer – I mean, are you kidding, Edgar? Are you a fucking child? Or do you think Chef Louis' food could use a little more chemical poisoning?" Ian laughed like acid. "It baffles me how you can be here for almost *three years* and still be..."

His voice cut off suddenly. Not trailed off like he lost himself in his own rage, but as if something reached into his throat and pulled it out with their bare hands. And then there was only silence. The current of Ian's breathing slowly calming. Edgar reluctantly raised his head, already planning on how he could revise his resume.

That didn't seem to be where this was going, because when Edgar looked ahead of him Ian wasn't vivisecting him with his eyes as he usually did. No, his boss instead had all his stunned attention focused on Scott, who stood beside him, his hands clasped tightly around Ian's.

"Don't," Scott simply said.

Ian Markov was a massive, beefed out maniac who had been known for destroying his employees so thoroughly that they not only left the hospitality industry, but moved town entirely. If he wanted to, he could grab Scott by the scruff of the neck and punt him like a tweed football. As far as Edgar knew, he was not outwardly homophobic – but if you trusted stereotypes, he definitely *could* be. For another man to touch him so tenderly before even introducing himself - that alone was so bold that it circled back around into stupid and dangerous.

"You're being mean to Eddie over nothing and it is unacceptable," Scott's tone had a numb calm to it that barely masked a deep well of strange rage. "He is a human being and you are a human being – so start acting like one."

By this point Edgar's mouth was agape in shock. Maybe he wouldn't have to do anything about this keyhole, because by now there appeared to be no other outcome than for Ian to murder Scott in cold blood.

Ian pressed his lips tight like wanted to protest. But then he just sighed.

"You're right," he said.

Wait. What?

His floor manager softened – visibly *softened* – and even moved closer towards Scott's touch. After some shy hesitation the man raised their clasped hands with inexplicable familiarity and grazed his thumb across the ridges of Scott's knuckles.

"My hands must feel pretty rough compared to yours," Ian remarked with a voice like a nice pillow.

Scott's face immediately went cold. Every outlet for expression fell slack aside from his eyes, which still radiated something tumultuous and overwhelmed.

"You're – fine," his eyes went to Edgar's, almost apologetic. "Now say you're sorry."

Edgar stiffened and waited for the vitriol, the immediate pounce and the tear of teeth against his jugular. Instead, Ian pulled away from Scott (who seemed immediately relieved) and faced him with genuine humility.

"I'm sorry, Edgar," he said. "Things have just been tense lately. We're really understaffed since you switched to the bar and Michael is being slow on letting me hire new people. I'm stressed. But I shouldn't have taken it out on you."

His manager's eyes were glowing with a faint blue residue. Ian's smile was faint – almost hopeful. This, in a very real way, was more upsetting than being yelled at. Still, Edgar cleared his throat and managed a nod.

"Sure," he said. "I get it. No - no hard feelings, I guess."

Ian seemed pleased by this answer. He looked back at Scott, clearly searching for approval, and Scott granted him a weak thumbs up.

"You're the musician playing tonight, right?" Ian asked, by now having entirely forgotten about Edgar's presence.

Scott didn't respond. He said nothing and remained perfectly still. He just stared at Ian with his unblinking doe eyes, and apparently that was enough to constitute a full conversation.

"Michael wouldn't stop raving about you this morning," Ian chuckled gruffly. "I thought it was weird, but – I get it now."

Edgar noticed Scott begin to waver slightly. Something was off. There was an energy radiating from this man that made the air around him feel thicker and heavier in a way that only Edgar bothered noticing.

Ian, suddenly unable to read even a fraction of the room, stepped forward and cupped a hand around Scott's waist. He pulled him closer, very slightly, but with an implication of only using a fraction of the force he was capable of.

"Maybe I'll just have to swoop you up myself before he gets a chance," he purred.

As soon as he said that Scott tore himself away from Ian, staggered over, and threw up into the sink. He retched until the only thing that came out was a long series of disjointed, low screams. The screams turned into a few sobs that wracked across his entire body. Then he just tried to steady his breathing.

Edgar looked at Ian, who wasn't reacting to any of this. Instead he just peacefully excused himself to go back to his office. Even once it was just the two of them Edgar still stayed where he was, staring at Scott in frozen panic. He waited as Scott gradually composed himself for a moment before breaking down again in another round of weeping. Then he adjusted his position and tried to gather his senses again.

He ran the tap to wash down his own sick, and after that he stood up straighter and tried to fix his hair. Once it was done to his liking, he faced Edgar again like none of that had just happened, even though his eyes were bloodshot and his
face flushed.

"That should work for a bit," he said, smiling weakly.

Move on. You can just move on. This really has nothing to do with you.

"What the fuck was that?" Edgar whispered.

"What do you mean? You have the same variant I have, I'm sure you know what -"

Edgar moved closer. "No. You just had a full-on *mental break-down* in the span of two minutes. What the fuck was *that*?"

Scott observed the distance between them and seemed confused by it. He twisted his hair.

"You saw that?" He smiled, regretted it instantly, and dropped it just as quickly. "People – People usually don't..."

Scott trailed off, but his lips still moved. He was talking to someone, or something – just not Edgar. And once again he could hear his mother's voice echo in the back of his mind. Keyholes are unstable. They're reflections of human beings with a power far greater than they're capable of understanding.

Keyholes are dangerous and should never, ever be trusted.

When Scott's eyes finally met his again, Edgar could see that he was afraid. He knew then that this odd, small, exhausted figure was just as scared and confused about all this as Edgar was.

Just let it go, Edgar, his mother's voice demanded from deep within him.

"Follow me," Edgar said.

New Orleans had a lot of old buildings - buildings that, in all honesty, had no business still containing people. A lot of them end up avoiding being torn down for historical reasons, until they're eventually more termite than drywall. In many cases the vintage architecture is adjusted slightly to fit modern needs. This commonly results in a few odd corners, some vestigial space left behind by time and ill-planned renovations.

For the Fairy's Den, on Royal Street and Bienville, that time capsule is what Edgar privately referred to as the *Weird Closet*.

The Weird Closet might not actually be a closet. It was a little too long – not long enough to classify as a hallway, though – and there was a door on either end that allowed someone to enter through the break-room and exit, for some reason, into the supply closet of the men's bathroom. But the first time Edgar stumbled upon the space he found an ancient, dust-covered mop abandoned on the floor, and since he was in the middle of a panic attack his brain just short of shouted the word CLOSET and cemented the observation in his mind forever.

"I've been meaning to bring a chair in here at some point," he idly remarked as he opened the door from the break room. "But I haven't, so -"

"This is fine, thanks," Scott mumbled, already striding to the end of the room sinking down to
the floor.

"There are – I mean this place is *full* of spiders."

"Thank you."

Scott sat, slumped up against the wall, one knee pulled up to his chest and the other leg splayed awkwardly in a position Edgar could not fathom being comfortable. Slowly, he watched the other man's vision lose focus. Not in any magical way, it was just as if he loosened his grip on the present moment and allowed it to drift lazily through his fingers.

There was a very real thought in his mind that Edgar would probably regret this, but that wasn't enough to keep him from sitting down beside Scott.

"Does this kind of thing happen to you a lot?" He asked.

Scott's attention was called back to him. He clenched his eyes shut, looked over at Edgar as if only now remembering he was there, and smiled as genuinely as one could through a thick veil of pain.

"Uh, it didn't used to," Scott sounded remarkably cheerful for looking like he was about to pass out. "I've found in the past few months that my abilities seem to be getting stronger, but – um – worse."

Edgar nodded and swallowed hard. "And the screaming?" He said.

"The screaming helps. Usually everyone's so wrapped up in my ability that they don't care, but..." He tapped the fingers of one hand against his knee, thinking. "But it's okay! I can still only affect people for a few hours," he said, but his good nature wasn't enough to fully mask a grimace. "I'm not sure how long the charm lasts these days. It shouldn't be too long. I promise no one who's met me tonight will remember me by the morning."

Magic is hard to detect unless you have a particular eye for the luminescent, oily residue it leaves behind. Edgar had enough education that, if he focused hard, he could spot that brand of manipulation when he felt it. The sheen that lingers after matter is shifted. The ripples from someone twisting the reality of another human being.

He did not feel any of that from Scott – not pointed in his direction, at least. That seemed to baffle the both of them. But if he left work today and woke up tomorrow with no memory of what was unfolding right now? That was hard to think about. That was oddly painful to think about. Edgar didn't know why. He didn't really want to question it. So he decided that he wouldn't.

"You have a weird name," He remarked instead, taking one finger to scrape the paint off the tile flooring beneath them.

"I feel like I've met a lot of Scotts over the past few years."

"Makes sense. I mean, it's an absurdly normal guy name. So it's just weird – I've never met another..." Edgar clenched his jaw for a flash and quickly rephrased himself. "I've never met a *genetic witch* before, but I always imagined they'd have some kind of weird, hippy sort of name."

Scott took that in very deeply and focused his gaze on the space ahead of them. But he didn't answer at first.

"That's probably rude to say," Edgar continued. "I don't mean to pry."

"My middle name is Skylark," Scott said in a soft voice. "Scott Skylark Kaufner."

Edgar frowned, his chest tightening. It was reflexive and stupid, but he couldn't keep it from happening.

"You shouldn't do that, you know."

Scott looked at him. "Do what?"

"You know I'm a magic user. You just told me that you think I must be powerful."

"Strong," Scott quickly corrected him. "I said you're *strong*."

"So you realize that knowing your full name is enough information for me to seriously hurt you."

He felt a new flush of sensation and looked down to see that Scott had taken this moment of absent skulking as an opportunity to hold his hand. In one instant he was warmed by inexplicable, bunny-soft wonder. Before he had time to dissect that reaction, Scott wrapped both his hands around Edgar's and clutched it to his chest, staring him down with his blue eyes burning deliriously.

"Then hurt me, Eddie," he said in a low, calm voice. "Hurt me terribly."

"W-What?"

"There's a ballpoint pen in my blazer pocket. Reach in and get it, and use it to command me to take the bottle of pentobarbital I've been keeping in my duffle bag."

Panic swelled through Edgar like a rolling electric current. Something in his mind screamed and begged to avoid a pull he could imagine tearing him into desperate shreds.

But nothing happened. He still felt like himself.

Immediately he tore his hand away from Scott's grip. "What the fuck are you doing?" Edgar said.

Scott paused for a few moments of shock before he closed his eyes and began to laugh. And it was a nice sound, but entirely wrong, with a joy to it that came off as septic.

"It didn't work," he kept saying, maybe to Edgar, maybe just to himself. "I can't control you."

"Listen, I don't know what the hell you were trying to do -"

"I can look at you," Scott whispered.

"You don't," Edgar attempted, "You can't just -"

Scott laughed dreamily. "I can *see* you."

He brushed the hair from his eyes and looked up at Edgar, making no attempt to wipe the tears openly streaming down his cheeks. Edgar wanted to run, but he didn't. Without knowing why he instinctively allowed himself to be observed with the same focus that Katy so often gave him, only in an entirely new direction.

What could Scott be looking at so closely? Edgar thought about his patchy semi-stubble that not even trendy expensive razors could fully get rid of. He considered the notch on the bridge of his nose and the scar above his eyebrow from a fall as a child. His shirt was stained from wearing it the shift before and putting off doing laundry. He probably smelled like absinthe and stale fruit juice.

It wouldn't have killed him to brush his hair this morning.

"You are *so pretty*, Eddie," Scott said with adoration.

Edgar blushed. Except it wasn't a blush, it was something else. Something that felt and looked like a blush, but was a different thing entirely. And he started to respond when there was a knock from outside in the break room.

"Eddie, I support you," Katy called out. "You can come out of the closet."

He rolled his eyes and quickly opened the door. Katy was standing there, twirling her vape between her fingers like people used to do with coins. She seemed especially nonchalant, though by the brief moments of worry evident on the outskirts of each glance, he could tell she heard what happened in the kitchen moments ago.

"I heard Ian use his big boy voice just now," she said. "Figured you might've come in here to...I don't know. *Re-calibrate*."

The word *pretty* still reverberated throughout Edgar's entire body in a way that made it incredibly difficult to hold a conversation.

"It sucks the way he talks to you. Are you-?"

Pretty? Absolutely not.

Maybe he had some kind of roguish, scruffy thing going on that certain women in the past had presumably found appealing for a brief period of time. He definitely had a charm, sure – most people have *some kind of* charm to them – but *pretty*?

Flowers are pretty. Old boats are pretty.

Was Edgar Gallows pretty?

Stop. No. Next question.

"I'm fine," Edgar insisted absently. "I actually just ran into tonight's musician, and..."

"You killed him," Katy said, looking over his shoulder.

Edgar looked behind him and saw Scott sprawled out and fully unconscious against the dirty floor. He gasped the first half of some kind of profanity and immediately went to his side

"What the hell happened, Edgar?" Katy asked from the doorway.

"It's – fuck," Edgar pulled him up into a seated position and stifled another yelp as Scott immediately slumped into his arms. "I think it's psychic fatigue or something. He's a magic user – Katy, help me pull him up, you're stronger than I am."

She took his other arm around her shoulder and got him onto his feet with virtually no problem. "He's a witch?" She asked. "He's like you?"

Yes.

"No," Edgar said. "I mean – kind of. It's – just help me get him to my car."

"To..." Katy's expression simmered into the dimly-worried outskirts of suspicion. "To do what?"

That was a very good question.

"He needs..." That was a *very* good question, Edgar had to admit, "he needs to rest someplace quiet. And it has to be private, because I think he's got some kind of charm effect that I don't think he can con-trol –"

"You don't seem charmed," Katy said. "You mostly look...confused. And maybe upset."

Edgar adjusted his posture in a feeble attempt to appear more in con-trol of the situation. "He can do things when you look at him, Katy. *In-fatuation*-type things, I think. Have you talked to Jess yet today?"

Katy thought about that a few moments before her eyes widened. She spoke, her voice much lower, even though Scott was still out of commission. "This is *that guy*?"

"Yes. And unless you want this place to turn into some weird, off-balanced orgy, I need to get him home."

Suspicion returned.

"*Your* home," she said.

He realized then how all of this sounded. Edgar presented Scott as some kind of semi-masculine succubus who drew in everyone in his vicinity, and his next plan of action was to remove him to a place where the two of them could be alone together. It felt so reasonable in his mind that he once again had to stop and check for signs of outward interfer-ence in his consciousness.

Did he want to have sex with this stranger he just met? Edgar was about as far from the random hookup-type as a person could get. Also Scott was a man. He might be a straight man, at that. There was a very real possibility that Edgar and Scott were just two regular straight men.

You are so pretty, Eddie.

Edgar fought so hard to keep the red from returning to his face that the heat seeped into his veins and warmed his blood. "I don't *think* I'm affected," he said. "I mean – you aren't, are you?" He faltered, then con-tinued. "He's a witch, Katy. Like me. I have to help him."

Her expression stayed neutral, but Edgar had the feeling she was fighting back a smile in a way that infuriated him. That didn't last long, though, when Scott shifted on his feet and raised his head slightly.

"Standing..?" He slurred vaguely.

He looked at Edgar and flashed him another groggy smile. Then he must've realized that there was someone else holding him up, and carefully side-eyed Katy without giving her his full attention.

"Uh, Scott, this is Katy," Edgar said. "Katy, Scott."

Katy, the people person that she was, took Scott's brief moment of awareness and motivation to stop being such a menace. Her voice got considerably more amicable, and she readjusted the placement of her arms in a way that implied holding a human being and not a bag of potatoes.

"You good, Scott?" she gently asked him.

He smiled and nodded. "Just...tired. It's so *cold*. It makes me tired."

"Yeah, the weather this time of year will do that," Katy reached out a free hand and brushed some dust and cobwebs off the front of Scott's suit jacket. "Uh, well, Eddie and I were talking, and he was saying that maybe you'd feel more comfortable if we took you to his place nearby to collect your thoughts and get some rest. Would you like that?"

Scott shifted his wavering gaze to Edgar again, looking at him the way Edgar looked at the crows that hung out outside his apartment. It was weird and scary and he wanted it to stop immediately.

"Are you friends with Eddie?" Scott asked Katy, still staring at Edgar. "I am."

"Does...he have a lot of friends?"

"Nope," Katy said. "Just me."

Edgar knew that she didn't say that to insult him. She was just saying something undeniably true. Edgar was never one with any sort of vibrant social life. Maybe it bothered him when he was a kid, but after enough time on his own he grew numb to the isolation. Be that as it may, as soon as he saw the flash of disappointment that crossed Scott's expression as Katy said that, he may as well have been a desperately lonely child again.

Katy started leading Scott towards the door. "Don't look too sad, bud," she readjusted Scott's arm and offered him an amicable grin. "Assuming you're unbelievably persistent, we could probably bump that number up to a cool, even two. Doesn't that sound nice?"

Scott sighed and leaned his head closer to the crook of Katy's neck.

"You seem really kind," he murmured. "I'm glad he has you."

Her face flashed from confusion to affection before ultimately settling on a mixture of the two. She crossed past Edgar and grinned.

I get it, she mouthed.

Edgar felt something tightly closed inside his heart stretch and ache against its bonds. This wasn't just manageable, human anxiety anymore. It was something else, a book written in a language Edgar never learned how to understand. And it frightened him. It was something that he acknowledged would probably feel good for someone else, but only left him feeling frightened and alone.

Even though he could be knocked over by a strong breeze, Scott reached out and lightly touched Edgar's forearm. The touch was so soft and tender that, at first, all it did was hurt. But he stayed in place, staring down at Scott's hand as it slowly lowered down his arm before wrapping around his wrist.

Suddenly he was calm. He didn't know why. He tried not to dwell on the shift.

"Come on," he said to Katy. "Let's go."

When Edgar first moved to New Orleans and finally found a job less than two miles away from his apartment, he was thrilled. No reason to keep slogging from one place to another in a car that constantly sounded on the verge of either gaining sentience or bursting into flames. Then he learned that, even though the city was slightly calmer outside of Mardi Gras season, there was still the perpetual danger of a parade forming at virtually any time or place.

It happened once, after a particularly grueling shift that left his hands raw and his back aching, that he made a wrong turn and accidentally landed in a throng of strangers that pooled over the course often city blocks. They turned what was supposed to be a fifteen-minute walk into a frantic flesh fumble that lasted almost over an hour.

Did he expect to add the constant risk of parades to his growing list of reasons not to trust the world? No, but things happen as they inevitably do. From that day on he stuck to making a far less convenient drive to work in a car that takes fifteen minutes off of the world's lifespan with every turn of the ignition.

It doesn't matter the season. You are never truly safe from the risk of parades.

"So you're just leaving in the middle of your shift?" Katy said as she opened the passenger's side door, then creaked it further with a clench of her teeth.

Edgar untied his apron and pulled it up over his head. "Tell Ian I'm sick. I have a feeling he'll understand."

"You think *Ian* will-?"

"Just tell him soon. As soon as I leave," he paused, frowning nervously, and added, "Like, immediately."

Katy carefully placed Scott into the car and buckled his seat belt.

She lingered, watching his face as he lolled his head from shoulder to shoulder.

"Don't look him in the eyes," Edgar warned.

"I'm not, calm down," she brushed back his hair and pressed a palm to his forehead. "Is this normal? Did he take something?"

The most accurate answer to this question was that Edgar simply did not have enough insight into the facts to have any goddamned clue what he was doing or what was going on. He made a sound that apparently substituted as a response, and Katy stepped back to allow him to get behind the wheel and drive off with the virtual stranger he was now bringing home with him for some reason.

Once the car rumbled out of the alley and onto the street, Edgar paused for a moment on the curb and risked a glance in Scott's direction. The other man was struggling to shrug off his poorly sized suit jacket, and at one point Edgar reached over and quickly undid the one remaining button. The blazer opened easily and Scott fumbled it off without a second thought. After that, he loosened his tie and undid the top two buttons of his dress shirt before slumping against the door and, apparently, immediately falling asleep.

His chest rose and fell in smooth tides. Even though this was his first time in Edgar's car, he had no problem with stretching his neck and shoulder and nestling even more comfortably into the side door.

He yawned and scrunched up his face like a street cat in the sun. Scott didn't sleep in the car like you were supposed to, with resignation and the steely anticipation of motion sickness. No – looking at him the way he was, Edgar could easily imagine him curled up in bed on a lazy Sunday morning.

But not *Edgar's* bed. And not necessarily on any particular time or day. It was just that, if Scott was capable of sleeping in a car that buzzed like a dirt bike, he may also be able to do the same on any other surface. Including a bed.

Yes, if there was anything Edgar could determine about Scott Skylark Kaufner with absolute certainty, it was that he was probably a man who had, at some point, slept in a bed. And that was all there was to be said (or implied) about that.

Scott's eyes opened halfway. He gazed at Edgar warmly and then faltered, head turning slightly to look out the windshield.

"Is it safe to drive like this?" He mumbled blearily.

Edgar smirked. "This thing has gotten me through the last few years well enough."

"But aren't you supposed to watch the road?"

He started to ask what Scott was talking about when he looked and realized that he was in the active process of driving, and apparently had been for a while. He immediately screamed and jolted the steering wheel to the side, swerving off the road and onto a large lot of dirt and dead grass. Without bothering to actually stop the car, he flung open the door and scrambled out onto his feet, panting with his entire body.

What just happened? Once he felt the shock and panic lessen its grip on his vision, Edgar took a look around to try and figure out where the hell his muscle control had taken him. And, as it turns out, he had been following essentially the exact path he always took to get home. He even recognized where he was now based on the sandwich shop across the road from the lot he had pulled onto.

He stiffly sat back in the car and stared at the dashboard. His teeth were gripped so tightly that it was starting to give him a headache.

"Are you okay?" Scott asked him.

"What do you want from me?"

Scott didn't answer him. For a moment Edgar felt an inexplicable swell of helpless rage. He wanted to take this dumb sensitive keyhole and shake him by the shoulder pads of his cheap suit until he could jostle out the man's actual intentions.

The keyhole reached over and lightly touched his arm again. And, again, the touch was immediately wonderful in a way that was difficult to force himself to ignore.

"You know my name," Edgar said, stiffening at Scott's touch without moving away. "You've done something to me."

"What?"

"I thought I was smart enough to know when I was being manipulated, but my skills are *clearly* rusty," the more he went down this train of thought, the easier it was to convince himself. "You... oh yeah, you used that goddamned *charm thing* on me."

Scott made a nervous attempt at a laugh. "No, Eddie, you don't understand."

"*Don't call me...*" Edgar wouldn't yell. He refused this intruder the right to his outrage. "Standing up for me in front of my boss. Getting me to *take you home* – I mean, do you realize you could've gotten us both *killed* with that stunt you pulled just now?"

"I didn't –" Scott stopped himself and closed his eyes, thumb tapping anxiously against his forefinger. "I wasn't *lying* when I said..."

He paused, and after that he unbuckled his seat belt and turned in his seat to fully face Edgar, pulling his feet up to sit cross-legged. His expression seemed calm, but something in his hands made it painfully clear how tense and tired he was. And, already, Edgar found himself struggling to maintain his current level of frustration.

"I know this is sudden," Scott began. "And I can't stress enough that this wasn't..." he trailed off, thinking, and then smiled faintly. "You're taking me back to your house?"

"I-It's an apartment," Edgar awkwardly corrected, as if what mattered now was tampering expectations.

Scott clearly had enough social tact to turn his head away and broaden his smile towards his lap. "Still more than what I have," he said with a chuckle.

His humor faded quickly and nothing took its place. For a brief and terrifying moment Scott seemed absolutely vacant, with even the glow of his eyes seeming to flicker briefly.

All at once he snapped out of it, and when he looked back up at Edgar there was a very present note of guilt in his face.

"Eddie," He cringed and rephrased himself. "No, sorry. *Edgar.* Edgar, you...you recognize me, don't you?"

Yes.

Yes Lark please Lark come on you can't mess this up PLEASE

A vivid chill ran down Edgar's spine. He couldn't place its reasoning. For a moment he remembered the feel of the thick quilt that covered his childhood bed as it wrapped around his small frame. That was the warmest, most comfortable spot in the house – which made no sense, because that blanket was itchy and smelled like rotting flowers.

The best part of his day growing up was the hour between crawling into bed and drifting to sleep. But how could that be true? Edgar never slept well back then and rarely had anything to look forward to in the morning. What could he possibly have been doing to make that stretch of time so treasured?

"Have we met before?" Edgar responded.

"I... don't know," Scott huffed, half-bemused, half-apologetic. "Probably not."

"Then why would you think I know you?"

"Do you *feel* like you know me?" Scott asked. "When we met, did you get the sense in any way that we had met before?" He furrowed his brow, deep in thought and also very confused and increasingly distressed. "Even – even in a *dream*, maybe?"

Outside, the sunlight was swallowed up by a veil of clouds. Everything darkened just enough to look a little uglier. Edgar was hit by a wave of tired melancholy. He leaned back in his seat, allowing one hand to fall limp against the door handle, and the other –

"There!" Scott piped up in a strained gasp.

"What?"

"Do you realize what you just did?"

Edgar stammered a bit. He turned away, absently squeezing Scott's hand before realizing not only what he was doing, but that he and Scott's fingers were already interlaced to begin with.

He stared at their hands. He looked up at Scott. The man appeared stretched so thin that if he stepped out of the car he'd dissolve in the oncoming rain.

For a while Edgar debated whether or not to stop touching him the way he was. The answer felt obvious, and yet when he considered making any effort to pull away something held him back. And as much as he wanted to say it was some metaphysical psychic force dictating his actions, it wasn't.

Once in a rare bout of bravery, Edgar stole a book from the local library that documented the first witch town in the mountains of Santa Cruz, California. Before they split the work of genetic witches into individual communities dedicated solely to social work and activism versus environmental and community work, the little town of Dullroar did all of it. They provided resources to those who needed it and constantly strove to improve the world around them.

If the same was described by the adult in his life it would be with derision. Because kindness isn't a choice if it's hardwired into your DNA, and if you don't have to constantly choose between kindness and cruelty then you might as well not be human.

It would make sense to Edgar later in life. Or, perhaps more honestly, he would come to the conclusion that it must make sense if it's an argument that people keep making. But hearing about it as a child, he found himself quietly comforted by the knowledge that there are people out there who would just prefer to be nice.

He was still holding Scott's hand. It had been a long, long time since Edgar thought that far back into his past.

"You've studied," Scott spoke in a hushed tone. "You probably know about bond magic."

There were a few hanging strands of dark hair blocking part of his face. It would be so easy for Edgar to brush them back with a sweep of his hand. He wouldn't do it, but he could fixate on it as much as he wished.

"Sure," he absently answered. "Archetypes and oil soaked twine. I've never been to a ritual but I read about them."

Scott was slowly moving Edgar's hand in his direction. Edgar watched it happen and did nothing. He thought about the black and white photos of smiling genetic witch children in Dullroar, climbing redwoods and tending to wildlife. For a book he only checked out once decades ago, he could still picture those images and the grief they provoked like it was happening right this very second.

"What about the other kind?" Scott pushed further. "The kind that doesn't need a ritual?"

"You mean – soul bonds, right?" Edgar relaxed his shoulders and thought about that. "Uh, sure. Not as much information about them out there since they're so rare nowadays, but yeah. I've heard of them."

"Can you...do something to – I don't know. Track them?"

Track them?

By this point Scott was holding Edgar's hand against his chest like something precious and fragile. And briefly, very briefly, and not even with a vibrancy strong enough to fully distinguish, Edgar felt that maybe he could be.

He clenched his jaw and shook away the dream. But he didn't move his hand.

"I...soul bonds are pretty much impossible to detect by outside parties alone," he said. "That's another reason why they're so hard to document. It's just something that's felt by the members of the connection."

"All of them?" Scott said.

"Yes," Edgar said.

Scott's face fell. "Always?" He said.

"Maybe?" Edgar paused, then shrugged lightly. "I mean – yeah. Yes. That's what I've been told, at least."

The silence that followed was so stark and startling that Edgar was suddenly vividly aware of the crashing pop of raindrops against the roof of the car above them. He got the feeling that he said something terribly wrong, not only from the look on Scott's face, but from the immediate ache that rippled in his chest like a new and hungry vein.

Scott let go of Edgar's hand in a way that likely intended no harm but still felt momentarily terrible for reasons he could not even begin to explain. By the time he had processed the sudden absence of his warmth, he looked up to see that Scott's demeanor changed completely.

There was a new confidence in the way he sat, his back straight and his head held high. The distance in his smile was very subtle, yet absolutely noticeable.

He no longer looked Edgar directly in the eye.

"Thanks for the ride," he said pleasantly. "I should really go, though. I have a performance tonight."

Before Edgar could track what was going on Scott opened the door and stepped out into the rain. He was unnecessarily gentle in closing the door, which was the last thing Edgar could recognize from the man he was talking to before. And then he was alone.

Alone. He was alone? Why was Edgar

holding the body of the fat brown bird in the palms of his trembling hands?

The little thing was so soft and so cold, and its black eyes no longer held the loving glimmer of a fresh rain puddle. Its neck was bent to the side at an angle impossible unless someone forced it.

His mother watched from the patio, her flask in one hand and a lit cigarette twisting twin tendrils of smoke into the crisp winter air. He looked up at her, too stunned for words, but something inside him pointed out that this would be the point in which a healthy person would start to cry.

"I had no choice," she simply said, unscrewing the flask and releasing the sweet fumes of the liquor inside. "Larks are an invasive species here."

Edgar flung open the car door and practically leapt outside. After quickly scanning the area he spotted Scott already a few blocks down, a great distance he rushed to meet as quickly as possible. Because suddenly making sure his shitty car wasn't stolen didn't matter nearly as much as stumbling through mud and puddles to chase after this sad, strange person.

Eventually the only thing that separated Scott and Edgar was a strip of asphalt and, somehow, every single driver in New Orleans zooming down the road one after the other. Edgar bobbed his head to peek through the gaps between cars, and at the first free moment he stopped thinking entirely and sprinted across the street.

"Hang on!" He called out, his voice starting to crack childishly. "Wait stop *don't leave again -*"

With his attention entirely focused on Scott up ahead, Edgar neglected to see the teen on the rented e-scooter until they slammed directly into him. Teens being teens, the kid was able to maneuver the fumble without coming close to crashing. They even had the skill to call Edgar an insult he could not recognize before continuing to zoom away.

He crumpled between the road and the curb – just limp. Tired. So much was happening.

It felt like hours in which he stayed in that fog of pain and confusion, though in actuality it was probably only a few moments before he felt a familiar touch on his shoulder.

"I hate those things," Scott remarked in a comfortingly flat voice.

At this point they were both soaked with rain, though Scott didn't seem to notice or be affected by it. He sat down next to Edgar, frowning and visibly worried, which to Edgar was much preferred to his previous demeanor.

"It seems they're in all the major cities," Scott leaned forward to adjust one of the straps on his shoe. "I tried to ride one in New York to get to a show I was doing, and I was so bad at it that I immediately got yelled at."

Edgar sat up, groaning softly. "By who?" He said.

"Oh, you know. Fast walkers. Mean elderly ladies. Little dogs."

Scott hesitated, then cast Edgar a weak smile. Was that a joke? There was an element in the man's face that expressed a wish for levity, a proverbial bridge built over the roaring rapid between them. Or, even better, an umbrella, since the rain around them was really coming down and only getting more fervent.

"I have this new tea blend at my place," Edgar said, very slowly starting to get back upright. "It's – uh – some kind of chai. I don't know. I actually haven't tried it yet, but the woman at the place I go to says it's her favorite and... she has a lot of tattoos. So I trust her."

"Okay," Scott took Edgar's arm and helped pull him up the rest of the way. "You should warm up."

"You're right. I think we both should, actually. So -" Edgar motioned back towards where he essentially abandoned his car. "Let's go."

It was hard, he quickly learned, to maintain a cool and casual exterior when your bones are suddenly wiggling and aching for sunlight. Still, Edgar held his ground, clenching his jaw as Scott's expression turned from an instance of raw delight to a low simmer of weary disappointment.

"I...I can't," he said. "I have to play a set."

"You don't seem thrilled about that."

"I'm not. But they might be there."

"Who?" Edgar asked in a voice that had to work a little harder to stay indifferent.

"...Eddie," Scott said, staring at his feet. "My soul-bond."

Once again something shifted inside of Edgar in a way that felt very good and very, *very* bad. Suddenly he lost interest in tracking the flow of rain drops as they sank down his temples. Instead he stared at Scott as he combed back his soaking wet hair with his fingers, which gave Edgar a chance to see the entirety of his face for the first time since they met.

He noticed, finally, the flecks of dark freckles that stretched over both cheeks and across the bridge of Scott's nose. The attraction he felt at the sight of them was so immense and overwhelming that for a good while he could only process it as a capital-F *Feeling*.

He heard his voice without realizing fully that he was speaking.

"Who's Eddie?" It asked.

Scott's mouth opened, but he couldn't quite push out a single full word. Finally he managed a breathy chuckle and a grand, defeated sigh.

"I don't know," he admitted.

The two of them both fell silent. It became clear in some blurry, symbolic way, that there was one of two choices he had in this very moment.

He could let the flashes of Feeling pass unremarked upon, leaving this keyhole to make the reasonable walk back to the Fairy's Den, play his show, and probably leave town forever.

Then Edgar could drive back home alone and go back to his life the way it was before. He would continue wasting leftovers because he could never figure out how to cook for one person. He'd be alone by himself and alone around people, day after day, year after year, until he ultimately died in his kitchen after finally attempting to make pesto and choking on an underground tree nut.

This was not the first time he documented that timeline for himself. It was, though, the first time that he bothered having an opinion on it.

And the alternative?

"Come home with me," Edgar said. "Please. Just until the rain stops, then I'll drive you back for the dinner rush. The crowds don't get around our age until later at night anyway."

Scott considered that. He gave Edgar a look that cut him deeply, yet so carefully and with such precision so as to not spill even a single drop of blood. It was just pure, deep inspection. Alchemy attempted through mere eye-contact.

And then it broke. He nodded softly.

"Okay," Scott said.

Edgar didn't live in a terrible part of town, and it wasn't like his apartment was a massive fringe of eviction notices and health code violations. It was an absolutely normal one-bedroom in a neighborhood not necessarily trendy, but with a decent amount of coffee shops and restaurants a short walk away. If he did have a throng of friends and lovers that wanted to hang out at his place, in theory they'd have a perfectly lovely time.

But he didn't. And if he did, he knew it didn't matter, because they wouldn't. Something about Edgar, about the way he engaged with other people or perceived his own home, gave his apartment the aura of a haunted house. Even his own landlord hesitated to come inside unless there was a prominent threat of property damage.

Why did he insist on bringing Scott over then? The thought hadn't occurred to him until he pulled into the gravel driveway outside his home. At the time all Edgar thought was that the man needed to be somewhere quiet and secluded, somewhere where no one else would even think of bothering them, and he automatically knew his house would be the best choice. Now, though, he could already feel his cheeks reddening in anticipation of humiliation.

Still, they couldn't stay sitting in his driveway forever if they wanted to get dry and warm at some point in the near future. Pride be damned, Edgar got out and prepared himself to welcome his very first guest in literal years.

They darted up the pathway and shivered outside the door as Edgar fumbled for his keys. Once the door was unlocked, he pushed it open and quickly pulled Scott inside.

Growing up his mother somehow managed to keep the house constantly freezing throughout the year. So when he got his first apartment in the city and the landlord explained that he had one of those fancy thermostats he could set on a schedule and adjust from his phone, he was ecstatic. No more clenching his teeth to keep from the embarrassment of chattering or having his legs ache from shivering so hard. Now on rainy, blustery nights like this he could just walk through the door to an immediately cozy household.

He was still anxious and confused, but as he took off his coat and hung it on the hook he took a break from his panic to enjoy the warmth. Much to his surprise, when he looked over at Scott he saw him doing the same thing.

"Wow," he breathed. "You *live* here?"

Edgar's heart tensed hard. "Um. Yes?"

Scott took a respectful look around at what he could see without moving. Then he grinned.

"It's beautiful!" Scott appeared to suddenly forget the circumstances of the day so far, completely lost in the glow and wonder of being inside a home. "Can you show me around?"

"It's maybe three rooms, there really isn't..."

Scott's attention had drifted from listening to the conversation, to staring at a framed print hung up above the little table where Edgar kept his keys. It was a black and white photo of a duck floating on the banks of the Mississippi that he bought at an arts fair a while back. Unlike most of the other decor in his home, Edgar displayed it because he liked it, as opposed to suspecting that it would make his apartment feel less unsettling.

Suddenly Edgar was wracked with anticipation. In that moment, the most important thing was what this stranger he dragged home would think about his duck photo. Scott gave it far more attention than a picture of a single duck likely deserved, and then he nodded thoughtfully.

"Classy," he said. "*Very* classy."

Once again Edgar was hit by that *Feeling*, in a wave strong enough to make him consider turning down the heat. He had to look away to collect himself and started to hang up his coat, just to have something to do. Then he realized he already took it off when he walked in. He froze briefly, genuinely startled for no apparent reason.

What happens now?

His clothes were soaked through with rainwater, and since he spent only half the amount of time in the rain that Scott did, he could imagine his were too. Wearing a wet old suit must be uncomfortable, even though Scott did nothing to suggest he was anything but generally okay.

He could technically leave things be, Edgar reminded himself. This was still a viable option.

On the other hand, Scott was definitely smaller than Edgar was. And Edgar just did laundry a few days before, so he definitely had some warm, clean clothes to loan him while he threw everything else in the dryer.

He imagined the way one of his shirts would hang on Scott and felt immediately like that was a thing he was not allowed to think about. The physical sensation it prompted was unlike anything he experienced before when being this close to another human being. It was raw. Humiliatingly vulnerable.

Edgar hated it. He also didn't hate it at all, which made him frightened of it even more.

From behind him Scott shuddered softly. Edgar didn't look directly at him, but turned his head enough to see him roll up the sleeves of his dress shirt and rub the pallid gray-brown of his forearms.
Fuck.

He gathered some pajamas from his closet before he had a chance to really think about what he was doing, came back, and offered the pile of fabric to Scott.

"Here," he said. "You can wear this while I dry our clothes."

Scott frowned. He smiled, and then he did a sort of strange, frown-smile. But still he didn't move – in fact, he stayed still enough for Edgar to notice that he was physically shivering.

"Come on, Scott," Edgar said, trying not to sound too desperate. "Things are much nicer when you aren't cold. Trust me."

"I know," Scott murmured. "And I – I *do*. I…"

A new emotion passed through Scott's eyes. His brow furrowed slightly, and he nodded. Then he took the clothes. For a moment his fingers brushed against Edgar's, and since it didn't look like Scott meant anything by – or even registered the touch – Edgar decided that he definitely didn't either.

Ian was right. Scott's hands were pretty soft. But Edgar didn't care or notice or have any opinion on that one way or the other.

He changed first and immediately insisted Scott do the same in his bedroom afterwards, which the man accepted with only some reluctance. Now no longer soaking wet and finally warming up, Edgar sat on the couch and waited for his new friend to join him.

His new friend, who was currently in his bedroom. Getting fully undressed. To dress himself again in Edgar's clothes, which to him felt far more intimate than just staying naked.

Once again, Edgar had to ask himself – was he still straight? Edgar was definitely operating under the assumption that he was straight. Much in the same way that Katy still claimed she was Catholic, even though she didn't practice any deeper than occasionally calling out to Saint Anthony when she was drunk and looking for her phone.

Deciding for no particular reason that he absolutely needed to keep preoccupied, he busied himself in the kitchen to make the two of them some tea. But he realized that, since he never had people over, he didn't have a reason to have more than one tea strainer. This insight was followed by fifteen seconds of pure, unadulterated panic before he decided to give Scott's cup the strainer and just pour loose leaves in his own mug.

He heard his bedroom door open as he was pouring water from the kettle, and that innocuous creak of the old hinges was enough for him to narrowly avoid spilling scalding hot water across the counter top.

Outside the rain pattered against the windowpane. Steam drifted from the surface of the water. The worry that someone or something would burst in and cut this moment short mixed with the fear of what would happen if nothing and no one did.

"That chai is strong," Scott's voice came from behind him. "I can smell it from here."

Edgar looked over and saw him sitting cross-legged on the tattered, presumably-pleather couch in the living room. He pulled his long hair into a sort of haphazard bun that still left some stray strands dangling around his face in a way that had to be either intentional, or at least done with his eyes closed.

But he looked better. He seemed comfortable – weirdly comfortable, actually.

If someone else was there, it would be easy to assume that it was Edgar who had been invited into Scott's home. That was a strange thought.

He didn't have the reaction he thought he might seeing Scott wearing his clothes. There were no shocking answers or life-changing revelations. Instead, all he felt was a low hum of relief. He knew now that the suit Scott wore previously was far bulkier than what made sense for someone like him. Now, in looser and thinner fabrics, Edgar could get a better picture of what he looked like.

His shoulders were narrow and his arms softly curved. He had even more freckles trailing down his neck and past the collar of the t-shirt Edgar gave him. Edgar stared until he realized he was staring and then quickly looked away. He tapped his fingers against the counter and mentally called himself a long list of cruel insults. Then he took a deep breath and brought their tea to the other room.

When he handed Scott his mug, he noticed the man still trembled.

"You're not warm enough?" Edgar asked.

Scott's large eyes got even bigger. "No! I mean – it's fine. *I'm* fine, you don't have to..."

His words trickled into silence as Edgar grabbed the quilt from the other arm of the couch, draping it over Scott's shoulders from the front. Midway into arranging the blanket to cover as much of him as possible, it occurred to Edgar that this was a weird thing to do on behalf of someone he didn't know.

Was he charmed? Sure, he could call himself *charmed*, but was he..?

"Thank you," Scott whispered.

By the slight vibrancy in his voice it seemed the both of them found themselves equal parts stirred and baffled. That made things a little easier. So Edgar took a seat and picked up his own tea. He bathed his face in the steam and sipped, quickly becoming much calmer than what made rational sense given the situation.

Tea always had a way of easing his anxieties. It probably wasn't the tea soothing him this time, though, since all the loose leaves made the mug nearly impossible to drink from.

Still, it was fine.

They definitely came in with a goal to talk about something important. Whatever their goal was, it was immediately left to the side as Edgar and Scott began to share their observations about the Fairy's Den, and other establishments of its ilk. He didn't expect to start talking about food service, but Scott had a surprising amount to say about the subject. Not only was he a traveling musician that spent almost every night in some kind of bar or restaurant, but he also made extra money between shows by helping out at smaller establishments.

"What would you do?" Edgar said, shifting on the couch to better face him.

"Oh, lots of things. I've bussed, washed dishes – I'm okay in the kitchen if it's a diner. Mainly I wait tables, though."

Edgar huffed. "I could never do that. I'm terrible with people."

"So am I," Scott smiled.

"Well you have your...eye-thing," Edgar looked away when he saw how his observation made Scott wince. "It must be difficult. But it must – I mean, it pays the bills. So to speak."

Scott made a weak blueprint of laughter. "I actually try not to use it on people when I don't have to," he frowned even deeper. "It's hard though. Like if I lock eyes with someone before I can find my sunglasses, or if they sneak up and grab me. Some people are really– *grabby.*"

Saying this saddened him. Edgar felt, then, the overwhelming urge to lift the spirits of the chilly stranger he dragged home with him. That wasn't a desire he felt often with other people, but this was a special case. Scott's sadness was not that of a regular human being. Instead, it possessed a potency that made Edgar's chest tighten.

"What – uh –" he wracked his brain for a nicer thing to talk about. "What's your favorite kind of pen? My best friend's a server and she has really hard opinions about the types of pens she uses."

Scott tweaked his brow, silent for a while before cracking a satisfied grin.

"Blue," he said.

Would he elaborate on that? Edgar waited and he didn't.

"Cool," Edgar said.

They talked easily for a long while – impossible to say how long as Edgar made no attempt to check the time. He felt too good, just entirely relaxed and comfortable in a way that was beyond rare for him.

So he was in the middle of saying something, or maybe it was Scott that was talking. Or it could've been that they were both being completely silent. Whatever the case, Edgar allowed his head to settle against the back of the couch and his eyes to close. Almost as soon as he did that, he drifted off straight into a deep and dreamless sleep.

He snapped back a few hours later. It was all but dark now, with only a faint ghost of light left to illuminate the shapes in the room. Next to him, Scott had curled up into a ball and was also peacefully napping.

They were supposed to talk about something important, weren't they? Edgar tried to rustle up some shards of urgency glimmering in the fog of drowsy serenity. He remembered Scott asking him about soul bonds. He remembered the look on the man's face as he brought up the subject, a sort of eager longing that had never been cast in Edgar's direction before.

It didn't feel bad when they were just chatting about nothing in particular. Sleeping concurrently was surprisingly refreshing. And yes, fresh out of a nap Edgar was willing to admit that Scott's touch did inspire a response other than directly negative.

He couldn't elaborate more on that before he recognized the silence settled around them. The rain must've stopped.

The promise he made before echoed in his mind and made his jaw clench involuntarily. This wasn't going to work. He needed more time.

Out of the dozen grimoires he collected growing up, he only brought one with him when he moved. It was your standard purple bound tomb, Academy-issued before they changed up their design, filled with incantations, sigils, diagrams and other information. One of the first things he did was collect the handful of spells he could see himself actually needing and transcribe them into a spiral-bound notebook. The original book was now kept in a locked case under his bed, while his new, less-formal equivalent went on to mostly hold poetry fragments and first-draft recipes.

No, it wasn't professional. But it was enough for a situation like this.

Edgar pulled the book from the junk drawer in his kitchen and thumbed to the section he needed in the back. He scanned the writing and crept around the house to get what he needed: a white candle, four stones, salt and a glass of water.

He slowly opened the sliding glass door to the patio with an armful of supplies and got to his work. First he lit the candle and dripped a few drops of wax onto the concrete so he would have a place for it to stand upright. With it still burning, he positioned the smooth stones to represent the four elements. Then he surrounded the setup with a circle of salt.

It was hard not to feel a little dirty working the way he did, especially since it came to him so easily. When was the last time he arranged a spell circle? By the way he moved you might think he never stopped practicing, and Edgar hated the thought of that.

But intent, right? Isn't that the source of all magic? So all he had to do was focus on the intent
of what he was trying to do.

The ritual came with an incantation that spoke of taking control of the elements and bending the winds of nature to the user's will. That was definitely not what Edgar wanted. He never saw himself as a
god, never wanted to be a god, and never wanted to associate with the kind of people who believed otherwise. So that begs the question: what *did* he want?

Edgar closed his eyes and poured the water in a circle around the candle.

"Help," he whispered. "Please help me."

The glass now empty, he set it aside. He very rarely was trusted to perform a ritual without any sort of supervision, and now that he was leading things on his own he realized he didn't know how to tell if
it worked.

When he looked down he saw that the water soaked into the circle of the salt, thickening it into a line of paste. That's a good sign. So where were his results?

Some more time went by. There was the distant honk of traffic and the rustling of rats in the alley beyond his patio. Maybe he messed it up. His mother always warned him that Academic magic was sustained through constant study and practice. If you go too long without connecting to the source, it's possible you'll be rejected entirely. Metaphysical amputation, so to speak. Which, at some point, was exactly what Edgar wanted.

He stood up and crossed his arms. It was cold. He was cold. His bad shoulder ached in the joint in throbs of dull pain. Everything in him was starting to hurt again. Edgar turned to go back inside, but stopped when he heard the hiss of the candle at his feet being extinguished.

By the time he looked down to see what happened, it was once again starting to rain.

An astonished smile lit up his face. He looked up and closed his eyes, for once happy to feel droplets of rain against his face.

Then the drops fell harder. A drizzle turned into a shower, and before long Edgar was ducking back inside to escape what wound up being a roaring thunderstorm.

He watched the barely-controlled chaos through the sliding glass door, cringing awkwardly. The older residents of NOLA were apparently in for a stressful night reminiscent of past disasters.

But this is fine. This was fine.

This would work.

Second Movement

Scott Skylark Kaufner sat in the back of an otherwise empty train car. He kept his head bowed and turned to the window, most of his face hidden by a pair of cheap and massive cat's eye sunglasses. His knees were brought up to his chest as he wept and prayed to god no one passing by would touch him or make him look at them.

"Just breathe, Skylark," Tenzin begged softly, her voice tinny through the speaker of his cheap flip phone. "Calm. Calm –"

"I can't do this anymore."

"Come home then. You tried – we all know you tried. Just come home."

"I can't," Scott hissed under his breath.

"Why not?"

Outside they were passing what looked like marshlands at dusk. The patches of water were black in the dying light, and the gaunt trees angling from the grasslands looked skeletal and laced with meat.

Hell. Scott was in hell. There was no other explanation.

"I don't remember how to get there," he said.

The line went silent, but he could still hear the static of what he imagined to be the sound of Tenzin's breathing. While waiting for her response, he unzipped his duffle bag on the seat next to him and dug for the bottle of medication he got from the veterinary clinic at the last town. The doctor didn't want to give it to him, for obvious reasons, and said that if Scott wanted to euthanize a pet he would have to make an appointment at the front desk.

Then Scott came closer and took the young blonde's hands in his. He flashed him a sweet smile, and suddenly it didn't matter that he hadn't slept in three days and couldn't remember when the last full meal he had was. His eyes could be bloodshot, glassy with tears and ringed with shadows – but they were still devastatingly blue, weren't they? And in the end, that was all that mattered.

He got the pills. The doctor even wrote his phone number on the side of the label. That was nice of him.

"You said you're going to Baton Rouge next," Tenzin said, very much not a question. "I'll meet you there."

"Ten -"

"No. Be quiet. I'll show Mom how to wire you some money. All you have to do is find a room and stay there for a night or two. Sleep in a bed. Eat something other than Twix and granola bars. Have a non bar-based dinner, Scott –"

Scott was crying again. "Tenzin, please."

"I'll take the next flight I can find and I'll bring you home myself. And it'll be fine."

The fragile certainty in his sister's voice was the most heartbreaking part of all of this. Tenzin was smart, the descendant of anthropologists and scientists who knew more about things than he could ever hope to. She knew what was happening to him. What would continue to happen if he ended his tour without finding the source of the name that's been haunting him for his entire life.

Of course. That's what she was guiding him towards. Scott couldn't be set loose on the world when he was no longer himself. He would need to be contained – through whatever means necessary.

"Okay," he said dully. "Baton Rouge. I'll see you there."

Tenzin breathed a sigh of relief. Scott had to physically swallow back a scream.

"I love you, Skylark," his sister whispered. "Take care of yourself, okay?"

He clenched the bottle of pills in his hand so tightly he could feel the label wrinkle under the skin of his palm. Still, when he spoke, his voice remained steady.

"I love you too, Ten-Ten," he said. "I love you so, so much."

There was a gap in his seat between the metal chair and the wall of the train that was the perfect size to drop in his phone. He buttoned up his mother's shearling coat, stood up on shaky legs, and forced himself to approach the conductor at the end of the car.

It was a taller woman with a uniform vest and short black braids. He somehow concocted a smile and started to reach out, then pulled back and instead chose to clear his throat to attract her attention.

"Can I help you?" She asked.

"Yes," Scott kept his head bowed politely as he spoke. "I...I was wondering what the next stop was."

"We'll be reaching New Orleans in a few minutes."

Scott was supposed to respond, but he got lost in the experience of staring as indirectly as possible at the space where the Conductor's face was supposed to be. When he was alone, and if he could focus very hard, he could imagine the concept of things like noses, eyes and mouths. It was just that at this

point it had been so long since he'd actually seen one that they sounded more mythological in nature, forbidden concepts you can think about but must never vocalize.

The front of her skull was a milky, twisting sludge of pigment perpetually mid-melt. It looked wet. Utterly terrifying. It looked like if he touched it, the substance would swallow up his hand and eat it to the bone.

Scott Kaufner was in hell.

He averted his eyes. He smiled.

"Thank you," he said.

The woman nodded and went back to checking tickets. Feeling like a ghost, and with his smile still clutching desperately to his face, Scott went back to his seat and grabbed his bag.

He went still for a while and stared out the window until the train ducked into a tunnel and the glass turned black and reflective. Immediately Scott recoiled as if someone had slapped him across the face. Quickly, he slipped his duffle over his shoulder and exited the train car.

The first thing Scott was aware of as he stepped reluctantly from sleep was the sensation of warmth. He opened his eyes, and in a haze of confusion, it took him longer than he'd like to admit to remember where he was.

There was what had to be that soft and cozy quilt carefully draped around him. It was dark out, new rain and wind howling, and the only light in the space came from where Edgar now stood at the stove in the kitchen.

He was hard at work, and by the looks of it he had been for a while. There was steam floating and at least two different kinds of sizzling, all of which was resulting in an aroma that reminded Scott for the first time in a day or so of how achingly hungry he was.

Scott stood up and briefly touched the sleeve of the soft, worn t-shirt he now wore. It touched against his bare skin with a faint tenderness – not hesitant or reluctant, just quiet. Shy, if anything. He fingered the material and felt his face start to warm.

A flash of lightning lit up the room, startling him out of his thoughts. Scott started to approach the window and quickly thought better of it.

"Oh," Edgar said from the kitchen. "You're awake."

The look on the bartender's face was easy to identify as a hesitant, nervous friendliness that made Scott want to laugh in delight. Everything about this awkward, mop-haired individual filled him with a sense of frantic relief – like the first few moments after a near-death experience, but stretched out over the course of hours. He took in the way Edgar's face rested naturally into an expression of numb distaste, yet warmed slightly whenever they locked eyes.

For the first time in Scott's life he had to make a conscious effort to restrain the emotions flooding through him. He could feel that he didn't have much of himself left to give to another Eddie, even if it was *his* Eddie, and there was a new part of him that had to push to be guarded. This could be a trick, after all. A grief-hallucination. Or he might have already taken his pills without realizing it and was now in some strange, but not entirely unpleasant sort of afterlife.

Either way, it was best to play it cool.

Scott nodded towards the window. "Weather manipulation seems like a bad taste in a town like this," he said.

Edgar's eyes widened slightly. They were large like his and a warm russet brown. They looked like the bark on every tree Scott ever loved as a child.

"Uh," Edgar stammered, stirring something in a pan. "I – I didn't -"

"Natural rain doesn't move like this," Scott craned his head to try and peek at the concoction brewing on the stove. "What are you cooking?"

He ventured a little closer, though stopped at the barrier where carpet turned to tile. Edgar relaxed, relaxed his brow slightly, and quirked his lips into a small and modest smile.

"Well I thought – with the storm outside..."

"*Your* storm," Scott added under his breath.

"I could use something warm to eat," Edgar kept going. "I thought you might too. So, uh, I'm just whipping up some Japanese curry."

The curry was a burnished gold stew, colored so deeply that it tinted the shards of chicken, potato and onion that bobbed along the surface. It smelled sweet and savory, with a soft bite that inspired without intimidating. More than that, it smelled nourishing. Warm. It had been ages since Scott had allowed himself a hot meal.

At this point he realized that he was very much drooling. He could remember buying a bottled cold brew and a mini box of oat cereal at the train station in Tennessee and mixing them together, allowing him to spend his ride nauseous and insane as opposed to insane and cramped with hunger. What did he eat before that? It would be impossible to say.

Edgar looked shyly proud of Scott's blatant gawking, though he at least gave Scott the dignity of pretending he wasn't watching once caught.

"There's rice in the machine by the fridge," he said. "Bowls in the cabinet above that. This should be ready in another minute or so."

Now Scott was faced with a bit of a conundrum. He did tell himself that he needed to go back to that dingy bar downtown and play for a crowd of handsy drunks, all in the vaguest of hopes that his mythical soul bond might be there.

But who was he kidding? All it took was the smell of one home-cooked meal to understand that he wasted the past three years of his life being miserable to no avail. How was he supposed to find one human being based solely on a name and the presumption of instant connection? If he had found the Eddie for him, they clearly weren't interested. Maybe they never even existed.

No, it was much better to take the rare touches of human kindness as they were offered. Scott would enjoy the company of this unhappy man in his quiet home. He would remember the taste of a delicious meal and the sight of a human face, find a way to get back to his bag at the club, and go find a bridge to die under. What happened afterwards would no longer be anyone's problem but his own.

The two of them sat on either end of a small, round table. Scott pulled up one leg onto the seat and imagined what it would be like to have a place like this of his very own. To collect the things he purchased, found, or received as a gift, and arrange them on his walls and shelves. He thought about what it would be like to be out in the world, surrounded by people you don't necessarily know, and feel okay because you will eventually go "home".

Home. Scott wanted desperately to go home. But, try as he might, he could barely remember what that place looked like. If it ever actually existed outside of his imagination.

"I usually add more chili flakes," Edgar said as he ladled curry over Scott's bowl of white rice. "I don't know. I try not to assume how spicy people like things."

Help me, Scott wanted to say.

"Thank you," he said instead.

The food in his bowl was a product of farmers, chefs and artisans. The fragrant sauce seeped into the depths of the rice and coated each grain in layers of gold. It took skilled hands and minds to understand how to take a seed or a leaf and turn it into a grain of rice, dried herb, or soft mound of spice. Even the bowl had to be made. The fork had to be crafted. The table and chair he sat at now was once the loving flesh of a mighty tree.

It had been long enough since Scott had seen cooked meat this close that it no longer looked real. Even the slight angle in which it was cut reflected a great degree of care. If he imagined biting into a piece and tasting the pooled combination of tangy sauce and the meat's natural juices. With only the flavor of the image in his head, Scott felt close to a faint.

He paused and took a deep breath, forcing himself to calm for a moment. "Thank you," he said to the curry, the table, and everything else in the room.

From outside his line of sight, Edgar laughed softly. Scott looked up at him, and he immediately silenced himself.

"I'm sorry, that was rude," Edgar swallowed his guilt with a long drink of water. "I'm sorry. I knew the gratitude ran deep with genetic witches, but...this is the first time I've seen it in person."

Genetic witches. That wasn't the first time Edgar had dropped such an official term.

"You're a genetic witch, aren't you?" Scott said, choosing to mimic his language.

Once again Edgar's face turned sheepish. "I mean – you know what I mean. Real genetic witches."

Scott frowned and ran the spoon against the surface of the rice.

"*You're* a real genetic witch."

There was so much he missed about being able to see faces, from the ripple of a person's smile to something as simple as being able to track where the person he was speaking to was looking. Even though he felt guilty for how uncomfortable he made Edgar with one simple observation, he couldn't help but feel quietly thrilled at how easy it was to notice his negative reaction.

The bartender clenched his jaw and darted his eyes from one place to the other. The corners of his lips tensed slightly, implying there was some way he wanted to respond but couldn't quite get out the words.

The whole thing was fascinating. The feeling of recognizing that he said the wrong thing was so familiar that he wanted to roll around in it like a feral cat in a sunny field. But he was also very hungry and decided, before anything else, he needed to address that first. So he scooped the spoon into his curry and brought it to his lips.

It is an impossible task to explain the feeling of eating an actual, hot meal after an extended period of time spent, essentially, scavenging.

And if that wasn't enough, it was a meal clearly crafted with *love* – inexplicable, and still so present that it washed over Scott like the warmth of the blanket that appeared over him when he first woke up.

The tears fell immediately, but they were different this time. Scott cried with the same tremor in the back of his throat that came whenever he saw something moving growing up and he had no concept of containing himself. He tried hard to give up that instinct long ago, and apparently all he needed was one nice meal to throw away decades of hard work. So he pulled up his feet onto the chair, balancing the bowl on his knees, and ate while weeping openly and freely.

Once he took enough spoonfuls to soothe the hunger pains in his stomach, Scott regained enough of his senses to remember who he was sitting with. It wasn't just another faceless entity he was in the middle of seducing into allowing him to pass on unharmed. No, he had to remind himself that he was eating dinner with the first person in years who could actually perceive him beyond the pull of his eyes.

Scott put down the spoon and awkwardly dabbed at his mouth with a napkin. He chuckled, looking everywhere but at the man in front of him.

"Wow," he said. "Bad manners. I hope I didn't..."

He trailed off when his eyes finally settled on Edgar, and Scott noticed the way he was looking at him. While Scott was already well into his meal, he had yet to touch his own serving. He just sat there, leaned forward slightly with his chin cupped in his hand. Up until now every look he cast towards Scott appeared to be expressed behind the cover of thick bulletproof glass. Now the fondness in the bartender's eyes was so stark and open that it was, frankly, a little shocking.

Eventually he must've realized that Scott was aware of his staring and blinked a few times. He sat up, raising the wall slightly.

"Do...do you like it?" He asked.

Scott was still tracing the residual vibration of Edgar's previous gaze against his skin. Nobody had ever looked at him like that before. Or maybe they had and he was unable to see it. Either way it was a lot to hold onto. He looked down into his bowl and smiled as he scooped another spoonful of rice and curry and ate it, feigning indifference so poorly he hoped it was clearly understood as a joke.

"It's okay," he responded.

When Edgar laughed a certain way, he closed his eyes and crinkled the bridge of his nose. Scott had no idea how terribly he missed just seeing another person laugh. He decided then, and with a certainty he did not know he was still capable of, that this night was worth however badly things would end for him.

His plan, once he realized Edgar was cooking, was to insist on washing the dishes afterwards. That's how he intended things to proceed, and yet at some point time flickered and wobbled, and the next thing he knew he and Edgar were at the sink doing the dishes together. Edgar would wash and scrub, and then pass the dish or pan for Scott to dry. He did this so naturally, like this is just how every dinner shared between them always ended. And Scott followed in the same path for some time before he became aware of just how strange things were.

This isn't how he ever imagined his night to end up. He was happy to be out of the cold, out of the rain that was now conjured into a frenzy beyond the walls of Edgar's apartment – but he wasn't supposed to be here.

He should've been seated at a piano, ignoring the weight of dozens of predatory eyes that he could not see. He should've been going home with someone too enchanted by his involuntary magic to comprehend his fear.

He should be in Baton Rouge.

He should be long dead under an overpass somewhere.

There was nothing in his cards that predicted he would spend his night in the warm company of a troubled, but very striking bartender. While Edgar hummed along to the music playing on his phone, Scott took a little extra time drying a cutting board so he could examine the other man. He recognized their shared touch in the shape and size of his eyes, which Edgar couldn't hide as easily as his coloboma.

The bartender's features were strong, yet boyish. Unlike Scott he was capable of growing some degree of facial hair, though he kept it par-tially-shaved to patches of dark copper stubble.

Edgar had a good face. Round and soft along the cheeks and jawline. It almost felt familiar, though Scott was grounded enough to admit that might be a conclusion he was forcing on his own behalf. He dried dishes and let himself enjoy the music, all while silently begging for any sign of recognition from the man beside him.

But what would that look like if he saw it? And what would he say in response?

Hey, Scott mused in dark amusement, *I know we just met – but are you the absolute love of my life Your answer is time sensitive and very much life-or-death.*

"So you think you're in a soul bond, huh?" Edgar asked offhandedly.

He took two bottles out of the fridge and handed one to Scott. Scott started to decline what looked like a dewy glass bottle of beer before he read the label and saw that it was, in fact, ginger ale.

So the bartender isn't quick to drink. What an interesting addition to his character.

Edgar crossed back to the couch and sat where he did before. Then he nervously looked from Scott's direction to the opposite end of the room, and gradually it became clear that he was being beckoned to sit next to him.

"I...I *know* I'm soul bonded," Scott clarified, doing as requested.

"That sucks."

That got a startled laugh out of him. "Yes," Scott said. "I guess it does."

Edgar sipped at his soda in a way so nonchalant that Scott considered he was faking it. "Do you know which kind?"

Scott blinked a few times. He frowned.

"I mean, they really gloss over it in school since it technically only applies to key -" Edgar cringed, paused, and continued a little more hesitantly, "To genetic...actually, it's 'birthright', isn't it? That's what you call yourself?"

"Birthright, yeah," Scott echoed, ears perked at a term he actually recognized.

"Right. So it's only been documented as a birthright thing, which means in the Academy they only tell us enough to – uh – keep an eye out," Edgar, once again, looked nervous. He moved on. "But there's a few of them, aren't there? Uh...there's Anima, right? Between people and animals. Then between people there's Ally, Nemesis, Kin -"

"I only know about the Lover's Knot," Scott said. "I know there are others, but that's – that's the only one that I really..."

He trailed off when he noticed Edgar's new, sharp tension.

"You think..?" Edgar looked away and whistled low. "Wow. That's heavy stuff."

Edgar fidgeted in his seat. Scott, now curious, decided to drink his ginger ale and watch him instead of making an effort to step in immediately.

"A Lover's Knot," Edgar repeated, nodding thoughtfully. "No, that's...wow."

"What do you know about it?"

By this point it was becoming clear that it was now Edgar who was now avoiding to look Scott directly in the face. And that insight alone was so amusing that it prompted a sense of affection for this anxious, non-drinking bartender. Scott felt that, perhaps if he wanted to, he could lightly tease the other man if he wanted to.

He didn't, so he wouldn't. But he could – and that's what mattered.

"I know it's rare," Edgar explained to the middle distance. "It's the most unstable in its early stages, potentially the most destructive. Um, but it's also the most powerful?" He thought about that and drummed his fingers along his knee. "I mean, that's why it's there, isn't it? You take two overwhelmingly *in-touch* magic users with abilities so strong that they could potentially destroy reality itself, and you pair them off with each other so they'll be too content to ever want to."

His face darkened. Something in his warm brown eyes turned cold and tired.

"Whoever your Eddie is," Edgar said. "He – *they* must be one helluva witch."

He took a long drink from his bottle in a way that suggested that the soda inside could still somehow get him drunk. Scott watched, unsure what to make of the response.

Is he...jealous?

His mind reeled at the thought. His focus drifted, staring at the faint stubble on Edgar's cheek. Scott wondered how it would feel against his fingertips.

"Lots of Eddies out there," Scott remarked, shifting the golden liquid fizzing in the bottle.

"Yup."

"Because there's Edward, right? But then there's also Edwin – not as common, but I've still met some."

"Edmund," Edgar added, perhaps a little too quickly. "Even, like, *Edwardo* could be a thing depending on what part of the country you're in."

Scott raised his bottle in agreement. "Exactly! And that's not even including the people who go by Ed or Eddie when it's not even the first part of their name. I'm talking Teds, Jeds – heck, I met a guy in Virginia who everyone called Eddie, and then I found out his name was *Zedekiah*."

"And you don't know if it's a man, right?" Edgar cut in. "It could be Edna or Edith -"

"You don't meet many of that type outside of retirement homes," Scott added wryly. He phrased it as a joke, but like most of his jokes, it didn't prompt a laugh so much as a swell of deep contemplation. Edgar spaced out for a while. Then he sipped his soda and put down the bottle, clearly regretting it once he realized he no longer had anything to do with his hands.

"So what – uh..." he idly clenched and unclenched his palms before deciding to fold his hands together in his lap. "What have you been doing when you meet a potential..?" He cut himself off and laughed weakly. "Like, you meet someone you think is your soul bond. What do you do? Have you constructed some kind of test to prove if -"

"I have sex with them," Scott said, light yet unsmiling.

In an instant Edgar's face went completely blank. Scott couldn't tell for certain, but he was pretty sure the man stopped breathing for a second. Then he took a deep breath, but still couldn't quite connect the dots to compose a full sentence.

Scott elaborated, slowly feeling weirder and weirder about his own strategy. "No one gave me any ideas. I sort of thought – I don't know – love at first sight and all. And maybe through physical intimacy we'd be able to awaken a sort of...mutual understanding?"

Edgar nodded, deep in thought. "So...assault?"

The shame was immediate. He didn't expect to ever hear another person call out the second biggest horror in his head so easily. It took some time before Scott found his voice again.

"I...I used to be able to control my variant," he tried to explain. "It used to just be...I don't know. Hook-ups. I know I wasn't using magic back then because some of them said no."

This was hard to talk about. Just saying it reminded him of every touch he somehow both invited, feared, and resented. But he had to say it now. He had to say it out loud to another human being.

"I try not to," Scott said. "I really try. I don't go in meaning for that to happen, and sometimes it doesn't. But I can't live the way I do and completely avoid anybody looking at me or touching me," he stood from the couch and wandered towards the window. "As much as I'd like to."

It was colder by the window. The rain reminded Scott of home. Home.

"They keep getting worse," he murmured. "Sometimes it's easier just to let it happen."

For a while after that he drifted in a hazy silence. And it annoyed him terribly. For the first time in forever he had the chance to actually communicate with a human being and, much to his character, he was so overwhelmed by his own emotions that he didn't know what to say. So trauma fed into self-hate, resulting in a full on, snake-cannibalizing pity party.

In the back of his mind he became vaguely aware of something approaching him. It was Edgar, coming to stand beside him. There was no discernible emotion in his face. At the same time, there was something about his presence that felt like a slow, pooling wash of comfort.

Scott felt a small amount of pressure and looked down to see that Edgar was holding his hand, his touch so light and hesitant that he could barely feel it.

"I – um," Edgar swallowed hard. "Should I stop?"

"Uh, no," Scott managed. "It's nice. Thank you."

Edgar nodded and settled his hand a little closer against Scott's own.

"I guess it explains the point of buffers," Scott added. "You know, affecting through something like music versus just...*affecting*," he cracked a dark smirk. "It also makes sense why I've never heard of another birthright that actually lived outside of a witch town. I've been so *exhausted*." Without thinking, he fully grasped onto Edgar's hand and gave it a squeeze. "I don't know how you do it."

Immediately Edgar stiffened, but he didn't pull away from Scott's touch. He sighed, softly.

"You're not what I thought you'd be like," he said.

"What did you expect?"

Edgar furrowed his brow, seemingly annoyed with himself for reasons Scott couldn't place. "I always figured...God, I don't know if this is somehow bigoted, but I just assumed birthrights would be – happier?"

He eyed Scott like what he said could've potentially offended him. It didn't. Scott just felt dimly confused.

"I don't know," he said. "We're still – people, aren't we? It's probably easier in witch towns, but...I've never been to another witch town aside from my own. Bluerose has been a pretty well-sustained community, though. There aren't a lot of refuge hubs left, but we do pretty well with the resources we have."

"So why'd you leave?" Edgar asked.

Scott's heart didn't drop as much as it fell slack and hung from its surrounding veins. He gazed at Edgar again, at his kind eyes and soft curls and hands that were both dead steady and buzzing with potential energy. By this point the sight of him was enough to make him ache with longing. To make him remember what longing for another person felt like.

And it hurt. Because that question alone was more than enough for Scott to be certain that this man was not his soul bond.

Edgar continued to hold his hand in a way that would require a little more force to break than Scott was willing to commit to.

"I wish I had some kind of advice," he said. "I don't exactly have people breaking down my
door demanding to sleep with me."

"Then what happens when you use your ability?"

"I..." Edgar turned away and frowned at the opposite wall. "I don't know. I've never done anything...innate. Not that I'm aware of at least. I might not even – I mean, I haven't ruled out completely that I'm not just a regular guy with a non-special birth defect. I wouldn't say I'm necessarily – like you."

"I would," Scott said.

Before Edgar could manage a protest, Scott stepped forward and gently turned the bartender to face him. Forgetting his feelings for the moment he touched his fingertips against each side of Edgar's face and turned his head to better stare into his eyes.

"It's the size of the eyes," he explained. "They're deep-set, but not hooded. That's rare. My sister tells me that's the primary signifier of the so-called *birthright gene*. Isn't that interesting?"

Edgar didn't agree or disagree. He looked conflicted in the way someone would be if tasked to solve an equation on a moment's notice. After some time he reached a conclusion. He sighed and relaxed slightly, settling his face against the palm of Scott's hand.

All it took was this small release for Scott to suddenly realize and feel weird about the way he was touching him. He was used to the kind of physical contact that people who approached him seemed to enjoy. A hand on the waist or small of the back, or his arm wrapped around the other's depending on how submissive or dominant he was perceived to be. It wasn't something he would say he was comfortable doing, but he'd done it often enough that he's long stopped feeling anything when it had to happen.

But he now held Edgar's face the way he used to touch the field cats in Bluerose when looking for cuts or signs of fleas. Not gracefully or in a way anyone would consider seductive. It was the kind of touch that said *this is what I'm supposed to be doing so just hold still and let me care for you.*

And that was a lot for someone like him to express to someone like Edgar. So Scott pulled back emotionally and gave the bartender's cheek a nonchalant pat.

His stubble felt pleasant against the skin of Scott's palm. He stood up and made his way back to the warmth of the center of the room. It was nicer there, that was impossible to deny.

"Have you considered…" Edgar piped up softly from the window. "Okay, so, uh, you do your thing when you play shows for people and it makes everybody want to – uh –"

There wasn't any other seating aside from the worn couch by the coffee table. So Scott decided to sit on the edge of the table to let him fully face Edgar. "To put it broadly," he said.

"Well that's a – *complicated* situation," Edgar's brow knitted in thought. "It seems like if you *really* want to sleep with an Eddie you should start by finding one one that's immune to your magic."

He realized what he said about a moment after he said it. Scott watched as he experienced a flash of sheer emotional turmoil that was then pulled back with both hands, presumably meant to be crumpled up and shoved in the trash can of his subconscious. Edgar darted to the kitchen, where he carefully opened up a cabinet and propped himself up on the handles of the bottom two drawers to reach a shelf he could easily access from the floor.

This sudden, but very vivid anxiety was not at all a new experience for Scott. Maybe it was the extra X chromosome, or the aura of gender nonconformity that slipped through despite the perpetual suit. What-ever it was, since Scott started traveling he found that anyone attracted to him – regardless of enchantment – had to go through a period of jus-tifying or panicking over their sexuality.

Scott had little opinion on the matter. He knew he was a man, and he knew most people perceived him to be a man – only more people than he would prefer did so with the double exposure of a thousand question marks.

Sometimes he fantasized about how many more questions these people would have if he still walked around in bare feet and sundresses like he used to back home.

God, he wearily thought to himself, *I wish I could stop wearing pants.*

He didn't assume Edgar to be any particular sexuality. Why would he, when he still wasn't sure what made people anything? If he had to guess, by the way he reacted whenever they touched, Scott figured the bartender was trying his best to be straight. But that could mean a lot of things.

Regardless, though Edgar may be immune to his ability, appeared the effects of what Scott has heard described as Gay Panic were universal.

Edgar pulled out a white paper bag of those fancy Italian cookies and unrolled the top. "So what's next?" He asked.

"What do you mean?"

"I heard you told one of my coworkers that you were only planning on staying here for the night. Where are you supposed to go next?"

Scott thought about the small-town vet that he charmed into helping poison him. It was so warm and dry and safe here. The feeling of not being tired and hungry settled over him with a reassuring weight.

Where *was* he going next?

Eating a single fancy cookie appeared to give Edgar the courage to sit back on the couch beside Scott. He chewed his treat and then offered the bag in his direction. Scott got himself a cookie and bit off small fraction of chocolate and shortbread.

"I was thinking," Edgar remarked while Scott quietly nibbled. "If you say you're tired, why don't you just stick around for a few days and rest?

The cookie was sweet and nicely textured. It vaguely tasted of mint. It was good. "From what I've read about New Orleans, it doesn't really seem like a restful kind of city."

"It can be. If you know the right places to go. If you have –" Edgar clenched his jaw and darted his eyes to his hands. "I mean, if you know someone that can show you the peaceful places."

Scott kind of felt as if he understood what Edgar was ramping off to offer. At the same time, since he couldn't remember the last human face he saw, he was still woefully inept at reading facial cues. So he decided to stay quiet for a while longer.

"You – you said that we're both sort of...I mean, we have similar –" Edgar let out a quiet huff, "*things*. Which, in a way, kind of makes us..."

"Family?" Scott offered.

"*Nope*," Edgar recoiled in inexplicable disgust that was quickly reeled back. "I'm sorry. That was weird. I just mean that, um, you could say that we should be able to...help each other out," he nodded, a little soothed by his own reasoning. "You helped me with my boss back there. Maybe now I can help you."

"How?"

Edgar shifted on the couch, eyes scanning the room. "Uh – you can stay on my couch. I like to play music, but other than that it stays pretty quiet. I work a half-shift tomorrow, so you'd have the place to yourself. You can sleep, take a bath. I don't know. My neighborhood's pretty quiet and it's good for walking around," he eased into a faint smile. "There's been tons of chickadees outside lately. It's pretty cool."

The weird downside of having another person capable of seeing him is that Scott was suddenly very aware of his reactions being observed from an outside perspective. Sure, he would do what he wanted to and weep with joy at the thought of someone caring enough to offer the chance for him to stop his never-ending search for nothing. The thought of taking a hot bath and lying down someplace soft and quiet, with no worries of trying to figure out what other people were expecting him to be, was something out of a fairy tale.

If he followed his instincts he would already be crying, burying himself in Edgar's chest and saying any sentiment of gratitude that he could think of. But that's a lot for a person that was still struggling to speak.

The last thing Scott wanted was to scare off his first, and potentially final, chance at honest human connection.

"And I don't know," Edgar continued, focused and flushed into the middle distance. "Maybe after work I can – uh – take you out. If you want. Like dinner. Together."

Scott waited for the familiar dread and nausea to twist knots in his stomach. The pain never hit him. He just stared, slightly curious, watching Edgar's nerve grow exponentially before he figured he should say something to keep the man from passing out.

"Are you asking me on a date?" Scott asked.

Edgar took a long time to form a coherent answer. "You know, it's funny you say that because – maybe? Potentially."

Scott frowned. "Why?"

That was enough to get Edgar to look him directly in the face. He went through a cascade of emotions one after the other, with each distinct enough for even someone like Scott to recognize. Shock. Frustration. Embarrassment. Pity for a moment, and then finally quiet determination.

"You seem...nice," he began carefully. "And I've – enjoyed talking to you tonight. You like my cooking," Edgar smiled nervously. "And – you know – you aren't...like, I'm sure you know you're handsome. And that's – it's not the *most* – but it's...yes."

This was not the first time Scott had been complimented on his appearance. It was, however, the first time he reacted to it. It, like the cookie, was pleasant and made him flutter slightly deep within himself. Even though he had no way of confirming whether or not it was true.

Something on his face must've teased some of that vulnerability, because Edgar relaxed his jaw and became a little more at ease. "I'll admit," he said. "I've never been attracted to a man before. But you don't really seem like that kind of man –"

"Oh," Scott said.

Immediate panic. "*Not to say that you aren't a man,*" Edgar quickly corrected himself.

"It's okay," Scott said with a sheepish laugh. "I just wasn't sure if it was that obvious that I'm intersex."

Edgar's face went entirely blank for a few moments. His lips tightened and he nodded.

"Mm-hm," he said.

"Is that...a problem for you?"

"No no!" Edgar insisted, his voice rising in pitch and intensity. "I mean, why would it be? I know Louisiana isn't the most progressive state in the country, but New Orleans is pretty liberal," he thought frantically. "Katy's gay! You met Katy, she's gay," he paused, frowning. "I maybe shouldn't have told you that. Don't tell her I told you that. All I mean to say is – sure, right? Why not?" He took a deep breath and smiled again. "I think it's very brave, actually."

The look on his face as he said that was honey-sweet and warm to the touch. Scott was surprised to see such immediate support from a stranger that came across as guarded as Edgar. He did seem to think that being intersex was a gender identity or sexuality, as opposed to a medical condition. But he did so with such earnestness that Scott couldn't help but feel endeared.

It wouldn't be terrible to actually make a friend, would it? An interesting, highly-skilled, very attractive friend who also happened to find Scott to be attractive and enjoyable to be around.

"Sure," Scott heard himself say. "I...yes. I would like that."

Edgar's eyes widened slightly. He opened his mouth, but said nothing, and continued to say nothing. Eventually he ate half of a second cookie and hummed happily.

"Cool!" he said, covering his mouth in the way that hid the crumbs, but not his smile.

After this initial moment Edgar launched fully into overdrive and began talking more than he had all night. He got them two more sodas and told Scott anything he could think to say about the neighborhood he lived in. It became clear very quickly that he was aiming to fill every potential silence with some sort of comment or observation. Like if he stopped talking for even a moment he would take back everything he said before and retreat into the earth like an anxious worm.

There was something very sweet about that. Scott considered stepping in to console Edgar somehow, to assure him that the current situation was a little more stable than the average house of cards. But how much did he actually believe that himself? So maybe it was better to just let things play out as he did.

And besides, it was nice to listen to someone talk. Just to get that honest insight into the way another person's mind operated. If he could, he'd ask Edgar to just talk and talk so he could fall asleep to the soothing tenor of the other man's rambling.

He began to follow Edgar around the apartment as he led him to all the major points of interest. The towels. The blankets. A brief stop in front of the duck photograph hung by the door, where Scott learned where it was purchased and was consulted on whether or not he should go back to the same booth and buy another one. Scott didn't answer – he didn't have to answer – and he only actually spoke again to argue with Edgar on whether or not he should take one of the man's two pillows.

It was odd enough to feel himself wearing Edgar's clothes – not bad by any means, just strange. And it was already such a kindness for him to allow Scott to sleep on his couch, he didn't need an actual pillow. He'd been resting his head on his own arms for so long that it was essentially good enough.

Still, somehow, Edgar ended up getting him to take the pillow. It was one of those squishy ones that he knew were expensive. Scott held it awkwardly to his chest and wondered how he managed to lose a fight this basic.

Soon they were standing between the couch and the doorway to Edgar's bedroom. It was the moment where the two would separate for the night, and yet neither of them did. By this point even Edgar had run out of things to say. He leaned against the wood of the frame, idly running his thumb along the inner crook of his elbow. Scott watched him do this. After enough time he reluctantly greeted the new desire emanating in his chest with uncertain courtesy.

He looked over Edgar's shoulder and into the open space of his bedroom. It was sparse, but a little more lived in than the rest of the house. Scott supposed he didn't bother crafting his room into something other people would approve of, allowing it to feel very much like the man lingering in front of him.

There was a loose stack of paperbacks on one bedside table. On the other across the mattress, a handheld game console similar to what Tenzin bought for the house a few years before Scott left. The comforter was plush and colored like honeydew, which felt like a surprising choice.

Scott's eyes shifted to Edgar, who by now had noticed him staring.

God, his eyes were *brown*.

Once again Scott considered this slow burn rising through him. And at the same time, he recognized the soft flush on Edgar's cheeks and the vague quiver of his lips.

What if he were to move past Edgar and make himself comfortable in the man's bed? Edgar might try and complain, but the odds were good that he wouldn't kick Scott out. They could have sex right now. Scott would be lying if he said he wasn't slightly curious about whether or not he was as good at sex as his previous partners would have him believe.

Frankly, he'd love to know if he even *enjoyed* sex.

At the same time, he was tired. It had been a very, very long day. He trailed his gaze out the window as casually as possible and heard Edgar let out a breath of what might have been relief.

"So, um... goodnight, I guess," he said sheepishly.

Scott smiled. "Goodnight, Edgar."

He stayed on the couch after Edgar excused himself into his room, with no intention of going to sleep just yet. And by the sliver of light that stayed illuminated from under the door, it was clear he wasn't the only one with things on his mind.

It was well into the night that Scott felt his exhaustion weigh on him and felt his eyes start to close. But when he sank his head into the pillow his senses were filled with sandalwood and coconut. Was it shampoo? Fabric softener? Whatever the source, the smell of it conjured an image of Edgar's pleasant, crinkle-nosed smile. The thought was enough to send a bolt of electricity straight through his chest.

He shot up from the couch, stood up, and immediately went to the glass door to the patio. Outside, the storm was still raging. The drops fell and interlocked in a fashion that was close to, but not entirely correct.

Rain didn't look like this. You don't watch rain fall and wonder how long the process took to rehearse.

On the dark of the patio Scott could make out a candlestick surrounded by a shape of small stones. Growing up with Tenzin, it wasn't difficult to spot a spell circle when he saw one.

He should be dead right now. Something pulled deep inside of him, tethering him to a particular kind of madness that he constantly had to pretend not to notice. Now that effort was more important than ever.

His first date. A completely normal situation occurring under the strangest of circumstances.

Scott went back to the couch and curled up under the warmest blanket in the world. He settled his head in the plush material of the pillow and closed his eyes with a sigh.

He was supposed to die tonight.

Edgar laid across his bed and stared up at the ceiling, making absolutely no attempt to even attempt to go to sleep. He kept asking himself – what did he do?

He rubbed his eyes and smiled, despite himself. What the hell did he just *do*?

In his mind he could imagine his mother warning him of magical manipulation. Of being played like a stupid, oblivious puppet, forced to bow against the ebb and flow of another will. He heard stories growing up of what it felt like and reacted to each with varying degrees of fear and curiosity. All these adults sharing stories of birthrights the same way children would talk about werewolves or boogeymen. Rumors and tall-tales meant to keep the lines straight and orderly.

Well tonight Edgar met a birthright for himself, and he was not at all threatening. Sure Scott was troubled and sorely out of his depths in a place like this, but other than that he wasn't too different from the any other average guy in town.

Aside from his soft features. The slight curve of his smile that arched like it was the very first smile being formed for the very first time. And how careful he kept his voice when he spoke, as if his words were a series of delicate glasses balanced on an unsteady tray. And his hands that, despite looking as if they could shatter at the smallest touch, were entirely steady and surprisingly strong –

Edgar snickered derisively and clutched his hands to his face. This was new ground he was treading on.

He rolled onto his side, cheek nestled in the covers, and thought about watching Scott cry just from eating his cooking. It was the kind of reception any chef would consider too unrealistic to even dream of. At first he expected that Scott must just be near starving, but he didn't shovel down his meal like you would expect in that case. Instead he ate gradually, occasionally laughing through his tears as he clearly enjoyed every bite.

Wasn't that enough reason to ask someone out, regardless of everything that led up to that moment? It would only be a one (or several – but limited) time thing, as Scott was already paired off at birth. All the curry in the world couldn't compete with the simple fact that he was matched in the proverbial aether with someone that was not Edgar.

But it *could be,* couldn't it?

Despite knowing next to nothing about soul bonds, Edgar was still pretty confident that he would be able to tell if he was in one. And as much as he enjoyed Scott's company, as much as the man's touch sparked an awkward spark in him that was strange to process, all of it felt – normal. Nothing otherworldly. Just a product of crossing paths with someone who fit so perfectly in his space that he kept having to remind himself that he hadn't always been there.

It would be a date. Maybe a few-day fling. Edgar was very lonely, and Scott, from what he gathered, was so isolated that it defied mortal comprehension. This would be a good break for the both of them before Scott continued on to where he was meant to go.

Edgar rolled onto his stomach and buried his full face, frowning deeply into his bed. Because Scott was looking for an Eddie, wasn't he? And up until he moved, that was who he was. People still called him that occasionally, but the chains of the nickname weren't nearly as tight. It felt silly to cling to that now when he's tried so hard to avoid the variation of his own names and everything attached to it. Was it really worth going back to that minefield if it meant potentially gaining the eternal affections of some tearful genetic witch that he only met that day?

No. Absolutely not. That's crazy.

Edgar got out of bed and slid open the door to the tiny bathroom in the corner of the room. He pulled the chain on the bulb that filled the room with a cobweb-y white light, closed the door behind him, and looked in the mirror above the sink.

His hair was a mess. He looked exhausted and flushed. None of that mattered right now. What was important was the smudge of his pupils that left them looking as if left in the sun to partially melt. With the plain dark color of his eyes they were harder to distinguish, allowing him to pass through his days with fewer unpleasant questions to answer about how he was born and where he came from.

Tired of looking and thinking, Edgar sighed and sat on the edge of the tub. He recalled, again, that moment in the hallway right before he left to pretend to go to bed. They were just standing, face-to-face, not saying much but still not fully willing to separate. Tired as he was, Edgar was still searching for anything left to ask or explain. Scott waited patiently while he pondered, also visibly sleepy but still pleasant.

Then his expression changed. He raised his focus slightly above Edgar's shoulder and into his bedroom, and Edgar felt his breath quicken at this gentle, contemplative scrutiny. Why did everything about Scott have to be so careful, so fresh-snow delicate? If the man swung his fist and punched him in the jaw he would've found the pain to be far more reassuring. He was helpless like this, standing and watching Scott undress the sight of his bedroom with his eyes.

Scott turned his focus to Edgar and looked at him more closely than anyone ever had before. It wasn't judgmental. It wasn't exploitative. It was just searching, searching and seeing, like how Edgar would pour over the pages of Rilke and bury himself in every individual line of a poem. Except it wasn't a poem – it was Edgar himself. And who would ever want to look at Edgar like that?

He kept staring. The city fell away from an instant. Edgar felt limp on his feet. The slight chill in the air of the old apartment touched every inch of bare skin with near-unbearable clarity, yet the cold was unmatched by the intense heat that was now actively burning him from the inside out.

This, apparently, was all it took to seduce Edgar Gallows. Enjoy his cooking enough, be genuinely kind and friendly for a few hours, and then give one singular steamy look to earn your place in his bed. Insane. Who knew that denying himself human contact for long enough would make him so goddamned *desperate?*

And what was he supposed to do? Ian was a dick, but he was way more attractive than someone like Edgar. From the rumors the other servers spread he was romantically and sexually capable – yet one touch from him made Scott literally break down in disgust. Would he really rather spend the night in the clumsy embrace of someone with little more than a vague understanding of the mechanics of gay sex?

For the first time that night he dared to imagine kissing Scott and felt his head spin. He remembered all the ways Scott had touched him so far and tried to picture all the ways he could go on to continue touching him, and the thought was enough to make him consider that he might actually pass out.

All of this panicked overthinking must've happened over the course of a few seconds before Scott's face changed, and the mood around them shifted back to calm. Edgar made no attempt to question and instead accepted the release of tension with overwhelming gratitude. He said goodnight and hoped to god that his face didn't betray the symphony of sheer terror screaming inside of him.

Thinking about it now as hid in the quiet of the bathroom, he still felt flecks of that warmth glowing inside him. A part of him wanted to scrape every emotional ember out of him and douse the remnants of the tap until the heat was gone forever. He also wanted to curl up with his arms wrapped around himself and burrow into the feeling like you would a soft blanket pulled right out of the dryer.

This sucks. This was terrible. It was too soon and too much, and not remotely fair.

Very conscious of the man hopefully sleeping on his couch, Edgar closed the bathroom door as quietly as possible. He crawled into the small tub and tapped the only name on his sparse contacts list that would be both still up at this hour and also maybe qualified to help.

Doctor Tate picked up almost immediately.

"Hello, Eddie," he said in a tone that didn't at all suggest that it had been years since their last conversation.

Edgar stiffened at the initial sound of his voice, then relaxed soon after. "Uh, hi Tate," he responded. "What's...what are you doing?"

"I'm mending a few holes in some of my sweaters," Tate said. "The days are getting colder, as I'm sure you've noticed by now."

Even talking about nothing, listening to his old therapist calmed him as much now as it did when he was a kid. Edgar leaned back and rested his head against the edge of the tub.

He wasn't much for phone calls, but he knew enough to get that if you called another person they were usually supposed to ask why. That's just basic human conversation. However, Tate was not a basic human. Suddenly they were back in one of their sessions, and Edgar has a very vivid memory of the doctor in his mind, sitting calmly in his armchair until Edgar chose to speak first.

"I met a guy today who says he's in a Lover's Knot," Edgar told him.

He clenched his jaw while waiting for a response. Which, with Tate, could sometimes feel like a very long time.

"Another birthright," Tate remarked after taking a while to think.

"Yes. I mean...yes."

Tate took a deep and measured breath. Waiting for Edgar to continue.

"It's kind of funny," he laughed in a way that he hoped reflected amusement rather than haunted uncertainty. "We actually met because I think he thought that – uh – he was in this Lover's Knot with..." Edgar exhaled sharply through his teeth. "With me."

He stopped talking. More silence. This was absolutely unbearable.

"Do you think it's true?" Tate simply asked him.

Now it was Edgar's turn for silence. Tate repeated the question, but this time a little softer, and maybe only for the doctor's own personal pondering.

"It can't be," Edgar murmured. "I'd know, wouldn't I? That's what the professors told us. It's a connection detected primarily through the members of the bond."

"Academic education of birthright culture is spotty at best. That's why I always regretted not pushing harder for your mother to take you to a witch town when you were younger."

Edgar imagined his mother in a witch town like Dullroar. He could picture her complaining about stains and pulling back with barely-masked disgust whenever anyone tried to touch her. He imagined himself with the other birthright children, learning about plants or meditating, while his mother nursed from her flask.

Like that could've been a possibility.

"I should feel it by now," Edgar said.

Tate sighed softly. When he spoke he did so at a measured pace, the way you might when explaining something crucial and potentially volatile.

"Eddie," he began, "I am an Academic witch. As much as I hesitate to identify with that particular set of politics, I cannot avoid that I've built and maintained a connection with the Outer through education under a very strict and precise set of parameters. In Academic witchcraft, you follow procedure to achieve an exact result. It's not unlike the foundations of science or mathematics."

This was not the first time Tate has given him this talk. It was a subject the doctor had a take on so passionate that, even as a kid, Edgar figured he couldn't share with other adults in the Academy. So he listened whenever he brought it up and allowed him to talk about it until he got to the point where he started to lose his cool and had to change the subject.

"I know, Tate," Edgar said. "I'm Academic too."

"*No*, Edgar," Tate stopped suddenly and started again, a little calmer. "No, you're not. You're not and – and you never were."

There wasn't much about home that Edgar ever longed for. If he missed anything, he missed Tate. The one adult in Shreveport who considered him worthy of trying to defend. Tate's breathing patterned shifted slightly, quickening for a beat before slowing down. This usually happened in the moments before the doctor unwound an analogy to fit the situation at hand.

Edgar closed his eyes and listened.

"We've been getting possums in the garden," he began. "My daughter likes to ask for me to bring one inside so she could have it as a friend. She draws pictures to make plans, like kids her age do, with all the things she would feed it and the little house she would build for the creature. And last night I told her that, we could bring this animal inside and give it all the resources and care we could. It might even accept it, since living things want to stay alive. But that wouldn't make it less of wild being."

"Am I..." Edgar's brow furrowed, struggling to follow. "Am I a possum, then?"

"Birthright magic is innate, Eddie. It's an actual, physical component of your being that's often as tangible as any of your limbs."

Edgar nodded. "It's his eyes, Tate," he said. "No one else seems to notice, but they glow -"

"What's his name?"

"Scott."

"I'm not talking about Scott right now."

From the other end of the phone Edgar heard a door open. Tate must be going outside. Once Edgar attempted to run away from home and ended up in his doctor's yard, where he and Tate sat in the rock garden and drank strawberry milk for hours of total silence. He wondered if the rock garden was still there. He wondered if Tate kept the same little brass rake that Edgar used to create triplicate circles in the sand.

"You were raised as a tool, Edgar," Tate grunted softly as he sat down. "The born livestock of Shreveport. But you escaped! You escaped. That's not your end anymore."

"Help," Edgar whispered.

"What?"

He wiped the tears not quite spilling from his eyes and said it again. "Please help, Tate. I have no idea what to do. Scott says he's been traveling all over looking for an Eddie –"

"Which is you," Tate gently cut in.

"I mean it *could* be. But I look at him and I feel...I mean, he's nice and he's pretty and I like talking to him. But it just feels...normal."

"Yes," Tate said. "Magic often does."

Edgar frowned and sank further into the tub.

"I can drive over later today," Tate continued. "I'm happy to provide an additional insight if that's what you need."

"Okay, that would be – wait, shit, it can't be today. I work a shift at ten and then after that Scott and I are going out."

He stopped. Saying that felt a lot more natural than he expected it to be.

"I see," Tate simply responded.

Edgar pressed his face against the porcelain of the tub to try and ease the burning in his cheeks. "I've never asked anyone on a date before," he said. "I don't know why I did it. I just want..."

He couldn't bring himself to finish his sentence. Luckily, with Tate he didn't have to.

"Well," the doctor clearly smiled, "that's a welcome change of pace."

"Maybe meeting you is more important."

Tate laughed in that faint way that only he could make work. "Actually," he said. "I don't think that's true."

At this point Edgar was fully lying along the bottom of the tub, his legs splayed out over the edge of the other end. He didn't even hold the phone against his ear at this point. With the weird shape of his tub he could just press it against his ear and the porcelain with the right angle of his head.

"You should get him flowers," Tate softly suggested. "When my wife and I first started dating, she would get me flowers sometimes and I'd think...wow. It's nice to get flowers."

The reaction to telling the one respected adult from his childhood that he was dating another man was both validating and befuddling. There was truly not even the smallest roadblock in Tate's thinking. Edgar may as well have told him that he was thinking of trying tapas or taking a new route home from work.

Then again, he didn't care. His mind was already on other things – like roses. No, daisies. Maybe? Something that smelled sweet. Something Scott could sniff every so often and smile quietly, like the smell could somehow tell him a funny secret.

Edgar's heart swelled. He felt, briefly, as if he might throw up.

"Try and get some sleep, Eddie," Tate said. "I'll drive down tomorrow and we can talk more then."

Edgar nodded. He realized after he did that he wasn't thirteen, sitting down for a physical session at Tate's office in Shreveport, and so he forced himself to manage a weak response.

"Thanks, Tate," he scooted upright in the tub and exhaled in a huff. "I'll do that."

They said goodnight then, and Edgar forced himself to go to bed and avoid another sleep deprived brunch shift. He nestled in the covers, irresistibly soft and warm, yet he still struggled to surrender to sleep, tired as he was.

It was so easy earlier, wasn't it? Edgar tried to manifest some mirage of what he felt sitting on the couch earlier that night. He turned his head to the side and thought about how, despite never sharing his bed with another human being, he still slept solely on the left side of the mattress.

As if he was expecting someone else to be beside him.

Frustrated by this new romanticism, he grabbed his phone and typed up a search on his web browser.

What does "intersex" mean?

The results were embarrassing for Edgar, but incredibly informative regardless.

Scott was still fully knocked out when Edgar got up later that morning to go to work. The man had arranged himself to take up as little of the couch as possible, and he slept face-down in the pillow, just as Edgar did on nights when he was particularly drained.

This was the first time since he moved in that Edgar had to navigate his apartment cognizant of another person's presence. It was an inconvenience to have to move as quietly as possible, and not to blast his before-work playlist the way he usually did. At the same time, something about having to think about not waking up Scott was strangely exciting.

He made extra coffee and left the remains in the press pot, next to a mug he picked out and carefully arranged. Edgar considered making an actual breakfast before reminding himself that he was woefully incompetent at cooking anything anyone would want to eat before lunchtime.

So he made sure his toaster was in full display and next to the bag of bagels he bought from the bakery in town.

As he ate his own bagel, he alternated between watching Scott on the couch and feeling weird and forcing his eyes to any other spot in the room. Everything felt uncertain. Not bad at all, but also not exactly good. Just strange – though strange in a way he wanted to see continue.

Part of him worried that he would leave for his shift and come back to find his apartment empty again. Not because Scott ditched him, but because he was never there to begin with. The last day could've just been some fantastical dream, or the product of Edgar's mind finally snapping under the weight of its own suffering. He could easily imagine driving himself insane and spending a quiet night in, having dinner and conversation, and absolutely swooning over nothing at all.

When Edgar opened the front door to leave, still deep in the imagining of his own psychosis, the latch squeaked louder than intended, and Scott shifted in sleep. He raised his head slightly and eyed Edgar through a messy web of black hair. His face was still. Focused. Surprisingly intense for having just woken up.

Edgar thought about the way he looked at him the other night and swallowed hard. "Morning, Scott," he quickly said. "I didn't mean to wake you. I'm just going to work."

A beat of pure nothing. Then the tension slid off Scott in one smooth motion. He grinned in a way that lit up his whole face and seemed to raise the temperature in the room up a degree or two.

"I – I hope you have a *really* good day…Edgar," he murmured before falling back against the pillow and, presumably, immediately back to sleep.

That one interaction, for reasons Edgar didn't have the strength or willingness to explain, was enough to allow him to essentially float to work in a giddy stupor.

Edgar knew his reputation at work was not that of a cheerful individual. It's why when he asked to switch front of house that they stuck him behind the bar. There, he could spend his shift either making drinks for the more personable servers or hanging out with patrons drunk enough to find him bearable. And whenever he came in for the brunch crowd, meaning every table was guaranteed to be exponentially more demanding and just as drunk, if not drunker, his mood was usually even more sour.

Today, however, he felt fine – good, even. The sleep he got was pretty restful, which means he didn't drink too much coffee. It helped that Ian was out till dinner, so there was no risk of being hunted for sport. His usual opening tasks were no more exciting than objectively mundane things were able to be, but they went by quickly. And every so often his mind would wander just outside the confines of the Fairy's Den and he would be hit by a shudder of excitement.

He felt like a kid. Specifically, he felt like how he always imagined kids were supposed to feel when he was one.

"Eddie?"

His breath hitched and his head shot up immediately. Katy was standing across the bar from him looking considerably less alert than Edgar felt. She watched him curiously, with a noticeable hint of unease. Because apparently it was nothing short of alarming for Edgar to come to work not feeling like absolute garbage.

"You good, Ed?" Katy said.

"Yeah!" Edgar frowned, suddenly hyper-aware of the pitch and volume of his voice. "I – no, yeah. I'm fine."

She didn't seem relieved. "How was last night?" Katy continued, her voice low.

He thought again about Scott's eyes boring into him. Large blue eyes, deep but not hooded. Just like Edgar's.

"Is that guy okay?" Katy scanned the surrounding area and then came back to him, her dread sharpened to a fine point. "Scott, right?"

"Sure, yeah," Edgar said, once again feigning indifference.

"His name was definitely Scott, wasn't it? About your height, crazy black hair, ugly suit?"

"Why are you whispering?"

Katy looked reluctant to speak. She took one last look around to see who else was nearby before ducking back behind the bar and leaning closer beside Edgar. From up close he was able to tell just how tired she was, tired and immensely perturbed.

"I *saw* that guy," she said. "I *met him.* I witnessed him talk to *other people l*ast night who are on shift today. But –" Katy took a harsh intake of breath. "*None of those people remember him. None* of them. At *all.* The same people who gushed at me about how he's the most incredible, enthralling man they've ever met now have zero memory that someone was even *supposed to play a set here last night.*"

Edgar remembered what Scott told him the night before about how long his abilities were able to affect people. It must not have hit Katy because he made a point not to look her in the eye. A small kindness that he probably extended not thinking it would trigger a paranoid episode.

"He's okay, right?" Katy said again. "Do you know what happened to him?"

"Scott? Uh – Scott's fine, he's -" Edgar was trying to look cool and probably failing. "I made him dinner. He's staying on my couch. It's all good."

Immediately Katy's panic came to a screeching halt. She just stared at him with narrowed eyes and waited for Edgar to inevitably jump to fill the silence.

"I mean...I have the space," he said. "He needs a place to stay. And, you know, I figure we could both use the company. Plus he's a pretty nice guy. A good hang. So, like, why not take him out on a –"

He shut himself up immediately and tried to focus so hard on filling champagne buckets with ice that it forced Katy to forget what he just said. Unfortunately, he was not a good enough bartender to work an ice machine that well.

Katy's voice came out ice cold. "On a *what,* Edgar?" She asked him.

"Because I know you aren't saying that you brought a stranger into your home last night and you're now taking him on a date."

Edgar awkwardly palmed the ice scooper. "I can date a guy if I want," he said.

"That's not – *that's not the fucking problem*, Edgar."

He laughed, mostly out of nerves. It was around opening time by then, and the first few tables were beginning to fill up, so he grabbed Katy by the shoulder and quickly pulled her back of house to try and calm her down in peace.

"You don't pick up random guys at bars, Edgar," Katy said. "You don't pick up *anyone*. Every girl I've ever seen you with has had to ask you out. And he's crashing on your couch? You barely let me into your place long enough to *use the bathroom*."

"You've been telling me to *get out there*," Edgar reminder her.

"This is different. This – this isn't you."

"No?" Edgar hummed, leading her down the quickest path to the dry storage pantry. "Please then, tell me who I am."

"You're a feral, grumpy guy who mainly just wants to sit at home and listen to the kind of music most weird uncles like," Katy said.

"That's fair."

"You're also completely emotionally unavailable to anyone who hasn't put in the time to prove that they won't hurt you."

Well shit.

Edgar stopped in the dry storage and stepped away from Katy, allowing her to back away from his rough touch if she wanted to. But she didn't. She stayed right next to him, scanning his body with hard eyes and a grimace.

"Did you fuck him?" She asked.

"What? No! Why do you think..?" Edgar clenched his jaw and pressed his hands to his eyes. "Katy, that's not a thing I've ever *done* before."

"Did you kiss him?" Katy rephrased herself.

Almost. Maybe? There were definitely a bunch of moments in which, if Edgar leaned forward and kissed Scott on the lips, it could've potentially gone perfectly. But what was he saying when he put it like that?

Katy's anger fell away then, revealing something underneath that surprised Edgar. It was fear. The emotion looked strange on a face as strong and striking as her own, and it was enough to immediately make Edgar feel very guilty. He watched her, mouth agape and without any useful words.

"Eddie," she said, soft and slow. "You're still...*you*. Right?"

"What are you talking about?"

She continued speaking, but her eyes shot to the open doorway at every small noise. "Scott," she said. "That guy that calls himself Scott. He – *did* something to the people here. You said he's..." she bit her lip and changed her train of thought. "I don't think you should be keeping him so close to you. I think he might be – dangerous."

He imagined calling the same guy that smiled at him this morning dangerous and tried not to laugh.

"Katy, he's not..." Edgar saw the shift lead pass by outside and immediately started grabbing cans of tomato juice. "He's a witch. He can manipulate temporarily with direct eye contact, and the effects fade after a while. That's all. No harm, no foul, and when you talk to him he's actually..."

He trailed off, arms full of aluminum cans.

"Finish the sentence, Ed," Katy said behind him, a little more level but still clearly on edge. "I'd love to be enlightened on your *type*."

Edgar shrugged as much as he could with his current baggage and started walking back towards the bar.

"It's hard to put into words," he said, an immediate lie. "I just find him to be –"

a figure so painfully familiar and yet entirely new and enigmatic that it makes me wish I could somehow undo and re-weave the strands of my past in a way that would make it make sense for me to be near him for as long as possible.

"He's cool," Edgar said. "He's done a lot of food service work. Same as you, Katy. I think you might get along if you actually got to know him."

By this point Katy had passed on his left and was now observing him with even more profound disbelief. He snapped out of his thoughts and met her eyes, immediately uncomfortable.

"You two must've made a *lot* of direct eye contact last night," she said.

The implication was easy to catch onto. "Katy, it's not like that," Edgar assured her. "We tested it, his magic doesn't work on me."

"Why not?"

Because I'm either a total idiot or maybe his predestined soulmate, Edgar thought to himself, feeling strangely calm about the whole thing. The ticket machine at the bar rang in. Five orders of the special blended mimosa for a table that hadn't even opened their menus yet.

Welcome to New Orleans on a weekday morning. He groaned warmly and switched on the ice machine for the blenders. Katy stayed a few steps behind him, radiating an energy that would be better suited on a sick wildcat aiming to pounce.

"Your section's looking a little lonely, Katy," Edgar said. Katy looked at him. She looked at his outfit, then back to meet his eyes. "Is this what you're wearing for your date?" She asked, motioning up and down the height of him.

He was wearing a checkered flannel shirt and brown jeans. His outfit for after work didn't occur to him up until now, and he realized meekly that he didn't have a single article of clothing in his closet that he'd consider suitable to be comfortable on a "nice date".

"I'll...I'll probably bring a jacket," he added.

"Which jacket?"

Whatever answer Edgar gave to this question would undoubtedly be the wrong one. Still, he decided to just be honest. "The green one," he said. Katy let out a sigh and nodded. His choice in outerwear seemed to comfort her somehow. She gave him a tired pat on the shoulder, fixed her hair, and dove to meet her tables with a near perfect smile. The sounds of several tables of happy conversation were soon to be drowned out by a melody of gears and blades from the trio of blenders on the counter. This was the soundtrack of the average brunch shift when you work behind the bar.

Through the din, he considered playing Devil's Advocate against his own growing sense of optimism. He had been telling himself that looked directly into Scott's eyes all last night and felt nothing. But that wasn't true, was it? Edgar felt everything so vividly that it terrified him, but all the feelings were his own.

Weren't they? Was knowing that Scott could control him enough to render him immune, or only allow him to be charmed with the illusion of free will?

It occurred to Edgar that Scott might be thinking this exact same thing right then. He must have this argument with himself in the aftermath of every conversation he's ever had. How lonely. How confusing and frustrating. If Edgar was in his shoes he'd just stop talking and looking and touching anyone – just to keep things a little easier to live with.

Gradually over the course of the rush he felt the thrill of last night beginning to fade. And then Katy's reaction to him this morning started to make more and more sense. Of course it would be concerning for him of all people to suddenly dive into a whirlwind romance when he'd spent the entirety of the past few years essentially lying face-down in the dirt and complaining.

Imagine Edgar Gallows with a boyfriend. *Oh, this is my boyfriend Scott. He's traveled all across the country having adventures and playing music. He radiates a kind, artistic intensity. He looks like the depiction of a beautiful artist in a Greek painting – unlike myself who, as you know, constantly looks like I'm nursing a mild tension headache.*

What a joke. Edgar lowered his head – not crying, but once again feeling like he was about to.

By the end of his shift he managed to simmer his despair into little more than a dull mental fog. Unpleasant, but manageable. He was about to head out the door empty handed before he remembered to check the green room in the back for Scott's bag.

For a moment he worried he wouldn't know what to look for. As soon as he opened the door, though, there it was – a large, worn duffle bag neatly positioned on the back of the small vanity table. The bag was unzipped, and Edgar repeated this fact in his head several times to justify the small peek he took inside at its contents.

He could see a hairbrush. A composition book that was worn enough to warrant being patched up several times over. A pair of women's sunglasses, the kind he could imagine Audrey Hepburn or Elizabeth Taylor wearing in a scene where they had to be particularly dramatic. And, most interestingly, two tattered paperbacks.

Edgar ventured a hesitant hand deep enough in to turn the smaller book so he could read the cover.

It was a copy of Homer's *The Odyssey*. Dual translations of both English and the original Greek. And in front of that, a larger copy of *The Streetmedic's Handbook*.

Hey, have you met my boyfriend Scott? He can maybe read Greek or something. And he probably goes to protests to care for the people fighting for societal change in the world. Do I go to protests? Oh, absolutely not. If I'm in a packed crowd of more than ten people I will start to sweat until I am essentially a human slug.

Feeling bad on multiple levels, Edgar forced himself to stop snooping. He was about to grab the bag and leave, then noticed the small sheet that had been carefully arranged to cover the vanity mirror. It didn't look like anything the bar would keep on hand, so he figured it had to be Scott's.

As he pulled it off he half expected something terrifying to be waiting in the mirror's glass. There wasn't. Just Edgar. He looked at himself and touched the collar of his flannel.

He looked fine. Certainly better than he did when Scott ventured to call him pretty.

With that justification firmly in his mind, he slid the strap of the bag over his shoulder and frowned at the weight of it. The pressure it created against his shoulder was imbalanced and uncomfortable. Edgar imagined having to cart this bag from city to city, day after day, and the weight seemed to triple at just the thought of it.

He gave one last nod to his reflection and left with the bag still dutifully holding him down.

Before going home he had to stop and pick up some groceries. He preferred avoiding the crowds of the larger supermarkets and instead chose to go to smaller, locally-owned grocers whenever he could. There was one by his apartment that he particularly liked, even though it was cramped and arranged like a well-lit catacomb.

It was so small that, no matter where you were, you could see at least a fraction of the floral display at the center of the store. The watchtower of a pantopticon. The laser sight of a rifle, following Edgar through every other aisle.

It said a lot that Edgar still made a point to shop there, despite the faint array of floral smells that seeped through the air of the store like a spreading cancer. Others found it nice. New shoppers commented on the wonderful aroma. Edgar endured it like a bad hangover.

After getting the items he needed he found himself standing in front of the display shelf of nut butters. Just standing there, musing about what his life would be like if he made the switch from peanut to almond. Who would he be? What kinds of things would he do with his days? His questions certainly weren't diversions from the fact that this was as close as he could be to the flowers without confronting them directly.

Eventually he gave up the ruse and crossed over to the floral display. He would try. He was going to *try* to try.

Even then, it didn't work. Despite their terribly nostalgic sweetness, the selection of flowers offered for purchase just *didn't work*. They were the type of bouquets you'd put on a tombstone, or give to a friend of a friend whom you got roped into visiting at the hospital. Was he really so dumb as to try and court a real-life fae child with a bundle of coldly perfect, possibly-bio-engineered roses wrapped in non-biodegradable plastic?

This is stupid. I'm stupid. Everything is stupid.

He paid for his groceries and loaded them into the back of his car. Instead of driving off immediately, he sat in the front seat with the doors opened and took a few quiet moments to try and brute force some calm. He tapped his fingers anxiously against his knee. As his eyes settled against the empty passenger seat, he thought briefly about the softly pleading look Scott gave him the other day. How soft his hand felt in Edgar's – soft, visibly delicate, but deceptively strong.

Edgar's face ran hot. The air in the car suddenly felt very stifling.

He got out of his car and feigned stretching his leg. A thoroughly performative action, playing to an audience of no one. Edgar took a deep breath, not expecting anything in particular. So it came as a surprise when he was hit with a wave of lush, warm scent.

It was like the flowers, but fainter. Less oppressive – almost grass-like. Edgar opened his eyes and scanned the lot to try and find the source of the smell. The last thing he expected in this industrial corner of the city was the presence of woodland wildflowers, but in the patch of grass near the curb he saw it.

He knew birds far better than plants. If these were flowers, weeds, or some sort of strange grass, Edgar had no way of telling. They were rather pretty in some light way. Cloud-like bulbs of bright yellow flowers clinging to the ends of pale green stalks. And as Edgar crossed the lot to take a

closer look he knew that perfume was coming from this splotch of soft nature.

Was this cool? He could offer his prospective date some mockery of nature, or he could show up with a handful of potentially-weeds plucked off the side of the road. Something that was *maybe* poisonous but *definitely* grew in the same spot where drunks peed on a regular basis.

One choice made sense on paper. One felt better in his chest. Both could be perceived as terrible ideas.

Edgar touched one of the flowers and was surprised by the way the petals felt between his fingers. When was the last time he touched a flower? Had he ever?

There was that ache again. A tip-of-the-tongue longing that was bubbling up in Edgar again and again lately.

He clicked his tongue, thinking quickly.

"Fuck it," he muttered.

Since he just had just clocked out, he still had his box cutter in his work pants. He was about to carve through a handful of stems, when suddenly he stopped. Edgar ran his finger along one of the stalks and felt the smooth ridges of its exterior. Even though he still had no clue what type of plant this was, he imagined it took time to grow as tall and wild as it was.

For some time it must've been a scruff of green, and before that just a scattering of seeds and roots in the ground. People, Edgar included, had to have passed by this spot day after day without paying this patch of growth as much as a second glance.

And then, suddenly, life. Color. It happens every day and it's so easy to forget how inexplicable and unbelievable it is.

"Uh..." Edgar cleared his throat and whispered to the flowers. "You know. Thanks."

Driving the rest of the way home, he kept taking glances at the bouquet of yellow flowers sitting on the passenger's seat. He found a stray scrap of twine in the front console that worked well to tie everything up into one neat bundle

The final product didn't look nearly as much like trash as he thought it would. It could pass for something sold in a farmer's market. Edgar was proud of it in a strange way. And, turning down the street to his unit, the thrill of the morning returned. A giddy, child-like excitement.

He saw Scott sitting on his front stoop, and the feeling swelled enough to make his head spin. Edgar fought back a goofy grin, but even just a tight-lipped smile was strong enough to make his face hurt.

That small voice in his head that spoke up in the walk-in returned. It sounded confident. Nearly smug.

He's been waiting for you, Edgar.

You've both been waiting for so long.

And now you're finally together again!

Even from a distance Edgar could tell he was in a good mood, his blazer pulled over his shoulders while he conversed openly with one of the stray cats that wandered the neighborhood. It was the fluffy, black and white cat with the bobbed tail that sometimes watched from the tree whenever Edgar cooked with the window open. The thing was wary of any attempt from Edgar to share his dinner with it.

The cow-looking cat was now gladly allowing Scott to run his fingers along the top of its head and under its chin. This came as no surprise.

Edgar got out of the car, grabbing the flowers and Scott's bag. He watched from a short distance for a few moments until he caught the other man's attention.

"Oh," Scott said to the cat. "That's him right over there!"

The cat turned its head to Edgar and, out of habit, he raised his hand in a weak wave.

"You can talk to cats?" He asked Scott.

Scott looked confused. "Sure I can," he said. "Anyone can."

"What – uh...what's it saying?"

"What do you mean?" Scott looked at the cat and thought about the question for a while, then laughed.

"Hah! This isn't..." he laughed again, a little softer now. "This isn't a *magic* thing. I don't know what he's saying. I just like to talk to cats and birds and stuff," looking fondly at the stray, Scott cracked a small smile. "They make good listeners."

The street cat noticed Scott stopped actively petting him and took it upon himself to furiously rub his face against the side of Scott's palm.

"He seems to like you," Edgar pointed out.

Scott was too distracted by the bouquet in Edgar's hand to respond to his comment. He didn't even notice as the cat took his lack of guard as an opportunity to climb up into his lap and get comfortable.

"Where did you get that?"

Edgar felt himself blush and grew immediately nervous. Not wanting to make Scott stand and disrupt the cat, he sat down on the ground in front of him and presented the mess of yellow flowers.

"I won't lie," he began. "I found them outside the grocery store. Nothing fancy. But I thought you'd like them, so, uh…"

"They're mustard flowers."

Scott said this with a tone that felt disjointedly serious for the situation. His eyes were still stuck on the flowers. After the initial wary anxiety, Edgar got the impression that he hadn't done anything bad or wrong. Just important. Strangely, inexplicably important. He tried to accommodate the reaction the best he could.

"Here," he took the flowers and gently placed them in Scott's hand. "I got them for you."

He watched Scott's fingers loosely wrap around the twine that knotted the stems in a bundle. His eyes remained in place even as their focus drifted.

"I haven't seen mustard in a long time…" he mused in a distant voice. "I didn't think it was supposed to grow this far outside… home."

His smile faded. Scott held the yellow blooms under his nose and took a long, deep inhale. His eyes closed, and when they opened he looked like a completely different person. Scooped out, weighed down, and thrown into the ocean. Just tired and sad and so, *so* lonely.

Edgar struggled to come up with something nice to say. "I thanked them," he tried.

That drew at least a fraction of Scott's attention. "Thanked who?"

"The flowers. You know – before I cut them," Edgar quickly lost the nerve to meet the other man's eyes and instead reached a hesitant hand to pat the curve of the tomcat's back. "I don't know. It was weird, but, uh... it felt nice."

The silence that followed that couldn't have been more than a moment or two, even though it stretched on in a terrifying eternity. So Edgar was startled, yet immediately grateful, when he felt Scott's hand on his arm. That relief quickly spiraled into heart-pounding breathlessness when that hand moved to touch Edgar's cheek and gently tilt his head up to look at each other.

There was no easy smile on Scott's face. No gentle, kind light in his eyes. Instead he observed Edgar with sharp, probing curiosity. Edgar could've very well have been some kind of mysterious spider that just stuck its teeth in his arm, and now Scott was holding him up by the thorax and trying to determine how much trouble he was in.

"What's something you don't like about me?" He asked.

Edgar let out a short, bemused huff. "What? Why would you want to know that?"

"I need to know I'm not controlling you."

"Will – that prove that?"

Scott's determination faltered. "I don't know," he said. "But it'll make me feel better."

By the way he spoke Edgar figured it wouldn't be a good move to claim that everything about the man ranged from good to wonderful. That's not what he was looking for. So Edgar made the strange choice to search his brain for things he didn't like about the person he was about to take out on a date.

"You're clearly unwell," he said.

Scott raised his brow. Edgar began swearing frantically inside his head. Did he really just say that? He just brought the guy flowers and called him crazy? What did he think he would accomplish here?

"How does that make you feel?" Scott asked.

"What do you mean?"

He leaned forward, deepening his attention with a quiet frown. "Do you think it's exciting? Sexy?"

"No," Edgar said. "It – well, I don't really know you, but it's a little worrying." he looked back at what he was saying and scoffed lightly.

"It's not something I *don't* like, I guess. It's just a thing that I noticed. Seems...seems like it's difficult for you."

Scott took a deep breath and let it out in a rush of air. Whatever he was looking for in his question, it looked like he probably found it. Then, once the air settled, he began to smile. It was small, but brought a peace Edgar could practically taste.

"Oh hey!" Scott exclaimed when he noticed the bag at Edgar's feet. "Thank you."
He knelt down, unzipped the duffle, and pulled out a bulky wooden hairbrush. Edgar watched him quickly run it through his hair, smoothing the hectic black mass into a smoother wave before tying it up in a loose bun. All of this was done in a few fluid motions, acted out so efficiently that Edgar didn't have time to consider asking if he wanted to go inside and stand in front of a mirror.

Scott's face was bright and freshly washed. He shrugged off the blazer and rolled up the sleeves of his dress shirt, smiling nervously.

"I don't really have any other clothes," he explained.

Edgar responded without thinking. "You look good. Very – *lovely*." He never in his life had ever called another human being *lovely* before. The word felt ornate and dusty coming out of his mouth. Based on the way Scott managed to visibly blush through the pallor and sunburn, Edgar figured it was the right adjective for the job.

Most people blushed in a striped cloud across their cheeks. This wasn't the case with Scott, who instead flushed almost fully scarlet in an instant. It only lasted for a few moments before fading to the previous, dark gray-brown hue, but Edgar saw. He saw and knew all at once that he would be willing to do nearly anything to see that color on his face again.
That Feeling returned, buzzing in his marrow like the pins and needles you get after sitting in one place for too long. He gave a small shake, as if that would be enough to knock out the sensation.

"Uh – I'm kind of hungry," he said. "Are you hungry? There are a few really good little restaurants around here."

Scott's expression turned worried. "Oh, you want...to go out to eat? At a place?"

"Yeah! New Orleans is a pretty big food city, so if you're here you sort of have to try the scene."

He stared as if he had just been offered a hard drug for the first time. Then he laughed nervously. "You know," he said, "I genuinely forgot that dates happen in...places."

"I find most things happen in places," Edgar teased gently, attempting playfulness. "Is that new information to you?"

"No, I know!" Scott paused and lessened his enthusiasm. "I mean, I go all *over* the place. I always have. It's just a little tricky because of the – eccentricities that people say I have," he frowned sheepishly.

"Especially in restaurants. It's not something I ever thought about doing with anyone other than family, or at least other birthrights –"

"Well, I'm a birthright," Edgar pointed out.

He froze as soon as he said that. Just shy of his thirty-first birthday, and he never once said that thought out loud. As a child he would think it, especially while studying in secret or staring at his reflection on sleepless nights, and even then he never dared vocalize the observation.

Yet in that moment, the words came out fine.

You'd think he was talking about the weather. It was cloudy outside. A little chilly. Edgar Gallows is a birthright.

Even Scott seemed startled by his statement. He brushed an already loose strand of hair behind his ear and smiled.

"I guess you're right," he shifted his mood to a fragile, yet earnest eagerness. "Well...sure, then! I would love to get dinner with you."

Edgar relaxed in a way that made him realize how anxious he was about not getting to this point. He smiled, and suddenly it was like starting the day over fresh.

As they walked, side by side down the street, Edgar enjoyed explaining aspects of his neighborhood that he never got to share with another person before. Even after years of friendship with Katy, he kept her out of his neighborhood as often as he could. He saw spot her coming out of a bar on the corner once and hid in a bodega until she was out of sight.

It didn't make sense. There was shame there, but towards what exactly? He really enjoyed the neighborhood he lived in these days, despite the circumstances.

There was the street art on the trash cans and the little gated dog park. The shop that changed storefronts practically every other month, and the haberdashery directly next to it that could've been as old as the city itself.

After a few blocks of walking Edgar was suddenly aware of how much he was taking. It wasn't his usual first date strategy to point out every spot where crows liked to congregate, to go halfway up an alley to present the tree where he once saw two squirrels sharing an entire tortilla.

Nobody needed to know all of this. And yet Scott listened – avid, absolutely enraptured at what sounded to Edgar like a complete nonsense.

The sidewalk was uneven. On this street there were a few breaks in the pavement that Edgar stumbled over almost every time he passed them. Scott followed him easily. He walked without his eyes ever leaving Edgar's and still didn't miss a single step.

Could he tell what he was doing? It didn't look like he did. It looked like he narrowed the entire scope of the world around them to whatever jabbering came out of Edgar's mouth. As if there was virtually nothing else worth giving attention to.

It was hard to *play it cool* with someone so open about their interest. Someone in a flashy city on a Friday night, surrounded by stylish people, who was choosing to give the whole of their focus to the chubby loser in the old flannel.

Edgar was immediately fascinated. A little disorientated with anxiety and excitement. Every so often he would notice Scott's eyes focusing specifically on Edgar's mouth – only briefly, but long enough for

Edgar's heart to pulse unsteadily in his chest. All of that probably played a big part in how much he was talking.

He anticipated some of the people around them to fall into Scott's inadvert charm. It only became an issue once. A woman at the crosswalk tapped Scott on the shoulder and asked for directions to the transit center. Scott blinked unsteadily, dizzied from the sudden outside call for his attention. But then he turned towards the woman and directed her easily.

It was clear midway into him trying to help that the woman was no longer listening. Edgar cringed at the sight of her grazing her eyes up and down Scott's body. He couldn't see Scott's face, but when he words trickled out it was clear he noticed too.

"*Damn*, baby," she murmured coyly.

The dread came like a new, rotting heat. The sweetness of something dead. Edgar couldn't see Scott's expression and was stunned to realize he didn't need to. The woman's pale brown eyes shimmered blue, and she hooked a few sly fingers into the collar of her shirt.

"You think you could walk with me?" She offered with a smile. "You wouldn't want me to get *lost,* would you?"

"I'm..." Scott's words were weak. Shameful. "I'm sorry."

The crosswalk sign ahead of them started to flash. In a moment of new boldness, Edgar gently clasped his palm to Scott's arm and pulled him into the street. He led them down the crosswalk and kept him close. Trying to avoid the blatant sexuality of a hand on the waist.

In the quiet after that interaction, Edgar worried that he might've made the wrong decision. Then he heard Scott let out a little sigh. He felt the release of his tension as the other man practically melted closer to him.

"Thanks," Scott breathed. "I'm – uh. Sorry. About that."

Edgar swallowed hard. *God,* his mouth was so *dry.*

"Do you like pet names?" Scott continued.

"Huh? Oh. I – I don't know," Edgar chuckled nervously. "I don't think I have an opinion on them."

"Sometimes when people call me a pet name I'm worried it's because they've already forgotten my name."

That was a horrifying thought that Edgar had no idea how to relate to. "Yeah, Scott that – that's crazy."

It was a wildly blasé response. And yet a beat after Edgar said it, Scott began to snicker wearily. He ventured to look over at his date and caught Scott eyeing him with a smirk and an affectionate glimmer in his eye.

"It is," he agreed. "You got that right."

With one poor attempt at comfort, Scott apparently decided everything was fine. It wasn't entirely convincing, but it was hard for Edgar to be at all introspective with this long-haired enigma happily grasping onto his arm.

If that wasn't enough, at the end of the block Edgar saw recognized the standee of his favorite Italian place set out on he street. It had been closed for renovations for months, but now it looks like it was finally back open. Without a word of explanation, Edgar grabbed Scott's hand and eagerly pulled him inside.

Il Bambino was a small venue that made use of every inch of space. The few tables were adorned with flickering candles and floral tablecloths. Lanterns hung from the ceiling in varying heights, providing intimacy for couples and a migraine-free dining experience for Edgar. There was opera music playing in the background that was dramatic, but not nearly as theatrical as the sounds and smells that flooded out from the window of the kitchen.

"This place is great," Edgar assured Scott in an excited hush as they waited in the lobby.

Scott looked around. He nodded and appeared to accept his claim, though couldn't hide the nerves in his eyes.

They waited by the empty host's stand for a while until a frazzled young man in an apron came by and greeted them. Usually the energy in the restaurant had a calm, quiet atmosphere. Tonight, though, Edgar could notice everyone he saw buzz with anxiety. He said nothing – it wouldn't fit the standard of a date. He just followed the host to a table.

As nonchalant as Edgar tried to be, it was hard not to flinch when the young employee practically bolted as soon as he handed them each a menu.

He avoided Scott's face for a moment and scanned the ornate card stock. The good news was that his favorite restaurant still offered all his most beloved dishes. The special was a Cajun Minestrone. Edgar had a particular reservation towards any restaurant who would claim *any* kind of soup as *special*. Other than that, things were comfortingly familiar.

That wasn't exactly true. Edgar had never shared a table here with another person. It was an adjustment to account for another pair of legs across from his own. Another glass of dewy ice water.

Another pair of eyes, worriedly darting across the dining room.

Edgar put down the menu. "You all right?"

"Oh! Oh, no it's – *sure*, I..." Scott trailed off as a server sped-walked by, paused, and ran even faster in the opposite direction. "The people here seem a little overworked."

Ah, right, Edgar remembered. *He's also in food service. He can spot something's up as well as I could.*

Il Bambino was closed for the better half of the year. While Edgar used to know the whole team by name, he could look around and see no one he recognized. It happens. Theirs was an industry with a lot of turnaround. But the restaurant was filling up quickly, and though it was a small space it was clear they were painfully understaffed.

Eventually he did notice the manager and co-owner of the restaurant. She was an easy figure to recognize – stout, hunched over, an aged face constantly tight with worry. She'd make people call her Nonna, despite being too young and not at all Italian.

She always looked a little sour, but now the distaste was even stronger. If it was food safe, he would absolutely expect her to be midway into a pack of cigarettes.

Nonna saw him and nodded curtly.

"Welcome back, Nonna," Edgar called out, attempting to override the tension in the room. "Is – Is everything good?"

"Half my team is out on the first weekend of symphony season," she looked like she wanted to spit on the floor as she said that. "I'm *fucked*."

Edgar heard Scott sigh heavily from across the table. He was distressed in a way that didn't make a lot of sense for the situation. Scott had somehow already finished his water and was now pouring a second glass.

"I mean this happens, right?" Edgar said, both to empathize with Nonna and comfort his date. "Especially with small restaurants. It's a stressful line of business, which is why I think places like this are so important to support – *right*?"

He held a smile to Scott that quickly went stale and awkward the longer Scott just stared back at him. It looked like he was desperately trying to transmit a message directly into Edgar's head – not through telepathy, but with sheer force of will. Unfortunately the message wasn't passed between them.

Scott finished his water and stood up. He approached Nonna and, in her presence, brushed his hair back and bowed his head respectfully.

"What do you need?" He said.

Nonna looked up to him, immediately confused and vaguely uncomfortable. "I need a server -" She began.

Scott looked her in the eye. "I'll do it."

"What?" Nonna scoffed derisively.

"I'll work as your server tonight."

He stared at her with unblinking, glowing blue eyes, and already the focus was affecting her. "Are you..?" She clearly wanted to look away and found she lacked the ability. "Are you ServeSafe?"

"It doesn't matter. Don't worry about it, Ma'am." Scott smiled calmly. "I'm going to work for you tonight," he said.

"But..."

He took her hand and held it between both of his own. "Please give me an apron."

Her brow quivered. She blinked a few times and slowly was able to regain some of her composure. Nonna stepped back and looked around, vaguely disorientated and visibly flustered.

"...All right," she said. "I still need someone to sub for my sous chef, though. You'll have nothing to serve if the food isn't ready in time."

Scott considered her position. His eyes met Edgar's, and he motioned towards where he was sitting.

"Edgar is a great chef!" He smiled. "He'll do it."

Horror burst from his veins and reduced his body into a puddle of shame jelly. He felt Nonna observing him from a distance and hoped to god that she would still have enough sense to recognize that Edgar, a man with a complete lack of any actual professional kitchen experience, was not fit to be a goddamned *sous chef*. By the faint blue light around the edges of her green eyes, he resigned himself to the fact that his night was about to be an entirely different kind of challenging.

"I guess you know the menu," Nonna considered.

Edgar thought about leaping out the window and retreating into the sewers. It was safe in the sewers. There were no opportunities for emotional development and little risk of parades in the sewers.

Finally, Nonna nodded. "Alright," she said. "Let's get you two suited up. We're fully booked all night, so get ready."

She disappeared into the back, and in their moment alone Edgar bolted from his seat and pulled Scott closer to the back wall. Scott seemed perfectly content at first, though his mood shifted when he noticed whatever face Edgar was making.

"Oh no," he said. "I overstepped, didn't I?"

"*Do you know what a sous chef is*?" Edgar whispered sharply.

"It's a...chef. A chef cooks things," Scott became less certain of this the more he spoke. "You cook things."

Edgar pressed his hands to his eyes so hard that his vision turned starry. Scott took his arms and carefully lowered them, which was very sweet. But no amount of kindness could make this less any less horrifying.

"I'm sorry," he said. "I just get upset, I...if someone in a restaurant is in trouble and I know I can help...It's just the way I was raised," Scott bit his lip and turned his eyes away. "I shouldn't have roped you into it. I'm sorry."

"Scott," Edgar tried to explain, a little calmer now. "A sous chef is the second in command in the kitchen. They don't just cook things, they oversee the *entire functionality* of the way food is prepared and plated."

"That's not the type of thing you'd want to do?" Scott said.

Edgar frowned. "I mean, of course it is -" he saw Scott's demeanor brighten and immediately added, "but it's a position that requires a *ton* of experience and luck and *skill*. You don't just walk in the back and start doing it."

Scott looked conflicted. He tapped his fingers together in thought and finally smiled when he came to a new plan.

"Then I'll do it," he said. "I'll serve *and* sous chef."

"Scott, you..." Edgar wanted to laugh at the thought. "You *can't*."

"Why not?"

"Because you'll die. Frankly, if you can't answer whether or not you're ServeSafe, you might not be qualified to wait tables."

A note of pride touched Scott's posture. "I'll have you know I've been waiting tables since I was a kid."

"What do you –? Does your family own a restaurant, or something?"

"No. What? My mom's a pianist," he smiled like he wasn't about to say something insane. "I just mean we'd usually offer to work at the diners we'd eat at."

"That's illegal," Edgar said.

Scott held up a triumphant finger. "Ah! Not if you don't get paid. We checked."

In his confusion Edgar was coming very close to being annoyed. "*Why were you an unpaid child server?*" He whispered harshly.

There was a silence. Scott's enthusiasm lessened considerably, and he seemed to fold slightly into himself and become smaller than he already was.

"This is a bad date," he lamented.

Was that true? Was that an accurate descriptor of what was happening between them right now?

Edgar ate a lot of meals by himself at Il Bambino, and with no one to talk to he often found his focus wandering to the kitchen. He always wondered what went on back there. Despite his own disastrous career in kitchen work, he fantasized about a hypothetical team where he could be allowed to work without the psychological warfare. It was likely an impossible notion. Something about his ideal career path depended on some degree of hostility, it seemed.

But for a chance to help make some of his favorite meals in the world? To do so with a pretty powerful safety net? It's not like Edgar was so incapable that his leadership would put a restaurant patron at risk. So would he do it? Would he give himself that chance?

"When people don't remember you…" Edgar posed carefully, "do they just not remember *you*, or does it black out the whole time you were around?"

Scott crossed his arms, lowering his head slightly. "I'll be honest, I don't really know. After I started relying more on my ability outside of performances, I stopped sticking around long enough to find out."

That wasn't a great answer. But would it stop him? Edgar *could* lead a kitchen. If it was a well-run team and a single night, it wouldn't be too far outside his skill set.

If Nonna ended up with a memory of Edgar waltzing into a temporary position of authority, she'd have to also remember that *she* was the one who hired him. So in a way, this would only be awkward for *her*.

Yes. Totally. I'm not delusional. Edgar narrowed his eyes in thought. *I'm officially not straight, so maybe anything's on the table. If this is a crime it's a new one, so I can't end up the first one to get in trouble for it. Maybe.*

While considering his options, he noticed Scott gradually sinking in despair.

"I messed this up," he said. "This isn't working out. You should just go, I -"

"Let's do it," Edgar said.

Scott paused. "Really?"

"Keep in mind I've never had this much authority in a professional kitchen. Never ever. I have no idea what I'm doing."

"Sure," Scott said. "I never know what I'm doing. I've found for people like us it doesn't really matter."

"Maybe I'll get to help make the shift meal," Edgar considered. "That'd be pretty cool."

Saying that made him doubt whatever prowess he thought he had a poet. It didn't even begin to uncover the depth of feeling he had towards the concept. The thought of making that meal himself and watching the team of exhausted staff members unwind with his cooking was an opportunity he couldn't possibly pass by.

Scott stared at him with the same expression he wore when they first locked eyes the day before. This time, though, whatever emotion that expression reflected built and bubbled up. Edgar had never seen the ocean, but from videos and photos he could compare the act to the build-up of a wave. Something inexplicable that climbed up, taller and taller, curving slightly as it rose. Then it crashed into white as Scott stepped forward, wrapped his arms around Edgar's neck, and kissed him.

A lot happened all at once. Something snapped in Edgar's chest and it felt like he could suddenly feel his entire body with greater and actual accuracy. He experienced every human emotion in rapid succession until they blurred together and became indistinguishable aside from static bolts of sensation. It lasted for an instant before Scott broke away and started to apologize for being so forward, but Edgar immediately fumbled to pull him back in. He needed another chance to taste what felt like sunlight bathing every inch of him.

He could feel Scott's fingers tracing through the shaggy curls at the back of Edgar's neck. He marveled at the weight of it all, the combination of warmth and chill. For the entire time they were that close to-gether Edgar had no past or future, or even thoughts of the present.

But it was more than that. As Scott kissed him, a spiderweb of cracks formed in the reality around them and stretched onward with a buzz of a billion drunken hornets. He no longer felt the ground. He no longer remembered the *sensation* of ground. There was truly nothing fath-omable keeping the two of them from falling into the unending scream.

Countless eyes peeled open from the nothing. Some were bloodshot, some bleeding, some entirely blind – and they were all angry.

They were *hungry*.

Reality returned. Edgar felt the world, felt his body, felt Scott breath-ing against the crook of his neck – sensations so sudden they, at first, were impossible to decipher. Whatever movement he made to pull Scott in for another kiss was so sudden it left a searing throb in the joint of his bad shoulder. Edgar didn't care. He was awash in wonder. He felt so much of himself and didn't find the awareness frightening – potentially for the very first time.

Sometime during their previous embrace Scott's dress shirt rode up slightly, and Edgar now had his fingertips clutched against the other man's bare lower back. It wasn't an explicit touch. The fact that it was barely anything somehow made it feel all the more tantalizing.

He didn't want to move away. He moved away and stammered an apology.

"It's okay," Scott's tone expressed a mild, amused surprise. "I – I liked that, actually. It felt...nice."

It felt nice. Edgar made Scott feel nice. He allowed himself a full, toothy grin and tried to gather himself for the night ahead.

"You'll, uh...you'll have to call me *chef* tonight," he explained, trying not to sound too excited at the concept. "Just as long as we're in here, I mean. It's a – sign of respect, you know?"

He worried that was too much. But then Scott let out the softest chuckle, a throaty, smoky sound that bolted straight down Edgar's spine.

"...Yes, Chef," Scott whispered.

Edgar could've died right then and there.

Going into town to eat never made much sense for Scott and his small family. Bluerose had the mess hall, a community kitchen with a regular calendar of meals available three times a day for employees and clients. There was also a small market restocked twice a week by truck, with employees on call to deliver right to the doorsteps of the people in town. There were a few small storefronts that had been passed from owner to owner run as a cafe or small restaurant. And if that wasn't enough, the lounge was just out of town with its own dedicated, semi-formal kitchen.

But Scott's father waited tables while he was still in med school. He was working in a little diner in Hillsboro when he met Scott's mother. So it was considered, perhaps, a way to pay tribute to the late Doctor Kaufner's memory. Regina Mustard Kaufner would take him and Tenzin to some little breakfast place – the kind that, if they were well-intentioned enough to offer vegetarian options, were rarely something worth trusting. And inevitably, after they finished their meals, Regina would warmly insist on helping with some sort of repair.

At first Scott and Tenzin would bide their time for the few hours until their mother had finished. Eventually young Scott decided that, if his mother was able to lovingly push her skill set and kindness onto strangers – why shouldn't he?

So he helped bus tables. He learned to *ask forgiveness and not permission,* as the saying went. Often no one would notice until he had already been working diligently for a good stretch of time, and at that point it usually was deemed too confusing to stop.

When he got older, he approached serving tables with the same mindset. Tenzin by then followed his lead in a way, though she much preferred helping their mother with her handiwork.

A part of him knew this routine of theirs was odd. Even if he didn't have friends informing him how weird a hobby this was, Scott was a clever kid and gathered this wasn't usually what families did together. But they *were* together while it happened. And the owners of their usual places were grateful for the help and attention that came from having two little temp workers who would accept payment in the form of free fries and desserts.

The whole *forced-assistance* routine was less fun when he was on his own. It was impossible to bare if Scott thought too hard about what *forcing* meant for him these days. It wouldn't be long until he would be as old as his mother was when she started raising him and his sister on her own. When that day came, would he still be around to see it? Would he still be doing physical labor and getting paid in free food?

He was given a striped half-apron with no pockets. Hard to think of a more superfluous accessory. Scott considered turning down the pen and pad offered to him, then decided with the current state of his memory he would need all the help he could get.

With a few minutes before the shift change in the main dining room, he lingered near the back where he could peek into the window. Edgar appeared determined. He also looked as if one wrong move would cause him to shatter from anxiety.

Their eyes met through the serving window. Edgar blinked uncertainly. Then his expression steadied and he flashed Scott a brave thumbs-up.

Scott's attraction hit him hard. The aftershock was a heady mixture of annoyance and worry.

This was supposed to be a brief rest before a prompt swan dive into the void. He had gone this way assuming it'd be a fun night or two and little else.

Some company, Skylark, he cynically reminded himself. *A hook-up, even. You know hook-ups? You've been gritting your teeth through a lot of them lately, it might've been nice to see if you'd like the kind that normal people have.*

He didn't plan to be this *affected.* That was the word that made more sense than something like "aroused". The way Edgar's touch so far had gone from careful to suddenly honest and needing still echoed against Scott's skin. That wasn't quite the intensity he had prepared for this late in the game.

Through the window he saw Edgar unbutton the flannel he came in with. He had a t-shirt underneath. It was worn and gray, with a collar that started to wilt a little lower than it likely was designed to hang. Scott could see a small tuft of chest hair peeking out. A darker brown than the burnished copper of Edgar's curls.

Scott stared longer than he meant to. He considered the whole of Edgar's chest, how it was broad and more heavyset. How it felt to be pressed against that chest when Edgar clutched him tight, as if catching him mid-fall.

There was a *heat* that radiated from Edgar. Scott was chilly almost constantly these days. He'd forced himself to avoid thinking about physical intimacy to the point where he'd actually forgotten a human body could *be* that warm.

A young server informed Scott that he'd be taking over for her section and filled him on the state of his tables. He listened. He thought about Edgar's fingers pressed tight against his back, and how they trembled slightly every time Scott breathed against his neck.

He had to work.

Maybe I can get out of having sex and just ask to lay my head on his chest and have him play with my hair.

No. Not the time. He had to get to work.

The next few hours of the night went by easily. It was the dinner rush. Luckily, this was a neighborhood restaurant, and a majority of the patrons seemed to be regulars. They asked few questions. In fact, they often already knew what they wanted before Scott could hand them a menu. Things went quickly, which worked out well.

Faceless diners cycled in and out. Some occasionally made flirtatious remarks, which Scott was too busy to linger over for long. A few people asked him for his number, to which he'd happily respond with a random string of seven to thirteen numbers.

One person asked him his name. Without thinking, he said it was Lark. Then he paused, cringed, laughed politely, and made an excuse to leave.

Even as the restaurant got busier – and it did get busier – he never lost track of Edgar's presence in the kitchen. He stole glances through the serving window whenever given the opportunity.

Edgar directed the other chefs and jumped in to work when needed. He expression was narrowed. Determined. His jaw pulsed and his hands shook terribly. Every so often he would pause and rub at what looked like a sore spot between his neck and shoulder, but only when no one was looking.

Scott wanted to curl up in his warmth and fall asleep like a stray cat. He wanted to feel Edgar's pulse against his tongue and chart the blood through his veins like how cartographers document riverbeds.

This was a lot to process all at once.

He was tapping in an order when Edgar's voice suddenly rang out from the kitchen, far stronger than it had been since they started working that night.

"*Don't –*" he cut himself off and tried to calm down. "That's the gluten-free fryer, right? You're about to cross-contaminate."

Scott pressed his lips tight. It was eavesdropping and a distraction from juggling the needs of his six tables, but he couldn't resist. He got a little closer and listened more.

Edgar became a little more meek, but continued talking nonetheless. "Semolina Flour *does* have gluten, actually. It's just made from a different kind of wheat. Have you – been putting these in *both* fryers?"

He listened to an explanation Scott was slightly too far away to make out. Then he heard Edgar suck some air in through his teeth and suddenly bolt back into command.

"We're 86-ing all fried food for the night. I can clean and change the oil before then, but it's not worth distracting the servers. Is..?"

There was a sliver of Edgar's face visible. He was frowning guilty. It was the look of someone who stumbled into an unearned position of authority and was suddenly aware of getting a little too comfortable with it. The other cook said something, and Edgar's frown lessened.

"No, it makes sense. Semolina looks a *lot* like cornflower, and your walk-in's not labeled as well as it could be. I've already started working on that a bit. Maybe when the rush thins you can help me – if you aren't too busy."

Scott couldn't hear the cook's response, but he saw Edgar warm into a shy smile. It could easily be gathered what the cook said. *Yes, Chef. Thank you, Chef. Your nervous disposition provokes an inexplicable sensuality that's very difficult to resist, Chef.*

Scott knew about chefs. He'd seen first hand the wick of their tempers. Some would strike out in rage at a moment's notice, while others would simmer darkly and slip out every so often to indulge in their substance of choice. Chefs, typically, were not happy and healthy people. But he knew immediately that Edgar was different.

Edgar's voice stayed calm, professional yet not unfriendly. He said "please" and "thank you" after giving requests to the other members of the kitchen. When he needed to make adjustments he did so gently, explaining the reason behind every change as he suggested them. Even better, when faced with something he was clearly unfamiliar with, Edgar asked questions with the mindset of someone who actually cared and wanted to learn and grow.

He thought about the touch of his authority. It was stern without authority. Just a person who knew a lot and cared about what they did.

It wouldn't be bad thing to be guided by a person like that. It wouldn't be a bad thing at all for a person like that to organize and direct, to keep things running efficiently. To graze their lips across Scott's skin, soft enough to make the baby hairs tremble in delight.

Skylark, Scott scoffed at the way his head swam. *Come on, Lark. Get a hold of yourself.*

Scott was fumbling to find his senses when until another server came up next to him and called into the window.

"Table eight wants to sub their red sauce for white!" They shouted.

Edgar responded while flicking switches at the base of the left fryer. "Got it, thanks! And we're 86-ing fried foods for the night, spread the word!"

The server gave a respectful *yes, Chef* and darted back into the weeds. Scott watched them go. When he turned back he realized Edgar had spotted him staring and was now staring right back.

He leaned against the worn counter top. His forehead was slick with sweat, with curls plastered to the side of his face. It wasn't the first time Scott had seen Edgar's bare arms and hands. With the heat and the work, they were now reddened in a way that highlighted every mark and burn scar. He was working his hands through a white rag, a playful brow cocked.

"How'm I doing, you think?" He asked.

Scott swallowed hard. Edgar was just trying his best doing something miles out of his comfort zone. He was rising to the ridiculous occasion Scott created, and all Scott had to do in return was match the friendly, lightly-flirtatious energy being brought to the table.

"I want you more than I have ever wanted another human being in my entire life," Scott said. "I want to feel you like standing outside in the springtime. Sunshine on every inch of me and flowers in the air. I...I, uh –"

LARK! Scott mentally screamed at himself. *YOU'RE BEING WEIRD! THIS IS THE WEIRDEST THING YOU COULD DO!*

Edgar's light humor was gone. He didn't look disgusted or fearful. His gaze was relaxed. Thoughtful. He blinked slowly at Scott, still toying his fingers through the rag as he observed Scott from through the window.

His eyes were brown. The hair on his chest and arms was a slightly lighter shade of brown. Edgar parted his lips slightly, then arched them into a smirk.

"You should get back to your tables, Scott," his tone was firm, yet giving. "That eggplant parm next to you is for your table four. You'll want to get that served fresh...*Scott.*"

Scott's cheeks burned. His chest burned. His *eyes* burned – when was the last time he blinked?

The only thing he said in response was the only thing he could think to say. He spoke it low, as gravely as his register was ever able to get.

"Yes, Chef..." he murmured dreamily.

The rest of the night was quick, busy, and hard to keep track of. By the time the flow of diners trickled into something more manageable, Scott was remorseful at the chance to catch his breath. He lamented any free space to think, because that inevitably filled his mind with disjointed mental images and imagined sensations that were difficult to know what to do with.

While closing down for the night, Scott didn't realize the other servers had accepted him enough to include him in the tip-out until he was handed a crumpled pile of bills and change. He took it like someone who had never seen paper currency before and wasn't sure what it represented. He wiped down tables in a daze, still hearing the work in the kitchen and thinking about the way Edgar managed to turn Scott's own first name into something so seductive.

A few servers were nearby, openly allowing him to do their work on their behalf. He was fine with that and welcomed the distraction. They traded some gossip and trash talk about some of the more troublesome patrons of the night, which Scott took part in reluctantly.

"So Lark," one blurry face in a high ponytail remarked. "You single?"

Scott struggled to think of an answer, thrown off by another person calling him by the name he'd essentially buried the day he left home. A few moments later the taller server beside her answered for him.

"Nah, I talked to Rachel in the kitchen. She said he's with Chef Edgar."

The first blurry face made a noise of playful disappointment. Scott kept his head down and continued cleaning the last table of the night, rubbing the washcloth to dry out the disinfectant.

The table was dry. It had been dry for some time now. At the rate Scott was going he ran the risk of polishing straight through the wood itself.

He's with Chef Edgar.

Scott continued rubbing circles with the dishrag.

Just as the few servers dedicated to actually complete the closing duties were finished, a few cooks from the back came out with steaming trays of food. The small dining room was flooded with the smells of fresh bread, and Scott noticed a big dish of spaghetti dressed with tomatoes and olives. It looked amazing and smelled even better.

Scott hadn't eaten that day. It had completely slipped his mind. This was the point in which hunger hit him, along with an additional flood of desire that made it very hard to function.

Edgar, he told himself. *Where's Edgar? Food can wait. Got to find my Edgar.*

Thinking that, he heard what Edgar told him earlier in the rush. *You'll want to get that served fresh...Scott.*

He had just finished serving himself a plate when he noticed Chef Edgar sitting in a booth at the far end of the room. The man practically glowed. He was flush with a happy exhaustion, a relaxed, sleepy ease that acted as an overpowering magnet.

He was already watching Scott. There were stains on his shirt and a little splotch of pesto on his cheek. He grinned like a kid might. Scott quickly filled a second plate and met Edgar at the booth.

"How was it?" He asked.

Edgar didn't answer. He didn't even look like he was struggling to think of an answer. All he did was take in the sight of Scott across the table, his chin supported on his hand. This was not an *in-public* type of look Edgar was giving him. This wasn't even an *I'm-openly-imagining-having-sex-with-you* kind of look. This was something primal and new.

This was something that Scott *would not expect* from a man who meticulously organized and labeled everything in his kitchen cabinets.

Scott was already talking before he realized it, resulting in a few stray words that made no sense. "I have..." his eyes darted from side to side. "Lot of...lot of *curtains* here –"

"Try the puttanesca," Edgar cut in.

Scott went silent. He looked down at the spaghetti on the plate and obediently spiraled a mouthful onto his fork to take a bite. It was immensely flavorful with notes of fish and garlic. It was immeasurably gratifying. It reminded Scott of the ocean in a way that made tears spring to his eyes. Scott resisted the temptation to pull his feet up onto the booth seat and eat the entire portion as quickly as possible. Instead, he wiped his mouth with a paper napkin and tried to enjoy food like anyone else would.

"You made this, didn't you?" He asked.

Edgar's grin broadened and his brown eyes shone brilliantly. "I wondered if you'd be able to tell," he leaned forward and lowered his voice. "The head chef had to pick up her kid, so for the last part of the shift I was the lead. Me. For almost *two hours*."

He spoke with a hushed excitement that was raw and rich. Scott fell straight into the lush color of his eyes and thought, in some part of his mind that was still semi-cognizant, that the quality of them was somewhat different now. The only word he could think of to describe it was *luminescent*, but that couldn't be right – could it?

The light flickered in and out. Either it was struggling to maintain itself, or Scott's mind was struggling to be able to perceive it for too long at a time. While he gazed and struggled to stand under the weight of his own unfathomable longing, Edgar poured two glasses of some ruby red cocktail.

He explained it was just Campari and soda water, and he was midway into explaining the flavor notes of this *aparteif* when Scott just shot it back in a single gulp.

The look on Edgar's face told him that this wasn't the kind of alcohol that was meant to be swallowed back as quickly as possible. Liquor was so arbitrary. Scott was tired and hungry and physically wanting in a way that was intimidating to try and approach.

"You don't drink much, do you?" Edgar laughed lowly.

Scott slid him his empty glass. "I'm used to vodka," he said. "Give me another, I'll try again."

They sat and began to drink together. Even after their plates were empty they continued to drink and talk. In the back of his mind Scott was waiting for somebody to kick them out. He stuck around for shift meals before and this was usually around the time when people would be eager to go home for the night. And yet, when he looked around, he saw the rest of the staff getting even more comfortable.

Cozy. *Weirdly* cozy with each other – but like the *something* in Edgar's eyes, it was difficult to pay attention to for too long.

Edgar and Scott somehow ended up on the same side of the booth. When did that happen? By the way Edgar was still up against the wall, it looked like it was Scott that moved to get closer. So once again he asked himself – when did *that* happen? He could now lean against Edgar if he wanted to. With the size of the booth they were already essentially touching. But he didn't. Not yet.

He was satisfied with just lying back and listening to him as he told stories about his shift in the kitchen. While he was technically listening, Scott was more focused on the new depth of emotion rising and falling in every word Edgar said. It felt like a buzz, but he knew his alcohol tolerance wouldn't allow him to get remotely drunk off of the amount he drank. The real intoxicant was the joy in his date's voice.

Scott felt so unbelievably happy. He had no idea that was still a possibility in his life, and yet here he was, fully content with the state of every atom in the universe. Even though the pain that followed him on a constant basis wasn't fully gone, it was able to be dulled to little more than a low ache. And that was amazing. Scott filled his chest with air and exhaled softly, closing his eyes for a moment when *the world fell away, torn like cheap tissue paper off a gift you open in a fit of rage. Scott was back in that place, that non-euclidean nightmare that made no sense and allowed for nothing but viscous drifting. It was nothing. Looking directly at it made his veins burn and his eyes taste like blood, but no matter if he kept his eyes open or clenched them shut the place was all he could see.*

No – fuck. Not here. Not now.

The infinite non-boundaries around him watched with desperate, mocking eyes and eyes and eyes. He could feel the negative space like a constricting mass entombing him, but also like the skittering legs of countless starving spiders. There was no one place he could look at, no singular entity to beg at with his eyes. His charm wouldn't help him here. There was no way to look something in the face that existed all around him, everywhere, all at once.

Then came the voice. It sounded like everyone Scott has ever heard overlaid in cacophonous unison. It rang so sharp and loud in his head that it made his eardrums wish for the mercy of bursting. Despite that, he knew that the thing speaking was still very weak.

Getting...distracted...Birthright, it murmured.

No. Please no.

Getting...hungry...Birthright...

No more, Scott screamed in his head, too far out to cry. Just end this. I'm so tired.

Want...More...

Scott's mind reeled and fractured. Please no no more I have nothing I have nothing else please god stop it stop it just let me die.

The noise in his head warbled. The voice, he realized, was laughing at him.

Never die, it said. You...will never die...not with...my help...

Scott came to suddenly, and for a moment his mind was an absolute blank. There were new shapes and colors in front of him that made less sense than the ones in the place. Slowly reality returned to him. The restaurant. Edgar. His very first date.

He was so, so happy. What a joke.

By this point he was sitting up in the booth. He never fell into that Somewhere Else around someone able to notice his absence. Whatever he did while he was preoccupied completely drained the color from Edgar's face. He faced Scott upright, eyes wide, looking ready to catch him if he were to suddenly pass out.

Scott tried to say he was okay now, but when he moved his mouth no sound came out. He figured that he just lost his words again – it wouldn't be the first time. Then Edgar said something, maybe a question or sentiment of concern. Whatever it was, Scott quickly realized he couldn't hear him. Then he focused and noticed that the tinny music, the quiet conversations of the other staff members, and the sounds of passing traffic were all replaced by the thump of his heartbeat and the murmur of his own blood.

Scott couldn't hear. He snapped a finger in front of his ear and the result was barely a thud. Just *thicker silence.* He was completely deaf.

This wasn't life-ending. He'd known people with varying degrees of hearing loss, hadn't he? But at this exact moment the realization of losing *this* along with everything else was simply too much.

He couldn't do this. Scott couldn't do this anymore. He couldn't keep pushing against something that proved over and over again to be far stronger than he ever was and ever could be. It was shocking at this point to think he'd lasted as long as he did.

If he ended it tonight, would that fix things? Would that save everyone he'd leave behind? Would his body rot as it should? Or would that *thing* swoop in and fill him quick enough for his heart to barely skip a beat?

Would he go to heaven if he died? Scott didn't think he believed in heaven. Would he wind up there anyway? That murky, colorful pit – was *that* the kind of heaven he'd end up in?

Scott didn't want an afterlife. He wanted quiet.

Quiet. He supposed that's what he had right now.

Hilarious.

Edgar touched his hand. Skin met skin, and all at once sound returned. The noise was welcome, though intense enough to spark a flinch and immediate headache. The lights felt brighter now. Scott winced softly.

"You okay, Scott?" Edgar said.

Scott looked at him. Edgar was beautiful and interesting, capable and intelligent, passionate and deeply-feeling. He was a lovely man, and it was very possible that he was the Eddie that Scott spent the entirety of his life looking for.

Or maybe he wasn't. At this point, who cared? At this point, what difference did it make?

It didn't matter anymore. But maybe Scott could allow himself a few more moments of comfort.

He leaned forward and settled his head into Edgar's chest. He smelled like basil and tomatoes, but if he turned his face to rest in the bare crook of his neck Scott could pick up the same scent he recognized from the bar of soap in his shower.

There was a strange dip the aortic arch on his neck that gave the vein an appearance of being two separate strands that could never quite meet. It didn't look natural. It couldn't be.

But, once again, he asked himself – who cares?

Scott kissed the gap and immediately felt Edgar shudder under his touch.

"What..?" He began in a voice already quavering.

Scott sat up and eyed Edgar, unsmiling. He grazed his hand over the other man's knee and slowly started to trace his fingertips up his thigh. It was an action he was taught early on and continued to do countless times on countless Eddies. Only this time he wanted to do it. This time he actually felt everything all his previous flings decided he must feel.

How beautifully and pathetically tragic.

"Take me home, Chef," Scott whispered.

He thought that would be the end of it, but it wasn't. Just as his hands were about to brush over Edgar's crotch the chef reached down and stopped them.

"Do you want this?" He said.

Scott stopped. He pulled his hands away and sat up, bringing some distance between them and allowing the blossoming heat to dissipate slightly.

"I won't lie," Edgar continued. "I mean, I've never done this before. I don't know if...but I want to. *I* want to. But we shouldn't if you just feel like..." he rubbed his eyes and sighed. "I'm sorry. I probably killed the mood, I think."

He was trying to help him. After how messy everything Scott brought him into was, Edgar still genuinely had his best interests in mind. Scott wasn't ashamed anymore. If there was any discomfort left inside him it was gone and gone for good.

"I don't know if I like sex," he was surprised at his ability to say that out loud. "I know that probably sounds crazy –"

"No, it makes sense!" Edgar jumped in, a little too enthusiastic. "I – I *totally* get it. I mean, it can be nice when it happens. But it's also *so* stressful. And you have to do *so much prep work*. And sometimes by the end of it I'm too tired to be anything but relieved it's over, you know?"

Scott related to that more than he expected to. He fought back a smile.

"Maybe we could...try it," he said. "You and me. I mean I *really* like you. And we wouldn't have to worry about the – uh...*prep work*. We can just – try it. What do you think?"

All it took was one shy look after this to see that his honest perspective left Edgar more breathless than when Scott was ready to hook up with him right in the booth. He gaped at Scott and struggled to speak.

"...O-Okay," he finally whispered. "Let's go."

By that time it was well past midnight. Some of the staff were fast asleep, touching hands or fully holding each other. A few people kept up a conversation in quiet, intimate comfort, turned entirely towards the other person as the spoke. Regardless of where they were or what they were doing, no one at Il Bambino noticed as Edgar took Scott's hand and guided him back on the street.

And when the sun rose in a few more hours, the team of this small restaurant would wake up, scattered on the floors and booths of their place of employment. They would be confused. They would question the empty bottles littered on the floor when none of them had a hangover.

They would have no memory of the shift the night before.

Etude no. 1

Two men share the same bed, unclothed in the first few hours of the morning. They are both warm with color and heat. They do not embrace, but overlay their hands atop each other, fingers intertwining.

The First watches the Other man, whose eyes are red and bloodshot. The Other catches his breath, worn from the aftermath of his small breakdown.

"I'm..." he isn't looking at the First, but can clearly sense him looking. "I'm sorry about that."

The Other takes in the silhouette of his body in the darkness. In his ugly suit it's hard to tell how skinny he is.

Fully nude, it's easy to miss how surprisingly strong he is. Just *solid*.

"I had a really nice night tonight, Scott," the First smiles.

The Other meets his eyes. The blue glows slightly in the darkness.

The First speaks again, his voice drifting even softer. "Can I come closer?" He asks.

"...Yes. Yes, please."

Satisfied, the First draws towards the body beside him in bed. He stays partially upright and allows a full examination of the star map of freckles falling down the Other's neck and splaying across the softness of his chest. Despite the sheer anxiety of their first night together, the First is fully at ease when he traces his fingers down the Other's side.

The Other shudders in a way impossible to hide in his current state. Putting his desires aside, the First pulls the covers up over them both and nestles against his bed mate. After some hesitance he feels the Other wrap his arm around him.

What a thrill. Absolute bliss.

Things will be different now, the First thinks to himself.

"We could try again, if you want?" The Other offers, reluctance and shame clear in his words. "I – I think I'm calm enough to...get *back on track.*"

The First snickers under his breath. "I'm actually *quite content* with the way things went tonight. Glad you're feeling better, though."

He adjusts and lets out a happy sigh. The Other suddenly feels both more relaxed than he'd been in some time, and an entirely new type of tense.

He's happy. He's *happy*? Despite the mess of all of this?

"Can I ask you something?" The First pipes up after some silence.

Already the Other braces himself for the question he's expecting. Why don't you like sex? Is it because you have the kind of body that gets you called *ma'am* by strangers until they see your face and cringe in visible confusion? Does it have anything to do with how you've avoided reflective surfaces for so long that you've entirely forgotten what your own face looks like? Is it that you're so desperate and touch starved that even physical affection you enjoy will apparently cause you to break down weeping?

"Do you think my puttanesca was *too* fishy?" The First asks, the question sleepy and thoughtful.

The Other lets out a breath. He swallows hard and adjusts the way his hand settles between the First's shoulder blades.

"It...has anchovies," he manages. "And capers. I don't see how it *couldn't* be fishy."

After a moment, the First snickers against him. "I'm probably overthinking it," he decides.

He nestles closer to the Other. It isn't long until his breathing softens and levels out. He is asleep. He is peaceful. He is *happy*.

The Other nurses something that feels like grief and affection. He relaxes, mainly to provide a pleasant nook for the First to rest in.

Things could've been so different, he thinks, staring at the sliver of moon visible through the open window.

Third Movement

Edgar was never much of a morning person. Today, however, he found himself up far earlier than usual. He stayed in bed, lingering in the warm silence of the morning, and watched Scott sleep beside him.

He told himself moving risked waking him up. And Scott Skylark Kaufner was clearly a man who needed all the restful sleep he could get. Therefore, the most polite thing he could do was stay exactly where he was and blissfully observe his companion's sleeping form.

Scott was like an oil painting. There were visible signs of sickness in the pallor of his skin and the angles of malnourishment. But at the same time there was a softness to him – the *capacity* for softness. A tangible strength more stabilizing than overpowering.

He was like no one Edgar had ever seen before. At the same time, seeing him as he was now felt remarkably familiar.

What if it was like this every morning? He mused blissfully. *What if I asked him to stay?*

Edgar scoffed at his own forward-thinking. That was ridiculous. He was being ridiculous. It was much more productive to move past thoughts like that and enjoy the good thing he was given.

Turning back to Scott, Edgar found he finally felt comfortable enough to carefully brush the hair out of the man's eyes and get a full look at his face. His nose was strong with a straight bridge. There were shadows rung under his large eyes. The aftermath of a sunburn across his cheeks.

It was hard to resist the urge to trace the curve of Scott's jawline. To spend at least an hour paying special, tender attention to every curve in his face. Just because he wanted to. Just because he knew from the night before that Scott would enjoy it. Just because he finally could.

He had to hand it to him – despite the lack of proper certification, Scott was a pretty good server. He was absolutely fine-dining good, and charming enough to double his wage in tips on any average night. And if it was a restaurant that pooled tips, that personable demeanor would be a raise for the entire staff.

Edgar could polish up his resume. If he caught Ian during the right hangover, his old boss might agree to be a reference. He could start at the bottom and work his way up. He'd done it before and he'd do it again. The struggles and anxieties and doubts would be nothing if Edgar could end his day curled up in the quiet stability of easily the most inexplicable, wonderful human being he had ever –

Eddie. Fucking hell. Get a hold of yourself, man.

He laid back in bed got a closer look at Scott, listening as the man hummed a quiet, unfamiliar tune. *Happy* wasn't a word strong enough to describe how he felt right then. There was an erosion of something deep and stagnant in his chest, a break that revealed blue skies and clean Winter sunlight. He felt a sense of freedom that he didn't fully understand and, frankly, didn't care to. It just felt *good*.

Some time into the morning Edgar heard his phone buzz. His immediate thought was to ignore it. There were far more important things to focus on. He had to think about something he could make for breakfast. Something that would cause Scott's face to light up in gleeful excitement. He had to offer to brush Scott's hair for him, and maybe twist the long, dark locks into a braid.

He remembered, suddenly, the conversation he had with Tate a few days before. His jaw clenched. Edgar fiddled with his hands, head instinctively bowing as it did in the presence of authority. He cringed, drew in a breath, and checked his phone.

Tate was messaging to say he just pulled into town. The doctor said he was stopping for gas and coffee, but would be at Edgar's apartment in the next hour or so, depending on traffic. Edgar sighed, put aside his phone and shifted in bed to gently shake Scott awake. As deep sleeping as the man was, he was easy to wake up. His eyes fluttered open and he stretched with a stilted yawn, rolling onto his back and looking up at Edgar in quiet contentment.

Immediately Edgar forgot the entirety of the situation and all the information he was planning to express mere moments ago.

"Hi," he said dumbly.

Scott didn't hesitate to raise his hand and touch Edgar's cheek. The touch lowered slightly and traveled, his hand coming to rest and lightly finger the curls at the nape of Edgar's neck.

Something was happening. There was something the two of them were supposed to be doing.

Oh, right! Breakfast.

From the bedside table Edgar's phone buzzed again. Edgar's mood fell immediately.

Oh. Right.

"Uh, there's..." he took the hand lovingly caressing him and interlaced their fingers, buying him a few moments of lucidity. "There's a doctor coming."

Scott's hand stiffened. He sat up slightly.

"Are you okay?" He asked, suddenly fully awake.

Edgar scoffed nervously. "No, I – I'm fine. It's actually...he's a therapist I saw as a kid back home. A really good guy. He's – *seasoned*, you know? When it comes to Academic magic. I thought he could help."

"Oh," Scott smiled sadly. "Oh that's really not..."

He trailed off, taking in Edgar in deep thought. Then he sighed, and after that he looked a little more cheerful.

"Okay," he said. "Can I borrow another shirt?"

Even just imagining Scott dressed again from his closet provoked a whole new reaction in Edgar. He tried to not look too eager, grabbing his favorite t-shirt from the closet before he left for the kitchen to allow Scott some privacy.

It might not have been the most important consideration since he and Scott already spent the whole night undressed together. Edgar just had a feeling that at this point in their relationship he'd still appreciate restraint in terms of physical intimacy.

Because I know him. Because I'm his soul bond.

Edgar decided to toss aside his aversion to actual breakfast and attempt to make them caprese toast. He had all the ingredients, and the recipe in his head didn't sound too difficult. So he took a little extra focus as he cut his tomato and mozzarella into rounds, drawing from the energy he generated as he rotated between anxiety and absolute confidence.

I'm not anyone's soul bond. What am I thinking?

I'm Eddie. I'm his Eddie. I have to be.

I'm so, so stupid.

From behind him there were footsteps as Scott approached, and Edgar quickly straightened his posture and tried to pretend as if he were normal and emotionally regulated. The sourdough popped out of the toaster and he started layering the bread with cheese and tomato. Because caprese toast was what mattered, not the way his heart apparently split open overnight and was now actively spilling out an entire life's worth of repressed emotions.

Scott came up close behind Edgar, settled his chin on his shoulder, and loosely wrapped his arms around his waist. In that moment, and if he had asked for it, Edgar would've ripped his heart straight out of his chest and shaved the flesh to top their breakfast. Still, he kept his cool. He kept something adjacent to cool, at least.

The two of them sat down for another meal, something Edgar had been looking forward to since he closed his eyes to go to sleep the night before. Soon, though, he picked up that something was wrong. Scott still thanked him for cooking. When he ate, it was clear he enjoyed it.

But he was quieter. His smile was outlined in something pained. Scott seemed resigned, as if he had let go of some kind of great weight and was now feeling the static of tension leaving his hand. Despite all that he still looked at Edgar with eyes that said *I like you, and I'm making no attempt to hide it.*

Wasn't that enough? Couldn't that override everything else Edgar was almost, but not quite intuiting?

Almost, but not quite.

Scott didn't look at Edgar like they were at the beginning of something new and exciting. He looked at him like a childhood dog that somehow knows it's about to be put down.

Edgar couldn't even ask if he was okay. It's obvious he wasn't.

"What can I do?" He said instead.

For a man who made his every emotion absolutely transparent, there were aspects of his expression that were still indecipherable. He took a bite of toast and smiled.

"You've done more than enough," he assured him. "I'm...I'm really glad you found me, Eddie."

No.

No, Edgar wasn't Eddie. Well, he was, but not in that way. Not in the way that meant he wasn't who he was when Scott kissed him. Scott was here for Eddie, but everything about him said that what he really wanted was *Edgar – and Edgar was Edgar.*

He thought about the way Scott's entire demeanor got buffed into pleasant nothingness. That's the way he sounded now, and Edgar wanted nothing more than to scrape off that layer of lead paint and scrub the name *Eddie* from his mouth once and for all.

But he didn't. Instead, Edgar reached across the table and took Scott's hands in his. He kissed one set of knuckles, and then the other, before carefully bringing their hands to his forehead and closing his eyes.

In the darkness he thought he heard Scott release a sob. It didn't continue, so Edgar stayed still. Scott stayed still. Everything was still.

After eating, they sat together on the front steps of Edgar's place, bathing in the sunlight of what was looking to be another warm autumn day. Scott was shivering, despite the temperate weather. But before Edgar could offer a hoodie, Scott had fetched something from his bag. It wasn't anything like the suit jacket he was wearing when they met. It was a fuzzy brown coat with a white trim. Scott slipped it on and smiled at the touch of it.

In a flash Edgar was hit with the overwhelming desire to take this man back to bed. Scott looked *tired.* He should be wrapped up in the covers, drifting in and out from a peaceful sleep. And Edgar should be beside him, picking music for them to listen to. Or maybe reading aloud something light and relaxing – like one of those old *Encyclopedia Brown* stories.

They just sat together in the sun. Neither of them said much. Scott's coat was soft to the touch, and Edgar found himself absently running his hands along the material of the sleeve.

That's how things were going when Doctor Tate Jensen pulled up.

Edgar recognized him immediately. The doctor was driving the same beat-up car Edgar knew as a child – only now it was slightly more worn down with age. It was surreal to see and think about how there were a few parts from his previous life in Shreveport that weren't immediately painful to think about.

The doctor stepped out into the day, and once again Edgar was startled to see how little he'd changed. Much like his car, Tate was a little more worn. But his clothes were still clean-pressed, his posture impeccable. He had the same wispy, pale blonde hair. Same carefully trimmed goatee.

For a while Edgar was so floored he could only stare at Tate while he approached. Beside him, Scott had yet to notice the doctor's presence. There was another street cat sitting at his feet, and Scott was quietly talking to it. The cat, inexplicably, seemed to be listening to him.

When Tate's shoes crunched on the gravel walkway Scott quickly excused himself to the cat and stood straight up. He bowed his head, tousling his hair slightly with his fingers. This still wasn't enough for him, and he dug through the pocket of his jacket to pull out the large sunglasses Edgar recognized from his bag.

They covered his eyes, which he supposed was their purpose. They also covered a good portion of his face. Perhaps an added benefit.

"Hello, Eddie," Tate said. "You look good."

"Hi Tate. You look the same."

He turned his attention to Scott.

"Hello, sir," Scott said. "Um. Doctor, I mean. My name is Scott, it's – good to meet you," he paused, and then added nervously. "I like your vest."

Tate observed him with a hint of hesitation that resolved itself almost as soon as it became visible. From that point on whatever problem he might've had was null and void. His expression shifted subtly, but just enough to imply that he'd known Scott for just as long as he had Edgar. His friendliness, even unspoken, was so immediate and absolute that Scott must've assumed it was his fault and quickly turned his face away.

"Sorry I'm sorry," he spoke quickly.

Tate cocked his head to the side. "Why?"

"I didn't mean to – uh – *control* you."

"You feel as if you're controlling me?"

Scott frowned at his feet. "You saw my eyes."

"No I didn't," Tate said.

"You.." Scott's frown deepened and his hands began to fidget. "So you just..?"

Edgar took one of Scott's trembling hands and gave the one closest to him as reassuring of a squeeze as he could manage. "That's just Tate," he assured him. "He's a nice guy."

He still looked uncertain. Such a visceral distrust based purely on making a naturally good first impression. It something deep in Edgar's heart ache terribly.

He didn't know what he could possibly say to make this better. He wasn't naturally thoughtful or emotionally vulnerable anymore. Luckily, with Tate around he didn't have to be.

"It sounds painful," he said in an even tone, "not to know when people's intentions are genuine rather than the product of your own intervention."

"It is," Scott softly agreed.

"How long have you been looking for your soul bond?"

Scott answered immediately. "Three years, one month and two weeks."

That was enough for even Tate to huff in mirrored exhaustion. "And I imagine you've been using your abilities on a regular basis? So often that you're now unable to exit Flow State?"

"Yes?" Scott cleared his throat and said it again. "Yes. I guess you could say that."

Tate stood there for a while. He kept perfectly still and observed Scott, his gaze steady and vibrant with focused thought. When he spoke again there was something even more careful in his voice.

"You're deteriorating," Tate observed. "How far as it progressed?"

Scott snapped out of his stupor and bolted up when Tate spoke. He was stunned, and standing beside him Edgar saw his eyes briefly glance in his direction. It didn't look like he wanted to answer. He did anyway.

"I can't see faces," Scott said. "I haven't seen my one since I was twenty-one, and I haven't been able to see anyone *else's* since..." he trailed off, gaze once again drifting in Edgar's direction. "He's the first human face I've seen in two years."

It seemed to relieve him slightly to say all of that out loud. Maybe that was the first time he ever admitted it to another human being. He certainly hadn't said it to Edgar.

Edgar remembered something Scott whispered to him the first time they met. It was barely distinct, the tone so earnest it jarred Edgar's psyche and made it difficult to listen well.

I can see you.

That was a strange thing to say, but coming from someone like Scott it could've been some kind of metaphor. Because he was a *keyhole*, right? A fanciful thing full of riddles and abstractions. That's what Edgar was taught to think. And sure, he was crying as he said that. But the tears could've been a product of – awe, maybe. Awe from the beauty of the universe.

As opposed to the other reasons why someone would openly cry to someone they'd just met. Desperation. Exhaustion. Abject loneliness. Trying to imagine it, Edgar realized that Scott wasn't the only naive one in this situation.

Despite just getting here, Tate was quick to lead the two back into Edgar's own apartment. He paused in the entryway and looked around the space. For a brief moment his expression warmed (Relief? Pride?), but then it changed and he was back to business. He motioned for Edgar and Scott to sit on the couch, and he dragged a chair to bring across the coffee table from them.

He arranged the small case he brought in with him on the coffee table. Edgar watched him unlatch and open the bag, and in a matter of moments he was hit by a painful wave of sense memory. He couldn't see what was in the doctor's bag, but he knew a lot of what had to be inside.

The distinct scrape of Academy Parchment. The smell of those little velvet pouches they'd sell in the University Supply Shop to keep more delicate materials safe. It didn't make sense how such innocuous things could be so easy to recognize. Edgar didn't want to think about how he was still able to recognize them so quickly.

"Scott," Tate said, palming through a variety of markers in different colors. "Do you know about sigils?"

"They're...symbols? Shapes, maybe. And they contain magic – some-how," Scott swallowed hard and frowned. "It's not the type of thing I was taught about."

Tate smiled, pleased. "Makes sense. You don't have much of a use for it. You made a good approximation, though!" Tate eased into the start of an explanation. "I like to say that sigils are intentions concentrated into line and shape. Some say they need to be formed under strict guide-lines, but I personally believe that anything can be a sigil if it is created with a purpose. Does that make sense?"

Scott looked very tired, even though he sat up right and remained physically alert and politely engaged. "I think so," he said.

"If you would allow me, I would like to try and draw a sigil on you," Tate turned his case to the side to better present its contents. "You can see I have some markers. The color doesn't matter much, but I find it helps if someone can pick the color and where I draw it."

From behind the sunglasses, Scott's brow tightened slightly. "What will it do?" He asked.

"I haven't drawn sigils on many birthrights, so potentially nothing. But my hope is that it would allow us to speak without you needing the sunglasses."

There was an instant stab of pain at the thought of any Academic magic being done on Scott. Edgar pulled back his reaction and focused on watching to see what Scott would do next.

He shrugged off his jacket and fixed his hair. Did he know? Scott offered his arm, palm up, towards Tate. Did he *know* what he was doing?

In the new focus, Edgar noticed a small pale scar, raised on the dark of his bare wrist. It looked like a burn.

He touched that wrist. He kissed that wrist. And yet, this was the first time he noticed that mark.

Tate saw it just as Edgar did. "Knight's Bond?" He inquired.

"What? Oh, uh. Yup."

He nodded, likely knowing by Scott's tone that he shouldn't press any further than that. Then he turned back to his markers. "What's your favorite color?"

Annoyance was a strange weight on Scott's face that he could only carry for a moment. Then he was back to utter defeat.

"Anything's fine," and then, thinking better. "Do you have blue?"

Tate nodded and got straight down to business. He took a metallic blue marker and removed the lid with absurd precision. Then he held

Scott's hand between his thumb and pointer finger and he slowly glided the tip of the marker along the expanse of his wrist.

He was done soon after, and Scott pulled back his arm to examine his new makeshift tattoo. As he did Edgar got to see it too – a small, blue smiley face drawn in the space right under this newly-apparent scar.

Weary confusion was woven into the muscles that kept Scott's expression tight with guarded respect. Still, despite everything, he slowly took off his sunglasses. He folded them in his lap and, for a while, kept his stare down low. When he finally did raise his eyes it was not to stare at the doctor, but next to him at Edgar.

"Notice anything?" Scott tried.

Edgar didn't respond at first. He was still staring down at his hand and seeing how Tate drew his smiley faces the same way he used to. The same overlap in the two ends of the circle. The same slight curve at the ends of the lines that made up the eyes.

He used to draw that on Edgar's shoulder at the end of sessions. He'd draw a little smiley face and cover it with a bandage. When he was a kid Tate told him it was so he could practice having something nice that was his and his alone.

By the time he was older and training to be an Archivist, he supposed he knew what Tate was *really* doing. Still, Edgar never brought it up.

When he finally managed to look up and into Scott's eyes, he found that the dark blue no longer emitted their usual unearthly glow. They weren't exactly flat and not at all lifeless. They just looked normal.

Edgar couldn't push out the words. He just nodded. Scott pursed his lips in thought and, not without some reluctance, shifted to face Tate.

By the way he carried himself it didn't seem like Tate feared Scott's eyes regardless of whether or not his sigil worked. When the two men looked at each other, Edgar expected his doctor to express some satisfaction from his spell maintaining its effect. Tate still just looked quietly contemplative.

"What do you see when you look at my face?" He said. "Would you feel comfortable putting it into words?"

Scott swallowed hard. He began to tap his fingers together in a motion that gradually became faster and more frantic. Edgar watched helplessly before realizing that he didn't have to be as useless to him as he used to be. If he wanted to pursue this it would mean growing and challenging himself. This wasn't a stranger hiding in the walk-in anymore. This was someone who helped him with the dishes and listened to him ramble about *Zelda* lore with inexplicable fascination. This is someone with expressive eyes and careful hands and a voice like old, solidly-constructed wooden furniture.

This is someone Edgar wanted to stay – if not beside him, than at least nearby.

So he steadied Scott's hands, gripping them together until they stopped trembling. Scott looked at him when he did that, and even though Edgar only saw him in those stylish sunglasses for a few minutes he knew he hated them and was glad they were gone.

He brushed Scott's hair behind his ear. "You're okay," Edgar said, even though he had no idea if that was true.

They looked at each other for a while longer. After that Scott turned back to Tate with a little more strength.

"It's..." his voice thinned for a moment. "It's soupy. Like paint water before you stir it into one color."

"You can't make out any discernible facial features," Tate gathered. "You can see my head, my hair, my body. Just -" a thought occurred to him, though he kept his revelation subtle. "nothing that would allow you to recognize me in a crowd."

Scott nodded. "Yes," he said faintly.

"It's trying to keep you from finding them."

Once again Scott looked startled.

"...Maybe," he agreed in a voice even more distant. "I...I guess so."

In a flash Edgar was a child again, witnessing adult Academic witches converse cryptically about topics he had no way to understand. That feeling of detachment, pretending to follow while also secretly lamenting that he absolutely didn't, was nauseating. Immediately he fell back into old habits: sit quiet, sit still, and wait for someone older and more qualified to allow you space within the interaction.

He could feel Scott watching him out of the corner of his eye, but was too ashamed to meet his gaze. So Edgar continued keeping his head forward and down. A part of him knew he was staying small on purpose. He hated how easily that came to him.

"If you grow up learning Academic magic," Scott broached the topic hesitantly, "do they still tell you about the Witch Eater?"

Tate made the kind of face he made when he was deeply annoyed but too serene to express it fully. "We're taught to describe its effects as a form of advanced mental illness," he explained. "Severe depression or PTSD. Things of that nature."

"It's a metaphor," Edgar added.

Both men turned to him in a way that prompted Edgar to consider bolting out of the room entirely. He stayed where he was, though, mostly because leaving would mean leaving Scott alone.

With a considerable amount of hesitation, he forced himself to explain what he knew about the Witch Eater, a concept he hadn't thought about since childhood. He recalled his mother explaining that Keyholes lack the capacity to connect with reality in any meaningful manner, and to cope with living they take human concepts they cannot understand and turn them into figurative equivalents.

"What's a Keyhole?" Scott asked.

Oh shit.

Even Tate tensed at the way Edgar could still drop a title like that with no problem, thought, or hesitation. The doctor wasn't angry, though for a while the he had to focus his attention on the surface of the coffee table.

"It's a slur the Academy in Shreveport coined," he said. "It's meant to refer to birthrights. Because of the coloboma."

Scott was not yet offended, just mildly confused. "That's...such an odd thing to think," he cocked his head to the side, drawing deeper in thought. "I've only met a handful of birthrights with colobomas. Most of them were related to me."

Tate sighed. He looked like there was a lot he wanted to say and just couldn't. This, Edgar realized, was not a new sight.

"Iris colobomas aren't even the only *kind* of coloboma," Scott furrowed his brow even deeper, trying hard to understand the bigotry of Edgar's upbringing. "That's what they mean by *keyhole*, right? Seems like they could make a far more applicable slur."

He was saying this so lightly. Of course he was. Scott never had to try and live a live in a community that knew how to see him and hated what they saw. By this point Scott had emotionally passed this completely without even a second thought.

"I interrupted you, Edgar," he said. "Please, keep going."

No adult had ever called Edgar a keyhole to his face. But Edgar learned the name from a very early age, and soon it played in his head in a constant loop. The worst thing you could call someone like him. The thing he called himself almost every day. For *years*.

"Do you still do your taps, Eddie?" Tate spoke softly through his intrusive thoughts.

"Huh? Oh."

Only half realizing what he was doing, he moved his hand out of Scott's and sat up on the couch. With his feet planted on the ground, he tapped the palm of his hand against each knee, left to right and back again, in a slow and steady rhythm. It was a skill Tate taught him as a kid that was either magic or psychotherapy, or some mish-mash of the two. The specifics didn't matter. All that was important was that it helped, even if only because it was something suggested to him by a person that genuinely wanted to help him.

"When a genetic witch is unable to cope with being alive," he continued through his taps, "they lose their minds, and since witch towns don't believe in medicine or therapy they just say that the person was 'taken by the Witch Eater'," Edgar slowly stopped tapping. "That's what my mother told me growing up."

Thinking back on this reoccurring conversation, Edgar felt a sincere disgust at his mother's behavior and the way he accepted with the blind trust that only a child can master. It was even a private joke between them during the times she considered him fit to joke with.

Finally, Scott appeared unwary. "We..? I don't know why she would tell you that. We have doctors."

"I know about healers -" Edgar tried to insist.

"No, *doctors*, Edgar. Doctors. *Medical* doctors, what the f..." the profanity died in his throat and Scott groaned in barely restrained frustration. "Birthright is a *disability* –"

"I'm sorry," Edgar whispered, feeling his hands clench.

"Do you have any idea how lucky us *keyholes* are to have a quirk in our makeup that ended up relatively harmless? I'm in constant pain, so I'm not exaggerating when I say that – smudged as they are – my eyes are the most functioning part of me."

"Scott," Tate cut in. "Be mindful, please."

By now Edgar was only half present in the moment. He couldn't stop the trembling that rattled him at the joints and made his eyes burn. It was stupid and humiliating, but there was no way of controlling it on his own. So he succumbed to the tight freeze, so cold that it burned, and adjusted to no light at the end of the tunnel.

"Hey."

He felt himself turned on the couch and taken by the shoulders. Edgar was steadied by hands that gently stroked his arms.

"I shouldn't have lashed out," Scott said. "Not at you. I'm so sorry."

Scott's face came in a little clearer. His expression was drawn and worried.

"I fucked up," Edgar said. "I didn't know."

"Edgar comes from a community that's almost as insular as I imagine yours is," Tate said. "It's not uncommon for someone raised Academic to believe they should get the entirety of their magic history and knowledge solely from the Academy."

Scott stared Edgar for a long while of steady, thoughtful silence. When he found his words his voice was low and soft, and very sad.

"You were taught to hate yourself, weren't you?" He simply said.

The first incantation his mother taught him was a physical illusion to make his iris whole. He used it so often when he first learned it that the physical exertion triggered a flu that lasted for six months.

"Were you?" Tate asked Scott.

"No," Scott took Edgar's hand in his. "But I learned."

Edgar was suddenly so, so tired. Without caring about what Tate could think he gave in to his needs and leaned fully against Scott, coming to rest his head against his shoulder. He didn't even care to consult his doctor's face to note his reaction. It simply did not matter.

"I think what Edgar is trying to express is that..." Tate trailed off, choosing his words with the same care that he chose markers. "In Academic studies, much of your birthright lineage taken at face value. There are generations of learned witches who don't realize that what they see as metaphor...can be a very real threat."

The thought of the Witch Eater surfaced again in Edgar's mind with a new clarity. He pulled up his head, now fully awake and engaged. "Wait," he said. "Are you *literally* being taken?"

There was that moment in the restaurant after their shift. Everything was going perfectly when suddenly Scott just vanished. He was still there right beside him – only not. His expression was slack. His eyes were dead. It only lasted for maybe fifteen seconds, just long enough for Edgar to consider that his date may have had some kind of seizure. Then Scott sprung back to life. And the rest of the night was such a whirlwind that Edgar completely forgot to ask – what the hell was that?

Scott stood up and meandered away from the couch. He didn't fully walk out of the apartment as his expression suggested he might. From the corner of his eye Edgar could see Scott standing and staring out the tiny window above the sink. He wondered what could possibly be going on in his mind at a time like this.

"Well…" his mind began to race, following the same desperate tremor as his heartbeat. "I guess that makes sense. If he doesn't have his soul bond than he's metaphysically incomplete -"

"I wouldn't say that," Tate corrected him.

"What I mean is that he's left open to all kinds of things. So if some incomprehensible…" he motioned vaguely. "I mean, it makes sense, right? But that's fixed now!" The hope in his voice shifted into a smiling plea. "…Right?"

He hoped for any sign of validation from the doctor. Once again, as it had been so many times before, Tate made no attempt to spread any nice, white lies. He leaned back in Edgar's cheap wooden chair and let his words drift thoughtfully out of him.

"Have you noticed the patch of freckles on the side of his neck?" Tate continued without leaving space for Edgar to answer. "I have a pregnant patient right now who is experiencing the same condition – same color, pattern and location. She told me it can happen to biological women who go through intense hormonal changes."

His eyes met Edgar's. He appeared genuinely apologetic, so much so that it was barely masked by his professional decorum.

"I'm not certain, but I've heard that birthrights can reflect traumas in magic connection through physical conditions or abnormalities that they should not be able to otherwise experience. If this was a healthy, unaltered Lover's Knot, he should've been able to find the other end of the connection with relative ease. Since he hasn't after so long, and considering the severity of his condition, I think it's fair to assume that something intervened and – severed the tie."

Scott was behind him now. His presence felt warm, yet somehow empty. Safe but lonely.

"So it's not him," he said.

"It could be," Tate told him. "It could not be. At this point it's very possible that your body no longer has the ability to tell."

News like this would be enough to break anyone. If Scott spent years making himself miserable, day after day, just getting sicker and sicker in a search that led to ultimately nothing – what then? What happens to a birthright with immense potential power after they lose all semblance of hope? Would a doodle from a permanent marker be enough to contain that fallout?

Edgar sat very still wand waited for the walls to crash around him. He waited to be hurt – for *somebody* to hurt. There was so much tension inside him that he almost yelped at the first touch of Scott's hands. Then they continued, resting gently around Edgar's shoulders in a way that was somehow both soothing and soothed. When he looked up, brave enough to try and check the look on Scott's face, Edgar saw him beaming with absolute peace.

"Okay," he said.

Scott crossed around the couch and sat back down, only this time he positioned himself close enough beside Edgar to easily cling onto his arm. He cuddled up next to him as if it was a perfectly normal thing to do after hearing the most devastating revelation someone in his position could possibly receive. And there was still an inkling of rationality inside Edgar that wanted to push the other man away and remind him how upset he was supposed to be. Unfortunately, it was impossible to access that common sense through the sugar-floss fog of infatuation.

He's dying, he tried to reason with this shitty romantic that was relishing the feeling of Scott's thumb grazing his skin. *Worse than death. The man is being absorbed by the void. Please – you have to calm down.*

"How long do you think I have?" Scott asked idly.

If Tate was jarred by this tonal shift he didn't express it. "It's hard to say," he mused. "I don't think there's a concrete timeline for being...consumed. From stories I've been told I believe it all comes down to how much you can take."

Something briefly illuminated itself in the blue of Scott's eyes. It wasn't a singular emotion as much as it was a physical embodiment of a prolonged, desperate scream. Even though he never made a sound, that one look was enough to echo along the inside of Edgar's skull.

He took a deep breath as he thought about that with the lazed indecisiveness that Edgar recognized from tourists choosing from the cocktail menu at the Den.

"I'd say another month," Scott concluded, apparently having no problem signing his own death certificate.

Tate leaned forward slightly. "What happens after that, Scott?"

Scott was the only person in the room immune to the grim dread that thickened the air. To him this was apparently a casual afternoon spent with the guy he slept with and his former doctor. He appeared to even enjoy the company. He took Edgar's arm and casually pulled it around him, and soon Scott was fitting himself quite naturally against the other man's chest.

Cute boy! A part of Edgar raved.

Dead, the rest of him despaired. *Dead doomed doomed dead.*

"I got a bottle of pills from a vet a while ago," Scott calmly explained. "I've been trying to learn more about technology, and the computer at the library told me that it's the drug people use to put down their pets. It said if I take enough I'll fall asleep and the medicine will stop my heart," he sighed again, sickeningly untroubled. "No pain. Nothing. The end."

Doomed dead doomed dead.

"I was supposed to use it the night I met Edgar," he added.

Just a charming, beautiful man on the knife's edge of suicide. For how long? How long?

Scott squeezed Edgar's arm. "It'd be nice to have a little more time, though" he looked up at him and smiled. "However I have left being myself...I'd like to spend it with you."

Edgar knew the sting of tears filling the surface of his eyes without ever actually falling and providing any kind of relief. It wasn't as if he didn't want to cry. He was certainly a drop-of-the-hat crybaby when he was a young child. After enough nights lying in bed praying that he could somehow (*sever*) separate the connection between his feelings and his tear ducts, one day his heart broke again and nothing happened. And from that point on he didn't cry. He couldn't.

At least, that's what he thought.

"I'll have to call Tenzin," Scott considered. "Or maybe I shouldn't. It might be better that she doesn't know where I end up," he looked at Edgar. "What do you think?"

Something hissed deep inside Edgar from the building pressure. Scott truly, genuinely did not care about his own death. And Edgar knew him for so short a time that it wouldn't be entirely unreasonable if he didn't either.

But he did. He cared so much. Edgar didn't want to know that Scott died alone in some alley or floating down the river. At the same time, he didn't want to watch him die in person either. He didn't want to touch a body that was once warm and find it cold, to run his fingers along the outline of his neck and feel the spot where the bone broke and jutted out. To look at the wings, so lifeless and limp, and wonder how they ever had the capabilities of flight.

And just like that Edgar was crying.

Scott's attitude towards death was probably the most outdated part about him. Most of his generation of birthrights, at least in Bluerose, no longer believed that the kindest thing you could do is give your body to the earth that chose to house you. Scott didn't believe he was better than other people for thinking that the greatest accomplishment of his life would be his ultimate death. It was just something he happened to think.

Growing up with a civilian like Tenzin he got to see how uncommon his perspective was. He remembered once when they were kids and they came across a cat who died giving birth by the bluffs. Scott was saddened by the loss, as young things deserve a caretaker they could relate to. At the same time he told Tenzin how lucky they were to have found the mother before she started to decompose. Now they could bring her body with the kittens back into town, where they can bury her in the field and she could eventually turn into more wild grass for her children to roam through.

Tenzin wasn't as excited about the concept. In fact, she broke down in bitter tears and ran back down the path to her house. He considered that a funny story for a long time after that until he finally realized how weird and distant she got whenever he brought it up. And then he watched her experience the grief of their mother's lost battle to cancer. His sister was the first person in his life who made him understand why some would consider death a cruelty.

Now he watched Edgar crumble at the thought of Scott's imminent destruction. He didn't cry like Scott did, or even how Tenzin cried when she was a young kid. His tears were raw and unpracticed. He wept like someone who had never seen a human being cry, but got a gun held to their temple and was commanded to mimic the experience.

He was usually much better at witnessing people break down emotionally. In fact, if he wasn't a walking cosmic horror he would've loved to joint the Witch Doctors as a therapist. But maybe not anymore, because watching Edgar sob gave Scott a new tension in his muscles. His breathing was shallow, and every inhale sent shock waves like hairline cracks along the arms of his ribs. His hands twitched erratically, and every thought in his head was reduced to shreds of dumb panic.

What do? Boy cry. Sad man! No good. Bad bad bad what do?

Tate tried to say something. It was probably insightful and very useful. Unfortunately, he wasn't Edgar and he wasn't crying as a result of Scott's behavior – so his words only registered as a calm, wordless cadence.

Scott darted to the bedroom and grabbed the plush green comforter off the bed. Then he came back and went about tucking it in around Edgar's shivering body. Was this the right thing to do? He had no idea. There was just an overwhelming urge in Scott to wrap him up in something comforting. So that's exactly what he did, adjusting his technique until Edgar was reduced to a teary head atop a mountain of blanket.

"Why did you do that?" Tate asked from behind him.

"I – I don't..." Scott winced. "I don't know what to do."

He'd always been small. Most people looked at him and assumed he was weak in a way that aligned with his height and body mass. For a long time this would be a completely accurate conclusion to draw. That's why, as soon as he left home, he started picking up jobs at warehouses and moving companies as well as restaurants.

A year later and he was much stronger. He could stack three full bus tubs in his arms no problem, which always impressed the older and gruffer dishwashers. And, if he needed to, he could support Edgar in his arms long enough to carry the chef back to bed.

Then he remembered Tate. He turned helplessly to the doctor and tried to find something reassuring in his particular spiral of flesh colors.

"I feel like I should bring him to the bedroom" Scott said. "I can carry him. He might be more comfortable there."

The doctor was silent. His face melt continued to drip. Scott whimpered audibly out of pure frustration.

"Oh!" Tate said. "I'm sorry. I forgot that you can't see it, but – I smiled at you," he said. "I'm smiling because I think that's a very kind idea."

Edgar was too wracked with the force of his own tears to protest as Scott bent down and wrapped his arms around his form. Scott picked him up, which was harder than expected but still doable once he balanced his weight. Once he knew he wouldn't drop the sad, sad boy, he swiftly maneuvered him through the other room and onto the bed.

He knew it was rude to completely abandon their guest with little to no explanation. That wasn't enough to keep him from pulling back the covers and getting into bed alongside Edgar. And as soon as he caught on to what Scott was doing, Edgar turned and buried his face to cry into his chest. Scott held him immediately and marveled at the low, wet warmth of tears soaking into the shirt he wore.

Scott did this. He did this to Edgar. The thought was something he expected to make him cry too, yet all it did was fill him with a deep swell of vacant shame.

Gradually, Edgar's sobs subsided and he fell silent. His breathing leveled. Maybe he was asleep, though Scott didn't dare check. He denied himself the time to so much as turn and see how much time passed since he left Tate in the other room. It didn't matter. Nothing mattered other than giving Edgar the comfort he needed to feel whatever he was feeling.

"It's not a death for a birthright."

Tate was standing in the open doorway with his hands clasped politely in front of him. Scott turned his head to see him as much as he could without disrupting the man in his arms in any way, shape, or form.

"Your first love is the Earth, right?" He said. "They're still studying the extent of the damage, but it's been confirmed that pentobarbital is terrible for the environment. It stays in the body after the death, and when the tissue breaks down it stays in the soil. It can even contaminate nearby water sources."

He didn't ask the computer many questions after learning about the medicine. Was the doctor right? If he was, then overdosing meant he wouldn't be able to arrange for a natural burial. If he did, he would be hurting the ground that supported him for his whole life. Finally the tears were beginning to well in his eyes.

"I don't know what to do," he said again.

He felt the mattress dip in the middle as Tate sat on the edge of the bed. Scott didn't speak, just softly stroked Edgar's hair to distract him from the anticipation of wondering what the doctor would say next.

Tate spoke again some time after that. "How are you?" He asked.

That almost got Scott to laugh. But laughing could potentially disrupt Edgar, so he pushed back the instinct.

"Uh – bad," he answered. "I feel insane. I'm tired constantly. It's so *cold* here. My..." Scott couldn't fight back a dark snicker, "my *mouth* hurts. I don't think it looks weird because no one's said anything but it's constantly sore. Isn't that weird?"

"I'm not sure. Are you anemic?"

"I've been wandering on foot every day for years and I feel like I haven't touched the ground the entire time. And no one can see me," Scott closed his eyes. "No one can help me."

By this point he was less holding Edgar to comfort him and more using the chef as a teddy bear to clutch onto and buoy him through his own turmoil. Tate, on the other hand, never strayed from calm. If Scott thought he was steadfast when he was a precocious tween, this actual doctor was working on a whole separate level.

"Were you a lonely child?" Tate asked him.

"Not at first," Scott said. "It was easier when I was a younger and didn't realize..." he struggled to find a way to describe it. "The coloboma was fine. People at home accept that some touches are easier to live with than others. But no one knows what to do with a soul bond."

Tate hummed in agreement. "I tried to find some stories of previous Lover's Knots once. There's definitely evidence that they've existed throughout documented history, the people involved just don't seem interested in talking about it," he hummed again. "I wish I could say how it feels when it happens."

"Well stick around, Doctor," Scott said. "And you'll see firsthand what happens when it doesn't."

Edgar roused from whatever rest he took and sat up in bed. His eyes were swollen and his face was red. He started to speak, only pausing long enough for Scott to wipe a curl from his face.

"When you opened your briefcase I smelled dahlia oil," he said to Tate. "Did you bring some with you?"

There was a profound pause. When Tate answered his voice was noticeably more solemn.

"I did," he said.

Edgar nodded and sat up more upright. "I cook a lot, so I have butcher's twine. That should work, right? I mean, it's probably thicker than the strand-grade stuff, but it's still cotton."

By then the plan he was forming became painfully clear.

Edgar was trying to get his childhood therapist to perform a bonding ritual on the two of them.

Scott shivered when he thought about the last time he felt the touch of damp, sweet-smelling strand against his skin. That night on the beach was so dusty in his mind that he could barely recall the details. It was the sensation of flame meeting flesh, creating a burn that hit on him and in him, that was still easily accessible in his brain.

The scar on his wrist had been there for most of his life, and by now he didn't think about it much. Looking at it now he was sure it was just as bright as the night it formed. Just as fresh as it will be the day he dies, even that moment somehow didn't end up coming for another few decades.

A soul bond is one thing. It's the biggest possible commitment, but since it's a metaphysical umbilical cord following you from birth it was a lot easier to let go and accept. Nobody plans to come into the world as one half of a prophecy, and once you discover the true nature of your existence it only makes more sense to accept it. What Edgar was suggesting was entirely different. The stakes were lower, but they were stakes *he* wanted to choose.

And that made things so much worse.

"You can't replace a soul bond, Edgar," Tate said.

Edgar still looked like he just finished crawling out of a full-on breakdown, but he spoke like he was back in control of the kitchen at Il Bambino.

"But couldn't it help?" He turned to face Scott and held his hand. "Maybe your bond with your sister was what got you this far. And if that's true, maybe bonding with me will keep you from getting any worse."

Last night Scott curled up against Edgar and listened as the chef explained the story behind every cut and burn on his hands. Every mark was a badge of honor, a point of genuine pride. He displayed even the dumbest cooking scar as if it were a crayon drawing from his a child he treasured. Fun as that was, Scott couldn't allow himself to become one more pain point on that man's body.

"I'm not sure you understand what you're considering," Scott spoke with far less authority than he intended. "You can't undo a bond once the ritual is performed. It would be permanent until the intention is fulfilled."

Infuriatingly enough, his warning didn't provoke much out of Edgar aside from a wry smirk. "Why do you know so much about this?" He asked. "Bonds are Academy stuff."

"Mom taught me," Scott moved on before either of them could consider the implications of that statement. "What would the goal be, anyway? Assuming we don't follow any set form."

Edgar pursed his lips in thought. "I haven't decided yet," he said.

"Well you should probably figure it out!" Scott tried not to shout. "If we end up agreeing to something you can't reasonably do, you'll end up psychically entangled to me for the rest of our lives."

Edgar tried not to smile, and then looked over to consult with Tate. "What would that mean?" He said.

The doctor took a deep breath and sighed. "For a basic binding, your existence would essentially be overlapped with his. You might..." he trailed off and bowed his head. "It could be that you share occasional sense fragments – something hits one of you and you both feel it, things like that. If you choose to separate physically it will be inevitable that you'll end up crossing paths again, regardless of where each of you attempt to go."

"Our fates would be connected," Scott added in a dull voice. "If you decided tomorrow that you hate me, we'd never be able to fully escape each other for the rest of our lives."

"We *do* keep talking about how lonely we are," Edgar said, grinning as he slid off the bed and strode into the other room.

Scott gasped, weakly outraged, and followed right behind him. Once again the two of them left Tate alone in the other room, but the doctor showed no signs of being even moderately offended. Which was great, because Scott had far too much to worry about right now to offer a sincere apology.

By the time he found Edgar in the kitchen he was rifling through the drawers and cabinets. When he saw Scott staring he stopped and pointed right at him.

"Name a band," he commanded.

Scott froze immediately. "What?"

"I played you a bunch of my music last night. Now I want to put on something you like to listen to. *So,*" he pulled out his phone and began swiping. "what do you want to hear?"

For the most part Scott knew that supporting this would mean allowing Edgar to get even more in the groove of his terrible idea. He didn't want to do that. On the other hand, if Edgar was looking to get music through his phone than the odds were good that he had that same music player that Tenzin did – the one that was essentially a Mix Tape of Alexandria. Which meant it was guaranteed to have albums newer and more obscure than what he could get access to on the shelves of any random library.

"Do you..." he crossed his arms and tried not to be too annoyed at his own weak will. "Do you have the newest Mitski album?"

Edgar's face warmed in the shape of a laugh that never made a sound. He huffed through his teeth, nodded, and began to tap at the screen. "Oh yeah," he said. "That explains a lot."

Soon after he said that, Mistki's familiarly heart-aching, ghostly voice began to resonate on the fancy little speaker Edgar kept on the kitchen counter. The moment it did Scott knew he made a terrible mistake. Now not only did he have to keep someone he already cared deeply about from making an honest effort to save his life, he had to do so while listening to what he already knew was going to be a *fantastic* album.

"Do you regret the ritual you did with your sister?" Edgar asked, stopping to pour coffee grounds into the French press.

Scott imagined Edgar being forcibly compelled to risk his life to get him out of danger. "We aren't doing a Knight's Bond," he said.

"You seemed okay with it once."

"I was a *child*."

Edgar stopped what he was doing. Silently, he took a wooden spoon from a container by the stove and stirred the grounds and water. He turned back to Scott, thankfully without a hint of humor in his face.

"...Okay," he said. "And now you have to protect her for the rest of your life. That's – a lot to put on a kid," as he continued he moved closer to Scott, only stopping when he was close enough to turn his hand and look down at the scar on his wrist. "So do you regret it? If you could break the bond somehow, would you?"

Scott talked about his sister. Tenzin began training in Muay Thai at the age of fourteen. She was practically two feet taller than him. She was stronger, faster, and intelligent enough to avoid most situations that would put her in the type of danger that could typically trigger their bond.

Still, she was his sister. Scott would do anything for her, bond or no bond.

Edgar brushed his thumb over the scar – very lightly, like it might potentially still be tender to the touch. It wasn't, but the intent was very sweet. There was a bright quality in his eyes that made his entire body burn with new strength.

"If you don't regret it," he said. "Why would I?"

"Because you don't know me," Scott tried to claim, even though as time went on he was becoming less and less convinced that that was true.

"Then I'll get to know you," Edgar volleyed. "But for that to happen there has to continue being a Scott Skylark Kaufner in this reality for me to know."

Behind them Scott heard Tate draw in a sharp inhale. Scott blushed slightly. Being called by his middle name at a time like this left him feeling even more vulnerable than he already was.

"Edgar," Tate warned from near the couch, "you realize that, if we enact a bond, the force feeding off Scott could transfer to you as well."

"Or it'll leave us both alone because there will be no entry point for it to attack through," Edgar shrugged at the both of them. "Intent and doorways, right? Isn't that what our whole line of business is all about?"

Up until recently Scott's entire life was dedicated to the fruitless pursuit of love from a person he could only barely recall. He spent countless nights imagining what it would feel like when he finally matched a face to the name. They feasibly be anyone that approached him, but when he met his Eddie it would be different. A switch would click in his head and suddenly his experience of the world would widen to include a second body alongside his own.

That isn't what he felt in this moment. Scott was still himself and could not expand his consciousness beyond the confines of his skin – at least, not on his own accord. He was able to be fully present while he stared at Edgar, tracing his gaze across the chef's bright eyes and tender, semi-pleading smile.

He thought he'd fall in love in a heartbeat. Turns out it took a few days. But the feeling was there now, stupid and absolute and *absolutely stupid.* But he knew at this point there wasn't anything he could about it.

"All right," Scott said. "If you're willing – I'll do it."

Edgar grabbed a bundle of butcher's twine from a nook beside the toaster. It wasn't clear whether he knew where he kept it the whole time, or if he narrowed down the location in the time Scott spent bathing in his feelings. Regardless, he had it now and seemed very pleased with himself.

"If you want me to do this it's probably best we follow the right steps," Tate said.

The two of them looked over at the doctor, who was standing by his briefcase and holding something Scott never considered he would come across again in his life. It was a bulb of wound, gossamer-thin string clinging to a scrap of redwood bark. Already he could smell the thick, bitter sweetness of the oil that would soon stain his skin. How didn't he notice it earlier?

After his ritual he reeked of ash and dead flowers and burning flesh for *days*. Just smelling the oil again made him kind of nauseous.

"Can we open a window?" He murmured, leaning against the counter.

Edgar quickly slid open the kitchen window and let in a brushstroke of cold winter air. It bit against the thin material of his shirt. Scott shivered until he ached, grounding himself in the familiar discomfort. Then he felt the radiating warmth of Edgar leaning next to him.

"It hurts, you know," Scott said.

"I figured. You're essentially setting yourself on fire, right?" Edgar bumped their shoulders together. "But you've seen what I do. I'm a chef! I burn myself constantly."

Scott laughed in weak disbelief. "Edgar, it's *different*. You're about to press a red-hot brand into a part of yourself that has never been touched before. If you suppressed all your natural instincts than there is a side of your brain that hasn't been activated, and by doing this you're allowing the first sensation those raw components feel to be *agony*," he tapped his fingers, focusing on the chill around them. "There was a point where my Knight's Bond was the most painful thing that's ever happened to me."

What was he doing? No, Edgar, stop trying to make show of affection to potentially save Scott's life. Stop trying to connect to a man who just now got slightly okay with going through life as an island. What part of the way Scott decided to live his life implied he was starved for affection? How on Earth could you possibly make *that* assumption?

Edgar got a strange new look on his face. "My mom dislocated my shoulder when I was ten years old."

The breath in Scott's throat turned into a choke. He lowered his head and coughed once into a fist that was immediately tighter than it needed to be. Something was wrong. While the cold air was a pleasant tether to reality for a while, as soon as Edgar said that it stuck to him and stung. He was freezing and burning, somehow all at once.

"It's not…" Edgar scoffed and rolled his eyes. "I phrased it badly. She didn't like grab me herself and –"he mimicked what Scott assumed to be an adult breaking the arm of a much smaller entity, complete with a soft *pop* of his lips. "No. That would be weird. Uh – she had my professor at the time do it."

"Fuck," Scott whispered without thinking.

"We were covering a mending incantation, and part of the way they test your abilities is by making you experience a small injury – you know, so you have something to fix," Edgar said in a way that sounded strangely like an attempt at justification.

Tate was still a part of the conversation and chimed in with words stone cold. "It's usually a cut on the palm," he said.

"But you have to do it yourself," Edgar added. "And I didn't want to do that. It sounded – " He laughed sheepishly. "I knew that if I was standing in class with my hand gushing blood I'd freak out and start crying. Even if it would only be for ten seconds, I just…I refused. I said I wouldn't do it."

He got that spacey look in his eyes that Scott never experienced from an outsider's perspective. It was frightening. More than that, it drew attention to that familiar current starting to crash inside him. That slate-grey, frigid madness that only got wilder by the moment.

It was now very hard to keep his tone level. "You didn't want to cut your hand," he reiterated. "So a grown adult broke your arm?"

"A *dislocation*, Scott. It's different."

"Yes, Edgar – it's *worse*," the current rose, striking with foamy fists against his bones. "You realize that, don't you? If you didn't get it properly treated you'd run the risk of permanent nerve damage…"

Scott trailed off when he noticed the deep darkness spread across Edgar's eyes. The chef stared down at his feet, the muscles in his jaws constricting in slow pulses.

When he looked through Edgar's kitchen the other day he saw that most of the man's cabinet space sparsely populated, with the upper shelves being entirely empty. At the time he figured it was an accommodation for his height. Edgar didn't seem one to drag a chair to climb onto, and as a cook it only made sense that he'd want what he used regularly to always be easy to grab.

That's what he thought initially, at least. Now, even just looking around the majority of the apartment that Scott could see from the kitchen, he realized that nearly everything was easily accessible, and mainly lower to the ground. He lamented the pinprick of his own limited perspective. It had just been so long since he'd been in an actual home that he didn't know to find it weird when the layout doesn't require you to raise your arms above your head.

"It was a really long time ago," Edgar said. "At this point it only starts to ache around this time of year – like a fun early birthday present," he flashed a grim smile. "I just mean to say that I...I know pain -"

"How long?"

Who said that? It couldn't have been Scott. Scott's voice never sounded like that in his own ears. It never glistened, razor sharp with pure rage. But Edgar looked at him when the question was asked, forcing Scott to consider that he might've been the one to ask it.

He held Edgar's stare until the chef broke away and let out a tight sigh. "It was most of the weekend," he said. "I think I got it by Sunday night because I remember being able to come out for dinner."

The ocean broke out of the sea and flooded the surrounding area. Massive waves broke down buildings like tissue paper and swept swarms of cars off the road. There was nothing left. There will be nothing left.

"It's mostly my fault," Edgar went on. "Academic magic takes so much focus when you're starting out, and I just wasn't good with psychic fatigue back then."

Around him Scott felt reality take on that oil slick simmer that he only knew from that Other Place. His feet were still on the ground, yet the feeling of pressure that came with touching the Earth was slowly slipping away.

This was bad. This was rapidly spiraling out of his control. Scott closed his eyes and practiced deep and measured breathing to try and calm himself down. He imagined Edgar as a child. In his mind he pictured an affable Southern boy in a flannel with clever eyes – a real *Encyclopedia Brown* type. If he thought very hard he could take that hypothetical child in his mind and bring him into his arms to hold him.

But then he thought too hard and imagined that release of pressure hands like his could create as they forced the bone of that child's arm out of its socket. He imagined that child alone, stammering incantations that would allow his arm to return to something other than a limp sock of flesh and bone. Did no one check on him? Did no one bother to care? Trying to find answers, Scott was right back to being so angry it terrified him.

The living void inside him laughed. It wryly offered him its help and Scott considered clutching his hands to his ears to drown out the noise. But he couldn't silence something that was coming from deep within himself.

"Where is your Mom now?" Scott asked. Or at least, he felt like he asked.

Yes, where is Edgar's mom? What's her exact address? How sentimental is she over the current state of her own shoulder sockets?

Scott winced. What a terrible, disgusting, abhorrent though. It doesn't matter how angry he was, or how ill-fitting that anger felt. He couldn't drop as low as to resort to hurting someone out of vengeance.

So I'll just make her hurt herself.

He let out the kind of hum his mother taught him. A low hum that barely resonated in the back of his throat. *No,* it said. *No no no.* The world shifted and he felt another wrack of pain that sent him staggering forward into someone's arms. It wasn't Edgar, though, but kind and faceless Doctor Tate. Scott knew this immediately based on the smell of the doctor's cologne and the feel of his sweater vest against his cheek, though he still allowed himself to be supported and ultimately steadied.

Sometime during his panic attack Tate led him onto the patio of Edgar's apartment. Scott wasn't sure when that could've happened. Once he was on his feet again he turned around and stared out at the view, which was really only a brick wall mostly overtaken by ivy. It was still nice.

Gradually he worked his way down to the ground and sat, cross-legged, his forehead settled against the railing of the fence.

"I don't have Petrichor," Tate said apologetically from behind him.

Scott raised his brow, surprised and then went back to tired. Even though his clothes looked expensive, or at least taken care of, Tate still sat down on the concrete next to him.

"I feel like it might've helped in a situation like this," he said. "Even though I know you need the good stuff. The real deal."

That was a weird thing to say. But maybe Scott was still just thrown aback at speaking this much about his own culture.

"You know a lot about birthrights."

Tate nodded. "When I started med school it was my goal to enroll in the Witch Doctors. I actually got accepted just out of med school. There's a good chance I'd be living the rest of my life near the Grand Canyon if my wife didn't get pregnant," he didn't shrug, but clasped his hands together in a way that expressed the same intent. "Private practice is more stable and well-paying, but it certainly lacks...well, you don't need me to explain the difference to you."

The metal felt good against his skin. Scott regretted losing grip on his sanity before getting his mother's jacket. While the cold was nice through the windows, being out in it with nothing but a t-shirt was maddening.

"Did you know my dad?" Scott, mostly to distract himself. "I'm named after him."

"Not personally," Tate said. "He interviewed me at the end of the application practice. Told me about the goals and ideals of his program," a note of humor reached his voice. "Clarified that he hated the name, but that it's what the Elders he communicated with insist they call it," he fell silent, breathing softly. "I imagine you didn't get a chance to meet him."

"The STEMI met him first,"

"Do you perceive that as a loss?"

He thought about that. He tried to think about his father. There were pictures in his head, though the faces were now blurry, but if he thought hard he could imagine messy blonde hair and handsome, masculine proportions. When he was little he remembered his mom telling mom that she missed the way he hugged.

"I look nothing like him," Scott murmured. "I don't really remember what anyone looks like at this point, and yet I know that much for certain. *That* feels like a loss."

Surprisingly enough Tate allowed that statement to hang in the air and drift like the first remnants of snow. He didn't try and say any empty platitudes to counteract the pain, instead watching it with him in quiet reverence. And even stranger, once it came to rest on the patio it slowly began to melt until Scott wasn't as hurt anymore. It was still difficult – it was just no longer painful.

"He did important work," Tate told him. "You know better than most the value of empathetic medical care and accessibility. To be able to get a good portion of it without leaving the safety of home must've provided so much comfort."

"Did you know?" Scott said.

He couldn't read Tate's expression, though could chart the dread by the stiffening of his shoulders (*shoulder shoulder*). Yes, he had the shape of a good man. He filled in the outline of a helpful person with all the prettiest colors, but was any of it real? When he saw an abused little boy in front of him, was he just one more larger and forceful figure refusing to help?

"One day I'd like to explain the full extent of Edgar's upbringing," he sighed and added, even softer. "To both of you. To get where I am in the Academy means either compromising your ethics, or..."

He trailed off and didn't speak for a long time. His faceless face turned, perhaps to look through the gaps in the fence. Scott thought he could read regret in his shoulders and lamented that he had nothing else to go on to determine what the doctor was feeling. Just as he thought that, Tate lowered his head and wiped a hand into the murk of his face around where eyes were supposed to be. When he spoke again his voice trembled slightly.

"I'm sorry," he said. "I kept him as a patient and slowed the process, buying him enough time to escape. That was all I could do," he fixed the collar of his shirt in a slow gesture. "Academics think that magic makes them stronger. They don't realize that we're often the weakest of humanity."

If Scott focused he could see the little scattered splotches where the rust on the fence started to rise and chip away. He touched the area to feel the texture and found it reminded him of the back of an old toad.

A nap would be good. A nap and some water. This was a lot of information to take into consideration and it was getting very hard to follow.

"Would you like to bond with him?" Tate asked. "Even temporarily, I feel as if you still know it's a massive commitment."

"I would," Scott answered without even having to think.

"Why?"

Scott faced the faceless man and, in a rare act of courage, expressed no emotion.

"He's kind," he said. "I think he's afraid to express it sometimes, but...I can tell he has a lot of love in his heart for the world around him. Plus you saw how daring he could be, just – brave. Heroic, even though it might scare him," Scott finally smiled as he thought about it. "He's a good person. I feel safe around him. I love..."

The words formed in his throat and almost escaped before Scott quickly swallowed them back. He wished desperately that he could search Tate's expression to see if he caught on what he was so close to saying. Unfortunately, all he saw in the doctor's face was the aftermath of an ice cream cake thrown against a wall.

"I'm relieved," Tate gently explained. "I thought that keeping regular contact with Edgar after he left would only slow his individuation. At the same time...I worried. I missed his presence," his words slowed and became more deliberate. "I'm glad to know he's found someone who wants give him the...*help* – that he's needed for so long."

"I think he's the one helping me," Scott muttered.

"Bonds go both ways, don't they?"

Scott leaned back and looked up at the slate gray sky above them. The clouds rippled softly in dark cracks and shadows. It would probably rain today.

"I've known Edgar for a long time," Tate told him. "It may not be my place to say, but I believe you should trust when he makes it clear that he wants to – *help* you. If anything, I don't think he fully understands how much he's invested in...helping you."

"Well maybe he's just that kind of guy."

Tate didn't respond at first. Then he lowered his head and chuckled softly. There was a soft whoosh of the sliding glass door opening, and Scott shifted where he sat to see Edgar standing in the entryway. He awkwardly clutched Scott's coat to his chest and attempted a smile.

"Uh, I – I thought maybe you'd..." he paused, eyes darting to the floor with a frown. "...I didn't mean to overshare."

Scott worked himself up to his feet and approached Edgar at the doorway. He carefully took his coat and slipped it on, immediately comforted by the feeling of the worn inner lining. Even though it still no longer smelled of his mother's perfume, the unquestioning warmth it brought every time he wore it still reminded him of her.

"I got upset thinking about you being alone in a situation like that," Scott buttoned up the coat. "But it's okay – because after today, you won't be alone anymore."

He looked up at Edgar and saw him watching with slightly widened eyes. Even though he no longer held Scott's coat he still had his arms clutched around him. He quivered the beginnings of a smile and let out a small, flustered laugh.

"So where are we doing this?" Scott asked.

"What do you mean?" Tate said.

"We need a testament to nature, right?" He looked back at Edgar, "I got bonded by the ocean last time and Mom always told me how she did her ritual during a thunderstorm. That kind of thing."

Tate stood up and brushed the sides of his slacks. "That's very beautiful, but Academic magic really doesn't require that kind of sentiment –"

"We have swamps," Edgar said, "but I don't really know any spots aside from the kind you need a tour guide to walk through. I – I've never been much of a hiker."

There was a short stretch of silence as Scott thought that over. Then Tate broke it with his own gentle suggestion.

"What about the Mississippi River?"

"It's mostly sewage right now," Edgar sighed. "I'm sure it's a testament, just...not to anything good."

More silence. Scott regarded the two men on either side of them, realizing that they were trying to find a solution with just as much focus and conviction that he had. It was very sweet. He put his hands in the pocket of his mother's coat and stilled himself in the warmth of it.

"Scott," Edgar said some time later, "you probably consider death a part of nature, right?"

"Of course," Scott said.

Edgar perked up slightly. "Well New Orleans has a bunch of historic cemeteries that I've been told aren't like anything else you can find in the country. I'm actually a few blocks away from one. We could walk there," he cast Scott a look both hesitant and hopeful. "Would that work?"

This man. It must have been so much work to guard a heart so big, so heavily, and for so, so long. Only to drop it all at once and offer to get their souls tethered together in a graveyard despite showing that he doesn't feel at all about death the way Scott does. What a beautiful human being.

"Yeah," Scott reached over and brushed his fingers along the side of Edgar's arm. "I think that would be perfect."

Edgar knew where the cemetery was because it was right down the street from a bakery that served his favorite hot cocoa during the cold season. He kept that connection in mind while he walked there. That steaming mug of thick Italian hot chocolate would be the perfect treat to reward himself with after standing adjacent to about a billion ancient corpses in varying stages of decomposition.

So, great news for him.

Scott and Tate didn't speak much as they followed him down the route just outside of his neighborhood and down Washington Avenue. Edgar didn't try to make conversation and mainly kept his eyes on the half-mulched, wet leaves that squelched under his boots. This didn't feel wrong. It just felt incredibly important and even more serious. Something in the weight of how much what they were about to do mattered so much to him that it drew attention to how little he cared about a majority of everything else in his life.

Lafayette Cemetery no. 1 made itself known through a massive iron gate now well-weathered after what must've been hundreds of years of burials and mournings. It was one of the most prolific graveyards in the city, known for tours and travelers, and all manner of goth. Luckily, and practically against all odds, the grounds looked sparse from what Edgar could see between the tombs.

He lingered by the opening, shivering despite the protection of his jacket.

"You two should go on ahead," Tate said, setting his briefcase on the top surface of a nearby generator. "I would like to ground myself and prepare the strand before I enter the space."

Yes, doctor, definitely let the two children enter the graveyard unsupervised. Nothing can go wrong there. You'd have to be a well-constructed skeleton to push aside those stone slabs that cover the doorways, and if Edgar ever crossed paths with a bone man that strong he was smart enough to just lie down and wait for death.

It was a beautiful afternoon in Corpse Town as Scott and Edgar walked down the grass pathways between the crypts. Edgar moved slowly and carefully, part of him expecting to accidentally crash an ongoing burial around every corner. His new companion, on the other hand, moved through the skeleton houses like he was pursuing the art in a museum. To him, this was apparently just a stop in his day before they got a bite to eat.

"Why are we here?" Scott asked at one point.

Edgar masked his shudder as a playful chuckle. "I was hoping we'd be past that question at this point."

"No, I – I mean…why are we *here?*" He held his hand out to motion across the alley of tombs they were in now. "You seem pretty uncomfortable."

At first Edgar felt the urge to lie and say he was fine. Or to dismiss his unease as immature or unreasonable. None of that felt honest. He stopped where he was, and Scott stopped a few steps ahead and turned around to look at him.

"Why aren't you?" Edgar said.

Scott stared at him. He was neither offended, ashamed, condescending or judgmental. He just stared and blinked at uneven intervals.

"We're surrounded by the dusty remains of, like, a *ton* of dead people," Edgar went on to say. "Doesn't that terrify you? Isn't that the point?"

Scott swallowed hard and turned away, his mouth working in silent, but intense thought. Then suddenly something made itself very clear, and he approached Edgar and took his hands in his. It looked like he would say something revolutionary before the nerve left him. He still held his hand, only now without the determination.

His silence forced Edgar to take in the atmosphere. Even though they weren't deep within the cemetery there was some energy that made them feel cut off from the city as a whole. Edgar could hear when a car passed without processing the noise the way he would from the sidewalk. Instead what made itself known were the croaking of bullfrogs and the distant trilling of insects. And, in some strange way, the silence itself had a noise. The clouds seemed to gurgle like a rushing brook. The moss hummed peacefully.

For a place of the dead, Edgar had to admit there was a surprising amount of life unlike anything else you could experience in the rest of the world.

Scott slumped his shoulders in quiet defeat. "I tried to think," he said. "I just can't put it into words that sound any good," he looked to the aisle of graves beside them and smiled faintly. "I just think it feels...safe here."

Ah, Edgar mused with affection. The poor strange man just wanted him to be good friends with the Bone Men. In a way he supposed there was no better person to be in a place like this with. Even if a zombie scrambled from the tomb beside them, they weren't likely to attack a man who would immediately offer them a helping hand and his own jacket to warm what was left of their flesh.

He wrapped his arm around Scott's and began leading them deeper into the cemetery. "I guess I get that," he said. "You could tell me more about it later if you think of anything else."

They didn't get far before Scott stopped again in front of a white stone tomb turned gray and black with age. The doorway was partially bricked over and covered with plaster, but after an indeterminate amount of time some of that paste had broken away to reveal the ancient masonry underneath.

"*F. Nolting,*" Scott said under his breath, reading the etched lettering carved under the arch of the roof.

He stepped forward and touched the lines between the brick. Scott took his first two fingers, the middle trailing after the index's lead, and traced gently over the grout plastered generations ago. Edgar knew that touch. Edger felt that touch last night. It was so goddamned respectful and fascinated, and seeing it from the outside felt like when a hummingbird feels safe enough to pause midair in your presence.

Scott looked over his shoulder at him. "Who do you think they were?"

"I don't know," Edgar scanned the front of the tomb and peeked his head around the walls on either side. "It looks like the plaque's missing."

"All this space for one person?"

Edgar took a few steps closer to stand beside him. "These usually house families, I think. Groups of people."

"But it's one name."

That was a good point. The name on the tomb sounded like one person, one body lying alone in the dark. Edgar didn't understand what neuron flared oddly in his brain to cause this reaction, but the thought made him feel a little sad. He realized then that it could be like how Scott described it – all that space for one person. In life Nolting might've been very important. Now, probably long-dead, the only thing they could be is lonely.

What a sincerely weird thing for Edgar to think. Something must've slipped in his brain and allowed him to slide and tumble into madness.

"We'll do it here," he said.

Scott looked at him. There was nothing complex in his demeanor. He just seemed really, really happy.

When Doctor Tate found them a short while later they were sitting on the ground outside of Nolting's tomb, their backs against the stone. Edgar looked up and locked eyes with this therapist, and the vaguest hint of surprise that was written on his face immediately made him feel awkward. He started to move to stand, but before he could Tate got on their level and sat down on the damp grass.

There was a small glass storage container in his hands. Based on the size of it, Edgar could imagine using it to hold salsa, or maybe excess brown sugar. But Tate now used it to carry a tumbleweed of thread floating in a small, amber pool of dahlia oil. The doctor shifted his position a few times and tested tilting his long legs in a few different angles. Eventually he found something comfortable and looked up at the two of them with a small smile.

"All right," he said. "Let's get started."

The smell of the oil filled the radius around them in a plume of scent as soon as Tate popped open the lid. When he dipped his fingers into the container the tips came out slick and stained gold.

"Which of you was born first?" He asked them.

Edgar and Scott exchanged a look, mutually realizing they had no idea how to answer that question. After a brief conversation they established that they were the same age, with Scott's birthday being in early spring and Edgar's being that same winter. That knowledge apparently meant that Scott got the honor to be the first to touch the wet, smelly string, which struck Edgar as kind of funny until it actually happened.

The red strand rested in a vaguely crescent-like shape across the palm of his hand. There were nearly no other imperfections on either of Scott's hands, but in a matter of minutes he would now have a very noticeable scar that he'd carry for the rest of his life. And he must have realized this too, yet he didn't have any reaction suggesting that this was something he didn't want to happen.

"It...only hurts for a little bit," Edgar clarified, staring down at the strand on Scott's palm "...Right?"

Scott's voice sounded distant when he answered. "It's rough, but it's only a second," he said. "You'll be okay."

Edgar wanted to laugh, because Scott apparently didn't consider that he wasn't asking for his own sake. Then, at Tate's direction, he carefully pressed his left hand against Scott's right and slid their fingers between each other. The oil was cold to the touch at first, but quickly warmed from their new, shared heat.

"I thought bonds had to face each other," Scott spoke softly while Tate started to wrap the strand around their held hands.

"A relationship exists in the world," the doctor explained. "This is meant to represent that you will live alongside each other, not just in the scope of the other's perception."

Edgar's chest was struck hard with the beauty of that sentiment. He anxiously darted his eyes to Scott and found the other man rendered equally as speechless.

They watched silently as Tate continued to physically bind their hands in the strand, working slowly and with a focused precision disproportionate to the task at hand.

"Scott," he said at one point. "Why don't you share something you've noticed about Edgar?"

Scott blinked a few times. The action was somehow thoughtful. "He closes doors very softly," he said. "And sometimes when he plays music he'll sing along to the melody instead of the lyrics."

"That's good. Eddie, now you."

Edgar's throat felt tight from hearing Scott's previous observation. Still, he managed to respond. "Uh – you talk in your sleep," he said to him.

"I do?"

"Yeah," the tension lessened as he remembered the night before. "Well – you hum. Only sometimes, though."

He didn't mean to imply anything when he said this. Scott, though, looked incredibly struck by the observation. He opened his mouth slightly, but then closed it and simply smiled.

When their hands were fully wrapped together it wasn't the total hold Edgar thought it might be. If he wanted to he could easily let go and yank his hand out of the web of string – the material was so thin it would take next to no effort. But even no effort at all was more than he was willing to expend to pull away from Scott's touch at that moment.

"Scott," Tate said again. "What is your wish for the relationship you're about to solidify?"

"I want you," Scott whispered, staring directly into Edgar's eyes.

He paused, then sank into that full-face blush that only made Edgar's head spin even quicker.

"I'm sorry," he laughed weakly. "Intention, right? I didn't...yeah," he cleared his throat into his free hand and tried again. "Um. I will be your friend. I will help you. I will –"Scott's face became very serious. "I will stay with you. Until you don't want me around anymore."

That will never happen, the child in Edgar's mind spat out frantically. *Stay forever. Let's buy a farm. Let's form a band. Let's build the safest, most comfortable nest in the world and never, ever leave.*

He shut up the kid as nicely as he could and found the nerve to smile and barely keep from crying.

"Eddie," the doctor said, his voice lowering. "It's your turn."

Scott's eyes looked so strange when they weren't glowing. It wasn't bad. They were still vibrant and deep – the kind of eyes Edgar would gladly stare at for an indefinite stretch of time without any fear of getting lost or afraid. They were a little glassy at the moment, perhaps welled with emotion at the potential of what he could say next.

Edgar took a deep breath and fought the temptation to turn to fully face him. "Scott," he said, "I promise that I will do everything in my power to make it so you can live a long and contented life."

Immediately Scott's face flickered between dread and affection and worry.

"Are you sure, Edgar?" Tate asked.

"I'm sure."

"Because you should understand that phrasing is important here. This is a connection built on your intention –"

"And this is my intention," Edgar calmly said, his eyes still on Scott.

Scott had the ability to cry without moving a single other muscle on his face. Tears just fell independent of him. And he continued to look as if what Edgar said terrified him, but after a moment his fear broke into a genuine smile.

Tate didn't say anything for a long time after that. Eventually Edgar forced his eyes way from Scott and saw the doctor simply staring at him with an expression warmed by sheer pride. There was no professional distance, and in that moment Edgar remembered that he was looking at a man who watched him grow up through the worst darkness of his life. The man who strove to try and protect him when no one else would, and who now dropped everything at a moment's notice just to help him again.

"Thank you, Tate," Edgar said.

The doctor nodded. He wiped his eyes with the back of his hand and, with the other, pulled out a small lighter.

"Good luck, friends," he said as he lit the other end of the strand.

The red string sparked with a flicker, and suddenly the entire web bust into flames. Edgar barely had a chance to visually recognize the sight of fire against skin before he felt the scorch. It wasn't just against him, it was *inside* him. His bones boiled. His veins charred and his chest cavity filled with smoke, and suddenly the world flickered around him like a cheap light bulb and

Eddie spent another night in bed, staring at the boy that laid beside him. He was there – he was definitely there, even though his entire being was sketched out in a sort of semi-physical, deep blue light. For a week they'd been like this, with him trying to go to sleep as if there wasn't another presence inhabiting the space inches beside him.

"What's your name?" Eddie whispered.

The blue boy didn't answer. He looked at him though, staring through long and messy hair with eyes that were even bluer than the rest of him. They were round, large eyes, with the black of both pupils dragged down slightly. Just like Eddie's.

"I – I..." He could barely hold onto his words through the sudden, frantic excitement. "I like your nose."

Up until now the blue boy's expression was tired, almost cold. With this one comment Eddie managed to bring some warmth to his face. He rolled onto his side and touched a shimmery hand to the front of his face. "You do?"

"Yeah. You look like one of the statues at school."

His bedfellow managed a small smile. It seemed shy. "Thanks," he said. "It's big and I'm still not sure how I feel about it."

"I like it," Eddie said again, then scooted closer and added. "What's your name?"

The blue boy looked hesitant. Than he looked sad again. Finally, he extended another smile.

"You can call me Lark. It's really good to meet you, Eddie."

The dream of a past he forgot up until now flickered out in an instant, along with the excruciating pain of the controlled burn in Edgar's soul. Reality returned, and he was back to being an adult in the graveyard in New Orleans.

But the memory stayed. Because that's what he saw – a memory. Every detail was familiar to him, from the pattern on the pillowcases to the large-eyed boy he shared a bed with. The sound of his voice, even as a child, even warped across some kind of indescribable enchantment, was unmistakable.

That was Scott. He met Scott before. And the more he dwelled on that moment in his mind, the more he thought it might be a continuation of something that happened far before that. Potentially, even, far after.

Why didn't he remember? What happened to make Edgar forget something this important?

Some of the initial shock began to fade from his brain. As things settled he became more aware of Scott's presence in a way Edgar could never feel another human being before. It was tricky to adjust to at first. It wasn't that the other man's heart now beat in his chest. More accurate to say would be that his life and presence resonated throughout Edgar's being with the perpetual buzz of static electricity. It was immediately intoxicating.

There was a very faint overlay that shimmered over himself. He focused hard on it, and as soon as he did he was awash with an array of feelings that were far more vast and vibrant than anything he had ever been capable of before. It was disorientating, and Edgar edged towards a panic before he forced his attention across from him and realized that it wasn't even his own feelings he was feeling.

They were Scott's.

His eyes were shut and his face was tight with concentration. His chest rose in fell in careful, composed breaths. Edgar didn't need to check to confirm that they were now breathing at the same rhythm.

"Are you okay?" Edgar asked him, because apparently he just now remembered he had a voice.

"It…It's gone."

He took his free hand and touched his temple. He pressed his fingertips to his chest and over his head. By now his hand trembled terribly, but he didn't seem afraid. Scott began to smile, and he started to cry. The shaking rose up his arm and across both shoulders, either indicating that he was terrified or in the middle of laughter.

An hour ago Edgar would think Scott was about to have a panic attack. And maybe he was. But now there was a strange new certainty inside him that said that he was okay. That whatever happening was good and safe. So he just watched and held his hand.

"What's gone?" Tate said, because apparently Tate was still here.

"The pain. The *feeding*. I-It doesn't -" he opened his eyes to look at the doctor and let out a loud laugh that surprised everyone but Edgar. "Oh *shit*, doctor. You…"

Scot shot his head to Edgar. He looked confused that he swore. Apparently he didn't realize that wasn't the first time he did so that day. That feeling passed, and his expression warmed back into dizzy, bemused tears. Scott struggled to speak for a while, then clenched his jaw and laughed through his nose.

"He…doesn't seem like he'd have a mustache, does he?" He finally worked out.

That was the first thing since Edgar came back to reality to genuinely shock him. And that must've shown on his face, because it was enough to surrender Scott completely to the will of his own emotions. He went limp, back pressed against the tomb and chin tilted up, and sobbed freely. Sometimes he laughed through his tears, sometimes he grinned so hard it looked more like a grimace. Mostly he just cried.

It was the perfect wail. Any mourner within earshot would envy his technique.

Edgar felt Tate watching him closely.

"You're smiling," he noted.

He was right. And Edgar felt no desire to stop.

"It worked," he said.

After Scott was through with his tears he gathered the strength to stand, and the three ended up gathered again by the gates. Scott gripped the bars with both hands, staring at every single person who passed by with absolute astonishment. This wasn't what most would expect to see outside a cemetery – a frantic man doling out extended, wide-eyed, un-blinking eye contact.

Time went on and he continued not to blink. Edgar made a private note to monitor that as a potential issue.

Tate stood beside him. His nice semi-suit was now splotched with mud, and he – like Edgar and Scott – stank of smoke and dead flowers. Still, he seemed pleased.

"There's a chance this might be overwhelming for him for a while," he gently warned. "Try to make sure he doesn't jump into things too quickly."

"I won't," Edgar agreed.

They both watched Scott watch the world.

"He seems..." Tate began, but let the sentence flicker out.

Edgar snickered. "Yeah," he said. "He does."

"And how do *you* feel?"

"*Everything is blooming most recklessly;*" Edgar quoted, "*if it were voices instead of colors, there would be an unbelievable shrieking into the heart of the night.*"

Tate hummed. "Glad to see you still know your Rilke," he looked back at Scott, turning contemplative. "And in regards to him?"

There was something. Something he was just thinking about him and Scott. But it was fading quickly.

No. *No.*

Not again.

You can't let this go away again.

It was like trying to grasp a downy feather carried on the breeze, but at the last possible second he snatched it up and remembered the boy in his childhood bed.

"We met before," Edgar whispered, sharp and hot to burn the words into his brain. "When we were kids."

He looked to Tate for surprise and found very little. It was rather anticlimactic. Then Tate reached over and gave him a physical pat on the back. It was a single touch the hand, very brief. Earnest and a little clumsy.

"I'm proud of you, Edgar," Tate said.

Those words cut through Edgar's exhaustion and provoked an immediate release of tears. He gasped slightly and awkwardly hunched his shoulders, lowering his head and wiping at his face.

"Sorry," he muttered to the doctor. "Sorry sorry sorry -"

He stopped when he felt Scott touch his chin and softly raise his head. Having some sort of insane C-PTSD flashback in front of people was one thing. He couldn't control it, and at least he was lucky enough to have it happen in front of people he trusted. But crying normally while looking someone directly in the eye was a nightmarish concept.

Or so he thought. Of course, when he looked up at Scott he found that staring into his eyes felt exactly as safe as Edgar did when he buried his head under the blankets and wept as a child.

Scott gazed kindly at him. He grazed a thumb along the base of Edgar's jaw, where the tears gathered and started to itch. Then some time passed, and his fondness faltered. Some more time after that and his expression was less romantic and more concerned and vaguely guilty.

"Six seconds," he said.

Edgar frowned. "What?"

"You should make sure to blink about every six seconds. Not exactly," Scott clarified, "you could make it four, you can make it eight. But that's annoying to keep track of, so – six. Just count to six," he smiled in a way Edgar supposed was meant to be encouraging. "You'll stop having to think about it eventually."

"What are you talking about?" Edgar said.

"I've probably stopped blinking too, right?" Scott sighed. "That's fine. I'll get the hang of it again. But *you* -" his voice turned surprisingly stern. "You got to get on that. Crying *hurts* if you go long enough without blinking. And, uh," guilt returned to his expression, "if you're anything like me you're going to be crying a lot for a while."

Edgar struggled with the concept that they both apparently forgot a human component as basic as blinking. But staring directly at Scott now felt the same as closing his eyes and being somewhere private and secure where these types of things couldn't matter too much.

"A lot for me or a lot for you?" He softly joked. "Because if it's the latter I could just give up blinking entirely."

Shock flashed on Scott's face before quickly joining Edgar in his weary amusement.

"I always thought that the blinking rule isn't for us," Scott confided. "Nobody admits it, but I really think most of the time we do it for the people that have to talk to us." He paused and grinned. "I've never said that out loud before."

Edgar smiled back at Scott, drunk off the closeness, ravenous for the attention of his previously unknown third half. Scott's eyes on his felt as easy and unquestioned as that of his own reflection – but if this is how he felt every time he glanced in the mirror he would be an entirely different person.

He touched Scott's face and pressed it against his in a kiss. It was nothing too passionate, as he still had enough sense to know that they were in the wrong place to do something like that. Still, just one structurally "regular" kiss and Edgar felt the rejuvenation of a perfect stretch.

Scott couldn't do anything but look at him. His lips moved slightly in the vaguest outline of words, but it was enough for Edgar to be able to read what he was saying to himself.

One.

Two.

Three.

Four.

Five.

Six.

Scott blinked. He gently tapped his fingers together and smiled. Edgar tried very hard not to laugh, mostly to be polite.

He felt Tate touch his shoulder and looked over at the doctor.

"I'm going to get back on the road," Tate said. "I have some notes to go over before my sessions tomorrow."

"Oh," Edgar said. "A-Are you sure? I thought maybe I could make you dinner. You know – to say thanks."

Tate smiled at him. "Next time," he said.

"But –"

"I came to help," Tate softly intoned. "I believe I succeeded. Now it's your job to explore how what we did has changed and expanded your world."

He buttoned up his coat and turned to address Scott. Edgar couldn't imagine the way his bond's perception of reality must've completely up-ended itself. If it was happening to him, and he could suddenly see other people after years of loneliness, he would be doubled over emotionally. And while Scott definitely looked like his attention was being pulled in a dozen places at once, the second he gathered Tate was saying his good-byes he focused on the doctor and with the utmost respect.

It looked like Tate noticed that effort too. "How is it, Scott?" He asked him.

Scott attempted bashfulness and stopped almost as soon as he started. He tightened his jaw and looked down, then frowned and faced Tate again with glassier eyes.

"It's beautiful," he said. "I completely forgot how fucking beautiful everyone is."

Tate arched his brow. "Everyone?"

Scott laughed. "Every single person I see."

The doctors eyes shot momentarily towards Edgar, seemingly look-ing for something. Once they turned back to Scott Edgar realized his therapist was searching for signs of jealously. Which made sense, he supposed. If anything, it was stranger that Edgar never considered even the temptation of the feeling. But that was probably for the best.

"Eddie has my number," Tate explained to Scott. "If you ever feel like you'd like to talk about anything, then I'm happy to –"

"You're private practice, right?" Scott asked. "Are you licensed in Oregon? That's where I live."

This didn't look like the response that Tate was expecting. It wasn't what Edgar was expecting to hear Scott say either. This was the first time he brought up where he was originally from.

"I...am, actually," Tate said.

"Do you take United?"

"I – I do."

Scott smiled. "Then I'd be very interested. I haven't had access to consistent mental health care in a long time. Can I call you in a few days to set up an intake appointment?" He hesitated before continuing. "I only have regular depression. I can't set up any time pockets or anything."

Tate was surprised, but still nodded as if that was a perfectly reasonable thing to say. Edgar considered picking up some kind of notebook to make actual bullet points of the things he definitely needed to bring up the next time he and Scott had a formal, sit-down conversation.

They parted ways with the doctor at the gates of the cemetery soon after that. Edgar stood and watched his doctor make his way down the street. His nice pale slacks were stained with oil, grass and mud. He was just going to get in his car and drive back to Shreveport, where he would go on with his life exactly as it was before.

Still, Edgar had to remember, he would probably keep smelling exactly as he did for a good few days. It would be easier for someone like Tate, though. Bonds were the typewriters of Academic magic – outdated, but it's not too weird and almost slightly charming if anyone founds out you associate with them.

He would be fine. That's what Edgar would just have to tell himself. Tate was older than he was and smarter than he was, and even though he'd never seen the doctor do a single incantation he had to assume he was good at them if he had to.

"This isn't what I thought it'd feel like," Scott said from behind him.

He was a step back from Edgar, once again looking around at the people that passed them on the street. His shock had settled slightly into intense curiosity. His blinking was unnervingly consistent.

"What part?" Edgar asked, looking down at the smiley face still drawn on Scott's hand.

Scott looked at him, giving him yet another searching scan up and down.

"You're not worried?" He said. "About what's going to happen to you now?"

"Not really," Edgar said.

"You might start doing what I can do," Scott said. "Hopefully to a lesser extent. Hopefully."

"We'll figure something out."

"Doesn't that scare you?"

"Did it really hurt before?"

Scott hesitated. "Yes."

"And it doesn't now?"

"No. Well – less so."

Edgar thought about what to say to that. "That's...an overwhelming beauty."

Scott's eyes widened. He seemed stirred by that. Then he frowned, searching harder. "You're really handsome," he said.

"I'm glad you think so."

"I'm serious. I thought I liked your face before but I've seen at least thirty other faces and yours is still my favorite."

"Yeah, Scott, I think we've established by now that we both have a very specific type."

They locked eyes, both frowning and close to laughter. Scott broke first, turning away to chuckle at his feet.

"Can I buy you a hot chocolate?" Edgar asked him, pointing in the general direction of his favorite bakery.

Scott gave him a look that reflected the same fatalistic happiness Edgar had been feeling on a near constant basis since they met. Did he always feel it too and he just never noticed? Or did their emotions and mannerisms truly muddle together into a slurry before being poured back into their individual psyches?

"Sure," Scott said. "I'd like that."

Death and Taxes was a small bakery built out of what used to be an auto garage. With it's proximity to some of the most known parts of New Orleans, Edgar rarely chose to actually sit down there and enjoy the ambiance. Which was a shame, because it was a rare business that was popular for the neighborhood without also selling blended cock-tails in yardstick glasses. It was black-owned, woman-owned and family-owned, so Edgar still forced himself to deal with the throngs of clueless people when he needed croissant bread or had a craving for sweet potato pie.

Now, though, was the rare few weeks in the winter where Death and Taxes was mostly only frequented by the sober and reasonably-pleas-ant. Lots of college students looking for a place to sit and study. A few scattered old folks reading the neighborhood paper or grumbling over games of backgammon. Maybe Lucy, the fat old bulldog that acted as the mascot, sleeping on the large couch in the back.

In other words, it would be perfect.

Walking there they were each moving independently. Pretty soon Edgar realized that this wasn't sustainable. While Scott could once move with expert ease across any kind of terrain without a single thought, he now couldn't go more than a few steps without getting distracted and tripping over a crack or being startled and almost knocking Edgar off the sidewalk. By the time they got to the bakery Edgar had his arm around his and was the one to physically lead him through the door.

"There's a lot of people here," Scott remarked, a little nervous.

This wasn't true. There was the usual clerk at the counter and two workers in the back kitchen, and other than that there were only a small handful of clientele. Of course, for someone who never once made a remark over the amount of people in much more crowded rooms, this must've felt like a lot more. Especially when he felt the new desire to look all of them in the face all at once.

He sat Scott down at the back couch. Much like Edgar's predicted, Lucy the Bulldog was working today, and she soon bounded over and began to sniff them curiously. The sight of her – and, perhaps, the damp touch of her slobber – managed to get Scott to pause the swivel of his head and unwind a little bit. He lightly stroked the top of her head, then fell back against the couch in a slump.

"Shit," he breathed. "I'm so tired."

Was the swearing a strange side effect of the bond? Edgar hoped it wasn't. He hoped it kept going all the time. It was fun.

"Yeah, I'd imagine," Edgar looked out the window and considered the time. "I'll call us a cab home in a bit. For now, though – a hot drink to warm up?"

Scott undid his hair and let it fall around his face. He brushed it back with his finger, a weak attempt to tame the black sea. As soon as he caught Edgar's eye and the word *mine* rang out deep within him. That wasn't the type of thing he usually thought. Was it a question, hope, or fact?

"Thank you," Scott said.

He thought of the blue boy in his bed. *Mine,* the word came again. *Mine and yours.*

They went to the counter and ordered two hot chocolates. Midway Edgar realized how gross and sticky his hands felt and, without thinking, grabbed the key off the counter hook and went to the bathroom. It felt good to run his hands under the warm water, scrub them with soap until they foamed. The act got off the residue without doing much to get rid of the smell.

The smell was bad. Sick and sweet. It made him think of his mother.

Rubbing his palms with paper towel he realized suddenly that he forgot to pay. It was embarrassing – frankly unlike him – but he figured since he was a regular there it wouldn't be an issue.

"Sorry, Mia," he apologized to the cashier as he came back out. "Weird day. How much will it be?"

Mia looked up at him, smiling amicably. "You're good, Ed. Your husband paid already."

"My..?"

Behind him Scott had his eyes shut, head settled against the back of the couch. Still, he made sure to stay awake enough to keep petting the dog that had now taken what should rightfully be Edgar's spot.

"Lucy approves," Mia noted.

He looked back at her. She flashed him a thumbs up. Edgar considered explaining her mistake, but he quickly figured it wasn't important he wasn't really concerned either way. Instead he just snickered.

Once their hot chocolates were ready Edgar took the mugs and brought them back to his bond, who sat up slightly and tried to stretch himself awake. He looked over at Lucy and made an honest attempt to nudge her off the couch. But, being a bulldog, Lucy had the density of a small moon.

"Oh," Scott murmured, trying and failing to push a little harder. "Oh no."

Edgar put down the mugs and clicked his tongue, which eventually was enough the attract the dog's attention and get her to reluctantly hop off the couch. She stood at his feet and looked up at him, all folds and wrinkles and wildly expressive eyes.

He scratched his fingers through her fur and cast the furry friend a nod. And then he took his seat.

The thing about Italian hot chocolate is that, even though it isn't a famous NOLA dish, it shares the similarity of depending on thickener. So while you do drink it, the cocoa is so thick it's more like slurping up the remnants of a melted chocolate bar. Edgar thought that this was something he could warn Scott about, just so he knew what he was go-ing into.

On further speculation, he determined not doing so would be fun-nier. So he didn't.

Scott sat up and took the mug with a grateful smile. He held it under his nose and smelled it, then let out a happy sigh. Edgar felt himself bub-ble towards a laugh as his bond tilted the mug to his lips and sipped.

"*Whoa,*" he whispered.

Edgar feigned innocence. "Is something wrong?" He saw Scott strug-gle to regulate his blinking and eased up with the teasing. "It's supposed to be like that. There's cornstarch in it. Try it – it's really good."

Even still, Scott was uncertain. But he still took a sip, and as soon as he did his eyes lit up. He smiled, leaned back with his feet on the couch, and continued to drink.

The hot chocolate was unbelievably decadent, just rich and buttery like something out of a children's book. It stuck to the inside of Edgar's bones and immediately insulated them. Soon he was warm. Soon he was incredibly sleepy. And again he remembered the boy in his childhood bed.

Did Scott know? Did he see what Edgar saw? If he did he wasn't telling. Or maybe he forgot like Edgar almost did back in the cemetery.

Edgar should tell him. He had to tell him.

He closed his eyes, which stung from how long he accidentally kept them open. In the darkness he was bathed in the fuzz and dust of Scott's fatigue. It was like being trapped in a massive dust bunny in the midst of some great darkness. The man had traveled for so long and was now be-ing granted with the opportunity for a rest that no one on Earth needed more than him.

This could wait. They gardener't going anywhere, right?

"You don't have to tell me," Scott said.

"Huh?"

"I can – I..." Scott wiped his mouth with his hand and grimaced be-fore reaching for the bottle of hand sanitizer on the side table. "I think

I can feel flickers of you. And I got a sense of – hesitance? I don't know. It wasn't from me, so I figured..."

"I know a lot of the staff here," Edgar quickly said. "The woman at the counter thought you were my husband."

What he witnessed in response to this was a complete lack of a reaction.

"Right," Scott said. "Sure. Okay."

He leaned back against the couch and kept drinking his hot chocolate. It was clear that, if Edgar chose as much, he could move past this situation entirely and never have it brought up again in the course of their relationship. Scott was genuinely indifferent. Still, if only for the sake of his own curiosity, Edgar pushed a little further.

"Did you tell her that you were?" He said, mostly without concern.

Scott, mid-sip and gazing sleepily ahead of him, shook his head.

"That doesn't bother you?"

Scott blinked. Six seconds passed. He blinked again.

"It makes sense," he concluded. "You know – considering."

He was a ball of nerves and tension when they met. Compared to that, the relaxation of today was night and day – even when Scott was faced with what he imagined to be his inevitable death. And now they were in an entirely new span of time. Now he was like an entirely different person. Same lines, same colors, same warmth and spirit – only with less pain.

The things that can change when a person is pulled from their pain.

Edgar put his mug down on the table next to the couch and slid closer to Scott. Without having to say a single word Scott angled his chest slightly and wrapped his arm around Edgar, pulling him close.

He didn't flinch or tense. There was no flash of anxiety or shame. There wasn't even a rush of any kind of overwhelming positive emotion. Edgar just settled his head in the crook of Scott's neck and buried his face in his hair. It felt as simple as crossing his legs and as thrilling as finding a new color in a rainbow.

"Yeah," Edgar murmured against his bond's neck. "I guess it does."

Fourth Movement

Katherine Nadine Delaney woke up to a pile of cat vomit partially drying on the covers. She wasn't surprised. In fact, the closest thing she had to a reaction was the weary relief of seeing that everything in the mess looked already digested. So Katy carefully peeled back the top blanket and crumpled it into a ball for the laundry, then stepped out of the bed and went to check on the offending party.

She found him curled in the basket of dirty hand towels in the bathroom. He filled the entirety of the surface area like a furry lid, with plumes of gray-white spilling over the edges. At first all Katy was able to to see was a mass of fur and creases. It was when she sat down on the cool, clean tile that the shape shifted and revealed the little head of Mister Wilford Brimley.

Wilford blinked his slate gold eyes at her in one slow motion that seemed to really tire him out. Katy sighed.

"I know, Princey," she murmured. "Mama usually waits till she's *in* the bathroom to puke, but you got the idea."

She picked him up and chuckled at his low, seismic grumblings. The next ten minutes were spend tending to him, wiping his face and crotch with a damp washcloth and warming a little extra chicken broth to pour over his breakfast.

"How about some yeast topper for a treat?" Katy asked him, shaking a small paper packet of nutritional yeast. "It's like a Cheeto for cats."

Her offer got no response. She turned and saw Wilford standing on her desk, idly sniffing his flat snout against one of the many new stacks of books. Involuntarily, Katy's eyes drifted and scanned some of the titles.

Modern Academic Witchcraft

Born Wild: Genetic Magic in America

The Official Academy Manifesto

Earth's Unwanted Garden

All of them were annotated to hell and back. She bought those dumb sticky note bookmarks that she hadn't used since college specifically to make sure she didn't lose certain pieces of information. To put it plainly, it had been a *super fun* weekend for her.

Katy turned back to her cat, who wavered his floofy tail in her direction.

"Come eat your Cheetos, son," she told him.

For most of her life Katy had no opinion on witches. The closest Academy to where she grew up in Massachusetts was all the way in Maine. The campus was in Rockport, since Academies tended to reside in smaller towns where the concept of learning magic could be shined up and presented as something worth the trouble.

In downtown Boston it just didn't seem as interesting. Sure, she remembered thinking it was amazing at first. She'd hyped it up for herself after acting as Dungeon Master for three younger siblings and all their friends. Katy owned campaign books official and independent, as well as a corresponding hat that has been immortalized in photos she has only ever shown to Edgar. But magic is duller in the real world. It somehow requires even more paperwork and diagrams than a tabletop role-playing game that at least allows you the illusion of pretending it's easy.

One Academy Representative that visited her high school spent fifteen minutes explaining the physical ramifications and three-month process to cast the closest equivalent to Vicious Mockery. Katy heard the man's droning voice as if he was still somehow talking, and her mind responded the same way.

Oh my god. So boring. No thank you.

From that point on the Academy's presence at her school was not unlike any other organization that wanted to control the lives of young people. And she just dealt with that in the same way she dealt with the particular type of student that obsessed over them. There were the ROTC kids. The Mormons. And then the Academy Junior Members, who Katy always thought would all look like dorks if they dressed as what she would always consider the prototypical wizard.

She had even less of a concept about genetic witches, or birthrights as they were more traditionally called. People she knew used to talk about a witch town in Canada or something where "everyone's all messed up and can do shit like the X-men". That's very much the overview of a shitty townie attempting to impress a girl to get in her pants. She didn't think any of it was true.

But honestly, who cares? It didn't matter. The subject didn't come up too often, and every time it did Katy was either studying or working to support her siblings. Was there a spell to add enough time to her day to make room for a third part-time job? Oh, there was? But it'll make her uncontrollably void her bowels every time she uses it?

Any other options? Be potentially very sick and in pain, probably forever?

That's probably fine. Katy would make do. She had so far.

Then she met Edgar Gallows. Meeting Edgar didn't start with their first conversation in the back of house at the Den. His first day was on one of her rare days off, and by the end of the shift nearly every other employee on staff who had her number shot her a text containing some piece of gossip. His eyes were weird in a way people didn't know how to explain. The sous chef just said they were fucked. He was described as having the energy of a street-tough orphan if that orphan couldn't throw a punch, but definitely had dead parents and was maybe also the Babadook from the horror movie of the same name.

Katy didn't know what to think when she read all of these opinions. They painted the picture of some sort of subservient gibbering mouther, a chaotic Eldritch mess that could somehow work out enough qualifications to get a job in a kitchen. Made sense that he would want to cook, she supposed. You had to put all those sticky, pinprick-haired tendrils to good use, right?

She always chose to depict the gibbering mouthers with sticky, pinprick-haired tendrils. Personal preference. Plus it was a hit with the tweens whose parents mistook her for a typical babysitter.

No, she didn't *literally* think that the new prep cook was a bubbling mass of protoplasmic eyes and gaping mouths. Katy had a very good sense of which people were people – and most people, at their core, are people. But from the way their coworkers described him they seemed to think he was more person *shaped* than anything else. Though they couldn't say any actual bad action or sentiment expressed, even when she pressed for details.

It was actually the opposite. Jess, her work wife, told her that the guy called her Beth for the first half of his shift. When she explained his mistake he apologized so many times that she lost count, and then he somehow got her to take his lunch.

She sent a picture. It was a lovingly-crafted baguette sandwich cut at an angle. Her review: *dude fuck wow,* followed by three fire emojis and a lizard.

At this point she didn't know what to think. Katy really only crossed paths with prep cooks in passing, so it's not like the mouther had to be a sparkling conversationalist. As long as he helped keep things moving during a weekend night he could undulate and wail to his hearts content.

Imagine her surprise when she clocked in at the start of her next shift and saw the new face putting on his apron. It was none other than Edgar Gallows, a completely regular human being. He looked like the type of guy who would spend most of his time in Katy's end of Boston trying not to look people in the eye. Sad. Nervous. Generally not a Babadook.

She started to introduce herself. But as soon as she put her phone in her locker and clattered the door shut, the sound of cheap metal hitting cheap metal rang out and Edgar full-body jolted. He shot his head up and stared at her, eyes wide.

What he would later explain to her as a coloboma didn't bother her. It was weird for maybe three seconds before she got over it. No, what rattled Katy to the core was the certainty that this shaky terrier of a man, this wreck that looked at her like he was waiting for her to bully him, this Edgar Gallows *was an actual goddamned wizard.*

It was so obvious. Something in the way he carried himself, like he was tensing something back to try and fit in and just failing spectacularly. Less wizard and more sorcerer if she was being technical. Regardless of the terminology, if anyone she had ever seen would fit the expectations of a cloak and pointy hat, it was the angsty motherfucker standing directly in front of her.

Edgar relaxed. He rubbed his eyes and sighed.

"Sorry," he said. "Nerves. I'm still learning what sounds mean what," he lowered his hands and smiled apologetically. "Hi. I'm new."

All Katy had to do was keep her cool.

"New...to *what*?" She asked, eyes narrowed.

Katy immediately did not keep her cool.

"Uh. Here?" Edgar offered, holding out his hand. "I just joined prep in the kitchen. I'm Edgar."

The hand she imagined he wanted her to shake looked normal. Cut to shit, but if he's a cook that was typical. His other hand was in plain sight against his thigh. Didn't look like he was hiding anything. There was no...*energetic field* radiating around the outline of his being.

Katy snickered at herself. She was being ridiculous. Treating him like an honest-to-god Merlin when he was more realistically just an absurdly well-fitting Academic would be giving his ego exactly what it craved.

"Katy Delaney," she said, giving his hand a quick handshake. "Nice to meet you."

Edgar risked a small, bemused smirk. "I'm sorry to hear the *Daily Planet* canceled your column."

Ah. Because when Katy introduced her name like that she sounded like a comic book character. This was nowhere near the first time she'd heard that joke. Still, she'd give Edgar credit – his delivery wasn't bad.

She waved dismissively. "Ah, it's fine. Got a great side-gig at the *New Frontiersman*."

As soon as she said that she regretted it. Edgar made a very baseline, surface level comic reference that everyone's grandma could chuckle lightly at. Katy responded by throwing out a niche call to a plot specific in a hyper-violent Alan Moore graphic novel. You buildup to talking about *Watchman*. It's divisive. Even if someone's holding a copy of the comic you have no way of determining how they feel about it based only on sight.

Exactly as she feared, Edgar looked uneasy. But then his expression changed. He was amused again, but in a shy and hesitant way that made the emotion come across as a whisper.

"Big Rorschach fan, huh?" He remarked.

Fuck he called me out so good.

Katy wasn't thrilled that this man could annoy her to easily to the extent where she was forced to confront her most problematic pop culture preferences. At the same time, though, she was deeply impressed.

"You want to see a picture of my cat?" She asked, already reaching into her locker to grab her phone before he got a chance to answer.

They were friends from that point on. This was a decision Katy decided on behalf of both of them. Eventually he must've realized she wasn't tricking him or trying to harvest his organs. Or maybe he didn't. If that was true, he still accepted his fate and allowed her into his life – with one exception.

It was about eight months before he mentioned growing up in the Academy. By then Katy already figured this was the case. Still, she jumped at the chance to ask him about it. Junior Members were so proud of the society they were striving to integrate into, but the moment she expressed interest he shut down and closed himself off with such force that it severed the end of her curiosity.

She didn't care at all about learning the inner secrets of Academic culture. Until then Edgar hadn't made a single reference to his life before moving to New Orleans. Despite that, he was clever and funny. He had strong opinions on arbitrary things and, even though he wasn't a cat person, he regarded Wilford with the stilted respect you would give to a coworker or a distant cousin.

He was a weirdo and Katy enjoyed him. She wanted to know more about him.

Katy didn't ask again after that moment. People don't react the way Edgar did for no reason. Whatever brought him to where he was now, he was clearly just preoccupied with rebuilding and moving forward. If Katy could do anything, she could support this small dork and be his friend. She would look out for the guy.

Yes, she had a permanent case of Big Sister Syndrome. And sure, she was parentified growing up in a household both loving and dysfunctional. But all of that was mostly worked out for her, and now she was mainly just proud she got to help guide her siblings into becoming contented and productive adults. Ben was in school to get his Masters in library science. Robbie did some stuff with computers that he was glad to explain but Katy did not understand. And Leanne was a goddamned *fireman. Hell yeah.*

If Katy could raise firemen and librarians, she could give a prep cook the support he needed to thrive. So for years she didn't think at all about magic in regards to her and Edgar's relationship. She just focused on being together.

Then that guy showed up. Scott. Another wizard.

Fucking *Scott the Wizard,* like a cartoon mascot for an off-brand computer game that teaches kids about basic math and bores them terribly in the process. To everyone else she knew he no longer existed. But Katy remembered him, his wild hair and his bad *Doctor Who* cosplay. The feel of his head against her shoulder as she carried him out of Edgar's little fort at work rang out very strong in her memory. His voice was low and gentle. He called her *kind.*

People were people. That was still true in her heart. But after seeing the wake of the Den after Edgar drove Scott away in his car, Katy wasn't entirely certain that the pleasant softie curled up in the passengers seat was actually a person.

Academy Representatives and friends that joined their ranks showed her a trick or two before. They used a staff, wand, or wand-shaped equivalent to transfer energy along the flow of an audible, spoken incantation. It was an entire thing. What Scott did was closer to the sorcery she imagined when she first learned about the existence of actual magic, and that was cool. Seeing it in person, though, and realizing how easy it would be to misuse a power that great, terrified her.

For a few days now she'd left Edgar in the presence of a man who could essentially rent out his brain to use as a mindless servant to his every whim. This was something she was immediately not okay with, but making an issue bigger than what she already did risked Edgar shutting her out entirely. She decided to stay back instead, taking the time to rely on her lesser-used, but still fine-tuned capabilities.

With that, she started researching. Katy Delaney had her very first scoop.

It was easy finding material to learn the basics of the Academy, both the organization as a whole and their locations across the country. And she got a lot deeper than that just by digging around on the right forums. Certain corners of the internet still consider the Academy to be a cult, and for a while it was a popular trend for users to enroll for long enough to gain access to certain private materials that they would then scan and upload before quitting the organization.

Obviously most of the surface level stuff got reported for copyright. No kidding. The Academy was a modern organization and they certainly wanted to keep their secrets secret. At the same time, based on a court case from fifteen years ago that documented the headquarters's attempt to sue the entirety of Reddit over a single dedicated forum, they likely didn't have anyone that internet-literate in their high ranks.

Now most of the important documents were heavily encrypted. Katy had to download them off of the kind of websites that kindly insisted on filling her computer with Trojans and her monitor with porn gifs. But it was worth it.

That's what she thought as she sat at her computer last night, waiting for a massive encrypted file of third-grade protection spells to download. Katy rocked from side to side on the seat of her cheap office chair, eyeing a banner ad above the progress bar that was just three super close-up shots of a penis going into a vagina, over and over again.

Katy cringed and thought it again. *It's worth it for Edgar.*

Now she was smarter. Significantly more exhausted. A specific corner of her apartment looked so insane that even Wilford paused while slurping his breakfast every so often to poke his head up and confirm that she was okay.

Which she was. Absolutely okay and moving on from that thought immediately.

It was hard to sift through the available information on genetic witches. All she could absorb with certainty were the basic historical facts. Anything further than that was either hearsay on forums, or Totally True Facts that just so happen to be only verified by members of the Academy. Out of desperation, Katy found herself starting to rappel down the same murky depths that lead the people to believe that the Holocaust never happened, or that 9/11 is still actively happening all the time.

But she wasn't stupid. Protective, maybe excessively so, but she had more common sense than most. That's why she had one stop to make before her dinner shift at work tonight.

The first thing she learned about Edgar was that he was a foodie, even though he hated the term so much that it prompted an audible gag whenever he heard it said out loud. But chefs usually like food – usually to a frustrating extent. Katy had an ex who worked as a line cook and they got in an hour-long argument over the consequences of different pasta shapes in which she eventually reached the opposite of an orgasm.

If there was anything that held Katy back from becoming friends with Edgar, it was his obsession with cooking.

Luckily, his tastes weren't extravagant or obtuse. Yes, if they bought cheese together he had to buy one of each density so he could mix the textures onto one cracker, creating what he called the "Omni-Cheese". But he at least had the sense to acknowledge that was an insane thing to do. Other than, he enjoyed cheap fried chicken as much as he liked anything artisanal or organic. In fact, he considered the best doughnut holes in the city to be found in none other than the corner store a few blocks away from Katy's apartment.

It's not an interrogation if you bring breakfast. It's not a bribe if it's to keep your buddy from being seduced into some kind of cosmic vessel. She was a woman on a mission, so Katy swept Wilford off his proverbial high horse on the desk and onto the couch in the other room. Lately that had been his new spot, right in the middle cushion, nestled in the folds of a robe that Katy supposed was his now. So she tucked him in within the fleece and knelt down to be eye to eye with him.

Vengeance on hold.

"Hello, Doodle," Katy cooed. "Mister Bing Bong. No brains in that head – no no. Just spaghetti."

Wilford opened his lips just enough to drool a little. He slowly closed his eyes and opened them again, then lightly bonked his fluffy head against her fingertips. Katy chuckled and leaned closer to kiss between his eyes.

"*Aw.* My son my son my *son.*"

Vengeance back. No, wait, one more pet on the head. Wilford blinked again and gurgled, which has always been his equivalent of purring.

Good, okay. Now back to vengeance.

She stopped by the market and gathered enough doughnut holes to grease over the fact that she hadn't been over to Edgar's place in years. The little pastries were made by hand by Louis, the leather-skinned French guy who owned the place. He wanted to talk. He always wanted to talk, and most of the things he said made next to no sense. Nonetheless, Katy was usually down to listen to his pseudo-riddles.

Not today, though.

"Katherine, my girl," Louis murmured as he rang up her paper box of doughnuts. "Ya' see the things these squirrels have been doing?"

Katy's grip on her card tightened as she put it back in her pocket. "Fuck," she whispered, then raised her voice to add. "You have *five minutes,* Louis."

By the time she made it to Edgar's place, she was still mostly disgruntled despite lacking any real reason or context. Yes, it was cute to know that the squirrels in her neighborhood have taken to riding atop slow-passing cars to get from place to place. And she could tell Edgar all about it, as soon as she picked up any additional offending party and threw him straight into the garbage.

Edgar's trash heap with wheels was parked in the drive. That was a good sign. She peeked through the windows as she passed and found little else but the usual clutter.

She smiled. It fell. Walking up the path she practiced what she would say as soon as the door opened.

Hi, Eddie? Are you possessed?

Forget I said that. It's me, Katy! I'm here to do something with you that only you would enjoy.

I have to go to that olive oil store on Dauphine and I need someone who knows what they're talking about.

There's a poetry slam going on right now at this coffee shop far enough away and if we go I promise I won't make any dismissive sounds.

David Byrne from the Talking Heads called me and said he wants to make love to you while sharing facts about your favorite finches. His only condition is that there be no equally short, Voldemort-y motherfuckers within earshot.

Standing on the front step Katy fixed her hair, took a deep breath, and smiled again.

Scott could hurt him. He might already have. He could easily hurt her too and there was really nothing she could do to stop it.

Her eyes still on the door, she reached into her bag and wrapped her fingers around her canister of pepper spray. It might not be magic, but it would buy them some time.

Katy smiled a third time, and this one managed to stick. She knocked on the door.

From inside there was some rustling. Music was playing, and the volume lowered before footsteps approached and the lock turned. The front door opened, and Katy braced herself for whatever she might find.

"Katy?"

It was Edgar. He looked fine.

By the looks of him he was fresh out of bed. He was wearing a worn t-shirt and the kind of pajama pants that she never considered, but was not at all surprised to see he owned. His hair was still damp from a shower. Edgar looked a little sleepy, but noticeably alert and present in the eyes.

He seemed confused. Not upset or unhappy, just confused. Which made sense.

"Uh, hi," Katy held up the box in her other hand. "I brought breakfast."

Edgar's eyes widened slightly when he saw the box. "Baby pink box," he noted happily. "I know where you've been. You – want to come in?"

His face went nervous for a second, and Katy's blood turned to ice. She kept her smile calm and forced the energy around them not to rise too high or drop too low.

"Do you think he'd mind?" She said, her friendliness noticeably strained.

He stared at her for a weirdly long stretch of time before blinking with a focus that also unnerved her. Then something hit him and he smiled and turned to look over his shoulder.

"Hey Scott!" He called out. "Katy brought doughnuts."

Scott's voice from deeper inside. Still gentle, but more solid. Considerably livelier. "I'll get my glasses, hang on!" The guy said.

Edgar frowned lightly as he watched some more movement going on just inside. He cast his eyes back to Katy. "He uses sunglasses to mask his thing. I tried drawing sigils, but I guess my markers make his skin itch," he smiled his way out of a dip in mood and opened the door wider. "It's whatever. Come in, though! Hi!"

She followed him inside. There was a vague memory of his place the one time she was invited over, and on an exterior level not much looked that different. If you give any sad, single guy their age a modest budget and directions to IKEA, they would end up with something akin to the layout she saw before her. The thrift store additions were more distinct to Edgar's personality. They turned this mediocre showroom into something she was able to identify.

It also didn't seem unusual. Katy was beginning to feel uneasy. She put the box of doughnuts on a rounded table and scanned the rest of the space, still gripping the pepper spray just out of sight.

By the sounds of it, Scott was in the only other room. Katy eyed the crack in the slightly-open doorway like a hawk. Every inch of her was primed for action. If someone gave her a few minutes she could count each individual hair standing straight up on her body.

From beside her, Edgar sat down at the table and flipped open the box, reaching for a doughnut hole and biting into it like nothing was wrong.

"You want some coffee?" He asked her.

She didn't answer. What was going to happen now?

"Katy?" Edgar said.

When she turned to him she imagined herself to have maintained a cool demeanor. But Edgar's expression fell immediately, and he let out a soft sigh.

"I get it," he said. "You're here to check on me, aren't you?"

That definitely seemed like something Edgar would say. And his eyes looked like Edgar's eyes. The way his muscles constructed themselves along the curve of his skull looked the way it always did.

But how would she know?

This wasn't a drunk slapping the ass of a young coworker. This wasn't Wilford getting spooked on Fourth of July or one of her kid siblings scraping their knee. Katy considered Edgar an additional brother, but she might have just put them both in even more danger by showing up here like this.

Her throat went dryer with every swallow. There was a presence directly behind her, an energy coming closer and closer with every passing moment. Then a voice struck through the air with a ringing earthiness like an oceanic siren's song.

"Good Morning, Katy!"

In an instant Katy spun her hand around and squeezed the lever on the canister in her hand, shooting an aerosol cloud of pepper spray directly into Scott's face.

About an hour later Edgar and Katy sat, side-by-side on his ratty couch. What felt like a noble act of heroic self-sacrifice quickly felt weird after the first ten minutes of hearing Scott cry-gag in the bathroom. He made no attempt to fight her when it happened, just crumpling immediately in pain and breaking down in panicked wailing. Now, since Edgar was refusing to say a word, the two of them were stuck listening to their quirky succubus cough and dry heave in the distance.

They had to fling open the windows and open every door. Katy should've probably paid more mind before using pepper spray inside such an enclosed space. Now they were stuck in a mixture of capsaicin fumes and cold winter air. Edgar sat with the collar of his shirt pulled up over his nose. He and Katy both had their eyes bloodshot and their faces slick with tears.

This was not a bad thing she did. Yes, Scott was doing a lot more whimpering than she expected going into this. But this was not a bad thing.

"I thought..." Katy had no idea how to finish that sentence.

Edgar didn't turn his head, but his eyes shifted in her direction. It was a weird feeling, being an independent adult and also a dog that had just peed on the carpet.

"You have to admit I have cause for concern," she attempted.

"Oh yeah," Edgar muttered, coughing hoarsely. "And you *have* to mace anyone that concerns you."

"It's...It's pepper spray. Mace is different."

Edgar doubled over and hacked into his arm. He grabbed a tissue from a box on the table and wiped at his nose, which was wet and running with thin mucous. His chest was trembling as he tried to catch his breath.

"You were farther away than I was," Katy noted. "I don't know how you got hit worse than me."

He smirked, then gagged.

Once the crisis in the other room settled into silence, Edgar excused himself and went in the other room to check on Scott. This was another thing that didn't seem particularly enchanted. If he was under a thrall, Katy figured he would either break out of it at the first moment of Scott's weakness or fling himself at her to protect him.

His dull, but very genuine anger wasn't really on either extreme. He seemed about as annoyed as he was on the average shift during Mardi Gras. Katy felt herself relax and become even more tense at the exact same time.

"Katy has something to say to you, Scott."

Edgar was leading Scott back out into the main room when he said that. The smaller man wavered slightly, his long hair even more of a mess and his every step a gamble. She couldn't see most of his face behind the sunglasses, but he looked *bad*. The general state of him on its own wouldn't bother Katy if not for the sheer, pathetic confusion that trembled off his very being.

If you took a baby possum too young to know aggression and kicked it square in its fresh, pink nose, it would understand what was going on more than Scott did at that very moment.

She shifted, shrinking under Edgar's steely glare.

"I'm sorry," She began.

"No," Scott interrupted, moving past Edgar's touch and slowly working his way to the table. "It's okay. You shouldn't apologize."

He palmed for the chair, hands still shaking, and sat down.

"She *pepper sprayed* you," Edgar clarified.

There was half a glass of orange juice on the table that Scott sipped at before grimacing audibly. "I don't know," he said. "She's your friend, right? How much have you told her about what's going on?"

She and Edgar caught each other's stare for a moment before he turned away.

"Well there you go," Scott continued. "If I was in her shoes, I'd...I mean, I can't say I'd do *this*, but – I'd definitely be worried."

Now Edgar was the one in the hot seat. He raised a hand to rub his eyes, but quickly thought better of it. Instead he crossed his arms tight against his chest and painted the space around him with a tired, dissatisfied scowl. Eventually he settled his focus back on Scott.

"Did you throw up?" He asked.

Scott nodded. He forced down another drink of orange juice and Edgar scoffed.

"You want me to make you some tea?"

Whatever face he made to react was almost entirely hidden, aside from a slight tightening in the corner of his lips. He nodded.

While Edgar prepared the kettle, Katy found herself taking the only other seat at the table. She was now almost next to Scott the Wizard, who leaned forward with his head in his hands and still tried to level his breathing.

"Does it hurt?" Katy asked, which was stupid because *of course it did.*

"Um. The glasses help?" Scott chuckled breathlessly. "You have some good reflexes. I'm jealous."

She smiled briefly, even though she really didn't want to. "I expected you to be angrier."

He raised his head slightly. "I have a sister. I consider myself a pacifist but if I thought she was in danger..."

His arms fell limp across the table. From the angle where they laid limp Katy noticed a small pale scar etched just below his wrist. Based on its placement it made her think of the chapter on bonds she poured over a couple nights ago, although the exact details were blurry through the veil of multiple Sugar-free Red Bulls.

"Right," she said, staring at the scar. "You have the thing. The thing that makes you do stuff."

At first Scott didn't know what she was talking about. Then he saw where she was looking and thought about what she said a second time.

He huffed, amused.

"Yeah," he said. "I have the thing."

Edgar came back a few minutes later with a steaming mug of tea that Scott accepted graciously. He sat up straighter now. He was able to smile, not with excessive friendliness, but with something more sincere that surprised Katy.

She could feel Edgar staring at her. "Can I help you, Eddie?" Katy said.

"You're in my seat."

"I'm a guest, aren't I?"

"I only own two chairs."

"And now you know two people," Katy smiled amicably at him. "Perfect fit."

Edgar looked at Scott, possibly searching the man for any sign of fear. He did that thing Edgar always did when he was upset, but not willing to put up a fight. Like when a child knows the *perfect swear* for the situation that was just too forbidden to say out loud.

He turned on his heel and started closing up the house again.

"Do the sunglasses really make a difference?" Katy said to Scott, who was lovingly tilting his head towards the mug of tea.

"I don't know," he murmured. "I'd say you'd have to tell me, but..." Scott sipped the tea and scrunched his mouth to the side. "I've never been able to talk to a non-magic-user about it."

The glasses were massive, cat's eye pieces of garbage. They looked like the kind of thing that Louis would sell on display at the market for three dollars. Katy couldn't imagine they helped in terms of protection from the sun, but they were tinted enough to completely obscure his eyes. Even still, he hesitated to face her directly.

She thought about what she read last night on genetic magic users. From cold facts to flowery myths, it all felt a little off when she was sitting right across from Scott. Katy started to ask another question when Edgar dove back to the table, grabbed her purse and her pepper spray, and went back to shutting doors and windows.

That made sense.

"I read..." Katy cringed and tried again. "Your power comes from your eyes, right?"

Scott tensed. "I guess. Eyes – physical touch – we aren't supposed to know the exact details."

He might not, but Katy did. Or she thought she did. Sitting across from Scott made it easy to question everything she read about birthrights that was actually penned by the Academy.

"It's weird that I can't see your eyes," she said.

Scott sighed. "I know. I'm sorry. It's just – It's safer, I think. For both of us."

Safer, sure. Still hard to hold an honest conversation. She could feel by now that she was past the point of blind, stupid rage. If she was willing to give the guy she pepper sprayed a chance to explain himself, the least he could do is give her the dignity of looking him in the eye while he spoke. How was she supposed to make an actual connection with him if she had no way to see his face?

By now Edgar had closed up the house and was sitting on the arm of the couch, watching them like a hawk. This didn't worry Katy at all. If she had to she could pick him up and maneuver him out of the room. She was just choosing not to.

"Can I have my purse?" She asked him.

"Absolutely not."

You know what? Fair.

"Okay," Katy sighed. "Can you open my purse and give me the sunglasses out of the side pocket?"

Edgar's expression tightened, and then released. He dug through her bag with the casual ease that only someone like him would be capable of and came out with her round-framed Windsor sunglasses.

"I'll be honest," she said to Scott as Edgar crossed the room to hand them to her. "They look like shit."

"That's...fine."

"You look like you're in a reboot of *Thelma and Louise* where they kill themselves before they even commit a crime."

From beside her she felt Edgar slap her in the shoulder. But that didn't matter, because as soon as she said what she said Scott broke out in a wide grin. He laughed softly and paused, then laughed even harder until it ended up in another round of hacking.

"Holy shit," he said. "It's been a long time since someone's spoken to me like that."

He certainly took that well. Even though she could feel Edgar's distaste coming off him in ripples of heat, her attitude soothed the rest of Scott's nerves. He now faced her with a smile distinctly familiar – hell, *familial* even.

It could be that he no longer deemed her as a threat. Or it could be that he was genuinely trying to be a friend. At this point it was incredibly difficult to tell.

Katy slid the gold-tinted sunglasses across the table and up against Scott's hands.

"Try these."

He faced her. Then he carefully looked down to pick up the sunglasses. He held them between two fingers very delicately, as if they were far more expensive than what they actually were. Even with his face obscured by cheap plastic she could tell he was hesitant.

"Do you trust me?" Katy asked.

Edgar still stood in the space of the table between them, shifting in awkward tension. "This is an insane time to ask that."

"Why did you come here?" Scott asked her in return, ignoring him entirely for the moment.

His voice was curious. Guarded. It was clear he wanted to know what she was thinking, but at the same time Katy understood the implication that her answer to this question was incredibly important. So she dropped her guard for a moment. Two could play at this game.

"I've never met a genetic magic user that actually – *uses*," she said. "I'm scared. I'm scared you might get Edgar hurt."

She heard Edgar exhale softly. He walked out of sight, and she didn't look to see where he went because her eyes were square on Scott. Katy watched as Scott took a deep breath and lowered his head to face his lap. He made sure his hair was fully obscuring his face, and he took off his garbage Barbie shades and folded them to rest on the table. Then he gently picked up Katy's sunglasses and folded open the legs.

He put them on. Scott raised his head slightly, allowing a glimmer of yellow glass to peek out through the veil of black waves. But then he stopped.

"Just let me see," Katy said.

She very rarely ever saw a person tense up so openly and with their entire body. For a while he didn't move, even though Katy was certain that he heard her. Finally he faced her, face drawn and heavy, and a few moments after that worked up the ability to fully look her in the eye.

The first thing Katy took in were how large his eyes were. They looked like Edgar's, and seeing that shape on someone else reminded her of how abnormal that look actually was. Through the glasses Scott's eyes were hued a matte ivy, and they glowed – literally glowed, like the hazy orb of light around a candle's flame.

At first the light terrified her because she knew exactly what it meant. But when she looked at it, she didn't feel controlled or manipulated. Nothing in her swayed too far in either favor or opposition. All she could really think at the time was that, by the look on Scott's face, his eyes scared him as much as they scared her.

"You don't want to be doing this, do you?" She said.

"No. Never."

She furrowed her brow. "Then stop it."

Scott stared blankly at her. She took the time to consider the mug Edgar had just dropped in front of her. It was pooled a light sandy brown that only came from her ideal mixture of creamer and coffee. Katy sipped and hummed, pleasantly surprised. Edgar definitely knew what she liked when it came to things like this.

"The sunglasses work," Scott remarked to Edgar, who was back to sitting on the couch with his arms folded along the back.

He looked back at Katy. Then the two just stared at each other. After some time Edgar tried to break the silence.

"The thing with Scott is that –"

Katy shushed him.

"You're very beautiful," Scott quietly observed. "You could be in a magazine."

It wasn't a come on. It was spoken with a distinct admiration, maybe even a little bit of pleasant surprise. She could feel him staring at parts of her face that weren't usually focused on when people wanted to hit on her. The shape of her eyebrows. The tilt of the tip of her nose. He looked at all of this like you would take in a painting in an art style you weren't familiar with, but certainly appreciated.

While it didn't feel unpleasant or dangerous, it was still weird.

"You don't look bad either," she admitted, giving his odd, almost ethereal features a once-over.

His lips quirked into a surprised half-smile. "Really?" Scott laughed softly. "I've had no way of knowing."

"Your hair needs a trim. Some shaping, maybe. But it looks pretty healthy for someone that's just been wandering around the country."

Scott beamed, very openly proud of himself. "I use coconut oil," he said. "And I try to sleep with it tied up most nights. You're right, though, my ends are split. I should've gotten a haircut months ago, but...mirrors."

Mirrors. Scott the Wizard doesn't want to look at his own reflection. When she said he wasn't unattractive, she was telling the truth. The average heterosexual, neurotypical female probably wouldn't gravitate to someone who embodied the pretty boy aesthetic in the sense of the sickly protagonist of a Victorian novel. But someone a little weirder, a little more neurotic, the appeal was easily apparent.

Her focus turned to Edgar. He was already staring at her. She was wrong when she said before that nothing changed in him. His face seemed more open. There was a quality in his expression that wasn't without worry or conflict, but generally more at ease with itself. No longer did she look at him and wonder if she would have to physically restrain his skeleton as it tried to scramble out of his skin.

Edgar's eyes were hopeful. That was new.

"What happens if you look in the mirror?" Katy asked Scott.

"It's – reflective? I don't know what..." He realized what she was trying to say and inhaled sharply. "Right. Uh – there's...you know, I've never actually tried to put it into words," Scott let out a weak laugh, both dismayed and bemused. "I don't know if it's an entity or another, separate plane of existence. I'm connected to it somehow – I think everyone that does this kind of stuff is to some extent. But. Um," his smile turned apologetic. "Whatever it is, it's been trying to crawl out of my face for the past decade."

There was a silence that followed that was long and strained and deeply confused. Katy tried to consult Edgar to confirm that *these* were the stakes they were dealing with, but when she checked he looked equally as stunned.

"You didn't know this?" Katy hissed.

Edgar looked between her and Scott. "I – I didn't ask. It seemed pushy."

"*The man has another dimension coming out of his body, I don't think rudeness is a priority for him.*"

Scott laughed once again, even more tired. He slowly slid the box of donuts towards him and picked out a small one. "It's not something that I think is – I mean, if I touched my face right now I wouldn't feel what I see when I look in the mirror. So to an extent you could say that this isn't happening. And it...well, it hurts, but it's a manageable hurt. Less than what you'd expect if you could also see it, which I don't think you can. Because you seem to be looking at me like I seem normal. Which means I probably do."

His voice quickly strained at the same rate that what little color he had fell from his face. He now faced Katy with a fear that was poorly masked, if at all.

"I look normal, right?" He said, calmly pleading.

"Yeah," Katy said immediately, without fully thinking. "You got – a nose. Two eyes. All the face things. I don't really know what I'd be looking for otherwise, but I'm not seeing any tentacles or weeping globs of protoplasm."

"Katy..." Edgar chided from behind her.

She picked up a doughnut hole and threw it at him, then continued. "I'm just saying that there isn't anything inhuman about the layout of your face. If I saw you on the street I would assume you were just...some guy. Just disheveled and artsy."

This morning Katy woke up with plans to rescue Edgar from the nefarious clutches of a charming, mind-controlling wizard. Since then she has succeeded in making him throw up, cry, and laugh in delight. He now sat, listening calmly as she spoke to him. There wasn't a single fragment of even repressed anger or offense anywhere on the man's body. He took small bites of his doughnut and watched her fondly.

"You're not attracted to me at all, are you?" He said.

Katy raised her brow. "Are you into women?"

"Are you into men?"

"Are *you* a man?" Katy smiled, which may have been in bad taste.

Scott met her mild amusement with a glint of his own. "Where it matters, I'd like to think."

"Well, unfortunately, that's more than I care to go for these days. I'd rather stick with a quality butch."

"What about a soft butch?" Scott countered.

Katy hid her surprise with a light scoff. "Do you consider yourself a soft butch?"

"I'm not talking about me," he said. "Like – in regards to the culture, sure, but I'm a guy. I was more thinking about my sister."

She didn't know what to say to the wizard she expected to confront now trying to set her up on a date. So Katy just started, momentarily as unblinking as the man across from her.

Edgar shifted uncomfortably from the corner of her eye. This must be a nightmare for a guy who she's pretty sure has never had more than one person care about him at the same time. That wiggling of guilt returned. The feeling that, while Katy knew her intentions were good, the execution may have been less than ideal.

"I need you to give me a weakness," she finally said to Scott.

He seemed politely confused, so she chose to elaborate.

"I can accept you being here," she clarified. "Ed clearly likes you, and it doesn't seem like you're actively harming him. But if that changes...I need to know there's something I can do to defeat you."

Part of her thought that phrasing things so dramatically would somehow make them come off as more casual, It could draw attention to the irony of taking a man who could be brought down by a too-hard high five and saying Katy might need to *defeat* him. Scott didn't laugh. He became deadly serious, not even looking away as Edgar nervously butted into the conversation.

"He's not like Academics, Katy. He doesn't know any incantations, all he has is what he was born with. And he doesn't want to use it like *this,* so what's the harm?"

"Bleach," Scott said.

Both she and Edgar focused on him when he said that. Everything around them seemed to slow, not through enchantment, but from the frigid effect of pure despair. It was so sudden for how extreme it felt that it took Katy some time to react. The first response she had was a sense of regret for giving him sunglasses that allowed her to see his eyes, because the absolute vacancy in his stare haunted her. He was still friendly and good-humored, only those qualities only applied to an outline of a human being with nothing filling out the center.

He swallowed hard and continued. "I made plans on what I would do if I..." Scott sighed. "I'll be honest, I don't know if it would work. This isn't really the kind of thing anyone I know had a way of preparing me for. But, uh, if you dumped bleach in my face it would probably blind me – at least temporarily – which I thought might stop my...energy field, or whatever they say. At the very least the chemical burns could distract my body enough to give you time to hold it down and gouge out my eyes."

The dread of his dissociation was a thick cloud that didn't, but felt as if it could slow down time around him and Katy. She was aware of Edgar crossing behind Scott and clasping his hands over his shoulders. He said something she couldn't hear, then sank forward and wrapped his arms around Scott's neck.

Strange. She'd never seen Edgar that openly affectionate without also being nearly blackout-drunk. If anyone had to bring that out, though, she supposed it might as well be a man willing to let himself be permanently maimed for the greater good.

If they were meeting under different circumstances Katy might make a joke about meeting the man Edgar would end up marrying. Saying that now felt uncouth, even for her.

"Would you really let me do that?" She said.

A degree of focus came back to him. He looked at her, not unwelcome or unloving, but still ice-cold.

"You'd be doing me a favor," he told her.

Edgar pulled his head up and Katy realized he was crying. It wasn't regular crying as much as tears just sort of seeping from his eyes. Still, it send a shiver of alarm down her spine. She sat upright and watched him pull Scott up from his chair.

"You should lie down," he said.

Scott shook his head, but still followed as directed. "It's good," he insisted vaguely. "This is good to think about."

"Yeah, but you have to divvy up your thoughts. Give everything it's fair share of focus, right?"

As soon as they were standing, face to face and physically touching, it suddenly felt as if Katy's presence had been entirely forgotten about. Not on purpose. Just in an instant nothing else existed. The shift was so sudden that she didn't even think to comment on it as it was happening. She drank her coffee, still reeling from Scott's recent request, and examined a side of Edgar that she was sure he would never intend for the public to see.

He brushed Scott's hair from his face and briefly lingered his fingertips along the side of his cheek. "Those sunglasses look really good on you," he said, smiling despite the tears.

"She loves you, Edgar," Scott wavered. "I love you and she loves you. That's why she wants to know."

Katy expected to feel more at the sound of this stranger that just showed up a few days ago now declaring his love for her pseudo-brother. Maybe after so much assault to her emotional senses she wasn't able to feel anymore. The room was swimming in feelings so strong that she practically had to hold her breath in order to maintain her baseline of numbness.

Her brother, on the other hand, drowned in the muck immediately. As soon as Scott said what he did Edgar sobbed and laughed and smiled and gasped, somehow all in the span of one single quiver of the face. It was a lush flourish of emotion, and once it passed he was left strangely still. His lips moved as if about to speak, though moving in silent shapes were all they were capable of doing. The shame that followed was child-like in its vastness. Luckily, it only lasted until Edgar took another scan of Scott's expression and melted back into what was essentially calm.

He kissed Scott, lightly, and with a tenderness that was surprisingly stark. Once he pulled away he spent a few moments just gazing into his eyes. Then he took a deep breath and stepped back, taking out his phone.

"You like The Talking Heads?" He asked Scott with a faint smile.

"I haven't heard of them."

"Wow," Edgar mused under his breath, tapping at his phone. "Have I got a treat for you."

She thought about how it usually only took four drinks to get Edgar to break out in his weird, David Byrne puppet dance. How he got so excited when they re-released the *Stop Making Sense* concert film in theaters that he saw it five times in two weeks. Katy went with him twice, even though she privately considered the band to be Grade-A Dork Music. She just wanted him to have someone to go with.

Edgar put Scott to bed while Katy lingered in the memory. She heard the strange, semi-poppy music start to play in the bedroom and realized that she recognized the song and album just by the opening drum and guitar riff. When did that happen? Katy has never in her life made the conscious choice to sit down and listen to The Talking Heads. But simply through knowing Edgar, she apparently absorbed the band's entire discography and history into her subconscious.

Focus returned to her as Edgar carefully closed the door. She sipped her coffee, watching him cross the room and sit at the free chair across from her.

He opened his mouth like he was going to say something. But then he just put a doughnut hole in the space and busied himself with chewing.

"You forgot to roll for initiative," Edgar pointed out some time after that.

Katy felt her cheeks redden. Much to her surprise, this was enough for Edgar to pull back the light degree of roasting.

"I know you thought you needed to do something," he said. "You were worried. And you don't know what's happening," Edgar bit back a laugh. "Hell, I thought I was getting on track with things and now you've gotten me more confused than ever."

That was strange to hear. From what Scott described before spiraling into the void, it made his situation sound pretty clear-cut. The first thing Katy stole off the internet was the initiation textbook for the Academy, and it put a description of where they believed magic came from in very simple terms. They called it Cassus, and it was considered a separate plane of reality that hovered just outside our own. The whole structure of the Academy exists to manually connect to the Cassus and feed off its energies.

Of course, nothing in what she read gave any implications of the Cassus being *sentient.* There was no threat of it wanting to move or manifest within a specific witch, much like how science textbooks don't warn about people too good at astronomy becoming bridges for distant stars.

She wanted to ask what Edgar was doing during the course of his education – because it clearly wasn't paying attention. And as much as Katy wanted that to surprise her, she spent the past few years as his coworker. He definitely tended to do little else aside from the things that interested him at any particular time.

"I don't really know anything," Katy said. "You know – about your life in the Academy."

Edgar tensed up. He nodded, but said nothing. Katy took a deep and awkward breath and let it loose through her teeth.

"I know you don't like talking about it –"

"What do you want to know?" Edgar said.

Questions reeled through Katy's mind. She considered asking for a pen and paper to help arrange her thoughts, but thought that wasn't a great strategy when getting someone to open up about childhood trauma. She kept a steady face and allowed her mind to calm slightly.

"What's your discipline?" She asked.

He rolled his eyes. "God, how much research have you..?" Edgar pressed his lips together. "I don't have one. I'm Legacy."

Legacy. So he was inducted into the Academy at birth. He didn't bother explaining what that meant, because he probably figured Katy already knew.

"If you didn't leave," Katy mused, "you'd probably be a professor by now, right? Isn't that how Legacy Academics end up?"

Once again, Edgar was simultaneously impressed and dismayed by the level of effort she put into finding out his history. He leaned back in his seat and reached up to twist a curl of red between his fingers.

Katy had never seen him do that before.

"They decided my coloboma meant I couldn't be an objective representation of the community's ethics," he said that like someone older and crueler was speaking in his voice. "But yeah, before I left I was working at the University library. Maybe by now I would've been close to starting Archivist training. You know – if I stayed."

"And you'd probably get set up with a nice girl to bear the next Legacy kid?"

Edgar scoffed. "Nope. Like I said, my DNA is tainted. The elders at Shreveport made a big scramble to figure out how to contain the Gallows fuck-up, and – uh..." something in him dulled near the point of indistinguishably. "They drafted a contract for my mother and I saying we would be taken care of for the rest of our lives, as long as our bloodline ended with me."

She had seen Edgar in many shades of angry. As a whole he was easily annoyed, disgruntled, frustrated, and occasionally flat-out enraged. This was different. It was like something took all the life and individuality inside of him and crushed it, smothering the remains with frigid, pitch-black oil. Edgar didn't look upset. He looked *nothing*.

"What else?" He sighed.

"Was your mom a birthright?"

Edgar shook his head.

"But then…" Katy tried to keep the curiosity from her voice. "If you didn't get it from her, then why –?"

"I don't know, Katy," Edgar murmured. "I don't know."

Silence. Once again she was hit by the feeling that she was way, way out of her depths.

"Do you…have a picture?"

Edgar blinked a few times. It seemed a little clumsy. He focused back on Katy and furrowed his brow. "Of what?" He said.

She managed a weak smile. "Of you? I mean, I've shown you tons of stupid pictures of me from my childhood. It seems…" Katy frowned and changed her plan of action. "You're a funky guy. I bet you were a cute kid."

His face was still, his eyes unfocused and gradually welling up with tears. Immediately Katy felt herself begin to vibrate with panic. Edgar noticed the shift in her expression and grinned, wiping at his eyes.

"It's fine," he assured her. "My fun new hobby is crying. I can't seem to stop. Uh – hang on."

He stood up and went to the kitchen, pulling out a particular drawer and rifling through a beat up notebook. Edgar gently leafed through the worn pages before coming to a particular spot. He stared down at it, distant and limp.

Feeling Katy's eyes, he looked up at her and winced.

"It's not very good," he said. "But it's the only one I have. I brought it because…I don't know. Certain spells. You probably get it."

Edgar hesitated a moment before picking up a small photograph and handing it to Katy.

It was a print from a digital camera, carefully torn down the middle. In the fragment that was left for her to hold, she could see a young Eddie Gallows standing outside a grim-looking building. He was wearing a uniform-style suit colored purple and gold. His hair looked more cropped and controlled than she had ever seen it – practically fit for boot camp training. Despite all that, he couldn't have been more than seven years old.

He was not smiling.

There was a slender hand beside him reaching out form the fray of the tear, pale fingers ghosting just above his shoulder. The way Katy has seen celebrities do on the red carpet when they want to seem intimate with other famous people they don't really know.

He doesn't want me to see this, she observed. *Why did I make him show me this?*

From beyond the scope of the photograph she could hear Edgar start to laugh. Katy glanced up and saw him barely trying to contain his snickering.

"I'm sorry," he said. "It's just weird to me that you're only now realizing that I've had a terrible childhood. Come on, Katy – I'm a trash person. You know that."

"*I don't...*"

Not entirely cognizant of her own actions, Katy folded the photograph fragment in half and stuck it in her hoodie pocket. She leaned forward and put her head in her hands, groaning softly.

This was a lot of information to take in all at once. And it drew attention to the fact that she and Edgar never spoke this openly about their struggles. Sure if Katy was having a bad day or dealing with a breakup, she felt comfortable venting to Edgar. But the things that kept her up at night, the deepest, darkest worries and thoughts that cowered in the corners of her subconscious? That just wasn't part of their relationship.

Not yet, at least. Apparently that was about to change.

"You don't take care of yourself," she said through her hands. "It frustrates me. You live like nobody sees you or cares about you."

Just by the sound of his voice Katy knew he found this funny. "Am I far off?"

"*Yes,*" Katy shot her head up at him and said it again. "*Yes,* Edgar. You are. You aren't the most popular guy in the world, but I've been around you long enough to know that you aren't the aberration you think you are. I'm aware of pretty much everyone you know, and I happen to know for a fact that they all think you're *pretty much fine,*" she felt her voice rising in her first honest show of genuine anger. "If you asked me, they'd probably like you even more if you'd let them have an actual conversation with you!"

As her voice became more enraged she noted a flicker of fear in Edgar's expression. That had never once happened before, and it immediately stopped her cold in her tracks. Because, even though she never saw him look that scared in the expanse of their friendship, Katy recognized that look on his face as soon as she saw it,

It was the same as the one in the photograph. It was fear, plain and simple.

Katy thought about the hand touching his shoulder. It looked poised. Rehearsed.

When Edgar first got hired he stifled panic at every loud and sudden noise, only calming once he was able to identify them. The first time a busser dropped a dish bin she heard he had to stand on the loading dock alone for a long time just to calm himself down. When he had to operate the shitty blender at the back, he leapt back and was on edge for the rest of the day. It only happened once. It always happened.

Katy thought at first it was because he was new. She thought it was because he was nervous. And then, after time, she just stopped thinking about it. Like an idiot.

Edgar was staring guiltily at the tabletop. He lightly drummed his fingers against the wood, only stopping his twitching once Katy reached over and took his hand in hers.

She didn't have anything to say. There wasn't a single shred of advice she could give to this witch recovering from what could very well be years of abuse. So she just held his hand.

He looked across at her, equally as silent. The sad, but grateful smile he built took a minute or two to fully form.

His eyes, near gold, shone brilliantly.

Nothing. That was all Scott wanted. And, in a way, that's exactly what he had now.

Things opened up immensely after his bonding with Edgar in a way he never expected to ever experienced. His sight was restored in its entirety and his feet were brought back to the ground. Basic laws of existence like gravity were no longer just theories he hoped would continue to apply to him. For the first time since childhood, Scott Skylark Kaufner felt like a human being.

Even when he laid in bed beside Edgar that night and closed his eyes, only to find out his tether to the screaming void was as sturdy as ever, he wasn't regretful. Things were still different. The sensory assault was raged on, but it now was strained through a mesh field around his psyche. It didn't gut him in the way it did before. It didn't scrape the marrow from his bones until he had no choice but to drift.

Edgar, once again having a mind for solutions, had the thought to keep music playing when it got unpleasant. That helped. He said that it must have something to do with keeping focus on one state to draw attention away from the other, and Scott agreed.

That sounded true. Scientific. What felt more real to Scott, though, was that hearing music reminded him of Edgar. It made him think of all the other things about him that now connected him to Edgar. So no matter how far out of existence he was pulled, as long as Shouty Suit Man kept yelling dadaist poems to synth keyboard, it was as if there was a constant alert in himself that just exclaimed *it's not how it was.*

That's where he was now – lying in bed, tucked unto the covers, objectively comfortable and also entirely not there. He could trace his eyes up and down the veins that webbed across the ceiling. His eyes told him he was in a small, contained room where the doors were closed and the windows were locked. And that information was able to travel from his eyes to register in his brain, though it could barely squeeze through the pinprick hole in an instance that just wailed *FOREVER VAST ALONE.*

Even the voice felt further away.

You are...foolish....Birthright, it warbled.

Scott clenched his eyes shut. As if that would help.

The voice continued. *The Child...is weak.*

"Fuck you," Scott hissed under his breath.

We are better...than such...broken spirit...

Anger swelled in the back of his throat like bile. "*Fuck. You,*" he spat again.

I can...show you, the voice cooed. *I...will...show you.*

Before Scott had a chance to protest the sensations began. Frozen in place, his muscles constricted in sudden spasms along the entirety of his body. He was wracked with a sickly chill that made his jaw clench until his teeth ached.

No. Not this.

Even though the surface of his skin stung and throbbed at uneven intervals, Scott forced himself upright and out of bed. Because he shouldn't be feeling this. He shouldn't know about these kinds of feelings yet. This was insight that was supposed to come from Edgar, not some otherworldly horror with no aim but to torture them. With no other choice Scott relied on base instinct.

His chest ached with an entirely foreign shade of sorrow, and he pushed through the pain to focus on palming across the wall until he found what he was looking for. Finally he felt it – a thumbtack left sticking out of the wall above the bedside table.

No time for thinking. Scott pulled out the tack and jabbed the sharp end into his now-limp shoulder.

Pain and grief. Shame and panic and unhinged isolation. Then, gradually, all of that faded and there was just the pain from the tack in his arm.

Scott wiggled the fingers of an arm no longer haunted by the ghost of someone else's injury. He breathed a sigh of relief and sank down to the floor.

That's where he remained when he heard the bedroom door open. It was Edgar.

"Well," he said in a tired voice, "I'd say you made a good first impression…"

He trailed off, probably seeing that Scott was no longer lying in bed. Edgar took a few steps to the side and found him on the floor. Even though he was exhausted, even though his body felt like jelly and his brain like dust, even though he jostled the tack in his shoulder at some point and could see a small line of blood dripping down his arm – Scott tried to smile.

It immediately didn't work. Because of course it couldn't. Not on Edgar. Not anymore.

"You're bleeding," Edgar observed.

He didn't give Scott a chance to explain himself, instead heading straight to the bathroom and turning on the tap. Edgar came back with a damp washcloth and sat down next to Scott and idly, but very gently pushed his hair over his shoulder and rolled up the sleeve of his t-shirt.

Once the plastic nub of the thumbtack made itself fully visible Edgar's demeanor made a quick shift. He didn't do or say anything. He just stared at it, one hand around the towel and the other still holding up Scott's sleeve.

"Blink, Edgar," Scott quietly reminded him after some time.

Edgar closed his eyes. He opened them. A tight, worried frown slowly stretched across his face.

"Why did you do that?" He spoke, words quavering around the ends.

Because I saw your hurt before you were ready to show it to me.

"It…helps," he said. "It's something I did when I was younger and, uh – everything got to be too much."

That answer didn't seem to ease Edgar much. "Don't…you shouldn't ever," he trailed off, still starting at the tack. "The music doesn't help?"

Guilt rose steadily inside of Scott. This was different than his perspective on death. He wasn't supposed to hurt himself on purpose and he knew that. That's why he kept the damage limited to things he could explain away to Tenzin. And it's why, even though his mother told him that he would have to do what he had to in order to survive, he never told her about things like this. It was a bad thing and he wasn't proud of it, and as the knowledge that he sank back to that old place only made him feel worse as time went on.

"I'd like to take it out now."

Edgar had a box of bandages now. Scott looked at them, and then at him, and he nodded.

A single stab of hot ice as the metal left his flesh. Wet heat. Then a warmth that was damp, but in a different way. Apparently Edgar took the means to make sure the cloth he cleaned Scott up with was soaked with warmer water. He felt the dry end of the cloth pat any remaining moisture before Edgar gently pressed a bandage against the pinprick wound.

Once he was sure there would be no more blood to avoid, Scott examined his work. The bandage was blue and shaped like a dinosaur. Scott smiled, then immediately took back the gesture when he looked up and saw the way Edgar was starting at him.

"There was a first aid book in your bag," he frowned, guilty. "I saw it when..." His guilt gave way quickly into more indignation. "Did you learn about all that so you could hurt yourself without any consequences?"

His words were an attack. Not on Scott – not necessarily – just a loose stab made to dead air. And there was nothing Scott could do to defend himself aside from point out that his theory made him out to be a lot more intelligent than he actually was. The shoulder was not a good place to be stabbed, even with a small, sharp implement. With all the nerves and veins he's lucky it didn't hurt a lot more than it did.

"I don't..." Scott swallowed hard, "I don't feel comfortable going to the hospital – like *this* – unless I absolutely have to."

His bond still looked upset, though he was now noticeably more sympathetic and a little annoyed about it. "Well it's normal to be afraid of that. Nobody likes going to the hospital."

Scott frowned, hurt. "I do," he said. "I love doctors. My dad was a doctor."

For a few moments the air was still and quiet. Then Edgar sighed and shifted to sit more comfortably next to Scott. He pressed their shoulders together, almost absently, then inhaled sharply and put the smallest bit of distance between them so he wasn't directly touching the new bandage. Still dissatisfied, he eventually moved his hand to lightly hook their pinkies together.

"It's still getting worse?" He said.

Scott took Edgar's hand and turned it over to see his new scar. "Not worse," he clarified. "Just different. Now that you're here."

Edgar furrowed his brow in frustration. "I haven't felt anything," he stopped and groaned under his breath. "I can make out all *your* feelings like they're coming from my own head, but I don't feel any of *that*," Edgar looked inexplicably disappointed. "I guess you're just stronger than I am."

"Not stronger," Scott corrected, sliding their fingers together and feeling the heat of Edgar's palm against his own. "Just more powerful."

His turned his gaze to the man beside him in hopes of finding comfort in the lines of his favorite face. The safety was there, of course, but with it came the realization that Edgar's eyes now wavered in a soft, unearthly glow.

It wasn't like Scott's eyes, or his mother's, or any other adult he knew in Bluerose. The light was still separate from the rest of him, a layer of fog that hovers over a forest before sinking into the trees. It was comparable, thankfully, to an adolescent. Someone able to form their abilities into a shape rather than a chaos of excess emotion.

Edgar smiled at him. Scott smiled back, but he couldn't help but feel a part of him flounder in dread.

It was still true what he told Edgar. Scott was more powerful.

For now.

Time slowed to a crawl. Edgar changed the upbeat music to something slower and more low-key, like hold music from the distant past.

He turned the lights lower, and the two of them laid back in bed together. With Edgar's face against his opposite shoulder, his breath warm against his skin, the mesh around his spirit felt near-impenetrable. Their hands still touched, fingers loose and thumbs intertwining.

Touching and being touched never felt like this before. Not better, just natural. It took no thought or planning to hold Edgar's hand a little tighter or for Scott to tilt his face and feel his curls against his cheek. It was the easiest thing in the world. He could've easily drifted back to sleep like this if Edgar didn't break the silence.

"Do you remember what you said before I made you lie down?"

"Uh, yeah," Scott said.

Silence. The rate of Edgar's breathing faltered against Scott's skin.

"...You said you love me," he said, a little stiff.

Scott felt his eyes drift shut again. "Yup."

The bed shifted as Edgar sat up slightly to stare down at him. Scott didn't get the look he was casting at first, and then let out a sigh as he realized what he accidentally just did.

He didn't need to spend years in civilization to understand the hangups most people have over the concept of love. He and Tenzin would occasionally go through phases of watching movie after movie of identical-seeming white couples that skirted and bickered for two acts before dramatically succumbing to the truth of their feelings. They wanted it, but they couldn't have it. And the reasons why they couldn't were very important and totally not worth shrugging off as ego.

The two Kaufner children were both fascinated by how fervently these made-up people refused an emotion. Sometimes their mother would catch them in the middle of one of their movies and watch for maybe ten minutes before muttering her frustrations in a mixture of hums and Greek and leaving to fix something in the other room.

"You love me?" Edgar said.

Scott could feel the breathless yearning that burned behind the doubt in his voice. Were they really going to do this?

"Yes," Scott said.

"You've only known me like this for a few days."

Weird way to say that, Scott thought.

"I know," he said. "I've been here too."

Edgar fought back a smile and sat up in bed, fixated on his own doubt. "You can't be in love with someone you've known for less than a week."

"Ah yes," Scott muttered. "The trial period."

"I'm serious Scott! That's not – love is something that develops over the course of experience and commitment."

"I agree. It's also a feeling that can happen instantaneously. I love your cooking. If you were to offer me a plate of something you made it wouldn't take me a week to decide if I wanted it."

He put down his eyes and checked how Edgar was registering that. The other man looked less guarded, which was good. But by the way his eyes shifted and his chest heaved it was clear he was still trying to find holes to poke in Scott's perspective.

"That's different," he said.

How? Because it paints you in a desirable light?

"Can't you..?" Edgar sighed again. "Can't you say it differently? Like say you *think* you love me, or that you're *falling in love* with me?"

This was close to laughable in Scott's eyes. "Nope. Absolutely not. It's already done."

Edgar took a deep breath and exhaled slowly. He sank back down to the bed, folding his arms over Scott's chest and settling his chin on his clasped hands. Edgar bore Scott's affection so reluctantly, and yet with immense gratitude that he clearly didn't yet have the capacity to put into language. It was so sweet that Scott just wanted to take him by the face and give him a gentle shake.

You fucking know what I'm talking about, don't you? He wanted to cry out to him.

Instead, Scott reached up and brushed his fingers through Edgar's hair. He picked out what he considered his favorite curl, ran his fingers along the entirety, and let it fall back into place like springing a coil.

Edgar warmed at the touch, near melting. Then he stopped. His face went cold, and without saying a word Scott knew where his mind was heading.

"I don't need you to say it back," Scott said.

"You don't think I can?"

Scott had no clue an acid could burn so guiltily. Acting quickly he decided not to act at all. He kept gently playing with Edgar's hair, working his fingers through individual ringlets. The shame of the man on his chest was smothering, though Scott tried to use that unpleasant sensation to further support his point.

"Say it if you want," Scott stated plainly, touching his fingertips along Edgar's temple. "Say it *when* you want. I'll enjoy hearing it if it happens, but...you echo in me now, Edgar. I already feel how you feel about me."

Fear. Relief. Joy. Self-hate. Edgar lowered his head and buried his face in his arms. Soon Scott felt his shirt begin to dampen, and he hoped the affectionate sympathy didn't read too heavily in his being.

"Will you say it again?" Edgar said, voice muffled by the shirt and warped by tears.

Scott grinned. He'd say it every goddamned chance he had if given the opportunity.

"I -"

"Never mind. You don't have to."

He waited until he was certain Edgar wouldn't interrupt again, then settled the palm of his hand against the back of his head. "I love you, Edgar," Scott said, clear as day and without any hesitation.

Edgar broke down weeping, his sobs like the old gold frame on an ancient painting. Something classical. Something in oil. Something that if people knew they forgot, they would regret it for the rest of their lives.

Etude no. 2

"I think," the First says, "that I don't feel enough."

He is in bed, nestled up against the Other, the nearest blanket loosely pulled up and over their bodies. Still, the Other has goose pimples running along the skin of his arms. The First wonders how he could survive in Oregon if a warmer winter's day in New Orleans is still too cold for him.

"You said you feel what I feel," the First pulls the other closer and attempts to make up for lost warmth with his own body. "And I do too. But you called it an echo or a flicker, and for me it's..." he smiled faintly. "It's like all of The Talking Heads being played at once."

The Other is softly stroking the First's back, but when he says that his fingers tighten briefly.

"I meant that as a compliment."

"I know. But doesn't that sound...tiring?"

The First looks up at the Other's face. He finds that he isn't upset – just drained.

"Maybe," the First rolls over to stare up at the ceiling with his hands folded on his stomach. "It's rare for me to be able to tap into that sense of passion. Before this the only thing that could help was..."

The words began unraveling in his head, moving on their very own like they did the first time he read them. *Yes – the springtimes needed you. Often a star was waiting for you to notice it. A wave rolled toward you*

out of the distant past, or as you walked under an open window, a violin
yielded itself to your hearing. All this was mission.

"Poetry helps," the Other says. "It – It can be soothing. Even the angry ones."

That observation comes downy-soft and perfectly cooled. It caresses against the First's skin and provokes a small laugh. He feels the Other's forehead press against his shoulder, and he moves his arm to fully wrap around him.

"You're right," he murmurs. "You're totally right."

Fifth Movement

"You're beeping," Scott said, sounding fully awake even though he was snoring moments ago.

Edgar reluctantly rolled over in bed and grabbed his phone, swiping to silence the beeping of his phone's alarm. He tossed his phone back on the table and buried his face in the pillow.

"What was that?" Scott asked from beside him.

"Nothing. Just my work alarm."

"Mm," Scott turned on his side and slipped an arm around Edgar. "You work tonight?"

"Nah. I'm calling out."

A beat of silence. Scott pulled away from Edgar and sat up to eye him worriedly.

"Are you sick?" He said.

Edgar smiled, cat-like, and stretched out in bed. "I don't know if you noticed, Scotty, but I can't stop crying."

His chest pulsed with nostalgia. The image of Scott as a child, bathed in a blue glow, illuminated his consciousness. Did he know? It was hard to parse anything concrete through the string lights of Scott's happiness that flickered as Edgar called him by a nickname. Even one as shoddy as that.

"You have to go to work," Scott said.

"It's food service. The best part of working at a restaurant like this is being able to skip a shift."

More frowning. A deepened furrow of the brow. "On a weekend night –"

"It's a Sunday."

"It's a *weekend night*," Scott reiterated, "and you're going to leave your servers without a bartender."

He left his words hanging like they proved how ridiculous Edgar was being. This was a fun new element Edgar was learning about Scott's character. He wanted to take it seriously, because this seemed to be a very important issue for the guy. It was just hard to really accept the gravitas he was proposing when it was in regards to a minimum-wage job he wasn't even good at.

If he didn't show up tonight, then Katy or Jess or one of the other servers would have to make their own drinks. And the worst thing that could come of that is that the customer gets one that actually tastes like how the Den intended.

Laughing inwardly at the thought, he didn't notice Scott roll out of bed and go to grab his dress shirt from off the dresser. He buttoned it up, vaguely pawing at his tumbleweed hair and cursing to himself.

"What are you doing?" Edgar said.

"I'm taking your shift."

He stood up straight and palmed some wrinkles out of his shirt. Then he looked back at Edgar – not angry at him, just unbelievably dutiful.

"Do you have a pair of jeans I can borrow?" He asked. "And – I don't know – a belt, probably?"

Edgar just stared back at him. He couldn't even pretend that Scott was bluffing, because he knew better by now. So he just lingered in his own disbelief

"You're not taking my shift, Scott," he said.

Scott raised a single brow like a warning shot. "Somebody has to."

"Do you know how to work a bar?"

"Do you?"

Fuck. Good point. Goddammit.

Despite realizing he was edging deeper into the wrong, Edgar still made a valiant effort not to appear like an asshole. "Wouldn't you rather just stay in bed? We can keep talking. I'll order Chinese food – I know a really good takeout place."

"Did you know that New Orleans is consistently ranked one of the top ten most alcohol-dependent cities in the United States?" Scott was now taking it upon himself to rummage through Edgar's closet – angry, but still very polite. "It's usually top three depending on the year, but lately crazy things have been happening in the Midwest. You have a *lot* of clothes."

"What are you saying?" Edgar asked.

He grabbed a worn pair of faded gray jeans and absently folded them against his chest. "You'll make things harder for the servers. A lot of them look younger and some of them told me this is their first job. And even if someone like Katy can handle it, she shouldn't have to."

Being honest with himself, Edgar could admit that the only thing that made him more qualified to serve liquor compared to Scott is that he could probably recognize more brands than him. And it didn't matter what qualifications he was lacking – meaning: all of them – because as soon as he fluttered his eyes Michael would hire him in whatever capacity he wanted.

"You're going to use your power to seduce my boss into hiring you?" He said.

Scott drew in a sharp breath. "They don't always want to sleep with me."

"But sometimes they do."

"Then I'll say no."

He said that with barely any conviction. His eyes were lowered onto the belt he found and was now working through the loops of his borrowed jeans. Edgar got a sick, itchy sensation all across his body and stood up, coming to stand in front of him. He wanted to touch him, to reach out and physically steady this gradually wavering man, but with what he was saying he wasn't sure a physical touch would be welcome.

"What happens when you say no?" He asked instead.

"Your boss is Michael Sinclair," Scott looked up at him through his hair. "Right?"

He was fully dressed now. He had the sleeves of his dress shirt rolled up to the elbow and the first few buttons below the collar undone. Any aspect of a suit before looked comically unfitting on him. In this moment, though, some mixture of determination and spiteful frustration made him look exceptionally striking. His eyes were dark and burned fiercely. His softness could cut diamonds.

At any other time Edgar would be a flustered mess. Right now all he could think about was how cold he looked. So Edgar dodged the question and grabbed his warmest zip-up hoodie from over the chair in the corner.

"Here," he said, handing it to Scott.

Scott looked annoyed that he didn't answer the question. Still, he took the hoodie and slipped it on. And then he seemed more like himself, only sadder and more exhausted. Scott felt it too. He sighed and slowly found his hairbrush, then sat on the edge of the bed to work through what was now a cacophony of tangles.

"Have you met him already?"

"No," Scott hit a tangle and winced. "We only spoke on the phone."

His voice was sour as he said that. Edgar recognized that slight hardening in his facial features – he saw it constantly at work whenever a patron hit on one of the servers.

"What did he say?"

Scott continued to brush his hair. "We talked about music. He asked me about my life," he paused the brush partially stuck in the midst of a knot of hair. "I sang for him. He said he liked my voice."

"You..." Edgar clenched his jaw in weird anger. "You *sang* –"

"He wanted me to play but I don't travel with a piano. I said singing was the best I could do," he sank even deeper into dread. "He said I sound like Hoizer."

High praise from Michael. More accurately, that seemed to be his go-to comparison to any man he found appealing. Edgar hated that he knew that. He hated that his boss heard Scott sing before he could, but that wasn't important right now.

Edgar sat beside Scott on the bed. He took his hand and lightly pressed it to the back of his bond's head to push him upright. Scott allowed himself to be led, though didn't seem to understand why. He sat straight, frowning gently at his hands in his lap, and stayed silent. The only sound he made was a soft noise of surprise when Edgar began slowly working his fingers through his hair.

"You have to separate it," he explained. "And work from the bottom up. You're not going to get far with a regular brush until you work out all these knots."

"W – Why do you know this?" Scott muttered softly.

"Katy and I go out drinking a lot. She's a pretty messy drunk but if I help her with stuff like this she doesn't feel as shitty the next day," Edgar shrugged. "I don't really mind. Figured it'd be a good skill to build."

Scott's took a deep breath, his eyes focused on Edgar's fingers. It was harder for him to work with the spiral of Scott's excitement and bewilderment twisting in him. He focused on making sure he could fully undo the mess of hair, but stopped when he actually noticed Scott's expression.

His shoulders were tight. His jaw clenched. Edgar pulled his hand back.

"Should I stop?"

"Oh!" Scott breathed in and blinked. "No that's...I'm sorry. I just haven't had anyone help me with my hair since I was a kid."

"Do you – like it? Am I being gentle enough?"

The smile on his face softened like warm mist. Scott settled his hand over Edgar's knee and grazed his thumb along the fraying material of his pajamas. His eyes burned brighter than usual – or maybe they glowed as they always did, and for some reason Edgar was now just more open to noticing the celestial quality. Either way, when Scott turned his gaze onto him – warm and anxious and loving – Edgar felt himself brushed in a buttery sheen of pure serotonin.

"You're being *very* gentle, Edgar," Scott spoke softly. "Thank you."

Was Edgar smiling? It's hard to tell. Whatever shape his face was making was not anything he was accustomed to.

"I'll go to work," Edgar assured Scott once he was able to run a brush through his hair without hitting a tangle.

Scott hummed. His eyes were closed and, unlike the tension he carried a few minutes before, every muscle in his body was now completely relaxed. He looked even more at ease than he did after they had sex. As far as Edgar knew, the only thing keeping him from falling limp like a dropped rag doll is the muscle memory of knowing that you have to maintain some rigidity when someone else is doing your hair.

The sight of it made Edgar want to laugh. He must've had his fair share of sister figures fussing over him in his time on the planet.

"I'm obviously not about to let you take my shift for me," he glided the bristles of the brush through the midsection of Scott's hair, then placed it a little higher up and repeated the action. "I only wanted to skip so I could spend more time with you. I don't know if you've realized that."

With his eyes still fluttered shut, Scott huffed out a small laugh. "The intention is sweet," he murmured. "But I could also just come with you."

"What," Edgar scoffed, "you sit at the bar and eat french fries while I mix bad drinks for assholes?"

Scott didn't answer, but grinned just at the thought of it. Edgar put down the brush to take a better look at his face.

"Really?" He said. "That sounds like a fun night to you?"

He opened one baffling blue eye. "Depends. Do you think I could try those truffle rosemary fries I saw someone in the kitchen plate the other day?"

"How'd you know they were truffle rosemary?"

"Come on," Scott grinned fondly. "I pretty much live in restaurants these days. I can recognize truffle oil from a block away."

God I love you, Edgar raved inwardly.

"Can I braid your hair?" He blurted out instead.

Edgar's before work routine usually involved spending a few minutes staring out the window in the kitchen. Once, the first winter when he moved in, there was a pair of cardinal newlyweds that nested against the frosted glass of the windowpane. He watched them every day, the brilliantly crimson husband and his pale brown wife. They had a trio of eggs, two of which hatched into chicks that were the size of their mother after about a week.

And then they were gone. Then they were all gone. And yet Edgar still stared at their old nest every day, tracing the pattern of twigs and petrified eggshell. Maybe part of him thought the birds might come back – or that *some* bird might return and need a safe place to rest. And until that happened, the sight of the old nest provided a great avenue to dissociate on so he could go into work with nothing in him aside from distant weariness.

But he forgot to do that today. After braiding Scott's hair he dressed himself quickly. He snatched a protein bar from the cabinet, and the next thing he knew they were out of the house and pulling out into the street. It was weird to be going to work with so much going on in his mind. Not all of it was good or bad, it just felt strange to be thinking so actively.

Traffic was pretty good today. It looked like it might rain later. From the corner of his eye he could see Scott bobbing his head slightly to the music playing on the radio. He looked very pleased with his braid and busied his hands by tracing the lines of each individual segment.

It was such a raw, unbelievable thrill to be able to see the entirety of Scott's face. The strong, straight line of his nose. The specks of freckles clouded over each cheek and the quirk of a boldly cheerful smile.

I did that, Edgar considered, shyly prideful. *I made him smile.*

"Mister Sinclair might have some questions," Scott said while they were stopped at a traffic light. "He's probably going to ask where I went and how I know you."

Edgar nodded, still mostly focused on how happy Scott looked. "It shouldn't be a problem. He's a busy guy."

"We should still think of something, right? Just in case."

"Sure," Edgar added absently. "What were you thinking?"

"Maybe you're my boyfriend."

Edgar felt about a dozen indiscernible things inside of him swell and burst and catch fire and explode into light all at once. He stood a little straighter and marveled at the new tingling current of static that was now rushing through his veins. This was amazing. This might be a stroke. If this was how Edgar would go out he gladly accepted his fate.

By now he knew there was no point in masking his feelings, as much as he wanted to by instinct. He glanced over at Scott and saw the man watching him, brow raised and lips slightly parted. They locked eyes for a few moments before Edgar remembered the road. Beside him, Scott was actually the one to readjust his posture and put on a casual demeanor.

"I mean, it's a good excuse isn't it?" Scott remarked idly.

What is he doing?

"Very – you know..." he darted his eyes to Edgar and started to smile. "Very *reasonable.*"

Oh my god. This asshole.

Edgar chuckled low. "Okay, okay."

By the way he beamed it was no secret Scott was proud of his ribbing. He leaned back into his seat, satisfied in his triumph, and touched the end of his braid.

"It could just be a story," he added, a little softer. "Just a think we say to make things seem less weird."

That was an even better joke. Did Scott really think he was going to get as far as he did and back out at the last possible second? Just throw out the concept of hand-holding, matching-sweater-wearing domestic-ity and pretend it wasn't something Edgar wanted immediately?

Adorable. *Hilarious.*

Edgar felt the ridges of the steering wheel under his palms. "I think it would be – um –"he cleared his throat, momentarily terrified, "real and accurate...if you were to say that you were my boyfriend."

Once again he caught Scott's face as it rushed fully scarlet. He blinked hard and grinned into the dashboard. His mouth moved as if he was about to speak, but he couldn't quite get out the words.

"*But,*" Edgar added, "I feel like...for me to say that I'm *yours,* I need to, like – do something."

"I cannot imagine anything more you could do for me."

When Scott said that Edgar went tense. He dug his teeth into his bot-tom lip and worked his mind through the ringer to put a very simple concept into human language.

Blink. Six seconds. Blink again.

"I'd like to write you a poem," Edgar said.

"I didn't think that was..." Scott trailed off, smiling confusedly. "I mean, I've never been in a relationship, but – I didn't think that was a prerequisite."

They pulled into the back of the Farie's Den and Edgar shut off the car. The two of them both stayed where they were, gazing at one another without staring directly face-to-face. Edgar felt good – more awake, more aware, even physically stronger in a way that probably wasn't actually real.

When Scott spoke his voice was plush. "I didn't know you wrote po-etry."

"I did. I used to, at least. And I'd like to try again."

By this point his bond had all but given up on pushing for Edgar to go to work. "I used to write songs," Scott said. "I filled a whole notebook with songs over the course of a few years, but one day it was just..." he trailed off, zig-zagging a finger down his braid. "What are some of your influences?"

Edgar unbuckled his seat belt. He fiddled with his shirt and checked to make sure he had his wallet and keys where they should be. All the things he would usually do before leaving the car, like he could somehow fool reality into thinking that he had any plans to leave just yet.

"I love Rilke," he said, gradually letting go of any hopes of restraining his enthusiasm. "I mean, he was my first poet that wasn't assigned to me in school. But he's in German – and I can't read German – and every English translation is slightly different, you know?"

He could hear his voice quicken in speed and rise in intensity. This was not the way he usually liked to talk to other people, at the risk of revealing too much of something already difficult to contain. But there wasn't anything in Scott's expression but adoring curiosity, which was good – but bad for any hopes Edgar had left of looking like a normal person.

Edgar continued, because fuck it. "There's this guy Stephen Mitchell who's translated a lot of Rilke and he's definitely my favorite. He doesn't do the most accurate, one-to-one between languages, but I personally like that because it better captures reading the poem in the way it was intended."

"Sure," Scott purred.

"So – uh – yeah. Rilke's a lifesaver. I read Letters to a Young Poet on a yearly basis and it's always amazing. *And,*" Edgar closed his eyes, calling to mind the writers that most affected him over the course of a lifetime. "Marina Tsvetaeva is so soothing, but like I said – it's hard to find a translation that resonates with me," he took a deep breath. "What else? I like Pablo Neruda. ee cummings is cool, but some of his work gets way too abstract for me."

Scott let out a dreamy laugh. Edgar paused his rambling to focus on him and his eyes widened slightly.

"Oh," he breathed. "I just – that's the first name you've said that I've recognized," Scott's eyes turned distant and soft. "Um...*Your slightest look easily will unclose me. Though I have closed myself as fingers, you open always petal by petal myself as Spring opens – touching skillfully, mysteri-ously – her first rose."*

He looked back at Edgar and smiled.

"Which one is that?" Edgar asked in a faint voice.

"I don't know. I can't remember. I'd know it if I saw it again, though."

They fell into a warm, peaceful silence so deep that it allowed Edgar to hear the softest pattering of rain as it touched against the roof of the car. The sound was like birds chattering playful secrets. Scott – Edgar's boyfriend – looked past Edgar and out the window.

"Katy spotted us," he pointed out.

Of course Edgar loved Scott. He was like the moon. Scott played piano and cared about things and people. He treasured Edgar's cooking and at the very least had a passing interest in poetry. Maybe he would soon reveal himself to be some variety of hateful, cruel lunatic, but for now Edgar was simultaneously being decimated and expanded from the ground up by the strength of his own sheer adoration.

So say it.

You know it's true, so say it.

It shouldn't be that hard, Edgar.

Scott's smile faded and a note of concern touched his face. "Do you have another pair of sunglasses?" He asked.

He felt it. Scott felt it. Scott could probably feel that *he* felt it, so in a certain sense he shouldn't have to say it at all. In which case *why couldn't he just say it?*

Scott took off Katy's sunglasses, leaned forward, and slipped them over Edgar's eyes. The world went golden. Edgar reached up and touched one of Scott's hands as they lingered over his temple.

"You picked a tough case," he softly spoke.

"Oh yeah," Scott said, smiling though still preoccupied, "because I'm doing *just dandy.*"

Any bad feeling left melted into the warm depths of affection. Edgar grinned, then he pressed Scott's perfect hand to his lips and gently kissed each individual finger. He could see his boyfriend teetering on the edge, swooning without quite falling into the glitter swirl Edgar was drifting in.

He'd get him. It couldn't possibly be that much harder.

There was a soft wrapping on the window behind Edgar. It was Katy, bent down slightly with her apron undone and held over her head. Edgar cracked the door open and she flashed him a look as pleased as it was vaguely confused.

His hand went to open the door when he heard a rifling coming from the next seat. It stopped suddenly, and Edgar looked over his shoulder to see Scott wearing one of the cheap sunglasses a brand ambassador left at the bar a few months bar. His boyfriend looked silly advertising artisanal gin, and he flashed Edgar a thumbs up before he left the car.

Katy looked between the two of them once they were all standing together in the rain. Her eyes went from Scott to Edgar, then back to Scott, before settling on Edgar with deep, analytical focus.

"You don't pull off the Windsors, Ed."

He touched the rims and frowned. "They're sunglasses."

"They're *statement* glasses. And right now the only statement I'm hearing is *too dorky for the opium den.*"

"All right," Edgar said, pulling off the sunglasses. "I guess that's reasonable."

Scott quickly touched the side of Edgar's face and turned it away from Katy. In one swift motion he switched their sunglasses, allowing only a glimpse of the pale winter gray before the world went tinted and glassy from cheap, dark plastic.

What was going on here? Something in the back of Edgar's mind told him this was worth being concerned over. It was that static, though, that strange new sparkle that made his muscles feel something other than tense or relaxed. An entirely new state of being. Compared to that, the type of sunglasses people put on his face didn't seem to matter.

"Jesus, is he – doing the thing?" Katy's voice asked, seemingly from far away.

He was more aware of Scott because the man's hand was physically resting on his forearm. "It's hard to hold onto." he said. "Even now I can't say how long it's been happening."

"Should he be here?"

Scott frowned. "I don't know. If I noticed before I wouldn't have – I didn't think...I don't know."

They both looked concerned in Edgar's general direction. What was wrong? He wasn't sick. In fact, Edgar felt the best he felt in some time. He took Scott's hand and interlaced their fingers, eased by the shared warmth of skin touching skin.

"It's harder to control when it first starts," he watched Scott explain in a strangely grave voice. "It will – it should – no, it *will* go away, it's just hard to say when."

Katy got a little closer. "He seems drugged."

Usually being talked over as if he wasn't literally directly in front of the speakers would unnerve him. It made him think of all the sessions he had with Academy doctors growing up, where they would poke and prod at him to see the extent of his general *wrong*-ness. But this was different, wasn't it? He wasn't a child on a medical table while his mother glowered from the corner. He was with his two favorite people in the world who only wanted to make sure he was okay. And the weather was so perfectly crisp. Everything felt good, inside and out.

"It happened a little later for me since I had to take hormones," Scott said. "But I remember the stage it looks like he's in right now, and it's kind of like an additional puberty that also sometimes gets you high."

It was so nice to hear them talk to each other without any suspicion. Just Edgar's best friend and his boyfriend, working together to figure out what was apparently wrong with him. Perfect.

"Did something trigger it?" Katy asked.

Scott sighed. "It's usually a strong emotional stimuli, so..."

"So it was you."

He was blushing again, his whole face turning pink for a few moments. "Shit," he whispered. "I...*shit*. Sorry, Edgar."

Sorry? Scott stumbled into Edgar's life and brought all the sound and color back into the world, warming his bed and his hands, warming *everything*, and now he was *apologizing* for it?

Man, I have a really funny boyfriend.

Edgar touched Scott's cheek, which was smooth other than a fine layer of baby hair. And he thought about how this was his boyfriend, *his* boyfriend who was very openly in love with him. Edgar was going to write him a poem so moving that it granted him the authority to be *Scott's* boyfriend. After that, they would be together for the rest of their lives.

Maybe they'd have kids. Maybe they'd open a cat sanctuary.

He had no idea it was possible to curl up within the soft, safe earth while also soaring into the endless opportunity of space. Edgar wrapped his arms around Scott's neck and settled his face against his chest. He closed his eyes and let out a soft sigh that released everything spinning inside him in a single, warm hum.

The next thing he heard was the crash.

Scott was standing upright one moment, and the next he felt himself knocked off his feet and pushed hard a few feet backwards. His back slammed against the side door with enough force for him to feel the car rock and the tires start to lift. He knew something like this was bound to happen eventually, but as much as he wanted to swallow back any reaction he couldn't keep from crying out in pain as his body hit metal.

His vision went starry and his hearing was swallowed by the screaming siren of the car alarm. He slumped to the gravel and tried to catch his breath.

Breathe. Blink. Focus. Blink. Breathe.

Edgar stood where he was before, frozen. Disorientated. Past him, Katy was slumped over up against the opposite brick wall of the restaurant.

She wasn't moving. At least she was breathing. The collar of her blouse was shifting with each shaky inhale, so Katy was definitely getting some oxygen. But Scott couldn't see her face and wasn't sure if she was conscious.

While he visually searched her body for signs of life, Edgar snapped out of his trance and fell down to his knees in front of him. He reached out towards him with hesitant hands, wanting to touch but fearing what doing so would lead to.

"W-What?" He breathed. "What happened?"

"Help Katy," Scott sputtered, still aching for air.

"Fuck, Scott, what the hell –?"

Scott took a gasp and forced out the words. "I'm okay. *Help Katy.*"

His vision stabilized enough for him to note that the golden fog in Edgar's eyes had temporarily dissipated. Scott focused extra hard and confirmed that, yes, the light was gone for now. His eyes were just brown and warm and, at the moment, deeply fearful.

Edgar stood, turned off his car alarm, and quickly went to tend to his friend. Scott stayed where he was until he could see Katy open her eyes and move her mouth to speak. Then he took a deep breath and helped bring her back onto her feet.

There are other kinds of birthrights then those that can effect emotions. But emotions, especially turbulent ones, can trigger – or even fuel an ability. That's just one more thing that makes puberty so turbulent. Scott had a dim memory of blowing out every window of his two-story home in a burst of childish rage. It was in the middle of the winter and they had to wait a week for the replacements to come. Even now the memory made him cringe.

It didn't look like Katy was limping when the two of them back towards him. Even though he hit a car and she a brick wall, it looked like Edgar's blast just knocked the air from their bodies and the thoughts from their head. Edgar steadied her. Once she was very much on her own feet, he still kept a hand on her arm like she could collapse again at any moment.

They looked at Scott as if he was the only one who could give them answers. The worst part of all of that was that their assumption was technically true.

So how do people stand when they know things? What do they do with their hands?

"Strong emotional reactions," he stated plainly. "Positive or negative. It's – a physical...response. Because you're discovering a new aspect of your physicality," he thought about that, and then added. "Like a sneeze."

Both of the individuals wavering in front of him seemed dismayed by this. Scott probably phrased it wrong. He wasn't able to grab onto figurative language in the way he could back when he used to write his own songs. Or like how he imagined someone like Edgar could do very easily.

When Edgar summarized his attempted explanation his voice was faint. "So this is just a thing that happens now if I feel too much?"

"If it's not – I mean, if you don't regulate it," Scott countered.

He stepped to the side and pressed his hands to his face. "What do I do? How am I supposed to control all this *right now*?"

"I learned to garden," Scott offered. "That's not...applicable here...though," he sighed and fidgeted his hands.

Katy tried to brush the mud off her arms with a frown. "You two should just get out of here."

"Just get home, Edgar," Scott said. "Go back to bed. I'll handle work and Katy can drive me back later."

This was Scott's fault. He didn't look for signs of magic outside of witch towns, so his guard was down and his eye inexperienced. If he noticed the signs he would never have allowed Edgar to leave the house and endure a bunch of drunk tourists. Scott had no desire to play bartender, but it wouldn't hurt him the way it could hurt Edgar in this state.

"Scott, I'm not.." Edgar clenched his face up in exasperation. "I can figure out a way to numb myself, I'll -" he cut himself off, an idea forming. "I'll get drunk."

Scott paused. He looked up at him. "How drunk?"

"How drunk do I need to get?"

Scott thought about the assortment of bottles he remembered seeing behind the bar as he first walked in.

"There's a medicine in witch towns that helps with this kind of thing. It's not technically alcohol but it has a lot in common with it," he said. "So if you drank enough hard liquor to dull your senses then you could be lucid enough to get through your shift without having to worry about manually controlling your emotions."

"It might work," Katy said. "You're not a clumsy drunk."

Scott hesitated, then pointed up towards his eyes. "I can blur the lines. I'm pretty sure if I work hard enough I can make sure all your boss remembers about tonight is that you were here, here on time, and that he decided to give you a few days off."

Where he expected jealously at that proposition, Scott only felt the burn of Edgar's defensiveness, a fire that situated itself somehow in front of all other sensations as if his heart was physically standing guard for Scott's. It wasn't what Scott intended or prepared for, and witnessing it immediately filled him with an underlying sense of gratitude.

"We'll go to bed together tonight," he said, softer now, "and sleep in for a really long time tomorrow."

Edgar didn't seem overly excited, but he still managed a small smile.

"Can we get out of the rain?" Katy said, scowling at spots of water along her white blouse. "I feel gross today and I don't need more people staring at my chest."

From childhood Scott was used to following servers. If someone was in an apron and dress shirt they could walk straight off a cliff and Scott would follow without question like some food service lemming. Even now the instinct was as strong as ever. If a skilled enough server motioned for him to follow, he was absolutely going to go wherever they led him.

So they ended up in the break room where Katy washed herself off in the nearby hand sink. Scott usually felt weird technically trespassing with two people who he intended to remember him. He tried to keep himself small, sitting on the edge of the couch and watching Edgar as he reluctantly clocked in and grabbed an apron for himself from the linen bag in the corner.

He felt sad. He felt scared. Edgar reflected a kind of winter Scott was unfamiliar with.

Once he was uniformed up he went to the couch, making a point to sit slightly closer to Scott than he needed to. His gaze was unsteady, possibly reflecting that he didn't feel entirely confident in looking Scott in the eye, even with the glasses.

Without thinking he made the same motion he did when putting his hair up and out of his eyes. Except he quickly realized that his hair was already out of his face, lovingly braided by the man who would soon feel fit to call himself his boyfriend.

Scott lightly touched the braid. Edgar did a really good job. It made sense – being a chef must require steady hands that could move with tender precision.

He only allowed himself a few moments to appreciate the man's handiwork before forcing himself to focus back on the current situation. But when he noticed Edgar was watching him, and specifically *how* he was watching him, Scott once again felt reality shift in an entirely new way.

It wasn't like being in the Other Place. The scary place. He knew where he was and who he was – in fact, the concept of his being resonated within itself with startling clarity.

Scott always said he didn't have a type. That was never true and no one close to him ever believed it. Privately Scott knew he never felt romantic attraction towards women, and that he didn't have much of a sex drive in regards to any gender. He liked passion and kindness, and was drawn to people who were easy to touch. Of course, none of that mattered compared to finding the right hand that could disarm him for the human time bomb he was.

Despite all of that, he was now feeling himself being looked at almost exactly how he always dreamed. Like he was someone that could be fully understood. The kind of stare that said *I'm here – I'm here, and I'm with you.* When he told Edgar he loved him he frankly assumed he was throwing the words into a wishing well and hoping for the best. And even though he didn't say it back in exact words, the way Edgar held his eyes echoed Scott's intention stronger than he ever expected.

Intention. There was a memory in the back of his mind the vow Edgar made in the cemetery during their bonding ritual, about promising Scott a "long and contented life". That alone felt like such a touching sentiment. It wasn't until now, though, that it became clear that Edgar had no plans for Scott to live that life alone.

Wait. Oh fuck.

Scott smiled, and he wanted to smile, but inside he felt himself began to spiral. Because *of course* the women at that bakery thought they were married. The whole world probably thinks they're married now, if only because the level of commitment the two of them created for themselves was so immeasurably deep that was the only reasonable point of comparison.

A bonding ceremony based on the terms of companionship, support, and contentment sustained for as long as possible?

That's marriage, Skylark. That's what a marriage is.

He was so afraid to call Edgar his boyfriend, when it never occurred to Scott that he had already *soul-married a man he barely knew like a fucking idiot –*

"Snack time," Katy said.

Scott snapped out of whatever he got pulled into as soon as he heard her voice. This came as a huge relief, as even though he considered himself in relative control of his emotions he was starting to feel that pressure of an imminent overflow. And if losing his cool as a kid blew out two stories of double-paned windows, he hesitated to see what the same would result in when he was far more powerful.

She was holding a bottle of dark rum in one hand and a glass in the other. This was presented to Edgar with that customer service panache of serving a steaming fajita plate, but she wasn't able to hold up the enthusiasm for long.

Her eyes went to Scott, and in the daze of the previous realization he forgot to not look away.

"This is our strongest booze," she said. "How much should he take?"

It was hard to consider. If he was comparing a common liquor equivalent to something like Petrichor, the best answer would be to put your lips to the bottle and drink until just before you throw up or black out. That obviously wouldn't be the call for someone who had a bar to run. And even if it was, Scott considered that it might not be the best call to give a full, adult Birthright's dose to someone who's never even had a taste before.

He balanced the numbers in his head. "Four shots, maybe?" He eventually concluded.

Edgar was thrown aback by this, Scott could feel it, but he made a point not to express the emotion. He clicked his tongue and raised his brow. Then, oddly enough, he started to chuckle.

"I don't even..." he shook his head in embarrassment. "I don't even know how much that is."

"Four shots is like six ounces," Katy paused, thinking. "Yeah – six ounces on the dot."

A few moments went by where Edgar just stared down at his lap and idly sloshed the bottle from one side to the other. Katy was still clearly trying to maintain a sympathetic front, but couldn't help but falter briefly in frustration.

"You're a bartender, Eddie," she reminded him.

He motioned with full hands in defeat. "I don't have the thing!" He attempted to defend himself. "The jigger! If I'm planning on jigging I need my jigger."

They started to quietly bicker in the sort of arbitrary way Scott had to imagine they did on a regular basis. Instead of interrupting, took his chance and carefully removed the cup and bottle from Edgar's hands. He screwed open the cap and poured what he could guess by eye to be the proper amount. As liquor hit glass the arguing stopped, and by the time he was finished both Katy and Edgar were watching him closely.

This wasn't fun. No one here was having a good time. Nevertheless, he tried to stay calm as he passed the glass back to Edgar.

"I'll get you some water," Scott said, standing up and heading towards the bar.

It might not have been a good idea for him to go out on the main floor alone just yet. But he didn't want to see Edgar shotgun almost a full measuring cup of hard alcohol just so he could numb himself to the world. So he would make himself useful. Scott was Edgar's barback for the night, and his primary job was ensuring his boyfriend didn't end his shift face-down on the floor.

He was filling up a second glass of ice when he felt a larger figure approach him. Dread ached in his chest. Time to put on the charm.

"Lark, right?" A man's voice called out to him.

Scott recognized the voice as belonging to Michael Sinclair, who he had only spoken to on the phone a few days before. He imagined Edgar's boss to be slightly older than they were, but other than that he no longer had an ability to match voices to potential appearances. So Scott manufactured some degree of a smile and turned with an excuse on the tip of his tongue.

The first thing he noticed about Michael is that he was huge – just a massive teddy bear of a man dressed in a Christmas sweater and Santa hat. He looked friendly, friendly and very handsome, but Scott couldn't get over just how much smaller he was in comparison. It unnerved him. He recalled the flirtatious quality of Michael's voice when they spoke before and suddenly started to regret going out here on his own.

"Hey!" Michael greeted him. "Katy filled me in on what's going on."

Scott furrowed his brow slightly. "Uh – did she?"

"Yeah, it's pretty cool of you to nurse our guy back to health. We just changed chefs, so I guess food poisoning is a possibility. I'm surprised he made his shift the next day based on how she made it sound," he shrugged. "Still sucks though. I would've liked to hear you play."

Michael was talking to him from a few feet away and didn't seem like he wanted to get any closer. He wasn't making any excuse to touch Scott blatantly or innocuously. Even his face expressed nothing but kindness and platonic concern. He looked like he was seeing Scott in regards to his relationship to Edgar instead of just a potential relationship to exploit.

And that was amazing. Scott still felt suspicious, mostly because if anything, this felt too good to be true. He almost wanted to check the mirrored wall at the back of the bar like it would allow him to see his reflection and note if his eyes were still burning.

"How's he doing?" Michael asked.

"He's...a little wavery," Scott said, hoping he could gauge Edgar's general alcohol tolerance. "Kind of nauseous still. He insisted on going to work today, so I said – you know – drink a lot of water."

Michael listened attentively to Scott's vague semi-lies. His dark eyes were rimmed in a vague blue glow that Scott almost completely forgot about, but recognized as soon as he saw it. That was him. He was doing that. And yet Michael did not look remotely aroused in any way. He was still treating Scott like he was nothing more than a good companion of a valued employee.

Was this actually happening? Scott relaxed his jaw, even though he didn't realize he was clenching it to begin with. His shoulders loosened slightly. As he continued to speak he felt his voice fall into that steady resonance he didn't think he'd ever try and practice again.

"I'm going to help him," he said. "I'm working behind the bar just to make tonight a little easier. You don't have to pay me. Think of it as like a – uh – training. For nothing."

This was an incredibly risky move to put on someone who wasn't actively aiming to get him into bed. And there was a second where Scott worried such a lazy strategy wouldn't work. Michael looked close to confused, and then he just wasn't anymore.

He nodded slow. "Right," he said. "I guess that makes sense."

Scott's boldness did not turn Michael on at all. His eyes didn't trace Scott from top to bottom in a way he could still feel even when he couldn't see the person's face. Everything was essentially normal and Scott was close to tears from just the relief of it.

"Behind," Edgar spoke hoarsely, squeezing past Michael as he stepped out of the way.

He went to the bar and started preparing his garnishes. Scott quickly searched his figure for signs of obvious intoxication. It looked like he was standing upright. He could bend down to pick up a jar from the fridge and straighten back up without pausing for sickness or disorientation.

Didn't he say that he and Katy went out drinking a lot? It made sense, living and working in a place like New Orleans. Maybe he wouldn't have any trouble working tonight at all.

He tossed some cut lime ends into the nearby trash, and then stuck his head in the sink. Edgar didn't throw up or gag, he just had his skull danging against the water-stained metal. A moment passed, and he began to groan sickly.

"*Oh god,*" his words echoed slightly. "*Oh my god. This sucks.*"

The death rattle continued. Scott quickly shot his head to Michael, but he didn't look at all alarmed. His indifference was polite, and there was an element of concern, but it was all entirely under the belief that what was going on was well under control.

Michael locked eyes with Scott and nodded. "All right – let me know if you guys need anything. I'll just be in the office."

"*Don't fuck my boyfriend, Michael,*" Edgar groaned, angry and half-coherent as his boss calmly walked into the kitchen.

As he was never much of an in-public drinker, the bar was the part of the average restaurant that Scott was the least familiar with. He could flip eggs or burgers, operate a sanitizer, run meals or return dishes. Hell, by now he could even run those fancy point of service systems that come with a touch screen. But when it came to alcohol, Scott could never wrap his head around anything more complicated that opening beer bottles or uncorking bottles of wine.

Still he figured it would be fine. Scott obtained his temporary position easily enough. As long as Edgar could take an order and fulfill it with something vaguely drinkable, he felt confident that he could charm a patron into accepting it without question. Other than that, Scott knew to keep the dishes clean and the right foodstuffs stocked. If he could make sure Edgar didn't pass out before he clocked out the night should go by smoothly.

Then he noticed the small, gray and black plastic device near the inside edge of the bar. It was one of those machines that prints out tickets as orders are placed. Which, Scott reminded himself, meant that there would be people at the bar as well as seated at tables who would have to accept the drinks they would make tonight.

Edgar was peacefully leaning against the counter, nodding his head to the jazzy Christmas standards being played by the costumed house band onstage. He looked to be in a better mood now, which was fine. Scott would carry the panic of their situation for both of them.

"How's it going?" Katy asked.

She stood near the gap in the bar and propped an elbow against the counter top. Scott noticed a small scrape just above her elbow, likely from the skin either being dragged along gravel or slammed against brick. He sighed.

"Edgar's going to teach me how to tend bar," he said.

Katy cringed. She tried to fix her face as if the gesture never happened, but Scott saw it.

"Uh, you're gonna," Katy craned her neck beside him and scanned the under shelf of the bar, "yeah, hang on."

She stepped behind him and grabbed a paperback kept by the sink. It was a mid-size paperback worn practically to the point of destruction. The cover was bent on the front and the back, and the spine was cracked through the text of the title. Still, he could make out the words *Bartender's Bible* laid out on the front in gold letters.

When he flipped through it he could see certain recipes that were highlighted, circled, dog-eared – or all three at once. It was the type of intense annotations that only could be deciphered by the person who marked it, if anyone.

He thought about Edgar reading this book multiple times a shift. Potentially before every new cocktail he had to mix. Scott looked up at him carefully shoveling out a single cube of ice from the small machine and popping it into his mouth.

"Is he not a good bartender?" Scott whispered to Katy.

"Good guy," Katy said. "Great cook. Terrible bartender."

Edgar noticed Scott watching him and smiled. He raised his hand and waved.

Scott had to pick a strand of hair out of his braid to give him something to twist. "Okay," he said. "Okay. Well then we'll work together. Whatever needs to get done, right?"

Katy didn't answer. When Scott looked back at her she was just meeting his eyes, searching for something he couldn't explain and didn't really want to know.

"Aren't I supposed to want to fuck you right now?" She said.

It was so easy to remember how to look people in the eye that he started to forget he wasn't supposed to. Even once he realized what he was doing he didn't look away. Because he wanted to know too, despite the dangers to them both.

"I think so," he said.

"But I don't," she looked deeper into his eyes and frowned. "Yeah. I still don't."

"Great."

"What changed?"

Scott opened his mouth to speak. He closed his lips without saying anything. He clenched his jaw and blinked a few times.

"I don't know," he said. "I feel like I keep saying that, but...I don't...know."

The new goal for the night was no longer to be a barback, but to hope that Scott and Edgar put together could do the job of a single, more qualified individual. Edgar approved of the plan with the relaxed indifference of someone who just ingested a lot of alcohol all at once and now decided not to regret it. He was in good spirits. He made a comment about wanting to find one of those fuzzy Santa hats that he saw Michael and some of the employees wearing, but before he could wander off to look for it three tickets beeped in on the machine and a couple sat down at the bar.

Scott forced himself to meet the eye of the red-nosed older gentleman taking off his coat across the counter from him. He looked disgruntled at first, but a few moments of eye contact eased his tension into vague concern.

"Uh, welcome to," in a moment of socially-induced panic, Scott completely forgot the name of the establishment they were now in. "Welcome! What can we get you?"

Beside him there was the whir a blender. Scott made a note to check the tickets as they came in, because if there's something Edgar should definitely *not* be doing right now it's operating heavy machinery. He held his smile to the man, who in return looked like he was trying to find a way to express his worry.

"Uh, I'll take a rum and Coke," he turned to the slightly-younger woman staring down at her phone. "You want a martini, right?"

"Yup," she agreed without looking up.

Scott stiffened awkwardly. There were so many kinds of martinis. "Right," he said. "So – olives?"

He expected the man to yell. To Scott's surprise, his first bar patron was surprisingly sympathetic. "She takes it extra dry," he said, then adding when he saw Scott's expression. "So less vermouth."

"Oh. Oh! I can do that."

Scott quickly turned to the paperback Katy directed him to. It was clear immediately why the book was as worn as it was. How was someone supposed to keep that degree of information locked in their brains at all times?

An extra dry martini means the least amount of dry vermouth. That's wet. That's still a martini just as wet as any other.

The earth loves me, Scott reminded himself, *but people are not on my side.*

While pouring a splash of orange bitters into a glass he noticed Edgar fill a pitcher with some neon-colored booze slurry. It appeared to come naturally to him. Though he wavered slightly as he handed the drink to one of the servers, his hands remained remarkably steady. Scott noticed this with relief and admiration before regretting noticing it at all when he realized he probably added too much bitters.

The orders came at a steady pace that only increased as the night went on. This, for Scott, was a different way to view the workflow of a restaurant like this. The bartender's guide was passed between him and Edgar and consulted for almost every drink they made, especially the ones that went out to tables Scott had no way of looking in the eye. Those who sat at the bar were understanding – weirdly understanding, actually – but he chose not to question it and instead take mercy where it is granted to him.

Like he imagined Edgar could, Scott was capable of losing himself in the work of his hands. And since it had been a few days since he played the piano, he was glad to have something to do with his body – even if it was something he was sorely unfamiliar with. After enough time of making the same drinks he was able to zone out slightly and drift above himself.

The holiday season started early here. The band onstage was going through vintage swing covers of classic Christmas standards, which Scott usually didn't have a problem with. He was rarely one to consider a song to be overplayed, even one that he didn't enjoy. If it was played well and with care, he had no problem listening to the same song on repeat for hours at a time.

Usually. *Usually.*

If this house band wanted to play all the holiday basics every hour, that was fine. What Scott had an issue with was the fact that the upright spinet piano being played was out of tone. Specifically, inexplicably, and infuriatingly enough – it was only the middle C key. So every C chord played in every song was slightly off in a way that made Scott want to die.

He told himself he was being over-dramatic. There were more important things he had to focus on, new measurements and techniques. The music was there, though. And if there was music in the room he had to listen to it, which meant that the slight incongruity with every other note soured in his mouth like biting on tinfoil.

By the time it got to be truly grating, Edgar was no longer having an easy time being drunk. He was moving a little slower and stopping every so often to lower his head and press his fingers to his temples. Scott was doing a majority of the work by then, plus constantly pushing Edgar to drink more water, and with the flat middle C and the constant eye contact he felt close to his breaking point.

When Katy approached the bar again Scott couldn't remember the last time he blinked and was either already crying or just about to. She must've been standing there for a long time, because Scott didn't notice her until she crumpled up a cocktail napkin and threw it at him.

"Lunch break," she said. "Come on."

Scott blinked hard and winced at the way his eyes stung. He looked down at Edgar, who was midway into sitting on the floor in a daze.

"C'mon," he echoed, holding out his hand.

He and Edgar ended up back on the couch in the break room, slumped up against each other while Katy got them all food from the kitchen. It wasn't exactly silent where they were, though the distance allowed all the individual noises to blur together into one indistinct rumble. This gave Scott a temporary break from what he considered to be torture severe enough to get him to admit to being a cold-war Communist. He breathed a little easier and idly rubbed his knuckle against his palm to ease the ache from where he held his paring knife.

"You're holding it wrong," Edgar commented.

"Hm?"

"The thing you do where you level the blade with the length of your index finger is a common move, but it's easier on the tendons in your palm if you pinch instead. You'll have more control over your cuts, too."

His voice sounded heavy. Tired. Scott questioned again why he was so obsessed with the state of every restaurant to the point where he would do something like this to a man who should absolutely be cuddled in some warm blankets right now.

If he realized what was happening he wouldn't have done this.

It isn't hard to keep your middle C key tuned. You use it in nearly every song.

The manual explained that dry alcohol meant less sugar, because bartending is designed to be a joke at only Scott's expense.

He settled his head against the back wall and closed his eyes. "I can't believe you do this," he murmured.

Edgar laughed weakly. "I know," he said. "I'm not good at it."

"Are you kidding? It's *so hard*," Scott sat up in a bolt, momentarily forgetting Edgar was leaning against him. "There's *so much* you have to remember. Every drink has a dozen variations and you're just supposed to somehow already know what they are. There's like a hundred different recipes in that book and you have to make them all on the spot with the person just *staring at you.*"

"And talking," Edgar smiled wearily. "Sometimes they like to talk."

"*Why do they talk so much?*" Scott hissed. "Don't talk to me. Don't talk to me! I'm mixing chemicals like a goddamned chemist, I do *not* want to have a conversation."

Edgar perked up a little bit. "Plus there's no fixing a mistake. If you're cooking there's usually a trick you can do to fix if the texture is off, or something."

"But what if you pour one of the fifteen liquors in a Long Island ice tea wrong?" Scott cut in. "There's no going back. It's all fucked."

"I like when you swear."

Scott, a little delirious from the shift so far, lowered his voice to a sharp whisper. "It's *fucked,*" he said.

Katy returned with a platter of steaming french fries and a few cans of Red Bull. This was the kind of cuisine Scott was very much used to. As much as he valued the actual, lovingly-crafted meals that Edgar was capable of, it was not something he would ever be able to fully adjust to. It felt much more natural to scrounge and grab what he could, eating it as quickly as possible in the quietest corner before going on with his day.

They huddled around the battered folding table in the corner of the room and ate what Scott felt Katy might've just stolen off the line. By this point, though, the specifics didn't matter. What could he do about it anyway? No one hit on him and now he has french fries. Those are two great things that are hard to make happen concurrently.

He thought about that with awe and dizzying glee. *No one hit on him tonight.*

"How you feeling, Eddie?" Katy asked, speaking over the rim of the can.

Edgar looked up with the end of a fry sticking out of his mouth. He blinked, stared for too long, and eventually squinched up his face to close and moisten his eyes.

Scott hummed approvingly. "He's almost got the hang of it, don't worry."

This wasn't the kind of answer that Katy would find comforting. But if Edgar hugged him a few feet closer to the building she could've easily broken a bone, so Scott hoped she'd accept it. And, after a soft sigh, she did.

They continued to eat.

"You can really hold your own, Scott," Katy said later. "I'm impressed."

"How many complaints are you getting from the tables?" Scott asked.

"Less than usual. Way less than expected, honestly."

That was surprising. For a tourist place that essentially required you to get plastered it would be unrealistic to want no complaints, but the fact that he was apparently mixing drinks well enough to be passable on their own accord felt pretty good. Close to good, at least. He was still primarily hungry and tired.

Katy took a fry and pointed it at Scott for emphasis. "You have a promising future as an actual bartender," she told him.

"Fuck off," Scott stopped himself, practically choking on his drink. "Jesus. I'm so sorry. That was mean."

From the swivel chair next to him Edgar burst out into sleepy laughter. Scott hesitated to gauge Katy's reaction to his unprompted outburst, but when he finally braved her face he found nothing but weary bemusement.

"You know, Ed," she said. "I couldn't picture the type of guy you'd go for if you went for a guy – but I get this. This makes sense to me."

So that's what it takes to get on Katy's good side. Take a face full of pepper spray and work a weekend dinner rush. Those were some maddeningly unreasonable circumstances that Scott would take without question. Because he could feel Edgar's response to her approval deep within him, and as soon as he did it was clear how important it was.

Edgar wanted Katy to like Scott, just in the way Scott would like Tenzin to like Edgar.

Tenzin, a natural judge of human character, would never jump to the kinds of conclusions Katy did. She would form her opinion on something arbitrary, like Edgar's favorite movie franchise or what he thought about Disney refusing the 2D animation medium. Maybe whatever obsession he had as a child – which, if Scott had to guess, would probably be birds.

Where did birds rank with Scott's sister? It'd be hard to say.

He thought about Tenzin. Tenzin, cross legged in her office chair, listening to Radiohead on her bulky headphones while her stylus dragged across the tablet on her desk. Or analyzing a recipe from one of their mother's books and making them all a meal so spiced it was inedible. Tenzin and Scott, running up the route from the mail room by the Bluerose gates with a box of Japanese candy ordered off the internet.

Tenzin getting on a flight to Baton Rouge.

A pang of regret hit his temples. *Skylark, you fucking idiot.*

Before they went back onto the floor, Scott and Katy ended up alone in the dish pit while Edgar laid down for a few minutes. Katy was standing in the doorway with the back door propped open, blowing out massive plumes of air from one of those robotic cigarettes. Scott watched her, leaning against the sink and attempting to fight back the guilt from his voice.

"You're pretty smart with the internet, right?" He asked.

Her eyes turned to him. "*Smart* is a weird way to say it, but yeah. Why?"

"I – I was wondering if you could maybe help me find someone," Scott shifted nervously. "My sister."

That piqued Katy's interest, even if she tried not to show it. "Is she okay?"

"Yeah! I mean – I think so. Uh – I spoke to her a few days ago and she said she was going to meet me in Baton Rouge to take me home," he began to speak quicker, because the more he summarized the situation the worse he felt. "Because I was supposed to go to Baton Rouge, but I decided to get off early to kill myself. So I ditched my phone and got off here to die, and then I...didn't."

Katy faced him fully now, vape hanging limply in her grasp. It was hard to read what she was thinking. In the back of his mind he remembered Edgar's reaction when Scott casually dropped the concept of his own death. People don't like it when you say you're going to kill yourself. Obviously, right? But some people tend to get really upset over the concept.

Obviously, right?

"Okay," Katy began as she slowly closed the door. "Well I'm glad you aren't dead."

"Sure," Scott muttered vaguely.

"But..." she pursed her lips and considered something in Scott's face. "You don't seem to be great at masking. Not without your eye thing, at least. So you were probably pretty freaked out the last time you spoke."

He thought about the train. The sting of hot tears on his face. The nausea and hunger pains and motion sickness.

"So if she's still in Baton Rouge she has no idea where you are and no way to contact you."

Scott thought about falling asleep with Tenzin in her bed the night before he left. Back when the plan was for him to be gone for only six months.

Katy put away her cigarette and went to wash her hands. "She's probably terrified," she said.

"I don't remember her phone number," Scott whispered. "She had to put it in my phone. I'm so bad with stuff like that."

"Yeah, I guess it's a lot of buttons if you weren't raised with it. Um..." she wiped her hands with a handful of paper towels and faced him with a calm smile. "I can find her, though. No problem. What's her name?"

"Tenzin – well, I mean, Tenzin is her middle name but she hates her first name so that's probably what she goes by online," Scott swallowed hard and tried again. "Yes, I'm certain. She's Tenzin Onyilogwu."

Midway into fixing her hair Katy paused. "That sounds African. Are you African?"

"No?" Scott frowned, glancing down at his arms. Did he look Nigerian? "I don't think I'm *that* dark. Why do you ask?"

"Oh – so she's, like, your step-sister."

"Nope," Scott said. "Regular sister."

"You have the same parents?"

Scott felt the small pull of a familiar tension headache burning be-hind his eyes. The same that always rose up when people started dissect-ing the relationship between him and Tenzin.

"Uh, no," he said, growing increasingly confused. "I mean, yes. We have…I mean, our mom died when Tenzin was younger, so she moved in me and – our mom?"

That sounded wrong. Why did that sound wrong? The headache throbbed tighter in pulses of electricity.

Katy's brow furrowed slightly. "Yeah, okay," she said. "It sounds like this might be another –"

"My sister moved to Bluerose when I was six," Scott tried to make it make sense in his head. "And I guess Mom – met Mom? And became friends?"

He glared down at the grime caked between the tiles underneath their feet. All of that sounded weird when he actually said it out loud, but the closer he looked at it the more it hurt to look at at all. It got to the point that Scott just started repeating the same facts, over and over, hoping to eventually decipher some actual sense out of them.

"Hey."

Katy touched his arm and jarred him from his turntable thinking.

"I'll find her," she said. "I'll get her number tonight and text it to Edgar," she trailed off, remembering Edgar prone on the couch in the other room. "Or I can text her myself and just say that I'm a friend and you're okay. If that wouldn't weird you out."

Those words rolled over him like a crashing wave, drowning out nearly everything else. Scott had a friend? Still raw from the strangeness of the previous train of thought, that casual offer struck him straight to the core.

Scott had a friend.

He once studied a book at the library on how to make friendship bracelets. It felt like an easy craft for someone terrible at crafts. Scott could easily weave a bracelet for a friend assuming he had a friend with wrists suitable for bracelets.

"Okay," he said, playing cool the best he could. "That sounds good. Thank you."

Somebody get me some goddamned thread.

At some point Edgar worked his way off the couch and ended up back at the bar. Scott found him sitting on two milk crates stacked on top of each other. He looked bad. His eyes were bloodshot and he was vaguely yellowed in spots that should not be yellow. If he hadn't thrown up already he was probably going to pretty soon.

Scott considered asking his bond if he was okay. But why? He had eyes, didn't he? And a consciousness that now embraced Edgar's? All it would take would be for one more table to order the crawfish special and Edgar Gallows would be knocked out entirely.

Instead of attempting conversation he just stood and rubbed Edgar's back, looking around the dining room. The rush was mostly over, leaving only scattered tables of diners milking the last stretch of time before the kitchen closed for the night. The band was done with their set, which meant Scott would be able to finish his shift with zero reason to go out and throw himself into the Mississippi. Despite the odds being stacked against them, it looked like they actually pulled this off.

"Your braid held up well," Edgar remarked to Scott.

Without thinking Scott reached up again and touched the tail of his braid. He'd done that a lot over the course of the night, either after brushing back hair that wasn't actually there, or just to feel the lines of it while waiting for the blender to mix. Since he got so used to playing with his hair the construction wasn't as neat as it was when they arrived, but for the most part it was still intact.

"It's weird," Scott said. "I never have my hair up in front of people like this. It was different at home, but for a while now I've only done it when I'm alone or at the piano."

"Do you like it?"

"It's nice to be able to see," Scott laughed weakly.

Edgar scanned his eyes across his face in a slow, drunken sweep. Even in the midst of a brewing hangover the quality in his stare was still potent enough to send a small shiver down Scott's spine. And once again he felt wary. If Edgar was struggling with his emotional control, it's possible that disturbance spread somehow to Scott's mind as well. So even though what he felt wasn't bad, it was slightly larger than he could comfortably handle – and that scared him.

"It's nice to see your face," Edgar said.

Because the thing is that Scott knew Edgar meant it when he said that. There was no underlying motive in the sentiment. In fact, he could feel Edgar's pride glowing in both of them. He felt *good* to have Scott be seen, and to also be seen with Scott.

Something in Scott lurched briefly. It was like a dry heave, but metaphysical. He tried to pretend it didn't happen and laugh it off.

"I'm – glad it isn't too much for you," he said, an off-handed comment.

Edgar took both hands on the counter of the bar and worked himself onto his feet. He took a few unsteady steps until he came to stand in front of Scott, and then he clumsily grabbed their hands together and pressed them to his chest.

He smiled, tired and sick, but somehow incredibly sweet. "You could never be too much for me, Skylark," he murmured.

Break. Burst. Shatter.

The break room reeked of a variety of liquors and syrups. Alcohol fumes made Edgar's eyes water, but he kept his stare steady and blinked consistently as he picked shards of glass out of Scott's hair. He had to undo the other man's braid, which was now slick with splashes of alcohol. The two of them were both splattered pretty thoroughly.

Scott glowered without a word, carefully removing bits of broken bottle from Edgar's curls. He was clearly upset. It was hard to focus on that, though, when the emotional buckshot that hit him moments before still rattled his bones.

"So that was crazy," he said.

Scott sighed through his teeth. 'I'm sorry."

"It's okay! You got – I mean…" Edgar picked out a particularly large curved piece of a bottle base and flicked it to the ground. "I surprised you, I guess."

"Do you..?" Scott tapped his fingers lightly against the side of Edgar's head, likely without thought. "You weren't raised as a birthright."

"I was not."

"So you don't know what it means. To call one by their middle name."

Edgar cracked a nervous smile. "I don't even have a middle name."

Scott turned even sadder, somehow personally hurt by the comment. His hand stopped picking for glass and came to rest over Edgar's shoulder. He stared down at the little bits of glass scattered and partially crushed on the hardwood below them.

Once again Edgar went back to the moment he spoke Scott's middle name aloud. As soon as he did every bottle lined on the shelves behind them burst all at once in a shower of glass and liquor. Startling as that may be, though, it was nothing compared to what happened inside of him. It was like a star going supernova. A single massive entity bursting into fragments of potential new life. It didn't get rid of his nausea and exhaustion, but it did wake him up better than any amount of caffeine.

"Is it bad?" He asked Scott.

Scott tried to smile and mostly pulled it off. "No, I…hm," he looked back at Edgar, hesitated a moment, and then forced a casual demeanor. "It's special. It's a – very special term of endearment that no one's known to call me outside of home. So you're right, it surprised me."

Edgar frowned, lightly guilty. "I just thought you wanted a nick-name."

"I – I do," Scott said. "It's not…I like it. I like it a lot. Really."

"I can call you something else," Edgar tried.

Scott held his face between each hand, careful of any stray glass pieces left in his hair, and forced them to face each other. "It's a special name," he repeated. "And you're special. Special to me. So you should call me that – if you want to," Scott smiled unsteadily. "I say you have the right."

He softened his grip on Edgar's head. Edgar took this chance to lean forward and kiss him. Or he tried to, at least, but Scott pulled away before he could get close enough.

"You're drunk," Scott said.

"Am I? Still?"

"I mean – probably."

Edgar wasn't about to push this particular battle with this particular person. He didn't need Scott to kiss him to know how he felt. The man experienced a mental solar flare at the mere sound of Edgar calling him the right pet name. Everything was fine. Things were good – *very* good, in fact. All the things have been better than they have ever been for anyone on earth, ever.

"You look pale," Scott observed.

Edgar nodded and stood from the couch, carefully stepping around the glass. "Yeah I'm gonna go throw up," he said.

He figured that after enough time in New Orleans his alcohol tolerance would adjust to the norm. Katy could handle her liquor so well that he could only judge how drunk she got based on the length of the hangover. Edgar figured that he'd become something like that – the kind of person who could easily knock out shots and cocktails like a champ while listening to funky jazz and eating a diet of mainly fried foods.

In a way that happened. If you took Edgar when he first moved to the city and force fed him six ounces of straight rum he would probably just die right then and there. Now at the very least he could get through most of a work day before throwing up all his internal organs. He wouldn't be as bold as to call that an improvement, but it was definitely a shift in behavior.

After vomiting he felt a little better, even though he stank of booze and still had small flecks of glass in his hair. He stared at himself in the

mirror, gently shaking his hands through his curls, and there it was –
flakes of sharp dandruff falling into the sink.

He wasn't cleaning that up. It was inconsiderate to the rest of his
team, but he just wasn't doing it.

When he stepped back into the break room he spotted Michael leaning against the doorway, midway into conversation with Scott still on
the couch. He stopped when he heard the door open and looked at
Edgar, concerned in that pastoral way that always made Edgar feel a little sick.

"I just told Kitchen Natalie to send you home with an order of
beignets," he said.

Edgar cringed. "You don't have to do that."

"It'll help the nausea. Plus, with the amount of booze you have in
your system you'll need some carbs to absorb it," Michael stepped inside
the room and softly closed the break room door behind him. "Trust me,
Ed, you'll thank me tomorrow."

"You told him?" Edgar said to Scott.

"Just the broad strokes. I didn't want you to get in trouble."

"Lark told me -"

"You can just call me Scott," Scott softly interrupted.

Michael paused and sat up against the edge of the table. "Scott told
me he was a birthright when we spoke on the phone," he said. "And
he was just explaining that you agreed to do some ritual thing to help
him out of some trouble, and now it's gotten you a little mixed up, So
you tried to drink because that would dull the weirdness and get you
through work – with his help, of course," he raised his brow. "Would
you say that's the situation?"

Thinking that Scott spilled the truth on his behalf was hard enough,
but knowing that he intentionally fudged the details in Edgar's favor
was even more annoying. And Michael called him Lark. It's possible
that Scott introduced himself to a lot of people as Lark when he assumed they'd forget him.

He quivered slightly, chilled to the bone. How long had that plan been put in place?

"It was my idea," Edgar said.

Michael smiled, a glimmer of pride shining in his eyes. "I hoped so."

Edgar swallowed back the rising tide of anxiety and forced himself to keep talking. "And he's not the only birthright," he said. "I'm – I am…"

Scott attempted to protest, but Edgar held up a hand to quiet him. Michael watched him closely, still holding part of an encouraging smile.

"Come on, Ed," Michael gently prodded. "You can say it."

"I'm a birthright too."

That marked the first time he ever said those words out loud to another human being that wasn't Scott. Edgar had no idea what to expect. To hire someone for years without knowing this core aspect of their very being must come as a shock – maybe even betrayal.

He adjusted his position and waited for the fallout. Would there be fallout? Is this something he even still had any reason to be ashamed of?

Michael took a deep breath and sighed happily. "I'm glad you finally said it," he said. "Good job, bud."

Time passed. Edgar's resolve lessened and his broad shoulders slumped. Scott got up from the couch while still keeping a safe distance to allow this conversation to stay insular, if not private.

"Did you not know I knew?" Michael said.

"Lots of people don't know anything about birthrights," Edgar attempted to reason.

"Right. Right," Michael scanned the ceiling and clicked his tongue. "Yeah, I guess you're a little too young to know about Daymoon."

From out of the corner of his eye Edgar saw Scott take in a soft gasp. "Oh wow," he said. "We're pretty close to where Daymoon used to be, aren't we? I didn't even realize."

"It was right in Mississippi – maybe a four hour drive from NOLA," Michael's face went sad and smiling as he thought about it. "They did a lot of really important humanitarian work for a lot of those run-down towns along the Delta. No one was willing to provide the resources for them to make any substantial change, but…they took care of people.”

Michael paused, fully lost in the dream. Sometime in this daze Edgar became aware of Scott coming to stand by his side.

“It wasn't great being gay in the nineties here,” Michael added after some time. “Ordinances were *just* being passed, but you know how long that stuff takes to matter to people. I was lucky to have the parents I did, but I had a lot of friends who were going through it. And it was just common knowledge for our generation that, if you reached the point where it was all too much, you go off and join Daymoon,” his smile was heavy, but still held on. “Some of us did. I was always really happy for them.”

He thought about something that finally dropped any remaining pleasantry from his face. For a while his stare lost all focus and it was clear he was somewhere else. Then all at once he returned, looking up at Edgar and Scott like they just walked into the room.

“It got flooded in the early 2000s,” he explained. “They had to abandon it. I kept in touch with a few friends there – one moved to another witch town, and the other said they got a job at the Southern Poverty Law Center, which is –“

“Wait,” Scott said. “Like they moved out of a witch town?”

“Yeah, she's living in Montgomery last time I checked. I haven't emailed her in a few years, though.”

Edgar shivered at the touch of Scott's icy, pitch-black confusion.

“Was she a birthright?” He asked.

Michael beamed. “Never spoke and had to walk with a cane, but sitting next to her was the ultimate painkiller. I never needed her gift the way some plenty people on the Delta did, but we liked the same music so we made friends quickly. I came to her birthday party once the year someone got her an eye control keyboard and she laughed so hard she threw up,” he hummed softly. “God I…I'll email her tonight. I bet she's doing some great work.”

So there are other birthrights that have not only left their witch towns, but started new lives in civilization entirely. Scott seemed shocked by this insight, and even sicker in the face than he already was before.

Edgar looked back at Michael and was immediately frozen by the affection in his boss's stare.

"So that's the only reason why you hired me?" Edgar said, his pride itching.

"No," Michael immediately answered. "I hired you because you had solid experience and your trial shift went well. You're quick with a knife and you work hard when you have to, and Ian told me that you reorganized the walk-in after a month of working here."

Edgar grimaced at the memory. He was so proud when he finally arranged the walk-in to a point where everything was visible and accessible. No more produce being shoved in available spaces and inevitably being misplaced and left to rot. Edgar brought in Ian, back when he still thought Ian would eventually warm up to him, and started to explain his new system. Ian was so enraged by his actions that he took a bag of carrots and threw them each in Edgar's direction.

He just stood there, taking each individual carrot, frozen and simultaneously terrified and completely understanding. Edgar had vivid memory of clocking out after work, driving home, and just crawling straight into bed to sleep when he hadn't eaten and the sun had just barely set.

On the one hand Ian kept Edgar's new organizational method. On the other, there just has to be a point where things like that stopped fucking mattering.

"Sometimes kitchen teams don't mesh," Michael said. "It doesn't mean you aren't good at what you do. You are – that's why I hired you. Then your ego and Ian's ego clashed and you wanted to get off the line, and I kept you on at the bar even though you're awful at it."

Edgar's heart slowed in a steady bass drum beat. "Why?"

"Because you're a birthright and I want to help you. Because you have real potential as a chef and I want to help you," Michael chuckled lightly and raised his eyes towards the ceiling. "Because you remind me of a lot of friends I had in the past that just gave up and...and I want to help you."

This was nice. Michael was saying a lot of very nice things to Edgar and he was, by proxy, nice for saying them. Yet with every hand reaching out to connect with him all Edgar wanted to do was dig himself deeper and deeper down. He wanted to pull the old floorboards with his bare hands, digging between the slats until his fingers were raw and bloody, just so he could drop into the crawl space and make friends with the spiders and overwintering raccoons.

Or he wanted to thank Michael. He wanted to say how much it meant to him to have a slightly older male figure witness him as an independent adult and genuinely care about his well-being. Edgar wanted to ask for advice on what he should be doing next, to get his insight on whether or not he was fit for an industry where anger and resentment was near obligatory. Or was it? Was it?

There was a lot he wanted to say and know. There was plenty he wanted to avoid and even more he wanted to embrace, but at the moment all he could do was stand in place and tremble.

Michael went from warm to worried. Edgar felt Scott's hands steady him just as he felt like his legs might start to give out again. His voice was low and calm as he addressed his boss, not unlike how Edgar was taught to speak when reciting incantations.

"I'll pay for the bottles I broke," he said.

"I told you, Scott, you don't need to do that –"

"Then I'll come back in a few days and fix your piano. I'll tighten pins, realign the hammers –"he cut himself off, probably sensing Edgar's vague doubt. "I have a repair kit in my bag. I'm self taught, but I can tune a spinet no problem. I'll even help you get a deal on way better piano that won't break down as easily as yours could and does and currently is."

This cold intensity, Scott's ghostly anger wasn't new to Edgar. It was the same way he spoke to Ian in the kitchen. And yet this time, Michael wasn't following along blindly.

"What – uh – what are you doing?"

"You're going to give Edgar a two week sabbatical to figure out what's going on."

"Yeah, that's –"

"And you're going to let Katy go early because Edgar's still drunk and I don't know how to drive."

"Okay but –"

"If you need the manpower I'll stay and cover her section for the rest of the night."

Michael let out a laugh. It cut off when he realized Scott was being entirely serious. He crossed his arms and leaned back, torn between amusement and curiosity, as well as a little bit of pity.

"I get it," he said. "Because that's your thing, I guess. You can mind control people a little bit."

Shock rippled off of fear and reflected into a mirrored prism of disbelief. Which emotion came from which body? No one knew and it really didn't make a difference.

"I can't say I haven't been around magic in a while." Michael shrugged. "Because who knows, right? That's the whole thing of it. So maybe when you tell people what you can do it doesn't hit as hard. A rain versus a hurricane, or something. I don't know."

He looked slightly amused with the situation, which was better than being afraid or angry. Eventually he caught on to the panic radiating from the two idiots across from him and took on a more serious stance.

"You don't work here, Scott," he said. "I guess you did a pretty good job at the bar – wow, I just...I just realized you've been working my bar all night," Michael scuffed his beard and sighed. "Shit. Yeah. So – sure, I'll let you tune my pianos. If you need ongoing work we can talk about that too. For now you should just get this one home and maybe come back and talk to me in a few days."

Edgar's perspective began to drift and lose focus. When he came back to reality he was sitting on the edge of the loading dock with Scott's arm wrapped around his shoulder. It was a comforting motion, but all it took was one look at the other man to see that Scott wasn't doing much better than he was.

It was a frigid, cold night. The only illumination came from the dirty yellow glow of the bulb above the door. There were no stars. No rain. No air, seemingly. The metal of the dock was ribbed, rusted, and caked with dirt.

"I thought I was the only one."

Scott's words were stiff when he spoke them aloud. He stared ahead at nothing in particular. He didn't blink.

"The only one that's left a witch town?" Edgar tried to elaborate. "Is that what they told you?"

"They...I'm so sick of saying this, but I *don't know*," Scott leaned forward and buried his head in his hands. "I want to say that they never taught me that much birthright history, but..." he looked up, suddenly haunted. "I can't remember. My mind, Edgar, it feels – *wrong*."

Edgar couldn't bring himself to think that he knew everything about birthrights. By now it was obvious a lot of what he knew wasn't right. Frankly, after a ten-hour shift and the shakeup in his brain, it was increasingly difficult to think about anything. Even so, he regarded what bare skin he could see of the man beside him.

Curses, as far as Edgar knew, were purely the stuff of Academy magic. They were considered an outdated practice, still taught in the form of history as opposed to instruction. This wasn't because of any ethical qualms. It's just that magic took energy and physical effort that increased in proportion to the effects. When it came to curse magic, anything just short of murder wasn't really worth the side effects, and if you were planning on murdering an enemy there were far easier and more effective strategies to do so.

He steadied his breathing and tried to remember what he was taught. Curses heal on their own and leave scars or burns that are impossible for the victim to detect, but can be used as confirmation by the caster that their work was effective. The placement would have to be something that the right witch can spot while passing them in the street or watching them from a discreet distance. The underside of the wrist, side of the neck, or even the middle of the forehead were all traditional targets.

But Edgar could see all of those spots of Scott's body right now, and they were free of any unnatural markings. Would he be able to see them, close as he was? He narrowed his eyes and tried to polish his focus to a precise gleam. Still nothing.

If Scott was moving place to place every few days, it would hard to imagine him staying still long enough to provoke the ire of an old-school Academic. So it could be the problem was that otherworldly entity, the proverbial *Witch Eater* that had been following him from the inside for most of his life.

Erik warned them that if they bonded it could pass, to some extent, onto Edgar. So why hadn't it yet?

By this point Scott was rubbing his arms and shivering in the cold. He rolled down his sleeves and buttoned the cuffs, but still wasn't warm enough. So Edgar stepped down off the dock and back to his car to grab Scott's coat. While staring into the floor of his backseat, his eyes involuntarily landed on his old car antennae still tossed aside after one ill-fated trip to the car-wash.

An idea formed in his mind. It was a bad idea. It might not even work, and if it did it was going to be incredibly dangerous.

From over his shoulder Scott was even smaller, curled further into himself. The world looked impossibly immense in comparison to his tiny, frightened form. Putting their small bodies together didn't make much of a difference in the grand scope of things, but it was something to push the scales. Edgar gripped his jaw tight and bent down to sweep the brown fuzzy coat in one arm and the antennae in the other.

He climbed back up the steps, came up beside Scott, and gently pulled him onto his feet. Scott allowed the repositioning without protest, only acknowledging the turn of events to smile when Edgar slipped his coat around his shoulders. Scott buttoned up the front and flipped up the light wool collar to bury his nose in the fluff.

"I miss my mom," he murmured.

Edgar frowned. That was quite the foreign concept.

The antennae was only about a foot in length when not extended, with a small black plastic bulb at the tip. Edgar was almost surprised at how easily how he carried it in his hand. He wielded it guided by the length of his thumb, just in the way he was taught but was never able to master or even fully process. But now, doing his second incantation in years and possibly the worst decision in his career in magic, he slipped into the technique without problem.

Scott didn't notice the stand-in until the bulb of the wand was pressed against the center of his forehead. He smiled, confused, and then his eyes went wide the moment he realized what Edgar was doing.

"Edgar, *wait*." he tried.

But it was too late. Edgar recited his incantation, words spilling like a gas leak in the cold of the air around them. Power surged through the length of the wand and ricocheted inside him. His body was broken open with a vastness, as if his sixty or so liters of human being somehow contained an incalculable degree of undetectable matter. His last conscious sensation was feeling the antennae drop from his hand and the toes of his feet leave the ground before

Genevieve Gallows pressed the switch of the electric razor and filled the room with the low sound of its buzzing. Eddie stood as still as he could, but even with the thin material of the towel wrapped over his shoulders he still shivered as his mother held him still. With one hand on his shoulder, Gen took the razor and pointed the blade towards his scalp.

In the reflection he could see a few lushly reddened curls falling in front of her eyes. Her face was focused and very cold, but despite all that her hair was still as glamorous as always. Eddie always imagined his hair would be that free and curled if it was allowed to grow. He would like to feel feel the weight of it, maybe even get the admiration he'd seen people give his mother time and time again.

She was very pretty. Eddie would like to be pretty too.

The razor approached, and the sound of the blade sent a wave of tingling between Eddie's shoulders.

"Wait," he said.

It stopped. His mother didn't look directly at him, but eyed his small form in the reflection like you would a stain that refused to wash out.

"I don't want you to shave my head," he continued. "I want...I'm going to grow my hair out."

A long silence. Gen switched off the razor and set it down on the counter.

"What do you think you're doing?" She said to her son in the mirror.

Her voice was a used needle on the beach or a baby shoe left on the side of the road. Edgar's chest clenched, but he didn't let go this time.

"I'm standing up for myself. I'm being brave."

She smiled. "But you aren't brave, Edgar."

"I want to do something good."

Gen leaned a little closer against him, a hand on each shoulder. "Of course," she purred. "But good is hard, isn't it? It's scary. It's going to hurt you. Wouldn't it be easier to just be quiet and keep your head down? Isn't that the Academic way?"

The hands on his shoulder traveled closer together. Edgar swallowed hard. "I don't want to be afraid anymore."

"You are, though. You're afraid of everything."

By now his mother hand one hand on his shoulder and the other rising to wrap around the base of his neck. Edgar blinked a few times. This felt wrong. This wasn't how the memory went.

Gen's face was just above the nape of his neck, but he felt no air from her nose or mouth. Her skin was against his, but it was pressure without the warmth of life.

And then, all at once, Edgar wasn't afraid anymore. He looked at himself in the mirror, so young and weak, and he found himself smiling. He laughed briefly, cutting it short mainly out of respect for the situation at hand.

"That's what you do, huh?" He managed through the pressure of his mother's hand on his chin. "You use people's fears to make them weaker?"

When he saw Gen's eyes in the mirror they were burning with a blind, seething rage. Edgar was nothing more than a gazelle with a broken leg, or a rabbit with no soft ground to bury into. And yet, in the presence of a threat that still considered him a fight, Edgar was very close to laughing again.

Gen pressed her lips to his ear. "When I claim him," she said. "I will make the last thing he sees be his pretty hands ripping out your throat."

That was just too much. Edgar began to snicker, and soon he was laughing with the release of an unfathomable degree of tension. The sound echoed off the walls, near-delirious. It only went silent as his mother tightened her grip on his chin and shoved her hand up, snapping his head back with a wet, thick crunch.

Sixth Movement

Edgar didn't wake up for a long time after his shift at the Den. Scott didn't know what he did. He didn't know why he did it. Edgar pressed the tip of some metal rod against his forehead, said something that sounded like human speech but also not, and just collapsed. Luckily, he was only cowered over the other man's body for a minute or so before Katy came out. The next thing he knew he was in the backseat of her much newer and well-kept car with Edgar's head in his lap.

She took them to her place and instructed Scott to help her tuck Edgar into her bed. Was that weird? Scott wasn't about to ask questions. He just positioned the covers just under Edgar's neck and brushed the curls from his face.

"He always said he felt more comfortable here," Katy weakly attempted to explain. "I don't know why. Maybe he was lying."

He wasn't. It looked pretty clear that Katy's comforter was the same as Edgar's, only colored rust instead of green. They both had the same white plastic orb on the bedside table – an oil diffuser that Edgar never once turned on, but Katy had a whole shelf of little smelly bottles for. It was undeniable that Edgar found some sense of safety here, something that he tried and failed to replicate in his own home.

Scott nodded. "It's good," he said. "You made the right choice."

Too wired to sleep, Scott followed Katy out into the kitchen. There was a little bar counter that he was able to take a seat at, though there wasn't much space to do much but settle the ends of his elbows on the tile. Everywhere else was occupied by empty cans and bottles, stacks of books, boxes of takeout and the occasional scattering of paper bills.

Katy took a bottle of beer out of the fridge and turned to Scott just as he held up a handful of singles and flashed her a quizzical look.

"Oh yeah," she said. "Those are my investments. I only deposit half my tips so I still have a little extra – just in case."

That didn't sound right. But Scott didn't have a debit card until his eighteenth birthday and barely understood how to use it, so he wasn't one to make judgments on peoples fiances.

"You want a beer?" Katy asked.

With everything Scott was feeling he could go straight to old habits and drink the nearest and hardest liquor until it dulled his senses to a soft, rounded point. But he didn't want to do that. The feeling of intoxication, which could only mimic Petrichor, was unpleasant and nauseating. Even though the withdrawals of habitual drinking were a slight sniffle compared to coming down from what birthrights can distill, it was only the terrible garnish on a drink he didn't want from the get-go.

"I don't like to drink," he said.

Katy smirked. "I gotcha," she said. "Give me *one* second...."

She dove back into her fridge and rustled some things around. Eventually she came back with a carton of orange juice. She sloshed the liquid inside and took a quick scan at the expiration date. Then she turned to Scott and raised her brow.

"That works," he said.

So he ended up sitting side-by-side with Katy, his new friend and Edgar's long-time companion. Work was hard, their mutual worry for Edgar in the other room deep and vibrant. With nothing they can do to help more than they have, now was a time for them to try and relax. They could have a conversation that would allow them to bond and forge a more amicable relationship.

Scott took a sip of orange juice. "How long have you been an alcoholic?" He said to Katy.

Katy stopped with her lips just above the rim of her beer. She put down the bottle and eyed Scott in a way that made him realize that he once again said the wrong thing. He clenched his jaw and tried to restrain his panic.

"I-I'm an alcoholic, technically," he said. "Or I was. A binge drinker at least, based on the definition."

"You used to do what Edgar did tonight?"

"Not at first. But I grew up taking Petrichor every day, and I only packed enough for – I don't even remember. Less than what I ended up needing. After that I had to improvise," he swirled the juice in his glass and relived the memories. "To get where Edgar was tonight, I'd need four shots and everything else in that bottle. For the first few hours, at least."

"Jesus," Katy whispered.

Clearly, having actual conversations was a skill that Scott would have to work on. Why couldn't he just talk about birds or food? Or, even better, get the other person to talk about themselves. That's always worked for every faceless individual he'd had to interact with over the past few years.

He just wanted to talk. He wanted to share all the weird shapes in his head.

Scott was selfish.

"What's your go-to?" Katy asked, still somehow curious. "I mean, are you a rum guy?"

"Not really," Scott laughed under his breath. "Everclear is quicker. It's hard to remember what states it's illegal in, though. Otherwise probably vodka. Anything that isn't too sweet or heavy. I don't – um – *enjoy* it."

Katy, weirdly enough, raised her brow and smiled at this insight. She took a swig of beer and nodded. "Man," she whistled. "It's a shame you stopped. Edgar's such a goddamned lightweight, I'd appreciate someone closer to my level."

You shouldn't be on my level, Katy.

"Why'd you quit?" Katy said.

"Shaky hands. I mean, I already knew my blood pressure was spiked, which I figured was just inevitable, but when I actually had to look down at the keys to play piano…"

He trailed off, staring down at his hands wrapped around the patterned glass.

"You play the piano," Katy said. "That's your whole thing."

Scott sighed in relief. That was easily one of the kindest things any human being has ever said to him. He turned to Katy and saw her point to the living room.

"Can I hear?"

He furrowed his brow, but when he followed the direction of her finger he recognized an electronic keyboard set up on a folding stand up against the wall. It stood like an electronic plateau, a structure of nature, strong and sturdy on what had to be a cheap plastic stand. His heart seized in his chest and he felt his face go flush with heat.

"I bought it years ago," Katy said. "I thought keeping it where I could see it would make me want to practice more, but it mostly just gives me another surface for Wilford to sleep on."

Right, Wilford. Katy's cat was still sitting where he was when they walked in, curled up on the couch and sleeping with the occasional gurgle. He tried to hold the thought of this adorable, kingly cat in his mind, but compared to the presence of the actual piano mere feet away nothing else could stick.

Already his hands were beginning to twitch. Katy finished off her beer and took the bottle to the sink. "I know it's late," she said. "and I'm sure you're happy to get a few days off from being some sort of dancing monkey or whatever –"

"*No,*" Scott spat out. "No no, I – no, this is…" he took a breath and blinked until the world turned staccato. "Please let me play for you."

The feeling of sitting down on a piano bench was universal, regardless of the location or quality of the seat. It was foreplay. It was the introduction to an ultimate release of all the pressure in his head. In all of his travels Scott never had an opportunity to play a keyboard before. That didn't even occur to him until he sat down in front of it, this strange hunch of plastic and metal.

He pressed a few fingers along the keys to feel the give. No sound came out aside from the soft click of pressure on plastic. Fascinating.

"You have to turn it on," Katy said from the couch.

When he looked over his shoulder he saw her pulling Wilford onto her lap. He was relocated without trouble, fluffy white arms splayed out in front of him, and eventually shifted slightly to the typical cat-loaf position once he was fully situated.

Suddenly Scott felt awkward.

"I'm sure you're used to a bigger crowd," Katy mused. "I can wake the neighbors if that would *inspire* you."

"No," Scott said, his voice surprisingly clear. "This is what I want."

He turned back to the keys, these jutting, careful appendages of black and white. The only safe constant that has followed him for his entire life.

"This is all I ever want," he said, a little softer.

Usually at his shows he would ask for requests. Pretty much any free time he had was spent listening to the radio or CDs at the local library, so he was loosely familiar with a lot of the major classics and current hits. Exact accuracy wasn't entirely needed. If someone suggested something he couldn't perfectly transcribe or found uninteresting, adding his own improvisational spin to it always went over well.

Runs and arpeggios are like the frosting of music. They hold things together and sound impressive enough to make up for what might be missing. And Scott definitely didn't think that only because they happened to be his favorite thing to play.

He found the power button for the piano and turned it on. There was a numbered list written along the top of the keyboard that displayed the sixty or so separate instruments contained in this one vessel.

Number thirteen was Spanish guitar. He slowly entered in the number and pressed the middle C, only to find the note played through the speakers in the brassy strum of a guitar. Shocked, Scott laughed loudly.

"Have you never played a keyboard?"

"I – I haven't," Scott said through his giggling. "It's unbelievable."

She snickered from behind him. "If you press the arrow keys you can cycle through the different sounds."

That's exactly what he did for the next few minutes. He went through each individual instrument, pressing the same key and marveling at the different ways this piano allowed him to communicate. The same note played thirty different times in thirty different ways, all on one machine – imagine that!

Then at one point his newest intimate companion made a sound that stopped his humor in its tracks. His hand left the arrow button, and he played the middle C again. And there it was, that woody, dusty sound that rang so devastating to his heart.

He read the words on the small screen. NUMBER 52: TACK PIANO it read.

"You like that one?" Katy asked from behind him.

She was so far away. Only a few feet in reality, but in his heart it felt like miles.

Still, Scott tried to smile. "It's the same kind of piano I had in my house growing up," he said. "It's...what I learned to play on when I was a baby."

"Very Wild West," Katy paused, then added. "Wait, did you just say *baby*?"

"You know, I thought more places would have them. And then I learned they're really only in silent movie theaters these days, which aren't as easy to find as..."

Scott drifted his fingers along the opening four notes of Liebestraume, which he played for his mother on her birthday one year. The beginning was really all he could remember without hearing the piece again. Tears pricked his eyes. His whole outfit reeked of booze. That suddenly didn't matter at much as it did mere moments before.

"Katy?" He heard himself ask. "Do you think you could..?"

"Yeah?"

It was stupid. It really didn't matter. He was a grown man in his thirties, he no longer needed someone else to keep him company on a piano bench. At this point he'd probably played more than his mother, an actual professional musician, and she was capable of doing her job on her own.

But wasn't that the point? It was a job for her. That was never supposed to be his life. Not for this long.

"Do you think you could sit next to me?" Scott asked.

"Oh," there was a rustling and a low, raspy meow from Wilford. "Sure, I guess. Hang on."

He was too embarrassed by his small request to do anything but stare ahead of him until he felt Katy standing just behind him.

"Scoot over."

Scott nodded and moved to one end of the piano bench. Soon Katy was seated on the other, the two of them close enough for their legs to be fully pressed together. That physical sensation grounded him at the elbows, allowing him to move his wrists far easier.

"I probably smell terrible," he remarked.

Katy scoffed. "You smell like alcohol, I smell like oil and remoulade. We'll shower off and go to bed soon, but first," she fanned out her hands to point at the keyboard. "You owe me a song."

She gave him a smile that resonated warmth throughout his chest. This was his friend, he reminded himself. Scott had a cool friend who didn't mind how sticky he was. His friend was going to let him use her shower because she cared about his comfort. He made a good friend tonight and soon they would have matching bracelets.

With that in mind, he stared down at the teeth of the piano. He positioned his hands and relaxed his shoulders in the way he could only do at a time like this. Then, his eyes drifting shut, he began to play.

The first few notes rang out through the speakers, and as they did Scott

sat on the shore of the beach, watching the waves crash. They dug their toes in the sand, smiling happily as they palmed more grains to cover their feet to the ankle. On a day like this, warm and placid, they could entertain themselves for hours just enjoying the products of nature. Press their skin to the sand. Eventually bob in the cold, dark water. Maybe make friends with a sand crab.

But today was different. They were perfectly fine, thinking of little only than when the right time would be to eat the lunch their mother packed for them in a little woven basket. Then they felt a hand touch their shoulder.

Scott looked up to see a woman, soft and rounded like their mother, only with near-black skin and piercing eyes. She had tight curls clinging close to her scalp and a thick necklace made up of large, pale red beads. The woman touched them gently and with concern, and though Scott was confused it didn't occur to them to be afraid.

"Hi honey," she said. "What's your name?"

"Scott."

She smiled. "It's nice to meet you, Scott. Are you lost?"

It was maybe a fifteen minute walk from the beach to their home. Just over the hills and through the field. They looked around.

"No," Scott said. "Are you?"

The woman's smile turned strained. She lowered her head slightly, but still regarded the sand with cool kindness. "Where are your parents, Scott?"

"My dad had a ST-elevation myocardial infarction and died before I was born," Scott explained, still thinking about the peanut butter sandwich in their basket. "My mom is at home. Or maybe she's working. I don't know," they looked back up at the woman and returned her smile with one of their own. "I can help you, though!"

"You can..?" The woman wasn't smiling anymore. "How old are you?"

"Six."

This appeared to truly bother the woman in a way that Scott felt weird and sort of guilty about. They kicked his legs out of the sand and crossed them awkwardly, palming the hem of the basic, sunflower-yellow dress they wore.

After a moment the woman regained her composure. She was back to treating them in that weird, sickly-sweet way that wasn't necessarily bad, just a little strange to comprehend.

"My name is Enoch," she stepped to the side and revealed a little girl about their age standing slightly behind her. "This is my daughter Tenzin. She's six too! We just moved into town, right Tenzin?"

Tenzin had the same dark skin and strong eyes. Her curls were just as tight, but there were more of them tied back in two twin bulbs of hair on either end of her head. She was wearing overalls with the pockets overflowing with rocks and picked plants and, when Scott looked at her, she immediately looked away.

"I'm going to go right over there," she said, pointing to a massive log of driftwood a few yards away. "I'll be right here and I'm just going to make a quick phone call. Tenzin, why don't you keep our new friend Scott company?"

She stepped away before Tenzin had a chance to agree or refuse the offer. That, to Scott, was also weird — to ask a question and then leave before the other person had a chance to answer.

Alone with Tenzin, the little girl worked her way to eyeing them cautiously. They stared back at her. What was supposed to do happen now?

"Are you a boy or a girl?" Tenzin asked.

"I have Klinefelter syndrome," Scott said.

She plopped onto the ground. "What does that mean?"

Scott wasn't entirely certain how to rephrase the way in which his mother explained it to him. "It means I have different — uh — chromosomes. Kind of different. Not like boys or girls. Well, the doctors say I'm kind of a boy but Mom says if I want I can be something else," they paused, pleased at their explanation. "Only later. When I'm a big kid."

Tenzin worked hard to understand that. Scott sympathized with the effort. That was the type of thing that weighed heavy on them if they spent too much time at once considering its implications.

She straightened up a little bit, still hesitant, but a little more open. Scott watched, curiously, as she dug into the front pocket of her overalls and pulled out a massive deck of worn, blue cards.

"Wanna' look at my Pokemon cards?" Tenzin asked them.

Scott did not know what a Pokemon was or what function it served. Tenzin took the top card from the stack and flipped it over, setting it on the sand so Scott could see the illustration on the back. And then Scott's world changed, irreversibly and for the rest of his life. They physically felt their perspective expand. They stared down at the card on the sand, struggling to describe, or even fully take in what they were looking at.

All they knew was that it was the most interesting thing they had ever, ever seen. They hummed softly in abject amazement.

Tenzin finally cracked a smile at their open gaping. "That's Jiggly-puff," she explained.

When Scott finally found their voice they were far louder than intended or appropriate.

"Wow!" They shouted.

The melody Scott played cut off suddenly, though he continued manipulating the keys for good ten seconds before he realized his pressings weren't creating any sound. It took him a moment to stop the momentum he fell into. Once he did, his hands reluctantly relaxed and eventually fell limp into his lap. Even once his body stopped moving his brain struggled to catch up to reality.

Soon he remembered the rare heat of a human body beside his own and turned slightly to look at Katy. She was sitting straight and looked as awake as she had been all day. He felt a stab of fear at the sight of her shocked reaction, but when she finally locked eyes with him there was no blue echo in her stare.

"Fuck," she whispered faintly.

Katy coughed into her fist and rubbed the back of her neck. She stared at nothing in particular with eyes that had to fight not to widen.

She spoke again and her voice was still vague. "Batteries. I didn't…I think that's the same set I used when I bought the keyboard."

There was the implication of a laugh there that never came to fruition. Katy and Scott just stared at each other. Scott could feel his fingers still twitching as if there were keys below them to dance with.

"I didn't expect you to play like that," Katy said.

Scott felt himself start to smile. "What were you expecting?"

"A...song? I don't know?"

"Oh," he turned away and traced a shy finger between the grooves of the keys. "If you want me to play a song you have to name one. I can't...think of them on my own anymore."

"You can't choose your own song to play?"

"Nope. That's why I take requests. Otherwise it's just – this," in a moment of vulnerability he dared ask what he always wanted to. "Do you think it sounds bad?"

Katy did that thing again where she spoke without speaking. Then she lowered her eyes and exhaled softly. He waited for her to assure him one way or gently let him down. She didn't do either. Katy searched his face, first avoiding his eyes directly, then staring straight into his soul. She did not smile.

"You're clearly very talented," she said.

Scott cringed. He always hated that word.

"So that's good," Katy's voice implied otherwise. "It's good to be...*good* at something. But your playing didn't make me *feel* good? God I sound stupid."

"How did it make you feel?" Scott said.

"Uh..." she clicked her tongue. "Just, like, a lot."

She suddenly seemed exhausted. Scott didn't feel great about that. There was, however, a dark satisfaction that came from pulling someone else into his head for a few moments. He recognized the drain in her features. *Yes*, he wanted to shout. *I know! It's the worst and it's like this all the time!*

"Do you have any clothes I could borrow for tonight?" He asked. "And – and a towel? I'd really love a shower."

Katy cracked a weak half-smile. It looked like she was about to make a joke before she thought better of it and changed her train of thought.

"You're a – guy?" She asked, a little stilted.

"Yes," Scott tried not to lean too deep in his own frustration. "I'm still a guy. I'm also *so fucking sick* of pants. If you happen to have some kind of nightgown so I can actually move around comfortably for the first time in recent memory it would make me very, very happy."

He regretted the even mild aggression in his voice. After starting this day getting maced and ending it with his bond collapsing into some kind of magic coma, Scott didn't have the energy to explain his thoughts on gender to another human being. Someone needed to provide him with nice-smelling soap and a soft dress and just let him catch his breath.

"It'll be a little big on you," Katy said.

Scott pressed his lips tight. "Most things are."

The world was a much kinder place after Scott was able to shower off a dozen exploded bottles of liquor and change into something more freeing. Before he excused himself to the bathroom Katy handed him a simple cotton slip, long and soft to the touch, and even offered to pair it with a silk robe colored with a bright floral design. It wouldn't add much in the way of warmth, but Scott gladly took it anyways because *colors!*

His suit was picked for him as a parting gift from the elders of Bluerose, none of which he could clearly picture anymore. They made the effort to give it color and style, but it was still terrible and Scott hated it immediately. He couldn't show it though, which hurt. Even more painful was that everyone he wore it in front of insisted they loved it. They called him *handsome.*

His family were the only ones that reacted with any degree of honesty. Tenzin looked him up and down when he first put it on and presented himself to her. He remembered the way she stepped forward and adjusted the silk tie back when it was still fresh out of the package.

"Well," she stated. "It's quite the costume."

When he stepped down the stairs his mother was waiting. Her steady expression darkened slightly as he came into view. She sighed – disappointed, but not necessarily at him.

"Try putting down your hair," his mother suggested.

He reached back and undid the knotted bun he liked to keep his hair in at the time. It fell along his back in tendrils of black. His mother touched his face in the way she did to brush the hair out of his eyes so many times before, only this time she moved in the opposite direction and pushed a few loose locks to fall in front of his face.

She stepped back, unhappy. "Is that better?"

He smiled, equally as thrilled. "A little," he said.

Now as he stood in Katy's bathroom, Scott looked down at his body and wished again that he had the nerve to face the mirror. He told himself it was fine, and that the feeling mattered more than seeing what he looked like. Scott wrapped his hair in a towel and twisted it before straightening up and balancing the towel knot on his head.

From the edge of the counter he could see the bottles of hair and skin products Katy collected. He wondered if it would be rude to ask her to borrow some once he dried off. His sisters back at Bluerose always gushed at the opportunity to share their products with him.

He would worry about that later.

Katy was sitting at a desk, her freshly-washed face illuminated by the light of two monitors. He took another look at the space around her and finally observed the notes and diagrams tacked along the walls.

"Wow," her voice chimed in as he looked. "You look cute."

It was a lot of magic stuff. He recognized some of the illustrations from things Tenzin offhandedly studied over the years. There were some written names of birthrights in the United States and some basic information. The script looked desperate. The angle in which they were hung and taped provoked a sense of panic.

Back to Katy. She appeared relaxed and pleasantly midway into another beer.

"I'm freezing," he said.

She flashed him a look that implied that the chill was actually his fault and not the weather. Then she focused back on the screens. "Thermostat's by the counter," she pointed off as she spoke. "Knock yourself out."

The thermostat was a fancy electric one, like Edgar's. It read that it was seventy-three degrees, which was not nearly as cold as Scott's body felt it was. That explained the look on Katy's face when he complained. He felt a little weird clicking it up a few more notches, but he did anyway.

"Wanna' help me stalk your sister?" Katy asked as the heat switched on from the vent above his head.

Scott clenched his jaw. He was starting to give himself a headache with how often he was doing this now. But that didn't matter, because he had to make up for one more fuckup of his. So he joined Katy at the computer, standing just behind her chair to watch her work. Doing this felt as familiar as putting on a reliable pair of boots.

"I have a few websites where you could run background checks," Katy said, clicking idly through an unreasonable amount of tabs. "Every search costs money though, so I don't want to do that unless we know we have the right name."

"I told you her name."

Katy hesitated. She spoke, her tone a little more careful. "You told me your memory's a little wonky, right?"

A chill of horror rippled down Scott's back. That couldn't be right. Was he that far gone that he could no longer remember his own sister's name? It was one thing for her face to blur indistinct, that was hard enough. But names are valuable. Names are identity.

Tenzin, right? It had to be Tenzin. He couldn't have made up a name like that from the ichor of his subconscious. He was not nearly that creative when it came with language. Tenzin. Tenzin, Tenzin, Tenzin.

"Do you know what witch town you're from?" Katy asked.

"Bluerose," Scott said, then grimaced. "I mean, I *think* so, but..."

After a flurry of tapping on the keyboard, Katy stopped. "This look familiar?"

On the screen was the homepage of the Bluerose Refuge Hub website. There were photos splayed alone the edges of the main block of text, and much to Scott's immense gratitude he found he recognized the locations. There was the arching wooden sign that displayed the name at the main gates. The dining room of the lounge with its massive curved ceilings. And the fields of mustard flowers! He would sit in those fields as a kid and pretend to be a beetle!

It was confirmed, Scott had a home. There was one thing that was concrete in the ever-changing universe.

Katy must've judged a response based solely on his reaction and began clicking from page to page. "There's a list of businesses," she noticed. "Does she work for any of them?"

"No."

"I'm pretty sure birthrights are registered like Academics – you know, for healthcare reasons – but the database must only be government accessible."

"Oh, Tenzin isn't a birthright."

Silence. Katy ghosted her hands over the keyboard, tapping her index finger over one of the keys without applying pressure. After a moment she nodded curtly.

"I could use some more info to go off of, then," she said. "Tell me about her."

Scott didn't quite understand what that would do to help, but he did as she asked. "Uh, she's tall. She knows a lot about video games..." he relaxed and started to faintly smile. "Ten's an amazing artist. So incredibly creative. And she's really...I don't even know the word for it. Worldly? We would watch a lot of this thing called anime – like the one where these sad children had to fight monsters in giant robots."

Katy laughed, low and dark. Scott continued.

"Tenzin's the coolest person I know," he said. "She doesn't like when I tell her this but she's pretty much an anthropologist – like mom was.

So she knows everything. And if there's something she doesn't know she definitely knows how to learn it.'"

"You said she's an artist?" Katy cut in.

"Oh yeah!" Scott grinned thinking about it. "She always drew these great little comics."

More frantic typing.

"- I must've had a dozen of them taped to the wall of my bedroom. They were so cute, but at the same time they really made you feel –"

"Found her."

Scott turned his eyes back to the monitors. On the left was a page pulled from a site called Webtoons for a comic called *Birdbrain*. *Birdbrain!* He started crying as soon as he recognized Tenzin's handwriting on the screen. What was the name of the main character, the little guy with the human body and the long-necked bird head? It had been so long and Scott couldn't remember. But it was so, so wonderful to see his tiny feathered face again.

On the other screen was a LinkedIn page for one Tenzin Onyilogwu. Good. Scott hoped dearly, in some strange part of his mind that he didn't like to dwell in too often, that if he could hold onto one piece of his mind it would be the knowledge of his sister's name. The Witch Eater could take everything else, as long as Scott was left with nothing but the memory of the family he once had.

The profile picture was outdated. It was taken right after Mom took her to get her hair styled in the crown of two-strand twists that would eventually turn into her massive grove of dreadlocks. The face was the same, though. Tenzin's face was the same and he knew it as soon as he saw it. Scott had to blink through the tears so he could just keep staring.

Her large, dark lips were stained plum. Her nose was wide with a single gold stud in the left nostril, and her eyes were strong and intelligent. She, like him, was never entirely comfortable in photographs. But while his awkwardness resulted in him avoiding any camera not held by a member of his family, she was able to make insecurity out to look pretty cool and calm.

His sister was the most interesting person in the entire world and he missed her with a desperation that could douse the sun.

"That's her?" Katy asked.

Scott opened his mouth to say yes and all that came out was a sob. He closed his mouth tight and huffed bemusedly through his nose. Katy visibly tensed up beside him and gave his arm a weird, single pat.

"There's an email on her LinkedIn," she said. "Let's draft us a message."

He stepped back to give his emotions some physical space and watched as Katy clicked the address on Tenzin's profile and opened up a new email. She typed significantly slower this time, narrating her words as she wrote them.

"*Dear Tenzin,*" she stopped and deleted the words, then replaced them with, "*Hello Tenzin! This is Katy Delaney – real name. I live in New Orleans just off of Louis Armstrong Park,*" once again Katy paused, highlighted that last specific, and deleted it. "*I live in New Orleans in the French Quarter, and recently I became friends with your brother Scott.*"

She looked over her shoulder at Scott and briefly scanned him up and down. Then she went back to her keyboard.

"*Scott is short with long black hair. He cries at things I don't really understand and if he's not crying he's saying things that make me want to cry,*" Katy faltered and then continued. "*He looks good in my pajamas. Scott is safe and alive. He doesn't seem to really know what's going on, but I'm pretty sure he didn't mean to be as big of a dick as you might assume.*"

"Ask it to tell her I'm sorry," Scott whispered.

Katy frowned. "Ask who?"

"The computer."

She turned around and flashed him a befuddled look. He blinked a few times. Was that wrong? From how Tenzin explained it to him a long time ago he thought that was technically right to say.

"*He thinks he needs to ask the computer to tell you he's sorry,*" Katy typed. "*If you're the one teaching him normal things you did a bad job. The man is a mess. I'm enclosing my phone number, please call or text and*

I can tell you more. Best," backspace, *"Sincerely,"* backspace, *"Regards,"* backspace, and then a solid fifteen seconds of staring at the monitor. *"Once again, this is Katy. Bye."*

Katy leaned back in his chair, staring at the text on the screen. She clicked a button and the whole message vanished, sent presumably into the sea of technological energy, where it will then be harnessed by all the tools capable of wielding such immense power.

"You realize the computer isn't alive, right?" Katy said, looking up at him from the chair. "It's a tool."

Scott thought about that. It took a while. Finally, he shook his head. "I don't agree with that"

"What?"

"It's unreasonable to decide what is and isn't alive."

Katy stood up, even more thrown aback. "We *made* computers, Scott."

He raised his brow. "Your parents made you. Are *you* alive?"

For a good long time Katy was unable to respond to that. She looked at the clock above her desk, and Scott did too, and soon they were both painfully aware that it was three in the morning.

"You're a weird guy," Katy said.

Scott was very pleased with himself. He stood upright and undid the towel from around his head, letting his partially-dried hair cascade down his back with a small shake. After such a long and treacherous journey, he was so happy to know that he was capable of still feeling like and being perceived as himself.

His eyes went back to Katy's screens. "Does your computer have LOLCats?"

"I..." Katy looked like she was fighting the urge to make a joke. She didn't, "Yeah. Yeah, grab a stool. I'll hook you up."

Katy and Scott planned to stay up for a while longer, just in case Tenzin saw their email and decided to respond. But a half hour later,

Scott succumbed to the inevitable and wound up sprawled out across the daybed in the living room. She felt weird doing it, but Katy ended up spending some time standing nearby and watching the guy sleep. He looked comfortable, but awkwardly so, like his body felt strange inhabiting the level of relaxation it currently lived in.

There was a knitted throw tossed over the armchair. Katy went to grab it and sort of dropped it over Scott's sleeping form. Just as she stepped back she noticed Wilford standing on the arm of the couch, fluffy white tail whooshing contemplatively.

"Heya Princey," she murmured.

Wilford turned his little snout towards the top of Scott's head and gave it a sniff. A small bubble of snot bloomed in front of one nostril.

"Yeah, man," Katy said. "What do you think?"

She waited to see what her cat would do. Wilford blinked very slowly and cocked his head from one side to the other. He reached out a hesitant paw – his *sneaky hand,* as Katy called it – and lightly batted the middle of Scott's forehead.

Scott scrunched his face, but didn't make much of a noise. This, apparently to Wilford this was the right answer to whatever question he was asking with his paws. He carefully stepped forward, pausing briefly right atop Scott's sleeping face before coming to curl up on his chest. Wilford wrapped himself up in the classic Croissant Position, but then raised his head slightly to stare at Katy.

"Oh," Katy said. "I didn't know that still applied when you do this to other people."

She stepped forward and gave her cat a soft scruff between the ears. She scratched under his little baby chin and gave his cheeks a single squeeze.

Wilford made a noise. Not any particular noise. Just a small, gruff sound.

Back at the computer she continued to casually cyberstalk Scott's sister. It got a lot easier once she found the webcomic this Tenzin had apparently been lovingly updating every week up until a few years ago.

Katy clicked through a few of the most recent pages and found a sort of semi-realistic, semi-cartoony style drenched in a pleasant 70s color scheme. It was cool. A little wordier than what Katy usually got into, but she could still see the appeal.

The account was made under the username *Pestobismal*. That got a chuckle out of Katy when she read it. She searched up the name on a whim and, much to her surprise and dismay, found that Tenzin was the type of person to make every account under the same name. And that meant *every* account, including a profile on Runescape that was last updated in 2009.

2009. Katy thought about Edgar asleep in her bed. At least, whoever this woman was, she had the sense to eventually stop playing Runescape.

There was a YouTube channel with a few videos. A limp handful of subscribers and less than fifty views a video – Tenzin was no influencer. Some of the thumbnails looked like home movies, and Katy recognized a few more videos to be of a young figure at a piano that she imagined must be Scott. Only his skin wasn't sickly and his smile was infinitely lighter.

He looked so young. Some of those videos showed him onstage, playing with a small band. Katy felt a little sick and too unnerved to watch any of them.

She did still want to snoop, though, and settled on clicking the newest video dated from the year before. It was in a studio of some kind, and there was a tall woman poised with her arms raised and her hands decked out in massive yellow gloves. A man was across from her, wearing those arm pads that Katy imagined were meant to be kicked and punched. But she didn't care about that guy, as she was far more interested in the figure he was facing.

Was that Tenzin?

Obviously that photo on her LinkedIn was taken of a girl maybe just entering college. So she was around Scott's age now. And when Scott said she was tall Katy partially assumed he meant in comparison to him. But she was definitely tall. Objectively tall.

Objectively tall and factually hot as fuck.

In the video Tenzin had bleached dreads tied up in a loose spiral that jutted out in fragments along the back of her head like a saw blade of hair. She was dressed in a t-shirt and athletic shorts, neither of which prompted attention. But the fit of the shirt allowed Katy to notice how broad and sculpted Tenzin's shoulders were, and the modest length of the shorts still allowed a clear view of her unbelievably strong legs.

This was a woman who could easily kick Katy's ass, no problem. She wasn't even show-off muscly either in the way some gym assholes tended to be. Tenzin was clearly trained for utility.

The younger Tenzin still watched Katy from her second monitor. Her eyes were deep and so brown that they turned the color into a challenge. Did the person with that body have those eyes? Even though dating was one of the last things on her mind these days, the thought made her chest throb.

Whatever. She was being stupid. Just because someone's kind of buff and has nice hair doesn't mean they're actually good at fighting.

To prove her own point, Katy played the five minute video on double speed, proving her indifference to the algorithm. There wasn't much to speak of at first. Tenzin would kick or punch without actually doing either, just practicing the technique. Sure. Once again – whatever. Then just before the last minute something changed.

The coach got the look on his face that straight men get before they do something that they think might be funny. And lo and behold, after one more move there was a flickering blur of movement that left the man writhing on the ground.

Katy leaned forward in her chair and scrolled back on the video, making some adjustments to watch it at regular speed. Then she could make out what happened. Apparently the man thought it would be a cool prank to do some kind of sneak attack and try and strike Tenzin with his elbow. With no other reaction than a slight deepening of her frown, Tenzin stepped back and slammed the coach in the face with her foot.

She kicked him. Foot to face. It was awesome and Katy watched that ten seconds maybe eight times before her phone began to buzz.

It was just past four AM. The sun would probably come up soon. The number on her phone was from an Oregon area code. Katy's eyes widened and she quickly minimized all the windows on her monitors, because for some reason her brain thought that would somehow lessen how creepy she was.

Since Edgar was in the bedroom and Scott was in the living room, and they both definitely needed to sleep, Katy ducked into the laundry room for privacy. So she sat between the dryer and the water heater, took a deep breath, and answered the phone.

"Hello?"

The voice on the other end was cold and fully awake. "Let him go."

Immediately the tone matched with the eyes and the body and the kick and the sudden electricity in Katy's chest. It was shouting without even the slightest raise of the voice. Katy struggled to remember how to speak, much less respond.

"Hi, Tenzin," she finally said.

"Let him go," Tenzin said again. "Call him a taxi to the Union Passenger Terminal right now or you will be spending the rest of your life evading the law."

"Uh, Scott's okay," Katy insisted, feigning calm. "I'm not...holding him hostage. Or anything."

"You know birthright is a protected class, right? And Oregon Penal Code states that it's a federal offense to murder a protected person."

"That's crazy," Katy tried to joke. "I thought murder was a crime for everyone."

The other end went silent. If Katy focused she could hear the sound of steady, leveled breathing. The breathing of someone so angry that it was now something different and even worse. Katy pulled her knees to her chest and thought about all the various branches of research she dug into over the past few days.

"I think you're thinking – well one, I imagine you misspoke. Because it's a weird situation," she took a deep breath and laughed softly. "There's a United States Code thing that works to penalize people who attack diplomats and anyone internationally protected. It's been brought up in a few cases when people were debating whether or not witch towns would stay company towns or get sovereign status. But even then it's really only a fine or a few years in prison," Katy half-scoffed. "Unless it's murder. Murder is still a crime, I think."

"Your name is Katy?" Tenzin asked.

Katy sucked in air because she was apparently still a teenage girl. "Yes," she said.

Tenzin didn't speak for a few moments. There was the sound of beeping on the other end of the phone. What could've been a voice on an intercom. It sounded like the ambiance of a hospital. Why would Tenzin be in a hospital?

"Listen to me, Katy," Tenzin said, both softer and even more intense. "I know your mind is telling you otherwise, but Scott does not want you. It doesn't matter what he said or what you interpreted – he does not want to touch you and he *does not* want you to touch him."

Something inside of Katy turned cold as she began to catch onto what Tenzin assumed was going on. This was not a very good first impression.

Tenzin continued. "Is he alive?"

"What -? *Yes,* Tenzin, I – I'm really not..." Katy's voice broke in her throat and she sighed, leaning her face against her fingertips.

"Where is he?"

"He's on my couch. He's asleep – fully clothed, I didn't – I'm gay, Tenzin, and I kind of assumed he was too. Gay or asexual or some degree of gender-something. But not a woman. He's told me that and I believed him was I not supposed to believe him?"

"Hey," Tenzin cut her off.

Katy did not consider herself a rambler. She also never thought she'd be in a position where she'd have to desperately convince another human being of her queerness. Katy was relieved to be stopped before listing the children's cartoon characters she was most fixated on growing up.

Tenzin sighed like someone having a way worse night than she was. "Please explain what's going on."

After some thought, Katy concluded it was best to keep things as surface level as possible for their first conversation.

"He showed up at my work last week and he's been hanging around ever since. We know – at least, we believe we have a sense of what's been going on, and we're just trying to help."

"Who's *we*?" Tenzin said.

"Me and Eddie," Katy responded without thinking. "Eddie's – another friend. He gave him a place to stay."

Tenzin made a noise that did not directly correspond to any specific emotion and somehow still stopped Katy immediately. The beeps and voices in the background across the proverbial phone line stopped with a whoosh, leaving only silence.

"Katy," she said after that.

"Yes?"

"I'm going to come to your home," Tenzin said. "I'm in Baton Rouge. Tell me where you live."

At first Katy had no problem saying her address. Then something changed. She knew she found Tenzin immediately attractive, yet it would be insane for Katy to let her libido override basic context. This situation was more nuanced than that.

Scott had plans in mind for in case he succumbed to Cassus, or whatever anyone else wanted to call what was trying to take him over. The way he described how to permanently blind himself was done so casually that Katy could imagine him saying it to anyone. He made it seem like this was something that could happen at any moment. How much did Tenzin know – or *think* she know?

"What will you do when you get here?" Katy asked.

"I'm going to fix this," Tenzin said. "For all of us."

Fear. That's all there was. Hot fear, burning, stinging, lemon-in-the-eyes fear. Katy was a ball on the floor, eyes wide and empty, every muscle tightened to the point of snapping.

Tenzin's voice returned. "Katy?"

Katy hung up the phone.

She found herself sitting on the chair in the living room, watching Scott sleep. He looked so peaceful. It made her think about how, even when he was presenting as smiling and happy, he was always a little bit on edge. If she considered the amount of time she spent with him so far, he was in a pretty good mood for most of it. At the same time, if she was brave enough to give him the right kind of hug, she was pretty sure he would break down into tears.

Not now. Now he was fine. He was cozy and resting, with Wilford standing guard on his chest ready to gobble up any bad dreams. Now he was safe.

Katy frowned. Now he would be safe.

Scott woke up midway into the morning. Katy was sitting with her back against the front door, scrolling on her phone through an online federated community she found for discourse and resources related to the Academy. On a whim she made a post describing what she gathered to be the circumstances of Edgar's last spell. She planned to consult the documents on her computer once Scott got up, but figured it wouldn't hurt to get insight from other practicing academics.

As he roused from sleep she was looking through the comments left on her thread that guessed the kind of incantation Edgar could've performed. The only specific she knew was that the sound Edgar made was longer, maybe two words, and that the focus was on what the Academy refereed to as the Indupero Point. Vainly, she hoped that could at least narrow things down. Maybe it did. It also definitely didn't.

"Is Edgar awake?" Scott called out in a bleary voice.

Katy raised her brow, eyes still on the screen. "Nope. Turned him on his side though – in case he pukes."

Sometime while he slept Wilford had relocated from Scott's upper chest to the empty space between his legs. That gave Scott the chance to sit up and look at Katy across the room without bothering the furry friend. She glanced up at her phone to see him take a hand and gently cup it along the back of Wilford neck, rubbing his thumb through the tresses of white fur.

"Hello, friend," he murmured.

She caught the gaze of her cat. He seemed confused, but mainly satisfied. A good pat is a good pat, after all. Katy went back to her phone, but Scott continued to talk. Not to her, she confirmed after another look – but apparently to the cat.

"You are probably the fluffiest cat I've ever seen," Scott softly remarked. "Your fur has some tangles, though. Are you old? You do seem very wise and noble."

Yes, Scott was having a full-on dialogue with Mister Wilford Brimley the Second. Usually Katy was the only one who ever wanted to do that. She peeked again – although her discretion made no sense as he wasn't paying attention to her. Wilford was hearing Scott, and arched up his head to stare at him. The curve of his tail and the angle of his ears expressed contentment. He carried himself the way he did after Katy treated him to a little morsel of cheese.

Scott scratched him just behind both ears at once. "Mister King," Scott cooed. "King of King and Lord of Lords."

"Isn't that Jesus?" Katy interrupted.

His eyes widened slightly. Then he smiled. "Yeah," he said. "Your cat is a classic Christ figure."

By now Wilford was fully melted in the fold of Scott's two arms. Scott held them practically nose-to-nose, whispering things that Katy couldn't quite hear. She just watched from a distance and thought about how much Scott knew about the Bible and how little he knew about the religions associated with it. A part of her considered asking that, if Wilford was Jesus, what did that make her?

Was she some combination of Mary and Joseph, archetypal parents and well-meaning sinners that Jesus still felt obliged to obey? Or was she God, Jesus's rightful father but also mainly regarded with submission on behalf of the son? She tried not to overthink it. Scott didn't talk about the Bible the way you do when you grew up going to mass in Boston once a week and for every major holiday. Where she saw a rigid structure for existence, he probably just saw another possibility that people came up with.

While Scott went in the other room, saying that he had to apply his testosterone gel, she decided to order takeout. Sleep was probably the better option, but that just wasn't going to happen. What also wasn't going to happen was for either of them to leave the house while Edgar was still asleep in Katy's bed. And he was still dead asleep – Katy checked on him and stood for long enough to see his face twitch mid-dream.

So she'd pay a little extra to get her breakfast sandwich delivered via smartphone. Scott was hesitant when she brought up getting food, then quickly changed his mind when she explained how maddeningly easy and contact-free the process would be. So in less than an hour, Katy found herself sitting beside Scott on her couch, eating breakfast together and watching the 90s Moomin anime. Courtesy and curiosity persuaded her to ask Scott what he would like to see, and despite apparently being able to see other human faces for the first time in a long time, Scott the Wizard decided he wanted to watch an old Japanese cartoon for toddlers.

He went on to stop her when she started to put on the dubbed version.

"Subs not dubs," he knowingly explained.

It was so weird to hear something like that being said by a person like him.

"It's the rule," Scott went on. "I'm not sure why. But that's what Tenzin told me and I believe her."

Katy heard the dry ice in Tenzin's voice, still smoking over the phone, and shivered. She kept her smile. She put on the right anime.

They ate in silence for a while. Katy tried to pay attention to the white squishy thing and his friends as they flew around on clouds, or whatever. It was immediately not that interesting. No, that wasn't right. It was interesting, as everything is with the right perspective, but its softness and quaint comfort made her feel uneasy.

She was getting old, and staying up all night without sleep now came with consequences. The main one being that she did not trust the chubby hippo freak talking on her screen.

"I wish this was happening under different circumstances," Scott said at one point.

He was staring fondly down at his sandwich, which he was savoring more than one would expect for the amount she paid for it. But his eyes were sad. He looked up at her, meeting her stare without hesitation, and once again Katy was awash in his faint blue glow.

It scared her at first. Then she realized that she didn't feel any different. There was an effect that couldn't be ignored. It felt like someone covered her mind with a thin sheet of tracing paper that they then used to trace an exact recreation of all her thoughts and feelings. Which is weird. But not really bad, and it wasn't enough to change anything.

"This is really nice," he said. "But I wish...Like, maybe we stayed overnight here because we caught up in conversation and fell asleep. And you and I got up first, but Edgar's fine and he's just sleeping in. And pretty soon he's going to wake up, and he'll complain we didn't order an extra sandwich for him...but then when he cooks something in your kitchen he'll still make enough to share."

Scott's stare turned dreamy. Faint fondness touched his lips, and he took a deep breath to exhale in a heavy sigh. With all of that, Katy was both startled and completely unsurprised. If there was any possibility left in her mind that he had some ulterior motive, that was gone and gone for good. Scott was a lonely mess in a bad situation who just needed a hot meal and someone to listen to him.

Out of the two of them it was Edgar with the most well-defined plan. What a novel concept – seemingly impossible. It's just that he swept Scott away so quickly, much to the confusion of everyone involved, that he must've known on some level that the man would fall for him in a matter of days.

"Extraction or Intrusion," Katy told him. "I asked some idiots online and people seem to agree those are the only two categories of spell he could've done."

"Oh."

Katy took a gulp of Redbull. "So he either took something out of your head or put something in. Does that sound..? I don't – fuck. Does that sound like anything?"

Scott looked like he knew the answer immediately but didn't want to put it into words. He bit into the last of his sandwich and chewed slowly, frowning into the carpet.

Something in the way he chewed actually managed to serve as an answer for Katy. And the answer was horrifying. Because Scott didn't seem worse than usual, and if Edgar imbued him with a positive sensation or insight thinking about it probably wouldn't upset him. Alternatively, there were only a few key things a new and potentially self-sacrificing lover like Edgar would think to take away.

"In extraction spells," Scott asked, "where does what you take go?"

He knew the answer. She knew the answer. Wilford, sitting on the windowsill and watching the cars, probably also knew.

"I still feel it," Scott closed his eyes hard and focused. "It's...fuck, it's *less,* but – he couldn't have taken all of it. I still..."

So it was settled. Edgar meets one nice guy and immediately goes and gets haunted for him. How sweet. How terrible. How terribly, terribly stupid.

"Well it's not all bad," Scott concluded, marginally cheerier. "Tenzin can help."

Once again, Katy tensed up. "What do you mean?"

Scott took the wrappers of their sandwiches and stood to throw them away. "Incantations are a language that takes years of practice, right? You have to get the pronunciation exactly right for the energy to be harnessed correctly. I can't do it. I imagine you can't," he nodded, clearly trying to convince himself more than Katy. "Tenzin can."

The person with a potential murder wish had the ability to practice magic? The kind you can control and actually use to attack, on top of being able to kick and punch far better than any of them combined? That didn't bode well at all.

"Are you close with your sister?" Katy began, even though the answer was obvious.

"Of course," Scott said. "She's the light of my life. Before recently I called her every day."

"Right. Right! And you told me that before recently you thought you were going to die."

Scott hummed softly. "Uh, no. I said I was *planning* on dying, because the alternative was going to be much worse."

Katy realized then that what she was thinking was not anything she'd heard anyone say aloud. Then she resigned herself to be the one to either shine a light on an unpleasant truth, or make themselves look like a total idiot.

"You're going to be – sort of – inhabited, right?" She said. "The entirety of Cassus is trying to take over your body."

She expected shock. There was none. If anything, Scott seemed pleasantly surprised. "Cassus," he repeated. "Is that the name you gave it?" he lowered his head slightly and let out a small laugh. "I mean, yes. Yes, that's what was going to happen."

"Why?" Katy said.

The feeling in Scott's expression thinned until it was near-translucent. "I'm a broken Lover's Bond, Katy," he spoke stiffly. "I'm very powerful."

While Scott's feelings were hard to carry at times, his lack of feeling was even more distressing. It only stayed like that for a short while longer, though, before he took a deep breath and smiled more genuinely.

"But it's okay!" He said, still tired but less nihilistic. "I don't know if I'm guaranteed a happy ending yet, but after meeting Edgar I'm pretty sure things aren't going to end up the way I thought. Plus, between the three of you I'm confident you can take care of it if things go South."

He crossed back to the side table where his coffee was and took a few small sips. Then he went to the window and stared out next to Wilford. It was a sweet sight, but it couldn't do more than float on the surface of a dark, bottomless pool of dread.

"You mean kill you?" Katy said.

Scott was unaffected by the question. "That'd be great, but you might not be able to. But if you could mutilate me to the point where I'm unable to use my powers, and then...imprison me, maybe? I don't know. Tenzin told me she has a plan."

Tenzin has a plan. Of course she had a plan. She was a human weapon who could definitely take a gust of pepper spray to the face and still bring all of them down, *and* she had a plan. Great.

"You don't care what happens to you," Katy observed. "Because it won't be *you* anymore."

"That's...I don't know," Scott turned his head slightly. "I hope not. But it doesn't matter. I'd rather be in pain forever than have a single person get hurt by my hand."

He looked back out the window. He raised a hand and grazed his fingers through Wilford's fur. The cat turned on the sill and gave the ball of his hand a soft bonk with his head.

Katy, weirdly enough, felt anger rise up in her chest. She put down her meal and reached to mute the little cartoon goblins on the television. In the silence, her distaste was fully present and stung acidic on the surface of her tongue.

"Do you think that's a cool thing to say?" She asked him.

Finally Scott looked at her. He was just as thrown aback by her tone as she was.

"It's not," she said, answering for him. "That's not healthy."

Scott looked as if he agreed. "I just meant that if I have to choose –"

"I'd prefer it if you chose to stay alive. That's an option too, isn't it?"

"Even if I manage to stay alive through this, I'll probably be in some degree of pain for the rest of my life."

"*No*," Katy heard the break in her voice and tried to calm down. "Not *everybody* has to hurt all the time."

"That's...not true, Katy."

His words were so calm that Katy was surprised how they could stop her spiral as immediately as they did. While one moment she was racing through feelings like a malfunctioning carousel, she was now suddenly still. She leaned back in her couch and sighed under her breath.

"Some of us have to live with pain," Scott said again. "Body pain. Mind pain.," he carefully approached Katy, smiling weakly. "It's just a thing that happens sometimes. Everyone has an individual outline that's meant to fit certain shapes and sizes of feeling. A pain that's small for me might be big for you, or it might also be small, but pointer. Does that make sense?"

Scott was sitting next to her again. He looked relaxed and comfortable, mainly concerned with Katy's feelings on on the whole conversation. And by now Katy was past being angry, especially knowing that her anger towards Scott was only half about the man beside her. Still, she wished he cared whether he lived or died.

"That's why I'm worried about Edgar," Scott continued, his calm sinking. "Because the pain I feel around – Cassus, I guess – it's a lot for me. It's unbearable. And he's clearly seen that and decided to help, but...I don't know if it's worth it."

"Can you do me a favor?"

"Of course."

Katy turned to him and took his hand. It looked dainty, but he had a strong grip and callouses across his fingers and the bottom of his palm.

"Imagine something with me," she said. "We somehow figure out a way to get rid of the hold Cassus has on you, On *both* of you. So you're fine, pretty much, for the rest of your natural life. You and Edgar just exist as a normal couple and you do whatever you want. What's the plan?"

As soon as she asked that she could tell that she was either posing a question Scott either had never considered, or never allowed himself to consider. He took a moment to collect himself. His process of thinking was so transparent that Katy could practically consider herself momentarily telepathic.

"Well...I would get to know him more," Scott said, words slow and deliberate. "We've only technically been on one official date."

"Where would you take him?" Katy prodded further.

Scott's smile was uncertain. It quivered with the tremor of a brewing daydream. "Maybe...a museum. Or a comic book shop?" He brightened slightly, "A park could be nice. With ice cream. Or – *ooh* – gelato. I like gelato."

Katy teetered on the verge of being slightly less upset. "And then what?"

"I imagine if we still like each other that we'd move in together. Officially, I mean," he paused, and then went on to add, "I'd get a job, I guess. I can repair pianos – I've worked with a lot of different varieties."

His voice was getting a little lighter. Not happy, but thoughtful – like he could see what he was thinking in his head. And that was good. Now they were getting somewhere.

"What would happen after that?" Katy asked.

By now Scott was so deep in thought that it must not have occurred to him to be embarrassed by her well-intentioned interrogation. He cocked his head to the side slightly and tapped each finger against his thumb.

"I don't know if Edgar knows about Sapling Ceremonies," Scott mused. "They might not be practiced outside of Bluerose. Even when I was a kid it was kind of outdated. But it still sounds romantic."

"Is that what birthrights do instead of marriage?" Katy said.

Scott remembered her beside him and caught her eye. He raised a brow, then huffed bemusedly. "Right, marriage. We could get married too."

Breathing was a little easier now. It was like a great weight that had settled over the entire room lifted slightly, and the negative space below could fill with a rush of fresh, cool air.

"I haven't gardened in a long time," Scott kept going. "I'm not a natural but I'm good if I study and I find it very peaceful. And if we have a garden Edgar could have all kinds of fresh herbs and produce whenever he wanted," he pulled his legs up and crossed them on the couch. "I also always thought it would be nice to volunteer at an animal shelter. I'm not grossed out easily or scared to get bitten so I feel like I could get pretty good at it. Plus I'd like to learn how to drive because walking around in bad weather sucks and I'm tired of public transportation."

Much to her relief, Katy realized she was smiling. "That's great, Scott," she said.

"And I'd get a keyboard," Scott quickly threw in. "And sometimes we'd gather everyone we love to come over to eat and make music together," he lingered in that, and finished with, "I want to learn ASL too."

"You do?" Katy said. "Why?"

Scott blinked hard. He laughed. "I don't know. That just popped into my head, I...I didn't know I wanted that."

They stared at each other. Scott's hair was down again, and it was an absolute mess. He brushed it after he showered last night, and already it was starting to tangle.

Katy kept her shear set in a black case under the bathroom sink. It was a nice set – nice for the time, at least – sheepishly gifted to her by her father on her first day of cosmetology school in Boston. After she moved she put it away, only pulling it out whenever Edgar or her current girlfriend at the time needed a haircut. By the looks of it, Scott was essentially a blank canvas. And though other things were far more important, Katy couldn't help but find that tempting.

"Have you thought about bangs?" She asked Scott.

Scott furrowed his brow a twinge. "Like – conceptually?"

"It looks like you pull up your hair a lot because it keeps it out of your face. Bangs would help."

"I – Sure, but..." he lowered his gaze and returned it far more discouraged. "It's also sort of a shield."

"From your eyes, right? The whole thing of it?"

Scott nodded. On the television the white goblin and his green hobo friend were hanging out on a bridge jamming to the harmonica. Great. Katy would love to meet the grown adult that developed from a childhood of this bullshit.

She brushed the hair from Scott's face and held it back with one hand. With the other she grabbed the back of his head and pushed it forehead until they were both forehead to forehead. Scott protested, but she was stronger. His eyes were wide and, after a moment, got even wider.

He whispered *no.* He whispered it until it turned into a pulsing hum that somehow expressed the same intent. Then the sounds fell to a trickle, and after that there was only silence. Scott stared at her and took in heavy, ragged breaths.

"I'm fine," Katy tried to not be audibly surprised by this. "I don't want to hurt you. I feel exactly like I did a few minutes ago."

"How?" Scott breathed. "I can see you –"

"You'd look good with bangs. You have the face shape for it. I know you like your long hair so I won't take off that much length, but I can get rid of the split ends and add a little bit of shape. It'd be really easy. Would you like that?"

Katy remembered they still had their faces essentially mushed together and pulled back slightly. Scott stayed upright exactly where he was, frozen with shock. Over time his breathing became steady and his eyes more aware.

He looked at her. He bowed his head in a single, solemn nod.

Scott was incredibly easy to maneuver, and he asked no questions as he was led into the bathroom and told to sit down on the folding stool she kept in the closet. She took a clean towel from the closet and asked him to hold up his hair while she wrapped it around his shoulders. By then Wilford realized what was going on and clocked in his for his job at the impromptu salon as a Professional Little Guy. He hopped onto the counter and filled up the sink with his fluff, his head slowly sinking into his own fur until he was nothing but an adorably-gurgling mass of hair.

"I wish I could pet him," Scott said from the stool. "Would he be upset if one of us pet him?"

Katy grabbed her supplies from under the sink, pausing to scrunch her fingers into his fluff. "He's never upset," she explained. "His only emotions are hungry and sleepy. And occasionally grumbly."

From behind her she heard him giggle affectionately. "He must be sleepy," he concluded.

She grinned as she stood with her basket and shear case. "Can you blame him? He's had a *long day.*"

Her shear set was well-kept and still slightly shiny, even after a decade of use. Katy was pleased to be someone Edgar felt comfortable geeking out with over knives, because he knew that she also understood the value of a quality blade. When they first met he came to work once after leveling his curls with street-grade kitchen scissors. Never again.

Scott immediately kept himself still in the way that people only do when they have their hair styled on a regular basis. That was also a surprise. Katy turned up the music and began to spray down his hair with water, nodding her head slightly to the thumping, RnB-styled bass of the K-Pop playing on Katy's phone.

His hair was coarse, thick, and slightly wavy. As Katy picked up sections to dampen them she noticed a slight red tint where there was otherwise just black.

In the mirror he could see his face and body was calm, but his eyes were closed. Then she remembered the glass in front of them.

"Oh shit," she said. "Sorry."

She turned him around and continued her work. But once he was facing her, occasionally locking eyes before nervously looking away, she couldn't help but notice how straight his nose was. His eyes were large and framed with eyelashes thick enough to swell her chest with bittersweet nostalgia.

Finally she had to ask. "Are you Greek?" She said.

Instantly Scott grinned proudly. "I am! Greek and Italian. A little Romanian too, I think. I'm surprised no one's brought it up yet."

Of course they haven't, Katy wanted to say. *You look like a page out a coloring book for someone with depression and two crayons. All your colors are wrong.*

"The first woman I ever dated was Greek," Katy said instead. "She had hair like yours. Lighter color, but a ton of it and it was thick as hell."

Scott's eyes went worried. "Will it be hard to cut?"

Katy flashed him a smirk. "I cut hers and I'll cut yours too."

She moved the stool so she could get behind him without risking him seeing whatever he saw in the mirror. Once she was there, hand palming the assortment of shears, she was faced with an entirely new kind of problem.

Her initial plan was to give Scott the most basic of haircuts. Just clean him up and get the hair out of his face. However, it was a very rare occasion for any hair stylist – lapsed or practicing – to come across this much healthy, virgin hair. Every strand read potential. The options of what Katy could do to his head were nearly limitless.

"What is it?" Scott asked, breaking her from her thoughts.

"Huh?"

"You're making a noise. Like – a groan of some kind."

"Oh," Katy said. "It's nothing," then, deciding to be honest. "I want to give you layers."

A beat of silence. "Why?"

"It'll be cute," Katy said.

More silence. Then, "Okay."

Katy scowled and leaned her head over Scott's shoulder to look him in the face. "I don't think you realize what I'm saying. This is a big proposition."

"I know what layers are," he said. "I trust you."

Unconvinced, she pulled out her phone and frantically opened an image search to zero in on the exact style she would want to go for. Not a wolf cut, that was way too mullet-y and closer to butch than she imaged Scott would want. Katy wanted shape, wanted Scott to want to want shape, and knew in the core of her being that would be best accomplished by a layered haircut.

"Something low-maintenance," she said to herself, even though Scott couldn't hear the first half of her thought. "You don't really have to put anything in it to make it look styled."

"That would be nice," Scott said. "I play with my hair too much to use hair products."

With social media now haircut trends surfaced by the week instead of the season. It was so exhausting Katy eventually had to stop trying to keep up. It's not like she had any reason to keep her feelers out before, since she found a haircut she liked for herself when she moved to the South and hadn't changed since.

Finally she found it – a model online who sported a long, slightly-feathered mane of arching layers that gave a naturally windswept style. It was *perfect*. Katy showed the picture to Scott and he laughed as if in disbelief.

"Wow," he said.

"Do you like it?"

"I mean, she's beautiful. But I'm not sure if I can really pull that off."

Katy's instinct was to hype him up. That was her favorite part of working back when she was able to work. Even now she could perfectly recall that moment where a client's face shifted from hesitation to determination. The exact pinpoint where they decide they're going to take a risk to make them feel better about themselves.

But Scott wasn't like most people. He said he lost his face at twenty-one, which meant by now he only had a memory of what he *used* to look like a decade ago – if anything. That meant he needed confidence more than any client she'd ever had, but for this to work Katy would need to change her strategy.

"She essentially has what I have right now," Katy pointed out the details on the screen as she spoke. "See? My hair's shorter, and you'd have bangs, but they both have long layers and a general floofy thing."

"Do you like it?"

Katy gave her head a shake and Scott cracked a small smile. "I love it," she said. "It's really fun. I like that it's got a kind of 70's glam thing, so it's simultaneously retro and current. It's kind of annoying to grow out if I decide to grow it out, but it also lasts a long time so I don't have to touch it up that often."

The look on his face was one she'd seen a dozen times before.

"It makes me feel pretty," she added, which was something she rarely admitted even in her head. "Really...soft."

She could tell that rang out sharp inside Scott. He lowered his gaze and briefly examined the phone. Then he took a deep breath.

"Okay," he said. "I'm ready."

"You sure?"

Scott looked at her – unsmiling, yet not unfriendly. "I trust you, Katy," he told her a second time.

That's the entire thing, isn't it? Hair is one of the only thing being can be assured to have control over, and even then it isn't a guarantee. And when it is, it's through the hand of an outside party. People care about their hair, no matter what they may say otherwise. From the regular community college dropout to the magical vagabond, everybody wants to look nice. They want to look what they consider to be nice, even if that standard only applies to them.

Usually Katy's texturing shears felt like small, silver scissors. Today they were a Sword of Sharpness Katy was tasked to wield in order to empower a damsel in distress.

She paused. Something still wasn't right.

Katy took her phone off the counter and opened her music player. After a few taps, the voice of South Korea's Little Sister was replaced by a super secret playlist dubbed only as KATY JAMZ.

It started with "Say It Aint So" by Weezer. The playlist was mostly Weezer. That's why she kept it a secret.

She put aside her phone again, picked up her shears, and began to cut. Rivers Cuomo on the speaker of her smartphone edged towards his dirty, dirty chorus, filling the small bathroom with the grit of guitars as

Katy refilled Edgar's mug with a few more loose glugs of whiskey. He stretched his back on the stool and groaned softly.

"You're going to kill me," he muttered.

She laughed and went back to her shears. "At least you'll go out looking good."

It was the first time Edgar had been over to her apartment, and she lasted almost a full half-hour before finally relenting and demanding she give him a haircut. She just couldn't take it anymore. The man worked in food service, he couldn't just be walking around with visible knots in his curls that she could pluck out like loose eyelashes.

This wasn't the first time she offered. But all the other times she did before they were both sober and at work. This time they were well buzzed. This time Katy didn't so much as "offer" as much as she let Edgar know that she was going to use sharp objects to make him look less he needed to be rescued by FEMA.

"Why do you have so many scissors?" Edgar asked as she snipped the tangles from his hair.

"I'm a hairstylist," Katy answered without thinking. "I cut hair."

"I thought you waited tables."

She paused, scissors mid-slice through a lock of red. Katy snipped the rest of the way, reached with her free hand, and knocked back the rest of her own mug of liquor.

"Ah," Edgar observed, drunkenly knowing. "I get it."

Katy scoffed. "Do you, now?"

"Yeah. You're a fuckup."

Katy froze. Something in her went thick like cement and she no loner had the capacity to control her muscles. All she could do was stare down at the tiles on the bathroom floor, which were now littered with little curves of red hair. Wilford watched her from the counter top and smacked his jaw, more concerned with the remnants from his bowl of tuna rather than Katy's emotional distress.

She could hear her mother's voice in her head. She wasn't saying what Edgar just said. No, she was gently assuring Katy that it's okay to fail. Everyone has limits, and there are some things we just don't have the capability to achieve. If you don't have the talent, you just don't have the talent.

Edgar was too drunk to be aware of anything that was going on behind him. "It's okay," he slurred. "I'm a fuckup too. Maybe that's why I like you so much."

He didn't mean to say something hurtful. Edgar was drunk on fried chicken, greasy waffle fries, and more alcohol than someone who isn't her would be capable of handling gracefully. It didn't matter how his comment made her feel. All that mattered was that she took care of his hair.

Once she was satisfied with her work the psychological bile in her mouth was old and no longer corrosive. Katy swallowed it back with another drink of whiskey straight off the bottle and pulled Edgar up to face the mirror.

She saw his face turn from woozy vagueness to surprise as soon as he saw his own reflection. He touched a curl that hung down against his ear.

"You kept my curls," he remarked in a voice soft with astonishment.

Katy frowned. "Of course I did. What'd you expect me to do, shave your head? All you needed was a trim."

He blinked. Then he blinked again. Then he closed his eyes hard, and when he opened them they were glassy and even more bloodshot.

"Uh," Edgar wiped at his face, laughing under his breath. "Sorry. Thank you. I'm sorry."

Tears were Katy's Achilles heel. Sadness, despair, anger – any dark and unpleasant emotion was something she could handle without a prob-

lem. But as soon as a person got all flushed and weepy she was just plain out of strategies.

She put her shears aside, staring anywhere but at the crying man shuddering next to her.

"I'll, uh," she cleared her throat and grabbed the bottle of liquor. "I'll just put this back."

For someone who hadn't practiced a shag haircut on a real life human being before, Katy was happy to see that she did a pretty good job. Scott's hair went from a singular current of doll-like plastic strands to an actual style with shape and variety. She peeked in front of him to adjust the strands on the fringe bang that now framed just above his eyebrows.

He watched her closely. "How does it look?" He asked, sharply anticipating.

Katy nodded approvingly. "You look so fucking cool."

Scott's eyes lit up at that comment, but the rest of his face only sank deeper into dread. He lowered his head and shrugged off the towel wrapped around him.

"Katy," he said. "You should probably step out for a second."

Did he hate it? Already he was touching the ends of his hair. Lightly palming over the front, perhaps to feel the smoothness of it all. It didn't seem like he hated it. Katy noticed his eyes drift reluctantly to the side, his head angling slightly as if considering what awaited him just behind his back.

By then she got what he was thinking. And as soon as she did Scott knew she did too.

"I want to see," he told her.

He may as well have told her that her search history got leaked online. Or that Wilford got hit by a car. Or that he had a fatal disease and was an hour past his predicted death date. Some sort of insurmountable, tragic news a little more groundbreaking than wanting to look into a mirror.

Every cell in his body was alight with fear, yet Scott stayed upright and confident. In fact, his back was a little straighter and his chin raised straight. He didn't cry and it was clear he wasn't going to. In the worst of terror he was somehow braver than he ever had been so far.

Katy leaned slightly against the door of her shower. "All right," she said. "Then let's see."

Scott stood up. He brushed his fingers across his face and realized that there was nothing there anymore for him to move, and there wouldn't be for a long time. Still, he did not smile. He looked at Katy in a way that told her that he wasn't sure about this and he didn't think she should be either. Yet he didn't force her to leave.

She told herself to keep cool and calm, and not to betray the anxiety that ate her up inside. It's hard enough for that split second before a client sees their haircut without also worrying about what might happen when they come face to face with themselves.

Time went still. The warm air blowing from the vents above the door screamed like an air horn. Scott turned around and looked in the mirror.

At first nothing happened. He didn't move, and Katy didn't move, so only Wilford had the nerve to shift his limbs within the confines of the sink, Scott just stood and stared, keeping his gaze steady and unblinking for a solid thirty seconds. Katy searched his eye line from body to reflection in an attempt to somehow discern some aspect of what he could be seeing.

She became fairly certain after some time that he was looking into his own eyes.

Then he began to move. He twitched his hand and raised it, traveling to let the fingers hover just above the skin of his cheek. The hand moved back, then forward again, and then finally touched his face.

Katy never thought she would find the sight of a man slowly and confusedly feeling out the confines of his own face to be so enrapturing.

"What are you seeing?" She whispered, because that's as loud as she felt she could be right then.

Scott frowned. The frown stiffened before shifting back into nothing. "Is this...me?"

"It could be."

"I got old," he got a little closer to the glass. "I'm so – I'm like *gray*. I look sick. When did that happen?"

Katy had no idea what to say to that. Because of that, she chose to stay silent. She stayed back and watched Scott as he continued to examine himself, stuck in a stutter between surprise and distaste. Whatever he was seeing, he didn't look too pleased with it. Not exactly disgusted – just confused. Which made sense. If Katy got the chance to meet herself from ten years ago, her younger self would also struggle to process the current state of things.

"Edgar's got weird tastes," he muttered, perhaps just to himself.

Well that was quite enough of that.

"Hey," Katy stepped in, physically worming her way into the identity crisis of the century. "You don't look bad."

"I've lost so much weight. I had no idea it got this bad. It's *awful* – I look like a ghoul, Katy."

"*No.* I know ghouls. You don't have sharp teeth and your flesh isn't rotting, so don't say that."

Scott shot her mirror self a puzzled look that she recognized immediately as the type of look Edgar has given her so many times before. Same boyishly furrowed brow, identical glimmer of dissatisfaction in the eyes. It was weird how uncanny it was, but because she was used to it Katy had no problem navigating the reaction.

She took his chin in her hand and turned it so they both faced the mirror. Scott allowed this with heavy resignation, and soon he was staring at himself again, and Katy was staring at him too.

Her first instinct was to comment on his eyes. That obviously wouldn't work. After what he'd been through, Scott could probably go the rest of his life without hearing anything good about his big, blue eyes. So she decided to take a different approach.

"You got a good face," she said. "Yeah you're a little malnourished, but it's a nice rounded bone structure. Once you gain back some weight it'll definitely soften up your features," she took a finger of her other hand and poked the apple of Scott's cheek. "Your cheekbones are higher than mine are, you fucker."

Scott pressed his lips tight. "Sorry?"

"Sonia – that's my first girlfriend – she had the same shape nose that you do."

"It's so weird," Scott lamented, running his index finger and thumb down either side of his nose. "All the other noses I've seen are regular-sized and curved, and this is just..." he flicked his finger down from bridge to tip. "*Bam.* Nose."

"Well first off – stop with the concept of *regular* anything when it comes to the human face. There's no gold standard here. And if you want other people to accept that you like looking at them, you'll have to deal with the fact that they like looking at you," she gave the tip of his nose a poke. "Plus, you sounded real proud to be Greek. You got the type of face of someone – fucking, like – Odysseus would hang with."

The smallest quirk of his lips in the right direction was enough to melt the freeze that Katy didn't even notice had taken over the small space. "Odysseus, huh?"

"It's the first Greek guy I could think of. Well, it was actually Zeus, but I had a feeling you wouldn't want me to compare you to him."

"He's not great," Scott agreed. "Most of the gods aren't. Except for – Hestia, maybe? I don't know."

Of course this would be the type of person with opinions on Greek mythology. Katy stifled a laugh as Scott looked back at his reflection, this time with far more kindness. He touched his nose, and then his cheeks.

"The T's definitely doing something," he said. "I don't look *manly*, but I do look like a man. Which I'd honestly prefer."

"You're a funky soft guy."

His eyes went to Katy. He narrowed them, then smiled. "I *am* a funky soft guy," he softly agreed.

To say a weight was lifted would be foolish. Scott stepping back from the void of insecurity for the moment was like a moon crossing past the sun and allowing everyone in the world to remember the concept of light all at once.

He ran a hand through his hair and gave his head a small shake. Once the blur of black settled, it revealed that Scott was smiling. Without saying a word he focused that smile onto Katy, and without needing to respond Katy understood that this was the greatest praise she had ever received in her life so far.

The rest of the day was rainy and dripped, slow and steady. Every so often Katy would check in on Edgar, mainly not going closer than standing in the doorway of her own bedroom. Or Scott would excuse himself to crawl into her bed beside the man and tell him things Katy couldn't make out from the couch, but understood she was not meant to hear. Otherwise the two of them mainly just watched the TV.

She made Scott pick something that wasn't a children's cartoon, just to see what he would pick. He ended up choosing Lars Von Trier's *Dancer in the Dark,* because he said Bjork was his favorite musician when he was a kid.

Midway into the saddest movie Katy ever witnessed, she turned and stared him down from the edge of the couch. "Are all birthrights weird, or are *you* just *really* weird?" She asked.

"It's hard to say," Scott concluded, calmly crying with a hand buried in the depths of Wilford's tummy.

When Katy was a kid she liked to listen to Christian rock. Her favorite movie was *The Rescuers,* unless there were no authority figures around in which case it was actually *Xanadu.* Apparently Scott spent his childhood enjoying movies that started with a poor immigrant woman slowly going blind and somehow managed to get *way more depressing.*

"Everything you like is either overwhelmingly sentimental or devastatingly sad," she pointed out as the credits rolled over Bjork's discordant wailing. "Don't you have anything normal that you're interested in?"

Scott wasn't offended by the question. He also definitely didn't understand it. He wiped the rest of his tears and smiled wryly. "So there's a gold standard for normal now?" He joked.

"Yes, actually. Something that doesn't make you feel any strong emotion."

"Is that –?" Scott was trying hard to imagine what she was proposing and couldn't get quite there. "I don't do that, really."

Now it was Katy's turn to not understand. "What do you mean?" She said.

"Everything results in an emotion or reaction. Most of those are pretty powerful, I find," just saying that made Scott tired. "I know that's not...well, I don't know what it's *not*, but it's just how I live."

He took a bite of salad from their second round of takeout. His chewing was thoughtful, and by the time he swallowed he was past guilty and now genuinely curious. "What makes you feel normal?"

Outdated business franchises. Escape rooms. Tapas. Jazz. Elevators. Self-driving cars. Most Western historical landmarks. All appetizers other than potato skins.

"It's..." Katy, now, felt a little embarrassed to share just how much she was indifferent towards. "It's different for everyone."

Scott thought about that very carefully. He closed his eyes to think even deeper. Then, after some time, he finally spoke. "You know what makes me feel normal?" He asked.

"What?"

"Moss."

"Okay."

Scott sighed. "I lied," he said. "I think about the kind of moss we had in Bluerose all the time. It's important and so beautiful and it makes me want to cry sometimes."

Katy pressed her lips into a line. She sipped at the glass of water Scott peer-pressured her into drinking and tried not to get too parental. "You must be tired," she remarked.

"Constantly. All the time. I don't know how I'm still able to function most days."

She laughed, and he joined. But the sound faded quickly, and once it was gone nothing took its place.

For some time after that nothing really happened. Scott shifted uncomfortably, and since Katy also didn't feel equipped to push the issue further she decided to change her approach slightly. So she pulled out her phone and flipped through her phone.

"I like you, Scott," she said, opening up her library of torrented movies.

Somehow she could feel the cozy warmth of Scott's happiness, even though she wasn't looking anywhere near him. "I like you too, Katy," he responded cheerily.

A soft twinge of uncertain vulnerability. "Yeah," she said. "So I'm going to do something I've never done for another human being before outside of my immediate family."

"Oh you don't – you don't have to."

"Yes I do," Katy pulled up a file and hovered a finger over the button on her phone that would cast it to her television. "I'm going to show you the one movie that has made me cry every time I've watched it."

She started the movie as soon as she said that, so neither of them had the opportunity to stop her. The name of the file appeared on the screen before it started, prompting Scott to gasp in delight.

"Oh, *The Muppet Movie!*" He said. "I love that one."

Katy recoiled in self-loathing. "Just watch."

"Who's your favorite?" After no response Scott smiled, pleased. "Mine's Gonzo."

She tried to explain his justifiable mistake when the movie started. As the opening scene played Scott enthusiasm didn't lessen as much as evolve as he realized he was watching something he had not seen before. His focus deepened and he leaned forward, causing Wilford to grumble from his spot in Scott's lap.

"Is this..?" He began.

"It's the reboot," Katy reluctantly finished.

Scott didn't give that confession the disgust it deserved. He just stared back at the movie as it opened and relaxed into the couch, grazing his fingers between Wilford's ears.

He sighed in relaxation. "I hope Gonzo's in this one," he declared to no one in particular.

Her daybed was bigger than the couch in Edgar's apartment, and yet she and Scott still sat close enough to be near physically touching. Katy was starting to scoot to one side of the couch when Scott made one small adjustment and settled his head lightly against the curve of her shoulder.

She thought about her sister Leanne. Before she got all bold, tough-skinned like a quality piece of leather, she was far too sensitive to grow up in a neighborhood like theirs. For some time she refused to speak to other kids, teachers, and barely their own parents. But every day after school she would come home and sit close next to Katy, just leaning against her and quietly whispering the events of her dreams.

Katy worked up to propping her head up against Scott's. It felt weird. It felt good. Her sister used to try and call her, but the average person only had so many tries in them before they wound up scooped out and empty. That was okay, though. She kept a close enough eye on Leanne's social media profiles to know she was alive and having a good time.

That's what mattered.

She yawned. What would come first – sleep or tears? Only time would tell.

Etude no. 3

Two men lie together in a bed that does not belong to either of them, in an apartment they should not have spent this much time in. One of them is awake and aware. One is beyond asleep, both there and somewhere else.

"Katy cut my hair," the Other says.

They are both on their side, facing each other. The First's eyes are shut. They twitch occasionally, reflecting an echo of whatever is happening where he is. His arms and legs are drawn slightly to his chest. When the other man braves to touch the First's temple it's hot with fever.

"You shouldn't have done this, Edgar."

He says that softer – not because he doesn't mean it, but because he doesn't want the First to hear it wherever he is. The Other unlaces the First's fingers from each other and takes them in his own. Their blindingly hot and twitching against his knuckles, but he doesn't mind.

"I'll take care of us," he says. "No matter what happens, I'll fix it. For everyone."

Part of him hopes for an answer. The rest understands that to be unreasonable and impossible. The Other settles for pressing the first man's hands to his chest, allowing the thump of his heartbeat to reverberate through him.

The other concentrates, hoping he can send a message to the other place where the First now inhabits.

Come home, Orpheus, he pleads.

After some time the Other drifts into an uneasy sleep. It is dreamless and semi-weighed, and in the depths he hopes to fall as far out of orbit as his First is. That Other Place with Cassus, or the Witch Eater, or whatever anyone who didn't truly understand chose to call it, was so frightening and forever. The First shouldn't face it as one body where there should be two. But as much as he wills himself to scatter, the Other remains reluctantly grounded in reality.

That is, until a tired voice wakes him up.

"Scott?" The First whispers hoarsely.

The Other forces himself awake and opens his eyes to stare at the figure across from him. The First looks bleary-eyed and slicked with sweat, but he is awake. He is awake and he is alive, and the Other can almost hear the earth welcoming him back in a tearful embrace.

"I'm..." the First sputters, trying hard to swallow. "I want barbecue," he said. "I'm so hungry."

"Yeah, I – I'll tell Katy."

He tries to move, but the First tightens his grip on his hand and holds him down. "Wait," he says.

"What?"

"Just...just wait."

It had been almost two days since the First ate or drank anything. If this wasn't a magic-related stupor he would be weak enough to warrant going to the hospital. In a strange irony, Cassus pulling the Other close allowed it to torture him indefinitely while his body stayed relatively sustained. He imagined the same must apply to the First.

He pulled his hand out of the First's tight grip and touched his cheek. The scruff was a little scruffier. He was still wearing the same clothes he had on when they brought him here from the Den and it made the whole room smell of sick and sweat and stale alcohol.

The First was a shaking, sweaty, confused mess. He was also the bravest, most heroic person the Other had ever seen.

"I get it now," the First tried to say, stammering slightly. "I understand, I..."

He didn't finish what he meant to say when the Other leaned forward and pressed their lips together. It was a long kiss, backed with the careful intent to tether and contain what was previously a vague cloud of human atoms in an ever-expansive void. The Other pulled back, gazing at his bond with tears of relief in his eyes.

"It's okay," he whispered. "Just rest now."

Seventh Movement

arah Tenzin Onyilogwu had not slept since she touched down in
Baton Rouge.

It wasn't like she was fighting off the desire with caffeine and constant movement. If you gave her meletonin, warm milk, soft ambient background noise and a perfectly dark room she would spend a solid eight hours unable to close her eyes for longer than a sustained blink. She would not sleep – of course not. More than that, though, was that Tenzin could. Not. Sleep.

That's how she knew Scott had to still be alive. They tested the range of their Knight's Bond early on. If they were kids and one of them was put in immediate danger, they could only help from as far back as they could safely run. Now, as adults, the distance they could stray while still being able to save the proverbial day was considerably greater – for Tenzin at least. It was just hard to say by how much.

She knew the feeling, though. It was like when you're not quite asleep and you can tell someone is watching you. Something more than intuition but less solid than a physical pull on the arm. By the weight of the sensation she knew he wasn't too close, but if Tenzin could feel it they still had a chance.

At first when Scott didn't answer his phone Tenzin was mainly only unsettled. Given the waver in his sobs the last time they spoke it wasn't a good sign, but lingering optimism reminded her that Scott was awful at technology and often forgot to charge his outdated Motorola. Or he would charge it, but accidentally end the call instead of answering it and feel too guilty to call back immediately. There were other possibilities, she told herself, besides the worst case scenario.

Then she still couldn't reach him at the airport in Louisiana, or once she got her rental car at the lot across the street. Tenzin sat in a spot at the nearby drive-in for a long time, staring blandly at the fancy stereo system she specifically requested in the otherwise bland hybrid she picked out. The silence was only matched in acidity by the burning sting of every vein in her body being twisted all at once.

Something was very, very wrong.

If he was *gone*-gone, she would absolutely know it. So the only options were that he was *here*-gone and wrecking havoc in some neighboring town, or he was just plain still here and somehow ended up *somewhere else*. Tenzin mechanically deposited chicken nuggets into her mouth and ran though the possibilities.

From their daily phone calls, it sounded like Scott was experiencing the same thing that was currently happening to their mother. But Tenzin couldn't say that without taking the Jenga tower of the last ten years and knocking into it, full force, with the entirety of her body weight. And these are all things she refused to throw onto Scott unless she was there in person to help bare the weight.

But that didn't mean she couldn't make theories. She brought her laptop with her, just in case there was an opportunity to pull out the many diagrams and graphs she developed over a frustrating amount of fragmented research. See, birthrights don't make a habit of recording a majority of their culture and practices. Theirs is an oral tradition taught face to face and left to either continue or fall into obscurity.

Academics do the data. If you want to know virtually anything about the Academy, it's history, or what they believe to be the definitive language of magic, there's a book to condescend to you. Unfortunately, Academics have an almost propaganda-like view of birthrights, turning any information on them into stories so inaccurate that Tenzin on multiple occasions thought they might've mistaken her brother for some kind of goblin.

So she asked around in Bluerose. She contacted the elders of other witch towns and asked them her questions too. Birthrights will tell you what they think they know, stressing that they only *think* they know it, because who are they to claim to be sure of anything with certainty? That was a different, less severe degree of frustrating, but through them she was able to get a few other case studies relating to what she was looking for.

Birthright magic, once controlled, is mild. And they all make a point to control it, that's just a part of the culture. And these mild abilities are done through a buffer that helps explain the effect to an extent and make it more palatable to civilians. However, if that same ability is abused without a buffer, it can potentiality revert to an inflamed state similar to that of early childhood.

A person who could sense intentions in those they interact with may fall into a state of near-constant telepathic exhaustion. Someone who can manipulate cells to heal small cuts and bruises might accidentally end up creating tumors in the people they try to help. Scott, or a birthright with Scott's diagnosis, could potentially go from projecting emotions to controlling far more than that. Potentially without even realizing it.

These were just theories at the moment. Maybe that's all they would ever be. When talking about birthright magic, even someone with the civilian equivalent of authority will always prefer to live in a perpetual shrug. She liked Scott because Scott was open to facts.

It's just that, as far as he knew, one of those facts was that his magic came from his coloboma.

Tenzin thought about the kinds of things he must be able to do now. She tried not to imagine him held captive in some basement or secluded bedroom. It didn't work. Music would help distract her, but that would break her vow to herself, so instead she just sat in silence and thought her bad thoughts.

Day and night switched positions as Tenzin drove silently throughout the streets of Baton Rouge. While their mother was seeing her off she made a quiet comment about how it might be nice to see a new city. It wasn't. Baton Rouge was awful. Everything was awful and *everyone* was awful, and all she wanted to do was find her brother and bring him home.

After her phone call with Katy Delaney ended prematurely, Tenzin was finally sinking into the sea of worst-case scenarios. Her brother, overpowered. Her mind, forced to destroy until he was saved.

She stared down at the pale scar on her wrist and touched a finger to it. *Calm,* she told herself. *Calm, calm, calm.*

If Tenzin were to drive the few hours between Lafayette and New Orleans, she could potentially pinpoint Scott's exact location based solely on the compass of their bond. That was its primary purpose, after all. She knew she couldn't do that, though. Because the closer she got to Scott the stronger the feeling inside her would become. It wouldn't be long until it would be *her* inside the sensation, instead of the other way around.

The thought of waiting any longer to get her brother out of there was painful. Physically painful, like needles under every nail. But if she left to save him now, in the state she was in, her body would end up a murderer. And that wouldn't be good for anyone.

Tracking the path to New Orleans Tenzin noticed a spot on the map called Prehistoric Park, located in the drive-through town of Henderson. It was almost sunrise and the attraction was closed for the next week. Be that as it may, with the circumstances of the given situation it was possible that a visit would do her good. When she and mom drove cross-country from New England to Oregon after leaving her father, they stopped to study many strange roadside attractions. It would be nice to remember that kind of thing, so she got in her car and pulled off.

The clear joke about Prehistoric Park as soon as you walk up to the gates was the Jurassic Park reference. She stood at the foot of the massive fence that would definitely, totally, absolutely keep out a dinosaur if a real one roamed inside.

She approached the thick wooden door. After palming the surface, which was sticky with cobwebs and the other consequences of being a place frequented mostly by children, Tenzin located the vague direction of the lock and hatch. She loosened her shoulders, closed her eyes, and centered the tip of her index finger in what she told herself was the right direction.

"Unlock, please," she intoned.

There was a definite click. Tenzin opened her eyes at the noise and managed a small, brief smile, growing only more satisfied when the door squeaked open as she pushed it. She stepped inside and made a point to close and latch the lock behind her. This would only be seen as an employee slip-up when they next open the space. More mischief than outright crime.

The trees were a little too tall and the air smelled wrong. Still, staring out at the woodland path in the dark reminded her of home just enough to strike Tenzin nauseous with dizzying homesickness. Back home in Bluerose it wasn't the point in the day where most people would bother getting out of bed. By now, though, the time could be considered early morning rather than very late at night. And besides, these days their mother's sleep schedule was erratic to the point where Tenzin could reach out at virtually any hour and have a chance for her to be up and reading somewhere in the house.

So she found a bench that faced a long-necked monolith and called home. Sure enough, Regina Mustard Kaufner picked up immediately.

Tenzin didn't speak. Mustard didn't either. When Scott left he took a majority of the words with him.

"I'm trespassing," Tenzin said, even though this was the first time she'd called in days and their mother probably wasn't expecting to hear that of all things.

"Okay," Mustard said. "Where?"

"It's a dinosaur park," she realized as soon as she said this that Mustard probably wouldn't know what that was. "That's a –"

"Park with dinosaurs. Fake ones," Mustard paused and said it again. "Fake ones?"

"Fake ones, yeah," Tenzin confirmed.

"All right. Good. Thank you."

The silence was not strained. Tenzin cherished her silences with her mother more than most anything else in her life. It was like being tucked into bed just firmly enough to feel safe and seen, even over the phone. She breathed deep and managed to take a single step away from the Murder Pit in her mind.

"What did you have for dinner?" She asked.

Mustard hummed softly. "They made pasta in the Mess Hall. Manacotti."

Tenzin smiled, relieved. Mustard found out about Tenzin's personal Lent-esc lifestyle change that occurred after Scott left and decided she would join by giving up food. She stopped eating entirely for three days before Tenzin feigned enough support to get Mustard to share news of her new commitment with Head Elder Noriko. Nori listened calmly and politely, then requested for Mustard to help her tend to Scott's old garden in the backyard. When the two of them got back the plan was now adjusted to incorporate two small meals, as well as water and juice throughout the day.

Everyone in Bluerose respected Nori, because Nori respected everyone in Bluerose. But as Tenzin packed to either bring Scott home to die or retrieve his dead body, she was fully prepared for their mother to snap completely. She confided that fear to Nori – because Tenzin also looked up to her guidance and insight – and she assured Tenzin that they would all do everything in their powers to keep Mustard healthy.

Manicotti is a fairly time consuming recipe, especially considering the volume of people the Mess Hall cooked for each night. So either Chef Renja made a ridiculous amount of stuffed pasta shells, or she was informed they were one of Mustard's favorite meals and spent extra effort just to make sure she ate.

"What are you going to do today?" Tenzin continued, leaning back to watch the bruised sky as it healed into morning.

"Nico from the Center is coming over for breakfast," Mustard said. "He has a few cases he wants my input on."

"Oh."

Tenzin frowned lightly. Despite how she still introduced him like a new acquaintance, Nico was a close family friend who had essentially acted as their main uncle figure for the whole of Tenzin's life. He was once Mustard's boss, back when she was a social worker for Bluerose. All of that stopped once Scott was born, Tenzin was told, but that didn't mean he couldn't use old tricks for a new distraction.

Or it could be added stress. The cases Bluerose handled weren't any less bleak than what was already happening – just more plausible.

"It makes me feel good," Mustard continued. "I would appreciate feeling useful in a way that I'm capable of. I imagine he knows that," she breathed in a way that wasn't a sigh to anyone else but Tenzin. "He's bringing donuts. From Sunny's."

Tenzin's heart ached terribly. She remembered the mornings when their mother would pile them in that massive convertible and make the drive to the dingy doughnut shop the next town over. The man who worked behind the counter would call Scott "boss" and her brother would revel in delight. He'd give Tenzin an extra doughnut hole if she could tell him a historical fact.

They stopped going there years ago. And now, with the state of their mother, it was physically painful for her to leave Bluerose at all.

But birthrights take care of each other. They take care of people, even when they struggle to take care of themselves. That's as much of a certainty as the dinosaur statue looming in front of her probably having a lot of penises and swear words carved onto the legs.

"Have you been eating, Tenzin?"

She blinked back into the present moment and stiffened. When was the last time she'd eaten?

There were the nuggets. That was when she got off her flight. That was practically a week ago.

"I don't think I can die," she murmured, almost as if in her own defense. "I mean – I will eventually, I guess. But I don't think the bond will allow me to pass out or die until I make sure he's safe."

Mustard was silent for some time after that. Usually when Tenzin made an observation about magic to her she let it pass with little remark in the positive or negative. This time, she retorted with something very close to frustration.

"You've mixed the order," she said.

"What do you mean?"

"You keep him safe *unless* you die. The choice is either fulfill the intention or get your body destroyed. That's why it was used in so many contracts."

The other kids at school used to tell her that she was so lucky to have a mom who never yelled or really punished. The kind of mother who wasn't okay with her and Scott cursing, but was easily convinced once they explained that they of all people should be allowed access to the most expressive form of language. Some kids would look at Mustard and see a maternal figure with no ability to make you feel quintessentially *in trouble.*

This just was not the case.

"You choose to be alone with fake dinosaurs instead of giving yourself food to sustain your body and improve your morale. This was a weird choice, Tenzin. You made a weird choice."

"I know, Mom," Tenzin managed, once again a child.

"You should've gone to a diner. You know what I've always told you two – most diners are open all night and they are all always a safe place to spend time in."

That's wasn't true. That was an insane factual inaccuracy, and Tenzin could easily point it out. But she didn't. Instead she weakly kicked her legs and lamented at how lame of a criminal she was.

Mustard continued. "You need to remember something, okay?"

Tenzin sat up. She readied herself for more berating or advice. Words of wisdom or an unrelated tangent filled with the occasional birthright abstraction.

"You start with bacon," Mustard said. "They might have other meats, but bacon is universal and tastes the same no matter where you go. Stick with bacon. Get two eggs, sunny side-up, and hash browns – but extra crispy. This is very important. You must clarify that with your server. Ask for Tabasco for the eggs – *always* Tabasco – and there's something else. Are you following, Tenzin?"

"Yes," Tenzin said dully.

"Request a pitcher of maple syrup. The server might be confused because people usually only order maple syrup with pancakes, but it's a fact that all breakfast foods taste better with a little bit of syrup."

"According to who?"

Tenzin could hear the soft smile in Mustard's voice. "Scott," she said. "This is Scott's favorite meal."

Once again – not true. Impossible. Scott would never make multiple off-menu requests to server in a restaurant.

"Levi, I mean," Mustard clarified. "The Great Doctor Scott Levi Kaufner. He used to work at a diner in this smaller town near Corvallis back when he was still in med school. Before the Witch Doctors."

"Huh," Tenzin said.

"It'll make you think of home," Mustard decided. "It'll remind you of your family. It will give you strength. And it'll be filling and delicious."

Tenzin smiled and said nothing. Mustard fell silent too. But this time, their peaceful quiet gradually became more and more sorrowful.

"You're hungry," Mustard said.

"Yes."

"Do you think he's hungry too?"

Because of Klinefelter's Syndrome Scott was born with weaker bone density. He didn't have much muscle mass or hope of defending himself. His memory was a puzzle with many of the pieces pulled out so harshly that it tore some of the nubs of the adjoining fragments. There was a ghost haunting him that he could no longer face or fully recognize.

The earth around Tenzin mourned for its love of the soft, feral child that had been lost to it for so long. He was designed to do little else but bob in the ocean and lie in the grass, but some malevolent force beyond anyone's control wanted to grab him by the scruff and force him into godhood.

What was she going to find when she found him? What would be left in his face that either of them could recognize?

Gradually, and then all at once, the sick feeling returned.

She left Prehistoric Park shortly after that and drove in a nothing daze through an endless stretch of swampland. The sunrise rippled off the water, changing the surface into colors that were beautiful and also not right. Tenzin didn't allow her eyes to stray from the road ahead of her. No beauty, no wonder – no music.

Soon she began to truly understand what their mother was trying to warn her about. Yes, her body had shut off its capacity for sleeping. That didn't mean it was immune to the effects of staying up for days at once. That would do something to anyone, magical bond or not. Tenzin became aware of a sort of flickering in her perspective of time.

A landmark far ahead of her would suddenly jut and pass by in a time span that didn't make sense. Tenzin would blink and the sky would go from deep Prussian blue to near-powder.

You should pull over, a voice in her head advised. *I don't think it's safe to drive like this.*

Tenzin adjusted her grip on the steering wheel.

You could get hurt. You could get someone else hurt.

She rolled down the window a crack and filled the car with cold, ugly air.

You aren't immortal, Tenzin.

Somehow she got to a diner. Somehow she ended up in the kind of ill-kept, retro-styled eating establishment that her family treated will more reverence than a church. The sense memory of sliding into the kind of vinyl booth seats that were always sticky regardless of how much you scrubbed them down rang strong in her subconscious. At the time she didn't mind, because she would be too busy trying to convince her brother to agree to see a more exciting movie at the theater, or listening as he struggled to explain the lore and mechanics of Runescape to their mother based on what he watched that day.

Now, alone, the whole thing place just felt gross.

Tenzin stared down at her plate, because apparently there was a plate on the table in front of her and she was in the middle of eating it. The steam rising from the plate carried notes of pepper, sweet maple, and cooked meat and potato. She ate, mechanically, acknowledging the way a drizzle of syrup across the dish changed its individual components without having any particular reaction.

Nothing felt as enjoyable or safe without her brother. Tenzin could only imagine that Scott was managing well enough before now, but she missed him so deeply that – in order not to drown in the feeling – she couldn't let herself feel much of anything at all.

She ate. She felt better after she ate. Tenzin paid, and tipped an amount that was normal for her upbringing but high enough to make the chipper server falter in genuine confusion. And then it was back to the road.

The feeling inside her got stronger as she followed the signs towards New Orleans. That's how she knew she was going in the right direction. It started with rising tide of pain as something deeply ingrained in herself was gripped in a massive fist and slowly dragged from her body. She knew the sensation well. It was why she stayed out of Bluerose's Mess Hall whenever Renja was preparing shrimp or chicken – or anything that needed to be *deveined.*

It didn't happen often. When it did, Tenzin was able to grit her teeth and move past the feeling to focus on a solution. Now, with age and experience and a fair deal of emotional strain, it was different.

It was excruciating. And the closer she got to New Orleans the worse it became.

Externally she looked normal. Exhausted, probably, but normal. Just below the surface there were countless reaching appendages clawing into her chest – pulling, pulling, pulling. A child's hand tugging at her wrist, only if the child had razor-sharp claws that were perfect for ripping through skin and flesh until it could wrap its tiny fingers tight around her wet bone.

Her bond burned around her as if the strand was still there and wrapped tight. But the feeling expanded, pulling from every part of her. Creasing her internal organs and making them bulge with pressure in spots previously ignored. It applied tension to her bones until they snapped in the middle, only for the strand to clutch onto either broken end and continue pulling.

Tenzin did not react. Her grip on the wheel was loose and her shoulders were relaxed. She breathed and blinked at regular intervals.

She was actively being torn apart from the inside out.

It was a struggle to think coherently and also drive safely. Tenzin tried nonetheless, just to focus energy on something besides the overwhelming pain.

She would find Scott. She would negotiate his safe release using aggression as a last-ditch effort. They would leave together, and they would never come back to this place.

By the time she pulled into the limits of the city her skin was a placid surface covering a writhing cataclysm of loose flesh scraps and screaming, pulsating bone. Tenzin wanted to throw up until she could get all the meat worms inside of her out and out for good. This was misery. This was hell. Tenzin was still driving fine – in fact, she was driving better than she usually did. She imagined this was probably because she was no longer fully in control of her own body.

She would save Scott. She would overpower anyone that tried to get in her way.

Her phone had the directions to the French Quarter pulled up on its GPS, but stopped looking the screen a long time ago. Tenzin just drove, allowing the bond to navigate on her behalf. It made a particular turn that resulted in a throbbing burst of agony so intense that a choked whimper finally escaped her lips.

At the studio, her coach told her recently that her Spinning Back Fist was getting pretty good. If she backed a single person into a solid, upright wall, she just feasibly just keep punching. And punching. And punching. Until her fist started to meet things deeper than skin and hair.

Tenzin closed her eyes tight, even though she was still driving. This wasn't good. She didn't like thinking like this. She focused on breathing in an attempt to calm herself down, something she remembered Scott doing a lot in the past, and found it did absolutely nothing. Breathing calms feelings. What she was experiencing was more like a cancer of the spirit.

When she opened her eyes the car was turned off and parallel parked. The fire inside her soothed enough to allow Tenzin to turn and examine her surroundings with eyes that could actually see.

It was a quiet neighborhood lined with barren oak trees. The side-walks were partially broken and ragged with moss and clumps of dead leaves. To the side of her car was a small, powder blue stucco building with white pillars. An apartment complex.

The right apartment had some crayon drawings taped to the glass of the nearby window. There was a potted cactus on a small table by the door. Staring at the exterior of the home made Tenzin feel nothing.

Her eyes went to the opposite door, unadorned and potentially va-cant, and she experienced a rage so intense that it blackened her vision entirely for a moment or two.

Calm. Calm, calm, calm.

She stood on the doorstep of this second apartment. The pain was gone, completely gone, which is how she knew for certain that she was in the right place. So Tenzin waited, ears perked for any sounds coming from behind the door.

There was none. Tenzin sighed softly and arranged her strategy.

Even though she wasn't a birthright, it does things to a person to be raised in a witch town like Bluerose. There were other civilians, but they were usually families or other children who were there to take advantage of the resources of a refuge hub for a span of no more than a year. That was, after all, what brought her and her mom there in the first place.

So her closest and most intimate relationships were with other birthrights – first by circumstance, but soon after by choice. Tenzin just preferred the company of people that lacked an interest in pretending the way others may expect.

A smile felt weird on her face, especially now. After a few tries she determined that just wouldn't work and instead chose an expression of cool calm. She grounded her feet subtly. And then she knocked on the door.

At first there was no response. But there was energy behind the lack of response that indicated there was definitely someone inside who was just choosing not to answer. Tenzin waited before knocking again, being sure not to slam her fist against the aged wood the way her brain was demanding her to.

Click. Turn. The door opened fully, revealing a shorter, redheaded man about her age. He was clean and well-rested, alert in the eyes, but still generally disheveled in a way that was hard to place.

The man didn't crack the door to hide something or hinder easy access. From how and where he stood she could easily just walk in and take a look around. It was so open and unassuming that she was close to thinking that something in her instinct could be wrong.

And then it wasn't. It clearly wasn't.

"Can I help you?" The man asked, perfectly friendly given the situation.

He was wearing a tailored shearling coat, pale brown material with a softer tan fluff around the edges. She recognized it immediately. Tenzin knew the wide pockets. She knew the exact jar where the out-of-place button in the front came from.

This man was wearing her mother's jacket.

The only piece of home Scott allowed himself to bring with him was that jacket. The elders worried him so greatly about looking like a target that Tenzin wore it herself as she drove him to the train station. It was his one comfort and this man was wearing it – for what? A trophy? Some sick thrill?

She would kick him in the throat, incapacitating him long enough for her to get that coat off of him and keep it clean. Then Tenzin would beat him until he was either physically ruined or ready to give her the answers she needed.

Tenzin found herself forging a small, sweet smile. "I'm a friend of Scott's..."

The man at the door now gripped the wood tightly. His face was slack and pale, and his eyes were wide with fear.

His huge eyes. Large, deep-set eyes that lacked a hood, but if she looked through the luminescent gold she could see the that the pupils...

"Oh *shit*," Tenzin murmured.

Without a word, the man closed the door in her face and locked it again. This immediately went terribly, and yet she was so thrown aback by the sight of the man's coloboma that it threw the pull of her bond out of whack.

She could be wrong. Some people just have a coloboma. But with the almost imperceptible glow of them, and the way he looked at her as if she said her violent thoughts aloud – what were the odds?

It didn't matter. She couldn't afford to debate herself.

The pull returned. The first thing it did was remind her the combat capabilities of a coloboma birthright. His ability was perceptive, so if willed right he could predict her next move before she executed it. That doesn't mean he could dodge it. He was one step ahead, but just by the looks of him Tenzin knew he was also physically weaker, likely slower, and definitely less intelligent.

What she felt was beyond anger. It was duty, like a solider in the trenches back before society gave real thought to questioning the futility of war. Tenzin raised her hand and touched the doorknob.

"Unlock this," she demanded.

She heard the click as the latch undid itself. When Tenzin turned the knob it opened easily and allowed her to walk inside the apartment.

The interior was cluttered and smelled like essential oil and cat urine. Tenzin's eyes immediately went to three figures at the far end in the kitchen. There was a glamorous blonde sitting on a stool at a bar with her hands around a mug. She was the first to notice the front door opening, and when she turned in her seat to face Tenzin all she did was sit and stare.

Tenzin spotted two men deeper in the semi-enclosed space. The first who answered the door had his head lowered and was speaking very intensely to the second figure across from him. They had their hands clasped together – firm, but gentle. Insistent. Worried.

She was ashamed to say that she didn't recognize the other man at first. Tenzin adapted so quickly to the family photos hung on the walls at home, where her brother was still an olive-skinned rapscallion with soft features and wild hair. Now his hair was shaped and styled into well-crafted layers that showcased his face rather than hid it away. His skin was the same sickly, ashen gray-brown that it became when they were eighteen. And a lot of the softness was gone – or not gone, just deeper inside and less readily apparent.

It didn't matter. It was still him.

Skylark.

She opened her mouth and no words came out. It might've ended up, however, that her presence was enough to turn his head her way. Scott looked at her. His eyes released some lock deep within herself. He took her in like the road takes in water after a long drought, and Tenzin got ready to hear him call for help.

He didn't. He just grinned.

Tenzin took a step forward when out of the corner of her eye the man from the doorway grabbed an empty beer bottle from the counter. In one swift movement he got into position, pointed the rim in her direction, and intoned an incantation. After that Tenzin couldn't even get out a protest. Her feet were off the ground as she was shot through the doorway and out onto the street.

Her back slammed against the steps of the complex and knocked the air out of her throat. She skidded across the gravel, tumbling onto her side and then her stomach. There was a scream. It came from someone. Somewhere. Maybe from her?

It didn't matter. Tenzin raised her head and swallowed the warmth of blood in her mouth.

She was going to kill this man.

There was an indefinite period of stunned silence after Edgar shot the intruder out of Katy's apartment. He didn't leave position, bottle still raised in case she tried to get back in.

"Fucking *hell,* Eddie," Katy breathed.

Hesitation etched through his composure. "I – I only meant to push her."

"Push her? You launched her, like, thirty feet."

From where he stood he saw part of the shape of the woman on the ground. She was moving slightly, but not getting up. He thought about moving to check if she was seriously hurt before he remembered that he definitely locked the front door when he closed it. And yet she got in moments later.

In the receding bone-headache of the previous incantation, Edgar noticed the slight glimmer around the lock of the front door. A shine that shouldn't exist given the lighting of the day.

She couldn't be from the Academy. Even the most powerful Academic witches have to speak their incantations clearly and distinctly. After his upbringing, Edgar was hyper-vigilant to that specific non-language and knew he could still pick it up from a distance.

So who is she? What is she?

Scott immediately started moving in the woman's direction. He stepped calmly, almost dreamily.

"Scott," Edgar said, "Stop."

He didn't. Edgar tightened his grip on the bottle.

"Please, Scott," he said again. "I'm trying to help you."

Scott didn't even react like he heard Edgar calling out to him. He leaned against the couch to put on his shoes, and with a clearer view of his face Edgar saw immediately that something was off.

It was his eyes. They were still bright, but the light was flat. It collected itself in a way that made his stare seem simultaneously focused and lifeless.

"*Scott*," Edgar said, a little louder. Then, with a nervous smile. "Skylark?"

Nothing. Scott put on his shoes and turned to walk out the door. While he was about halfway between the couch and the doorway, Edgar raised his bottle again and said a second incantation. Two so close together were difficult for someone out of practice, and he slumped to the side of the counter to try and bare the strain.

Katy's voice made its way through his haze. "What did you do, Edgar?" She asked.

He looked up and, through bleary eyes, saw the small circle of energy that now surrounded Scott. It was roughly the radius of a hula hoop. The field it created was mostly translucent aside form a very soft, bubble-like shimmer that concentrated at points of contact. And Scott stood in the middle of it, still and seemingly calm.

If Edgar wasn't hurting as bad as he was, he'd be proud of himself for getting a field hold right on the first try.

"It'll contain him," Edgar explained through the stabbing in his veins. "No one gets out, no one gets in. Until I break it, at least."

Edgar stumbled to the sink and quickly splashed water on his face.

"She's just lying there," Katy observed from behind him. "Just staring at the ground."

He turned and moved past Scott to where Katy watched out the window. "Close and lock the door when I'm out there," he instructed.

"What are you talking about?"

"You and Wilford hide in the bathroom. I'll come get you when it's safe."

Katy's face shifted in a surprising display of actual fear. "No – shit – Ed, you can't *fight* this woman."

"I'm not afraid."

"No, Edgar, you don't get it –"

From out the window Edgar picked up on the shape of the woman shifting as she got off the ground and back onto her feet. From that point on whatever Katy said didn't matter. He left the apartment, bottle in hand, and prepared himself for battle.

He and the woman stood on either end of the driveway, and already they were both pretty beleaguered. The woman breathed heavy with her lips slightly parted, and though her skin was dark Edgar could still make out a line of what might be blood.

She wiped her mouth with the sleeve of the sweater she wore and stained a streak of red. Yes, that was blood. Edgar drew blood from this woman. Now he felt sick as well as frightened.

"Declare yourself," she commanded him.

The words came before Edgar could stop them. "Acolyte Gallows, Generation Four, Shreveport Academy Mantle Layer."

The shame that followed as soon as he finished was so great that he almost let the bottle fall from his grasp. Even after all this time, and no matter how much he could try to improve himself as a human being, there was still a knee-jerk part of himself that would always be innately Pavlovian.

The woman seemed disinterested. "Sharp tongue for a Mantle Layer Academic."

"Thanks," Edgar grimaced. "Why are you here?"

That actually stirred through her intensely serious front. Her brow furrowed slightly. "You don't know?"

There was blood streaked on the floor at his feet. It still looked wet. Edgar bit back a shiver and remembered why he was here.

"I know," he said. "You want to hurt us."

"Hurt...*us*?"

He looked up at the woman and saw that she was distracted from whatever mission she was one. She peered at him as if Edgar suddenly started speaking in a foreign language. And then that passed and was replaced with a strangely gentle frustration. Apparently she was trying to figure out where to go from here.

"Okay," she murmured. "That is...what you know. Now can I tell you what – *I* – know?"

She took a single step forward. Edgar reacted in a way that didn't push her back, but stopped her from going any further.

"I know you call yourself Eddie," she said, softening her voice into a thick fog. "And if you left your Academy, I know you must be lonely. Which I can understand."

"Get away from me," Edgar warned.

The woman got closer. Her hands were raised, which revealed that she had no wands or anything to act as a stand-in. So how could she have done what she did to unlock the door?

"You met someone you believe you could relate to," the woman lowered her voice even graver. "And now you've become attached. I know."

"Stay *back*."

By this point the woman was within arm's reach and still getting closer. "I also counted two incantations in a row, so if you use a third on me this soon I know you'll pass out from the pain."

Edgar stared up at her and spoke through gritted teeth. "You think I care about that?" He said.

"No," the woman spoke low. "I guess not. Maybe all you care about is him. So if that's true, you should trust me when I ask you to *give me the bottle*."

In a heartbeat Edgar remembered every time he gave up. Every instant where he should've been brave and instead chose to retreat. A thousand memories overlaid on top of each other until it was just a blur of color and sound that filled every inch of Edgar's mind as he wound back and slammed the beer bottle into Tenzin's temple.

In the movies that would send her crumpling to the ground and out of commission. That's what Edgar assumed would happen. And while it definitely threw her off her guard, she only staggered to the side before grounding herself enough not to fully collapse. That left Edgar with no stand-in and an opponent who was far angrier than she was just a few moments before.

He scanned the ground around them for a substitution. Then there was a flash of motion as the woman wound back and slammed the bone of her elbow into Edgar's face, just above the eyebrow. The result was a gray, agonizing nothing that rang out throughout his entire body and sent him immediately to the ground.

If you asked him before, Edgar would say he had a pretty good pain tolerance. And maybe he did. Maybe what the woman did to him was supposed to hurt way more than it was supposed to. It still was incredibly painful, so much so that he couldn't even bring himself to scream out or cry. He just stared in shock as his face became warm and his vision darkened with a gush of blood.

Though the mixture of blood and tears that welled but did not fall, he saw Tenzin staring out towards Katy's front door in deep focus. Edgar clenched his jaw. He couldn't let her get back in there. He *wouldn't*. From where he was he could grab her by the ankles and maybe wrestle her to the ground. Edgar was just now forming a very convincing theory that punches like that were much harder to execute when you weren't standing upright.

She said something to him that was immediately drowned by the ringing in his ears. He made a face, probably, and she frowned. The woman pointed a finger at him and he immediately tried to scramble away, but the disorientation of the hit temporarily turned his limbs into jelly.

Then she mouthed a single word Edgar was able to make out.

Mend, please.

A different warmth wove its way across the gash on his face. It was tingly, like someone spilled TV static over the open wound. Then it faded. Edgar reached out a hesitant hand and found, much to his re-signed amazement, that the cut was gone. He was still in pain. His face was still dripping in his own blood. But he no longer had any active head wounds.

That was not an incantation. It was not the type of unspoken ability he'd seen any birthright do. That was just *magic,* plain and simple.

His hearing gradually returned to him and he was able to hear what likely gave the woman so much concern. Katy was shouting, near screaming, a constant stream of dialogue that Edgar couldn't entirely make out. There was a lot of swearing. Between the profanity was the occasional clear word.

PLEASE

NO

Edgar groaned and struggled to get back upright. Every bend in his joints felt like pressing directly into the center of a fresh bruise. The woman, already standing, was staggering her way inside.

"You can't get him!" Edgar shouted. "I put him in a containment field and only I can break it!"

SCOTT

STOP

The woman broke out into a run.

Now it didn't matter how badly it hurt. Edgar sprung onto his feet and staggered after her, ignoring her blood, ignoring his blood, paying no mind to how each step stung all the way up and threatened to make his legs give out again. Ahead of him the woman flung open the door with a point of the finger and bolted inside. Edgar was close behind, close enough to grab her by the collar of her frayed and bloodstained sweater and yank her backwards.

"Let her go."

That was Scott. Was that Scott? It couldn't have been – Scott would never talk to Edgar like that. But when he looked he saw Scott looking directly at him with a stare as cold as the tone of his voice. The same man who nestled peacefully in his arms, who wiped away his tears with a complete lack of judgment, now looked at Edgar as if he were stranger.

A dangerous stranger.

A stranger he was ready to take down himself.

It was then that he noticed the faint splatters of blood on the wall of energy in front of Scott. They didn't bead quite enough to be entirely noticeable, as if they were a scribble of marker drawn on plastic film. The outline, the vague shadow, was enough to draw Edgar's attention downwards as his eyes followed the drips.

"Skylark," the woman said. "Look at me. I'm fine. I'm okay."

Scott's hands were clenched in fists now misshapen, slicked red and caved in at spots like two beaten lumps of wet clay. They trembled with how tightly they were held. Between the dents and on the ends of both hands, fragments of stark, white bone escaped the flesh.

Edgar's heart dropped. "Oh my god."

"He wouldn't stop," Katy said from nearby, where she watched in horror from behind her armchair. "I – I think he was trying to break through it."

She was truly terrified, close to tears and visibly shaking. This was the first time Edgar had ever seen her this upset. It sparked some protective outrage that made no sense and fizzled awkwardly in light of day.

"Look at me," Scott demanded in a voice that inspired only dread.

The woman immediately jumped in to protest. "No wait *don't* -"

Edgar looked at him. Scott was not mad in anyway that he had ever experienced before. He was perfectly calm, so settled in his absolute vengeance that it appeared to relax him.

Once again, it was the look in his eyes that scared Edgar the most. There was not a hint of recognition. Scott's were the eyes of a shark that just tasted blood and was now hungry for more. The sight was starkly terrifying in a way the struck Edgar straight in the lungs and made breathing a laughable concept.

"Go to the kitchen," Scott slowly said. "And bring back a bottle of bleach."

The room was silent and deathly tense. All, of course, except for Edgar. Because, even though he was clearly in a grave degree of danger, he was no longer afraid. He knew this wasn't Scott talking to him. This was some lingering magic from his childhood. Or it was Witch Eater, maybe. Either way, Scott didn't want Edgar to hurt himself – it was some greater divine force speaking *through* his boyfriend that wanted Edgar dead.

And that was much easier to handle. It was pretty much fine, actually. So he took it all with a degree of curiosity.

The woman physically put herself between Scott and Edgar. When she faced Edgar her eyes were pleading. "Don't listen to him," she said.

"Wasn't planning on it," he tilted to the side to get a better look at Scott. "You should move out of the way."

"Why? What?"

Edgar sighed and elaborated without taking his eyes off his bond. "You're a magic user. He's being hunted as a vessel for the Witch Eater or whatever. As far as I know he still can't get out of this, but it might be unstable."

The woman didn't answer. She stayed where she was and lowered her arms. Katy was the next one with the nerve to speak up.

"Edgar," she said. "That's Scott's sister."

Scott's sister. Tenzin. The Knight's Bond.

Edgar let out a breath. He had no idea an archetype bond could result in a pull this strong.

"Did he tell you that?" Tenzin asked him. "He told you about the Witch Eater?"

Half his face was covered in dirt and blood and it itched terribly. "Lots of people have been implying it," he remarked idly. "There's a few different names I've heard so far. But I've tethered myself to the source of magic, so it sort of confirmed things personally."

Both Katy and Tenzin were shocked by the way he said that. Edgar kind of surprised himself as well. Everything changed so quickly that he still didn't have time to process everything he'd seen over what only ended up being a day.

He lost his focus staring at Scott's bloody, broken hands. The man was a pianist. "We need to get him to a hospital."

Tenzin stopped him as he moved to grab a comb on the nearby table. "Lower that field and he kills you," she warned, razor-sharp. "Your friend tries to stop him and she's next."

"I don't think he knows who I am right now," Edgar said, matching the level of her voice. "If I tell him I won't hurt you he has no reason to believe me."

Fix this was what that meant. It was an awful way to go about it, but Edgar could see no other option. Based on his own narrow scope of understanding, Scott's perspective was limited to his sister and people who could potentially hurt his sister. There was nothing he could do on his own to fix that aside from seeing what Scott would want him to do with a bottle of bleach.

Tenzin was not excited about Edgar's implication. She narrowed her stare like doing that would be enough to reveal something that she couldn't already see from less than a few feet away.

"What *are* you?" She asked.

That's a weird question to hear. That's a complicated question to even begin to answer.

"Well," he took the comb and put in his back pocket. "I actually go by *Edgar* these days. Let's start there."

"...No," Tenzin furrowed her brow and said it a few more times. "No, no. You don't."

Edgar was still trying to figure out what she meant by that when Tenzin awkwardly linked their arms together and turned back towards Scott. He stared Edgar down, a viper just about to strike, but with Tenzin as she was he held back.

"Scott!" Tenzin spoke with an exaggerated cheer. "I'm so glad that I finally got to meet Eddie! You didn't tell me that *Eddie is here.*"

Scott's death stare remained steady. Tenzin continued, tightening her grip on Edgar's arm to the extent where, even if he wanted to reach for the proxy in his pocket, he wouldn't be able to. She continued, fluidly and unnaturally happy.

"*Eddie* was showing me some of the cool stuff he can do. Can't he do some *cool stuff*? He really knocked me off my feet, but he was *so nice* in helping me up and making sure I was okay. *Isn't Eddie so nice?*"

Something in the man's eyes began to shift. He blinked. Six seconds went by, then a few more, and he blinked again. It wasn't until now that Edgar realized he hadn't blinked at all for their entire previous exchange.

Tenzin was on a roll now, talking quickly and picking up a more genuine passion. "Remember when we were really little and you used to tell me how kind and smart he was? He'd tell you all those facts about birds, and then you'd tell them to me, and we'd be like *yay! Birds!*"

Edgar could tell Tenzin's words were having an effect, as every time Scott blinked a little more emotion came back into his face. But what bothered him were the things she was saying, because he had no memory of them. He knew they spoke as kids, and apparently so did Scott, but from the way Tenzin described it they had an entire relationship. If that was true, why didn't Edgar remember?

If that was true, why hadn't Scott said anything yet?

"Yes, you're absolutely right," Tenzin concluded, agreeing with no one. "Eddie is nice, and clever, and he would *never hurt us.* Because he loves you remember?" She added more emphasis. "*Eddie is here, and he loves you.*"

"I love you, Scott..." Edgar whispered limply.

Scott sank out of rage and into deep, cloudy exhaustion. Once he said that the final switch was made and he was once again himself. He blinked rapidly and twitched his brow. Edgar knew Scott was back on the ground once he could feel the man's flickering emotions sparking deep in him.

"Okay," Tenzin said, jarring Edgar from his own internal realignment. "Take it down."

He was a ghost of himself as he took out the comb and spoke the incantation that sent the shimmer of energy dissipating into the air around them. Scott didn't pounce in attack. He just stood and trembled. Edgar's first thought was the fuzzy coat thrown over the counter, but if offered it to him now it would likely get stained with blood. Unsure where to go, Edgar just stood and watched.

Tenzin stepped forward and caught Scott just as he started to slump forward. She took his shoulders and got him upright, picking up his chin and brushing his hair back.

"You got a haircut," she remarked.

"Ten..." Scott murmured.

"It looks good."

"My hands hurt."

"I know," Tenzin nodded. "I'm sure. Can I see?"

Scott held up his bloodied, busted hands. They appeared to startle him when they came into view, though he was too tired to do much with his panic.

"Now put them together," she softly directed. "Careful. Thumbs touching. There we go, just like that. Good job, Skylark."

"How did this happen?"

"Don't worry about it right now," Tenzin gently tapped her finger in the space between the thumbs and spoke. "Mend, please."

The same shimmery, slightly-lit phosphorescence rippled across the surface of Scott's hands. He closed his eyes and winced, though his pain expressed no surprise. Edgar watched, mutely horrified, as the exposed bones burrowed back into open gashes that were then fused back together. The rivets of his knuckles expanded with a crackle that Edgar hated and knew he would struggle to forget. Then the energy faded.

Tenzin lowered her hand and examined Scott's fingers, apparently having no problem with the blood still soaking his skin. He stretched out his hands and arched his fingers upwards.

They looked fine.

"We should get you to a piano," Tenzin said.

Scott nodded. He twitched his mouth without quite getting to the point of speaking. And even though Edgar knew this was a family moment, even though he had a billion questions about what was going on, none of that was important to him. It might be rude and it might result in another elbow to the face, but Edgar was not about to let that stop him from stepping to Scott's side and making sure for himself that he was okay.

He came up and pressed a gentle hand to the small of Scott's back. As Scott's eyes met him he was about to say something comforting when Scott spoke before he had the chance.

"Edgar what..?" He drifted his eyes shut and let his shoulders fall limp. Then he was back. "Tenzin you hit him."

Did all bonds work in way close to how the one between Scott and his sister did? Edgar couldn't say for certain. He also didn't think he could bring himself to take that risk at this point. So, perhaps to make up for the terrible welcome he gave Tenzin when she first showed up, Edgar jumped in to lie.

"Uh no," he quickly said. "I – uh –"

"I did," Tenzin said. "He took a direct elbow strike to the face. It hit well, too. I'm surprised he's still conscious."

Scott frowned. It wasn't entirely proportional to the situation – it was just a regular frown. "Ten...that's a bad first impression."

"Well, you didn't exactly set him up for success."

He looked distraught. Then tired. Then amused, and then tired again. Eventually he took his hands and wiped them on the hem of Tenzin's sweater. She stuttered a gasp-laugh, but didn't make an attempt to get out of the way.

"Wow," she said. "Thanks."

Even in pain he smiled. "These aren't my clothes. I don't want to be rude," once his hands were sufficiently clean – or at least no longer wet – he got closer and pulled her into a hug.

Watching from the outside Edgar knew exactly the type of hug Scott was giving his sister. It was the type of embrace that would easily reduce Edgar to a loose pile of feelings that would just drift away in the wind like dandelion blossoms as soon as they pulled apart. He wondered what something like that would do to a person who grew up with him. Someone who wasn't unbelievably, whole-heartedly in love the way he was.

Tenzin kept her cool for the most part. She even managed to hold onto a scowl until the charade became impossible. Then she wrapped her arms back around him, one hand between the shoulders and the other on the back of the head. It was protective. Assuring. Maybe a little possessive, but that last observation could've been a projection rooted in Edgar's own jealousy.

Because he was jealous. The strange story Tenzin made up while Scott was still in his trance echoed deep within him – this weird painted farce of the two of them being legitimate friends as children. He couldn't stop thinking how, if he got to actually grow up with Scott in his life, he would've ended up a completely different person.

He'd be braver. Definitely happier. Maybe he could be touched by other people without freezing or flinching, drifting towards vomit or holding back tears. Imagine that.

Scott pulled away, a little brighter yet still very bad.

"You should lie down," Tenzin advised.

He ignored her, tuning her out without question in that way that only siblings know how to do. His attention turned to Katy, still standing just behind Edgar. He took her in, sinking back into a deep well of tired fear.

"Which of you was it?" He said.

Katy pushed out her voice, stronger yet still ringed in strained terror. "What do you mean?"

"Who did I attack?"

Tenzin carefully took Scott by the shoulders and started leading him towards the couch. "Let's not focus on this now."

"It was me," Edgar said.

He said this because he knew how hard it was to exist with so much in the world left as a question. Still, the response was hard to take. Scott's face recoiled as if hit hard. All of the guilt was plainly visible with his face in plain view, which was both assuring and somewhat shameful. Edgar was seeing something he wasn't supposed to – they all were, now.

Tenzin bristled like a shock traveling through an electrical current as soon as he stepped forward to touch Scott's arm. Edgar ignored her, despite the danger. He took Scott's hand, the blood dried off and left with only a faint sticky residue, and he held it against his heart.

"You didn't touch me," he assured him. "I had you restrained to the point where you'd definitely hurt yourself more trying to break free. I'm okay."

"Was it frightening?"

Edgar smiled. "Maybe at first. But not for long."

He saw Scott press his hand against his chest a little harder. The bond stared into his eye, searching him for signs of well-meaning deception. When he found none – because there was none – he lowered his eyes and sighed wearily.

Tenzin pulled Scott back and led him to sit down on the daybed. He allowed this and immediately sank into the cushions. This time he didn't curl up to take less space. Scott let his eyes flutter shut just as he was, sprawled out like a rag doll.

"Did I scare the cat?" Tenzin said, addressing Katy without looking directly at her.

One look confirmed that Katy was clutching Wilford to her chest. The cat was entirely unaffected by the conflict that was only now leveling off. While his mother was ready for a tall, stiff drink, he was gradually falling asleep in her arms.

Katy swallowed hard. "No," she said. "He's fine. He's strong."

"Good. Do you also think I'm trying to kill my brother? Is that why you hung up on me?"

No one spoke. Twitching his newly-formed hands, Scott sighed again like he was relearning how to breathe. Eventually Tenzin lowered her head and hummed, seemingly disappointed in herself.

"Okay," she said. "That's probably my fault. I'm not very good at...*expressing* things like that. Especially not now."

By now Scott's sister was a completely different person. The air of military-grade, stoic hostility revealed itself to be a facade. Despite the ache of her elbow against his brow still throbbing, Edgar knew she wouldn't be a threat unless he made himself to be one first. Now, Tenzin was a sort of stilted figure that mainly just came across as worried and tired. In that way there was a lot of her brother in her.

Again, and a little bitterly, Edgar wondered what the two of them were like as kids. Under better circumstances.

While he thought about that he saw that Tenzin was staring at him again. It wasn't angry, which was convenient. That deeply examining gaze that could excavate an archaeology site without any equipment must be a trait that ran in the Kaufner household. Scott was better at it, perhaps more practiced, which led Edgar to assume that if he ever met Scott's mom she would be able to see every dream he's had and sin he's committed in the blink of an eye.

There was a little nagging sensation in the back of his head, a buzzing voice that spoke through the feedback of his pain.

I need to know that I can trust you, it said.

He blinked a few times and it went silent.

"This is a long shot," Tenzin paused to see if Scott was listening. "Do you have any iron supplements around here?"

"I...don't," Katy said.

"What about juice? Apple, orange –"

"I have OJ, yeah."

Tenzin's stillness had flaws. Her right knee jiggled slightly as she stood. She rubbed her index finger very slowly with her thumb, so subtly that it would be hard to notice for someone not looking as closely as Edgar apparently was.

Maybe he would fit in better with the Kaufners than he thought.

"Try and get him to drink some if you can," Tenzin's requests were a lot looser now. "Just orange juice and water until he's fully conscious again. If he's not holding his end of a conversation in an hour or so I have some connects just out of town we can take him to."

Edgar had to step in. "Wait," he said. "What are you talking about? Does this happen every time your bond gets triggered?"

"It's not the bond," Tenzin became strained as she forced herself to keep talking. "He hurt himself. He lost blood, and..." she took a deep breath and softened her voice. "He's anemic."

He immediately looked over at Scott on the couch, who was drifted somewhere between awake and asleep. Edgar remembered seeing his naked body for the first time and immediately diving into an ocean of emotion and sensation. But there was something else, right? Something that hit him before losing grip and slipping away into the everything.

A thought. An observation.

Wow. His skin doesn't look healthy.

No matter what time it was he always looked ready to go down for a nap. He was constantly chilly, despite it being a warmer winter for this time of year. Once it had a name the signs were so immediately obvious that Edgar could only think of one possible reason why he didn't see it until now.

Before he extracted a piece of Scott's demons into himself, he looked for signs of a curse. That telltale physical mark that most malicious academics would see as a badge of victory. Edgar thought it would be impossible to ignore. Edgar also thought that a non-birthright couldn't transfer magical energy without a conduit. If someone could, they could easily curse another human being without leaving a single physical mark.

He looked up at Tenzin and felt strangely steady. "What did you do?" He asked her.

She reeled in guilt with the same pinpoint accuracy as when she hit him in the face. That, not the bottle to the side of the head, was the closest Edgar got to knocking her off her feet. Tenzin regained her footing and sighed, fumbling for indignation in a way that felt exclusively civilian.

"Orange juice and water," she said to Katy again before turning back to Edgar. "If you show me to your bathroom I can wash off your face."

Another Kaufner quality. She and Scott looked to be about the same age, so who influenced whom? Whatever the case, and even though it reflected a lot about Edgar's character and the way he expected to be treated by the world, Tenzin's small sort-of kindness comforted him. Not a lot, but enough.

Scott's hair still littered the floor of Katy's bathroom when he led Tenzin inside. Her shear case was left open on the counter next to the sink. Tenzin paused in the doorway to take in the scene.

"Uh. Katy cuts hair," Edgar grabbed a clean washcloth from under the sink. "She cuts mine too. When I let her."

Tenzin let out a vague noise that implied surprise, and perhaps a slight degree of respect. She stepped inside the room and didn't close the door fully behind them, instead leaving it cracked just enough to get a view of Katy and Scott on the couch. Edgar observed this with a new, muffled focus that overlaid across his previous sense of attention. It was the same feeling he had when he opened the door to her for the first time.

There were the concepts of the present moment – the whir of the fan, the buzz of the light, the smell of bathroom cleaner and floral shampoo. Tenzin near the door and Edgar closer to the shower. The low white fluff of Wilford peering in from just across the door, proving that the trash goblin was prepared to either defend Edgar or help a stranger take him down. All of that was there – and there was even more.

If he could see it, it would shine like the wall of an energy field. If he could hear it, it would rumble like the kind of thunder sheet they wobble for sound effects in movies. In a way he could see it, and he could also hear it, but both of that was also not true. It was like Tenzin's voice and his voice speaking over each other, each expressing the similar sentiment.

I want to know who you are
what you want
why you're here
why you left
if you left
what happened
what happened
what happened???

The questions continued layering in that odd, warble-whisper. His first thought was to call it intuition. Edgar knew that was wrong. He didn't ever have this degree of insight into other people and didn't expect a skill like that to pop up overnight.

"You're telepathic," Edgar said.

Tenzin shook her head. "Excuse me?"

"You're putting your thoughts in my head."

Tenzin took the rag from Edgar's hands and absently sat him down on the toilet. "That's you," she said. "You're doing that for yourself."

"What are you talking about?" Tenzin didn't answer and Edgar fought with a childish frustration. "Scott told me what's going on."

"My brother hasn't taken his anti psychotics in over a decade."

"He *what*?" Edgar blurted out.

Tenzin frowned, watching the tap running water over the already sopping towel. "You must know by now that he isn't well. Beyond the lack of medication, there's no way of knowing what he retained and what he forgot after – what happened."

The grief took the lines of her body and turned them into stone. She looked miserable. But considering what she just said, and what Edgar sensed she was skirting around, he struggled to manifest the pity it looked like she was trying to evoke.

"You seem pretty torn up for someone who cursed their own brother," he said.

She turned off the water and let the towel drip into the sink. "You have no idea the choice I had to make."

Harsh words wrapped in blankets of exhaustion. That somehow made them more effective to Edgar, who suddenly had a memory of sitting across the table from his mother with a shot glass of sweet-smelling, clear liquor in his hand. Her voice in his ears, telling him that they were equals now. Inviting him to take a drink with her.

The choice he had to make.

The choice he ended up making.

He shook away the image as Tenzin wrung out the towel and began gently dabbing it to clean up the side of Edgar's face. She worked carefully, moving every so often to wash out the blood and return with a clean – albeit now pink-tinted – cloth to work with.

"Is your name really Edgar?" Tenzin asked, not meeting his eyes directly.

"It is. Edgar Gallows," he frowned. "You won't find me in the register, though."

Tenzin paused, carefully sweeping the end of the towel across Edgar's eyelid in a single, delicate motion. "You have any ID?"

"I tossed my Academy Card a long time ago."

"I imagine you have a driver's license."

For a while Edgar wondered if he was about to get mugged on top of assaulted. Then that bubbly feeling returned as it occurred to him that Tenzin didn't care about his status in the Academy. She barely reacted to knowing he could wield a wand. There was another question in her mind that was clearly far more important.

She was trying to see if his name was actually Eddie.

Without another word he shifted in his seat and pulled his wallet from his back pocket. He opened it, fished out his license, and handed it to Tenzin. She was partially resigned to how easily he bent to her will, yet still took it and read over the contents.

It was impossible to read the look on her face.

"No middle name?" She said.

"Nope."

The first twinge of emotion was sympathy. It was gone as soon as it appeared. "That's cruel," she said, handing the ID back to him.

"Do a lot of people lie about that?" Edgar asked while putting his wallet back in his pocket. "They pretend like their name is Eddie when it actually isn't?"

Tenzin frowned and went back to cleaning the blood off his face. "I'm not sure. I always suspected. He used to specifically ask anyone that went by the name to approach him after his shows, so – I figured if someone took a shot he'd accept it without question. Especially once things got exacerbated."

Edgar winced even though Tenzin's touch did not sting. "That's awful."

"It doesn't seem like you fell for it the same way others have."

She paused again, towel resting against Edgar's skin. With her so close, and after denying eye contact for so long, the single stare she granted him was particularly piercing. Edgar thought about the shared scars on his and Scott's hands. That would be hard to explain to someone who already barely liked him and proved to be way better at hitting than he was.

"Well I'm a birthright too," he said. "That's probably why."

That wasn't technically a lie. It could potentially be true. A lot of things about he and Scott could potentially be true.

Tenzin continued to clean. She looked unconvinced.

"You're the first, you know."

"The first to not be affected?"

"No," Tenzin said. "The first Edgar. As far as I know, at least. He gives me the full name and address of anyone he goes home with and there's never been an Edgar," she rinsed out the bloodied towel for one last time before tossing it with the other dirty linens. "You've also lasted the longest. From what I gather he stopped even spending the night after the first few hookups."

Was that suspicion Edgar was hearing in her voice? "I didn't do anything to him," he said.

"I believe you. I do. In fact, I don't think you could."

She stepped away and Edgar looked at himself in the mirror. His face was clean and damp, half rubbed pink from the material of the towel. She definitely did a thorough job. He touched the fresh area around his brow and thought about where he felt the skin and flesh split open.

"Does it really matter if I'm the first Edgar?" He asked Tenzin. "Scott never brought it up. I don't think he cares."

In the reflection Tenzin's expression weighed heavy. "He wouldn't know. But it makes a big difference."

Her attempt to leave on an emotionally profound statement was halted when she spotted Wilford standing right outside the door. She stopped midway into opening it, hand still on the knob.

"Oh," she said flatly. "...Hey."

Wilford shot out a wet sneeze and slowly slunk away.

When she and Edgar left the bathroom Scott was sitting upright, slowly sipping a glass of juice. Katy was next to him, arms crossed tight in continued worry. He was talking to her in a soft, faint voice, and she clung to every word until she heard the two of them approaching.

Katy raised her head and looked to Edgar first. That waver returned and spoke again.

I need to know you're okay.

By this point Edgar had no idea what was happening. Still, he cast her a nod, and she seemed to appreciate that.

"Oh – fuck," Scott said weakly. "I guess...all that really *did* happen, huh?"

Tenzin and Edgar got closer, and once again seating became an issue. Both of them moved to where Katy was, because both of them wanted to sit closest to Scott. It's not like it was something he needed – Edgar just had the overwhelming desire to feel his bond's presence next to his own. Apparently Tenzin felt the same way.

Which made sense. Edgar was only out of commission for a day and a half, while Tenzin and Scott had been apart for years. On one hand, it would be a polite show of courtesy to allow the sister of his boyfriend to properly reunite with her long-lost brother.

On the other hand – fuck that. Edgar was terrified and had no idea what was going on. His head ached physically and his entire body ached psychically. All he wanted to do was lean his head against Scott's arm, close his eyes, and attempt to undo the knots of dread in his stomach.

"Give me your keys," Katy said to Edgar.

"My – excuse me?"

"I talked with Scott about it, and I'm going to take him back to your apartment," she said.

Edgar perked up, mostly grateful and a little bit smug. "I can just take him home myself."

"You aren't coming with me."

His satisfaction drained immediately. He looked over at Tenzin to either judge her level of aggression or see if she was willing to stop this and didn't find much in the way of either. She looked over at Katy steadily, still mostly inexpressive. She just stared.

"I don't like wizard fights," Katy said, eyes vacant and pointed ahead of her. "I had to watch Scott beat the bones out of his hands. And I know being friends with a cook means that you're going to see some blood, but...not *that much*, Edgar," she leaned forward and rubbed her hands across her face. "It shouldn't be that much."

Tenzin spoke up now. "I have to talk to him," she said. "There are things he needs to know –"

"*His bones,* ma'am. The guy just reformed his skeleton, I really don't think now is the time for more life-shattering revelations."

Scott opened his eyes slightly. "More?" He murmured.

A ripple of hesitation rang out in both Tenzin and Edgar, which Katy noticed and took with bland annoyance. She didn't wait for the two of them to confer whether they should relay the insight Tenzin shared before. Instead she looked back at Scott and gave his arm a soft shake, jostling him awake.

"You're anemic, Scott," she told him.

Silence. Edgar tried to summon up that bubbly feeling he got with Tenzin. It didn't come. There wasn't a block in rising tide, there just wasn't any of that kind of ocean when he looked at Scott.

"What kind?" He said after some time.

Katy looked hard at Tenzin. "What kind, ma'am?" She repeated.

"...Iron-deficient."

Silence at first. Then a soft sigh from Scott.

"I think I lost a lot of blood, then," he raised his hands slightly, looking at either side of his palms. "I should...go to the hospital."

"Scott –" Tenzin attempted.

"You want to go to the hospital, Scott?" Katy interrupted, speaking loud enough to dissuade even Tenzin from trying to fight back.

Scott tried to sit up, which looked like an incredibly difficult effort that ultimately wasn't worth pursuing. "I wanted to go to sleep," he took a moment to catch his breath, "But if I do that...I don't know. I think – I might...go into shock? Or maybe – die. I...mm."

Katy gave Edgar and Tenzin a look that Edgar knew quite well. She polished her *you fucked up* look so well over the years that at this point it barely came across as outwardly aggressive. It was a friendly smile that inexplicably left its victim with a shame immense enough to smother any potential protest. Edgar wasn't immune, but he knew to expect it at times like these.

Tenzin, though, was instantly baffled.

"Cool," Katy said as she stood up and carefully pulled Scott up with her. "I'm going to take Scott to the hospital. You two are going to stay here and hash out your Main Character Syndrome bullshit until you figure out that the Pretty Sad Boy loves you both equally, just in different ways."

Edgar stayed back and watched Tenzin scoff and step forward. "That's not what this is."

"Because you know what it would be if he didn't?" Katy asked her in that pointed, distinctly customer service voice. "If he loved his sister the same way as his boyfriend? You know what I would call *that*?"

Tenzin didn't answer. Katy pulled Scott's arm around her shoulder and leaned towards her, eyes sharp and voice finally disdainful.

"*Gross,* Tenzin. I would call it *gross.*"

It was very close to funny watching Tenzin stand, shocked frozen while Katy took Scott out of the house and into her car. He heard her engine kick off and saw her car pull off the curb and down the road. Once they were fully alone, Tenzin turned her head enough for him to see the look on her face. That empty stare that expressed stunned disorientation. Which was *hilarious.*

"Why did I let her take him?" Tenzin asked, mainly to herself.

"Katy has a way with people."

"She's *terrifying,*" said the person who elbowed him the face hard enough to potentially kill him if she kept on going.

They lingered in a home that was now far more silent and secluded than either of them were comfortable with. At least Edgar could say that he was more at ease than Tenzin was. He knew how to handle Katy when she was happy-mad, a combination that was far more intimidating than just being angry. He wasn't pleased to push her over the edge like this. At least he was able to navigate the situation with relative grace.

Tenzin was typing something on her phone. "She didn't say, so I'm assuming you know what hospital they're going to."

Shit. Fuck.

He heard her scoff at his reaction before dropping the subject and going back to her tapping.

"Are you just going to storm through every hospital in the area?" Edgar asked.

"Does your friend have baking soda and vinegar?"

Edgar didn't answer. A few moments later Tenzin looked up at him from her screen. "I looked it up and it says that can get blood off of hardwood. The flecks might be hard but the puddles aren't fully dried yet – if we clean it up now we can keep it from staining."

His eyes went to the twin splattering of blood where Scott once stood. In the back of his mind he tried to see his bond pounding his fists into a pulp, absolutely maddened by a need for violence. The image didn't come in entirely. Even after seeing a hint of that anger Edgar just couldn't picture that degree of darkness from a person like Scott. And he wasn't going to try.

Katy lived primarily on a diet of alcohol, frozen food, leftovers from work and takeout. Edgar occasionally took it on himself to clean up enough of her kitchen to make a homemade meal that was bulky and substantial enough to provide leftovers for a week. Because of that he knew her kitchen had some basic staples, including a dented box of baking soda and half a bottle of white vinegar. At Tenzin's request he fished a roll of paper towels from behind the sink and came back to meet her with his supplies.

There was a cleaning guide pulled up on Tenzin's phone, and by the color scheme Edgar knew it was from WikiHow. That told Edgar a few things. It said that this was almost certainly an entry on the first page of results in whatever she searched. Which meant that Tenzin didn't naturally know how to clean up blood, and was potentially too wary of the subject to put real research into finding the answers.

He thought about this as the two of them blotted the remaining wet blood off the floor.

"So," Edgar said. "You cursed him with anemia?"

Tenzin's features twitched without fully breaking into an emotion. She continued blotting. "I suggest rephrasing that question and you might get a better answer."

That was fair. "What curse did you use?"

"...Draining."

He balled up a red-stained ball of paper towel and threw it in the rest of the pile. "You realize the name isn't literal, right? You're draining memories, not plasma."

Tenzin went still. She stared down at the blood stain under her fingertips, this flower of deep crimson-brown that wept through the grain of the wood. Her eyes closed and he lips move the silent shapes of what could be prayer.

Calm, she kept saying, over and over again. Just *calm, calm, calm.*

"Sorry," Edgar said. He mostly meant it. "I – I don't know. I didn't know any of this was going to happen, I..." he let out a faint laugh and hoped that she of all people would be able to hear this without doubting his sanity. "I think I've sort of been in a cosmic trance state for...well, I guess it's been less than two days. It felt like a *lot* longer than that."

"Tell me more, please."

It was a calm, perhaps even indifferent request. But when Edgar looked across at her her eyes were wide and fixed intently on him. He swallowed hard, unsure how to continue.

"How much do you know about what's happening to your brother?" Edgar attempted.

Tenzin answered immediately. "What do *you* think is happening?"

Everything fell to pieces so quickly after he woke up that he didn't have the time he'd prefer to sit and process the place he was just in. The Other Place. The things that it showed him. The way it whispered and mocked. Inside him every second there was entirely vivid. Putting it to words, though, was difficult.

"There's...a place," he said. "I think it's a place. If it's a person – like, a god or an alien or something, then it's big enough for you to be inside of. And it's not that it has magical energy, it...it *is* the energy." Edgar furrowed his brow the more he thought about it. "I don't know if that's common knowledge. Is it?"

"I wouldn't say *common*," Tenzin took a deep breath. She picked up the box of baking soda and began liberally sprinkling it over the dried blood splatters. "People in Bluerose know, but that's just because of

Scott. Beyond that, the other towns don't seem to want to think that hard about it."

The next step on the guide was to let the baking soda sit, so they did. They stared down at the white powder, mutually silent. Tenzin, Edgar quickly learned, was great at silence. She accepted it with no question and not a single protest, diving so completely in the absence of stimuli that it was possible she forgot Edgar's presence entirely.

"You go there too," Tenzin said some time later.

It sounded like she was speaking from deep within herself, resulting in a voice that sounded miles away. She wasn't upset or happy. There was no fear in her voice, though no excitement either. If anything the only solid emotion he could decipher in her was disbelief.

Edgar, suddenly, felt inexplicably sheepish. "This was the first time."

That could be the end of his response. He didn't need to go into detail of how he got there, of what exactly getting there required. There was no need to explain what it felt like to lose all concept of body and ground only to be forcibly pushed back into confines that now felt slightly misshapen. Even though she wasn't in the process of actively beating him up, Tenzin was still a stranger.

But she was Scott's sister. And from the way Scott spoke of her he loved her dearly and trusted her with every fiber of his being. Edgar watched her open the bottle of white vinegar and blot some of the sour-smelling liquid onto another wad of paper towels. She began to scrub at the dusting of powder, cleaning the way people think they're supposed to when they don't have much experience in more specific work.

Tenzin brushed a golden loc behind her ear. She wasn't looking at Edgar, but he knew she was still listening.

Right before he accidentally blasted Tenzin out the door, Edgar saw the look on Scott's face as soon as he caught sight of his sister. It was an entirely new kind of joy. Scott was a child again, happy without any context of the world at large.

"I did an Extraction spell," he told Tenzin, soaking his own handful of paper and joining her in scrubbing. "It took some of whatever has Scott and put it into me."

Tenzin stopped cleaning. It looked like whatever they were doing was helping, so Edgar kept on working for the both of them. He scrubbed the baking soda with vinegar, which soaked the powder into a bubbling, pink paste.

He would need water.

There was a pitcher in the cabinet that Katy sometimes used to make margaritas when she got bored with winter. Edgar ran it under the sink to fill with water. He looked out the window nearby, which was bigger than the one in his place and had a better view.

A smattering of crows on a nearby roof conversed and flapped their wings. There was an old neighbor in Edgar's building who used to toss some mixture that left the yard haunted by bevvies of crows and ravens throughout the year. She died recently, and over time the birds stopped coming. Edgar considered taking over her role on his own. But after three hours researching the best combination of seeds to fit the needs of the right birds he got far too overwhelmed and had to lie down.

He would do it now. Edgar would fill the space outside his home with birds.

"How much do you remember of your childhood?"

Tenzin was still sitting on the floor. She was talking to him without looking at him, which was something she apparently did a lot.

Edgar held the pitcher of water in his hands and settled slightly against the counter. "Not a lot. Hopefully soon I won't remember any of it."

"What did Encyclopedia Brown charge to take a case?"

The answer appeared in his head immediately. "Twenty-five cents an hour," Edgar frowned, and then laughed. "What – why do you ask?"

"How'd that guy steal that painting?"

"What are you talking about?"

Tenzin finally faced him. "In that *Encyclopedia Brown* book. The art thief stole his friend's priceless painting. How?"

Once again Edgar struggled to follow what she was talking about. Then it hit him. He grinned, so amused by this nostalgia-bait that it momentarily made him forget his troubles.

"Oh god, right!" He said. "*The Case of the Supermarket Shopper.* He told his friend to buy four – I think it was things of toothpaste? And with the rest of his cart he couldn't use the express checkout line at the grocery store. It bought him extra time," Edgar chuckled. "I haven't thought about that in forever."

"He told me it was your favorite case," Tenzin said.

The enjoyment in him grew stale. Edgar held the pitcher a littler closer to his chest and once again wrestled with distrust. Because Tenzin – or, at least, this woman who somehow passed as Scott's sister – was saying something impossible. Worse than that, she was saying something untrue.

"Then he's lying," he gently clarified. "That one really upset me, actually. I spent so much time trying to solve the mystery on my own, and when I flipped to the back the answer made no sense to me. Because at the grocery store my mother took me to the express lane was twelve items, when in the book it was only ten. So I felt cheated," he looked away, embarrassed. "I think I cried going to bed that night."

"I know," Tenzin's voice said, a little closer now. "He told me when it happened."

Edgar heard that, but didn't really process it. He shifted his feet and thought about a child so stupidly sensitive that missing the historical context of a children's mystery series from the 1960s would reduce him to tears. It felt so far away, and yet at the same time part of him was still wearing that formal-cut, purple and gold blazer.

"Your mother beat you," Tenzin told him.

When she said that the statement rattled down his spine and he bolted his head up. Tenzin was standing directly in front of him now – with reservation, the way a new zookeeper would approach a wild animal. She adjusted her expression, perhaps to accommodate the shock written all over Edgar's face.

"No," she corrected herself. "Not beat. Not exactly. But she was abusive, right?" Tenzin did not leave room for an answer. "She would shave your head. Grab and pull your arm until it left bruises. Sometimes she'd stay out all night without making sure there was dinner ready. And there wasn't food in the house that you knew how to make. You went to bed hungry a lot back then."

Edgar's voice was a stranger's in his own ears. "How do you know all this?" He said.

Inexplicably, Tenzin smiled. Not a big grin and not for a long time, just a slight spasm in the mouth that reflected immense, almost overwhelming happiness.

"Oh my god," she whispered. "It's you. He found you."

A slow cyclone started brewing inside Edgar. He backed away, step by single step, but no matter how far back he got Tenzin's attention left him feeling incredibly claustrophobic.

She shook her head slowly. "No one thought...I mean, statistically it's impossible. Especially with the amount of information we had. Our elders were willing to give it a shot, but I know a few of them who weren't even certain you existed. Even after what mom did."

Apparently his body was backing him away in the wrong direction, because eventually Edgar ended up pressed against the fridge and couldn't move away any further. He tapped his fingertips against his thumb desperately, not knowing what else to do.

Tenzin noticed this before he realized what he was doing. "You even stim like he does," she laughed breathlessly. "And I was ready to kill you. I'm...I'm *so* sorry, Eddie."

He took in air, the cyclone threatening to pull his organs from their rightful places. No longer able to handle existing in this reality he closed his eyes, and then he was back in bed in Shreveport. Edgar was a child, lying beside the glowing blue boy with big, sad eyes. But it wasn't him, was it?

Well, it was Eddie.

And Edgar was Eddie.

In the darkness Tenzin continued speaking. "You go by Edgar now," she corrected herself. "I'm sorry. I'll call you Edgar," she paused, and then said, "Hello, Edgar."

He tried to touch the blue boy once. His hand met no physical matter. There was only a warm hiss like dipping into a bath of warm carbonated water. Edgar felt that same sensation in his heart when he felt Scott's body fully pressed along his own. Not even in sex – just to sleep.

"...Hi," Edgar responded.

They stared at each other, Neither smiled. Neither really breathed. A simple question hung in the air just above both of their heads.

What happens now?

Eighth Movement

Scott loved the hospital.

Maybe *love* was the wrong word. He loved old diners and taking walks in the clean peace after a rainstorm. Scott loved to touch things that were soft or old and well-constructed, and to spend the occasional night sleeping in a bakery while the overnight staff prepared the bread for the following day. Chunky sweaters. Cats with chubby cheeks or a tendency to chirp. Edgar Gallows, and to a more ghostly extent Eddie.

Things like that.

It was just different in the hospital. They all looked the same, even when they didn't. From massive, labyrinthine buildings to intimate clinics, there was an aura of clinical comfort across each location. A sterile warmth that could still suffice when there were no other options.

He knew people like him who hated having to wear the Kelley green hospital bracelet that signified a birthright patient for the hospitals in witch town regions. Scott never minded. The color was pretty, calming to the eyes. And it was a great way to tell everyone who saw him without a single word who he was and the type of care he needed. Whenever a doctor or nurse walked into the room, their eyes only went to the flash of and they would already understand what they would need to do to help him.

And so he always knew he would be helped. He couldn't hurt anyone here. He allowed himself to trust that they would take the precautions to make sure they wouldn't hurt him either.

Everything was hazy for a long time. The world was blurred in places and darkened in others, and Scott couldn't hold onto thoughts for long before they fell out of his grasp and into the murk. The Other Place was there too, but farther way – much farther. Still, where he was he could just hear the voices.

You are...dying, Birthright.

You...fools.

The presence was at a distance he could ignore with relative ease. So Scott focused what energy he had on staying at least partially conscious.

Eventually the world reformed. The first thing that became clear was that, at some point, Katy put her sunglasses back over Scott's eyes and bathed the world in golden hour shadows. He was in a fresh hospital gown, one of the nicer cloth ones they usually give to patients they don't consider to be on the verge of death. That was a good sign. His body felt thick with tension that cried out in pain when he shifted under the crisp sheets.

"Hey," Katy called out, sitting in a chair beside his bed. "Don't do that. Your IV."

Scott couldn't talk yet. He followed where Katy was pointing and saw a large bag of red-black fluid hung up on on a stand. There was tubing coming out from the bottom that snaked around the metal and branched into a needle stuck into the crook of his elbow. The fog was pulling back enough for him to see that they put in his IV close to his brachial artery. They probably wouldn't do that unless they struggled to find any other, more suitable vein. When was the last time he drank water?

The needle was actually just above the crook in the elbow, which wasn't a location he ever saw before. It confused him. Then again, everything felt confusing right now.

"You got the O."

"Huh?" Scott murmured.

Katy was trying very hard to lighten the mood of the situation. "You're getting a Type-O transfusion. Universal Donor, baby," she paused. "The doctor said it's standard."

Scott sighed. He read every paper his father ever wrote on birthright physiology, and at the time of his death there was no proof that birthright bodies were substantially different from non-magic users. It was frustrating to learn that people on a wider scale still reuse to believe that. It must be so much more appealing to assume that Scott was a special boy who got his good boy special superpowers from somewhere in his body. He must have a chamber in his heart or gland in his brain that stores all his magic like a tumor.

If only it were that easy.

Scott remembered enough to know he was a universal recipient. He knew that meant there could be people in this hospital who needed this blood more than he did.

Katy scooted her chair a little closer to him. She touched the railing of the bed, which was apparently as close as she was willing to get. Or at least that's what they both thought before she leaned forward a moment after that and clumsily clasped a hand over Scott's wrist.

When she spoke her voice was soft. "Are you okay?"

"I have to be."

"You're allowed to be upset about this, Scott."

Finally Scott laughed. The sound was rough and it left him coughing so hard he almost threw up. "I – I can't, actually," he managed once he calmed himself down. "Not yet, at least. Not here. You saw what Edgar did at work when he got overwhelmed by emotion. And that was something *positive*. Our negative reactions tend to be a lot more destructive," gathering a little more of his faculties, he focused better on Katy. "Did they give me any benzos?"

"You were unconscious. Were they supposed to?"

That wasn't a reassuring answer. Then again, he shouldn't be experiencing what he was at his age.

Scott tried to smile, but he couldn't really manage the effort and definitely didn't want to. He shouldn't have to smile in a place like this, where the status quo is to be sick and in pain. So he sighed and quietly asked Katy to go get a nurse, and maybe because he didn't make an attempt to look unaffected she quickly obeyed.

A few minutes later she was back with a new staff member trailing behind her. His scrubs looked fresh and his smile manufactured, two qualities that led Scott to assume this person was either still in residency or fresh out of the nursing program.

He clenched his jaw. This would have to be approached carefully.

"I need a benzodiazapine, please," he said.

The nurse blinked a few times, his cheer carved from friendly concrete. "I didn't see on your chart that you had a prescription, Mister Kaufner."

Panic. Even through the sick it rocketed like lightening. That filling, near-tipping feeling was already starting.

"Our doctors are still meeting for shift change. If you don't mind waiting for another ten or fifteen minutes I can ask them what they think."

"You're doing your job," Scott carefully observed. "I can respect that. But I'm telling you that something bad is going to happen soon if somebody doesn't sedate me."

He knew the way that the nurse was looking at him now. He was examining Scott for signs of addiction. Maybe physical mannerisms that can be linked to mental illnesses like schizophrenia. Most people beg for benzos for the lull of the high. It wasn't as common of an occurrence to take them to keep blasts of psychic energy from rocketing out of you when you're pretty sure you're a floor below a maternity ward.

Scott lowered his head in defeat. Then he noticed something – a familiar flash of green on his free wrist. He raised it slightly, looking at the birthright medical bracelet that had apparently been put on him while he was spelunking in the void.

It's here, he thought, mystified. *They do it here too.*

Without saying a word he held his wrist higher so the nurse could see the green. He waited for a reaction that never came.

"Are you okay, Mister Kaufner?" He asked.

"He's birthright," Katy said from her spot near the window.

The nurse at least by now had the sense to adjust his customer service face and make it slightly more apologetic. "I don't know what that means."

Oh no. Oh no, no, no.

Scott let out a low, repetitive hum. This is why he only went to clinics. This is why he learned to stitch up his own gashes if he ever got hurt on the job. This is exactly why he never even considered medical care unless it was to pick up hormones or get a goddamned *flu shot* –

Another figure in a white coat rushed into the room, pushing a small cart in front of them. She was an older, feminine-type with a small cloud of silver coils clinging to frame her amber brown face. The doctor didn't acknowledge anyone in the room and immediately loaded two separate syringes. She injected them each into Scott's IV bag, one immediately after the other. He began to question why he let them get this far without asking what they were doing when he felt that familiar full-body warmth seep over him.

Instant nightfall.

"I am so sorry," the doctor said. "I was waiting for you to wake up. With the size of the transfusion we're doing nausea is a big possibility and I couldn't have you too drugged up to not choke on your own vomit."

Scott settled his head against the pillow. It was starchy. Soft things are good, but there's something about a starchy pillowcase that gave off the impression of truly being cared for.

Whatever the doctor gave him, it was fantastic and he wanted it in him all the time forever.

"My name is Doctor Zula Landry," she said. "She/her pronouns. It's a pleasure to have you with us, Scott."

The nurse still lingered by the doorway. He no longer smiled. "Did you give him Ativan *and* Klonopin? Isn't that dangerous?"

"He's a birthright, Duncan, he needs the side effects." Zula eyed Scott like an old friend. Specifically, an old friend she was aiming to gossip with. "Duncan is the skeptic of the unit," she said.

Speaking felt like digging out of a mountain of gelatin with just his mouth. "Of...what?"

"Of genetic witches," she said. "He's of the newer generation, and you know they like their doubting."

Scott raised his eyes to Duncan the Nurse. This was a new development. It never occurred to Scott that he would have to exist in a world where some people straight up doubted his status as a human being on the planet.

That was pretty much the only thing he was taught that he was able to count on, wasn't it? He wasn't guaranteed happiness or safety. Birthrights were entitled to nothing but the knowledge that the earth wanted them there, wanted to provide a home for them to exist in. If something could give Scott control over his mind and a place to stay alive for few more decades, he wouldn't ask anything of anyone ever again.

All he wanted to do was live in cotton dresses with people that he loved, drinking hot drinks and making music until it was his turn to die. Instead, there were assholes with bad goatees who would rather risk countless lives because they refused to see him as anything other than a goddamned *cryptid.*

"Duncan," Scott called out. "Hey, Duncan."

He looked at him.

"You gotta help me, Duncan," he said. "I'm not a genetic witch."

Duncan was now frowning. He didn't answer. Scott sat up slowly, steadying his hands behind him to keep from toppling over.

"I'm a Sasquatch," Scott grinned madly as he spoke. "I'm a gay, intersex Sasquatch, and if I don't figure out my shit soon I might just wind up being your next god. What do you think about that, *Duncan?*"

Scott fell back then, exhausted by his efforts, but laughing the best he could and feeling very pleased with himself.

The doctor took his vitals. Or, at least, that's part of what Scott assumed she was doing. With the drugs coursing through his system, causing the lines of the room to waver slightly as if bathed in heat, it was hard to pay attention. So hard, in fact, that he didn't bother.

When was the last time he felt this utterly relaxed? It was before leaving Bluerose, much longer before that. It had to have been sometime in his childhood, as that was the only time he could think of when he could tell himself that everything was going to be okay and have his body believe it.

Doctor Zula touched Scott's shoulder, a touch he barely felt through the depths of the white and fluffy cloud that his body felt encased in. "Scott," she told him. "Your friend Katy tells me you've been having problems with your memories."

"Yup," he said. "I mean...Yes, Doctor."

She nodded, grave yet kindly. "I can't speak on any supernatural influences, but once we stabilize your iron levels over the next few weeks it should help. You'll also get some color back in you, and definitely have more energy to work with," Zula glanced at her nearby monitor and sighed. "Frankly, I'm surprised you managed to last as long as you have."

"What do you mean?" Scott said.

"Well you were diagnosed with iron-deficiency anemia thirteen years ago. Your chart says you got a single transfusion that day, but it looks like it was only enough to keep you conscious. Apparently your Doctor Park prescribed iron tablets, but he put a note in your chart saying they were never picked up."

Scott fell silent. That wasn't right. That couldn't be right. What was he about to do, assume that his family neglected his physical health so severely that, even if he managed to get the god out of his system, he could die from organ failure at any time? No. He wouldn't even start to acknowledge that as a possibility.

There had to be another answer.

"Doctor," he asked, pushing through the high for focus. "What else does my chart say?"

She pulled the monitor closer to face her and pushed up her glasses to scan the contents. "Well, let's see. You started testosterone treatments at thirteen years old. Your pediatrician and your last GP actually both rave about how much of a pleasure you've been as a patient, which I don't think is something I've before," Doctor Zula hummed, continuing to read. "You've been on a variety of anti psychotics and mood stabilizers since early childhood. Eventually you were established on Lithium, but you haven't had a blood test since your anemia diagnosis. I imagine that means you stopped taking it. Which probably the smartest choice to make," she raised her eyes over the screen to look at him. "What are you taking now?"

"For what?"

"For your Bipolar."

Something pushed from deep within Scott. It thrashed at its walls, clawing at every surface with fingers that quickly turned torn and bloody. It threw its full body weight against the surrounding confinement until every bone bruised. The walls moved, maybe just a little, but refused to fully give way. Eventually the feeling got tired and retreated to a corner, burying within itself like an animal about to die.

"Scott?" The doctor asked.

"Nothing," Scott said flatly. "I'm...I'm taking nothing."

The easy charm of Doctor Zula quickly waned. It fell into a doctor's competent determination, a quality Scott could fall into as easily as a warm bed. She pursed her lips thoughtfully and got a little closer, lowering her voice so only the two of them were able to hear it.

"Have you been keeping up with the new standards of the Witch Doctors?" She asked him.

So that's how this woman was so attuned to his needs. Scott wanted to smile yet couldn't really find the energy. "I haven't," he said instead.

"You should. Your – I mean, Doctor Kaufner's work – has truly changed the game over the past forty years," Doctor Zula restrained her enthusiasm and continued. "They have advocates for birthright patients outside of witch town regions now. To help explain their situation and all potential options. Would you like me to call one for you?"

That was something else to think about. Another scoop of slop atop a pile on a plate already filled with hairline cracks. Not only was Scott not the first birthright to leave a witch town, there were apparently so many that their major medical organization had to create new procedure to accommodate them.

He thought he was the first. Why? Did anyone tell him that, say those exact words? Did they even *imply* them? Scott closed his eyes hard and tried to think back, but going backwards in his memory was difficult. It was grinding two gears in an unintended direction that threatened to make the whole mechanic burst.

"It's okay, Scott," the doctor tried to soothe him through his thoughts. "With all of this going on you must be exhausted. I'm sure it's difficult to think straight about things like this."

Tears escaped his closed eyes. He wiped at them, groaning softly. This was miserable.

"I'm his advocate," Katy declared in a strong, but unconvincing voice.

He forced himself to look at her, as the doctor did now, and between both of their attention Katy shirked back further against the window.

"I mean, I don't have..." she held up her hands like she needed to prove she was unarmed. "If there's paperwork involved I don't have it. But I can...listen. Explain things. I don't know."

Zula turned back to Scott and shot him a questioning look. Scott wiped at his eyes again. He nodded.

While the doctor and his advocate talked about the apparent state of his mental health, Scott stared up at the tiles on the ceiling and allowed his mind to drift. Through the haze he felt that imitation-headache twisting behind his eyes. Like the rain Edgar summoned it was almost, but not entirely correct. As intoxicated as he was, he was able to detect the feeling as evidence of magic.

He was bipolar. Early onset, by the sounds of it. Straining his imagination, Scott could see the blurry image of a psychiatrist's office decorated in a way that could appeal to children. But maybe that was all that was – imagination.

People in Bluerose don't introduce themselves with their most significant quirk or hardship. Ultimately a disability is a disability, regardless of whether or not it granted the person some rare, unearthly power. And there were times when that wasn't even the case. Sometimes someone with depression just has a chemical imbalance. Sometimes a person with Hemophilia is just born into a body that struggles to clot its own blood.

Sometimes a coloboma is just a coloboma.

It didn't really make a difference. He could think back on his mother and someone he knew to be the head Elder of Bluerose sitting him down and explaining that his genetics were only the foundation of the person he would ultimately become. Because of it, his tools for living were slightly different than others, but that didn't mean he wouldn't be able to have a long and happy existence. Scott was still a human being worthy of love and deserving of respect.

In retrospect, this is a very strange thing to say in regards to a slight dip in his pupils.

It didn't make a difference.

But it *did*, didn't it? Scott carried so much weight in his head that it astonished him that he was able to walk upright. Before he met Edgar, the only time he was able to achieve a sense of calm was through dissociation or exhaustion. That wasn't normal. That's not supposed to be how he lived his life. Once he raised the iron levels in his blood and got back on some kind of mood stabilizer, imagine how much better he could be feeling.

Scott would be healthier. Stronger. He would

sit on the edge of the dingy bed in his dingier motel room, phone held limply to his ear. Tenzin was on the end, not taking, but breathing steadily to let him know she was still there. Waiting for him to speak. Hoping he would be the one, once again, to break the silence.

"I didn't know what else to do," she told him after a very long time.

"It's okay."

"No, Skylark, it isn't. We..." Tenzin took a deep breath. Her sigh was shaky enough to rattle straight in his heart. "We failed you. All of us."

Scott sank back onto the mattress. "You did what I asked. What else could be done?"

"I spoke to Doctor Park and he sent a prescription for iron tablets to a pharmacy near your next bus station. And he gave me the number of a psychologist who said she could have a session on the phone and figure out a new medication for you," Tenzin's voice grew terminally hopeful. "It won't fix everything but it should make it easier."

Easier. Scott ran his fingers along the word like the chamber of a revolver. Easier for who?

He considered the spiral of writhe twisting just under his skin. It pulled in every direction. He threw up so many full meals that at this point he was considering living off of bread and juice.

Scott wished he was dying. What he was edging towards was so much worse.

"No," Scott said.

A beat of silence. "What?"

"I thought getting physically stronger would make me feel better and it didn't," he closed his eyes, regretted it, and went back to counting the water stains on the ceiling. "If I stay like this I'll be easier to overpower."

"Scott that's insane," Tenzin said. "Someone could seriously hurt you."

That's the idea.

Checking in the lobby a fellow traveler knocked into Scott as he was exiting the front door. The man didn't apologize. Scott stood outside and watched him through the glass, imagining how his hair would feel as he gripped it hard enough to slam his skull against the counter, again and again, until discreet facial features were reduced to wet putty.

The man was twice his size and visibly much stronger. But Scott could kill him easily, easily and painfully, and the thought of that terrified him.

"Could you?" Scott asked Tenzin through the phone. "You know – seriously hurt me?"

Tenzin didn't answer. By now he couldn't even track her breathing.

"You're the only one willing to talk to me. You don't pretend like I'm out on some noble pilgrimage for the good of the universe."

"Skylark –"

"I'm trying. I'm definitely trying, but..." he wasn't crying. Why wasn't he crying? "If you see me next and I'm not – me – anymore, I need to know you'll be able to take care of it. I think you're the only one in Bluerose powerful enough to pull it off."

A long, tense silence. "Please, Scott," Tenzin whispered. "Please take your meds."

"Do you feel it? Can you feel what I feel from over there?"

"No. You're too far out and you don't always tell me where you're going next, so I have no way of knowing where to go to help. Did you mean to..?" Tenzin huffed. The sound turned into something resembling a scoff. "I'm still upset. I don't need magic to empathize with you."

That was some small gratitude from the earth, and even though it was extended onto his sister instead of him Scott would accept it gladly. He would bare this poison alone. It would sicken his body to the point where it was useless to even the most starved scavenger. The damage would be there, but it would be far more limited. Sometimes sacrifices like that are necessary.

"I'll call you tomorrow, Tenzin," Scott told her.

She had more to say. In fact, she was in the middle of protesting when Scott flipped his phone closed and tossed it aside. At that moment the heat on the rusted mini-split across from him switched on, filling the room with the whir of a fan very close to death. Scott sat up and thought about the previous conversation. He tried to remember the turning point event from their shared childhood, a pointless effort that ultimately came up eroded and indistinct with the wet tides of nothingness that crashed against it.

Scott thought of Eddie. He leaned forward and focused every amount of energy towards even remembering the outline of his face. The color of his eyes. Anything at all.

Nothing. He apparently had it once but it was long gone.

The grief was nauseating, and because it originated from this plane of existence it was actually a lot worse to deal with. Scott went to unzip his bag and rifled for his last bottle of Petrichor. Just by shaking it he could hear that he had a little more than two doses left.

He'd take it all now. Clutch onto the insights and tear them straight out of his head, buying him a night of dreamless sleep. That was the one scrap of mercy he was willing to allow himself at this point.

As soon as he unscrewed the lid of his flask, the smell of the substance inside filled the confines of the motel room. It was coldly sweet like a fresh rose. Musty in a way that seemed to thicken the air around it. Scott crinkled his nose in distaste and dumped the contents into a paper cup from a stack by the coffee maker.

Staring down at Petrichor, it looked like being handed a glass of water that you just know is poisoned. The fumes already had him buzzed. Scott took a deep breath and downed the two doses in one gulp.

Don't puke. Please don't puke.

Scott fell limp to his side on the bed and clutched both hands to his mouth. He was hoping that, after now drinking actual alcohol like a normal person, he would have a slightly higher tolerance for birthright medicine. Obviously that was wrong. What was he thinking? A handle of Everclear nursed over the course of a month was not enough to prepare him for what he now understood to be an overdose of Petrichor.

His mouth was dry and sticky and burned madly. He needed water. But when Scott sat up and reached for the bottle on his side table he turned the wrong way and collapsed onto the carpet. The noise he let out as his back hit the matted fibers was thick. Choked.

The world sparkled with mad clarity. He took in the oily residue of reality, all the shapes he was not supposed to be able to see. What if doing this gave whatever was in him a chance to take over once and for all? Would Scott wake up again? If he did, where would he find himself?

Tears flowed from his eyes. Breathing was getting increasingly difficult, and every time he exhaled the flow of air pushed up a little bit of stomach acid. Scott blinked madly, trying to cough, trying – for some reason – to stave off death for a little while longer.

You okay, Scott?

No. I'm scared.

Yeah. Me too.

I don't know what I'm going to do. Everything hurts.

I'm sorry. It wasn't supposed to be like this.

What do you mean? I don't understand.

It's okay. You'll figure it out! You're always so brave.

You think?

Yeah. Do you remember my last birthday with you?

No. I'm sorry.

That's okay! Because I still do. You saw my bruises and told me you'd come and save me.

Oh.

I think you still can! I think you can find me and we can save each other. Just like how we promised.

Lying on the dirty motel carpet, Scott trembled an unsteady smile, vision blurry from tears and insanity. "Y-Yeah, Eddie," *he breathed.* "I'm coming. I...I promise."

"You with me, Scott?"

Scott blinked back to the sensation of lukewarm liquid filling his mouth. It was water. He was sitting upright and drinking from a paper glass of water. Soon the cup was empty and he slowly crushed the damp material in the palm of his hand.

There was a new blood bag on his IV stand and a heat pack on his arm. A distant sense of clarity let him know that he asked Duncan the nurse for that, because he was feeling a chill at the injection site from the temperature of the blood. He knew this happened. He had no memory of it.

Katy was sitting next to him with her phone in hand. There was a digital clock on the wall above her head. They'd been there for a little over three hours.

The density of the high was mostly gone and left only a vague nausea and the grumblings of hunger.

"I zoned out," Scott said. "I'm sorry."

"Yeah, you looked pretty spacey for a while," Katy glanced over at the clock. "You were able to respond to things for a bit, but over the past hour you were just *gone*. Moving, looking around, just *nothing* behind the..." Katy saw something in his expression and frowned. "You probably don't want to hear about that right now."

Sitting up and lying down felt essentially the same. Every angle he could arch his head made absolutely no difference. He could close his eyes and interpret the same amount of information as when they were open and scanning the room. Some people stand on the ground and look ahead of them and actually feel like they're standing on the ground and looking ahead of them.

That must be nice.

"I almost died," Scott said.

"Fuck. What – just now?"

He huffed a small laugh. "No. I don't know when, but – a while ago. I think I almost asphyxiated."

Katy leaned back in her chair. She sighed under her breath. "Fuck," she said again.

"It's actually – it's kind of jarring. Because I was just lying there, you know? I was thinking that everything was over for me, and..." Scott felt the words pale as they left his lips. "I didn't want to go."

He breathed in and out, blinking back tears like that could do anything to stop them from coming. God, he was so sick of crying. It didn't even mean anything anymore.

"You don't want to die," Katy said.

"No," Scott whispered. "No, I don't."

He thought back to the motel room, and the comforting weight of the blurry child sitting on his chest. Just remember his face. Just pull back the fog and find something recognizable to match the voice that felt so familiar to him.

"Kind of throws a wrench in your whole life perspective, doesn't it?"

Hearing that surprised Scott, and he laughed. "It really does."

He examined the crumpled remains of the cup, the wrinkles of damp card stock coated with something people might not be intended to ingest. It was like a tiny brain held in the palm of his hands. Something flawed. Something created essentially by accident. It wasn't supposed to be here, and yet now it was and there was no way to undo its existence without destroying it entirely.

"Scoot over," Katy said.

Hospital beds weren't meant to accommodate two people. Luckily, Scott was small enough for him and Katy to squeeze together and perfectly fill the space between either railing. Maybe perfect was a bit of an overstatement, but Scott was willing to overlook the hard plastic digging into his hip in exchange for the warmth of a safe human being.

"Apparently you had a child psych in Oregon who prescribed you Wellbutrin. Doctor Landry said that she called the office and your sister picked it up. So that might be part of why she's here."

He tried to remember the phone call. It was Tenzin on the other end – wasn't it? Already the memory was dipping back into the tar pit pooled over his brain. Scott despaired at losing something so important after so short a time and pushed himself to remember the one important insight from that memory.

Scott didn't want to die. He didn't want to die.

"She also thinks your testosterone treatments probably saved your life," Katy said that with a casual simmer that neither of them were convinced by. "Apparently studies have shown it raises hemoglobin in some men. She isn't sure if that still applies to someone with Klinefelter, but she said that's the only medical theory she has so far on how you went on a road trip essentially running on empty."

"Hm."

Katy tilted her foot and tapped Scott from over the blanket. "Wellbutrin's great. It can make you a little edgy sometimes. Maybe a bit twitchy. But it helped me a lot."

"You've taken it?" Scott said.

"Oh yeah. Apparently they use it for a bunch of different conditions. I was Seasonal Affective as shit back in Boston, and Wellbutrin was the only thing that really worked for me."

Scott stared down at his hands. "If these pills make it harder to play the piano I'll kill myself," he paused and smiled limply. "I don't mean that. I don't think it's true. I just wanted to say it out loud."

He thought, maybe hoped in some way, that Katy would mock him for how over-dramatic he was being. There was a perfect opportunity for her to make a joke about how, if those were the types of thoughts he had on a regular basis, then he should've gathered he was bipolar much earlier. She stayed silent. He looked across at her and saw that Katy was gazing distantly out the window.

She fluttered her eyelashes and darted her stare to him, perhaps noticing that he was watching. Then she went back to the window.

"I'm not worried about you," Katy said.

"You're..." Scott turned the best he could to face her more directly. "You're not?"

Katy shrugged, almost indifferent. "Not really. Don't get me wrong, this whole situation looked pretty crazy at first. But the more I learn, it's just...not that interesting."

"Oh – am I *boring* you?" Scott asked, already breaking out in a grin.

"You are, actually."

Maybe it was the new sobriety or the newer blood coursing through his system, but Scott suddenly felt more aware than ever. He was stifling giggles now, toying with a strand of hair with his free hand as he listened.

"I bet you know a lot of guys being possessed by a god," he said.

Katy hummed. "I went to school with a few anemic kids. My mom's bipolar – and she's fucking *crushing it,* by the way. Uh – I know gay people. I'm a gay people. Plus my best friend at work is on the ace spectrum. I can't even say that you're the first intersex person I've met, because I heard once that a lot of people are and don't know it," she leaned forward and thought deeply. "You're more into Edgar than anyone I've met. And that's great, but it's not...I mean, it's not *Batman: The Ride,* you know?"

This was the funniest thing any human being has ever said to him. Despite Scott's tired rolls of laughter, Katy kept a stony demeanor, still acting like she was delivering news that he would find hard to hear.

"I hate to be the one to tell you this, Scott," she said. "You're just kind of dull. Right now the most unusual thing about you are your medical issues, so once you get that under control you'll be indistinguishable from every other queer artist in New Orleans."

"I'll probably be shorter," Scott added.

"Probably, yes."

"And *magic.*"

"Oh *who cares*?" Katy declared to the otherwise empty room. "Who cares! I know a card trick, I'm just as magic as you are."

In that moment Scott knew he would do anything for this steely-faced blonde cuddled up beside him. There was no ritual bond between them and it did not matter. He would fight for Katy. Watching the slight satisfaction in her face from her final claim, Scott could physically feel himself mark off the part of his brain he would dedicate to maintaining her well-being for the rest of his life.

At that moment, Tenzin appeared in the doorway. She changed her clothes and left her dreads damp and loose around her face. He looked at her, so close to him after so long, and it was like seeing her again for the first time.

They really grew up in the time that they spent apart. He didn't even realize that when he thought of Tenzin he still saw the child from his past. That was the image of her that comforted him the most, but neither of them had been a child in a very long time. Staring now, Scott was forced to remind himself that the person in front of him was a full grown woman, strained and terribly lonely.

A ghost of her voice echoed in his ears. *I don't need magic to empathize with you.*

Scott swallowed hard. "I'm so sorry, Ten," he whispered.

Tenzin practically ran to his beside and pulled him into her arms. With his face buried in her t-shirt he was hit with the smell of the home-made laundry detergent that his mother used since he was born. It was light, but musky, warm like hay but wet like leaves after the rain. The sensation was so immense that it left no room for any kind of reaction. He just let it wash over him.

From the darkness of the fabric he heard his sister's voice. "I couldn't fix it," she spoke into his hair. "All I wanted to do was fix it and I couldn't. If we told you how sick you were you might remember everything else you were trying to forget, and you could've ended up in even more pain."

He sat up and smiled at her, his sister, his light and anchor. "We've been managing the best with that we could work with."

"Well that's over now. Ask me any question you want answered and I'll tell you. I'll tell you everything I know, Scott."

Why did you say that I was the one trying to forget? Did I do something to myself or did someone else do something to me? Is it reversible – and if so, do is it something I should want to reverse? If I gave my medical chart a closer inspection would anything else surprise me? Did no adult in Bluerose stop me out of helplessness or a sense of duty, or am I not actually at home at home as I thought? Do I still even have a home?

What happens now? What happens now?

"Where's Edgar?" Scott asked her.

Tenzin glanced to the doorway. "I...don't know," she probably realized the implication of what she was saying and quickly continued. "We drove together! He gave me the address because he said Katy took him here to get stitches when he had an accident in the kitchen."

From beside him Katy scoffed. "*Ratatouille* can't use a goddamned whetstone to save his life. Never again."

"Do you think the rat in the movie is named Ratatouille?" Tenzin said, brow furrowed.

Katy met her uncertainty with an equal degree of bold assurance. "The rat gets it as a nickname, Zinzin. Because he's really good at cooking."

Sometimes when they were growing up, Scott would propose a philosophical concept that was so abstract that Tenzin would have no idea how to react. Or he would have a dream and insist on telling her every detail until she was absolutely lost, because he had the bad habit of telling stories from his waking and sleeping life with the exact same tone and cadence. He knew the exact moment his sister mentally concluded there was no point in attempting to respond. Just a blank look of clarity and a slight quirk in the brow. Exactly what he was seeing right now.

Was he still high, or was his sister and his best friend going to get married?

Hopefully both. He hoped it was both.

"Hey."

Edgar carefully walked in. He, too, got the chance to clean himself up and change his clothes. Everything went wild so soon after he woke up out of his trance that Scott barely got a chance to actually look at him.

He looked good. *Really* good. Was that also the blood, or any of the other fluids that Doctor Zula had steadily pumping into him over the course of the last few hours? Edgar just looked different. Just as Scott was able to feel himself steadily – and perhaps reluctantly – regaining his strength, his bond was following the same incline.

There was no beacon of pure joy radiating from deep within his being. But his eyes were more alert, somehow richer in their shades of brown. His face was steady. It didn't look like a noise too loud or movement too sudden would cause him to even waver, much less topple over. The angles of his body would express perfect ease to someone who didn't know him better. For Scott, the main thing he read was a sincere sense of preparation.

This was Edgar the Birthright. And god, was he a sight to look at.

"That thing with the whetstone," Scott said. "That's how you got that scar across the bottom of your thumb, right?"

Edgar didn't hear the first part of their conversation, but was immediately willing to join in. "I saw a lot of fat. It was gross."

He looked like he wanted to retell the story, thinking back on it almost fondly. But he thought better of it. Edgar raised the tote bag that Scott didn't even notice he was carrying in one hand.

"I don't know when you'll be able to do this," he said. "But we brought you a change of clothes."

There was a glimpse of soft blue chunky knit peeking out from the top of the bag. Katy narrowed her eyes at it. "Is that my sweater?"

Immediate tension between both Edgar and Tenzin. They exchanged a look, which – given the previous events – felt to Scott like a fantastic sign. For a few moments they silently prompted the other to speak, until finally Edgar broke first.

"My clothes suck, Katy," he said.

"No, I – I don't think..." she snickered quietly. "I don't care. I have siblings – I was taught young to accept that my wardrobe is a shared resource," Katy scooted further forward and tried to peer into the bag. "What'd you pick?"

Suddenly Edgar was stricken a little shy. He poked at the bag and shrugged. "There's that sweater you wore back when you dated that Christian girl. And a sort of flowy, crinkly skirt thing. It's brown."

"*Pleated,* Edgar. The word is *pleated,*" Katy looked pleased, and leaned back in the bed. "That seems good! It's not even stuff I wear anymore. All my grandmas are dead so I no longer have any reason to own a cable-knit sweater."

The energy in the room was light and affectionate, yet Scott found himself drawing inwards. It was unfamiliar territory to be surrounded by so many people who cared for him in so many ways. Being in the depths of it felt safe – and it also stung in its potential impermanence. Since when did the society decide he was fit to exist in this degree of comfort? When was he supposed to be wanted by more than just the ground under his feet?

"You've never seen me in feminine clothing, Edgar," Scott pointed out, a test and a plea.

Edgar's mouth tightened, but not in disgust. Instead, when paired with the soft blush on his cheeks, he looked more embarrassed.

"It isn't – I mean – It's really not –"

"He picked the outfit," Tenzin said.

"I don't care if you want to wear a skirt or a dress – or anything like that. Really," Edgar established, quickly regaining his cool. "I just – don't really know anything about them. Especially when they aren't on a...person," he took a deep breath. "I tried to think about why I would want to wear a skirt, and my first thought was that spinning around in one and making it go all big probably feels pretty nice."

"It does," Scott quietly confirmed.

"So I picked the only one that I thought you could do that in. If you wanted to. And, uh, it's not tight-fitting, so you can still cross your legs if you want," Edgar shifted his feet anxiously, eyes briefly lowering to scan the floor. "I also...um, I got you a treat."

He came a little closer, rustling through the bag as went to stand beside Tenzin.

"When Katy took me to get my stitches I was kind of freaking out," he scowled sheepishly to himself. "Still scared of blood, you know. Uh, and there's this vending machine in the lobby that has the Cookies and Cream Hershey's Bar. Which is crazy, right? A niche flavor in a vending machine? It's my favorite, though, and she bought it for me for being brave," there was a muffled crinkle from the bag. "White chocolate is divisive, though. Luckily, I peeked in your bag when I first grabbed it and saw three of the same candy bar wrapper. So – here."

There was a twin Twix bar held in his outstretched palm. Two hundred and fifty calories. Objectively unhealthy, but able to provide a small burst of energy during a caffeine withdrawal. There's two of them, so you can save the other for later with less mess. They're also a simple combination of textures that can fill your stomach without provoking that inevitable nausea. If you throw up after eating a Twix, your mouth will taste primarily of stomach acid and not an ultimately failed attempt at sub-par nutrition.

His heart twisted in his chest, pained and self-loathing. *Some people just enjoy a candy bar, Skylark.*

"Thank you, Edgar," Scott said graciously, taking the bar and setting it down in his lap.

The four in the room lingered in silence. Edgar's attention was focused solely on Scott, which Scott observed graciously and warily. A lot was going on all at once. The negligible weight of the wrapped chocolate bar resting on his thigh felt like it could leave a bruise if he kept it there for long enough.

"Katy," Tenzin said, poised in a way that felt slightly off. "Do you think you could show me where the bathroom is?"

"There's one here. It's behind you."

A brief, vaguely frustrated pause. "I'm making an excuse for both of us to leave."

Scott could actually hear Katy grind her teeth in contemplation. She locked eyes with Edgar, who looked away from Scott long enough to cast her a nod. It looked like they were silently negotiating how to handle a threat. He knew his sister wasn't a danger to anyone, unless they mishandled her tablet. Or if they jumped on a pop culture bandwagon without knowing enough about what they were talking about. Or, perhaps most of all, if someone put Scott into immediate danger.

There have been a few occasions where he's witnessed the change firsthand. The way her usually placid, serene face suddenly shifted into something akin to the feel of a gun between your eyes. If that's what they saw then they definitely didn't see Tenzin. No wonder Katy was so wary now.

At some point his friend reached an internal decision and pulled herself out of the hospital bed. "There's a little patio on the roof. You can get a pretty good view of the city."

"That sounds good."

Katy paused putting on her coat and shot Tenzin a sharp look. "They keep a security guard by the door. Sometimes two of them. What I'm trying to say is – fight me and you're outnumbered."

She probably said that expecting her comment not to genuinely hurt Tenzin's feelings. She didn't express the pain as openly as Scott would. But he saw the subtle reshaping in her eyes and knew Katy's suspicion upset her.

"Yes," she said, looking away. "Noted."

They left then, Katy leading the way and Tenzin following a few steps behind. It was the same posture she took when following one of the elders in Bluerose. In her brain it expressed a sense of respect to make it clear that the other party was more capable of leading. Their mother explained that youth were taught that they had just as much right to walk alongside their leaders, but apparently she was unable to fully grasp onto that.

Alone, Edgar got closer to Scott's bed. He left the bag at his feet and settled a hand on Scott's leg. Through his touch Scott was hit with a rush of sanity. Floor under him and ceiling above him. Walls on every side. A window to his left. A television in the opposite corner. The heat pack on his arm was gradually becoming lukewarm.

"Did I do something wrong?" he said.

"Huh?" Scott saw Edgar point to the Twix bar in his lap. "Oh. No. I mean...It's a Twix bar. Can't put a lot of malice in a candy bar, you know?'

Scott frowned, toying with his hands so forcefully that he was even more aware of the needle in his arm. He could still feel Edgar watching him. Waiting, undoubtedly, for a more honest response.

"I can feel your heart, Skylark. I know it upset you," Edgar bent down in an awkward position so he could catch Scott's gaze. "I'm just trying to figure out why."

This was insane. How much of love is the other person actively trying to understand the few emotions you don't feel comfortable sharing? Scott didn't want to wrap himself in a cocoon of his own misery and rot in its fluids until there's nothing left but fragments of bone. He also didn't want to share just how badly he had been treating himself over the past few years, because the more he looked back on what he remembered the more he became disgusted by his own behavior.

He picked up the Twix bar. It looked like it was in solid condition. Occasionally the bars would crack or break coming out of the machine or sometime during transit, which was fine but threw all his plans out of whack.

"Can we split it?" Scott offered to Edgar.

Edgar worked his way into bed alongside Scott. For some reason he felt as if he and Edgar might fit in this slightly-larger twin bed with zero problem. Obviously that made no sense, but they too ended up managing. Scott pulled up the blanket and tucked it over Edgar's legs, offering him a modicum of hospital-grade warmth.

To say that he leaned against him would be inevitable, as with the space they had there was nothing else for them to do. But Scott fully supported his weight on his boyfriend, letting his eyes fall halfway shut as he undid the wrapper of what he truly, deeply hoped was the last Twix bar of his life.

Edgar nursed his Twix bar and considered the gentle mixing of cheap caramel and biscuit cookie. It was sweet, but not the sweetest candy bar on the market. He didn't know the exact reason why Scott latched onto them the way he did, and he probably wouldn't try and ask for a long time. There was no need to. Edgar understood.

"I had an image in my head of what abuse looked like," he said. "I think she knew that. It wouldn't surprise me if they all did. Paint a picture of child abuse as a spectrum that starts with a closed-fist punch to the face and it leaves a lot of wiggle room that kids might struggle to dispute."

Scott mowed down his half of the chocolate bar so quickly that Edgar barely noticed. He ate Twix like he drank alcohol, with the express intent to get the process over with as quickly as possible.

"She used to cook, but not often. Sometimes she'd make a basic meal – usually a canned soup or stew. But most nights I'd have to ask, which is…I don't know. Weird when you're that young," he took another bite and thoughtfully chewed. "But she'd stay late at work sometimes and I wouldn't know until I found out in the middle of the day from one of my professors. And I'd spent the rest of class just…dreading. Because when I got home that night I'd have no idea what to do."

It was hard to think about, even now. That slight touch to his shoulder as the teacher who saw him more than his own mother informed him of his solitude, perhaps knowing everything it meant for him. Some of them were kinder than others, but none helped in any way. Which – maybe they couldn't. But they could've tried.

"There was food in the house," Edgar said. "Well, there were things that could *be* food. Like raw meat, or…you know, flour and spices. It was good stuff – put me in that kitchen now and I'd make a great meal, no problem."

"But you were a child."

"We didn't even have a *step stool*. I couldn't reach the bread," he thought of something, frowning. "Maybe she was expecting me to practice my incantations. I knew a basic matter manipulation spell by then, but – it *hurt*. I didn't like to do it."

He could feel Scott's breath gliding evenly against the sleeve of his shoulder. It was measured. Every touch of warm, damp air soaked against Edgar's skin and dripped pure grief down his bones, cool and pungent.

"You chose hunger," Scott said.

Edgar nodded. He didn't know what else to say about it.

"The hunger stopped bothering me after a while," Scott said. "It kind of hurts and – itches, maybe? But I learned if you wait it goes away. Then after a while you just...don't get hungry anymore. You just forget about it. That's the worst part."

That was a great way to describe the experience of watching Scott eat. Whenever they shared a meal together his bond ate like he was just now remembering that food and eating was a thing he was able to do. Edgar forgot their conversation in favor of recalling every time he's seen him eat since they met. He knew he was overcompensating. He was immediately jumping to a greater degree of worry than what might be necessary.

But Edgar knew that experience of hunger pains slowly fading. The moment your own body loses faith that you'll make an effort to keep it alive.

There was a really good po-boy place not too far from the hospital. Whenever Scott was released, that would be the first place they would go. They would get a po-boy and some potato chips and Scott's body would know that there were people looking out for it.

"You're hiding something from me," Scott said.

Tenzin told him a lot of information in the few hours after they cleaned up Katy's place, and every insight still rattled inside him. Of course Scott could tell. Considering that the guy wasn't on an express train to the panic attack of the century, the exact details must not be clear.

Or maybe this had nothing to do with their bond. Edgar assumed he came in here with a pretty cool front. Sure, he was worried – Scott was in the hospital, of course he would be worried. But there's a difference between *boyfriend hurt* worried and *potential brain-damaged soul bond* worried.

Scott sighed. "Tenzin must've told you I'm bipolar."

Edgar blinked a few times in a row. Right. That was also new.

"I know it's a lot," as he continued his words were heavy. This was very difficult for him, clearly ."I get if it...changes things."

Don't laugh, Edgar demanded himself. *You're both in a really weird place, but if you laugh it'll make everything so much worse.*

He adjusted his position and wrapped an arm around Scott's back. With that small change he could get even close to his face, acting like he was aiming to tell him a secret. "You know what C-PTSD is?" Edgar said.

"Complex Post Traumatic Stress Disorder? I do."

"Right!" Edgar smiled. "You told me about all those medical text-books you've read. Do you remember the symptoms?"

Scott drew into his own thoughts. It would be interesting to see how much written information he'd be able to recall when he was missing a majority of the first half of his life.

"Hyper-vigilance," he began. "Irritability, depression, general anxiety – all kinds of mood swings, really," Scott closed his eyes to focus further. "Issues with sleep. Oh, and flashbacks. Lots of flashbacks."

Impressive. "Who does that sound like?" Edgar gently prodded.

"Me?" Scott furrowed his brow slightly. "You too, actually. I guess it fits both of us."

"Well, you met Erik – he diagnosed me before I left," Edgar scanned the ceiling as he recalled the faults of his being thus far. "I have severe C-PTSD, chronic pain, I'm allergic to shellfish – which, living here of all places is *the worst* – and..." he lowered his voice to a whisper. "I'm terrified of dachshunds."

The way he said that, as well as the slight dart of the eyes, got a small smile out of Scott. "The dogs?"

"They're slightly too long. It feels wrong to me."

Scott took that in, likely imagining the complete non-threat that was the average wiener dog. As that happened, a smiling doctor strode into the room. She had her eyes on a chart in her hand until she closed the door behind her and looked up, pausing when she saw her one-patient bed now contained two.

Edgar could move. That would be the responsible thing to do. He'd probably have to do it anyway for the doctor to do her job. And yet he stayed exactly where he was, head tilted to brush his cheek against Scott's shoulder. Almost like a challenge.

The doctor huffed a smile. She was tired, yes, but still pleasant. "I imagine you're Edgar. I'm Doctor Zula."

"Should I move?" Edgar asked, with no intention to do anything.

"I can work around you," she went beside Scott and took a thermometer from a machine to take his temperature. "You're almost done for the day. Assuming nothing's wrong, I'd like you to pick up those iron supplements and take them over the net two weeks. Then come back and we can see how you're adjusting."

Scott mumbled a response through the thermometer held under his tongue.

Doctor Zula poked and prodded around Scott for some time. Scott took this scrutiny well, without questioning or hesitation. He just knew instinctively how to angle his body in a way that would best suit her goals. Sometimes it looked almost as if he could predict what she was going to do next, and if he needed to roll up his sleeve or take a deep breath he did it all without being asked.

The environment of a hospital like this reminded Edgar a little too much of the Academy for him to ever be fully comfortable. When Katy took him there for stitches the two of them ended up splitting the cost after he revealed that he didn't have insurance. This still nagged him with guilt years later, because it wasn't true.

Edgar had insurance. But it was Academy insurance, and if he ever used it it would immediately notify Shreveport as to where he was living now. Katy still chided him sometimes, as he worked enough hours at the Den to qualify for their employee health plan. Whatever excuse he gave her as to why he couldn't was so dumb that Edgar couldn't even remember it anymore.

The real reason was just too complicated to admit. Too pathetic.

Edgar Gallows did not have the legal power to remove himself from his own health insurance. He tried not to think about that, as if he thought about that for too long he began to think about everything else he couldn't do because of his remaining ties to the Academy.

He wouldn't be able to rent an apartment unless he could find another landlord willing to house him without signing a lease agreement, because he was unable to do so himself. And forget about ever going through all the paperwork needed to buy property. Edgar couldn't even get legally married without attracting the attention of his Academy's board and getting himself dragged right back home.

It was enough pressure to snap his spine like a twig. And so far, no one else in his life in New Orleans knew anything about it.

But everything's changing now.

He locked eyes with Scott and saw the man flash him a small smile. His eyes were affectionate behind the round lens of Katy's sunglasses. He appeared to be truly enjoying himself.

Later, Edgar told himself as he touched Scott's hand. *I can focus on that later.*

When the doctor was satisfied she took a seat and started swiftly typing into her computer. Scott continued sitting upright, only gradually relaxing back into Edgar once he gathered he no longer had to be a model patient.

Katy and Tenzin returned just as the Doctor's furious typing slowed to a human speed. They were in the middle of quiet conversation – or, at least, Katy was talking and Tenzin was listening. This was a dynamic Edgar recognized in an instant.

Doctor Zula looked up when she heard them and smiled. "Ah," she said. "You brought the whole fam, Scott."

Edgar felt uncertainty flash across the room. The feeling skipped fully over Scott. "Hah!" He laughed wearily. "I guess I did."

She turned in her seat and addressed all of them at once. "You'll have to keep this one in bed tomorrow. Make sure he's stocked with drinks and snacks. Recovery time might take a little longer at first, but he's reacted well enough that I imagine he'll be able to fight and frolic in about a week."

"I do love to frolic," Scott murmured bemusedly.

Tenzin frowned. "Could he get through a flight?"

"Well – I wouldn't. Not if you can help it," Zula shot Scott a wink. "You got a lot of new blood, Scott, you can't afford to waste the oxygen."

Scott nodded, trusting immediately. But then his eyes went to Tenzin, and his eager smile fell.

The doctor instructed Scott on scheduling his next appointment. She went through possible symptoms and gave him a card that had a nurse's hot line, open twenty-four hours a day, that he could call in case he needed advice. She said a lot of useful information that was suddenly incredibly difficult to fully listen to. Edgar dearly hoped that Scott was following along, which – given the alarming degree of new focus in his face – might not be at all of a problem.

She shook his hand. She cracked a joke that went over lukewarm. And then the doctor excused herself from the room – quietly closing the door behind her, as in her line of field she probably knew when something was wrong.

Scott waited, perhaps until he knew that the doctor was out of earshot. When she spoke it became clear just how tired he was. "I'm not going back to Bluerose, Tenzin," he said.

She recoiled slightly. It must come as a shock to hear him shift like that so quickly, face-to-face. She looked, briefly, at Edgar, then cringed and turned away. "What is your plan?" She simply asked, eyes to the ground.

"Please look at me, Ten," Scott answered, now much kinder.

She did.

"I'm sick. In a lot of ways. I saw myself in the mirror for the first time in years yesterday and I know that if Mom saw me looking like this she'd freak out. I'm safe here –"

"*Safe?*"

"*Safer.* For now. Between Edgar and Katy's knowledge of magic there's a chance they could help me make a plan to actually beat this."

That was the first time Scott actually spoke that much hope aloud. Edgar felt this confidence and determination buzzing warmly in his chest and knew that he meant what he said. Tenzin must've felt it too. Still, she couldn't quite let it go.

"I know you don't want to leave him," she said. "And I respect that! He can meet us in Oregon after we get there. I just need *two days* alone with you –"

"It's not that easy," Scott protested.

"You just found each other, there's no way you're already at that point."

"I don't..." He frowned, confused. "I'm just saying that the situation is a little more nuanced than that."

Tenzin's tone started rising in passion. "How could things *possibly* be –?"

Scott raised his palm in her direction, revealing his bond scar and silencing her protest in one fell swoop. The room fell frozen. Edgar wondered in a quiet part of himself if he was about to get hit in the face again.

He felt Tenzin focus on him and shuddered inwardly. The look on her face wasn't outright anger, but something uncertain that drifted towards several different extreme reactions.

"Tenzin," Scott warned. "I consented. I had to or it wouldn't have worked – you know that."

She closed her eyes hard and took a deep breath. "It's *so superfluous*," she whispered.

"It tethered me. We're pretty sure the bonds I have now are the only things still keeping me here."

"Have you tested the radius?"

"I haven't had any reason."

"So you literally *can't leave?*" Tenzin scowled, seeming to swallow back her words. Then she tried again, a little more controlled. "We'll take him with us, then," Tenzin turned to Edgar and said it again. "You're coming with us."

Edgar nodded. "Okay."

"Wait," Scott attempted.

Tenzin pulled out her phone. "I'll get the tickets right now."

She didn't do much aside form unlock her phone when Katy reached over and snatched it out of her hand. Tenzin didn't fight back. She made absolutely no attempt to resist and only watched as Katy tossed the phone into the depths of her purse. Then once she did that Tenzin continued to stare, perhaps processing.

Katy went to the hospital bed and unlatched the railing on Scott's side. "Doctor Zula said you're good to go," she said. "Do you want to get out of that gown, or do you feel like showing off that ass to the city?"

"I –"Scott huffed a semi-laugh, still concerned. "I'll pass. Clothes sound good."

"Would you like help getting on your feet? You might be a little dizzy at first."

Scott nodded, agreeing to taking Katy's outstretched hand and using it to steady himself while he swung his legs over the edge of the bed and onto the floor. He stood up, but something shuddered and he fell back onto the mattress. Tenzin took an immediate step forward, only stopping onto the weight of Katy's glare.

At first Edgar was smug about the reaction. Like he was so much better for not immediately leaping to rescue Scott as soon as he so much as faltered. Then he realized the way he had his hands positioned, ready to prop him up if he so much as leaned back slightly farther than he was right now. To literally catch him.

He forced himself to reposition.

Soon Scott was walking in careful steps towards the bathroom. Katy handed him the tote bag with the clothes Edgar picked out for him, smiled encouragingly, and closed the door behind him.

Immediately she spun to Tenzin. "*You gotta' fucking cool it, lady,*" she hissed under her breath.

"You don't..." Tenzin looked at the door and stepped away, lowering her voice. "You don't know what you're talking about."

"The man just got two buckets of blood funneled into him. He just found out from a doctor that he's been bipolar *forever*, apparently –"

Tenzin's eyes widened in a pulse. "He knows? Well if I could've just –"

Katy shushed her so aggressively that it was close to a threat. "You love your brother. You miss him. You're a pretty statue with big feelings and that's *super cool*. But if you take the guy who's been alone for that long and suddenly love-bomb him it is *not going to help*."

"She's got a point," Edgar attempted to add.

He ducked to the side as Tenzin grabbed a plastic packet of tissues and lobbed it in his face. "Here's what's going to happen," she said. "His life is *his* choice. If he wants to go back to the commune he can. If he doesn't – guess what? He won't."

Finally a note of anger invigorated Tenzin's expression. "Or what?" She said.

Katy, this time, had zero reaction to her growing rage. "What's the alternative? You take the highly unstable witch with a potentially steadily-progressing god powers and force him to do something he doesn't want to do? That's fine. It's not like he has a historical lack of agency in his life."

"So you're afraid of him," Tenzin decided. Possibly grasping for any sense of an upper hand.

"No, Tenzin, I'm fucking *sad* for him. He deserves to get a vacation from the magic trauma to feel like a regular goddamned human being. See a movie! Check out one of the Jazz clubs on Frenchman Street!" Katy looked over her shoulder, briefly listening for noises in the bathroom behind them. "I know a few boutiques by the river where he can get clothes of his own that he might actually *like* wearing. That would be a start."

Tenzin, at this point, had little to work with in terms of an argument. Her face was more active then ever, twitching nervously as she tried to defend herself despite having no recourse. Eventually she pulled herself together.

"What's your motivation here?" She said.

Katy stood straight. "I'm Scott's advocate."

"You're -" Tenzin frowned, tilting her head slightly to the side. "You mean that Witch Doctors mandate? That only applies to medical issues."

"Not for me," Katy smiled.

The bathroom door cracked open. "Are you done arguing?" Scott called out through the crack.

Katy didn't answer. She didn't look like she had any plan to. Instead she focused on Tenzin, and even from where Edgar sat he could read the look on her face with utter clarity.

Are we? It said. *Are we done arguing?*

Hesitation slowly faded from Tenzin's body. She stood a taller – a lot taller, actually – and took on a new steadiness. "Yeah, Scott," she said. "We're done. Sorry."

It would be good to leave the hospital. Even only being there for a little over an hour, the commercially abstract paintings on the wall and the softly buzzing lights above them were making his skin crawl. So he pulled himself out of the bed and put on his jacket. Stopping to stare out the window, he pulled his attention inside himself to see how Scott was feeling.

Tired, mostly. Overwhelmed. Confused. But something else – it was weak and shimmered luminescent, but it was there.

It was hope.

Edgar breathed in and out. He buttoned up his jacket and turned to join the others, then jolted inwardly as soon as he saw Scott standing by the door.

Scott, his mind breathed dumbly. *Whoa.*

With his pretty features and long hair, Edgar partially figured that Scott would pass as any other girl dressed in Katy's clothes. That wasn't something he was dreading or anticipating. It's just what he assumed would happen and he figured he wouldn't know how to feel about it until he saw it.

And now he was seeing it. And now he was *feeling*.

Scott leaned against the sink next to the door and slowly sipped water while Katy got her things. Her pale blue sweater hung on the large side against his form, coming to hug just below his hipbone. The collar was loose and exposed the a jutting peak of collarbone.

I wonder what color his skin actually is. Maybe it's like caramel. Or bourbon. Or bourbon caramel.

The skirt was the color of aged dark chocolate, and it fell to about the ankle. The material practically floated around him, as if he was swimming gracefully on solid ground. He shifted from foot to foot every so often, and every slight movement echoed in the expanse of softly sparkling fabric.

Growing up in Shreveport Edgar assumed that men were meant to wear certain clothes and women were meant to wear others. He figured it was a simple matter of tailoring, and even though the University uniform of his female work colleagues looked more appealing he always believed if he put it on people would know something was missing. Of course, expanding his world meant expanding his mind. He couldn't claim to understand the full scope of sex and gender and sexuality, but he definitely knew it was far more vast and complicated than he ever imagined.

Still, to see a feminine man dress in feminine clothes and somehow end up looking more masculine than Edgar had ever seen him was an entirely new insight. He looked more like a man than Edgar ever felt, and he made sure to always dress solely in the things online research has assured him that men sometimes wear.

It would be stupid to say he understood. He was hit by his lack of perspective with a jarring force, and the consequential realization of the sheer scope of humanity shook him to his core. Academics are supposed to understand the inner workings of the universe, aren't they? And yet all it took was a slight twist of preconceived gender norms to rocket Edgar into a panic.

Edgar didn't want to wear a skirt. Or, maybe, he didn't want to wear that particular skirt. It wasn't like he wanted the world to perceive him as a woman, or even a man who dresses like a woman. He hated that those seemed to be the only options, as he felt the same way about either label as he did the jackets he continued to buy and replace from the sporting goods store downtown. They worked on other people, in photographs and on the mannequins. So it must be fine for him. It just had to be.

His heart was pounding so loudly in his chest that he heart every beat ring in his ears. And if he could hear it, obviously Scott could do. He turned his eyes to Edgar from across the room and watched him curiously.

Those eyes. That hair. Those perfect hands. Scott may have been the one with a lot of new blood, but it was Edgar that suddenly had to sit back down on the edge of the hand to avoid a faint.

Tenzin was the first person outside of him or Scott to be certain that the two of them were in a Lover's Knot. It was validating in a way, because if you wrestle so deeply with something that important it feels good to have someone agree with you. This was more than that, though. It was hard not to think that every time they started to form some foundation of the world around them, any answers were framed again as new, impossible questions.

He had understanding for the holes in Scott's memory. That was easy. Being as kind to the gaps in his own apparent timeline was a lot more difficult. If Edgar was going to start repressing things, there were many far better places to start.

The stiff mattress dipped just beside him. It was Scott. Edgar turned to face him, partially realizing that they were now alone in the hospital room.

"I told them to meet us outside," Scott said. "I can feel you're a bit —"

"I think I'm your Eddie, Scott."

Fuck, Edgar didn't want to say that. He knew Scott already had so much he was juggling with, and to throw that alongside everything else was cruel. Edgar simply couldn't bare the weight of the possibility of his own anymore. So not only was he being cruel, he was being selfish as well.

Scott wasn't blinking. "Oh?" he said.

"I'm sorry. Fuck, I – I'm so sorry."

"Is that what you've been so spinny about?"

That was a good way to describe it. Ever since Tenzin showed up his mind and heart have felt like that carnival ride that spins so fast it sticks you to the walls. If Scott could succeed in talking him down from something like this, Edgar would likely experience what it felt like for his feelings to throw up in a dirty trash can.

"It doesn't matter anymore," Scott tried to assure him.

"Wait, what do you mean?"

"I'm just saying you shouldn't worry about it. I don't care who Eddie is now."

It was hard not to feel hurt. Is that something the blue boy would say to him? Would that child be so quick to abandon him – or sometime who could potentially be him?

Scott put a hand on his knee. "I will always love Eddie. For the rest of my life the biggest regret I have will be that I wasn't able to know that I found them. But I..." the hand tightened, because a grasp for solid ground. "I can't do this to myself anymore. I need to move on and focus on staying healthy. I – I *want* to stay healthy. To be *happy*. I think that's what they'd want too."

Edgar had questions. Edgar wanted answers to those questions. He wanted certainty and solutions and for every inciting incident and conclusion to be emailed to him at least two days in advance. To not understand so much was abject misery.

But his bond wanted peace – that's all. If Scott was able to recover and live a quiet life well into old age without ever understanding what happened to him, it was clear now that he would. And by the way he looked at Edgar, and how he essentially held his leg like a security blanket, Edgar understood that his ideal quiet life involved the both of them.

What else could he do rather than fulfill the terms of their bond?

Of course I want you to be happy, Lark.

He leaned forward and caught Scott's lips in a gentle kiss. He lingered afterwards with their foreheads touched together.

"You're right," Edgar said. "Let's drop the subject then."

The tension faded quickly and completely. Knowing he could do what he did just then with two simple sentences was more satisfying than any incantation. Edgar felt Scott's gratitude like the first moments of dipping into a bath. Even with the day so far, he allowed himself some time to enjoy the sensation.

"I – I forgot to say," he added, a little gentler now. "You cut your hair! I like it. It looks –"

"I know," Scott grinned, almost slyly. "I know how you think it looks."

Edgar's cheeks reddened. He continued to flush while Scott stood from the bed and offered Edgar his hand.

This morning those hands were bloodied and beaten out of shape. Edgar could still envision the spores of bones sprouting from the flesh, the dents where the natural skeletal structure was pounded into wilted defeat. After whatever his sister did, they looked exactly as they were before. Long-fingered. Tender. Infinitely capable.

He held Scott's hand, and the anemic pulled him up with barely a struggle. Scott touched his forearm, first affectionately, and soon after for support. He touched his forehead to Edgar's shoulder and sighed softly.

"Let's get out of here," he said.

Edgar was more than happy to comply.

Po-boy sandwiches were, at least between Edgar and Katy, a frequent topic of debate. Edgar preferred the roast beef variety, like when it was first sold to working class folks. His best friend, on the other hand, raved constantly about the flavor combination of a fried oyster po-boy and an icy Budweiser, because she was a monster and someone he probably shouldn't be hanging out with.

They approached the rusted food truck, and Edgar waited on baited breath to see what Scott would order. The man darted his eyes to him every so often while looking at the menu, but Edgar wasn't about to order on his behalf. Edgar had a feeling Katy's speech to Tenzin partially applied to him as well, and he was determined not to let his hard opinions on food override Scott's free will.

"Is the roast beef sliced or shredded?" Scott asked him, staring up at the menu.

Edgar feigned indifference the best he could. "Uh, shredded. And it's tossed in gravy."

"Gravy? Wow," Scott nodded, approvingly. "I think I'll have that."

Beside him, Edgar heard Katy suck in some air. He stared at her, long and hard, knowing damn well that he just won a landmark victory in a years-long battle.

Once they got their food they sat at one of the scattered picnic tables scattered in front of the truck. They were under a flimsy umbrella that barely stood a chance at protecting them from a hard rain. But that didn't matter, because the skies were clear and cloud-broken in partial cracks of blue. Not that Edgar paid much mind to that.

Never in his life had he watched someone eat a sandwich with such intensity. The most important thing in the world at that very moment was seeing Scott react to his fourth favorite sandwich and determine how the man ranked it himself. Compared to that, everything else was trivial.

First bite. "Oh man," Scott chewed carefully and swallowed. "That's really special."

Yes, Skylark, Edgar thought to himself. *Yes it is.*

"The hot sauce is a nice touch," Scott said. "You know, I really like New Orleans hot sauce. I think it's some of the most flavorful in the country."

Edgar tried not to shout. "A lot of the brands here ferment the chilies. Isn't that interesting? It makes a big difference."

"Have you told him about the time you tried to make hot sauce?" Katy piped up from across the table.

A wave of retroactive nausea spiraled in his stomach. Edgar put down his sandwich and thought back to the weekend his spent essentially camped out in the bathroom, so sick that he started typing a last will and testament into the notes app of his phone.

Tenzin sat beside Katy, digging a spoon into a paper cup of baked mac and cheese. "If you poach the peppers before you use them then you kill off a lot of the food-borne illness."

He shot her a look of mild surprise. She shrugged. "I taught myself a few basic African recipes. Mostly sauces," she glanced down at her spoon of golden pasta and did something similar to a smile. "I make a pretty good pepper sauce."

"How's my Scotch Bonnet plant doing?" Scott asked, now midway into his sandwich.

A degree of strain crossed Tenzin's expression, but only the edges and tips of it were visible from above the surface of her reassurance. "Your garden is thriving. The only guaranteed way to get Mom out of the house is when we have to harvest and distribute the bounty," the tide of positivity ebbed, revealing more pain. "I'm still an awful gardener, but Nori comes over almost ever morning to tend to things."

Now it was Scott's turn for his mood to sour. Edgar noticed him clench his jaw slightly and tighten his smile until it was no longer cheerful. "That's..." he took a breath and let it go slowly. "It's kind. That's a kind thing for her to do."

As soon as they finished eating it was clear that Scott was ready to go to sleep right there on that rickety tabletop. Edgar knew he had to get him home. That would be difficult to navigate with the other two sitting across from him.

"We should..." Edgar was carefully wrapping up the rest of Scott's sandwich. "I can bring him back..."

He thought about what Katy said in the hospital. It was a frightening concept, but Edgar wanted to know that everyone here had the agency they deserved. So he leaned down and shook Scott awake. His bond sat up and grumbled blearily.

"Hey," Edgar asked him. "Where do you want to go now?"

Scott blinked – one long, hard blink. "Can we go home?" He mumbled.

Tenzin sighed from her end of the table. "We aren't in Oregon, Scott."

"Yeah I know."

With how tired he looked he'd have no reason to put on a ruse for Edgar's sake. He probably would never talk like this at all, based on how Tenzin reacted. It was the look on Tenzin's face that stifled him from being utterly overjoyed. Because she looked hurt, and it made sense. She must've put herself through hell for so long, only to now feel like her own brother chose someone he met a week ago over her.

Although, if she was right, Edgar's connection with Scott was formed at birth and he technically had known him for longer than she had.

She turned away and rubbed the ball of her hand against her eyes.

Who am I kidding? Edgar thought to himself. *None of that matters.*

The four walked back to where Edgar and Katy parked, Tenzin and Scott leading the way. Their footsteps squished through grass and damp leaves. Thinking back on what he and Scott talked about in the hospital room, and the warm weight of fullness in his stomach felt a lot more profound.

Still, he couldn't stop looking at Tenzin. She led Scott so diligently. Edgar barely had to make an effort to sense how Scott felt about her. The pure strength of faith and adoration was more powerful than anything he'd ever inadvertently shared with Edgar. Even looking at him Edgar could tell he was at peace. Just limp with contentment.

Tenzin could see all this too – couldn't she?

Katy bumped his shoulder, jostling him back the moment. "You good to handle this on your own?" She asked.

"Huh?"

"Well I do technically have work tonight. I have to give Mister Man his wet food and take a shower. That is, unless –"

"No," Edgar said.

There were a few moments of pause. Then Katy stuttered a laugh. "That's it?" She said. "Just – no?"

"I can handle it."

"You aren't planning any wizard bullshit, right?"

"Do you trust her?" Edgar said.

Katy's face turned contemplative. She cocked her head to the side and examined the back of Tenzin's head.

"You're that unsure?" Edgar scowled in slight worry. "What'd you talk about on the roof?"

"She fell asleep," she said under her breath. "From the moment we sat down until you texted me that the doctor came back, she was just *out*. Fully shut down."

Scott pointed at something off in the distance. Tenzin turned to get a better look, allowing Edgar to see an actual, sustained smile.

He raised his brow. "Huh."

They parted ways at their car under the agreement that Katy would visit tomorrow and check up on them. As soon as Edgar unlocked his car, Tenzin immediately opened the back seat and helped Scott inside. By the time they were back on the road Scott had his head in her lap, and happily slept as she stroked his hair.

There was a moment where she looked like she expected him to protest at this, and he made an extra effort to present himself as supportive. He asked her if she needed him to adjust the temperature. She said no. She started to say something else when Scott started to hum quietly to himself, another symphony of semi-musical tones and notes.

Tenzin looked down at him and widened her eyes.

"Oh yeah," Edgar said. "He does that a lot."

She looked up at him with another trembling semi-smile. "H-He does?" She managed.

He didn't know how to answer that, and it didn't seem like Tenzin expected him to, so he just decided to start driving. And he went through traffic with only the usual problems, nothing he couldn't navigate easily. At the same time, though – he was distracted.

Scott was fine without answers. Give him enough blankets and he could make a cozy nest in the nook of any existential crisis. That was admirable. It was also deeply frustrating.

Edgar tried to think back on whatever he remembered regarding his education on bond magic. The details were so blurry. By the time they started teaching about bonds Edgar already knew his life path in the Academy as someone who would have little to no chance of actually practicing the education he was getting. Between that, and everything that went on in his life before and after school, he just couldn't bring himself to pay attention.

There was an Academy downtown. It supposedly had the biggest library in the southern branch of the system. Back when he still allowed himself to care about things like that, it sounded impressive. If he became an archivist he probably would've gone down to that library quiet often to take advantage of their resources. He heard rumors that there was a projection room with Super 8, and even 35mm capability.

That meant roughly a century's work of magic documented. Heavily guarded, the type of footage that no one even bothered digitizing – which meant nothing to leak online. As far as Edgar knew, the only people with any knowledge or interest in the content of Academy libraries were Academic librarians.

Edgar could talk to an Academic librarian. They weren't mean or pretentious, instead possessing barely enough ego to sustain basic human function. The average Academic of his ilk mainly communicated through email and paperwork, but if you put in the right amount of effort they could be surprisingly talkative.

Getting there would be the hard part. Convincing Scott it was worth the struggle would be even harder.

He was still thinking about this as he parked outside his apartment. Tenzin swept Scott into her arms and carried him easily. She followed Edgar inside and paid zero mind, good or bad, to the layout of his apartment. As soon as the couch came into view that was exactly where she went, and she laid him across the cushions, pulling off his coat and bundling it behind his head as a pillow.

She lingered there, slightly knelt down. Edgar could see how tired she was.

"Hey," he said.

Tenzin looked up at him.

"Do you want to lie down?" Edgar closed the door and hung up his coat. "I can change my sheets. I don't know...I mean, I have a shower. If you want to – like – shower," he frowned. "You already showered. You can shower again. If you want."

"Right," Tenzin mumbled.

Scott shifted on the couch. He sat up, first in a jolt, and only calming once he looked around and gathered where he was. His eyes went to Edgar, deeply sleepy.

He smiled.

"C'mere," Scott called out to him.

There was space for Edgar to consider how his next actions would look to Scott's sister as she watched from the ground beside the couch. He didn't. It didn't matter and he didn't care. Edgar went to the far end of the couch, and immediately his bond scooted towards him and buried his face against his chest. Scott wrapped his arms around him, his hair falling almost fully in front of his face. Within seconds he was asleep. And within seconds, the tension assaulting every cell in Edgar's body soothed and went still.

Things were peaceful. Gloriously peaceful. Edgar felt safe and grounded, and in the moment where he brushed a lock of hair back behind Scott's ear and out of his face all was right with the world.

"Wow."

Tenzin was sitting on the floor now. She observed what was happening in front of her quietly, partially amazed and part despairing. Which was fine. Everything was fine.

"I..." she darted her eyes to Scott and lowered her voice. "It's strange. To see you change like that."

He touched a palm to Scott's upper back. "I figured it was the bond," he remarked.

"You don't know about Lover's Knots, do you?"

Edgar smiled. He just smiled.

Tenzin leaned back and sighed. "Yeah," she said. "I didn't either. For a while I was able to get documents from the Portland Academy, but once they found out my ID was a forgery they blacklisted me."

"Okay. You know Scott loves you, right?"

Her brow twitched in surprise. She didn't answer at first. Edgar was thrown aback by his own straightforwardness, but decided to continue going anyway.

"He talks about you constantly," he said. "I was kind of surprised to learn you were the same age. He has big, *idolizing kid brother* energy."

Tenzin stared at the ground. She pivoted between a smile and a grimace.

"You aren't losing him," Edgar continued, a little softer. "If he has a choice he won't let that happen," he settled his palm against the back of his head and let out a faint huff. "Honestly, I think if he had a choice all four of us would live together and platonically share a bed at night."

That made Tenzin laugh. It was only a little sound, but it still counted.

I made Tenzin laugh!

She did that thing where you fight back a yawn but still make a stifled noise. Looking at her without the threat of violence, he could see that Katy was right in her perspective. This woman was clearly worn down to scraps. Even just sitting in one spot she still wobbled slightly. Her stare was unsteady, like focusing on any one thing for more than a few moments took considerable effort.

"...Take my bed," Edgar said. "Please."

She looked close to arguing him over this. But by now, after all of this, whatever effect her own bond had on her faded enough to allow her human needs to take priority. Magic users as still human, after all.

Well, as far as he knew, at least. But maybe it didn't matter.

He heard Tenzin fall into his bed with the bedroom door left open. Edgar stayed where he was and idly palmed the individual knots of yarn on the back of the sweater Scott wore. He could feel the pressure of his chest push against him every time he inhaled – a steady testament to nature. The total relief Scott experienced as he slept was so strong it made it hard to sustain the flame of uncertainty.

Edgar closed his eyes and let the feelings wash over him. It was a quiet place, quiet like the cemetery. The life of it washed out everything else around him. In the dark place in his mind he heard footsteps, and then felt a whoosh of air as Tenzin settled his bedspread over him and Scott. With the added warmth, the soft touch of worn cotton, Edgar surrendered to the static in his limps and drifted towards sleep.

Far away – very, *very* far away – he heard piano. A song he remembered. Edgar hummed along to the melody as he drifted off to sleep.

Etude no. 4

Two souls lie, curled up on a couch in the early hours of morning. The First is drawing out of sleep, while the Other is deeply resting against his chest.

"You called me Orpheus, didn't you?" The First whispers.

The Other does not respond. The First shifts an arm from under the comforter and grazes his fingers just under his companion's sweater, enough to allow him to touch the bare skin of his lower back. He isn't sure if that is right to do with the other still asleep. After a few moments the First pulls back and settles for holding him closer.

"It makes sense you'd know your Greek mythology," he says, faintly amused. "So much tragedy. So much beauty. But I'm not Orpheus and you aren't my Eurydice. Neither of will die here. Not for a long, long time."

He feels a little better when he says that. The Other relaxes even deeper into his arms. In a burst of inspiration, the First leans forward and whispers in his ear.

"I hope you dream about cats. Lots of cats. And you have a whole block of cheese to share with them."

The First kisses the top of the Other's head and sighs, happy. He closes his eyes again.

Ninth Movement

According to the Respectable Doctor Zula, Scott Skylark Kaufner was not to get out of bed for two days. He didn't tell her at the time, but he was sure that would be impossible.

He had a great respect for any doctor. To Scott, medical professionals ranked second on the scale of important human professions, right above food service worker and before librarian. It was just that he was now fully adjusted to living a shark's lifestyle, constantly moving forward and never staying in one town for long. If he wasted extra precious moments on pursuits like *rest,* he might feel better, but he'd also start asking himself questions.

Why did he think this could possibly work? What was he planning on doing if it does? How the fuck did he start off with so much potential on life and end up in *Florida*?

It was a welcome change to be in New Orleans for this long. Scott secretly enjoyed the concept of getting to know a city, the thought of finding a really good coffee shop and knowing that he could actually come back the next day if he felt like it. But even as he imagined staying in town for an extended period of town, the thought of staying home (*Home?*) all day was foreign to him.

What was he supposed to do, lie on the couch for twelve hours and listen to music? He couldn't even imagine what that would feel like. Nice, maybe. But was it worth the risk?

Scott worried vaguely that if he allowed himself to lie down for too long he would lose all resolve to get back up and keep moving. And that theory must have some sort of logical grounding, as he spent the entirety of his bed rest drifting in and out of sleep.

It was sleep like he never knew. Deep, vast, cave-like and semi-dreamless. Scott was aware of being fully supine across the couch, the soft blanket tucked back over his body and squishy pillow under his head. He knew he was more comfortable than he thought one human body was capable of. And through a fading veil of vision and darkness he was aware of voices and movement.

Edgar touching his hair. Tenzin helping him drink some water. Katy sitting on the floor beside him, watching something on the television. And something else.

Something else.

You must've been really tired.

Yeah. I am.

It's good this is happening then.

Tenzin sitting on the floor at his feet, head settled on his legs. Edgar cooking in the kitchen. Katy cracking jokes.

Is it? Is it good?

You have to get rest to be strong.

I don't want it to get stronger.

It won't get stronger, Scott – *you* will.

Huh.

Letting go felt so good. He hoped this is what his body would experience when he died – a pure release of every muscle, all his fears and aspirations. Just gathering every aspect of his identity and letting it fall as grains of sand between his fingers. It left nothing, but a good nothing.

Are you him?

I thought it didn't matter.

It doesn't. But is it?

At one point he was aware of being spoon-fed from a perfectly warmed bowl of miso soup. Miso soup isn't hard, it's just hot water and fermented bean paste. Through every spoonful, though, he could note the presence of finely sliced vegetables. Green onion and mushroom. Something squishy that might've been tofu. Clearly Edgar's personal effort.

Just focus on them, Scott. Focus on getting better again.

Slowly, the disorientation faded. It was like a wave that pulled back over him, farther and farther, and this time it didn't rev up to crash forward again. The feeling just left. Scott woke up just before dawn in a quiet, dark house, and he didn't hurt at all.

His chest didn't ache and his head didn't throb corrosively. Not only was he not freezing cold, he was actually overheating. His mouth still stung slightly, but it didn't burn the way it usually did when he thought about it too much. And Scott was awake. Fully awake. If someone said he could lie back down and go back to sleep, he'd politely decline. He just didn't feel the need, and that amazed him.

Thin blue light stained the walls. There was a warm silence settled over the apartment that only came when you occupied a space with other people. Scott saw a glass of water on the coffee table and, even though he wasn't nearly as thirsty as he thought he'd be after sleeping through the day before, drank the whole thing in greedy, messy gulps.

He wiped his hand over his mouth, marveling at the lack of regret he felt at such an action. He touched his fingertips against his bottom lip and pressed. It was fine.

Oh shit. I can't wait to kiss Edgar again.

Scott got up onto his feet and felt the way he fit so perfectly within his own body. The material of Katy's skirt brushed against his legs, allowing freer movement and a cape-like swoosh with every step he took.

Good. He hummed the word as he thought it. *Good good good.*

The bedroom door was cracked open. Scott pushed it forward a little more and peered into the room. Tenzin and Edgar were asleep on the bed, each at an odd and uncomfortable angle. Since he knew them both to be a little chilly with new people, they probably weren't friends yet. Still, sharing a mattress was a promising start.

He watched from the doorway for a while and smiled. Safety was such a foreign feeling for him, and yet there it was. It strengthened the plasma in his new blood.

Outside the neighborhood was just waking up. Distant birds conversed in the tall oaks lining the street. Cars passed, quieter ones than what Edgar drove. The sky overhead was ripe with the potential for more and brighter light, so Scott sat down on the front steps and decided to greet it himself.

Across the street he saw a cat he recognized. It was the one he spoke to the day he met Erik – Scott imagined the little guy must be a resident of the area.

He waved and smiled. The cat sauntered off and ducked under an overgrown shrub.

When Scott was young his mother told him that it was important not to watch nature too closely. A flower preferred to open its petals in the morning in private, and cliffs would rather erode without the attention of prying eyes. Scott listened. That didn't mean he agreed. If left to his own devices, he would absolutely lock eyes with the sky to track every hue it shifted into as time passed.

It was his personal opinion that the Earth didn't mind. Sunrises and sunsets were apparently acceptable to appreciate, maybe the planet would get a sense of satisfaction in knowing there was someone enjoying the less-seen beauties it created on a daily basis.

The reflection of sunlight through certain trees – because it always looked slightly different depending on the trees. Or the intricate patterns in even just a single patch of moss.

Scott missed moss so goddamned much. It wasn't the same in the South, as much as they touted their claimed equivalent.

He heard a small, muffled *merp* from just in front of him. It was the street cat, now sitting with the wrapper of a partially-eaten meat stick clutched in its front teeth. Once he saw that he caught Scott's attention, the cat dropped the stick at his feet and eyed him expectantly.

"Oh!" Scott smiled. "You found the trash can! Good for you."

The cat looked down at the meat stick. He looked back up at Scott.

"Do you need help getting that open? Here," Scott took the meat stick and unwrapped it further, offering the softer, chewed end towards his friend. "There you go. Munch munch."

His companion did not eat. He just kept staring at Scott, and eventually he pressed the tip of his nose against Scott's hand and pushed forward.

Scott furrowed his brow. "Oh it's – for me? That's very kind, but..."

This was a time to be honest with himself. If a street cat offered to share its food with Scott a week ago, he would take it and snack with the cat without question. It was never a good idea, but he wasn't about to deny such kindness from a fellow beleaguered creature of the earth. He had no exact memory of doing this, but with the urge as strong as it was Scott had to imagine it happened before. Probably a few times.

However, the blood transfusion and solid chunk of sleep was enough to allow his mind to function more efficiently. So while he did see this as an act of gratitude from animal that trusted him, he was also aware that this cat was asking him to eat garbage. And Scott didn't want to eat garbage. Today, in fact, he felt weird thinking that there was a recent time when he would.

He could also just eat the other end.

No. No, that's still weird.

"I..." Scott looked down at the cat, "*I* am a vegetarian. Isn't that crazy? I don't eat meat. For health reasons."

The cat did not respond. He slowly blinked in Scott's direction.

"But I wish I could," he tore off a piece of the meat stick and offered the chunk to the feline. "Maybe you can show me what it's like?"

His friend stretched out his neck and gave the morsel a hearty sniff, and then a little lick, before finally pulling the whole piece into his mouth. He chewed happily and swallowed.

Scott chuckled as he scratched the sides of the cats face. "Yeah." he cooed. "I bet that's good."

The cat stayed with him a little while longer before scampering away while Scott was distracted by a passing V of what sounded like seagulls. He figured it would be a blow to the cat's pride to ask him to take the meat stick back, so instead Scott crossed the street and hid the treat under the bush where he saw the cat hide. So his little buddy could come back to it later.

Through the small-leafed branches Scott got a glimpse of a makeshift cat nest, complete with a little bowl of water some kind soul must keep refilled. There was a ratty child's blanket and a few bits of food and crinkly wrappers good for batting around.

We all need to have fun, Scott concluded, happy to see this.

He put the meat stick on the blanket and pulled back, wiping his hands against his skirt. It was a beautiful day! He spent some time wandering up and down the block and taking in the sights, all the colorful, Southern-style architecture. Some homes had French flags in the window. A lot of gardens were barren from the climate, but there were the occasional bunches of cold-season plants. Pansies and violas, star-like petunias and long bell towers of foxglove.

Scott had a deep respect for anyone who knew how to keep flowers alive. That was always his weak point in gardening.

"Skylark!"

His heart swelled joyously. That was Edgar, calling out to him from a few houses down.

"Good morning!" Scott shouted back, casting him a wide wave.

"What are you doing?"

"Just moving," Scott felt himself grin as he walked towards him. "I have so much energy!"

Edgar lowered his eyes and frowned. "Shoes would've helped."

He was worried. There was good reason to be. New Orleans had an open container law, and because of that, broken beer or liquor bottles were a common sight. This wasn't Bluerose. Even walking barefoot in Bluerose has caused him to step in something gross or painful before.

And it was sweet to see Edgar worried. Pretty Edgar, standing on his porch looking like he was waiting for the moment Scott finally woke up. Knowing someone was waiting for him who he could meet so easily was just about the most delightful thing in the world to experience.

Scott picked up the edges of his skirt and sped up the pace, cutting across two yards of damp grass and hopping directly onto the porch – not a big jump, but still an accomplishment in his opinion. Edgar blinked, astonished.

"You look good," he said.

He held the hem of Edgar's shirt and pulled the man towards him. "I feel good," once Edgar was close enough Scott wrapped his free hand around his waist, smirking cat-like. "*You* look good."

"Oh – I – thanks, uh..."

"I'd like to kiss you know," Scott said.

Edgar flushed red and nodded "Yeah sure okay."

They kissed. It didn't hurt. Scott pulled Edgar closer, engulfing himself in the warmth of his body, and it was amazing. There was no otherworldly horrors of present, physical discomfort. It was just a kiss so normal that it made Scott burn madly.

He felt Edgar graze his fingers down his spine. Edgar tasted like toothpaste and he was steadily and shyly working his way to hook his thumbs under the hem of Scott's sweater.

Scott was swimming in delight. He pulled back and kissed Edgar's forehead. Each of his cheeks. The tip of his nose and the gap between his neck vein and then just below the neck. Soon they were back against the wall, Edgar laughing in confused amusement and Scott continuing to kiss him at odd intervals and locations.

"T-Tenzin's awake," he said through gasps. "Tenzin's awake, Scott!"

He growled against Edgar's neck, his way of saying that had nothing to do with what he was currently busy with. Scott felt Edgar shudder underneath him, then gasp, then snicker again before further squeezing his arms around him.

Once he got that out of his system – for the time being at least – Scott happily followed Edgar back inside. They found his sister in the kitchen, pouring a cup of coffee. She looked up at the two of them when they walked in.

"We looked through your things," she told him.

A quick mental note of the things Scott remembered he packed in his duffle bag. Something about knowing his sister rifled through his belongings worried him briefly. It was a silly fear – it's not like he had a diary for her to snoop through like a sibling in an old sitcom. He barely carried anything on him at all, so what was there to hide?

He frowned. There wasn't a diary, but there was the book where he tried and failed and tried again to write actual songs like he used to. Worse than that, there was –

"Where is it?" He spoke, barely audible.

Tenzin didn't speak. She turned her head to Edgar, who Scott felt hold him by the wrist and turn him around. His bond, his boyfriend, the man he almost missed out on in favor of falling into death, now gazed carefully at him.

"The pills, right?" Scott nodded, and Edgar sighed. "I have them in the lock box with my grimoire. That's not to keep you from getting to them, I'll give you the code, it's just – it's a dangerous medication to keep lying around."

"Did you use your magic to get it, Scott?" Tenzin asked, tight in her courtesy. "Charm some kind of...I don't know, vet or hospice worker?"

Scott's voice was heavy in his throat. "It was a vet," he said.

He heard his sister take in a deep breath. "They could get arrested if anyone finds out."

"We don't have to talk about this now," Edgar touched Scott's cheek and turned his face back to him. "Hey. I looked it up and there's a pharmacy nearby with a drop-off box. I can leave it there if you don't want to. It's your call, no questions asked," he drew inward before adding. "But we shouldn't – we don't have to worry about it right now, okay?"

Did just getting a hold of the pills count as a suicide attempt? He came close to being close, and as much as Scott might tell himself that didn't matter, the look on his loved one's faces told an entirely different story. To them, the only difference between him taking the pills or not was that, because he didn't, there was still a person they could worry about.

Scott didn't want to be worried about like this.

Even he feared for the man who flirted his way into a bottle of poison. It was like that person was someone separate from who he was now now, and Scott could see how badly he needed any form of help.

"I was actually digging for these," Tenzin clarified as she grabbed a packet off the counter and tossed it to him. "Here."

Scott caught the small white packet immediately. Another surprise.

"I didn't want to strip you while you slept, so you missed a dose," she paused. "C'mon, Skylark. Get to it."

There were people here now with the express intent of making sure Scott was taken care of. It made him happy. It made him feel gross, but that could also be the sweat from his brief coma. Emotional trauma be damned, a shower would be nice right now.

And what a shower it was. Scott thought that maybe, because he felt warmer naturally now, he would no longer find enjoyment in a shower hot enough to melt steel. It was actually the opposite. Standing underneath the shower head, a rush of steaming water running over his body, he felt the heat against himself in an entirely new way. And the longer he stayed he could trace the spots in which his skin began to flush.

He stood there longer than he needed to. Once he finally stepped out, the temperate air of the bathroom touched him with a refreshing chill. Scott smiled, grabbing the towel and gently scrubbing it through his hair.

His eyes went to the mirror so easily, like his body already forgot about avoiding the act for the past decade. The Scott in the mirror already looked so different from the one he saw a few days before. His cheeks were deeper in color and his eyes as large as Edgar's. He was an odd-looking figure, but looking at him it made sense that at least a few people would choose to love him of their own volition. The man in the mirror touched the ridge of the nose and smiled, thinking of Odysseus finally returning home to Ithaca.

So he found himself familiar. That wasn't surprising. Or was it more than that? Scott looked closer until the lines of his face lost their intended meaning and blurred into something else. A landscape. A bar of sheet music. A melody on the piano written and played by someone that wasn't him.

And then he understood. Scott smiled. He wasn't seeing himself in the mirror – he was seeing his mother.

Scott looks like his mother.

His smile broadened. *Good,* he hummed.

He walked out of the bathroom and found Edgar at his open closet, digging through his clothes. He stiffened when he heard Scott open the door and turned around. They locked eyes. Edgar's stare lowered to his bare chest and, after a brief contemplation, he grinned.

"You're already less pale."

It felt good to be looked at like this. It felt like the shower. Edgar met Scott's gaze again and pulled back his enthusiasm with a soft blush. Edgar was blushing a lot lately.

"We really need to get you some new clothes," he said. "I'm trying to find you something to wear, but – I don't really have..."

Scott sauntered easily to stand beside Edgar in front of the closet. He dug through his closet before, but looking at it with a little more attention he found that it was a surprisingly vast wardrobe. There was a strange variety that implied the man took a few trips to the local thrift store and just grabbed every article of clothing in his size.

"Do you wear all of this?" Scott asked.

Edgar scoffed. "Oh no. I – considered a lot of looks when I moved. Then I found, like, three flannel shirts. That sort of became my whole thing."

There were a few Hawaiian shirts in varied colorful patterns. A few cool-toned cardigans. Chinos, weirdly enough. Scott rifled through the hangers and pulled out a deep green rugby shirt with a white stripe across the middle. He held it up, feeling the material. It was soft. Probably vintage.

"I didn't think that'd be your style," Edgar said.

"It's not for me," Scott held the shirt up in front of Edgar's chest.

"Oh, I – I don't –"

"You bought it, didn't you? You must've thought you'd wear it at some point."

Edgar raised his brow, attempting a rebuttal. "How do you know I haven't?"

"Have you?"

He didn't respond. Scott softened. "You look very handsome in your flannel. But I think you'd look handsome in lots of stuff," he looked up at Edgar, analyzing the doubt in his expression. "Do you like it?"

"...I do," Edgar admitted.

"You like the color?"

"Yes."

"It's very smart. Like something a doctor would wear."

"Yeah. That's why I like it."

Scott smiled and fully handed Edgar the shirt. "Then it's settled."

He left Edgar standing near the closet and grabbed the packet of testosterone gel off the bedside table. Usually applying his gel was the worst part of his day. He needed to sit in one place with his t-shirt rolled up like a greaser until the goo on his shoulder dried. It needed to be someplace clean, but also someplace where he would be in anyone's way, so he usually ended up in the far end table of a chain coffee shop.

Now the whole world was different. Scott could just relax in peace for the five minutes he needed and then go on with the rest of his day.

"I haven't seen you do this in person before," Edgar said. "Are you supposed to do it every day?"

Scott tore open the packet and squeezed the pale substance onto his two fingers. He rubbed it in a small circle on the skin of his upper shoulder. "Twice a week," he said. "For the rest of my life."

There was some more rustling from the closet and then Edgar came to sit on the bed beside Scott. "Wow. That's a lot."

"Eh, I'm used to it. If I transitioned to be more feminine I'd have the same relationship with estrogen," he got up and went to the bathroom to wash his hands. "It's a low dose, not a big deal."

Drying his hands, Scott turned to see Edgar changing into the shirt he forced upon him. He slid his hands through the sleeves and tousled his curls. The muted, olive green was the lightest color Scott had seen him wear so far, and the tone allowed him to see the slight caramel tint in Edgar's auburn hair. Edgar touched the chest of his shirt, expression twitching thoughtfully. He laid back on the bed with his hands folded on his chest.

He was smiling very faintly. Then the smile faded, and once again he appeared deep in thought.

Scott sat, cross-legged on the bed and stared down at him.

"Was it hard to choose?" Edgar furrowed his brow, perhaps trying to imagine what he was thinking. "All it would take would be a different course of medicine and you'd be living in a completely different body."

"Not completely," Scott corrected. "But I see what you mean."

"So how did you know you were a man?"

People have asked him this question before. He's heard different people answer and knew that many times it involved a long and complicated journey. That just wasn't the case for Scott. And he knew that made him incredibly lucky. He was raised gender neutral and told early on that he would eventually have to begin a regime of some kind of hormones to keep his bones and brain healthy. After learning his options, Scott decided he felt like a guy and everyone went on accordingly.

It was anticlimactic. Nothing worth crafting any art over. It wasn't even something he usually liked to bring up in conversation because of how simple the whole process was.

"How do *you* know?" Scott answered instead.

He overheard this volley in a conversation some folks were having in a gay bar in New York before a show. It seemed like a clever way to simplify an otherwise infinitely complex situation. It sounds unusual to an outside observer because it's different, and with that one simple question many are able to realize that sometimes these core elements of identity are just things that quietly exist until we notice they're there. Scott knew he was a man in the same way that any biological, cisgender man knows. Plain and simple.

Or at least, it should be. But a few moments went by after he asked and Edgar never responded. Scott became aware of a low rumble in Edgar's subconscious, the warning signs of a psychic drain about to overflow.

Edgar stared up at the ceiling. His jaw didn't clench, but his brow furrowed. He blinked, unsteadily and in rapid succession, and he continued not to answer.

Scott's first thought was that, however the person lying beside him identified, it didn't effect the way he felt about him. And he thought it might help to say that out loud. But then he went on to think that, if Edgar was living his life under the assumption of being a normal straight guy, the last thing he probably was ready to deal with was the knowledge that he was wrong on all three accounts. By the looks of it the thought was so far beyond his understanding that he was barely able to properly panic over it.

"You look so pretty, Edgar," Scott quickly said.

Eventually Edgar was able to bring his attention back to Scott. Scott touched the chest of his shirt and ran his thumb along the material. He wished he could think of something he could say to calm a person with these kinds of questions, but he just didn't. Maybe it would be worth taking Edgar back to Bluerose, if only so he'd have access to the many books on gender identity Scott collected from seemingly every other adult he knew.

"It's probably fine, right?" Edgar weakly wondered aloud.

"It doesn't make a difference."

"Doesn't it?"

"Well – it does as much as you want it to. And whenever you want it to. So if all of that amounts to nothing, right now…"

Scott trailed off, confused by his own sentence. As he parsed the phrasing in his head he felt Edgar's chest vibrate from laughter. He looked down at him and found that he was smiling. And that made Scott smile too.

He took his hand up from Edgar's chest and touched his fingertips to his cheek. "Your life must've made so much more sense before you met me," he said, half-joking.

Edgar moved so easily to meet his touch that one would think he'd been waiting for it for a lifetime. "It did," he said. "And I hated it. I prefer this."

It wasn't easy to bend down and kiss his curly-haired lover without getting any excess goop on him, but Scott made it work.

Once the gel dried, Scott dressed and joined Tenzin back in the other room. She was leaning against the counter, now with a second mug of coffee that Scott imagined was meant for him. He paused, midway into buttoning up the last few buttons of the flannel he stole from Edgar, and took a better look at her.

Tenzin was still wearing a handmade dread cap big enough to cover her braids. There was a demographic in Bluerose, made up of the oldest and youngest adults of the community, that practiced crochet as a buffer. Because of that, the town had a seemingly endless supply of any form of yarn-based hats, scarves, shawls and blankets. Some stitches were basic, while others were so elaborate that they were featured not only in American publications, but in overseas magazines like *Pom Pom Quarterly*.

The older crocheters were kind to Scott because he admired their techniques, and he would eventually stop talking if you put him in front of a piano. But they all loved Tenzin. Tenzin was cool and still, growing inconspicuously like the vines of a bean plant. She would sit in their circles with her sketchbook and spend hours quietly sharing words of wisdom with people old enough to be her grandparents. It was clear that's how they all saw themselves in relationship to Tenzin, and that's exactly how they treated her.

Putting it simply, the crocheted items gifted to Tenzin were like nothing else in the world. They were made not only with love, but with expert insight. So if someone were to make a yarn-based cover meant for her to sleep in, they would absolutely made sure to line the inside with silk.

Tenzin reached out one mug of coffee, even though Scott was still a few yards away. He came closer and took it, but his eyes couldn't stay off the hat for long.

"Do you recognize it?" Tenzin said.

There were visible knots in the pattern where it switched between stitches. Some sections of the hat were felted into one swatch of material, while others had open gaps that offered virtually no protection. It wasn't even closed in the back. The hat was literally unfinished.

But it was supposed to be, wasn't it?

Oh no.

Scott frowned. "You found your present," he said.

"I was wondering if you'd remember," Tenzin laughed under her breath.

He totally forgot up until now. For months before he left on his tour he would meet with what he determined to be the most patient members of the crochet circle and tried to learn enough to make his sister something as a parting gift. But god, was it hard. And he was awful at it. His hands would move so clumsily, like they were appendages crudely grafted onto him and left to spasm as they wished. Eventually he got frustrated enough that he shoved the project in the corner of his bed and just gave up.

Scott looked over his work once more for the first time in years. "I did a really bad job."

"You did," she sipped her coffee and finally cracked a smile. "It's really itchy. But also...sharp, somehow?"

"Maybe you shouldn't wear it."

Tenzin's eyes went mischievous. "Not an option. No take-backsies, Skylark."

"I didn't even – you *stole it.*"

"Hm."

He watched her take another long, leisurely sip of her coffee, clearly indicating the end of the conversation. Scott couldn't beat that. Something about Tenzin's particular hum was utterly impassable, making any attempt at protest a non-starter. She would be a spectacular elementary school teacher.

After one more scowl at his terrible, terrible hat, Scott leaned against the counter next to his sister and sipped at the coffee she made him. She kept it black, as he preferred, but when he took that first drink he was hit with the harsh impact of nostalgia.

Scott drank until he could no longer bare the heat of the coffee and then swallowed with a sigh. "God dammit," he breathed. "You make the best coffee."

From beside them Edgar came in and poured the rest of the French press contents into a cup for himself. He started to drink, then stopped.

"Where'd you get these grounds?" He said to Tenzin.

"From your cabinet."

"It smells –"Edgar sniffed again. "I don't know. Not bad. But different."

Tenzin nodded. "There's salt in it."

"Salt?"

"Yes."

"There's salt in the coffee?" Tenzin nodded and Edgar put the mug back on the counter. "How...How much?

"Just a sprinkle over the grinds. Before I added the water."

Edgar thought about that. His suspicion grew, and then paused at an apex. "Which salt did you use?"

Tenzin shifted and eyed Scott with mild confusion. "He's a chef," Scott clarified.

"Ah. Uh – just the table salt."

Edgar approved of the response. He was still incredibly uncertain. Eventually, though, that gave way to curiosity. Of course it did – knowing Edgar as Scott did, he knew a new flavor would entice him. So he took his cup and smelled the steam again.

It had to smell normal, didn't it? Scott only knew the kind of coffee Tenzin made, and in his opinion it didn't smell that far out from what you'd get at any diner or cafe. If anything, the aroma was more refined. It was like a more concentrated, yet less bitter version of what every other cup of coffee was trying to taste like.

He drank. Scott watched closely and noticed the exact moment when his brow slightly raised.

"Wow," he said. "That's actually really good."

Coffee was more fun with friends. That was the only way to describe it – Tenzin huddled by the sink, staring out the window, while Edgar scrounged for bagels. There was a slight creak coming coming from a pipe in the wall that rang out delightfully. Scott had his elbow propped up on the counter beside him and found the sleeve of his shirt sticking against a stain that was indeterminably sticky.

Adorable.

The only thing that would make Scott happier is if his mom was there. She wouldn't even have to be piloting a conversation. All he would need is her presence, the knowledge that he could see something interesting and turn to point it out to her. The sight of her smile. It was hard to imagine now – her face, her eyes, the curve of her lips – all that remained was feeling all that evoked in him.

"Is mom still mad at me?" Scott said, just to say it out loud.

Tenzin's silence immediately went tense. "What are you talking about?"

The toaster popped behind Scott, but Edgar didn't move to pick up his bagels. Everything was still. Scott wondered again if this was something else he got wrong. Another non-truth his brain wove to make up for the countless gaps between his synapses.

"Why would you say that, Scott?" Tenzin said, near-angry.

Scott held his coffee closer to his chest. "She never calls me. I haven't spoken to her since I left."

Braving the odds to look his sister in the face delivered surprising results. Even though her voice teetered close to outrage, when he looked at her he saw an expression of deep hurt. Despite being twice his size and far stronger, Tenzin faced him like he just punched her in the gut and she was more than ready to surrender.

In the back of his mind Scott heard Edgar pick his bagels from the toaster with greater hesitance than any human being has ever touched a bagel before.

"Scott..." Tenzin began.

He quickly felt the desire to retract everything he just put out there. "It's okay," he said. "I know I'm wrong. I'm probably wrong."

"If you could've seen her. If you had any idea the pain she feels."

"It'd be worse if she kept in contact. I know I'm not doing well. It's fine, I...I just miss her."

Tenzin put down her coffee and stepped in front of Scott, taking his cup and putting it aside as well. She held his hand in both of hers with the kind of fluidity he was pleasantly surprised to see she was still capable of. The touch was welcome. He once led Tenzin around town like this, hand in hand, him pointing out every sight he decided was interesting on that particular day.

How times have changed.

Reality returned to him with the feeling of a weight at the base of his palm. Tenzin released her hands and he unwrapped his fingers to see that she slipped him her phone, the screen turned on, and his mother's contact card already pulled up.

He stared down at the screen for what felt like a very long time. It dimmed, which smartphones usually did before going black. Knowing that he wouldn't have the nerve to ask Tenzin to unlock her phone a second time, Scott quickly tapped the number and started a call.

"Do you –?" Edgar quickly lowered his voice. "Should we go?"

Before his bond could act on that thought Scott awkwardly grabbed onto the hem of his jean's pocket, keeping Edgar in place. With his other hand he held the phone to his ear, already shaking, already hearing the cracks form in his voice before he even had a chance to talk.

One ring. It might take a while for her to answer.

Half a ring more, and then: "Tenzin."

His mother's voice was smoky. No, that wasn't right. Smoke was dirty and toxic to the lungs, this was something far cleaner. It was cool to the touch and instantly refreshing. Damp wood after the rain. The spray of saltwater during a storm.

"Hi Mom," Scott said – two words that came out far easier than he ever expected.

There was a small intake of air on the other end, something that could've been a stifled gasp. Scott pressed his lips tight together and clenched his hands, inadvertently drawing Edgar closer beside him. He waited like he wasn't the other half of this conversation. What else could he do?

Tell her how afraid he was? Apologize, because by now he was pretty sure there was something he was supposed to be apologizing for? Beg for her to mix him a mug of hot lemon water with honey and rub circles on his back?

Please, he inwardly prayed. *Please want to keep loving me.*

He felt tears pricking at his eyes. Then, maybe because she somehow sensed this, his mother began to hum.

Before Scott and Tenzin, the Kaufners were a line of birthrights who worked as social workers and therapists for the clients that came through Bluerose. His mother learned everything about social work from her own mother, Scott's grandmother, who he never got the chance to meet. Among this breadth of knowledge was Tone Speech, a sort of variation of pidgin language that is comprised of varied tones and melodies. It was originally developed to communicate with children and adults who enter the system and find that their trauma has limited or completely depleted their will for verbal communication.

It was never fully implemented across the other refuge hubs, as they preferred the versatility of ASL – an established language most have at least heard of. But Scott's mother Regina loved the emotional depth of every simple phrase. She got her mother to teach it to her, and then when Scott was born she passed the language down to him.

Tone Speech was useless in its current scope. It was everything to him.

She hummed the same two notes, the first longer and the second slightly lower. It was the melodic phrase that corresponded to the words *I'm sorry.* There was no quantifying descriptors in Tone Speech, and because of that emphasis in statements was established through repetition. His mother repeated the notes, over and over, only gaining speed as they continued.

I'm sorry. I'm sorry. I'm sorryI'mSorryI'msorryI'm –

"Mom, it's okay," Scott wiped at his eyes and swallowed a laugh. "I'm not..."

SorrySorrySorrySorry –

I love you, Scott hummed, the sound trembling as his tears began to flow. *I love love love you.*

Please love, there was a small hitch in the tone. Maybe a sob? *I love you please love.*

Scott found Edgar's hand clasped around his arm, and the other supporting him by the waist. He was almost fully holding him, looking around in a way that suggested he had no idea what was going on. Tenzin, meanwhile, watched from a slightly further distance. Something in her gaze felt just as physical as the touch of his newer bond.

You hungry? Scott hummed.

His mother scoffed. *No.*

You happy?

No. NoNoNoNoNo –

Please happy.

No. Miss you. No happy. Miss miss miss miss.

Miss you, Scott hummed through his sobs. *Miss you Mom.*

Home. Come home Bird.

Mom.

Home. Home. Miss you. Love you. Please home. Please Bird.

This was too much. He felt the weight of his mother's sorrow from halfway across the country, and it was gradually grinding each vertebrae in his spine down to a powder. Scott felt his knees start to buckle. Just before his hand lost its grip on Tenzin's phone, Tenzin stepped in and grabbed it herself. That left him free to fall completely into Edgar's chest, weeping like a ghost.

"Hey Mom," Tenzin said. "Everything's fine. I have it handled. I'll call you later, okay?"

She paused, listening. Tenzin sighed. *I love you,* she hummed softly.

Pain hitched in Scott's chest. Since when did Tenzin understand more than a few basic words of Tone Speech? How often was this familial dialect being spoken in his absence? Has his musical kamikaze mission driven his own mother mute?

He lost himself to his darkness without even realizing the risk of dragging Edgar down with him. With his face in his chest, Scott had no way to chart the spread of his emotions until it was already too late. Edgar crumpled under the weight of it, and so Scott did too, and they both ended up huddled against each other on the kitchen floor.

In the murk of emotions there was no separation between what was Scott and what was Edgar. There was just one expanse of turmoil that wrapped around both of them, plush and damp like moss after rain. So much stored that could be released from the softest touch.

They were the same in the pain. Everything was.

Tenzin touched the feeling and it wailed.

"Shush," she said steadily. "Calm. Calm."

She gently rubbed the backs of The Pain in a small circle just below the shoulders. The Pain breathed in deep and exhaled in a shudder.

"She still talks," Tenzin assured it. "I think she just got overwhelmed. We caught her off guard."

"He didn't know," The Pain wept.

Tenzin started to speak, then let out a semi-baffled breath. "You're right," she said before turning to the feeling's second head. "We've clearly kept too much from you, Scott. I'm sorry."

There was a rise in the feeling, that familiar build-up of tension right before the release. This was bad. It was hard enough to track his emotions, and now those cracks have only deepened with the brute force of Edgar's inexperience as a birthright. Their pooled repression was cracked and faulty, breaks growing wider with every passing second,.

He closed his eyes until his jaw clenched and the apples of his cheeks started to ache. At any point in time his mind was only loosely clinging to the confines of his body. All it would take was one strong enough tear to separate the two and spare his loved ones the fallout.

So Scott tore. He ripped himself out of himself, pulling with both hands and feeling the give gradually continue to give and give and

The planes of the apartment ripped through like thick webbing, sending Scott plummeting out of reality and straight into The Other Place. He fell, faster and faster, so fast that the ribbons of luminescent color stretched into many open-mouthed screams.

Then slowness. Then stillness. Soon Scott was back to drifting in place, breathing in the oil stick and feeling it burn in his lungs with every inhale.

He knew where he was. But things were different now.

There was a lack of active presence. Being there felt like occupying a stranger's bed while they're asleep beside you. There-ness, yet not-there-ness. He felt the eyes, but couldn't see them. Maybe they weren't watching him. Maybe they were closed, or somehow not seeing.

Without the cacophony of voices Scott expected silence. What he got instead was low, babbling brook comprised of a million whispering voices, each saying something different. It was strange to experience knowing that this space was occupied by him and him alone.

But then Scott realized he actually had the strength to move his head, and as he did it became clear just how wrong he was.

He was not the only person in the oil slick. Everywhere he looked he saw a mass of static in the rough shape of a human body, some stagnant and others flickering in and out like a dying bulb. Each of them dangled in the dense nothing just as Scott did, tethered in place by a thick, ropy tendril extending from their middle.

The tendril reminded Scott of a length of ritual strand, only if the strand was as thick as a telephone wire and made of meat. He was a fair distance away from the closest tendril, but even that was close enough for him to see that the individual veins throbbed slowly with the passing of stimuli.

He stared for a long time. Unsure what to think. Unsure how he could think so clearly. Wondering, vaguely, and not really wanting to know the answer, why his tendril looked so different from the others around him. Malformed. Underdeveloped, even.

A new awareness came to him of his body existing within this body of space. He focused enough to feel his arm, and then his hand, and then to slowly lift his arm and hand in front of him. Scott reached out to the nearest body without any plan of what to do if he managed to touch it. It didn't look like he'd be able to, but he shouldn't be able to see it so clearly either — so why not?

His fingers peeled thick rivulets through the air and came back feeling like grease. Gross.

Scott looked down and touched the deformed rope coming out of him with curiosity. It wasn't wet, but it felt wet. The ridges of veins were hard like wood. At every point where his fingertips met the surface of the new flesh, the touch echoed somewhere inside him that he recognized without understanding.

His bond did not move as freely as the others. One look at the meat strand and it made sense why. It looked, somehow, as if the space itself was somehow eating the flesh of his tendril. Part of the material was slowly being absorbed into the nothing, bit by bit, through the efforts of countless tiny invisible mouths.

The feeding, Of course. It was so obvious that seeing it in actuality made Scott feel very little. However, that changed when he saw the limp fork in the tendril just beyond where the feeding started. He realized immediately what it was.

His bond. His Lover's Knot. But something split it in two, turning one solid strand into two weaker ones. There was another misshapen meat tendril that split off alongside his own. Scott traveled his eyes up the free stretch of strand until he could see the figure tethered in the end in plain view.

Joy. Sorrow.

Edgar.

It was him. It's always been him – Edgar was here. Edgar shouldn't be here. He was drifting close by to Scott, same cord keeping him in place, same look of immense confusion.

You shouldn't be here, Scott lamented in his head. But of course you are. I brought you into my pain and now I brought you into my hell too.

He watched Edgar look from side to side. His feet still shifted, trying to find solid ground, just as Scott did his first few times here. Eventually he turned his head and found Scott treading nothing beside him.

At first there was no reaction on his behalf. But then his lips rose into the beginnings of a smile. Because he trusted Scott. Scott was his soul bond. And look where that's taken him.

"Where are we?" Edgar asked, the words clipping like they were being played back on damaged speakers.

Finally the fear came. Oh no, he thought. He tried to find the tone that matched the sentiment.

No. No no no nonononononono –

Tenzin carried Scott and Edgar back to bed. Each of them were mostly lifeless in her arms, but since their bodies were only about a tenth the weight of their thoughts and feelings Tenzin had no trouble holding them up.

She pulled back the covers and tucked them in. It didn't look great. Tenzin's nurturing nature was cobbled together from what she read in books and saw in movies, and even then everything she did was only an imitation. But how badly can you mess up putting two emotional train-wrecks to sleep? What could she do wrong – wrap the blankets too tightly?

Potentially asphyxiate them from the tightness of the wrapped blankets?

She loosened her tuck slightly until it was more to her liking. Then she sat at the foot of the bed and watched the two of them for a while. As soon as they were both lying side by side, Edgar and Scott huddled up against each other, face to face with their hands held together. They didn't look like passionate lovers as much as lost children maintaining morale until the grownups come.

This was her brother. If what she learned so far was correct, then these two individuals in front of her were both technically her brother. One soul forced to adapt into two. Some modern iteration of Janus, a singular god that just happened to have two faces.

It wouldn't be like it was now for long. As soon as they stabilized and overcame whatever trauma was currently unfolding, they might latch on as they should and emerge as a fully-intact Lover's Knot. They'd be contented with each other for the rest of their lives. It would be a life Tenzin wouldn't see much of, but if she was willing to be utterly delusional she could tell herself she was okay with that.

Her illicit studies informed her that soul-bonds between humans are almost always connected in childhood. They're meant to develop together, just the brain of a human being is meant to develop alongside its body. So inevitably they end up forming corresponding identities that overlap, eventually completely. The eldest member of her crochet circle once described it as a hivemind before they realized Tenzin was in the room and quickly changed the subject.

There was nothing about what happens when a soul-bond grows up into what Tenzin could see as two completely distinct people. A deeply feeling, inadvertent iconoclast like Scott. An emotionally repressed, head-bowed conformist like Edgar. The two didn't make sense in the same body. Everything about this was just very slightly off. And yet there they were, literally clinging to each other.

She watched. She just watched them. Tenzin would've kept standing guard if she hadn't gotten a text from Katy.

Outside, it read.

And then. *Coming in.*

And after that. *Don't hit me lol.*

A few moments passed before Tenzin heard the front door of Edgar's apartment unlock and open. Her alarms didn't go off, so she could only imagine it was Katy letting herself in. She reluctantly moved from her post and left the room, closing the door as gently as possible behind her, as if the two in bed were only asleep and not deep in some sort of transcendental fugue state.

She caught sight of Katy just as she was coming inside. As with every other time they'd met so far, she was dressed strangely enough to jar Tenzin from whatever thoughts she was fixated on before she walked into the room. Her hair was meticulously brushed and styled into little waves of gold, but all that effort was paired with an outfit consisting of jeans and a worn t-shirt printed with the poster of the first *Evangelion* movie. To top all of that off, she donned what looked to be an actual slap bracelet on one wrist, colored with the stripes of the lesbian pride flag.

Tenzin observed more than long enough to draw Katy's attention. Instead of recoiling or mocking, she smiled and gave a little turn. "You like it?" She motioned to the shirt. "You're the weeb, right?"

The last thing Tenzin expected to start her morning off with was hearing a woman she barely knew call her a weeaboo. She furrowed her brow and debated whether that was worth having a conversation over.

"Yeah," Katy said, agreeing with nothing. "I hope that guy keeps ret-conning his anime every ten years till he dies, just as one big *fuck off* to the fans who didn't appreciate it the first go-around."

Her smile turned expectant. It could be that she was hoping Tenzin would agree with her statement, or use it as the basis for one of those impossible-to-settle pop culture arguments. She was trying to make a connection, clearly. Or determine Tenzin's general attitude regarding something she was still unable to trace.

"Are the lovebirds still asleep?"

By now Tenzin realized she'd gone this entire time without saying anything. "They're in a state of psychic dissociation," she said.

Katy's face fell. "Oh."

"It's..." She was tempted to call it fine, but that felt disingenuous. "It's happening."

"Yeah," Katy said. "I can imagine."

Tenzin suddenly felt very, very tired. So tired that it weakened the joints that kept her bones held upright, so she meandered to the table and sat down. Katy watched, coming closer, but starting and stopping intermittently.

"Are you okay?" She paused and palmed awkwardly at her slap bracelet. "I know I don't know you that well. We didn't make the best first impression, but – yeah. Are you good?"

"I'm just tired."

Somehow Katy ended up in the chair across from Tenzin. She even sat down with a degree of style that made no sense. "I can imagine," she said. "You look like you've gotten some sleep now. You're with Ed, so I'm sure you're eating well," Katy blatantly looked Katy up and down. "You could use a bath."

Tenzin straightened up. "Why? Am I – do I smell bad?"

"No!" Katy let out a nervous laugh. "No, you just – you look tense. When I'm that tight I find a bath calms me down. I thought it might help you."

"I'm six feet two. Do you see me in a bathtub?"

She said that sharply enough to shut Katy down immediately. And that felt good for a little bit, until it didn't anymore. Tenzin always knew she had a tendency to spark – especially lately, especially now – but it didn't have the same sense of satisfaction when the other person asked for nothing and offered no aggression or danger. So Tenzin took a deep breath (*Calm, calm, calm*) and forcibly unwrapped some of the knots in her shoulders.

"Listen, Katy –"

"What about a massage?"

Tenzin faltered. "What?"

"Don't ask Edgar for suggestions, though," Katy snickered quietly. "Every time he's tried to find a place it's ended up being a hand job parlor. *Every time.* It's not entirely his fault – there's a lot of them here. But still, you know, what are the odds?"

The insistent goodwill in Katy's tone forced Tenzin to imagine Edgar walking into a massage parlor without realizing they'd end up offering that proverbial "happy ending". It brought up a lot of follow-up questions. At what point did he realize where he was? Is that the type of thing you'd check on intake paperwork, or do you get the offer at the end of what must be a pretty mediocre massage?

"The rub-down before the rub-down," Tenzin murmured, following her own thoughts.

Katy's eyes widened for a moment. She laughed, shocked, and pressed her hand to her mouth. That managed to calm Tenzin even further, that sudden burst of positive energy. She leaned a little more comfortably in her chair, still unhappy, but not quite as wound up.

"I can't," she said. "I'm sort of on-duty –"

"For what?" Katy cocked her head to the side. "No one's in danger."

"We don't know that," Tenzin's focus drifted a little closer to the tangles of fear right on the edge of her vision. "We don't know much of *anything* for certain, which to some degree means that we're *all* in danger..."

She trailed off when she saw the way Katy was staring at her. There was a strange knowing in her eyes, a vivid sense of exact understanding that unnerved her. Because their individual lives couldn't possibly be more different. Katy was a non-magic user, a civilian who grew up in civilian society and lived a normal life, while Tenzin –

"When'd your parents get divorced?" Katy asked.

Tenzin's chest tightened. A giant spotlight was shone directly on something quiet and vulnerable inside her, and the new attention forced it to stop crying for the moment.

Katy lessened her vague smugness and put on an expression that was more sympathetic. "I just figured. Some people have a certain degree of constant tension that I feel has to come from some massive rug-pull early on in life," she leaned forward, settling her chin on the ball of her hand. "Something that tells your squishy, dumb kid brain that being safe is a luxury and it remembers that forever. I have a good sense for that kind of thing."

Her eyes were a pale green that reminded her of the glass bottles used to use for Coca Cola back in the day. They weren't glowing. Tenzin focused harder. She knew birthright disabilities to be physical or mental, external or internal, engaging or perceiving. At the same time, though, Tenzin knew that if she ever found a way to detect birthrights the knowledge would be useless at best and deeply offensive at worse.

She still tried. She still looked. She found nothing.

"I was six," Tenzin finally said.

By now Katy wasn't smiling at all. She just nodded. "That's awful."

"It was a good thing. My mom –"

"I mean for you. It's awful for you. A kid needs stability at that age and, whatever happened, I'm betting you didn't have that."

These were the types of things Tenzin tried not to think about. Because she was lucky, wasn't she? She still had a family that cared about her and a community that wanted her to succeed. If she was ever in trouble anyone in Bluerose would drop everything to help her in whatever way they could. She still sometimes wondered if any of it was real. Or if it was the type of thing she was meant to have.

Her life. Her home. Her friends. Her family, even.

No. Calm. No.

"Are your parents divorced?" Tenzin forced out the question, just to fill the air.

Katy sighed. "No. It would've really ripped off the Bandaid, though. You can thank the Catholic church for decades of strained Americana," she locked eyes with Tenzin and smirked darkly. "It does something to you, doesn't it? Because kids know when something is wrong. *Babies* know – I've read studies. And to have that sense of worry without being able to imagine why – or maybe you can and *no one's* talking about it...it's exhausting."

She grazed the thumb of her other hand over the table, lost in thought. Tenzin considered how much a person's intention effects their expression and the way they carry themselves. The desire to protect. The urge to confront. The want for connection. When you take all of that away and see the dust that remains, it's hard to look at.

"Sounds like you need a massage," Tenzin remarked in an attempt to joke.

Katy smirked. "I do have a guy. I see him once a month."

"You have a guy?" Tenzin said. "Why doesn't Edgar just go to your guy?"

"He's too *talky*, he says."

"I guess I wouldn't want a chatterbox getting me off either."

Katy laughed again. "Fuck, you're clever. You..."she broke off again in giggling. "God *dammit.*"

Tenzin felt herself smile.

A short while later she sat back and watched Katy rifle through Edgar's fridge, only raising her head to make the occasional comment to no one in particular. She muttered something about him never getting "the cool kind of hummus" before grabbing a bell pepper from one of the drawers and biting into it like it was an apple. Katy closed the door with her hip and turned back to Tenzin.

"You drink?" She asked.

Tenzin shook her head. Katy went back to the table, still chewing on a chunk of raw pepper.

"Never?"

"Never."

Katy ripped a portion of the pepper off and slid it across the table towards Tenzin. "No interest?"

"Nope," Tenzin said. "No booze, no drugs. Even caffeine is a rarity for me. Just coffee once or twice a week."

Saying this aloud was never something she paid any mind to. That was because her view of the world was limited mainly to witch towns and birthrights, people who were known for just taking others as they were and for what they required. It's substantially difficult to surprise a birthright. If you told one that you never tried alcohol and never would, they would have no opinion on the matter.

But people – what some would describe as *normal* people – some of them drink. Or they smoke. They might even do recreational drugs. And they definitely have a lot to say about people that don't do any of that.

It was weird to feel nervous about what another person might think of you.

"You're straight edge," Katy said, using another chunk of pepper to point at Tenzin.

"I...guess so."

Katy bit into the crunchy green flesh. She nodded approvingly. "That's cool."

She continued eating the vegetable, and after a few moments it looked that that would be the end of that conversation. Tenzin was in Katy's house and saw the many bottles of alcohol piled on the top of the fridge. Living in New Orleans she probably hung out in cool clubs, or within the rowdy crowds of a boozy parade. And yet this individual, with her hip clothes and fluffy hair, appeared genuinely impressed that Tenzin chose to spend most of her time dead sober.

"Why do you ask?" Tenzin braved and carefully took the chunk of bell pepper from off the table.

Katy shrugged. "I was going to see if you wanted to get a drink."

"Right now? It's ten-thirty."

"*Mimosas*, baby. I know a good brunch place."

That's right. People like alcohol so much that sometimes they'll get themselves buzzed for breakfast. They gather at well-lit, trendy cafes where they serve diner food, but for triple the price. Tenzin had driven past them before, both in the Pacific Northwest and in her time in Louisiana. It always sounded intriguing, but at the same time she knew it was the type of place that Scott would find uncomfortable and their mother outrageous.

A mimosa was a cocktail, wasn't it? And didn't they make virgin cocktails? Or, in this case, would that just be orange juice.

You know, I don't hate orange juice.

She bit into the pepper. It was cold and crunchy. Then Katy gasped.

"Got it!" She said. "Let's go to the Cardinal."

"Is that a bar?"

"It's a tea room! Little sandwiches, porcelain cups and saucers, *little sandwiches...*" Katy paused, frowning. "You can't tell Edgar, though. He's been trying to get me to go there with him for months."

Tenzin swallowed back the rest of the pepper. "Why haven't you?"

Katy thought long and hard. "I'm worried I'll laugh," she finally concluded. "He's really into it and it's a little *Jane Austen* for my taste. I mean it might be cool if it's done well, but if it's cheesy I know I'll make fun of it and he'll get pissy."

An image of frilly lace doilies on polished wooden tabletops. Those three-tier stands for delicate confectioneries. A general musty smell. Soft music – based on Katy's vague descriptor, probably something like Schubert or Liszt.

God, Tenzin missed Liszt. She missed an opportunity to just sit and enjoy a piece of music, even a classical piece she really only liked out of nostalgia.

"Okay," she said. "I'll go."

Katy brightened, glass-green eyes filling with excitement. She pulled herself out of the chair and tossed the remains of the pepper in the vague direction of the trash can. It missed, but her enthusiasm didn't falter.

"Great! You ready?"

"Oh – did you mean now?"

Tenzin looked behind her towards Edgar's bedroom. The door was closed and the room behind it was silent. There really wasn't anything she could do. Frankly, Tenzin wasn't even certain she knew what the two of them were experiencing right now.

Her only goal was to get her brother out of danger. He wasn't, though. Well, he was, but there wasn't a lot she could do about that with what she had right now.

"You have your Spidey Sense, right?" There was a small rustling as Katy picked up the stem and seed pod of the pepper and properly threw it in the trash. "If things were bad I imagine you'd be way less calm."

A good point. "That only applies to Scott," Tenzin said.

"I've done my research. A lot of the stuff that applies to him applies to both of them, right?"

She was being very nice. It wasn't like Tenzin spent her entire adult life not talking to non-magic users and other more conventional people. Her title in Bluerose was Design and Communications Coordinator, which essentially meant her job was to design materials and connect with businesses that could potentially work with the witch town. And back when she had the energy to develop her webcomic, she found that she was able to grow a modest fan base online.

But patrons, clients, colleagues and fans each spoke with a specific agenda in mind. Tenzin was able to interact with them without an issue, but none of them spoke to her like she was a normal person.

None of them spoke to her like she was a friend.

"You shouldn't trust me so easily," Tenzin said.

Katy didn't respond to that. Tenzin slipped off her knitted cap and let her locs fall over one shoulder. There was a fair bit of multi-colored lint scattered along her braids, and she made an honest attempt to pick out the pieces of fluff before quickly giving up. She tossed her dreads over her shoulder and took a deep, pained breath.

Apparently Katy watched all of this closer than she had any reason to. The tone of her voice when she spoke after that was different. Caring and surprisingly serious.

"You're a baby, Tenzin," she said.

"Excuse me?"

"You're a big baby. More than one, actually. You're just a big stack o' babies."

Tenzin wanted to feel defensive over her own abilities. She was mainly just confused. "I could hurt you very easily."

"That's nice."

"I'm serious, Katy. I'm a Khan 10 in Thai kickboxing. That's the equivalent of a black belt."

Katy still wasn't concerned. In fact, she looked closed to disinterested. "So what," she said, "you're gonna kick me in the face in the middle of a tea house? That seems...assault-y. Plus I doubt you'd have the space."

"You saw me use magic."

"Oh yeah. You have a whole different thing going on."

That was one way to put it. "Does it concern you?" She asked.

"Not really."

"It should."

Katy blinked a few times. The rest of her expression did not change. "What's oolong?" She eventually said.

Tenzin had no idea how to answer that. The fluffy blonde elaborated.

"There's black tea. Green tea. Those are two colors. So what's *oolong*?"

"I guess it's just...a different type of tea."

Katy's grin broadened. "Right? But *how*?"

It could be that it's a different type of leaf. There might be an oolong plant, and that's where they harvest the blend from. Or maybe the name describes a type of production process, an aging or smoking that makes it distinct from other teas. Tenzin wasn't sure. She'd had oolong tea before, but it just tasted like tea.

As much as she enjoyed it, most teas just tasted like tea. Unless it was matcha or chai.

"We should go," Katy said. "I want to go. I want to try it."

Over the last day or so she spent alone with Edgar, Tenzin found him to be polite enough, though generally unsettled and a more than a little distracted. He was tired, which Tenzin understood. He was afraid, which Tenzin related to. He wasn't thinking about the next opportunity to have a really fun time, because *why would he do that*?

This was different. This was strange.

At the same time, and in a way that was frankly more concerning, it tempted her. This woman was very tempting. When Scott woke up, she knew he wouldn't be offended that she left them alone. He was always near-aggressive when it came to her making friends. Even if he didn't remember that, the instinct could still be there.

"Sure," she said. "Let's try it."

The architecture of New Orleans was way different from what Tenzin was familiar with in Oregon. That's all she could really think about as she followed Katy down the street, past wrap-around porches and brightly-colored townhouses. It reminded her, vaguely, of something out of a Tim Burton movie. A satire of a society as depicted through design.

It was really pretty. Everything was warmer here, despite the season. Even the air had a certain floral heat to it with every breath she took.

Tenzin thought about Scott back in the apartment. She wondered when she should call their Mom and make sure she was doing alright.

Even a second of peace felt like a parasite in her head that had to be extracted as soon as possible.

Beside her Katy rambled about nothing in particular. She spoke with the unspoken implication that Tenzin was welcome to join in, but she would keep talking regardless of whether or not she actually did. Every so often her eyes would shift in Tenzin's direction like she was seeing if she would be commanded to shut up – as if she were waiting for it, even. Then she'd see that it wasn't going to happen, and go right off to explaining her opinions on the latest advancements in artificial intelligence.

Or the drama between mainstream social media platforms and open-source alternatives. Or the latest Netflix true-crime documentary that she claimed to be *bait-and-switch, without the bait*. Tenzin used to be better at keeping up with the never-ending stream of news and cultural landmines that went off every day. Now she barely understood a word of what Katy waxed poetically on.

When did she allow her life to get so isolated?

Eventually they ended up at a gray and red-painted Victorian on some street corner. A Victorian! Tenzin never expected to be so happy to see something she was able to recognize from home. A wooden sign hanging on chains over the stairs read *Cardinal House* in dark red lettering. Little red birds were painted at the head of each white step.

There was a bay window looking out over the street, and through the glass Tenzin could see a few round tables, each with a different color tablecloth and floral arrangement. The place looked popular without being too crowded. Patrons of varying ages came in and out through the doors.

"It's cute," Tenzin observed.

Katy frowned. "It is," she said. "You're right."

She faltered, staring up at the sign and humming thoughtfully. Tenzin thought about what she said before, about how Katy was coming here now with her instead of Edgar. At the time Tenzin assumed that meant she didn't hold sentiments like that in high regard. Now, though, it was clear how this quaint little tea house now posed a serious ethical dilemma.

"We can go somewhere else," Tenzin offered.

"*Mm,*" Katy pursed her lips. "No. No, I think it's fine. I'll get him a teapot," she nodded, pleased. "Yeah, he's been saying he wants one for, like, a year. We'll see if we can find one with a bird."

With that she started up the stairs and towards the front door. Tenzin followed, pausing briefly when Katy held open the door for her before reluctantly going in first.

The inside of the Cardinal House was made up of two large rooms with tall ceilings framed in dark wood. Each had four tables (*four-tops,* as Scott explained to her once), but the young host in the frilly shirt informed them that there were a few more tables in the back garden.

"We'll sit there," Tenzin quickly spat out without giving time for Katy to think.

She felt Katy look at her in a way that made her cringe to herself. Other than that, her new friend stayed silent, and neither of them spoke as they were led through the house and down the steps into the backyard. There were paved stone paths that wove through grass and hazy splotches of multi-colored flowers like a veins. The host sat them in the corner table, closest to the massive, ivy-woven wooden fence.

After she handed them their menus and left, Katy finally felt permitted to speak. "You can't stop thinking about him, can you?"

Tenzin tightened her grip on the menu, denting the delicate card stock. "I think it's reasonable," she said. "Given the circumstances."

"Well, it's been years, right? So have you just been...worrying about your brother the whole time? Just lying in bed, staring at the ceiling, imagining how fucked he is twenty-four hours a day?"

Of course not. Thanks to her nightly dose of Prazosin, Tenzin slept without dreams.

"It seems unreasonable to expect me to relax knowing my brother as I know him is dying," Tenzin put down the menu and paused to keep her voice calm. "He's been alone, I have no way of knowing anything other than what he chooses to tell me – and I can't even be sure that what he tells me is true. Are you saying I should keep all that in my head – and then what? Go bowling? Mini-golf?"

Katy cracked a smile that she, at the very least, had the decency to then pull back. She stared down at the menu, fingering the lace-like designs on the edges. "I guess I've never been on the other side of that," she mused.

Her face went cold. She seemed drained. Tenzin wasn't surprised, considering the amount of effort it must take to be that peppy all the time.

"Do you tell them?" Tenzin asked.

"Who?"

"The people you're hiding from. Do you tell them how you're really doing?"

Katy shifted in her seat. She looked incredibly uncomfortable, even though her natural charm. "It's – okay," she said. "It's fine, actually. We talk on major holidays like clockwork. And it's not like –" she let out a sharp, singular laugh. "I mean, there's nothing magical happening on my end."

"There doesn't have to be," Tenzin said.

"I'm not...I'm really not – I mean, maybe I *was*, but..." Katy smiled again, perhaps bemused by her own anxiety. "I feel like I'm probably a better liar than Scott. I just get that sense."

It was new for Tenzin to see a smile so sweet armed like something that could kill her at a moment's notice. It was a threat of violence and a quiet request for mercy. Katy's smile was beautiful and distantly upsetting.

Tenzin tore her eyes away and onto her menu. "Yeah," she said. "I bet you are."

Katy ended up ordering a pot of strawberry peach Oolong tea and Tenzin the orange chai. They got suggested the Crows Nest, which was the house special of sweet and savory tea cakes, and Katy agreed with another slight frown.

She didn't need to explain the reason. Tenzin remembered when Edgar pointed out the crows in the yard the first morning she spent at his place. His whole face lit up with excitement and he just sat and watched them for almost ten minutes. It was weird to look at. It made her feel the same way as she would if he started undressing in front of her.

Now Tenzin felt guilty. She supposed Edgar could use a new tea blend to go with the pot Katy was going to buy him.

The conversation fell silent while they waited for their tea. Tenzin, still calm, still in control, dimly felt herself teeter towards a panic. She was not a naturally sociable person. Maybe online, where there was the mask of the screen and an anonymous profile picture. If she was talking with someone online and she couldn't think of anything to say, she could just send them a funny Youtube video or a meme from her folder to keep the conversation flowing despite anything meaningful being said.

"What, um…" Tenzin sipped anxiously at her ice water and debating taking one of the biggest risks of her life. "What do *you* think about memes?"

Katy raised her brow. She wasn't following, but still looked intrigued. "Like – memes? The concept of memes?"

"I saw your desktop setup when I…" It no longer seemed like a good idea to bring up anything to do with their first and second interactions, "You seem techie. I thought maybe you'd have an interesting take on the subject."

"You'll have to narrow it down a bit. Memes are just cultural fragments passed from one person to another – they've been around a lot longer than modern technology."

Tenzin raised her head slightly. "Well they say that, but what about deep-fried memes? The ones that are just random pictures put through dozens of filters until they're practically indecipherable?"

"What is this?" Katy laughed. "Why are we talking about this?"

"What I mean to say is – what fragment of culture is something like *that* exchanging?"

Katy scoffed in disbelief. Still, she leaned back in her chair and crossed her arms, seriously considering what Tenzin was saying.

"Absurdity," she finally said. "Incoherence. Online culture ate its own tail a long time ago and now the national sport is laughing at the creation of digital litter," Katy smiled again, deviously. "Sometimes I just send Edgar stock photos of old men eating spaghetti. Like, thirty at a time. It makes him so angry."

"It's not really fun unless it's fun for everyone," Tenzin said.

That did feel a little silly coming out of her mouth, and Katy looked at her like she was the puniest narc at the drug den. Then she was back to wry curiosity.

"Tell me, then," Katy said. "What's a meme you think is *fun for everyone*?"

"Business Cat," Tenzin said.

"That...that fucking macro series from – what – 2010? Do you know how much cooler shit has happened since then?"

"I do," Tenzin shrugged. "I'm not a fan."

By now Tenzin could tell Katy was more aware than ever of the other people in the space surrounding them. She fidgeted like she wanted to yell but knew she couldn't. So, forced not to overreact, she focused all her excess energy in staying calm to the point where her stillness actually buzzed with energy.

Tenzin continued, perhaps knowing she was aggravating her table-mate and choosing to push the limits. "You're right – the landscape of the internet changes so frequently that I just don't have the time to keep up with what's now considered funny. So I've decided to stick with the things I genuinely like, which usually tend to have a lot more structure to them. So advice animals, LOLCats, doge stuff –"

"Runescape," Katy piped in.

She paused. It was easy to imagine that, unless Scott somehow remembered how to spell her last name, Katy might've had to scour the internet to find her contact information. Doing that much was probably easy for a woman who acted like she already explored the dark web and lost interest in it a long time ago. It wasn't a shock if she found Tenzin's Runescape account.

"I shouldn't tease you about that," she said. "I know you stopped playing when you were a kid."

"Oh – no I didn't."

Katy's olive branch quickly rotted. "What do you mean?"

"You must've found my old account," Tenzin said. "I pretty much maxed it out and got bored so I quit for a long time, but then when they brought back the classic server people started to – oh, do you know what an Ironman run is?"

The waitress came back with their order on a tray. When she was here last Katy paid her special attention, but she now ignored her entirely. Instead she had her attention fixed solely on Tenzin, watching her like a new kind of life form that could either cure cancer or spread an entirely new and more fatal disease.

"I do not," Katy said.

"It's a game mode where if you die you lose your inventory, or sometimes your whole account. Runescape players will do modified Ironman challenges with additional restrictions, so for the past few years I've been working on a shrimp-locked Hardcore Ultimate Ironman –"

"Hang on – *shrimp-locked*?"

"I can only go to places in the game where you can fish for shrimp. Shrimp is the only thing I can cook and eat as a food source. And if I die I'm dead forever. Just like in real life!"

She was smiling at Katy. If Katy's smile was a switchblade meant for self-defense, what was Tenzin's? She hadn't thought about it before.

Something inside Katy released. She picked up the small teapot that was handed to her and poured a stream of reddish-gold into her delicate saucer. Then she picked up the cup and smelled the steam, not really relishing in it, just curious to see what would happen.

"I think most of what your brother knows about the normal world is what he gets from you," Katy said. "Would that be fair to say?"

Not true. Scott stopped playing Runescape as soon as he accidentally killed a dog.

"That's a big responsibility," Katy took a few tiny, loud sips of her tea. "I was a big sister, so I should be able to say I know the feeling. But I don't. None of my siblings ended up like me."

"Mom comes from an old line of birthrights," Tenzin explained, pouring a little sugar into her chai without bothering to taste it first. "She's a social worker, which for a refuge hub like Bluerose is one of the most valued titles to have."

"Ah. She's important."

Tenzin sighed wistfully. "No one's more important than anyone else in a witch town. You get respect and regard when you do respectful things that are worth being regarded. But because of that they tend to be so dedicated to their work that they don't really bother learning about civilian culture."

"Civilian. I kept hearing that reading Academy stuff," Katy rolled her eyes slightly. "That's such a weird thing to call people like us. Like all magic-users are cops or soldiers."

"It's not too far off. I can't speak for the Academics, but birthrights consider magic to be a responsibility. Their abilities are like a chronic illness that has to be managed, only theirs has the capability to help the world around them," Tenzin scoffed. "Besides, what would you prefer? Muggles? Mortals? We're still people."

The mood around the table became a little heavier. Katy put down her cup and stared across at Tenzin, a little more serious. "Are you?" She said.

"I – I mean..." Tenzin sighed, newly anxious. "As far as I know. Scott's dad wrote a lot about the physiology of birthrights and Academics, and...they can definitely get hurt. They can die. Many birthrights have conditions that significantly cut down their lifespan, so some die even sooner than they should. We've lost a lot of..." Tenzin felt her eyes start to tingle and quickly changed the subject. "I know the whole soul-bond thing complicates the issue, though."

"You didn't answer my question," Katy said.

"I'm trying to."

"Are you?" Katy leaned forward and lowered her voice. "Are *you* a person?"

Tenzin was midway into drinking her tea when Katy posed that question. After the words left her lips she paused with the cup still poised at her lips. The smell of the chai was sharp and spicy, with a cold sweetness that reminded her of home. Tenzin focused on the smell, because trying to think of an answer to what Katy was asking was a lot more difficult.

Between them was a knotted platter resembling a maroon nest of individual twigs. There were little cakes and sandwiches arranged along the surface, beautiful little things that almost looked too captivating to eat. One of them had cut strawberry and whipped cream – Tenzin's favorite. But it was also the only one of its kind on the plate, so she took the knife from her own place setting and started to carefully slice the small cake in half.

"Scott told me you aren't a birthright," Katy's breath hitched, like she was struggling to put her thoughts into words. "And the Academy handbook says that magic has to be transferred through a wand or – or proxy, or something."

Tenzin put half the cake on her plate. "What's the alternative, you think?" She said.

She spooned out a portion of cake and ate it. It was really good. Soft and pleasant. She could probably eat a dozen little cakes if they all tasted like this.

"I don't know," Katy admitted, staring down at the plate between them. "I don't really know what's out there."

That strong murmur of disappointment in her voice was strikingly familiar to Tenzin. It was exactly what she experienced when she first started her studies into magic and found how inconsistent and confusing everything was. Basic qualities of birthright magic had different names depending on the witch town and the individual birthright. Academics had their own terminology for everything, it seemed, including things Tenzin had so far been unable to verify and might possibly be made up.

The people born with magic didn't want to talk about it. The people who spend their lives studying it will fill textbooks with things that might not actually be true. Make any effort to compile a comprehensive overview of magic in the world and you're guaranteed to be frustrated. And Tenzin, wandering onto the scene with an entirely new technique, must only make things that much more confusing.

"It was a practice the Witch Doctors tried to develop," Tenzin said. "It's hard to pick up, so not many people caught onto it."

"So you weren't born with it."

"I was not."

"And you don't study it."

"I got my start reading some of mom's Academy books, but I switched to this and haven't done an incantation since."

Katy seemed suspicious. She seemed doubtful. She also was undoubtedly interested. "So you just..?"

"Meditation. With this birthright medicine called Petrichor. It was pretty intense," Tenzin's mind echoed back to that memory and she felt an icy chill in her stomach. "I can maybe tell you more about it another time."

"Sure, sure," Katy murmured. "And now you can just – do magic?"

The floral display in the center of the table was starting to wilt. Tenzin didn't have a natural eye for plants, but she recognized the limp, sickly-yellow tissue of a lifeless daffodil. She pointed her finger until the tip just but touched the skin of the flower and whispered.

"Bloom, please."

There was a shiver of movement in the bouquet. The daffodil shifted like some living thing, stiffening with the color returning to its petals. In a matter of seconds it was fresher than fresh, newly-bloomed and over-whelmingly fragrant.

Tenzin heard Katy gasp as soon as the change happened. Once it was finished she stared at the resurrected flower, lips parted. She looked astonished. Like her mom and brother were the first time she brought home a bag of Doritos.

"How badly does that hurt you?" Katy asked.

"Huh?" Tenzin hummed, lightly amused. "Oh. No, it doesn't."

Katy poked at a sandwich. "You can do stuff like that without pain?"

"I can. I don't it often, though. It's sort of like...a relationship, maybe."

She didn't say anything after that. And Tenzin wasn't surprised. Back when she managed to teach herself incantations from her mother's Academy textbooks, one spell would leave her writhing in shocks of agony along her body. It would feel like a knife twisting in her gut, only without the blood of the wound. Just a full-body wracking of *wrong bad no.*

Academic magic felt like trying to pull the skin off your flesh with your bare hands. The tactic outlined by the Scott's father and the other Witch Doctors felt like nothing at all. There was zero physical effect, positive or negative. And that was strange, wasn't it? It was close to aggravating. Tenzin didn't spend enough time around non-magic users to have to think about it that often.

"It's cool," Katy said.

Tenzin was focused mainly on eating the rest of her cake when she said that. Katy was smiling very faintly, a gesture that expressed a sense of pride that Tenzin didn't fully understand and wasn't sure how to feel about. She approved of what she saw, but not in a way that raised her opinion of Tenzin. And because of that the reaction was a lot easier to swallow.

"That's what I always wanted magic to be," she lowered her eyes, her smirk turning sad. "I mean, it's not a fireball or anything, but...it's cool and it doesn't seem shitty. Assuming there's no other terrible side effects you haven't found out about – it's nice to see."

She picked a little cake off the plate with her fingers and bit into it. A small dollop of chocolate cream dropped onto the plate in front of her. Katy took her thumb and swiped some frosting off the corner of her lip and smiled.

"Yum," she said.

Tenzin sat with her spine settled easily against the back of her chair. Her shoulders curved easily and her arms were heavy, hands folded loosely in her lap. A soft floral chill brushed against her cheek. Her eyes went down to the new life blooming in the bouquet on the edge of their table.

She hummed, so faint she hoped it wasn't audible. Three tones, the first higher, the second lower, and the third at a slightly different register. Tenzin took a deep breath and smiled as she let it go.

As Edgar regained a grasp on his consciousness, he realized he was sitting at the long dining room table in his childhood home. It was exactly as he remembered it – hard as he tried not to – from the antique gold and purple table runner laid across the center of the tabletop, to the dark and ornate crown molding snaking out above him.

He was at his usual middle seat on the left side. His head was slightly lowered, staring down at the snifter glass placed on the table in front of him. Edgar knew exactly where he was. This night stained his bones like the aftermath of an atom bomb. The smell of the clear liquid pooled in the glass was stifling, its sweetness filled the indentations in his throat and made it difficult to breathe.

The panic could not reach him. If he focused hard he could feel the buzzing warmth of Scott's touch against his palm.

It's different now, he told himself, over and over again. *Things are different now.*

"Drink with me."

His mother's voice was wrong. It, like the liquid in the glass, was syrupy and far too cold. If he ever thought this mirage was real that impression would be the first thing to break his immersion.

She was sitting across the table from him. At first glance it was like looking at a photograph from a family album, but the longer she stared the more off it became. The lines of his mother were slightly too thick in places and too thin in others. There was a drift to her curls, like they followed a slightly altered law of gravity.

"Come on, Eddie," she said again. "Drink with your mother."

Edgar pushed the glass away. "I'm not thirsty."

The mother curled up her lips and released a loose imitation of a chuckle. "No," she said, drawing out the word. "Isn't this what you want? To forget? To wipe your mind and keep feeding like the glutton you are?"

"I...don't know what you're talking about."

"Of course not," the smile unraveled off her face and she stared off into a place Edgar couldn't sense. "Of course not..."

She didn't speak for a while after that. The world around them went slick with oil, vaguely luminescent and softly flickering in spots. Then, as quickly as it started, the altering stopped and the illusion returned.

"What do you want from me?" She asked him.

Edgar blinked. He counted to six. Did time move the same way here as it did in other places?

"Are you hungry for power, Edgar? Even more than what you already have? Do you crave vengeance against those that have wronged you?"

"I want you to leave," Edgar said.

"And yet you brought me closer," she leaned forward and lowered her voice. "Take your medicine, Child."

"No."

The smile returned, like an animal gleeful in death. "How do you know you didn't take it the first time?" She said. "Maybe your life these past few years has been nothing more than the fantastical delusions of a thoroughly fried brain."

That wasn't true. That can't be true. He dumped out the glass into the soil of the potted ficus in the corner of the room and left as soon as his mother fell asleep. This thing was trying to get inside his head by pulling at every vulnerability it could grab onto.

Edgar fought to keep the fear out of his face. Because this wasn't real. This wasn't really happening.

"You had your chance," the mother said. "They built an altar between us and the Birthright took your place. Why try and steal more now?" She spoke louder now, her words tightening with barely-restrained anger. "There is no *room* for you here, Child. I do not have more of myself left to harvest."

The instinct returned. That little voice that said to bow his head and keep his voice low. To be small. Docile. Then he thought about what the contradicting concepts the entity was proposing. There was the taunt of Edgar being in some sort of psychosis induced by the drink his mother tried to share with him the night he left. Moving to New Orleans, meeting Katy, finding Scott – all of that was just a fantasy world created to keep him alive while he numbly stocked books at the University library.

He knew that couldn't be true. Edgar could observe, note, taste, consider – but he lacked the imagination to create anything like this. Not on this own. So that left the only other option, the alternative this figure in him brought to life, perhaps without even realizing it.

That this was real. Edgar did have some sort of madness in him now, torn off from a vaster poison residing inside Scott's consciousness.

Only all that poison was supposed to belong to Edgar from the very start.

His jaw tightened. He begged his eyes not to widen and hoped there would be no way to cry within yourself, or wherever the hell he was at this very moment. There was no way of telling, but Edgar hoped dearly that he was able to maintain a calm and emotionless demeanor.

All while thinking – it could've been him.

"I lied before," his mother told him, staring at the ficus with a bored expression. "I won't kill you. I can't. If I kill you his body dies as well. I'm sure you've counted on that."

She stood and walked to the plant in the corner. Her fingers brushed against a single, glossy leaf, and she tilted it to catch the light of the chandelier hanging above them.

Edgar wasn't listening. He was still running this new insight in his mind. Because it could've been him.

"I'll have to restrain you, somehow," she plucked the leaf, leaning against the wall to examine it closer. "Paralysis should do the trick. I could arrange for a nice facility to maintain your health while the Birthright and I do our work."

It should've been me.

"Don't worry, Edgar. I'll make sure he gets *plenty* of opportunities to visit."

He turned to the mother at the end of the room. With the leaf slowly crushed in one hand, she was eyeing him with a menacing cruelty that – for some reason – evoked no reaction in him. Edgar lifted his glass and took a brief hit of the nauseating fumes radiating from inside.

"Do you think it lived?" He put down the glass and looked back at the plant.

The creature looked vaguely annoyed at his lack of discernible fear. Still, she complied. "The plant you poisoned?" She looked down at it and scoffed. "Nothing will grow in that soil ever, ever again."

Edgar frowned lightly. "All from a splash of liquor?"

"You think that's liquor you almost drank?"

Wait. What?

The sensation of his hand being held became stronger. It lowered and concentrated until it became a strong pressure around the circumference of his wrist. Though his body stayed limp in position, something visually imperceptible was being pulled up and out, up and out.

He somehow knew what was happening and who was behind it, and he wanted to tell Scott to stop. The cancer he was speaking to now had no other aspirations other than drawing out their torture for as long as possible, but it also had *answers*. Answers to things that no one else would be able to enlighten Edgar on.

If this was true he wanted to know. He couldn't move on and build from nothing like Scott wanted to. Edgar wanted to understand who he was and what happened to him, but there was no more time to make that happen before the mutilated memory dissolved before his eyes. There was a flurry of sensory disorientation as his body experienced several planes of gravity all at once.

His lungs pulsated frantically in an effort to breathe. The rest of his body struggled to remember what parts were meant to hold tension and what were designed to remain relaxed. Edgar panicked at the feeling of some thick, bumpy tumor writhing in his mouth before realizing that it was actually his tongue.

Scott touched his face. Good. He pushed himself closer to it in a hungry attempt to fully wrap himself in the feeling like a frightened child under a blanket.

It should've been me.

No.

Edgar forced himself to move away from the touch, away from the feeling of comfort and wholeness and everything peaceful in the world. When he was finally alone and fragmented, though, Scott grabbed his shoulders and pulled him back to his chest.

"*Shh*," Scott whispered. "Calm, remember? It's okay."

When Scott first came into into Edgar's life it was less of a casual stride and more of a weak and very sick stumble. He was a tangled, desperate, pallid and starving mess that wretched at unwanted human touch. The sound of Scott puking in the sink after Ian came onto him, moaning in despair in the way you only do once you stop hoping help will come, was something Edgar would never forget.

Maybe he would've at one point. But not now. Not after knowing that all of that was his fault.

Don't cry, Edgar.

He was pulled back and forced to look Scott in the eye. Much to his dismay, the man was welled up with tears. Scott took a trembling hand and brushed back Edgar's hair before taking in a slow, unsteady breath.

"Do you know who I am?" Scott smiled, tears falling. "It's me. It's – it's Lark."

You don't deserve to cry, Edgar.

He ignored his thoughts and broke down anyway, practically throwing himself at Scott and sending them both tumbled back onto the bed. They laid there for a long time fully collapsed against each other. Their chests rose and fell against each other, each out of sync with the other. Edgar's face was buried in the Scott's hair, which now smelled like his own shampoo.

"I'm so sorry, Skylark," he sobbed weakly.

Scott wrapped his arms around him and held him close. His entire body shook with each breathy shudder of tears. He hummed the same few notes, over and over again.

Edgar tilted his head to feel more of Scott's warmth against his face. "I forgot for so long."

"I didn't," Scott managed in a faint voice. "Even when I forgot I didn't forget. Not really."

To think that someone would spend so long thinking about him. And then go out and just wander around, night after night, living their entire lives in the hope of crossing his path. Despite the fear and regardless of the pain. To push forward when everything else pointed out how much easier it would be to throw in the towel.

"All this for just a name?" Edgar asked.

Scott laughed without parting his lips. "More than a name," he shifted out from under Edgar and made it so they could face each other. "The name had a feeling when I saw it in my mind."

"Yeah?"

"Yeah. It was..." Scott closed his eyes and smiled. "It made me feel warm all over. And soft, like being under the blanket on the couch. When I thought about it I felt safe, and – and strong," he opened his large blue eyes, made even more luminescent with tears. "You make me feel the same way, Edgar. That's how I know now. That's how I know it's you."

They stared at each other, blue meeting brown, manic light settling against a calm expanse of soft earth. Edgar knew this has happened before – not just since they met, but for countless nights across years of his childhood. The exact images were still hard to reach, like Scott explained, the feeling was there.

Only it was different now, wasn't it? The sad Blue Boy was a man now, and Edgar could actually touch him. So that's exactly what he did.

He brushed his fingertips against Scott's forehead, and then trailed the touch down the side of his face. Edgar pressed his palm against his chest in a few different places until he picked up the thumping of the man's heartbeat, and then he paused and tracked the song for a while.

Scott was warm. He was soft. He was alive and he was here, right here.

And Edgar wasn't alone. In a sense he never was.

"I love you, Skylark," he said, low and serious.

He worried a moment that saying that would trigger a blast of some kind. It didn't. Scott parted his lips slightly and let out a tearful, happy murmur. Inside, the tides between both of them were calm and clear enough to reveal small stones and shells. And when Edgar finally said the sentiment in his head aloud, he felt released from some final binding and finally, fully free.

It was coming back into himself and realizing there there was still a self to come back to. It was coming home for the first time and feeling the warm air inside hit you just as you walk through the door.

If Edgar drank with his mother it would've meant extinguishing the warmth inside him – potentially for good. Considering how he lived his life up until then, it would make more sense if he had done it. Stayed small. Followed the path. But, right on the precipice of thick, sweet fog, Edgar pulled himself back and escaped.

He saved his own life. When no one was able to provide the help he needed, Edgar stepped forward and helped himself. Now there were others in his life that valued him.

You're really strong, you know.

You've worked so hard for this.

You should be proud of yourself.

But was he?

"I..." Scott blinked. "I don't know what happens now."

They stay in bed forever. Run down the streets until their limbs burn with use and then find a spot of warm sun to bask in. Get more hot chocolate.

From beside him, his bond (his *soul* bond) sat up in bed. He was still happy, but less overjoyed and now considering something concerning. His feet shifted in the covers and his hands fidgeted as he thought.

He didn't speak for about a minute. Then he nodded, all business, "We have to go to Bluerose."

"Really?" Edgar sat up too, wondering whether it was excitement or hesitation he was holding back. "Now?"

"Absolutely. I think the Witch Eater wasn't expecting to handle us both at once, so it would have no reason to pretend that..." a bewildered smile touched Scott's lips, but he pushed it aside. "Something has been keeping us apart. I knew my memory's a non-starter, but it doesn't make sense to me that you..."

He stopped talking. Something in the air began to knot with increasing density.

"What did it want you to drink?" Scott asked, eyes still boring holes through the bedroom doorway.

Edgar sat up too, hesitant to return to their previous encounter – even only in his memory. "Mom tried to drink with me the night I left. I think it was just mimicking the memory –"

"Alcohol?" Scott said that a little tersely. When Edgar didn't answer he rephrased himself. "Your mother wanted you to drink *alcohol*?"

You think that's liquor you almost drank?

Scott must've been able to sense the shift in Edgar's confidence. He touched his hand, and then his arm. Even though there was still intensity in his eyes, he smiled and spoke a little quieter.

"You work behind a bar," he said. "You have for some time. I know it's hard to think about, but I bet if you focus you could try and recognize the smell." Scott looked down and clenched his hands for a flash. "Please, Edgar. It's important."

"I don't know," Edgar said, cringing at how little he questioned growing up. "It's clear. You can't buy it in the stores. I assumed it was moonshine, only I guess it smelled more...sweet?"

Suddenly Scott scrambled out of bed. He stood still on his feet and wavered slightly, then regained his stability and strode out of the bedroom.

"Scott?" Edgar called out.

No response. Reluctantly, Edgar got out of bed and peeked out through the doorway. He found Scott pacing through the rest of the apartment, scoping the space with an increasing frenzy. His bond opened the front door and looked outside. Then he did the same out towards the back patio. Scott even opened the pantry as if someone could be hiding in the closet-sized space inside.

"Where's Tenzin?" He said.

They were the only ones in the apartment. "I don't know," Edgar found his phone on the counter and checked for any notifications. "Katy told me she last night that she wanted to come over today. Maybe they went out together someplace."

"Do Academics use Petrichor?"

Scott practically shot out the words. Edgar looked up at him, regretting being clueless given how serious this situation apparently was. Petrichor was a pretty distinct name in his eyes, mostly because it was far more beautiful than any term the Academy would adopt. If it was somehow something that linked their cultural upbringings, they would change it. They'd suck the meaning and life out of it and give it a new, more scientific-sounding label.

"What's Petrichor?" Edgar asked.

"It's starch and water and sugar fermented with adapted plant matter –"

"You mean EV? You know about EV?"

"*The Pokemon?*"

A startled laugh escaped Edgar's lips. This was getting them
nowhere. For there to be any hope of them overlaying their shoddy
timelines and making some sense of their lives, it wouldn't happen while
they were both so worked up. They'd need to calm down before going
any further.

With some prodding Edgar managed to get Scott to sit down on the
couch. He put on the kettle and prepared two cups of herbal tea.

"What's EV?" Scott called out from the couch.

Edgar pulled out his phone and scrolled through his music library.
"It's Ethanol Viridis. The Academy uses it as a painkiller, mainly for
more practiced witches."

"And you've taken it."

"What do you want to listen to?"

"Have you taken it, Edgar?"

They needed something to lift the mood at least slightly off the
ground. Edgar tapped his playlist of the best bands he'd seen in person
during his time in NOLA. It was still in progress, the track list mainly
made up of his favorite songs from funk bands like Tank and the Bangas
and Mia Borders. Now was the perfect time to put it to the test.

With a few taps and swipes, the room was filled with the low, rhyth-
mic strums of bass guitar. Edgar adjusted the volume so it was loud
enough to enjoy without fully swaying what was still a very important
conversation. Then the kettle beeped, steam rushing from its mouth,
and Edgar poured the boiling water into each of their mugs.

"Edgar..." Scott attempted as Edgar passed him to walk back into the
bedroom.

"Hang on."

He got on his knees and reached down for the lock box gathering dust under his bed. His fingers brushed against the steel of what was, at the time, the most expensive thing he ever bought for himself, and he dragged it out with both hands. Not because it was too heavy for one, but more out of an irrational desire to not jostle the contents inside more than necessary.

The man at the store he bought it from said this was one of the highest-quality lock boxes on the market. Was that true? Fresh out of the Academy Edgar still relied on trusting any other human being with even the slightest bit of authority over him – even if that just meant a name tag and key ring. Either way, it's served its purpose so far. He tapped in the code and opened the lid.

The grimoire he stole, bound and wrapped in the box at his feet, was not the only copy. It was standard practice to transcribe the same spells across multiple tombs – it was a form of studying that, as a young Academic, Edgar participated in to create his own book of family spells. But that wasn't what he took. No, the grimoire he grabbed in a last-minute impulse as he walked out the door for the very last time was the one his mother displayed on a stand in the living room.

It was not his. It was not hers.

It was his father's.

Edgar undid the bindings and unwrapped the layers to reveal the aged leather book. It felt smooth and cool to the touch. Even after all this time, the book was in good condition. It wasn't worn with age or use. This wasn't a spell book that had seen any substantial action.

Even as child he wasn't allowed to rifle through his dad's grimoire. It was spite that prompted him take it with him rather than his own copy – but that was fine, as his spite's first suggestion was to empty the liquor cabinet and set the whole house ablaze with his mother still inside. But once he copied down the spells he thought he might need at some point, he didn't open the book again.

Now he carefully peeked into the inside of the front cover. There was small-script words written on the upper corner. Presumably his father's handwriting.

Novice Gallows, it read *Generation Three, Shreveport Academy Mantle Layer.*

That gave him pause. Even though his father left when he was still very young, he remembered him working as a researcher. He visited him in his office once and knew it was far from where the Mantle Layer academics worked. Promotions were not a common practice in the Academy. Growing up in the community he did you are assigned a role based on ability, and from that point the only direction you can go is down.

At least, that's what he thought. At this point, though, who really knew?

Edgar huffed low, rolling his eyes. If he would go through family secrets, it was best to take it one at a time.

By the time he stepped back into the other room, Scott found the mugs of tea in the kitchen and had them arranged on the table by the couch. He sat on one end, polite and distressed. When he noticed Edgar he straightened up and awkwardly patted the empty spot beside him.

"Here's what I know," Edgar sat down on the couch and put the book in Scott's lap. "I have never taken EV. They're pills you get at Academy pharmacies. I know they work – I've *seen* how they work. And because of that I decided not to take them."

It made Edgar a little sick to see his father's grimoire held so respectfully in Scott's hands. He watched him fan through the pages like you would an unfamiliar book in the library.

"I know how to make it, though," Edgar said.

Scott stopped. He blinked a few times. Edgar looked away.

"It's near the back. Right before the pages go blank."

There was the soft rustling of Scott going through pages, and then the noise stopped. Silence, and then a sharp and stifled noise that could've been a gasp had more air been allowed. Eventually Edgar had no choice other than to turn back and see how his bond was fairing.

Scott had the book open on his lap, flipped to the recipe for EV. But that's not where his attention was. His eyes were fully closed. With his head slightly bowed it was hard to make out what his face was doing, but Edgar could hear him struggle to level his breathing. His shoulders shook slightly and his chest rose and fell unsteadily.

"Uh – here," Edgar took Scott's hands and folded them so the man was hugging himself, with a hand placed just below each shoulder. "Tap on each side. Left, and then right, over and over again."

"What?"

"It's EMDR. Eye-Movement…" he stopped, scowling. "I can't remember what the rest means. It's good for self-soothing, though. Gives you something else to focus on. Doctor Tate taught it to me when I was a kid. Remember when I did it on my knees the other day?"

The model patient he was, Scott nodded curtly and immediately started tapping one shoulder after the other. It was too fast at first, and then too slow. The speed stuttered for some time until it leveled out, and soon after that it stopped.

By this point Scott was breathing easier. He unfolded his arms and put aside the book, still keeping it open to the right page, and then propped his elbows against his thighs to put his head in his hands.

"Fucking hell," he whispered.

Edgar let whatever he was experiencing continue being processed. Some time after that Scott sat up, composed again, although considerably more exhausted. He leaned forward and took his tea, drawing the mug to his lips and allowing himself a few sips.

He blinked rapidly for a moment longer, and then was fully calm. "Do you have Tenzin's phone number?"

"I don't – yeah, actually, I think I do. Should I call her?"

"Yes."

By the way he spoke now there was something big he had to say. Edgar quickly took his phone and pulled up the contact card he made for Tenzin – the newest addition in a list of ten or so phone numbers.

He dialed her number and handed Scott the phone, but all he did was stare down at it in dull resignation.

Edgar wasn't sure what to think. "You talk in here," he said, pointing at the bottom of the phone. "This is the speaker –"

"I know how phones work. Put it on speaker, please."

If he put the call on speaker, was he supposed to set it on the table and walk out of the room? Or was he just supposed to stand there and hold it while Scott and his sister exchanged whatever revelations they had to share? Edgar decided to hold the phone between them in the hopes that the other man would push him one way or the other.

It barely rang once before Tenzin picked up. "Edgar," she said.

"Ten, it's Skylark," Scott said, all business. "Where are you?"

There was a rustle on the other end. He recognized, very dimly, the muffled cadence of Katy's voice in the background. And after that, weirdly enough, the two of them shared a small laugh.

"McDonalds," Tenzin said, an audible smile in her voice. "Are you okay?"

Scott didn't answer that immediately. He struggled so hard to speak that it appeared to physically hurt him. Tenzin asked the question again, no longer smiling.

"I'm fine," Scott said. "It's – you and Katy researched Academy structure, right?"

"Sure. Yes. Why?"

"Do you know about..?"

He turned to consult Edgar. Edgar frowned, but still leaned closer to the phone. "Ethanol Viridis," he said flatly.

"Oh," Tenzin said. "Hi. Okay, uh – EV, right? Academics opioids."

Fear struck strong in Scott's face. "Did you take it?" He asked. "Back when you practiced Academic magic – *did you take it?*"

"No. It's impossible to find legally unless you're registered. That's part of why I stopped practicing – it hurt too much," she paused. "What's going on? What did you see?"

"It's Petrichor, Tenzin," Scott said. "EV is Petrichor."

As he said that he stood from the couch and began to pace around the room. It seemed he couldn't keep himself still, couldn't even stop his hands from clenching and tapping. That was when Edgar understood why he was instructed to put the call on speaker. Holding one thing in one place must be hard when such strong emotions apparently demanded immediate movement.

Tenzin was still there, though. She was communicating through the phone in Edgar's hand while Scott was back near the duck photo by the front door behind him.

"Scott?" Tenzin waited and tried again. "Scott, what –?"

"He's...moving," Edgar said. "He's moving around."

On the other end Tenzin sighed. "Of course," she said. "That's fine. We're only a few blocks away. But I need you tell me what's happening."

"*They've been giving him Petrichor,*" Scott called out, having now apparently relocated to the kitchen near the washing machine.

"What makes you say that?" Tenzin said. "Petrichor requires a Distiller with ARFID – It needs a birthright."

Scott came back to the couch – not to sit, but to stand just behind Edgar. "It's the same recipe."

"Are you still there, Edgar?" Tenzin said.

Edgar nodded. "Um. Yes."

"Read me the recipe."

He took the book from the table and tried to make out his father's small, cramped written words. "Let's see, it's a mash made from Psychotria viridis leaves and flaked corn. They say to mix it with crushed barley, and then ferment the solution and –"

"Distill it?" Tenzin finished, sounding very tired. "And then – I don't know – spray dry it and put into capsules?"

Everything in the world suddenly felt freezing cold. "It's infused into sugar, actually," he said. "And then made into tablets."

The sounds of movement behind him stopped suddenly. Scott's emotions in his chest were like scanning through the dial of a radio at top volume. Thinking felt difficult, and it was hard to be afraid of a story you only know every other plot beat of.

"I didn't drink it," Edgar said – to Tenzin, to Scott, and to himself. "I didn't, I dumped it out."

"You're a Birthright, Edgar," Tenzin cut in, clearly trying to comfort him. "Petrichor can't hurt you."

"That's *not* true!" Scott cried.

"Not like it would hurt me or Katy. You know that, Scott," Tenzin took a deep breath. "Now sit back down."

It was definitely sibling behavior that she knew he was still looming adjacent to the conversation at hand. Scott clenched his jaw, clearly upset, and yet he still circled around to sit where he did on his end of the couch. He was still for the most part, aside from one foot that bounced madly against the hardwood.

"It's not like what you're thinking," she explained. "Because it's not Petrichor."

Scott frowned. "It's the same recipe."

"Same structure, different ingredients. Distillers use all kinds of leaves, remember? You you bought me my first Prismacolors by selling them the clippings from your garden."

Anger simmered into a heavy grief. "I...I think that sounds familiar."

Katy murmured something from too far to make out. Tenzin hummed.

"That Psychotria stuff is apparently what they use in Ayahuasca. Which is an interesting substitute for people unable to actually imbue regular plant matter. It could be considered a synthetic equivalent, I suppose. But it would be more accurate to say that's just an incredibly dangerous, psychotropic intoxicant."

Neither Edgar or Scott had anything to say to that. Edgar felt the static warmth of contact as Scott touched his hand and interlaced their fingers.

"What bothers me," Tenzin continues, "is that it looks like it has a lot of the same effects."

"Like what?" Edgar said.

"It would explain the gaps in your memory, Edgar," Tenzin pulled the phone away at the sound of Katy speaking. "Yes, I think so," Katy said something else, and Tenzin sighed. "I don't know. Hopefully."

Edgar wrestled with a new, sudden anger. "Tenzin, I *didn't drink it.*"

Immediately he regretted the outburst. But Tenzin responded, completely unaffected. "Yes," she said. "You didn't drink it *then.*"

"I recognized the smell," Scott spoke up from beside him. "It's like rotting roses, isn't it? Kind of chokes you up. That's Petrichor – or something like it," he tried a smile that felt incredibly inauthentic. "I've been taking it since I was a baby. I know I'm not wrong."

Edgar absorbed that description in his mind and considered how incredibly accurate it was. He knew that smell the way children of smokers know the stench of nicotine. So familiar that he eventually stopped recognizing it as it clung to his clothes and skin. Then someone else in the room would comment on the aroma and he'd be hit with the ghost of home that never washed off.

Yes, he knew that smell from the blankets that covered his bed. The cushions of every piece of furniture in the house. And sometimes, when his mother served him a bowl of chicken noodle or tomato soup, he could swear there was something else behind the faint metallic undertones.

Something rotting.

Something *floral.*

Oh god.

He dropped the phone and sprinted through the bedroom and to the bathroom. Edgar fell to his knees in front of the toilet so hard he felt the bones of the caps buzz in pain, but that didn't matter right now. He flung up the toilet seat and threw up into the bowl, heaving until everything was bile and buzzing and pain.

This shouldn't surprise him. This is the same woman who let him go hungry and cold, who physically bruised him and arranged for stronger professors to do far worse. He already knew for a fact that his mother was emotionally and physically abusive. Now there was the potential for her to have drugged him – poisoned him, even – possibly on a regular basis. Why does that make a difference? Why would learning of that possibility still hurt so badly?

Nothing changed in him since the age of ten. Edgar Gallows was still a helpless, stupid child.

With his eyes clenched shut he heard the sink start running. Then the sound stopped, and Edgar felt Scott brush the curls off the back of his neck and brush a cool, damp washcloth against the skin. He shuddered at the sensation at first before feeling the full-body release. It was like having a comforting weight settled over his psyche, pressing it into the earth after the rain.

He sat up from the toilet and offered Scott what he hoped was a reassuring smile. It was hard to remember what faces were meant to do when they felt okay. In his mind Edgar searched for something to say to offer insight, connect, or even just fill the silence. But he was tired. He was just so tired.

Scott helped him up and handed up a glass of water he had apparently filled up ahead of time. Edgar took a swig, spat into the sink, and started gulping down the rest.

"Small drinks," Scott advised.

Small drinks. Right. Edgar slowed his pace, but still stayed where he was until he finished the glass. Once it was empty he placed it on the counter top and stared at his trembling hands.

He rubbed his eyes. He nodded, unsure as to why.

Things got a little blurry in the haze of feeling, and when he came to he was sitting at the table and staring at the wood grain underneath his fingers. There was a ring stain, slightly sticky and glistening in the daylight. For a chef Edgar was not great at wiping down his surfaces.

Scott was leaning against the counter and watching him.

"Did you say something?" Edgar managed, throat aching with every syllable.

He shook his head. The toaster sprung up, and Scott turned to tend to the pieces of newly-browned bread he apparently was in the middle of preparing. Edgar wasn't sure what to make of the situation, so instead of spending any more energy trying to answer any more questions, he folded his arms on the table and settled his head in the darkness.

Shortly after that the front door opened. Edgar didn't bother getting up. If it was a home invader, Scott would have to handle it himself.

Voices in the warmth of darkness.

"Are you making cinnamon toast?" Tenzin asked.

"I am," Scott said. "I only made enough for me and Edgar, though."

"That's fair."

The chair in front of him was pulled out and Edgar heard someone sit down. Then he felt a hand touch the top of his head – stiff, a little clumsy. Probably Katy. Something inside him fizzled, a pulse that radiated partway outside of his skin. Katy didn't say anything, and yet he was able to hear a shadow of her voice inside his head.

I'm trying, it said.

He didn't move or speak or do anything in response to the kindest gesture he experienced from his friend in recent memory. Edgar was thoroughly out of commission.

There was the soft clatter of a plate being set down beside his head. Edgar could feel Scott's stare so vividly that there was no point in the man reaching out to physically touch him. And yet he didn't get up. He was so unbelievably done.

Something clawing and frantic started thrashing madly inside his gut, which was strange since the energy in the room was calm and quiet.

"Scott," Tenzin said. "Come outside with me for a moment."

Silence like the moment before a gun goes off. "Okay," Scott responded, voice flat.

Two pairs of footsteps left to the front door, which opened and closed as softly as possible. Did everyone think Edgar fell asleep? Did they think he was dead? Is this how people would react if he had some kind of massive stroke and died against the tabletop?

The hand on the top of his later turned into a finger prodding the center of his head. "Hey," Katy said. "If you don't eat that then I'm going to."

The toaster. The comment about cinnamon toast. The faint smell of butter and spice swirling in the air. Edgar was so preoccupied with being a pile of broken shards that he didn't even fully realize or appreciate that Scott made him something to eat.

Somebody cooked for him.

Edgar raised his head just enough to see the plate and the single piece of toast it lovingly supported. Scott probably had the other piece, having split the portion between the two of them to keep Edgar's stomach settled.

The toast was sliced clean through in a diagonal line across the middle. It was an even, olive-toned brown, which was slightly less cooked that Edgar typically preferred when toasting his own bread. Each triangle was gleaming brilliant with an amount of butter he'd personally consider downright unreasonable, and the sheen of melted fat was speckled with two layers. The first was fine grains of white sugar, and above that a dusting of cinnamon.

If he gave any more than the bare minimum of thought to what was happening right now, tears were inevitable. Edgar felt as if he'd experienced a lifetime's worth of emotions in the span of a few days. So he decided not to think more than he had to and just pick up one of the triangles and take a bite out of the corner.

Bread was so much better when cut at an angle. It varies the experience, be it baguette or sliced bread, and with the right strategy it can offer new anticipation to an otherwise simple meal. And meals with fewer ingredients are sometimes the most impacting. As he chewed his toast, Edgar noted that the thin layer of bread blended with the butter and spices to create something with a unique savory hint to its sweetness. It tasted how Edgar imagined an old blanket at a loving grandmother's house would smell like, assuming he had any of those things in his life.

Edgar realized he was smiling. This didn't fix the situation by any means, but a single piece of bread managed to fill him with such immense gratitude. In that moment it was a more powerful comfort than a long embrace. Edgar was so blown away that by then he couldn't even cry if he wanted to. He just settled his head against his other arm and ate his toast half in tiny bites.

Katy was watching him, half-smiling with sad eyes. Edgar took the other triangle of toast and held it up for her.

"O-Oh," she said. "You don't have to do that."

"You should try it. It's really good," Edgar softened more into his comfort. "I don't know where he thinks up this stuff."

"You mean you've never..?" Katy, briefly, looked pained by his comment. Then she pulled it back. "Yeah" she said. "Thanks."

They ate the toast together.

It didn't seem to hit her nearly as hard as it hit him.

Tenth Movement

"What do you need, Tenzin?"

Scott and his sister stood outside Edgar's apartment in the late afternoon. Blue skies, warmer air – nothing that felt like how the season this time of year should. Scott was even comfortable with the sleeves of Edgar's flannel rolled up to the elbows. He rubbed his arms, still pulsing with excess energy. His bones felt agitated. His blood bubbled.

It was weird to feel so warm where he once would swallow shudders.

He noticed Tenzin staring at him and paused.

"Can I feel your arms?" She said.

"Uh. Sure?"

Tenzin gave his upper arm a slight squeeze, and as soon as she did her eyes widened slightly. "Wow."

"What?"

A small smile touched her lips. "That's some serious muscle mass."

It was wrong to consider pride at a time like this. "Really?" Scott managed, despite it all.

"Well – comparatively."

That was still something, he supposed. He thought about the compliment, and then Tenzin stepped back and positioned herself in front of him. She took a stance he found familiar and held up her palms in front of him.

"Punch my hand," she directed him.

"Are you kidding me? No."

Her smile went from impressed affection to something far more daring. "Come on," she said. "It'll help."

Scott physically backed away a step. It made no sense to be threatened by the concept of someone else wanting him to harm them, but that's how he felt and he couldn't back out now. "Hurting you won't help anything."

"But you can't hurt me. I'm stronger and faster than you are, guaranteed. And that doesn't even matter, because our bodies would hurt us before we could ever put each other in danger," Tenzin's fire blazed with excitement. "Face it, Skylark – we're each other's ideal sparring partner."

That made a lot of sense. And Scott didn't want to admit it, but the offer sounded incredibly tempting.

With everything going on inside him, the urge for destruction was ready to ruin him and everything around him. He wanted to break something. He wanted to feel the impact of one force slamming against another.

Scott was so, so fucking *angry*.

That was bad – right? It was a feeling he'd spent years actively repressing out of risk of opening floodgates he would never be able to close again. So he should just go ahead and keep them closed.

Right?

"You forgot," Tenzin said, lower now. "You've been mad about this since we were kids. A feeling like that doesn't just *go away*. This won't solve anything, but it'll let you start to accept it."

His fingers tapped against each other. Then Scott felt his hand clench shut at his side.

"Thumb outside the fist, Scott," his sister advised.

He groaned, but still did as he was told. "I've never thrown a punch, Tenzin."

Something close to relief and sorrow flashed across Tenzin's face. He had an image in his mind for a second of his hands drenched in his own blood, but he couldn't quite hold onto the how and why of the memory. Then her reaction was gone, replaced by a strict professionalism. Scott remembered that his sister was skilled enough in her sport to teach it herself and felt a little better about the situation.

"Relax your shoulder," she said as she stepped forward and raised his right hand. "Keep your fist loose, too. Don't tighten until the moment of connection. Start with your wrist sideways – keep it straight, though – and snap upright as soon as you hit," Tenzin pulled back and motioned towards him. "Show me."

Scott physically went through everything he just showed him before raising his fist and awkwardly striking the air. It felt ridiculous. Somehow a show of aggression from a body like his own felt all the more useless.

"No," Tenzin said, like his reaction was an audible comment. "That wasn't bad. You're bending your wrist, though – that's dangerous. Try again."

He did.

"See if you can hit straighter. I can tell what knuckles you'd hit with an angle like that and it would really hurt."

Now deep in focus, Scott stopped thinking and just adjusted himself accordingly. He continued to strike the air a few more times, with Tenzin making small suggestions on where to shift the weight on his feet or how to pivot his hips as he moved. And the more he refined the action, the better it felt. Not better, maybe – but more satisfying. Like he was actually doing something other than a caricature of an action.

Soon he had to stop to catch his breath. There was a layer of sweat sticking his bangs to his forehead. A part of Scott reminded himself that he was supposed to be in bed rest. That just wasn't going to happen. He could regret going against doctor's orders later – for now, the priority was getting this rage under control. If nothing else, then for the sake of the one other person who was forced to carry it with him.

Tenzin stepped back in front of him and raised her palms. She didn't say anything, just stared him down, stone-eyed. The look was so unfamiliar to Scott that it frightened him, but only for a moment before he remembered who he was with and what they were doing.

He imagined being a child and having someone look at him with that kind of attitude. A person that was meant to care for him – someone he literally depended on to keep him alive. He'd have no other choice but to absorb that poison. There would be no where else he could go.

No one there to keep him company.

Scott raised his fist and slammed it against Tenzin's palm. There was the thick slap of flesh meeting flesh, and an instant static of physical sensation against his knuckles. There was the impact, and it ran all the way up his arm.

"*Shit*," Tenzin breathed.

"Fuck, are you okay?"

"Huh?" She looked up at him and laughed. "Of course. I'm fine. I just...you've gotten a lot stronger."

Scott stood up straight. He was aware then, of each breath as it traveled in and out of his body. The physical activity didn't ache as much as it would've before. In fact, it seemed to expand him within himself, opening up his ribs and allowing the trapped muck inside to start to seep out.

"Can I try again?" He said.

His sister smiled.

He stood and punched Tenzin's hands, changing which palm he struck and with what hand he hit with. Scott compared the feeling of each hit and thought of how to tweak his strategy to make the next one tighter, faster – *stronger.* After that he stopped thinking. He just kept punching until his whole body ached with effort.

Through the hits he heard his own voice, but different. From a long time ago. He could make out fragments between the slap of each strike.

He's just out there on his own, and they're saying there's nothing they can do to –

Hit.

– am I supposed to do? We're meant to BE together. If we aren't, isn't everything in danger? Doesn't anybody care?

"Good, Scott," Tenzin grunted. "Keep going."

It's not fucking fair, Tenzin.

Scott hands throbbed. The static of each punch was making every nerve in his arms spasm. It didn't matter. He kept going.

I miss him. I miss him so badly.

His cheeks burned with helpless tears. No, not helpless. Not right now. Not anymore.

I think I'm forgetting his face.

Scott hit until his arms were useless and he had to sit on the gravel to catch his breath. He palmed the rocks, gasping for air.

"You should take a class," Tenzin sat down with him, more winded than Scott would've expected. "Kickboxing, maybe. You have great endurance for a beginner."

Even through his exhaustion and grief, Scott wrestled with pleasure. He tried to laugh, but the sound came out choked and breathy. Soon after that he slid backwards and fully sprawled out across the ground. The individual pieces of quartz and stone dug into his back, but they were cool enough to the touch for him to not really mind.

"I want..." Scott swallowed and hitched his breath in his throat. "I want Edgar and I to go in a Fog Bank."

Tenzin didn't say anything in response to that.

"That's what they call it, right?" Scott tried to raise his head and failed. "The steam treatment of Petrichor? I want that."

"I heard you."

"I'm so tired of not remembering," he took a deep breath and sighed, chest settling. "I know it's a lot."

"No," Tenzin touched his ankle and gave it a small squeeze. "Well, yes. But it's time. I'll make the flight for next week."

Scott grimaced. "Make it tomorrow."

"No."

"Yes."

"If you're doing a Fog Bank you need your second blood transfusion. You can use all the strength you can get."

"I want to go home, Ten," Scott said. "I want to wear my clothes. See the beach. Eat a meal with my siblings. I want…"

There was no point, he hoped, in finishing that sentence. If Tenzin knew him more than he knew himself, she had to know what he was aiming to say.

I want Edgar to meet my mom.

Scott sat up to look across at Tenzin. "I have a doctor in Bluerose, don't I? We can just do my transfusion there."

He tried to give Tenzin a look that expressed this is what he decided and what needed to happen. Assuming she still refused, he had a debit card and tested memory of the bus line in New Orleans. Scott never flew in a plane before, but he could get to an airport. He could check a bag and provide money for tickets. Edgar should be able to work his way through the rest.

Tenzin came over and offered a hand for him to take. Scott held it, and she pulled his full body weight back up onto his feet with zero strain. He steadied himself, then crossed his arms.

"Your eyes," Tenzin stated plainly.

He looked down at the floor. "I know."

"Do you? You understand what's happening to you?"

"Of course. I told you over the phone, it's the reason why so many people just want to sleep with me."

"Not everybody."

Not everybody – that was true. There was Tenzin, obviously. Katy, Edgar's boss – hell, even Edgar to an extent, as he never sexualized their interactions together, even after they had sex. All of that was only within the past week or so, though. Only after the bonding.

Or was it? The woman who ran the Italian place they had their first date at didn't try to sleep with him. In fact, none of the people that Scott pressured into employing him made any attempt to get in his pants. He didn't even consider it an option at the time, because those moments were separate in his brain from his shows. There were the times he played music in an effort to evoke his Eddie, and there was every other moment he spent working odd jobs or holing up in the library to kill time.

Tenzin picked at some colorful fuzz sticking along one of her dreads. "There's something I haven't told you about Mom," she looked up, saw Scott's face, and quickly added, "She's okay. Well – she's not dead, or anything."

Scott let out a tense breath. That moment of worry jarred him enough to draw attention to how badly his fists stung.

"Her eyes are like yours," Tenzin noted under her breath. "She has a coloboma. Only with her...do you remember what she could do?"

He tried to think hard. His mother looked like him – Scott knew that, even though he was only just now adapting to a full awareness of what he looked like. If he imagined himself, but older and as a woman, the whole picture got muddled in his head. His mother's name was Regina Mustard Kaufner, she had a passion for classical music and spontaneous home renovations and design. She used to be a social worker, but for as long as Scott knew her she made her living by playing three nights a week at the Lounge and assisting in construction projects around town.

That was all he knew.

Tenzin drew in that small intake of breath she did just before ex- plaining something she learned or theorized about their culture. Some might find the gesture patronizing. He knew other birthrights their age that would immediately shirk at the sound of it. Scott accepted this pre- lude without question. He was ready to learn.

"The source of magic is intention," she began. "I've documented every birthright ability I could find, and they all are either engagement or perception-based."

"What do you mean?" Scott said.

"You're bipolar, which means that you struggle with strong and quick changing emotions. I think that's why your variant can generate a sort of forced empathy at will. It's the intention of being understood, and it helps engage with those around you."

Scott tried to follow what Tenzin was explaining. "I can make people feel my feelings," he summarized.

Hearing what he used to be able to do rang familiar. He could almost grasp onto a hazy memory of being able to throw a sob like a ventriloquist could throw voices. In times of barely-hinged buoyancy Scott could recall making a party out of any new room he walked into.

Yes, it was becoming clear to him. For so much of his life Scott was not celebrated, mourned or pitied. He was, instead, a celebration and funeral dirge in and of himself. An embodiment of emotions where others remained a vessel.

It was hard not to be saddened by that thought. All of that felt so far away now.

He stood and watched Tenzin wander down the path, each step slow and exaggerated. She wandered a lot when she was deep in thought. There was large stump at the end of the driveway, another oak on the street that must've succumbed to enough damage to warrant cutting down. Tenzin sat on its jagged surface and stared out into the street.

"Then there's flow state," Scott said, remembering what Doctor Tate told him before.

Tenzin shook her head. "Flow state is what Academics use to describe the period when you're actively connected to magical energy. Like the time directly before and after saying an incantation. If it applies to you then you've been in it your whole life," Tenzin's voice took on the quality of an eye-roll. "All birthrights have."

It's official – there's not a single person that actually understood the laws of magic in this plane of existence. Scott might just be the best bet to obtain some actual answers, being that he lived from birth with a direct line to Cassus or the Witch Eater, or whatever people chose to call this *source* they were so keen to speak of. Unfortunately, he had no intention of becoming a cartographer for his own personal hell. And since he wasn't about to push Edgar down this particular path of research, the next best bet was his sister.

Scott sat on the edge of the stump, squeezing in beside Tenzin to face down the rest of the sidewalk. From so close he could smell the lavender and argan oil of the moisturizer she used for her hair. It was a different brand from what he remembered the last time he saw her. Still, she made the conscious effort not to use a product that smelled like roses, even though rosewater was a main ingredient in so many moisturizers and Scott hadn't even been living at home.

"Your ability is engaging," Tenzin's mind was so focused Scott could hear the gears turning in every word she said. "Mom's is perceiving. Because of her coloboma she could..." Tenzin chewed gently on the edge of her bottom lip. "Remember how she'd get these *feelings* about people?"

"Vaguely," Scott said.

"I see that as a way of sensing the intent of others. But then – after you left..."

She trailed off. Tenzin wasn't good at his kind of thing. Even with his mind scattered Scott understood that. If there was bad news to be shared, if someone had to hear something that would be sad or upsetting, that was Scott's job to handle. Tenzin was the person with plans. She was the support to any sentiment Scott had been able to uphold throughout the entirety of his life so far.

"What did I do?" Scott breathed, already dreading her answer.

Tenzin folded in on herself slightly. Her palms clutched her elbows and she cringed at her feet. "She kept getting triggered. More and more, she just couldn't stop from peering into anyone that tried to talk to us. Eventually it just turned on once and...didn't stop," she looked at Scott out of the corner of her eye. "Like you."

Terror sank deep into Scott. He felt it pull at him like a riptide, and though he tried his best to keep his body still the way he was taught he was inevitably thrashed and tangled in the icy depths of it.

"I'm not sure how to describe what's changed," Tenzin toyed with a loc as she spoke. "She won't talk about it for long. As far as I know, Mom's gone from sensing intentions to...sensing thoughts," she slumped her shoulders at the concept. "Everyone's thoughts. All the time."

"Jesus."

"It's not as bad in town!" The genuine attempt at enthusiasm in the way Tenzin said that only broke his heart even more. "Those of us who understand her condition are less...*loud* to her. And I seem to be a blind spot, which bodes well for when you get back. Still...she doesn't leave the house most days."

After hearing the state his leaving put his own mother in, Scott let his vision lose focus and patiently waited to die. There must only be a few breaths left in him before his lungs caught up with the tone of the situation and shut down entirely.

Tenzin kept on going, perhaps rehearsing for her eulogy for him. "I've been trying to think of a way of navigating it," she said. "It's hard to imagine that it's just this fixed, inflamed state with nothing that can be done about it. So far I haven't been able to figure out a viable way to help her," she paused, then quietly added. "I think I've thought of one for you, though."

Scott didn't care. It was a nice sentiment, but it didn't matter. He had no interest in being less miserable if his family remained remotely as unhappy as he was. With his big toe he dug into the softer, sandy soil by the roots of the tree stump – the beginnings of what would soon be a perfectly acceptable grave.

"If your aggravated states are the natural heightening of your basic abilities, it would make sense that yours would be some sort of –"

"Mind control," Scott finished under his breath.

"But that's not quite it, is it? How many of those people you slept with did you actually *want* to sleep with, Scott?"

"None," Scott frowned and pulled at his hair. "I don't know. Maybe sometimes I felt like I could've – like, conceptually. I wanted to want to. Sometimes."

Tenzin adjusted herself on the stump so she could face him better. "Let me put it this way: when you spoke to people after your shows, were you thinking *I want this person to fuck me?*"

"*No,*" Scott gaped. "No! If I was thinking anything it wasn't much other than *please work.*"

"What would that look like? What would it mean for you if it *worked*?"

He thought of the way Edgar touched his fingers against his face like astronomers once mapped out the stars.

"Intimacy," he simply said.

"So sex."

"That's not what I mean, Tenzin."

"For most people it is. So if you were going into these interactions with the *intention* of general intimacy, it's possible your targets translated that into their own interpretation."

Scott felt sick to his stomach. "Don't say it like that. Don't call them my *targets.*"

"They didn't all want to have sex. Not in the beginning. Maybe even more of them offered something else at first and it just led to sex because that's what a lot of people consider the next step to be," Tenzin didn't linger on that terrifying concept for long. "We could test it."

That was Tenzin. Naturally curious, ready to chart everything considered too sacred to record on paper. Tenzin wanted to understand where Scott would be happy to simply exist undetected. That was their fundamental difference. And though he often tried to support the instinct, now in particular it just wasn't possible.

He tried to think of how to get out of this. While he did Tenzin's eyes were scanning the street, and they settled on an older man coming down the block with his dog. The man looked like he could be the same age as is father had he not died before Scott was born. He had twists like

Tenzin used to, only his were kept shorter and streaked with gray, and his pit bull was a bulky slab of dog in a sweater.

"How about him?" Tenzin said.

"Tenzin, Edgar is my soul bond. He's my *boyfriend*," that last fact was something Scott handled like a religious artifact. "I don't want to be with anyone else."

She squeezed his knee a little too tightly in her enthusiasm for science. "You don't get it. If it's intention, you decide how the interaction go. If you want you can approach him with no intention at all," Tenzin focused her gaze, an idea forming. "Yes. Have the focus be for him to *not* react in any way and see what happens if you say something weird."

This wasn't where Scott thought she was going. Even so, he didn't like it. "I don't want to play with you like this," he said.

"Consider the implications, Skylark."

She'd told him that before, hadn't she? In fact, isn't that something she often asked of him, all the time, for the whole expanse of their lives together? *Consider the implications.*

What if magic was a modern evolutionary trait representing the next stage of mankind? Consider the implications, Skylark. Why are birthrights offered government-funded healthcare when there are Academics across the country with the same diagnoses? Do we really exist in a world where the stuff of fantasy is actually a disability for the already disabled? *Consider the implications, Skylark.*

No. He didn't want to. It was privileged, maybe even selfish, and that was fine. Scott's body ached and his mind deafened him, and all he really wanted to do was live quietly with those he cared about. Let the others ask the important questions, and additional, smarter people than him could look for answers to their heart's content.

"He's almost past us," Tenzin quietly updated him as the man approached.

The theory now, from what Scott understood, was that he could now influence with his social objective rather than his feelings at the time. Knowing Tenzin, this one statement was backed up by the indirect intel of his every conversation with her, as well as countless hours of ze-roed-in research. And if he thought about it, it made sense.

In the grand scheme of things, the Eddie he was looking for could've been virtually anyone. But Scott couldn't think of it like that or else he would immediately pass out and go insane. He provided needless structure that really only hindered what he was trying to achieve. Even though the hostel clerk, laundromat attendant, and restaurant manager could all potentially be his Eddie, since he regulated his search for dur-ing shows his mind blocked out that possibility.

And since his date with Edgar he didn't go there at all anymore. Someone his age who called themselves Eddie could come along and in-troduce themselves, and Scott would grant them an accommodating de-gree of kindness without considering anything more.

Nobody hit on him since his night at the Italian restaurant. Since he no longer had a way to hide his face, he was forced to admit this was a theory worth testing.

The man and his dog had just passed them on the stump when Scott spoke up.

"Excuse me," he said.

The man stopped and looked over at him. He wasn't pleased, but he wasn't angry either. This stranger looked about as confused as someone in a city like this would be if a man like Scott called out to them.

"Uh – yeah?" His voice was slowly becoming tinged with a low amusement. "Are you lost, son?"

Scott stood up and took a quick look at himself. He was still wearing Katy's skirt, but he had a feeling the comment was referring more to his unbrushed hair and bare, dirty feet. Even though there was nothing to brush back, he still started to sweep his fingers across his face. Then he raised his head and looked the man directly in the eye.

The tide in him trembled. He kept his stare, wide and unblinking, and made a rare effort to actually think of what he wanted out of a social interaction.

Don't freak out. Please don't freak out.

The man shifted his weight from one foot to the other. His brown eyes simmered with a deep blue glow.

Scott wondered what to say next – for the good of science.

"How do you know if you have daddy issues?" He said.

Scott held his breath and waited for the man to recoil. Instead he just furrowed his brow and seriously thought about what he was asking.

"I know a few people who you could say got them when their folks divorced," he looked Scott up and down. "Did yours?"

"No. My dad died – I never met him."

The man clicked his tongue. "That'll do it."

"Is it bad, though? I mean, I'm sure it's bad. I mainly just like it when older men call me *boss* or *champ* or –" Scott pointed at the man. "Or *son*, obviously."

"You mean – in a sexual way?"

"More like in a *I'm-thirty-but-still-please-adopt-me* kind of way."

The man nodded. "Ah," he said. "I get it."

This was working so well that it was incredibly off-putting. Scott was even starting to relax into the interaction, so much so that he forgot his weird conversation with someone he didn't know was part of one of Tenzin's grand experiments.

She spoke up for the first time from on the stump just behind Scott. "This isn't working," she said. "Be weirder."

"I have a gun," Scott told the man.

Fuck, he screamed in his head. *Oh my god.*

"*Weirder,* Scott," Tenzin whispered sharply. "Not more threatening."

The man was not afraid or angry. He had no reaction at all, even though he definitely heard him. Scott turned to Tenzin and flashed her a helpless look, silently begging her to step in and direct this to whatever she was trying to use him to accomplish.

She didn't help him. Tenzin just looked up at him, observing. Like a scientist charting the oncoming demise of the world's most socially inept lab rat. Scott faced the man again and swallowed back a whimper.

"Can I pet your dog?" He asked.

The man smiled. "Sure thing. Her name's Bella."

Scott bent down and looked at Bella the Pit Bull. Her large nose twitched as it sniffed the air around them. He held out a hesitant hand in front of her snout and giggled softly at the feel of her whiskers brushing his skin as she inspected him. She licked his hand once, bobbed tail wiggling.

"Good girl," he leaned forward and whispered, "I don't really have a gun."

Bella took her opportunity and licked the side of Scott's face. He laughed.

Moments after that Scott and Tenzin watched the man lead his dog down the street, exactly as calm as he was before the two of them spoke. The man wasn't any happier or more upset – if feelings existed on a gauge his dial was virtually unmoved. And then he turned the corner and eventually exited out of view, leaving Scott alone in his astonishment.

Now Tenzin deemed herself able to stand and touch his arm. "You can control it," she said.

Scott could control it.

His hands began to tremble. *He could've controlled it.* This whole time, through every terrible night spent tumbling with faceless people. All that time he spent wondering if he was someone they actually ever wanted in the first place. They could've been monks. They could've been *married.* After navigating all of that guilt, folding it up and storing it as neatly as he could, he now had it all spilling out into the realization that none of it had to happen in the first place.

"I hurt people," he whispered.

The hand on his arm squeezed. It snaked around him until Tenzin was half-holding his side with her chin resting on the top of his head. "You didn't know," she said.

"Nobody knows anything. That doesn't excuse being reckless."

"You didn't want it."

"Neither did they. Potentially," Scott sight and closed his eyes. "It's dangerous how little of this is actually documented."

Tenzin let out a short, dark laugh that vibrated through Scott's skull. "I've contacted every witch town in the country. None of them have any interest in the work I've done so far," she went softer, a little more respectful. "They all thanked me, but they said it shouldn't make a difference."

"But that's not true," Scott pulled away and eyed her with growing passion. "You just helped every person I'll have to interact with for the rest of my life."

"I helped *you*," Tenzin said. "And if I was right about you, maybe we can find a way to help Mom."

She looked at him hard before pulling out her phone and doing all the little gestures a person does when they have a phone like hers. Soon after that she found what she was looking for and exhaled a curt huff.

"There's a red-eye tomorrow morning," she told him.

Scott wanted to tell her to book it. But it wasn't that easy. If there were only a few people who had full free will around his presence, he wasn't about to make any decisions on their behalf.

When he and Tenzin came back inside, Edgar was seated on the floor by his record player, reading the sleeve of whatever vinyl was playing. Scott wanted to get straight to business, but when he heard the music he had to stop for a moment and take it in.

The tremor of the vocals let him know it was The Talking Heads. He couldn't get any more precise than that. As much as Scott enjoyed the band, he still operated under the belief that all of their songs sounded pretty much the same.

"*Fear of Music*," Edgar said, holding up the all-black cover.

That meant nothing to Scott. "Good," he said.

Katy was smoking on the balcony. Tenzin gave Scott a final scruff of the hair before she crossed the room towards the back door to join her. She leaned down to fold her arms over the top of the steel fence. It was a more nonchalant gesture than Scott was used to seeing from her. A leather jacket kind of cool that didn't fit, but he supported it.

He shifted his focus to Edgar. The bouncy, strummy, aggressively funky music playing on the record player wasn't doing much to raise his boyfriend's spirits. It looked like he was reading the lyrics – not lip syncing or singing along, just quietly following with his eyes.

It was harder through the beat of the music to sense his feelings. Through the bridge was still there between him and Edgar, the novelty of experiencing another person's emotions was now less remarkable. His mind had long-accepted the extra limbs grafted onto his body. But with new attention he was able to make out a faint impression.

Empty. Cold. Dusty. Lonely.

Scott quickly sat on the floor, beside Edgar, close enough to press their shoulders together. He felt Edgar sigh, gradually unwinding to release a slight degree of tension. But he didn't look at Scott. Maybe he refused to, or wouldn't allow himself the right – Scott had no way to be certain. What he did know was that Edgar, as soon as he was touched, stopped blinking.

Six seconds went by. Then fifteen. Soon it was close to a minute of open-eyed sorrow.

"Oh Edgar…" Scott murmured.

Edgar clenched his eyes shut and winced. He turned down the music. "Sorry," he said. "I…"

The word hung heavy above them, filling the air like smoke. Edgar, his eyes still closed, sighed and pressed his temple against Scott's shoulder. Good. Finally.

Ahead of them Scott saw the patio door slide open. Katy and Tenzin filed in, both the picture of action. They headed towards the front door and Katy left first, already pulling the keys out of her jean pocket.

Tenzin was coming towards where Scott and Edgar were sitting on the floor. She crouched down and lifted the needle off the turntable, silencing the music.

"You're leaving again?" Scott said.

"I need Katy's laptop. We'll just be outside," she reached into her pocket and pulled out her smartphone. "Here."

Scott took the phone without fully understanding what was happening.

"I started digitizing the albums in the living room earlier this year," she explained. "The first two are all on my phone. The app is already pulled up – Edgar will know how to use it."

Scott felt weird. Uncomfortable. The expensive phone in his palm wasn't sticky, but he had the same response as if it was. Soon he was close to refusing her outright when Edgar pulled himself out of his self-cocoon and took the phone from him.

He thanked her, low and half-hearted. Tenzin smiled faintly and turned away to follow Katy out the door, and soon they were alone again.

Over enough time Scott got used to silence. Living here, with constant conversation and inviting music playing, quickly destroyed that tolerance. Now without the music and with no one talking, he squirmed. He felt too small to exist in such an empty space.

"You can see faces?" Edgar asked.

Scott looked at him. He nodded.

"All faces? Even in photos?"

He nodded again. Edgar cocked his head to the side. "And you said you see your face too, now?"

It occurred to Scott that he never got the chance to directly tell Edgar that new and profound change in his life. It was a massive hindrance in his life, and every time he mentioned it had been incredibly nonchalant. It was there and ruined him. Now it was over with, and though it hadn't been solved for long the time when it ruled over his life felt far away. He could imagine his reflection quite easily now.

Scott thought about what he looked like and quietly checked in to determine how he felt about it today. When he focus came back to Edgar he found his bond was gazing at him, warm even through his own pain.

"You are *so* pretty, Scott," he whispered.

Warmth flooded his body. He slumped his shoulders and echoed that sentiment over and over again, so charmed that he didn't even notice Edgar unlock Tenzin's phone to start swiping and tapping. Scott only caught on that something was happening once he saw his bond's face flicker with happiness, a wide smile breaking out on his face.

"Oh my god," he said. "Look at you."

Scott scooted a little closer, anxious to see an old photo but also wanting to see what could bring Edgar any joy at a time like this. It was a photograph taken at the beach by their home. It was on a rarer, blue-sky sunny day, and his mother was smiling faintly, eyeing the camera like she was happy but didn't know how to relay that to a lens. Scott was being carried under her arm, although most of his face was obscured by webs of seaweed. The only part visible was his massive, laughing grin.

"Yup," Scott said. "That sounds about right."

"Where's Tenzin?"

"Probably with Mom. I think around this time she was the one that mainly took the photos of us."

Edgar faltered. When he answered his voice was slightly stiffened. "Sure," he said.

There wasn't much desire to question that response when Scott could instead focus on remembering what his mother looked like. He was right in a lot of his presumptions. The two of them shared an identical strong, straight nose and striking brow. Scott could see himself in the shape of her lips. And her eyes were large, like his, only instead of blue they were a near-black brown.

She looked strong. If she were an actress she'd be perfect for a black and white movie. All the colors would still have the exact intended effect. Her stomach was plush and rounded, and her arms looked like they could only be soft – though he'd seen her install a floating cabinet on her own with few instructions over the course of a single day. She lifted him up like that a lot in childhood, holstering him like a piece of carry-on luggage. And Scott was fine with that. He felt safe there.

He looked over at Edgar and saw him staring at the photo with equal intensity. He seemed uneasy in a way that made it seemed like he struggled to grasp what he was seeing.

"Is she nice?" He finally asked, very hesitantly.

Scott warmed. "She's *kind*. Quiet. My mom's the best listener in the world."

"She seems – familiar."

"To you?" Scott sat up, leaning in closer. "Do you know her? Have you met my mom?"

Edgar's face twitched. Unknowing confusion sputtered within them like Edgar's car when he dared to try and make it drive. Eventually Scott decided to stop things from getting too far down the road and placed a soft hand against his thigh.

"Show me another one," he said.

Edgar tapped the photo back into a gallery and scrolled down a few rows. He spoke again. His tone was moon-glowing with affection, which clashed against his bottomless undercurrent of pain flowing between them.

"You look rowdy," he expanded a poorly-angled picture of Scott as a toddler, crooked on his feet and triumphantly clutching a hammer in each hand. "Did you get in trouble a lot?"

"Well – kind of."

"What does that mean?"

Scott mimicked the taps and swipes he watched Edgar do and managed to pull up a family photo of the four of them: Scott, Tenzin, Regina and Enoch. Scott and Tenzin were wearing matching Ankara dresses, though young Scott appeared much happier with the garb than his sister did. Enoch was smiling calmly, the way people were supposed to smile in photos. His mother, meanwhile, was completely ignoring the camera in favor of looking down at the open binder in her lap.

He knew that binder. It's where Enoch kept the papers she published in various exclusive scientific journals over the course of her career.

"We would make some weird choices," Scott said, paraphrasing his mother's words. "And she'd talk to us about them. Ask us what we were thinking and how we felt."

"And that's all?"

Scott knew what Edgar was really asked him and it was like a knife to the gut. He tried to keep himself calm.

"Yes," he softly spoke. "That's all that would happen."

They stared at one of the only full family portraits of them all in existence. Scott was lost in the moment, separated slightly from this time and this place versus all the other times and places that existed in his head.

He remembered Edgar. There was someone else there too, an overlaying presence that was as familiar as it was not physically present.

It still hurts, doesn't it?

It does. I don't know why.

I think sometimes things hurt for a long time before they get better.

What are you supposed to do until then?

Wait, I guess. Do something else.

"Are you trying to talk to me?" Edgar said.

Scott wasn't sure how to answer that. The answer he came to was *no*, but was that because it wasn't him he was talking to, or because he didn't have to try? He didn't want to keep secrets. For this to be a secret, though, he'd have to understand what it was he was holding back.

He looked down at the phone. "I think I know what album this is from. If you keep looking you might find the photo they took after Mom curled my hair."

They looked at photos for what felt like a long time. Whatever Tenzin and Katy were doing outside, they weren't apparently in any sort of rush. At first Scott looked at each picture alongside Edgar, seeing and recognizing memories that had been long wiped for years. After a while his attention drifted to the face of the person beside him.

Scott's mind went back to the Other Place where he saw that he and Edgar were physically connected, each sharing halves of one tether where everyone else around them had their own. It could be said that made them soulmates – in a sense so literal that Scott struggled to comprehend it.

It wasn't fair. Scott wanted to see a picture of Edgar as a little kid. He wanted to stare into the young face of someone he loved so deeply and feel that sense of protective gratitude. And he would know then, wouldn't he? All he had to do was match the shapes and voices to make sure the voice in his head was not just a projection of his own disease.

It doesn't make a difference, right?

I don't know anymore.

Do you love us?

Us?

Yes.

I do. But in different ways. I think.

Try not to worry about it, Scott. It's a good thing that's happening!

Scott took Edgar's hand and lowered it, taking his eyes away from Tenzin's phone. He gazed over the tired calm of his bond's expression, the way his large brown eyes shone drowsily and the limbs of his body hung loose where they laid.

He felt tongue-tied then. The romantic speech he wanted didn't aim to come out in coherent sentences, and unfortunately Edgar had no knowledge of Tone-Speech. So Scott blinked a few times and brought Edgar's hands to his chest. Then he spoke.

"Come home with me."

"When?" Edgar asked.

"Tonight. Tomorrow, actually. Early tomorrow, I think."

He didn't respond at first. Then he smiled. "Okay."

"I know it's a lot to think about –"

"It really isn't."

Edgar slipped his thumb and index finger between the buttons of Scott's shirt and idly touched his chest. It stabilized Scott, even though he had to draw in a breath from the chilled touch of his fingertips.

"I think I have a way we can restore a lot of our memory," Scott whispered. "Maybe all of it."

"I've never been to a witch town before," Edgar frowned gently and brushed his hair back with a furrow of his brow. "Should I not tell them I'm Academy?"

"Some birthrights our age might make an issue out of it," Scott shrugged. "You meet anyone in Bluerose who knew me growing up and I promise it won't matter."

"Why not?"

"Edgar..." Scott laughed, vague and weary. "Edgar, darling, we've been waiting for you my whole life."

That was the first time he'd called Edgar by any pet name other than "Chef". It fell out of him so easily that he wasn't sure what to expect in response. The slight quiver in Edgar's brow confirmed that he heard him. The shimmer of red across his cheeks and nose, all above a faint, bewildered smile echoed the sentiment. With that alone, Scott began to wish he didn't have such easy access to the cavalcade of fireworks going off in his boyfriend's chest.

Edgar's hesitance made him look younger. The shy heart throbbing on his sleeve was something Scott knew well, a snapshot memory from lives and lives ago. A lot of the picture in Scott's head were still indistinct, too much so to fully recognize what it is he once saw.

There was one thing he was certain of in that moment: Edgar Gallows must've been an adorable child.

"Do you do that a lot?"

Katy sat on the curb outside Edgar's apartment, vaping thoughtful plumes of English Breakfast-flavored smoke into the late-afternoon air. She was hitting the stick a little harder than she probably should've, but the soft buzzing in her brain that it resulted in was perfect for dealing with the stress of today.

People sustain nicotine addictions all the time, sometimes for no reason at all. They don't need wizard death marches or otherworldly terrors. As far as Katy was concerned, what she was doing made perfect sense within the context of the situation.

"Smoking is cool," she said. "It's cool and fun and feels good and makes you look more interesting."

Tenzin was sitting in the open backseat of Katy's car, typing on her laptop. The flicker of keystrokes paused a moment when Katy said that.

"Can I try?" Tenzin asked.

"Nope."

"That's what I thought."

She continued typing.

Katy kept a cheap laptop and mobile hot spot hidden in her car at all times, just in case. Because you never know what might happen. Maybe she'd have an hour to kill waiting for an appointment. Maybe she'd complain to someone about a game she was stuck on and they'd make the mistake of claiming they could do better. Or perhaps an entirely new kind of magic user will need to send some emails and buy plane tickets without accruing too much roaming data.

Shit happens.

"Oregon, huh?" Katy remarked, the verbal equivalent of dead air.

"Yes," Tenzin said. "Near Portland."

"Is it snowing there right now?"

"We don't get much snowfall. Maybe a little bit for a few days in January. Witch towns tend to be fairly temperate though."

Katy sucked on the end of her vape until her head spun. She held the vapor in, then blew it out through her nostrils. "Sick," she said.

More typing.

If Tenzin could tell Katy was upset, she didn't care enough to actually address it. On the other hand, maybe she didn't realize. Growing up with Scott as a brother, creating a door between herself and her perception of emotion could very well be a very viable coping mechanism.

Otherwise you're left aimless every time the man broke down – which, Katy guessed, probably happened a lot.

It's not like she wanted to say how she was feeling. At this point it no longer mattered. Plus, it was mostly a good thing that was happening and she didn't want to get in the way of it. The situation wasn't even about her to begin with, it was about her scruffy, smaller companion. It didn't matter what she thought of it. What mattered is that Edgar Gallows was unhappy and now he wasn't. He had no hope or motivation to pursue a future for himself, and now he did.

Katy had a friend, and now she didn't.

Ugh.

Why was she acting like this? She was an adult woman who paid her bills and nurtured a living animal. And it's not like Edgar was her one and only friend in the world. People were always offering to hang out with her. So what if he runs off to Oregon and she never sees him again? She could just call up Jess and meet for a drink.

Or go to the bar with Lee from the drag club. Or see Marta and do Jagershots long past the point where Jagershots stopped being fun. Which was *one*.

Katy suddenly felt a little sick to her stomach. She sighed.

"Will it be hard to take time off work?" Tenzin asked.

"Uh, no. Michael's a chill guy. Plus he already put Edgar on a sabbatical –"

"I mean for you."

The two fingers she used to wobble her vape in place went still. Katy turned her head and looked at Tenzin, who regarded her with no pity and only the calmly stern demeanor of someone making travel plans.

Still, Katy faltered. "What – do you mean?"

"Oh," Tenzin quirked a brief smile. "I assumed you were coming with us."

Very carefully, Katy felt herself slip her vape back into the pocket of her jeans. She stretched out her legs into the road and tried to reform the shape of the feelings she experienced just before this. Beside her she could see the edges of Tenzin's body as she turned in her seat to put the laptop aside.

"You're angry," she said.

"What?"

"Or – sad? Thinking..." Tenzin frowned. "It's hard for me to tell. Everyone I've grown up around has had years of therapy so they just describe what they're feeling as they feel it. I find that to be far more helpful."

That sounded like autism, but Katy didn't know enough to delve into that particular subject just yet. Instead she shifted to press her back against the large stump on the curb, allowing her to see more of Tenzin as she spoke.

"When you take Edgar to Bluerose," she began, "I don't see him wanting to come back."

"I wouldn't worry about that."

Tenzin said that so quickly. And she didn't seem like the type to tell nice white lies to make someone feel better.

"You don't think he'll feel better there?" Katy prodded further. "A witch town, surrounded by people that like and accept him. Isn't that kind of – I don't know...where he belongs?"

"Well...you know him better than I do. Do you think he'll be comfortable in a relatively small town where nearly every single person thinks they know exactly who he is? Where there's zero chance for anonymity or personal identity?"

A shiver of by-proxy dread ran down Katy's spine. That was bad. That was not going to be fun. Anytime they've been out together and ran into someone on the street that recognized Edgar and wanted to rope him into conversation, he got through those interactions by the skin of his teeth. For someone with aspirations of being a chef, he had zero interest in fame – or even a strong degree of recognition.

"I can't say he won't want to move at some point, but I doubt he'll stay in Bluerose forever," Tenzin shrugged lightly. "And it's probably for the best, considering how near he is to Shreveport right now and the hold they have on him.”

Katy frowned. “What do you mean?”

“Maybe if Scott really wanted to stay there,” Tenzin mused, a touch of sadness in her face. “At this point I don't think that's likely either. I tried to contact the right people and let them know what's going on, but when he finds out he finds out that he's technically been leading a team in town…” She laughed, once, and very strained. “He says he remembers Bluerose is a refuge hub, but I guess he didn't connect that all the birthrights that live in refuge hubs are *employees,*” Tenzin leaned forward and rubbed her face with her hands. “If I had Scott's email I could make sure I notified the proper contacts. I don't, though, so…I messaged his assistant and hoped for the best.”

This was another horrifying concept. Katy tried to imagine someone like Scott realizing that he'd had an entire career that he had zero memory of. Did he write schedules? Did he sign paychecks? And he had an *assistant*? It was hard to imagine Scott delegating tasks he didn't feel like doing to any form of subordinate. Or even just referring to someone he worked alongside with as a *subordinate.*

“How many people?” Katy said.

“In the Ambassador program?” Tenzin stared up to calculate the numbers. “Well, Mari made some changes since he left and split off the minors into a subgroup with a different lead…people graduate or transfer every year,” she closed her eyes and mouthed a few near-silent numbers. “I'd say on average – around a hundred? Maybe slightly more?”

Katy cringed. “He's going to hate that.”

“I know.”

“Did he like it before?”

“He was good at it. He knew it was important.”

“That's not an answer.”

Tenzin looked at Katy, gentle and weary and kind. “You're welcome to come,” she said.

Was that an invitation or a request? Did Tenzin want Katy to feel included in this budding adventure, or was she sincerely asking for her help? Wanting help would make sense. Katy had enough confidence to know that her customer service sensibilities could manage most forms of conflict. Dealing with exposed social anxiety as well as a full-fledged existential crisis would be a lot for a person who can't distinguish emotions unless they're properly labeled.

It would technically be a vacation. Katy could certainly use one. Only...

"I can't," Katy said.

"Oh. Okay."

Tenzin took the laptop again and went back to typing, because apparently her answer didn't actually matter. And Katy was about to believe that response until she spoke again.

"Why not?" Tenzin asked, her eyes still on the screen.

"My cat isn't doing great. He's old, I..." Katy sighed through her teeth. "If something happened to him while we were gone –"

"Say no more."

"I know it's stupid."

"No," Tenzin cut in, slightly sharpened. "He's your cat. He's important. You should be with him."

Katy built up a small smile, despite herself. She shifted her eyes from her hands, to the stump behind her, and then up to the cloud-scattered sky.

"Hey..." she hesitated, but forced herself to continue. "If you get back after Black Friday – uh – Edgar usually makes a meal for Wilford's birthday."

Tenzin looked up from the laptop. "You throw a birthday party for your cat?"

"I do, yes," Katy watched Tenzin look down and go back to clicking furiously. "It's not a serious thing, I just – what are you doing?"

"I'm changing the date of our return flight."

She clicked a few times and then smiled. Tenzin shut the laptop and slid it back into its discreet case. When she finished putting it back in its hiding spot, she crept out of Katy's car and closed the door behind her. All Katy could think to do was stare, just look at what was going on and try and figure out what was happening.

"You don't think unraveling the mysteries of your brother's life is more important than celebrating my cat's birthday?" Katy said.

Tenzin paused. "Probably," she said. "But I'm not going to be the one to tell Scott he's not invited to a kitty-cat birthday party," Tenzin shot Katy a look that was simultaneously emotionless and very amused. "Are you?"

In the back of her mind Katy thought about Scott cradling Wilford and burying his face in his fur. She remembered that the cat allowed him to do this, too. Wilford just let Scott nuzzle him, looking off into the distance with an expression that reminded Katy of a crucifix that hung in her childhood church.

The Christ figure comment made a lot more sense now.

Tenzin held up a hand to help her up. As soon as their palms were clasped Katy had to notice just how powerful Tenzin's hands were. The knuckles were slightly calloused, but her nails were well-manicured and painted over with different pastel glosses. Katy put in no effort to be pulled up, and Tenzin needed none at all to get the job done perfectly.

Christ, Katy blushed. *She's strong.*

Standing closer together, Katy took a moment to reexamine the steady slopes of Tenzin's bare shoulders and upper arms. In photos she looked so serious. You'd never expect her baseline to be a sort of quiet, uncertain confusion.

"Do I have something on my shirt?" Tenzin said, looking down at the material.

Katy considered avoiding the subject and hiding her blatant staring. If she did that Tenzin might not question it. Wasn't she the one that said she struggled to recognize emotions that weren't directly pointed out to her? If that were the case, Katy could potentially eye her up all she liked without her ever catching on to the fact.

She took in a small sigh forced herself to meet Tenzin's eyes. "I'm admiring your muscles," she said.

Tenzin didn't respond.

"I can already see that you're strong," Katy continued, bracing herself to keep direct face-to-face contact. "But there's a lot of discipline in your body. You have a physical strength that I'm pretty sure you can only get when you're also incredibly intelligent," she awkwardly tucked her hands into the pocket of her pants and finally broke away from Tenzin's inquisitive stare. "I don't know. It's attractive."

"Are you flirting with me?" Tenzin asked faintly.

"Maybe. I – I'm not sure, actually," Katy furrowed her brow slightly. "You're fun. I enjoy you. You have some interesting things to say. I think I – I'd like to hear more of them."

"But you think I'm attractive?"

Tenzin said that like that was the only thing she retained from everything Katy said. And that was sweet in a way Katy couldn't really explain. But it also settled the deal for her, so she opened her phone and pulled up a page for a new contact.

She handed it to Tenzin. "You should give me your phone number."

Katy was prepared for hesitation and found none. Tenzin took Katy's phone with almost excessive care and typed out her phone number. When she handed it back her number and name were filled out, complete with a pigeon head emoji entered as the surname.

Another bird person. Katy had such a knack for attracting the bird people.

The two of them went back inside and found the front room empty. There were sounds of life coming from the bedroom, though, and soon after Tenzin latched the front door shut Edgar poked his head out.

"Scott has your phone," he said to Tenzin. "He's out on the balcony I think."

Tenzin made a small sound of affirmation and drifted towards the back door to join him. Before she opened the glass, though, she paused and looked over at Katy. She didn't say anything. She just stared.

"You're into women, right?" Katy asked.

"Yes."

"And you're still this bad at interacting with them?"

Tenzin nodded. "I am, yes."

From the corner of her eye Katy saw Edgar start to smile. As if he could consider himself more competent than anyone who struggled with their social skills. Or was he expressing a kind of happiness that said he was glad for her to be interested in someone not obsessed with motorcycles or nightclubbing? Was he really so ready for her next potential girlfriend to not try and talk to him about cars that he'd instead prefer the woman who almost KO'd him in one blow?

Maybe that was reasonable. Katy didn't know anymore.

Inside Edgar's bedroom, his bed was overlaid with a variety of clothes – most of which Katy had never seen for as long as she'd known him. The clothes had enough variety that it made her realize how he only wore maybe four different outfits just mixed and matched depending on the day.

She stood with him at the foot of his bed, looking out at the sea of unfamiliar fashion.

"You see my problem," Edgar said.

There was a polo shirt. A pinstripe vest. *Fake leather pants.* It was as if an alien had to pick a style of human male fashion and settled eagerly on all of them. Katy didn't want to laugh, because it really wasn't funny. Edgar was trying so desperately to fit into the mold of Stylish Man Guy, and it clearly wasn't working.

She thought about that. It really *didn't* work. Even the flannel he practically deemed his uniformed didn't read as *man*. Not that it read as *woman* either. It never occurred to her that she silently perceived her best friend as a genderless amalgamation of opinions and anxieties. All of the clothes that made sense on his body were just *Edgar* clothes.

And there were some more along the bed that she could make out, even though she'd never seen him wear them even once.

Once again, she reminded herself not to laugh. But the more she imagined Edgar walking around in a lace dress shirt and leather pants the funnier the image became.

"Katy..."

She turned her head away to hide her snickering. "I'm sorry," she said. "I – I just...*hoo boy.*"

"I never shopped for myself before when I got all these," Edgar said, defensive and also audibly smiling. "I literally searched online for *things men wear* and just bought one of whatever I could."

A sudden insight flashed into her brain, stark in its simplicity.

Oh hey, he's trans. That's a thing trans people do.

After everything else that had happened, Katy wasn't sure how to broach this. By the lack of fear in his face it didn't seem like this was his way of coming out to her. It seemed like he had no way of reading into the subtext of his own explanations. This complicated things, since Katy was absolutely not equipped to guide another human being through any sort of repressed queer awakening.

Edgar read into her expression. Apparently, though, he was reading the wrong page.

"I will accept three questions," he said.

Have you seen how many different kinds of pronouns people use these days? Do you have any names you like better than your own? Can I still call you my brother?

Externally Katy put on an expression of playful ribbing. "Did you..? Have you worn the leather pants in public?"

"Once. They're pretty squeaky."

"I'm seeing a lot of vests here. Why don't you ever wear vests?"

"They make me think of being at work," Edgar said. "One more."

Katy thought long and hard of what her final question would be. "What's something here you've never worn but secretly think you'd look good in?"

She tracked Edgar's cringe, though almost imperceptible. He looked down and took a deep breath. "I mean, I like the flannels. But – I have a few floral shirts that I always wished I could wear."

Her expectation was for that answer to be a lot more embarrassing. By the way Edgar watched her, it seemed he was thinking the same thing, and was now waiting for her to laugh at him. Katy turned back to the mess of laid out clothes and found a nice, short-sleeved Hawaiian shirt – black and scattered with sunflowers. She picked it up and held it against Edgar.

"Oh yeah," she said. "You definitely pull that off."

Edgar grimaced slightly. "It's the Pacific Northwest, Katy. I'm heading into *actual* winter."

"Layers, Ed. Long sleeve underneath and a jacket on top. You'll be golden."

"That's…" Edgar furrowed his brow and drew his lips briefly into a long, straight line. "You know, that makes sense."

Katy sat, cross-legged at the head of his bed and watched as he packed. They made lighthearted, unimportant conversation, as if this was just a regular day and not Katy's first time hanging out in his bedroom. She knew better by now. His anticipation was evident in every movement of his hands. Edgar smiled a lot, but his eyes were wracked with attention.

She wanted to say something to make him feel better, even though she really didn't know what that would be. Because there was still a part of her that worried he would find himself happier on the other side of the country and find no more use in New Orleans and those who inhabited it. And that made her feel so selfish, so sour in the pit of her stomach.

"It'll be quick," Edgar said at one point while folding a pair of jeans. "Two weeks, but I guess a lot of it is going to be rest. So I should be fine – right?"

"Right," Katy said. Then she toyed with the edge of the comforter and added, softer, "Are you nervous?"

"He says there's a ritual they do to undo the effects of Petrichor," Edgar added another shirt to his suitcase and looked around the room. "So if I lost memories by taking something similar, he thinks it might be able to restore them. For both of us. But it sounds like a rough process, so – yeah, I guess. Kind of."

Katy grabbed Edgar's Switch from the bedside table and handed it to him. He took it and smiled gratefully before adding it to his backpack.

"This is your first plane trip, right?" Katy said.

"As far as I know."

"You want an Ativan? I have some in my purse," she shimmied her legs under the covers as she said that. "I'm sure I don't have enough to help Scott, but it could chill you out for the flight."

Edgar paused, midway into shoving a paperback into his carry-on bag. "I have aberration in my head, do you think I'm going to have the mental space to be afraid of flying?"

"I can't tell," Katy mused. "That definitely sounds like you."

"It...does. Good point."

Once he was fully packed, he put away the rest of his discordant wardrobe and straightened up the odds and ends of a mostly bare bedroom. Somehow, in a turn of events that made little sense to her, they ended up in bed together after all of that. She was under the covers, and he above them, and they both stared up at the ceiling. They stayed like that in silence until Edgar pulled out his phone and started playing music on the nearby speaker.

Weezer. *OK Human.* What a weird choice for a time like this.

"Don't buy water at the airport," she told him soon after. "It's crazy overpriced. Just bring an empty water bottle and fill it up after you get through TSA."

"Okay," Edgar said.

"A little moisturizer helps during long flights. Sky air is, like...dry. Somehow."

"Nice. Thank you."

"You're coming back, right?"

Katy didn't mean to say that. She didn't want to say something so vulnerable and pathetic. She bored her gaze into the speckles of what was one a popcorn ceiling, avoiding the man – the *person* beside her, and denying herself any comfort or judgment he might have to offer.

"Of course I'm coming back," Edgar laughed, very faint, like the ghost of a ghost. "Why would you say that?"

"I don't know," Katy said to the ceiling. "Destiny or some shit. Maybe you don't want to spend the rest of your life a parish away from where you were abused."

The silence where Edgar thought about that was the first thing in a very long time that made Katy want to cry. And knowing that it brought her that close to tears was so embarrassing that it only heightened her sadness.

Edgar turned on his side to face her. He looked far more sure of himself lying in bed than he ever did standing on his feet. "Just say you'll miss me, Katy," he said.

"I'll miss you, Edgar."

She answered immediately and felt a small satisfaction at how easily that knocked the smile off his face. He looked at her closely, perhaps seeing the bags under her eyes or smelling the vape fumes still clinging to her clothes. After that he reached over and touched over the covers, just below where Katy's elbow was.

"Then we'll miss each other for a while. I'll send you pictures and you'll send me stock photos. Then I'll come back and cook Wilford a nice quiche for his birthday," he gave her arm a gentle squeeze. "We'll see what happens after that."

Their relationship seemed to change so much in such a short expanse of time. When she met Edgar in the break room she never would've expected to just be lying beside him in bed like she was now. Even a month ago it would still be impossible. Their floodgates had been closed for so long that the mechanisms had rusted over. Teens sprayed graffiti on the bare and rocky wall. And, as nice as this was, Katy still considered whether or not it was better that way.

Not better, but easier. Safer.

His bedroom looked a lot like hers did. Was that on purpose?

Edgar packed quickly, and Scott and Tenzin didn't seem to ever have unpacked. There wasn't much else to do in terms of planning for the trip. Edgar mentioned that it might be fun to walk down Decatur Street just to move around a little and see some of the city. It wasn't that Katy was invited so much as it was assumed she would come with them.

"I can't," she said, smiling amicably. "Jess called me earlier and said she needs me to cover dinner tonight."

It was a blatant lie that Tenzin immediately saw through. Even Edgar didn't entirely convinced, but he let it slide. They ghosted through their goodbyes at the door until there was nothing else left to push forward, and Katy was ready to crawl back into bed.

She reached out a hand to bump Edgar's fist, only to be met by a small paperback book.

"Here," he said. "Some homework while I'm gone."

Katy recognized the book as something she'd seen Edgar reading before at work. And like every other book Edgar cherished, it was beaten to the point of almost falling apart. *Letters to a Young Poet,* the cover read *by Rainier Maria Rilke.*

"I'm not reading poetry, Edgar."

"It's not poetry, it's letters about – well, poetry. But also life. Being alive," he unwrapped her fist and forced the book into her hand. "Just read it. For me."

Behind him Scott was sitting, cross-legged on the couch, animatedly exchanging words with Tenzin. They sat, shoulders touching. Everyone here was always touching.

She thought about Edgar's hand on her arm through the covers and Scott's head on her shoulder. The physical affection Katy has received in the span of the last few days drastically outweighed what she had in years.

It made her hungry. Lonely. Sick. Angry.

Tired, mostly. All of those, for her, were different words for tired.

Something inside her craved escape. She needed to be alone, so she put on her best smile and separated herself from that love-filled household.

Once she walked through the door of her own, empty apartment, she found Wilford curled up over a splotch on her hardwood floor that was now far cleaner than everything around it. No blood anymore, which was nice. Just a constant reminder of her inability to mop consistently.

Her cat lifted his head slightly at the sound of the latch and blinked his gooey eyes.

Katy dropped her bag on the floor and slipped off her hoodie, letting it fall nearby as well. "Hey, Pizza Pie," she murmured.

She bent down and started to pick Wilford up, and in response he made a low grumble. Katy paused and tried again at a different angle. More grumbling. She patted him across his body to look for a particular pain spot. Finding nothing, Katy sighed and just laid down on the floor beside him.

"I'm good at loving you, aren't I?" She asked him.

Wilford sniffed the air. He stretched out his head and sniffed his nose just in front of Katy's.

"It's hard, you know," Katy closed her eyes. "Actually, I don't think you would. Lucky."

Her eyes tingled, warm and damp. She groaned and rubbed at them with the balls of her hands. Rolling onto her back she wondered how it could be possible to feel mostly fine so much of the time, and sometimes drop off into pits of despair for no reason at all.

She should've gone with Edgar and the others. Why did she choose to sulk on the floor when she could be having a nice time with her friends? That's the kind of behavior she indulged in as a teenager.

Katy pulled out her phone and switched to her contacts. It took more scrolling than she was proud to admit before she found the number she was looking for. Was she really about to call it, though? Didn't she isolate herself with the aims to avoid growth and make things *easier* for a night?

Scott came back into her mind. The way he looked at himself after she cut his hair. How, when he rested his head against her, she could feel his body move slightly with every breath. Just that trusting, unquestioning, platonic closeness.

She called the number. It rang longer than she'd prefer, although if it went straight to voicemail Katy wouldn't be surprised.

Then a voice. Older now, but still very young. Harder now, a little gruff, but still sweet. Genuinely uncertain from just one single world. "Kitty?"

Katy's heart twisted. It had been so long since anyone called her that. She breathed a little quicker now and closed her eyes, trying to calm herself. Her sister spoke again.

"Kitty, are you all right?"

"I'm fine," Katy forced out the words on the ends of a laugh. "I – yeah. Um...hi," she swallowed hard and opened her eyes, tears finally escaping down the sides of her face. "Hi Leanne."

Nocturne

Tenzin was old now. She was eighty-three years old.

Her dreadlocks were long since cut, and she now kept her hair maintained in short, white curls similar to what her mom had before she died. But that was a lifetime ago. Tenzin's face was relatively unwrinkled for her age, but her hands trembled, fingers bent and hardened from arthritis. She hadn't trained in some time, stopping the art shortly after Mustard died. Now she can barely draw before everything just aches.

Regina Mustard Kaufner was long dead, having passed away peacefully in her sleep years and years ago. Katy died too - lung cancer. Or liver damage. Maybe heart failure. She couldn't be sure yet. What mattered was that most of people she loved were gone. Soon Tenzin would be gone too. The doctors told her that the same kind of ovarian tumor that killed Enoch was now back to take her too. They tried hard, but there was nothing they could do.

Tenzin wished they didn't make such an effort. Not much reason to at this point.

She gathered what strength she had left to meet Scott and Edgar one last time, driving or flying, or even just taking a walk to wherever they now inhabited. They met at a diner. As Tenzin hobbled through the door, she recognized them immediately and was stunned by how little had changed.

They hadn't aged. Well, that couldn't be entirely true. They were starting to gray and wrinkle as all inevitably do. Only, while Tenzin aged over fifty years since they last saw each other, Scott and Edgar couldn't have aged more than twenty. They sat in the corner booth and leaned against each other, faces drawn together in hushed conspiring.

The menus laid in front of them were untouched. They probably wouldn't order anything.

They didn't acknowledge her until she slid in across from them. Then, moving in sync, Scott and Edgar turned to look across the table with an expression of mutual idle curiosity.

"Hello, Scott," Tenzin said. "Hello, Edgar."

"Hello, Tenzin," they said. "It's been a long time."

They both said that as if it were some sort of inside joke. The wry tone in their double-speak silently enraged her, but at this point in her life such emotions were hard to hold onto for long. Soon it left, and she was just empty inside.

Do they know? Do they understand what's happened to them?

"What have..?" Everything she planned on saying fell away from her, and she now found it difficult to speak to the entity sitting with her. "How are you?"

A server greeted them with a tray of ice waters. Edgar handed one to Scott, who took it without moving his eyes away from the cars passing by outside. Scott did not thank the waitress, or even acknowledge her presence. The sight of this made Tenzin fists make a futile attempt to clench.

"We're doing well," they said. "Work gives us lots of time to think."

Look at me, Scotty, she begged in her mind. *Please look at me.*

He didn't. His eyes, like Edgar's, were foggy with peace and glowed a soft, dark green. At one point he reached over to pull a hairband off from around one of Edgar's wrists, and Edgar turned to help tie up his hair while he took a sip of water. Four hands operating to perform a task done fine by two for thirty years.

Tenzin forced herself to hold onto that image of the young child on the beach in Bluerose, awe-struck by a single Pokemon card. She leaned across the table and touched his hand, and when she did he finally met her eyes and smiled.

Smiled politely. Like you would an old woman you give your seat to on the bus. Tenzin's heart rotted in her chest.

"Scott," she began, "are you still practicing?"

Edgar, meaninglessly listening from beside him, cocked his head to the side.

"Practicing what?" They both asked, innocent as anything.

When Tenzin answered her voice felt warped in her mouth. "Your piano. Do you still play the piano?"

The two looked at each other. Their brows twitched, both un-matched and in perfect alignment. Tenzin watched them commune and wondered what was information was being shared between them. If what you could even call what they had *sharing* after so many years. Finally they regarded Tenzin again with a dual smirk.

"What part of us used to be Scott?"

Tenzin would die soon. She was old and she was wise, and she was now also alone. A diner like this was no longer a welcome space for her. It wasn't home – she had no home. But none of that mattered anymore, because in a what could be considered a moment in the grand scheme of things she would return to the earth.

Her brother told her often that the earth would welcome them all. Hopefully he was right.

She sat in the booth and felt the riptide of a life lived. Across from her Scott paid no attention to her turmoil, focused now on leaning his head against Edgar's shoulder with their hands intertwined. They were in love. They *were* love. Consumed within the prison of it.

A presence lingered all around her. Boundless eyes watching, oily and voyeuristic. And then a voice, like all the voices warbling over each other.

Is this really...what you've all been working towards?

When she opened her eyes Tenzin was back on the ratty fake leather couch in Edgar's apartment. Her body did not hurt. She was not veering on the precipice of the end of her life. She blinked a few times to reestablish her presence in this reality, then turned onto her back to stare up at the ceiling.

She wanted to cry. She didn't. She wanted to scream. Tenzin didn't do that either.

There was nothing she could for now but follow the tide. With that thought centered in her head, she buried her face in the back nook of the couch and tried to get a few more hours of sleep.

Etude no. 5

Two lovers lie in bed, holding each other, bare chest breathing deep against bare chest. They are warm under blankets and through the veil of darkness. The First closes his eyes easily, soothed by the tides of the Other's breathing against the crook of his neck. He can picture his bed fellow in his entirety based solely on the map of his body heat pressed against his own.

But something is off. His lover's breathing is a little quicker than his own. His limbs fidget more than they usually do. The First is worried at first, then remembers something and chuckles low.

"I told you not to have that second cup of coffee," he says.

The Other's voice smiles when he responds. "It was *good.* I've never had coffee that tasted like that before. What did you say was in it?"

"Chicory. And *caffeine.*"

"I'm okay," the Other wraps his arms around the First's neck and pulls himself closer. "I'm having a nice time."

They stay like that for a while longer. After some time the Other's breathing slows down to a reasonable pace. And though the First is tired, though he only has a few hours to sleep before they get up for their flight, he now has no hope of fully drifting off. Not when he can smell the woodsy herbs of the other man's leave-in conditioner and feel his toes grazing up and down his inner calf.

"I have a game," the First finally declares.

"Do you?" the Other sounds intrigued and not at all tired. "Let's hear it."

"Would you rather serve a bachelorette party or empty grease traps for a week straight?"

"Easy. I'd rather kill myself."

There is an instance of hesitation at what might be a poorly-timed joke. Then the First starts to laugh in quiet, barely-restrained giggles. The Other man feels it rumble against his chest and in the hands that twitch in his hair. He joins the First in his laughter, and together they try hard to keep their amusement audible to only them.

Eleventh Movement

Regina Mustard Kaufner spent most of her time these days watching home movies. Especially now.

Her capabilities with technology weren't to the standards of her daughter, but they were certainly better than her son, which meant she could hookup an HDMI cable from her laptop to the television without an issue. So she sat on the floor, picking a the rest of the pumpkin muffins Chef Renja made her while she watched ghosts of the family that may as well no longer exist.

First there was Levi – permanently young and effortlessly ashy-blonde. His smile, carefully composed in public spaces, was brilliant whenever the two of them were alone.

His eyes were so, so blue.

Even though she was raised in that old Birthright philosophy of radical death positivity, Regina preferred to watch clips of Levi from before he got dedicated himself to the project that would ultimately end his life. His colors were so much brighter then. It was good to be reminded on the expanse of movement and energy that used to be held in such a handsome, broad body.

Sometimes she would see herself in this footage, which made sense as her camera was originally her husband's. She would be practicing piano or at the table in the kitchen, surrounded by mountains of paperwork. However Levi filmed her he would focus so lovingly, slowly zooming in on her face as if it possessed some gravitational pull.

Then there would be Scott. Dark-haired and wide-eyed from birth. A perfectly large head and four wonderfully chubby limbs that wiggled as he screamed and cried. The footage of him before they started Petrichor treatment was blurry and hard to make out. Regina could still remember how exhausted she was at that time. Grieving from the death of her love, sobbing as baby Scott sobbed and wracked with joy as he laughed. And despite the heart-pain and magic-pain, she was still trying to create memories like any new mother would.

Things stabilized quickly. Soon there were many long shots of the camera balanced on a tripod in front of the tack piano while Regina propped up her two-year-old son on the bench in front of it. What started off as clumsy pounding turned into basic scales. It wasn't long until he was elegantly handling the highs and lows of Liszt's *Liebestraume* – the only classical piece she could get him to play before he lost interest in the whole genre.

Then, soon after that, appeared Enoch and Tenzin. Both of them were still visibly hesitant at first, deep in the shells of the domestic violence they escaped. By the time she met them on that beach she hadn't been a social worker for several years. Luckily, the instincts were still there. And when she found Enoch lovingly standing guard while Scott and Tenzin played in the water, Regina knew any effort to get them to open up would be worth it.

For a long time Tenzin avoided the camera. As soon as it pointed towards her she would duck behind the nearest hiding spot. Lucky for her she already caught the attention of Bluerose's greatest Case Ambassador. From the first day they met Scott was enraptured with her quiet self-assurance. His infatuation was so strong that, had Regina not known better by then, she would think this little girl was the other half of his ill-fated Lover's Knot.

The two of them were inseparable, even before she moved in and officially joined the family. It wasn't uncommon for Enoch to call saying her daughter was missing, and for Regina to take one look and find Tenzin drawing in Scott's bedroom while he napped.

She gradually got older. Braver. Stronger. Even more intelligent, somehow. While Regina proposed the bond thinking that Scott would always be there to protect Tenzin, she quickly proved that it was more likely to be the other way around. On more than one occasion, and long after childhood, Regina would still find them together – Tenzin with her headphones on, sketching or reading one of her comic books while Scott slept nearby.

Sometimes Regina would think about what Enoch told her shortly before she died.

You'll take care of them. And they'll take care of each other. I'm not afraid anymore. Maybe we didn't even need your bond – we were already a family.

Enoch was beautiful – like that Venus of Willendorf statue she saw a picture of while flipping through one of Levi's mythology books. Every smile of hers was moon-like, be it first quarter or waning crescent. There were many clips of Enoch holding the camera while Regina, younger and more present, explained the steps of the latest renovation project she was working on. Just by the way she held the camera it was clear Enoch was listening with the utmost attention, and as she filmed she would shift the shot to follow along with her, step by step.

Watching the little ghost of Enoch on her television, she often wished her dearest had a middle name. Sometimes when she thought about her in her head, Regina called her Venus.

This reoccurring eulogy took a few hours. If sometime tried to call or knock at the door, Regina chose to ignore them in favor of catching up with the phantoms of the past. The only way to pull her from her grief work was to do so directly and physically. Because of that, the only ones in Bluerose with a chance at getting her attention were the ones who knew where she kept the spare key.

Today that well-intentioned home intruder was her old coworker Nico Harbor Mackenzie. Regina knew it was him because he was the only person who locked the door again behind him after he entered. She head the careful footsteps of his his logger boots approach her in the living room, and then smelled the faint sea mist of his cologne.

More than that, she *heard* him. His affected dwarfism, which allowed him to soothe questions and judgment for a brief period of time, also meant his mental presence was one of the least overwhelming in town. Still, it filled the room like smoke from a fire. Regina sat up from where she sat on the carpet in front of the screen and mentally prepared herself to pan for coherence from the stream of nonstop stimuli.

Good morning, Mustard, Nico thought to her.

"Good morning, Harbor."

shelooksbad lookshungry mightbe sick

Regina closed her eyes and touched two fingers to lightly rub her temple.

Sorrysorrysorry – the cacophony stilled slightly and became a bit more clear – *should I put on the foil?*

A smile touched Regina's lips. The only thing worse than handling the aftermath of people coming to visit her was the guilt they felt just by being here. Once a person realized that they couldn't truly think one thing at a time for long, the layers of mental blabbering tended to bloom exponentially. With all of that, Regina would be quickly exhausted.

It was Tenzin who came up with the idea of making anyone who comes into the house wrap aluminum foil around their heads. She explained it was something conspiracy theorists thought could prevent external brainwashing and mind reading. At first Regina didn't think anyone in Bluerose would believe a science-fiction plot device could possibly work to neutralize magic no one has ever bothered to explain.

Apparently most were willing to stretch their suspension of disbelief if it meant feeling better about themselves and the world around them.

No, the foil did not work. It didn't make the exposure worse, but it also did nothing to improve it. However, as she adjusted the height of the kitchen table and pulled out two of her shorter chairs from the side closet, watching her mid-sixties ex-supervisor create a cone of crinkly aluminum around his head was very funny. It cheered her up while also making him think that his presence wasn't painful to her, which meant everyone wins and that this was a good and clever idea.

"I brought croissants," he said, sitting across from her and pushing the box in her direction.

The croissants were likely from the community kitchen. They were uncovered, still warm, and perfectly crisped. Lately everyone had been so nice to her that it was starting to make her kind of sick.

Regina wondered if this man assumed her children to be dead.

She bit into the end of a croissant, tasting nothing and feeling nothing. After chewing the baked dough into a paste, she swallowed the fat and carbohydrates and formed a small smile.

"Have you..?" Nico trailed off, newly anxious.

"Tenzin will call me when she needs to."

wedon't haveaway to fighthim

Regina held her smile, but dug her fists into her palm underneath the tabletop. There were people in her life that could handle this situation far better than she could. Levi would crack a joke and offer him a drink. Enoch would explain that his concern was appreciated, but that there wasn't much any of them could do other than hope for the best. Tenzin would stare at him in absolute silence until he was forced to leave the house to catch his breath.

Scott would tell him to fuck off. Then he would also probably offer him a drink.

"I was wondering if you needed help in the garden," Nico said weakly. "It might be good for you to get some air. Plus it looks like the endive is ready to be harvested."

"Did Nori send you?"

His eyes widened. The gray of them flashed brighter for a moment before he shook off the light and turned his face away.

Regina was so shocked that she struggled to hold onto anger at first.

"I'm sorry, Mustard," Nico murmured.

"Did you really think that would work on me?"

"I don't know, I – I panicked. Once I heard what happened between you two –"

She took another bite of her croissant. "Nothing happened between us."

"You threw a glass at her head."

"And I missed," Regina said.

Nico gave her the kind of look that knocked the smugness out of her head in a heartbeat. The kind of stare that expressed his belief in a higher standard of behavior that currently wasn't being expressed. When working for the Center she didn't get it often. It was strange that, decades later, it was still just as effective.

He leaned back in his chair and rubbed his graying beard with one hand. "Listen," he began. "I can't pretend like I understand what you're going through."

"I believe you do," Regina got up and went to the fridge. "I know you love your ferrets."

"Do you really want me to compare my ferrets to your human children?"

She picked out a protein shake and closed the door, leaning against the textured plastic. "You *love* your ferrets. You commission them sweaters in the cold season. A new one every year. If something were to happen to them and you were useless to help, it would destroy you."

As she unscrewed the lid of her shake she waited for Nico to correct her. She gave him a decent opportunity to call her unreasonable, and he chose not to take it. When she looked up at him again he was staring thoughtfully out the double doors into the yard.

"I could bring them over, you know," he said. "Bing and Bong. Bong's already tearing a hole in the new couch, but...I mean, you raised a bipolar kid, I'm sure things like that don't surprise you much."

Regina took one drink of her protein shake, which was flavored strawberry-banana but really only tasted like chalk. She grimaced. "Oh yes, as soon as Scott gets hypomanic he loves to burrow into the furniture."

She heard him chuckle under his breath and felt a small satisfaction that her attempt at a joke landed successfully. Her eyes drifted out the window and she took in the light of the early morning. The sky was made up of overarching cliffs done in varying shades of gray and white, and a slight breeze animated the limbs and leaves of the ever-growing garden.

From far ahead of them, Regina could see the slimmest glimpse of the ocean. It was so deep and dark, and colored in a way that made her heart ache terribly.

"Hey," Nico said.

She looked at him in his Journeyman shirt, his dignified, salt-and-pepper hair covered mostly by a ridiculous wad of aluminum foil.

Nico hopped out of his seat and brushed the croissant crumbs off his pants. "I think I'm ready for you to teach me how to make a sunny-side up egg."

Regina frowned. "What are you talking about?"

"Remember forty years ago when you teased me for not knowing how to make a sunny-side up egg?"

"Do you remember every comment a dumb child tells you?"

He smiled. "I do. And you said I needed to know just in case I ever had an important date."

Since they first met a few years before she started assisting in the Center, that was before she learned that Nico was aromantic as well as asexual. In her opinion he was incredibly handsome, so being young it wasn't absurd to think he'd be interested in things other than social work and squiggly rodents. It wasn't absurd, but it was incorrect.

Slightly incorrect. Nico also had a passion for puzzles.

"Well I'd say today in an important date. So how about it?"

Some examination drew Regina to the conclusion that this was a ploy to get her to eat actual food. Or maybe indulge in cooking, which at one point in life was a great love of hers. Regardless of the specifics it was obviously a grab to get her to be *her* again. Coming from anyone else it would be quickly shrugged off, but this was Nico. They spent practically their whole lives together.

If anyone had a vested interest in seeing her be more like herself again, it was him.

So she got out the step stool from under the sink and set it up in front of the stove. Regina switched on the gas and picked out a pan to place over the burner.

"I'm using truffle oil," she explained. "Any will do. Others might actually be better. But I'm sick of this oil and I want to get rid of it."

She opened the tall bottle and poured a drizzle into the pan in one smooth, circular movement. Nico stood beside her, and the two of them watched the consistency of the liquid change as it heated up.

"I don't know why you waited for me," Regina took the carton of eggs from the fridge. "Forty years is a long time to avoid such a basic recipe."

"Well I'm an avoidant guy."

"You're secure and you know it," Regina let out a snicker while she cracked two eggs into the hot pan. "You paid so much for that *official* attachment style assessment. Then you framed your results and kept it up in your office for years."

He flashed her a bemused look. "Ah – so your memory hasn't failed you completely."

Regina rolled her eyes. With the eggs now sizzling in the pan, she covered them with the lid and set her handheld timer for two minutes. Behind her, Nico was still staring thoughtfully through the glass as it shielded the cooked eggs.

"So that's how you do it," he murmured to himself. "That's how you cook the sun."

She left him with directions to slide the eggs onto a plate when the timer went off. Then she excused herself upstairs, where she ducked into the bathroom adjacent to her bedroom. There was a sheet draped over the mirror, which served no purpose now. Regina still kept up the habit in case her son needed it when he came home.

When she folded it up she was greeted with a woman far different than what she saw in the home movies. Her dark skin was creased with wrinkles under the eyes and at the side of her mouth. Her cropped black waves were flecked with strands of silver. A few locks by her face were almost entirely white.

Regina was old now. That was inevitable, and on its own it did not bother her. She craved being old and knowing she was living a life that stretched like fresh-woven silk.

The loneliness was harder. The pain made it even more unbearable.

Her eyes, so brown they were practically onyx, glowed visibly like the red of a hot coal. The sight of it depressed her.

While examining herself Regina felt her smart phone buzz in her pocket. She pulled it out and saw that Noriko was calling. Hesitance rolled over her like a crashing wave. Thinking back on their last interaction, Regina had to admit that – even though Nori was a close family friend – she was also the Head Elder of Bluerose and Regina did attempt to assault her.

It was only right to accept whatever punishment Noriko felt was needed. One of Regina's strongest qualities at the Center was having thick enough skin for anyone to get out their aggression before coming to the core of their actual problem. The Kaufner pain tolerance was hard to match.

"Hello, Elder Ninokata," Regina answered, attempting formality.

"Hey Mustard. Got a minute?"

That was a much different tone than Regina expected coming from the old woman she almost concussed a few days prior. Unnerved by the reflection in the mirror, she pulled she sheet back over the glass and went to the bed in the next room.

"I imagine Nico is with you," Nori continued.

The audio on her end was a little warped. It sounded like there was a lot of wind. Was she calling from her car? Where could she possibly be going this early in the day?

"He is," Regina confirmed, shoving down her curiosity.

"Good. I felt as if you might need the company, at least for most of today."

She couldn't read thoughts over the phone. That was a mercy most of the time, but now she wished she couldn't. Regina tensed her index finger against her thumb. "Why?" She ventured. "What's happening today?"

Silence. Hesitant silence. The silence before you say something that could potentially upset someone.

"Well," the wind tunnel sound went still. Maybe Nori pulled to the side of the road, "Tenzin emailed me yesterday."

An email. So she had something too big for her to comfortably explain over the phone. Regina swallowed hard and watched helplessly as each breath came in more and more strained. Nori waited for her to speak, and when she determined she wasn't going to kept on going.

"It's good news, Mustard," she said. "Well – maybe not good. But it isn't bad. They're safe, they're...they land in PDX at 10:45," Nori added then, with more intention. "All of them."

All of them. *All* of them? Could that mean –?

Regina's lips moved, but she couldn't get the word out. She refused to say that name aloud until she knew it was being directed at the right person.

Outside the scope of her turmoil she saw Nico standing in the doorway with a plate of eggs and two forks. The way he looked at her made it clear that he understood instantly who was calling and what they were saying to her. He looked around, briefly hesitating, before just walking into the bedroom and sitting on the floor by the nearest wall.

He took one of the forks and stabbed it directly into the yolk. Once the yellow pooled over the white, he carefully sectioned off a fragment and ate it.

Nico nodded to himself, very serious.

"She's almost certain it's him," Nori said. "He's immune to Scott's magic and they shared a vision where they were attached to the same tether. That sounds like the best we could get given the circumstances –"

"Him?"

Nori paused. "Tenzin didn't write anything about...pronouns. He – they – were very young when you..." she stifled a protest that cut off into nervous silence. "It's possible things changed. That happens."

It's not them. It couldn't be.

"She says his name is Edgar Gallows," Nori paused like she was trying to remember. "No middle name, I don't think."

Nico got up from the floor and brought him and his plate of eggs across the room to sit on the rug at the foot of Regina's bed. He continued to eat, not making any attempt to comfort through means other than proximity.

Regina repeated the name for the first time in over twenty years. "Edgar Gallows..."

"That's them, isn't it? I could get a picture. I'm sure you'd know if you saw a picture of them."

She checked like clockwork every year to see if they had any form of online presence. Every year she found nothing – at least, not on the surface level. There was no online registration for Academy legacy members, and even if there were every IP address in Bluerose was blocked from any Academy website. So that was an avenue not worth pursuing.

Tenzin tried to push a widespread use of VPNs to mask their IP address, but that didn't get far beyond their household. Her daughter could easily take the full name of Edgar Gallows and track down the individual's current location, be it residence, psychiatric facility, or cemetery. But Regina refused, even privately, for only her own sake.

Most days she figured they killed them when Scott has his first major break in reality. Some of those days she looked on that concept with a sick sense of gratitude. Because the alternative was that she left that wide-eyed child with the patchy dark red curls alone in a society that treated them so cruelly.

Nico raised the plate with the second egg and other fork. Regina shot him a look and he shrugged before beginning to eat it himself.

It probably said a lot about the way Regina lived her life that this man was the second choice when it came to comforting her.

"I'm picking them up now and we should get back around noon. That gives me enough time to explain to them your condition, so hopefully their effect isn't as overwhelming."

"That's all right," Regina said.

"If it's easier I could stagger visits and send them in one at a time."

Are you kidding me? Bring me my children – immediately and all at once. Surround me with them. I'm so sick of all this cruel silence and emptiness. Give my fucking family, Nori.

Regina put on her most audible smile. "You don't need to worry," she said. "I'll take a half-dose of Petrichor. It'll be fine."

More silence. "Nico is with you now?"

"He's eating eggs," Regina said.

"Is that – a metaphor?"

"No."

"...Okay. All right. I'll – text you that photo when they come in. Try to wait to take the Petrichor until then."

After Regina got off the phone she let the expensive device fall out of her hand and onto the floor. She followed soon after, sliding off the bed and ending up cross-legged beside Nico. Nico, who by now had finished his eggs, put aside the plate and looked her up and down.

"I feel like I've dodged a bullet by not having kids," he said.

"It's great, Harbor. I never knew there were so many ways to get punched in the gut."

He reached over and picked a few pieces of lint from the bedspread that stuck to Regina's sweater. "Scott's a smart kid. Give him some rest and the right medication, and he'll be back in his office before you know it."

"We sent him off with enough Petrichor for six years and he went through it in three," Regina trembled inwardly just saying that allowed.

"We have no way of knowing what that did to his long-term memory, but from what Tenzin tells me he's retained...very little. About his old life."

wellhe mightnot needit right?

Regina bit the insides of her cheeks hard enough for them to burn electric. She lowered her legs and splayed them out in front of her.

"Well," Nico leaned forward and gave her upper knee a small pat. "He'll figure it out. There are memories that could still be stored in the body, you know. For years and years, even if they're no longer accessible in the mind. So as long as he gets healthy and isn't overwhelmed..." he took a deep breath and smiled at Regina. "We can handle this, Mustard."

Ican dothis Icando this I candothis

Regina hadn't been big on shows of physical affection for some time now. However, in a rush of uncontrollable feeling, she took Nico's hand in hers and held them towards her chest.

He looked confused – not by the intimacy of her action, but by her ability to still be this intimate with someone outside of her family. She felt close to the same way, and for a few moments the two of them sat, closely touching in befuddled silence.

"You should spend more time with your other friends," Regina said.

"I can't," Nico whispered. "You're the only one who knows about eggs."

Regina laughed. The sound was as unfamiliar in her mouth as the emotions that prompted it. She pulled away from him and lolled her head back against the bed, guffawing loudly.

Somehow Nico persuaded her to spend some time outside in the garden. His intent was for the two of them to pick the endive and carrots that were ready. After touching the rain-moistened leaves of one singular carrot, Regina immediately decided that this wasn't the way she was meant to kill time. So she left the gardening to Nico and decided to take the wet weather as an opportunity to finish cleaning the two vintage riding toys she was in the process of refurbishing for the Center.

Her focus was on the Cozy Coupe because it was the dirtiest and that always made for more interesting work. It was already taken apart – hard plastic hood overturned on a layer of canvas with the grimy wheels arranged above it. She had the good sense to leave her bucket of cleaning supplies by the door where the rain couldn't easily flood it, so she grabbed it by the handle and sat it down by the hood.

Diluted dish soap was the best solution she could think of to get rid of the decades of dust and dirt that accumulated between the cracks of the textured surfaces. She had a spray bottle half full of the mixture, and she sprayed a generous shower of the stuff onto the hood before going at it with her scrub brush.

She would spray and scrub, then pour over with water and scrub again. It was monotonous work that allowed her mind to drift to other things, like the smells of the soil and saltwater mixed with man-made chemicals. This was the closest Regina ever got to a meditative state, and as she watched the shades of brown wash clean off the plastic she thought

"I'm going to take them."

"What?" Enoch said from the other end of the phone. "Mustard, no. That's kidnapping."

Regina leaned back in the car seat and kept her eyes on the doors to the University. "Yes," she confirmed. "I'm going to kidnap them."

"Fucking hell – that's…" Enoch trailed off, and when she spoke again she was much calmer. "We'll call the police. If we have proof of abuse we can call the police."

But we don't have proof, Regina wanted to point out. All we have are the visions of my son and some bruises that'll be covered up by an organization with authority near to that of the Catholic church.

Enoch clicked her tongue anxiously, as if she were right beside her waiting for class to get out. "I don't like this," she said. "You said the parents refused to meet with you. What if they've tracked your license plate?"

"I'm being very discreet," Regina tried to assure her.

"Well if you're still in the Doctor's car then no, you aren't. Regina, you can't keep taking these kinds of risks. You have children to think about."

The doors pushed open and released a sea of purple-suited children all around Scott and Tenzin's age. Regina immediately stopped paying attention to what her love was saying. She shifted the phone into her opposite hand and got out of the car, standing to peer through all the faces and dissect the crowd into parts. Looking for the smaller body. The larger set of eyes.

Because yes, Regina did have children. And right now, one of them needed her help.

Once the crowd started to thin Regina began to worry. Did she miss her chance? She was starting to consider pulling off and circling the surrounding city blocks, but before she went any farther with that line of thought she caught sight of a familiar face she was seeing for the very first time.

They were smaller than the other kids and walked a little slower – not from noticeable depression, just deep in thought. They had a young face that was still slightly older than what made sense for their age, with large, deep-set eyes hued a warm shade of brown.

This child matched Scott's description of Eddie. What identified them for certain, however, was the feeling that flooded Regina's system as soon as she caught site of them. Her love for those around her came in varying colors. For Enoch it was a bright emerald green, while Tenzin was more of a comforting blue-gray. It was always different for everyone – always – and yet when she looked at the child absently making his way down the stairs she felt the exact color of love she felt whenever she looked at Scott.

Sunflower yellow. Every single time.

It had to be them. Eddie.

Enoch was in the middle of explaining some kind of Louisiana legality when Regina hung up on her without a word. She got out of the car and fidgeted, unsure how to do this. She had no intention of stealing them if they didn't want to go with her. It would help to find a way to explain who she was in a way that would make sense to the child – but in a way that didn't encourage them to strike up conversations with frantic strangers in the future. Everything that made sense before Eddie walked outside now felt just as wrong as everyone had been trying to tell her.

This wasn't Scott. Regina had to remind herself that. This was the other fragment of the being that ended up developing into her son. Was she truly as responsible for this half of his spirit as she was for him?

Not seeing a gap in the sidewalk, Eddie stumbled and scraped his knee against the concrete. From across the street Regina could see the wound, a grating of skin just deep enough to swell blood. It was the type of thing Scott would proudly show off before washing clean with a hose and bounding back off with his day. Eddie, however, stayed still. They did not move. Staring down at the blood, they broke down immediately in quiet tears.

No one was helping them. A few purple-suited adults looked at them as they passed, but did nothing. Regina bore this sight for maybe ten seconds before she grunted in annoyance and ran over to their aid.

"Oh wow!" She exclaimed. "You really tumbled, didn't you?"

Eddie shrank even smaller on the ground and turned his face away from her. Horror weighed her heavy in place, and Regina knelt down and adjusted her attitude.

She started by speaking much softer. "Does it hurt?" She asked.

"It – It's scary."

"The blood?" Regina glanced down at the trickle of red running down just below the hem of his shorts. "Yes. You don't like blood," she smiled vaguely. "It's kind of spooky isn't it? Do you think it means that something bad happened?"

The child nodded. They lowered their arm away from their face, though still kept their eyes focused down from Regina's direct line of sight. A sign of respect from Academy children, she learned some time ago. It disgusted her to think about.

She rifled through her bag and pulled out a few paper packets. "I keep sanitary wipes on me," she said, tearing the top off of one. "They're for my son. I don't think he would mind if I used a few to help clean you up, though. Would that be all right with you?"

At first Eddie didn't respond. He wiped at his eyes and took a deep breath. Then he nodded.

"The thing about scrapes like this," Regina told them as she gently wiped away the blood up his leg, "is that they feel a lot worse than they actually are. You've really only hurt a few layers of skin – and you have many layers of skin, Eddie – so you haven't gone deep enough to cause any permanent damage on it's own. This might sting a little bit, buddy."

Regina pressed a fresh sanitary wipe over the wound. Eddie's face scrunched up without making much of a sound, and once again she felt the sunflower yellow of adoration for her child.

"You're being very brave," she murmured. "Anyhow, it hurts because under your skin has things called nerves. And that's how you feel things – most things, at least," Regina was quickly reaching the borders of her medical knowledge. "You didn't hurt your body. It's more like you triggered the alarm system that lets you know that something bad could've happened. Does that make sense?"

Somewhere in that explanation Eddie gathered the nerve to look at her. They seemed uncertain, and yet more than a little curious. She got a better look at his eyes, and at the iris coloboma that gave them the quality of something antique and wise.

She supposed that meant they could see hers as well. She wondered if Eddie would ask about them.

"How do you know my name?" They quietly questioned her.

Regina's eyes widened slightly. Did she call them Eddie? Was she so preoccupied with comforting them that she forgot to make any effort to do things subtly?

She thought about Enoch. She should've let Enoch come with her.

"My name is Regina," she said. "But you can call me Mustard if you'd like. Wouldn't that be funny? It's like the flower, but it's also a sauce."

Regina stood up and pulled her wallet out of her purse. Eddie followed her lead and got up on their own accord. Still, they didn't drop the issue. "Do you know my mother?" They asked.

She thought about the cold voice that spoke to her on the phone and shivered. "No," she said, forcing a smile. "I'm actually...I'm Scott's mom."

"...Scott?"

There was a photo in the inner fold of her wallet. It was new, printed by Enoch only a week before Regina drove off on this terrible road trip, but already the creases were well-defined from folding and unfolding. It was of Scott and Tenzin, each only half-visible and under a pillow fort that collapsed over them mid-nap. Regina smiled at the image, then turned it to Edgar and pointed at Scott's laughing face.

The recognition was stark. For a moment it was frightened. Then that broke away, and Eddie's brown eyes once again welled with tears.

"He's real?" They managed weakly.

"So what would you say, Mustard?"

Regina looked up from the now clean toy car parts laid out in front of her. Nico was standing near the edge of the garden's soil, carrying a full basket of carrots with both hands. He was splattered with dirt almost up to the elbows and smiling about it in the way crazy people do when they enjoy that kind of thing. She blinked, counted until her friend made a face, and blinked again with her internal timer now calibrated.

"Did you hear my question?" He asked her, dimly playful.

"Of course."

"Really? What did I ask, then?"

She scanned the area around them and thought to herself, sparking any hint of deductive reasoning hopefully developed over fifty-six years of avoiding awkward social situations. It could've been a comment on the weather, the way it teetered unsteadily between stillness and rainfall. Or he could be searching for validation on his gardening skills, which would be a ridiculous thing to ask of her.

Maybe he wanted some carrots. He could take all of them as far as she was concerned. Regina no longer wanted to live a life where human presence was severely outnumbered by produce.

Nico scoffed and rolled his eyes. "I didn't ask anything," he said.

"What do you mean?"

"I was just testing that trademark Kaufner hyper-focus," he went to put the basket by the door and stood by the canvas of toy parts. "Where do you go when you do stuff like this?"

Regina could still sense the way Eddie felt as they nestled into her arms after a bad dream. Just tired and trusting, like an old tom cat learning to open up its heart again for the very first time. They made themselves so small as they whispered their fears – all of them – until they ran out of whispers and worries and were left exhausted enough to fall asleep.

Eddie was grounded where Scott was lost. Scott was hopeful when they were despairing. Eddie liked poetry and knew so much about birds, and the fact that it took so long to bring this one soul together was the greatest shame of Regina's life.

She picked up the clean hood of the Cozy Coupe. "Help me carry this inside?" She said to Nico.

There was a large keg of Petrichor kept in the corner of the kitchen. The crafting team in town had it specially made for the family shortly after Scott was born and the need for it became clear. It was elaborately made out of Douglas Fir stained deep red. There were carvings of fat little birds and garlands of leaves along the rim. It must've taken a very long time to make, and the friends that made it did so intending loving present for the family.

A present that inadvertently celebrated the chronic illness that now plagued both mother and son.

Regina got a glass from the cupboard and held it under the tap to twist out a single dose. Immediately its stench filled the room, and all it took was the beginning of her groan for Nico to open the sliding glass door and let in the fresh air.

"Sorry about that," Regina flipped on the nearby switch that turned on the air filtration system she installed many years ago. "I'm usually better about that. I'm a little distracted."

She turned and set her glass on the counter. Nico was back at the kitchen table and watching her stand there, just taking her in with neither judgment nor exact understanding. Regina opened the fridge and paused, meeting his gaze. Suddenly very tired.

"You take that every day?" He said.

"No. Only if I have to face a lot of people."

He looked down at the box of foil still sitting on the tabletop. His face became sad in a dark and ghostly way.

The foildoesn't help

Regina peered down into the variety pack of hyper-caffeinated, obscenely-sweetened energy drinks that Tenzin left in the fridge before she left. There was cotton candy and something called Peach Squizzle. She settled on the cotton candy.

"It doesn't," she confirmed as she filled the rest of her glass with translucent pink chemical sweat. "But it makes me laugh."

She saw him touch the side of his tinfoil hat and assumed he was about to take it off. Instead, he pushed the tip of the cone forward, turning the whole thing into a kind of antennae. He poked at the end and smiled slightly.

This man could be a grandpa to human children. Instead he was a grandpa to generations of ferrets scattered about Bluerose. Regina hoped those little fur worms knew just how lucky they were.

Nico carried the conversation while Regina nursed her makeshift cocktail. He spoke quickly, filling her in on the latest cases moving into town. Telling her the kinds of details that weren't invasive to know, but definitely should've been reserved for other Center employees. Once there was nothing left to say on that subject, he moved on to talk about all the reasons why he regretted accidentally trying to teach his ferrets how to take off neckties. While he described all the more formal house guests who came to his place and now risked getting choked, his eyes would dart every so often to Regina's steadily diminishing glass.

The more she drank, the farther his thoughts got from her own. Things became smaller and clearer all at once. These energy drinks were practically syrup on their own, which meant they were perfect for masking the horrible taste of the medicine mixed into it.

"You don't even react anymore," Nico remarked at one point.

"It's a little easier when you understand it," she forced down another sip and sighed. "Understand and accept it."

"You could drink me under the table, couldn't you?"

"There's not a direct correlation. Still – I'm sure I've built up a tolerance to...*something*."

Nico nodded slow. "Makes you wonder how Scotty must be now."

Regina's mouth went dry and sticky-sweet. It took her a few times before she could pull back a satisfying swallow. She tried to imagine Scott's natural liveliness, his boundless energy warped by years of exhaustion and abuse. It was something she could only sustain for a short while before she had to abandon the effort.

She spoke to him on the phone. He still knew his Tone Speech. He still was able to cry.

He was still her son.

In the center of the table her phone buzzed. It was a text from Noriko – just the words *ON OUR WAY!* It expressed the kind of excitement that implied things hadn't gone wrong so far. There was an icon above the text that Regina was meant to click to download a photo attachment. Her finger hovered over where it was meant to click without fully touching the screen.

Inwardly, she recited Nico's thoughts upon first seeing her. Looks bad. Looks hungry. Might be sick. Even though not looking at it wouldn't make the issue any better, Regina wasn't sure she could handle seeing Scott – or any of her children – in such a state.

A sigh escaped her lips. Regina was selfish.

She pushed the phone towards Nico. "Look for me?" She requested. "I don't think I have the nerve."

Nico quickly accepted his task and tapped the screen with little hesitation. She studied him fiercely as he looked at the screen and regretting finishing her Petrichor so early. His eyes were focused in one place. The twin caterpillars of his brow were knitted close together. He didn't look worried. Whatever he was seeing was clearly provoking a lot of different thoughts.

Finally he looked up at Regina. He cracked a half-smile.

"What is it?" Regina breathed.

"He got a haircut," Nico said, now grinning.

He offered her the phone. With only a little force to the mechanics of her body, Regina took her device and looked down at her son's face for the first time in three years.

Scott lost too much weight. He was closer now to his original skin tone of varnished driftwood, but still clearly iron-deficient. His cheeks were gaunt enough to the point that his large eyes looked even more unnatural. He must've had to answer so many questions. Regina hummed unhappily.

"Look closer, Mustard," Nico prodded.

She closed her eyes and took a deep breath. Then she looked again. Somehow Scott got a hold of a skirt that resembled a dress he still had in his closet. He had her coat held over his arm, which meant he wasn't too cold. His hair was clean and maybe even styled, with bangs that kept the whole of his face in clear view.

He was smiling. Not a blurry smile captured in the middle of him talking. Not something so fake it make the rest of his face look plastic. Just a regular, slightly sleepy smile. He seemed calmer than she ever remembered him being.

Tenzin stood beside him. From what Regina could see she didn't look hurt. She still maintained that sense of duty in her expression that was so well-known in their town, although now it was riding backseat to other, more prominent things. Like the tube of Pringles she was in the middle of eating. Regina's daughter was obsessed for months with the mission of rescuing Scott, driven far past exhaustion, and now she was just casually eating potato chips.

Scott's other arm was interlaced with that of a third figure. They were older now, and their short hair was grown out into beautiful spirals of copper curls. Still, Regina knew those eyes without hesitation. Even from pixels on a screen she could feel the sunflowers open inside her.

"Eddie..." she whispered.

They were also looking at the camera – not smiling, but looking like they were probably about to. Their hand was frozen in a small wave. Relief came first, because the child was alive. Then came guilt, because they had been alone. That turned into anger, and sorrow, and finally confusion so strong it mixed wrong with the Petrichor and made her head foggy.

She stood up. From the back of her mind she heard Nico's voice. "You want to listen to some music, or something? I can pick up some food for when the kids get here."

Regina ignored him. She walked towards the front door, slipping on her sandals and grabbing her coat. Nico called out again before starting to follow her, but by that point she was already halfway out the front door. Instead of bothering to close it, Regina kept on down the path and pointed her index finger behind her.

"Keep closed, please," she said.

The haze of Petrichor made it easier to actually feel the magic energy as it coursed through and out her body. From behind her there was the sound of the front door obediently slamming shut and locking, seemingly all on its own. She heard Nico testing the knob and calling out from inside. First a questioned murmur. Then a shout. The knocks turned into poundings, but still she didn't stop.

It wouldn't trap him. He'd realize eventually that he could go out the back. But his confusion should buy her some time.

The Bluerose burial grounds was an expanse of natural land that everything else surrounded. It served two purposes: the first was for lovers to plant and tend to their saplings as a testament to nature and their commitment to each other, and the second was for those with a connection to Bluerose to be laid to rest. It used to only be Birthrights. Recently, though, as Refuge hubs have started to become more open to civilians in their official ranks, so have their cemeteries.

Regina liked to think her family played a part in that.

She walked in a daze until she made her way into the grove. There were no signs, no markers, no identifiers of any kind that would allow anyone outside of those already in the know to be aware of who was buried where. New clients in town often just thought this to be an esoteric garden showcasing an assortment of trees. It was an unspoken rule not to explain more than what was directly asked of them.

The olive tree was easier to spot. It helped that it was a strong, short, fat little thing, its trunk knotted and strong. But Regina went one step forward and tied two colored ribbons around the base. She said it was decor, which wasn't technically looked down on. No one needed to know the reason for the tribute.

The first ribbon was colored a strong orange reminiscent of a ripe tangerine. The one above it was edged with lace, and emerald green.

Regina fell to her knees in front of the olive tree. The soil was moist and soaked cold through the thin material of her pajama pants. It was a frigid day, and the veil of tiny leaves wouldn't do much to cover her from the new rain.

But it didn't matter. None of that mattered. Regina opened her lips to laugh and the sound was delivered wrapped in a sob. Her tears were hot and her blood burned in anticipation of spring coming early.

"Loves," she sobbed in a voice trembling with life. "Levi, Venus, my loves. It's finally happening."

She got closer to the olive tree and clutched the cool wood against either palm. Her forehead met the ribbons, both of them, and they were as smooth and brightly hued as the day she tied them on.

Regina smiled. She made a noise that didn't sound like it, but felt to her like laughter.

"Our children are coming back," she whispered.

When Nico finally found her she was curled up on the damp earth, spooning the trunk of the olive tree. Her clothes were wet and muddy and there was clumps of dirt in her hair. She was fast asleep, because even once you accept the Petrichor into your life there was truly no way to stay dry in the storm.

But she was smiling. Smiling, deep in sleep, with the ghosts so close to laid at rest.

Nico rubbed his hand hard across his face and sighed. He couldn't blame her. That would have to wait until she was conscious again. Until then, he left to find some stronger bodies to help carry her back home.

He decided that's what he would do. But first he stood in place and watched his old friend, deep in her dreams. Her eyes twitched in sleep and she hummed what he recognized as Tone Speech but couldn't translate. She did it all through a small, barely distinct smile.

It had been a long, long time since he'd seen Regina that happy.

Acknowledgments

hello friend! it's good to see you. i'm sure you're tired after reading
a novel that ended up being infinitely longer than i planned it to be, so
you don't have to stay if you don't want to. but if you'd like to sit, i'd
love the company. i got some tea – earl gray, iced. i'm trying to be mindful of my caffeine intake these days.

i started *blind trust* during a time of immense trauma and revelation
and finished it in three months. in that time i actually wrote almost fifty
thousand extra words, maybe more, that were lost in various software
errors. i think i gave myself tendinitis and for a few days just opening a
door hurt. one book quickly turned into two, and now two have bal-
looned into four. this is by far the most ambitious project i've ever done
in my life, but people seem to be enjoying it so i'm happy to do it.

none of it would be possible without my wife riley, the person who
casually proposed me seriously pursuing a career in published writing
and not really being swayed at all of my arguments on why that would
be so hard. they later on went to sit through multiple one-sided conversations as i tried to logic why a human being would want to spend
real currency on a book i would've just given to them for free had they
asked. i've written maybe fourteenth-length novels and i stopped seriously considering publishing, and now because of them i have a physical
book of my actual words.

riley, your patience and quiet devotion are unmatched and astounding. i love you steadily and consistently enough to forge a new grand canyon, and as soon as i finish writing this i'm going to come home to you and we are going to build a hot dog car in the computer video game *space engineers.*

going back even further i have to thank my childhood friend samuel marion schultheis, who i have known since the second grade. he was my first reader. he wanted to be an editor until i told him that editing involved more than reading my stories, giving them back, and saying "i really liked this". i have memories of giving him my second novel a chapter at a time and getting frantic texts as he got to certain plot points. i don't think he realizes how much that fueled my creative passion when nothing else could.

he kept a copy of that novel on a shelf with other books by traditionally published, adult writers (i think we were fifteen at the time). When i asked why it was there, he said that was the shelf where he displayed *all his favorite writers.*

sam, if you ever read this, i will never be eloquent enough to put into words how much that means to me. how much *you* mean to me. i have been so lucky to have a person like you in my life, and i still kind of think you could be the next pope or president if you wanted to be.

finally, well – can I scoot a little closer? hi. i'd like to thank you – like, *you*, the person who bought and/or read this. i don't care about the format you have or the amount you paid for it. you read my book! that's really crazy. it's so hard to read anything these days and you chose to read about scott and edgar trying to figure stuff out.

that's really cool. you're really cool for doing that and i appreciate it greatly.

i hope you liked it. that's a fun thing i feel like most writers consider themselves too *writerly* to admit, but i'm pretty sure we all think it. i hope you liked my story. i hope it made you feel safe and comforted most of the time. i'm very attached to creating a genre of *soup lit* that provides adventure without feeling overwhelmingly cynical and also pairs great with crackers. yum yum.

i'm midway-ish into book two of *songbird elegies,* which i'm calling *migration patterns.* a lot of things are happening. questions will be answered pretty quickly and more will be asked. you'll meet some more people who i am very fond of. i'm going to try and release it as soon as i can, but until then i welcome you to search me up on bing or askjeeves (or, like, google or something) and keep up with my personal website. you'll find my tumblr through there because i am a vonnegut protagonist thoroughly unstuck in time, and through there it's far easier to snoop on my progress.

that's all i have to say. Sorry i didn't really let you get a word in edgewise this time. maybe after you read this you can find me online and tell me how your day's been going. provide no context as to why you're telling me this or who you are. i have pretty bad memory issues so i'll almost certainly forget that i gave you permission to do this to my future self. let's consider it a secret between friends, okay?

thanks again. i hope i see you in the next one. get home safe. have a nice snack. i love you dearly.

best,

clover jean gardener

april 26th, 2024

www.ingramcontent.com/pod-product-compliance
Lightning Source LLC
Chambersburg PA
CBHW062100290726

48975CB00001B/49